Sometimes you find more than you bargained for
when you're

LOOKING FOR TROUBLE

Sometimes you find love and romance...

Relive the excitement...

Three complete novels
by one of your all-time-favorite authors

Anne Stuart has, in her twenty-five years as a published author, won every major award in the business, appeared on various bestseller lists, been quoted by *People, USA Today* and *Vogue*, appeared on *Entertainment Tonight* and warmed the hearts of readers worldwide. She has written more than thirty novels for Harlequin and Silhouette, plus another thirty or more suspense and historical titles for other publishers.

When asked to talk a bit about herself, Anne once said, "Anne Stuart has written lots of books in lots of genres for lots of publishers. She lives in the hills of Northern Vermont with her splendid husband and two magnificent children, where it snows so much, she hasn't much else to do but write."

ANNE STUART

LOOKING FOR TROUBLE

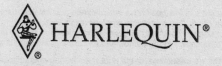

HARLEQUIN®

TORONTO • NEW YORK • LONDON
AMSTERDAM • PARIS • SYDNEY • HAMBURG
STOCKHOLM • ATHENS • TOKYO • MILAN • MADRID
PRAGUE • WARSAW • BUDAPEST • AUCKLAND

HARLEQUIN BOOKS

by Request—LOOKING FOR TROUBLE

Copyright © 2000 by Harlequin Books S.A.

ISBN 0-373-20172-9

The publisher acknowledges the copyright holder of the individual works as follows:

CINDERMAN
Copyright © 1994 by Anne Kristine Stuart Ohlrogge

CRY FOR THE MOON
Copyright © 1988 by Anne Kristine Stuart Ohlrogge

CHASING TROUBLE
Copyright © 1991 by Anne Kristine Stuart Ohlrogge

This edition published by arrangement with Harlequin Books S.A.

Visit us at www.romance.net

Printed in U.S.A.

CONTENTS

Dr. Daniel Crompton was HOT! But Suzanna Molloy was determined not to get burned.

Cinderman

Chapter One

Nancy Drew, she wasn't. She was a far cry from Brenda Starr, as well. Slinking through the sterile corridors of Beebe Control Systems International, her head down, her eyes focused on her battered sneakers, Suzanna Molloy could feel her heart pounding, her adrenaline pumping, her brain going into overdrive. Maybe she wasn't cut out for undercover work.

If anyone recognized her, she would be in very deep dog droppings. She was persona non grata around here, having been impertinent enough to ask questions about the corporate structure and political affiliations of the mysterious megacorporation that had sprung up out of nowhere in the last few years, and having compounded her crime by asking those questions in print. Not that a huge multinational complex like BBCSI should be threatened by the small trade newspaper she worked for. After all, the *Tech-Sentinel* had an excellent reputation for hard-nosed reporting in the scientific field, but that field was, in fact, quite small. BBCSI could squash the *Tech-Sentinel* flat, if they wanted. And if they made the mistake of thinking no one would notice.

So far, they'd been smart enough to do no more than offer a few warnings, and to refuse to grant Suzanna any interviews. But she wasn't the mild-mannered sort that took rejection lightly. Not when she had hints of exactly what Dr. Daniel Crompton was working on.

Now she huddled into an oversize lab coat, reminding herself that she needed to walk like a dweeb. Keep her head down, shuffle her feet, maybe even mumble underneath her breath. She'd spent enough of her life among the computer nerds and scientific misfits to be able to pass herself off as one. Just long enough to get herself into Crompton's private lab. The lab that no one, not even his bosses or assistants, was allowed to enter.

Suzanna Molloy hadn't gotten where she was by taking no for an answer, she thought, darting a surreptitious glance down the hall. Not that she'd gotten that far by most standards. A two-room apartment in an old Victorian house on the edge of a northern California town, a bank account that kept her in yogurt and a car that had seen better days did not amount to impressive accomplishments in the scheme of things. But they were things she'd accomplished herself. Everything she had, she'd earned—including her reputation.

She wondered if she'd be quite so determined if it were anyone other than Daniel Crompton. She'd met the great Dr. Crompton on several occasions—all public receptions when the BBCSI hadn't been able to keep the press at bay—and it had hardly been love at first sight. She'd decided early on that Crompton was one of those men whose ego was almost as large as his intellect, and in Crompton's case that was saying a great deal. The man was legendary— for his brilliance, his youth and his chilly manner. The fact that he wasn't half-bad to look at only made him better copy.

She whipped around the corner, breathing a sigh of relief. It had been difficult enough getting past the security guards in the first place. One would have thought BBCSI harked back to cold-war technology, given the almost hysterical level of protection the fortresslike complex boasted. Fortunately she had friends in low places: the picture ID with its computer scan code was meticulous enough to avoid detection, and the blueprint of the building would enable her to make her way to Crompton's fortified third-story lab without any betraying hesitation.

Once she got there, it would be up to her to get inside. She had no illusions. The place would have security that would make Fort Knox seem like a public park, but she wasn't about to give up if she got that far. She had in the capacious pocket of her lab coat a handy-dandy device that would take care of any computer-coded lock. She'd only be in trouble if they went in for something as archaic as a dead bolt and key.

She'd chosen her time well. Even the most dedicated security freaks and scientific geniuses liked to get home to a hot meal, and it was just after five-thirty. Most of the employees were too intent on getting the hell out of the place to notice another white-coated employee, and BBCSI was vast enough for her to simply blend in.

When she reached the third floor, she found it deserted. Crompton must have already gone home, and the computerized lock on his unmarked lab door would be child's play for the circumventor one of her friends at the paper had set up for her. Taking a deep breath, she walked to the door of the lab, listening for a moment. Not a sound within, and if she could trust her instincts, which she usually could, the place was empty. Doubtless, there were security cameras all over the place, and she moved closer to the door, the white coat shielding her actions as she quickly, efficiently tripped the lock and then stepped inside, closing the heavy door silently behind her.

DR. DANIEL CROMPTON stood inside Henry Osborn's plush inner office, impatient as always.

"For heaven's sake, Dan, have a seat," Osborn said,

using his usual boisterous charm, something he'd perfected during his twenty years in the corporate high life.

Daniel was immune to charm. And he hated being called Dan. "I'll stand," he said in his deep voice. "I won't be here long."

Osborn didn't let his irritation show, but Daniel knew he was feeling it. "Hell, Dan, you make me feel like a principal calling a recalcitrant schoolboy onto the carpet."

"That's your problem," Daniel replied with exquisite rudeness.

This time he did manage to ruffle Osborn's cheer. The older man's small eyes darkened for a moment, and then he showed his teeth in a semblance of a smile. "We need results, Dan."

"When I accepted your funding, I did so on my terms." Daniel found this all quite tedious, but then, most of his life outside his lab involved wasting his time with fools like Osborn, and he'd grown inured to it. "You provide the money and leave me alone."

"Yes, but we need something. A sign of progress, of good faith. You know, if it were simply up to me, you'd be left to your own timetable. But we've got a board of directors, stockholders, demanding results. General Armstead has been on my tail for a week now, about you."

Daniel simply shrugged.

Osborn got up and came around the desk. He was a trim man in his early sixties, impeccably dressed, impeccably mannered. He was also a snake and a liar.

He put his hand on Daniel's shoulder and stared up at him earnestly. "You know what we're after. And you're the man to do it. Half the scientists in the world are trying to create cold fusion, but our money's on you. If anyone's going to do it, you will."

Daniel stared at him. "At this point I'm not particularly interested in cold fusion."

"Damn it, how could you not be! I'd heard you've been

concentrating your efforts on physical chemistry, and that's going to get you nowhere. The only way you're going to create cold fusion is with lasers, with—''

''If you want to create cold fusion, Osborn, I'm sure you can find space for a lab,'' Daniel said.

Osborn's hands clenched for a moment, then relaxed. ''You know, you're damned annoying, Dan. If you weren't so brilliant, someone would probably wring your neck.''

Daniel looked down at him. ''They could try.''

''We need some results, Dan. At least a preliminary report. I trust you—''

''If you trust me, why do you need a preliminary report?''

''I said *I* trust you. I'm just the lowly CEO. Armstead's head of the board of directors, and after spending thirty years in the army, he's used to having his orders obeyed. Just give us something. Anything.''

Daniel considered him for a long moment. He didn't trust him, but then, he didn't trust anyone. Trust was a human emotion and a waste of time, and Daniel Crompton never wasted time. It was too precious a commodity.

He'd already wasted more than enough with this man. ''I'll have one of my lab assistants write you a report.''

''Your lab assistants don't know diddly. You don't let them anywhere near your experiments, you just keep them glued to computers, running theoretical tests.''

''It keeps them busy,'' he said. ''I'll have Jackson do it.''

Osborn didn't even blink, something Daniel could respect. Robert Jackson was Osborn's spy and stooge, and they all thought Daniel was too involved in his work to realize it. Daniel didn't trust anyone, but Jackson's yuppie friendliness had made him more suspect than most.

''You know what the stakes are, Dan,'' Osborn said. ''You know what cold fusion could do, I don't need to remind you. Don't you care about providing unlimited, safe energy for the world? Don't you care about ending our reliance on oil-producing nations? Don't you want to help make the world a better place?''

''Not particularly,'' Daniel said with complete honesty. ''I'm only interested in my work.''

''Danny—'' Osborn began.

''My name is Daniel,'' he said, ruthlessly interrupting Osborn. *Dan* he could barely tolerate; *Danny* was going beyond the pale. ''Or Dr. Crompton, if you prefer. And ask Jackson what I'm doing. I'm sure he can come up with a reasonable guess. For a spy, he's quite intelligent.'' He turned on his heel and started toward the door.

''I'm not finished,'' Osborn said, sounding petulant.

Daniel didn't pause. ''I am,'' he said. And he closed the door quietly behind him.

The whole thing was incredibly tedious, he thought as he let himself back into the lab. He was so damned tired of dealing with the corporate mentality. He'd accepted Beebe's offer several years ago for a number of reasons, including the fact that they seemed to have more money and fewer restrictions than anyone else making an offer for his services, and the offers had been plentiful. The government had wanted him, of course, but he'd never been fond of bureaucrats. The defense industry's offer had been tempting, but in the end he decided he disliked generals even more than bureaucrats. Private industry gave him the hives; academia was impoverished. BBCSI had seemed the perfect solution, a young multicorporation whose right hand didn't seem to know what its left hand was doing. Apart from Osborn and the deceptively avuncular General Armstead, they were an innocuous bunch. The corporation was large enough to hand over all its vast resources and leave him alone.

Until the last few months. They searched his lab at least every other day. It was usually Jackson, but sometimes it was one of the other brilliant but completely uncreative research assistants Daniel had been given. He wasn't particularly concerned—there was no way they were going to find what he was working on. They were still convinced he was working on cold fusion, and as long as they were looking in that direction it would take more than all their puny intellects put together to figure out what he was up to.

He'd present his results to Osborn, Armstead and their confederates sooner or later. After all, they'd paid for it. But not before he'd finished with his obsessive checking and rechecking. He'd been able to duplicate the results a half-dozen times. He wasn't about to make his discoveries public until he was convinced, and he needed at least a half-dozen more trials.

He'd been at the computer when Osborn had issued his summons. He headed back in that direction, then stopped. Something wasn't right.

He turned around slowly, surveying the sterile, obsessively neat confines of his spacious lab. He hadn't been working at the hood—that section of the physical lab used for dangerous experiments—for days now, and yet it looked different. There was a definite odor, something burning, and he started toward it, then halted.

"Who the hell are you?"

The intruder had been in the middle of sneaking toward the door. He turned and glared at her as she stood like a deer pinned by a set of headlights. Except there was no fear in her steady gaze.

"Er—I'm new here," she said, sounding embarrassed and innocent. Except that he didn't believe her. "I'm looking for Dr. Smith's lab, and I thought this was it."

"There is no Dr. Smith at BBCSI," he said flatly.

"There has to be. Do you know how many Smiths there are in this country?" she asked.

"No, and I don't care. And you're no lab assistant. I recognize you. You're that reporter. How did you get in here?"

She straightened her shoulders, meeting him glare for glare. He couldn't remember her name—it was something like Samantha—but he remembered that look. He supposed she was pretty enough, if she weren't so damned interfering. He didn't like interfering women. He liked them plump, passive and silent, content to feed him and stroke him and leave him alone when he was working.

Unfortunately he had yet to meet such a paragon, but Samantha or whatever her name was had to be one of the worst.

"I'm not *that reporter*," she said, her voice as cool as his. "I'm Suzanna Molloy. And if you ever agreed to an interview, Dr. Crompton, I wouldn't be forced to go to such extremes to find out exactly what it is you're doing."

"Your curiosity justifies breaking and entering, Ms. Molloy? And just how did you get into Beebe in the first place? Someone must have been helping you."

"I'm not about to reveal my sources, to you or to anyone. I've heard rumors that you're working on cold fusion, Dr. Crompton."

"Just about everyone in my field is working on cold fusion. That isn't news." He moved to the telephone, picking up the receiver and pushing a button.

"What are you doing?"

"Calling security."

"Wait." She moved quickly—gracefully, he had to admit—and disconnected him before the call was made. "Just a few answers, Dr. Crompton. I've heard that there's something very wrong going on here at Beebe. That you're working on something extraordinary, something well beyond cold fusion, and that there's a good chance it might fall into the wrong hands."

He stared down at her. She was tall for a woman, taller than Osborn, and her eyes behind her wire-rimmed glasses were a clear, intelligent brown. Intelligence. He hated that in a woman.

"Where did you get your information?"

"Is it true?" she persisted. "Are you working on cold fusion?"

"No," he said flatly.

"Then it's something even more important. Though I can't imagine what."

"That's the problem with people nowadays, Ms. Molloy," he said. "Not enough imagination."

She had a wide mouth, one that curved in a reluctant smile that he found oddly fascinating. "People usually say reporters have too *much* imagination."

"Don't try to charm me, Molloy," he snapped. "I'm immune."

Her smile vanished as she stared at him in shock. "Charm you?" she echoed. "No one's ever accused me of having charm before."

"Don't expect flattery from me. What were you doing in here?"

"I'm certain you're incapable of flattery, Dr. Crompton," she shot back. "And I was simply observing. I didn't touch anything. Though if I were you, I wouldn't go off and leave an experiment like that."

"What experiment?" The burning smell was stronger now, and all his instincts were on the alert.

"In the hood. I couldn't tell what you were doing—you didn't leave your lab notebook out—but I would think—"

"I wasn't working on anything," he said, whirling around and starting toward the hood, just as smoke began pouring out. It was thick, oily and green, accompanied by a noxious odor.

"Where's the fire extinguisher?" Suzanna Molloy shouted through the fumes. Within seconds, they began to engulf her figure and the room itself.

"Get the hell out of here!" he said, slamming the hood down over the bubbling, roiling mass.

"Where's the fire extinguisher?" she shouted again.

There was no way he could stop the heavy fumes from escaping, no way he could even begin to guess what concoction had been brewed on his bench during his absence. All he could do was get out of there and take Suzanna Molloy with him.

He could barely find her through the swirling darkness. Her body was warm, strong, solid when he bumped up against her, and though she struggled for a moment, he was a great deal stronger than she was, and he simply dragged her over to the door. Only to find it inexplicably locked.

The only other exit to the lab was dangerously near the hood. He heard a sudden roaring sound. "Get down," he shouted, shoving her.

She had the gall to slap him, something he could almost admire, but he shoved her down on the floor, anyway, covering her with his larger body, shielding her, as the force of the explosion rocked the room, shattering the windows and showering them with broken glass and something warm and fetid. For a moment he absorbed the feel of her body beneath him. And then the hot gluey substance began to leak through his clothes, burning his flesh, and he let out a muffled howl of pain.

SUZANNA WAS FLOATING. It was dark, hot and choking, the stink all around her, yet somehow she was safe. His body was pressed down on hers, covering hers, and he was strong, large, keeping her from the evil that surrounded them. She could feel something hot and wet begin to ooze through her clothing, through the jeans and the lab coat, small patches of burning fire, but she couldn't move to brush it away. Crompton was pinning her down.

She put her arms up, to push him away, then drew them back in horror when she realized they were covered with a greenish slime. He was moaning quietly, and through the greasy smoke and darkness she could see that his eyes were closed. He had a cut on his forehead, probably from the flying glass, and blood was pouring down the side of his face.

Distantly she became aware of other things. The brightness of the emergency lights filling the darkness, the sounds of alarms echoing through the complex, the pounding on the locked door. Their bodies were blocking it, and Crompton was too big for her to move, too big for her to crawl out from under him.

She reached up and caught his shoulders, grimacing at the slime that coated her fingers. "Dr. Crompton," she shouted, but her voice came out hoarse and strained from the smoke. "Daniel." She shook him.

He opened his eyes and stared down at her. He looked dazed, almost innocent, and she was suddenly very much aware that he was a man, an attractive man, even bleeding and covered in green slime. Then his eyes focused, his mouth curled in disgust, and he scrambled off her, staggering slightly.

And then he reached down and hauled her to her feet, out of the way, just as the door slammed open.

A moment later they stumbled out into the hallway, assaulted by noise, by voices. Hands were touching her, poking at her, trying to make her lie down, but she wasn't about to lie anywhere, not with all these people milling around, shouting at her. She'd be trampled. She searched through the crowds for Crompton, and for a moment she couldn't spot him. Then she saw him, towering over the others, swaying slightly, his lab coat coated with the same green slime that was burning her skin.

She slapped the restraining hands away and started toward him, through the crowds of people, coming up behind him just as he caught a young man by the lapels of his spotless lab coat and slammed him against the wall. "Jackson," he said, his voice raw with smoke and fury. "What the hell did you do to my lab?"

The man caught in his grip was white-faced with terror

and babbling something incoherent. Crompton bounced him off the wall again, and the man collapsed in what appeared to be a faint, just as Suzanna reached him.

"Leave him alone," she said hoarsely. "You've been burned."

He turned to glare down at her, the blood oozing down his face. With his smoke-streaked face, his long hair, the absolute rage in his expression, he looked more like a pirate than a research scientist. "I'm not absolving you," he snarled. "You probably helped set this up, and then it backfired on you. You're in it with them, and it was a damned lucky thing you weren't killed."

"You're crazy," she gasped, rubbing her slime-coated hands down her legs, trying to get some of the burning ooze off her skin.

"Am I?" He reached out for her. His hands were coated with the stuff, as well, and for some reason she thought of old science-fiction movies, and bad colds, and all sorts of other disgusting notions.

She didn't know what he was going to do to her, not with all those witnesses surrounding them. Daniel Crompton didn't seem the type who gave a damn about witnesses, and he was in a truly towering rage. She stared up at him, trying to look pugnacious and failing entirely, as his hands caught her shoulders. Surprisingly enough, they were gentle, not painful.

"Who sent you here?" he demanded. "What were you doing in my lab?" He gave her a small, impatient shake, enough to rattle her already impaired equilibrium. "Are you going to answer my questions?" he demanded, ignoring the BBCSI employees that crowded around him and the paramedics who'd arrived on the scene.

She looked up at him, into his dark, brooding eyes, and that dreamy, spacey place danced over her once more. "Eventually," she murmured. And felt herself begin to slide into a graceful faint.

Chapter Two

Daniel caught her as she fell. His lab was now an inferno, the flames belching forth from the broken door, and he realized if Suzanna Molloy hadn't distracted him, he would be a dead man right now. And he wondered why.

The paramedics took her away from him, and he let her go, noticing at the time that he didn't want to. He filed that unlikely reaction in the back of his brain, to be considered later, as he reluctantly allowed himself to be bundled onto a stretcher. While he had every intention of walking out of the building, of driving himself to the hospital if and when he deemed it necessary, the strength in his legs seemed to give way, and his entire back was burning and throbbing from the green goop that had covered him. Out of the corner of his eye he saw Osborn leaning over Jackson's collapsed form, and there was no mistaking the air of collusion between the two men. Daniel added that to his mental file. He was about to lift his head to look more closely, when he felt the prick of a needle in his arm, too late for him to protest. With one last glance at Suzanna Molloy's unconscious figure on the adjoining gurney, he closed his eyes and went to sleep.

He'd spent some time in pre-med, when he wasn't busy with his other studies. As he lay facedown in the emergency room, while a group of physicians dealt with his back, he decided he was well to be out of that branch of science. For one thing, he didn't seem to have the requisite sadism. They were scrubbing the skin on his back with what felt like steel wool and talking about sports, for God's sake! They assumed he was still knocked out from whatever they'd pumped in his arm, but he had always been resistant to drugs, and he'd regained consciousness just as some helpful female had stripped off what remained of his pants.

"He doesn't look in such bad shape," a female voice observed, while someone took what felt like a razor to his shoulder blades. He didn't move.

"Actually he looks quite luscious," another female said. "What happened to him?"

"Lab explosion," a male voice, the one interested in football, chimed in. "He's in worse shape than the patient in L-4. She only got the stuff on her hands. What do you suppose this junk is?"

"Slime," a woman said with heartless cheer. "Don't you think we ought to turn him over and see if his front's affected?"

"Get your mind out of the gutter, Sophie. His front's just fine, and it's nothing you haven't seen before." More scrubbing along his backbone, the feel of it like raw coals being dug into his skin. He didn't even quiver, interested to hear how this conversation was going to continue.

"Oh, I don't know. He's pretty cute. Lab explosion, did you say? Does that mean he's going to turn into the Incredible Hulk every time he gets angry?" Sophie asked.

"Very funny. We're almost finished with him. Why don't you check his pupils while I see about getting him upstairs for observation?"

He felt her walk around him. Her hands were cool on his face. She started to pull open his eyelid, and he glared at her. "Get your rubber-gloved hands off me, woman," he snapped.

She jumped back with a startled shriek. She was just the

kind of woman he usually found attractive—blond and pretty and stupid. He wondered how Suzanna Molloy was faring.

"You're awake," she said needlessly.

A white-coated doctor pushed Sophie out of the way, trying to look efficient, as if he hadn't been obsessed with football a few moments ago. "That dose of morphine must have worn off too quickly. Are you in much pain?"

"Not when you keep your hands off me," he snarled. "Where are my clothes?"

"Er—we had to cut them off you. Someone from Beebe Systems was going to see about getting you some new ones. You won't be needing them for a while. We're admitting you for observation."

"The hell you are."

"Dr. Crompton, you've been through quite an ordeal. We need to make sure you've suffered no head trauma, that the goop on your skin won't cause a reaction. We need—"

"I need my clothes. If someone doesn't provide me some within the next two hours, I'm walking out of this place naked."

The doctor looked at him warily, trying for a cheerful smile, only to have it fade again. "You're kidding."

"You can't keep me here against my will, and you know it as well as I do."

"It's my professional opinion—"

"I don't give squat about your professional opinion. Two hours." He lay back down again and closed his eyes. Damn them and their drugs! As if his body hadn't been through enough, he still had to fight off the effects of the narcotic they'd pumped through his system. "Get me Osborn," he said.

"I'm not sure if Mr. Osborn is still at the hospital."

"He's here," Daniel said grimly. "Tell him he's got five minutes."

He was there in less than three, and he didn't come alone.

Daniel didn't bother to lift his head, but he knew that Osborn had at least two people in tow. Doubtless General Armstead, and either Jackson or maybe one of the Green Beret types that mysteriously wandered the halls at Beebe. He didn't care—he was too busy concentrating on the strange feelings that were sweeping over his body. Not unpleasant, they seemed to be seeping through his abraded back, sending little electrical charges through the surface of his skin.

"How are you doing, Dan?" Osborn's hearty voice boomed. "You gave us quite a scare."

Daniel considered his options for a brief, satisfying moment. One of those included throttling Osborn, a sorely tempting fantasy but one which, in the end, would avail him nothing. He'd never been a man who was prey to his emotions, and he wasn't about to become one now.

"What happened?" he asked in a deceptively neutral voice, opening his eyes. He'd been right. Retired General Jack Armstead stood a few feet away, his bulldog face creased into a look of concern, one that was belied by the alert, dangerous expression in his colorless eyes. The Green Beret type was a man named Cole Slaughter, and he didn't look any friendlier. Daniel wondered idly what happened to Jackson.

"One of your experiments must have gone awry," Osborn was saying. "Unlike you, of course, but you must have forgotten what you were doing. Jackson said he smelled something burning. If he hadn't alerted security, we might not have been able to get you out in time."

"Ah, yes, Jackson. A useful man," Daniel murmured, not bothering to deny Osborn's convenient theory. "Where is he?"

Daniel wasn't a sensitive man, but he was an observant one, and even in his current state he recognized the quick shift of communication between Armstead and Osborn. He filed it away for later examination.

"Slaughter drove him home," Armstead said. "He was pretty shaken up this afternoon after you attacked him."

Daniel didn't bother to deny it. "How is Ms. Molloy?"

"The woman who was with you? No one knew who she was—she didn't have any identification on her, apart from a Beebe tag, and that was phony. What'd you say her name was?"

"Suzanna Molloy."

Henry Osborn swore with more emotion than he'd shown since Daniel's lab had blown apart. "The reporter? What the hell was she doing there?"

"What's going on here, Osborn?" Armstead demanded. "Your security sucks. I'll have that woman arrested for trespassing."

"No, you won't." Daniel levered himself up to look at his three visitors. "She was there at my invitation." He wasn't quite sure why he lied—it merely seemed the next logical step.

"You invited her?" Osborn said. "But why? We don't want the press involved in our work. She's too nosy as it is. How do you know she didn't set the explosion?"

"Was it set?" Daniel asked pleasantly.

Osborn recovered quickly. "Damned if I know. Industrial sabotage isn't unheard of, and you're not the type to make careless mistakes."

"No," said Daniel. "I'm not."

"We'll have the security staff question her as soon as she regains consciousness," Armstead announced. "Slaughter, see to it. I want answers."

"You'll leave her alone," Daniel said evenly.

"Daniel, be reasonable," Osborn pleaded.

"I always am. Ms. Molloy is a friend of mine. An intimate friend of mine. She was there to spend time with me, and for no other reason." It was a flat-out lie, but for the time being his only defense against Osborn's trickiness was to lie, and sex was the one thing the man would find believable.

"Do you think it's wise to sleep with someone in her position?" Osborn asked with great disapproval.

"It depends which position she's in."

They didn't even crack a smile. "This isn't like you, Daniel," Osborn said.

Crompton considered it as the door swung silently shut behind the three men. No, it wasn't like him at all. And he was feeling oddly playful for a man who'd just survived a murder attempt.

He had no doubt whatsoever that that was what it had been. He wouldn't have left a volatile compound simmering if the pope had summoned him. He'd had his share of lab explosions in the past—what research scientist hadn't?—but what he was currently working on involved nothing more dangerous than potential eyestrain and carpal tunnel syndrome. He'd been glued to his computer for months now, checking and rechecking. The only work he'd done under the hood had been to keep the legion of spies off the scent.

He sat up gingerly, staring around him at the sterile examining room, flexing his sore muscles. Maybe it was something as elemental as surviving death that was making him feel so unnaturally energetic. The sense of well-being was thrumming through him. God, he almost felt like smiling.

First off, he needed to find Molloy, to see what kind of shape she was in. Now that he'd identified her, he didn't trust Armstead and his goons not to harass her. Besides, even though he'd taken the brunt of the explosion and the green slime, apparently she was still unconscious. He wanted to see what she felt like when she woke up. Would she have the same sense of well-being? The same tingling, burning sensation in her skin?

And he wanted to see if she still had the same inexplicable effect on him, a combination of fury and attraction. No one was going to stop him from finding out.

AT LEAST THE ROOM was relatively dark. Suzanna could hear the sounds of the hospital behind the curtained alcove, the quiet hush of rubber-soled shoes on polished vinyl floors, the hiss and thump of medical equipment, the muffled murmur of voices. She'd been awake for a while, alone in this anonymous room, but no one had come to check on her.

Just as well. She felt odd, disoriented, and she wanted time to herself, to consider what had happened to her.

She'd fainted, like some damned Victorian heroine. She'd collapsed gracefully in Daniel Crompton's arms, and it wouldn't have surprised her if he'd dropped her on the ground. The man was not equipped with the most advanced set of social graces.

But she didn't think he had. She could still remember him holding her, she could still feel that strange, wrenching sensation, when they'd taken her away from him. He hadn't wanted to let her go.

Now where did that absurd thought come from? If Crompton hadn't wanted to let her go, it was because he'd wanted to shake the truth out of her. Hadn't he practically accused her of sabotaging his lab? Brilliant the man might be, but when it came to common sense he seemed to be lacking. If she'd set him up, she wouldn't have waited around, arguing with him. She would have gotten the hell out of there.

Her hands were burning. She glanced down at them. They looked the same—strong, long-fingered, with no jewelry. She'd seen those hands all her life, and yet suddenly they looked different to her.

The door opened silently, and a shadowy form stepped into the dimly lit room. She recognized that shape, even before he stepped into the light, and she let out a sigh of relief.

"Uncle Vinnie," she whispered, holding out her hands to him.

He advanced into the room, a short, squat figure, no more than five feet three inches tall and almost as round, wearing a suit that probably cost more than the entire contents of Suzanna's closet. It didn't help. His thinning gray hair was pasted across his scalp, and his own rings made up for Suzanna's lack of jewelry.

"I blame myself," he said morosely, taking her hands in his.

"Don't be ridiculous, Uncle Vinnie," she protested, ignoring the pain his grip caused her. "You gave me a tip. I followed up on it. It just goes to show you were right— there is something funny going on at Beebe."

"You might have been killed," he protested, releasing one hand and heaving his bulk into a seat beside the bed.

Suzanna managed a wry smile. "Only the good die young."

"Don't be ridiculous, *cara*. You may be able to fool the others, but you've never been able to fool your Uncle Vinnie."

"You're not my Uncle Vinnie," she pointed out. "You're Francesca's Uncle Vinnie, and I've told you a hundred times I really don't need you to watch out for me."

Vinnie waved a plump hand, dismissing her protests. "You let me be the judge of that. A young girl like you, on your own in a man's world…"

"I'm not that young. Twenty-seven," she pointed out.

"You're young for your age. Now my Francesca, she marrried right out of that high-priced college the two of you attended, and she's got her husband and her husband's family to look out for her. I'm a lonely old man with too much time on my hands. I need someone to fuss over, you know that as well as I do."

"Uncle Vinnie," she said gently, "you are neither old, nor lonely, and you certainly don't have too much time on your hands. I don't understand why you persist in thinking I need watching over."

"I promised Francesca. Besides, since I've retired, I need something to keep me busy."

"You haven't retired, Uncle Vinnie," Suzanna said.

"I haven't been down to the restaurant in more than a month," he protested.

"You may have retired from the restaurant business, but you haven't retired from your career. Let's face it, Uncle Vinnie, you're a crook."

"I'm a businessman," he corrected, not the slightest bit offended. "My friends and I, we have investments—"

"Rackets," Suzanna supplied.

"And we look after our own."

"I'm not your own, Uncle Vinnie."

"Once you became Francesca's best friend and college roommate, you became family. And nothing's going to change that. You won't let me help you, but at least you'll let me warn you. And what do you do? Instead of keeping away from danger, you walk right into it with open arms."

Suzanna managed a tired grin. "I'm hopeless."

"I don't like what's going on at Beebe, Suzanna. Even with my connections, I can't find who's behind the organization, but it doesn't look good. You need to keep away from them."

"At least I don't need to worry about BBCSI being run by organized crime," she said.

"Very funny," he said stiffly. "There are worse things than our little fraternal organization. You're out of your league, there, Suzanna. Leave it to the experts."

"I don't even know what it is I'd be leaving."

"It's big," Vinnie said.

"I imagine so, considering the way people are reacting. Someone tried to kill Dr. Crompton today."

Vinnie's pouchy eyes narrowed. "You're sure of that?"

"Reasonably sure. They almost sent me with him."

Uncle Vinnie muttered something in Italian he assumed Suzanna was too innocent to understand. Fortunately Francesca had taught her every dirty word she knew, and the force of that expletive did more to convince Suzanna how desperate things were than anything since the lab had first exploded. "So it's gone that far already," he muttered, half to himself. "And now everyone knows it."

"Everyone knows what?"

"That whatever he was working on, he's succeeded. No one would risk that man's life if he hadn't come up with something worth vastly more. You know what his reputation is, don't you? America's secret weapon? And if they're ready to sacrifice him, rather than let him cause trouble, then he must have come up with an even more effective weapon."

"Weapon?" Suzanna echoed, shocked. "You think he was working on some kind of weapon?"

"Everything nowadays can be used as a weapon. If he was working for the good of mankind, do you think someone would have tried to blow up his lab, with him in it? No, Suzanna," he said sadly. "What about a little trip? Have you ever been to Venice?"

"I'm not going anywhere."

"It's not just up to me. I'll protect you if I can, but even I have bosses. People to answer to, and they're all far too interested in what's going on at Beebe. I can't be sure I can keep you safe. The stakes are too high."

"And exactly what are the stakes?"

Uncle Vinnie shook his head slowly. "I don't even want to guess. My people will look out for you, *cara*. To the best of their ability. But if you have any sense at all, you'll stay as far away from Dr. Crompton as you can. The man's living on borrowed time. Whatever he's discovered has already fallen into the wrong hands, and he's too knowledgeable, too dangerous, to let live.''

''Wouldn't that be killing the goose that laid the golden egg?'' she argued.

''Not when they've got the formula for making those golden eggs. Who needs a goose that you have to feed and take care of?'' Uncle Vinnie said philosophically. ''What about Paris?''

''I'm not going anywhere.''

Uncle Vinnie just looked at her. ''I'll put the word out. No one will touch you. But you keep away from Dr. Crompton. I don't want any accidents. If and when he gets his, I don't want you within range. Do you understand?''

''Vinnie...''

But he'd already moved toward the door, silent despite his bulk. ''Watch your back, *cara*. And keep away from that man.''

He was gone before she could utter another protest, and she leaned back against the pillow, letting out her pent-up breath. Ever since Uncle Vinnie had come into her life almost ten years ago, he'd been mysterious and beneficent, a wise, almost comical figure, there when she needed a shoulder to cry on, an ear to listen to her problems. It had taken all her determination to keep him from pulling strings for her. If it had been up to Vinnie, she'd probably be managing editor at the *Washington Post* by this time.

But she'd made it brutally clear that what she had in this life she intended to earn. She'd had too easy a life. She was the only child of doting parents with too much money. When they'd died while she was still in college, all Uncle Vinnie's protective instincts had come into play, but Suzanna needed to fend for herself. After twenty years of having things handed to her, she was suddenly out on her own, and she'd been determined to make her own way, without Vinnie pulling strings. She'd accepted his friendship, and even the occasional tip, but she wasn't about to let him tender any offers on her behalf that people couldn't refuse.

Keep away from Dr. Crompton, he'd said, and she'd be wise to listen when a man like Uncle Vinnie spoke. If Vinnie said Crompton was a doomed man, then it was highly unlikely Suzanna could do anything to save him, and she wasn't quite sure she wanted to. The man was overbearing, unpleasant and too damned smart for his own good. He was just the kind of man she found most irritating, and she preferred thinking of him as the enemy.

Unfortunately, it wasn't going to be that clear-cut. Somebody else saw Daniel Crompton as the enemy, someone who used noxious fumes and sneak attacks and who didn't care if someone besides Crompton got killed, as well.

Suzanna had the choice of siding with Crompton or siding with the forces of darkness, which meant she didn't really have much choice at all.

Of course, Vinnie had meant for her to steer clear of the whole thing. But she couldn't. Not with an organization like Beebe Control Systems International in her backyard, one shrouded in secrecy and security worthy of national defense. Crompton might work for them, but she wouldn't put it past them to be behind that lab explosion.

Maybe it wasn't a murder attempt. Maybe it was just a warning. But a warning against what? And how in heaven's name was she going to find out exactly what he was working on?

The lab was trashed now. She hadn't found anything of interest in the few minutes she'd had before Crompton's precipitous return, but she suspected he didn't keep his most important work there. Whoever bombed the place wouldn't have dared risk destroying it.

His home was the obvious place to check. She needed to get out of this hospital and go check out the place. He had to be in worse shape than she was—he'd been covered with that revolting green slime that had burned her hands.

He'd be in the hospital for days, but if she didn't get moving soon, someone would get to his home before she did.

She swung her legs over the side of the bed. She was wearing one of those damnable hospital nightgowns. It was slit up the back and chilling her spine, and the bathrobe looked as if it were made out of ancient dish towels. Nothing, however, compared with the foam-rubber slippers. Suzanna wondered whether she could fashion a sari out of the sheet.

She wasn't alone. There'd been no sound, not even a whisper of noise, but the air around her shifted, and she looked up, staring at the tall figure in the doorway.

Another damned doctor, she thought wearily. This one in hospital greens, as if he'd just come from the operating room, or was about to return to it.

"Go away," she said flatly. "I've been poked and prodded enough. You're not doing any more tests."

He moved forward, into the pool of light, and she had an unpleasant shock as she looked up into Daniel Crompton's dark, cool eyes. She realized that those eyes were traveling up her long, bare legs with far too much leisurely interest. And that the feel of his eyes on her skin burned almost as much as the green slime had.

"What are you doing here?" she demanded, wishing her voice didn't sound slightly husky.

"They said you were unconscious."

"I'm not."

"No, more's the pity. Are you always this pleasant?"

"About the same as you," she replied tartly.

He ignored her taunt, moving across the room so silently it took her a moment to realize his feet were bare. The sight of his long, narrow feet was so startling that she didn't realize he'd picked up her hand in his and was busy taking her pulse. He began tapping her wrist.

She tried to yank away, but his fingers tightened. "I just want to test your reflexes," he said in an irritated voice.

"'Trust me, I'm a doctor'?" she murmured. "My reflexes have been checked plenty, and they're just fine, thank you. How are yours?"

"Fast."

"Jolly."

"Too fast," he said enigmatically, still holding her hand. She only wished she didn't find an odd sort of comfort in it. "How do you feel?"

"Like a wall fell on me."

"That was me."

She felt a moment's compunction. "I didn't thank you for saving my life."

He shrugged. "I'm not sure I did. Have you had any visitors?"

Suzanna thought of Uncle Vinnie and was glad she never blushed when she lied. "No. Were you expecting anyone?"

"If a man named Osborn tries to talk to you, refuse to see him. The same goes for Armstead, and just about anyone else."

Curiouser and curiouser, Suzanna thought, staring up at the man. "Isn't Osborn your boss? The president of Beebe?"

"He wants to know what you were doing in my lab at the time of the explosion. He doesn't trust you, Ms. Molloy. He thinks you might have rigged the explosion."

"And what do you think, Dr. Crompton?"

He reached out and put his hand along the side of her neck, his fingers long and cool and deft against her heated skin. "I think your pulse is racing, Ms. Molloy. I think you need a good long rest, with no visitors."

It was no wonder her pulse was racing, she thought irritably. Daniel Crompton was a vastly irritating man—he was enough to stir anybody's blood.

"What about you?" she asked abruptly.

"I'm getting out of here. But if I were you, Molloy, I'd stay put. At least here you're relatively safe."

"Why wouldn't I be safe?"

He shrugged, an abrupt, oddly appealing gesture. "I don't know. But it might be wiser not to ask anyone."

A moment later he was gone, and she was alone once more in her hospital room, using the very curses Uncle Vinnie had as she stared at the closed door in frustration.

Chapter Three

Daniel wondered why his feet weren't cold. He tended to be oblivious to physical discomfort, but right now he was intensely aware of every minuscule reaction his body was going through, and walking barefoot down a sidewalk at half past five o'clock on a late spring morning in northern California should have been downright chilly. Particularly since he was wearing nothing but the loose green scrub suit he'd stolen from a locker at the hospital.

It wasn't particularly warm outside—he knew that. His instincts told him it was hovering around fifty, and yet he felt entirely comfortable, almost hot. His skin no longer burned, but it tingled, pleasantly enough, and he felt an odd tickle between his eyes.

His arms were hanging loosely by his sides as he moved along, and he contented himself with twitching his nose a couple of times as he stared absently at an old VW bug parked on a side street.

The VW burst into flames.

The fireball of heat threw him back against a building, and he stayed there, dazed, uncomprehending. It usually took a great deal to surprise him, but the explosion left him in a state of shock, and it took him a moment or two to steady himself, glance around to see whether someone had lobbed a grenade, or a mortar, or whatever it was people used to blow up things.

The streets were deserted. Lights were coming on in the buildings surrounding him, but there was no sign of anyone around. In the distance he could hear the faint wail of a fire alarm, and decided it was time to make himself scarce.

He ducked down a back alleyway, disappearing into the night. He wasn't in the mood to listen to questions, particularly when he hadn't the faintest idea what the answers were. While he'd never been one to let the stresses of ordinary living get to him, the last twenty-four hours had been enough to rattle the most phlegmatic of men. He'd had his lab invaded, he'd been sabotaged, poked, prodded, and now it seemed as if someone had set off a bomb just as he was walking by, and he could hardly count that a coincidence. To top it all off, he felt strange, restless, edgy and in a towering bad mood.

He moved through the early-morning light swiftly, away from the devastation of the burning automobile, trying to shake the sense of uneasiness that was plaguing him. He lived as anonymously as possible, in a box of a condominium in a box of a building, and by the time he neared his neighborhood he was running, at the comfortable loping jog he'd perfected. It was getting lighter by the minute, it was now close to 6:00 a.m., and he wondered whether the hospital or Beebe had anyone out looking for him.

The enclave of bland, architecturally atrocious buildings came equipped with a security guard and gate, something he'd never thought much about in the past. In his current position, he wasn't in the mood to talk to anyone, answer questions or even have to put up with someone looking at him strangely. All he wanted was to get back to his apartment, lock the door behind him, lie down on his futon and clear his mind. Until he could come up with a reason why someone would want to kill him.

He decided to wait until six, hoping against hope that

the guard's shift might end, and he could slip through when he wasn't looking. He still had his watch, a fact which surprised him, and he stared at it, willing it to move to six.

When it did, he almost wished it hadn't. The prickling sensation that had been nagging at him suddenly washed over his body full force, and a blinding pain shot through his head, so fierce he thought of the VW and wondered whether his own brain was going to explode. His stomach cramped, and he sank to his knees on the pavement, no longer caring that the guard was going to see him. The man would probably call the police, or at least an ambulance, and Crompton would be back where he started, his escape for nothing.

Slowly, slowly, the pain began to abate. The rush that spread over his body settled into an edgy kind of heat, and he managed to lift his head, expecting to meet the security guard's curious gaze. Or perhaps even his gun.

The security guard was standing in his little box, guarding the gate. He was smoking a cigarette, glancing idly in the direction of Daniel's hunched-over figure with all the interest of a toad.

Daniel staggered to his feet, both relieved and incensed. Not that he wanted the man to pay attention to him, but he might at least have shown some concern for the security of the building. Not to mention the welfare of one of its tenants.

He advanced on the man, angry enough to brazen it out, only to come up short. The security guard had his name, which was Doyle, emblazoned across his pocket. And Doyle was looking straight through him as if he wasn't even there.

The hell with him, Crompton thought, circling the security gate and striding past the oblivious guard, fully determined to ignore any belated questions or calls to stop.

There was no abrupt shout or even a tentative question

as Daniel reached the door of his anonymous building. The guard didn't seem to realize he existed.

It wasn't until that moment that Daniel realized his keys were somewhere back at the hospital, along with his slime-splattered clothes, his wallet and his shoes. "Hell and damnation," he muttered, wheeling around, prepared to go to the oblivious Doyle and demand that he open the door for him.

Doyle was no longer oblivious. He looked like a bloodhound who'd scented a juicy pheasant on the wind. Alert, head cocked, listening, he stared just over Daniel's head.

Was the man blind, or drunk, or just abysmally stupid? Daniel neither knew nor cared, he simply wanted to get up to his apartment, get out of his stolen scrub suit and take a shower, to wash the hot, prickling feeling from his skin.

The door opened, and an early-morning jogger stepped out into the cool air. Daniel grabbed the door before it could swing shut again, muttered a terse thanks and disappeared into the building.

His fourth-floor apartment was an easier matter, since he was smart enough to leave a key under a loose section of the carpeting in the hallway. Within moments he was safe inside, the door locked behind him.

He was oddly breathless, shaken, and his brain was awash with a thousand anomalies, too many things that made no sense, particularly to his own orderly mind. The way that car had burst into flames. The guard's oblivion. The brief flash of shock on the jogger's face when Daniel had brushed past him.

Not to mention the odd, fuzzy look of his hand as he'd opened his front door.

He stared down at his body and knew something had to be wrong with his vision. He looked foggy and slightly out of focus but when he raised his head, the apartment was clear and precise. It was only his body that seemed blurred.

He rubbed a hand across his eyes, but it didn't help. The

morning light was filling the ascetic confines of his apartment, but he didn't bother closing the curtains. They might
be looking for him, and his home was the logical place to
try to find him. Since Doyle and the jogger had been too
sleepy or hung over to notice his return, he might be able
to remain in hiding for at least the few hours he needed for
a shower and a nap.

The hot water spat like tiny needles onto his skin, but
he was inured to the discomfort. He stood in the shower
for what seemed like hours, trying to wash away that odd,
heated sensitivity that covered him, but it was useless.
Turning off the water, he stepped out into his steamed-up
bathroom, grabbing a towel and wrapping it around his
damp body. Maybe a shave would wake him up.

His bathroom mirror was completely fogged. He reached
out and rubbed the condensation from its surface. And then
he rubbed again.

There was no reflection whatsoever in the mirror, not
even the towel that was wrapped around his torso.

There'd been a phrase he'd read long ago, in some melodramatic novel. Something about one's blood running
cold. Suddenly he knew exactly what that phrase meant.

He slammed open the bathroom door, heading for the
bedroom and the mirror over his dresser.

Nothing. He could see the plain, white-covered bed behind him, the unadorned white walls, the pile of books on
the nightstand. But he couldn't see his own, slightly out of
focus, shower-damp body at all.

"Oh, no," he murmured, utterly fascinated. "I'm invisible."

SUZANNA CONSIDERED following him. Daniel Crompton
had simply disappeared from her hospital room like a
wraith, and if she'd had just the slightest bit more energy,
not to mention a slightly more modest outfit, she would
have climbed out of that hospital bed and gone after him.

As it was, her feet barely touched the floor before she sank back, groaning. Her head throbbed, her skin tingled, and her temper was not the sweetest.

Nor was it improved by the sound of voices breaking the early-morning hush of the hospital corridors.

"I'm afraid I must insist, nurse," the man said. "There's been a serious breach of security at Beebe, and a question of sabotage. If you won't let me question Ms. Molloy then I'm afraid I'm going to have to take action."

"You can question her all you want," came the tart reply, "during visiting hours, and if her doctor gives permission and she's willing. Until then, Mr. Osborn, you'd better leave."

There was a moment of silence. And the unmistakable sound of crinkling paper that was undoubtedly green. "Five minutes," the nurse said, her shoes squeaking as she made her retreat.

By the time the door opened, Suzanna was lying in perfect stillness, her eyes shut, her breathing shallow, not a flicker betraying her awareness. She would have liked to steal just a tiny glance at this Mr. Osborn who was so determined to get his own way. He was one of the people Crompton had warned her about. An odd thought, an SOB like Crompton looking out for her. It could almost make her smile.

"Are you awake, Ms. Molloy?"

Suzanna didn't move.

"They told me you'd regained consciousness several hours ago, and no one mentioned giving you any additional drugs to help you sleep. Open your eyes, Ms. Molloy. I have no intention of leaving until I talk with you."

Suzanna managed a faint, very believable snore.

To her dismay she heard Osborn seat himself in the plastic chair beside her hospital bed. "If you prefer, we'll play it that way," he said. "Allow me to introduce myself. I'm Henry Osborn, CEO of Beebe Control Systems. I imagine a clever girl like you already knew that. What you might not know is that I can be a very dangerous man to cross, or a very helpful man, if I'm feeling generous. You've been a boil on our behind for the last six months with your incessant questions, but we've been forbearing, believing in the right of a free press.''

Osborn was the kind of man who believed in total control of the press, but Suzanna managed to keep from voicing that opinion.

''I want to know what you saw in Dr. Crompton's lab before the unfortunate accident. Your help in this matter could be invaluable, and we're known to reward those who help us.''

It was no accident, Suzanna thought, and you know it. She let out another gentle little snore, wondering whether she was overdoing it.

''On the other hand,'' Osborn continued smoothly, ignoring her act, ''you were trespassing on private property. You had a phony ID tag, and we haven't ruled out the possibility of industrial sabotage. We could push it as far as attempted murder, Ms. Molloy, and you're our obvious suspect. I don't believe what Crompton told me about you for one moment.''

He was good, Suzanna had to admit it. She was dying to know what Crompton had told him. It took all her formidable willpower to keep from reacting.

He rose, and she could feel him move toward her. ''We'll be watching you, Ms. Molloy,'' he said softly. ''If we can't get to you here, we'll wait till you leave. Sooner or later you're going to tell us what you know. What you saw.'' And she felt his hand on her breast, squeezing it painfully thruogh the layers of hospital cotton.

She couldn't control her start of pain, but she played it through, opening her eyes for a deliberately dazed moment, then shuttering them again, uttering no more than a plaintive moan before she ostensibly drifted off again.

"I could almost believe you, Ms. Molloy," the nasty little sadist murmured. "If I were just a little more gullible. I'll be back."

Suzanna almost snorted. She couldn't imagine anyone less like the Terminator than the brief glimpse she'd had of elegant, white-haired Henry Osborn. Except that he might be just as merciless.

The door closed with a sigh, but Suzanna didn't move. She held still, waiting until she was certain he was truly gone. Uncle Vinnie had been right, but then, she'd never had cause to doubt him in the first place. There was something extremely nasty going on at Beebe Control Systems, and while sabotage doubtless had something to do with it, she put her money on the deceptively charming gentleman who'd just mauled her breast. If only she knew what Crompton had told him!

Doubtless nothing flattering. But it hadn't been the truth, either, or Osborn wouldn't have hesitated in having her arrested for suspected sabotage, as he'd threatened to do. Obviously Osborn had his secrets, and he wanted to know exactly which ones of those Suzanna had been privy to.

She let her eyes drift open, still keeping her breathing regulated. The room was empty, the early-morning light sending strange shadows against the pale green walls. It was just after six, and in the far distance she could hear the wailing sounds of a fire siren.

She sat up, moving quietly, and slid from the bed. One thing was certain: she wasn't going to stay there and wait until Osborn could summon his goons to watch over her. Assuming he had goons to summon. She needed to get out of this place, and she needed to find out what was really going on with Daniel Crompton. She'd almost been killed, just because she was in the wrong place at the wrong time, and her breast still throbbed from Osborn's nasty grope. She wanted to know what Crompton had told him, she wanted to know what the man was working on, and she wanted to know whether either of them was still in danger.

And there was only one way to find out.

She had to ask him. No, scratch that—she had to sit the man down and force him to tell her what was going on. Exactly how she planned to do that was still a mystery, but she'd always relied on her ability to improvise when things got a little complicated. First things first.

At least they'd brought her clothes back, a little the worse for wear, her ratty running shoes still usable. The great Dr. Daniel Crompton might have no qualms about going out barefoot in stolen hospital garb, but Suzanna was a little more discreet.

Her borrowed lab coat had taken the brunt of the slime assault. Suzanna dressed quickly, grateful that apart from the tingling in her hands and an odd heat at the back of her eyes, she seemed to be in fairly good shape. As a matter of fact, the worst of her discomfort still came from where Osborn had mauled her. Interesting.

The corridors were coming to life as she stepped out of her room, but she'd already learned that the best way to get away with something was to look as if you knew what you were doing. She strode down the hallway quite purposefully, not dodging when she passed an orderly's curious gaze, and a moment later ducked down a deserted stairwell. She was free.

If she'd had any sense at all, she would have headed straight home, barricaded herself inside her second-floor apartment, put something cool and jazzy on the stereo and gone to sleep.

But she didn't feel particularly sensible. The old Victorian house she lived in was more than a mile away, on the far side of town, her car was presumably still at Beebe, and she knew for a fact that Dr. Daniel Crompton's apartment was much closer—only a brief walk away.

He might not be there, of course. But if she'd gotten into

a place with security as tight as BBCSI, then she had little doubt she could get into his apartment. There was no way she was going to rest until she got some answers.

DANIEL WAS ENJOYING himself immensely, not in the slightest bit disturbed about his new body. He could feel himself, see himself, albeit slightly out of focus. If he dropped the towel on a surface in front of the mirror he could see that, as well. If he picked it up again it seemed to float in midair. If he draped it around him, it disappeared.

It made no earthly sense, in terms of physics or any known science. He tried it with various other items. Any piece of clothing he held would still be corporeal, but once he put it on it vanished. He wandered through his apartment, wearing only a pair of old jeans that he usually preferred not to be seen in. At least this time he wouldn't have to worry, he thought with dark humor.

Once he put food in his mouth, it disappeared, and he swallowed half a quart of his special multivitamin energy drink that usually sufficed instead of regular food, washing it down with at least a gallon of coffee. He turned on the news, something he seldom bothered wtih, but the brief story about the explosion at Beebe was the company line. He stared at Henry Osborn's cool, concerned face and muttered an expletive.

Which reminded him. If people couldn't see him, and that doubtless explained why the guard and the jogger seemed to be ignoring him, would they be able to hear him?

All in the nature of scientific experiment, he dialed Henry Osborn's unlisted number. His ruthlessly elegant, ruthlessly slim wife, Doris, answered the phone. He'd never liked her, either the insufferably smug way she moved through the few social functions he'd been forced to attend, or the way she'd delicately, unmistakably come on to him on one of those same occasions, letting her slender, bejeweled hand rest high up on his thigh. She was a barracuda, well-suited to her husband.

He started with a little heavy breathing.

"Is anyone there?" Doris demanded, cool and imperious as ever.

He kept his voice low, husky, unrecognizable, as he murmured a couple of graphic suggestions he would have been far more interested in trying with Ms. Suzanna Molloy.

There was a shocked intake of breath on the other end, leaving him in no doubt that even if people couldn't see him, they could certainly hear him. And then elegant Doris Osborn said, "I told you not to call me here, Dorfio. We'll meet at the health club, as always." Before Daniel had time to recover from his shock, she'd hung up the phone.

Dismissing her with a reluctant laugh, he went about his experiments. If he was invisible, perhaps he had other gifts, as well. One thing was certain—he hadn't been invisible in the hospital. Suzanna Molloy had looked up at him out of those distrustful brown eyes, and there'd been no mistaking the hostility in them. Nor the reluctant fascination. While Daniel didn't usually waste time paying attention to how people responded to him, in Suzanna's case he didn't consider it a waste. For some reason he had yet to fathom, she fascinated him. It only made sense that he'd be interested in her reaction.

He must have been visible as he walked through the town. That car exploding couldn't have been an accident, not after the events of the day. Someone must have been waiting for him, armed with some kind of heavy artillery.

But by the time he'd reached his apartment building, he'd been gone. He could remember that strange, tingling feeling, like a hot flash, that had spread over him just as it neared 6:00 a.m., and he could only guess that that was when it had started. The question was, how long was it going to last?

He flicked off the television, then held very still. Someone was outside the door. Knocking, with a fair amount of insistence. He wasn't in the mood for visitors, or for answering the door. It would only be someone from Beebe, trying to harass him again.

If it was someone from work, it was someone who had few qualms about breaking and entering. Whoever stood outside his door was fiddling with his lock.

He glanced around him, considering where to hide, and then realized he had no need to. He could stand right there, motionless, soundless, and whoever was attempting to break into his apartment wouldn't even know he was there.

He hadn't set the security lock when he'd first come in, a major oversight. He waited patiently as the lock finally gave and the door opened. There were any number of people who'd made a recent habit of breaking and entering his personal space, but he could only hope it was the one person he was interested in seeing at that particular moment.

It was. "Dr. Crompton?" Suzanna Molloy's faintly husky voice heralded her entrance. "Are you there?"

She knew damned well he wasn't, having knocked loudly. He watched as she stepped inside, closing the door quietly behind her, her brown eyes sweeping over the living room of his apartment, looking right through him.

"Typical," she muttered in disgust, stifling a yawn. She moved through the living room, glancing at the plain white walls, the piles of professional magazines, the lack of anything like a stereo or even a rug on the floor. Even his old small TV was probably black and white, a rarity in this modern age.

"He must be some kind of monk," she muttered, glancing at the narrow futon he occasionally slept on.

Not exactly, he thought, surveying the long sweep of her legs and the firm, gently rounded bottom beneath her faded jeans. She wasn't his type. But maybe he was ready to change his type.

It happened so fast he had no warning. She turned

around, heading into the kitchen, and barreled, unseeing, right into him.

She fell backward, onto that luscious bottom he'd just been admiring, staring up in shock, staring at nothing. This could have its advantages, he thought, wondering whether he dared to so far as to touch her.

She shook her head, as if clearing cobwebs from her brain, and struggled back to her feet. "Keep your shirt on, Nancy Drew," she muttered out loud. He controlled the urge to offer her a hand. She wouldn't see it, and if she felt it, she'd probably scream.

He managed to avoid her as she moved tentatively into the little kitchen area he seldom used. He heard her open the refrigerator, then her remarkably graphic curse as she discovered just how empty it was.

"I'm starving," she moaned to herself. "And all the man seems to eat is moldy cheese and beer."

He didn't bother correcting her. He moved back against the wall silently, so she wouldn't run into him again. The small electronic clock signaled it was now eight in the morning.

He felt that same, strange flush sweep over his body, and he leaned against the wall, trying to control the sudden weakness in his knees as the pain shot through him. He was shivering, praying for the moment to pass, when through the fog of pain he heard her strangled scream.

"How did you get in here?" she demanded, her voice filled with horror. And he opened his eyes to realize that for the first time in hours, someone was staring directly at him.

Chapter Four

For a moment Suzanna couldn't move. He stood only a few feet away from her, in the middle of his soulless living room, dressed in a faded pair of jeans that clung to his narrow hips and long legs. He wasn't wearing a shirt, despite the coolness of the morning air, and Suzanna decided then and there that a scientist shouldn't have such a chest. He should have been pale and soft and flabby. Not toned and tanned and subtly well-muscled.

He hadn't bothered to tie back his hair, and it hung around his strong-featured face, making him look like a pirate, not a biochemist with a Ph.D. in physics on the side.

She managed, just barely, to pull herself together. "Where did you come from?"

"I live here, remember?" he replied in an even voice. "You're the one who's not supposed to be here. Where did you learn to pick locks?"

She could feel just a faint trace of color heat her cheeks, but she simply tilted her chin with a defiance she didn't completely feel. "I do what needs to be done."

"Including going to jail? Breaking and entering is a crime, last I heard, and you've done it twice in the last twenty-four hours. Were you planning on planting a bomb here, as well?" He asked the question with cool disdain, wandering past her shocked figure to stare out the window, giving her a full, distracting view of his back. It was almost sexier than his chest.

"Being able to pick a lock has nothing to do with being able to set a bomb," she said, tearing her gaze away reluctantly. "Why should I want to blow up your lab? Or your apartment, for that matter? I'm a reporter, not an industrial spy."

He glanced back at her over his shoulder. "It makes a good story."

"I'm not that desperate for a byline. You don't believe it, either," she added with sudden assurance. "What did you tell Osborn about me?"

Daniel turned and leaned against the wall, seemingly at ease in his partially dressed state. If only he'd just pull a shirt on over all that gorgeous flesh, she might be able to concentrate a little better. "So Osborn came to see you? I thought he would. What did he want to know?"

"What I saw in your lab."

"And what did you see in my lab?"

"You," she said.

"Is that what you told him?"

"I pretended to be asleep." She remembered the brutal feel of his hand on her, and she couldn't control a slight shiver of distaste.

"What did he do to you?" Crompton asked suddenly.

"What makes you think he did anything?" she countered, acutely uncomfortable.

"The expression on your face."

"You don't miss much, do you?"

"I'm a scientist. I'm trained to observe. Did he hurt you?"

For some reason she didn't want to tell him. Tell him that the CEO of a multinational corporation groped her breast, that an elegant, middle-aged businessman hurt her. It was both embarrassing and unbelievable. "Do you think he's the kind of man who would?" she said instead.

He stared at her for a long moment. He had really wonderful eyes, she realized, but then, that was in keeping with the rest of him. They were a dark, mesmerizing blue, almost black, and yet she could almost imagine tiny pinpricks of golden light, almost like flames, at their center. Scientists were supposed to be nerds. How come she got trapped with the one gorgeous one?

"I wouldn't have thought so," Crompton said, dropping down on the uncomfortable-looking futon. "But you're acting like he molested you."

"Hardly," she said in her driest voice. "And you still haven't told me what you said about me. Whatever it was, he didn't believe it."

"You had quite a conversation, considering you were pretending to be unconscious," he observed.

"He was doing all the talking."

Daniel considered her for a moment, and she wished there was some place she didn't mind looking. His chest was too distracting, his eyes, his mouth, his hands were far too strong and elegant. She concentrated on his left shoulder, trying to ignore the bone and muscle. She'd always had a weakness for slightly bony shoulders, and Daniel Crompton's were just about perfect.

"I told him you were visiting me," he said after a long moment, stretching his legs out in front of him. "I didn't want him to jump to any conclusions if he heard you'd broken in."

"Why not?"

"He'd be more than happy to concentrate his energies on prosecuting you, when I know perfectly well you didn't set any kind of incendiary device in my lab. Whoever did it would get away scot-free, while you languished in jail."

She pushed her hair away from her face in what she hoped was a suitably no-nonsense gesture. "I never languish."

The smile was small, only a faint quirk at the corner of

his mouth. It nevertheless managed to transform his entire face, from the austere, elegant beauty to something infinitely more approachable. "I imagine you don't," he drawled.

Suzanna didn't want to approach him. "You think it was set?"

"I see that journalist's mind of yours clicking away. If I had any sense I'd kick you and your questions out of here."

"I haven't quite figured out why you haven't," she admitted.

He surveyed her with a clinical air, and it took all her self-control not to glance down at her own appearance. She knew perfectly well what she looked like, and she'd never been one for spending needless time fussing with her reflection in a mirror. She had bluntly cut, dirty-blond hair, though her mother referred to it as wheat-colored, which certainly sounded a lot more attractive. Her nose was unimpressive, her brown eyes large but disguised by the wire-rimmed glasses she wore. She seemed taller than average, her figure the typically ten-pounds-overweight American female figure, and she wore an exclusive uniform of baggy jeans and rude T-shirts. The current one was a faded fuchsia with the logo Eat Quiche and Die emblazoned across it. She had never been the type to incite men's passions, and she doubted the estimable Dr. Daniel Crompton even possessed such passions. Even if, looking at him stretched shirtless across his futon, she wished he did.

"Neither have I," he said, shattering any irrational hope she might have had that he harbored a secret passion for her. "Maybe I'm putting up with you for the same reason people say they climb mountains."

No woman liked to hear herself mentioned in the same sentence as a mountain, but Suzanna swallowed her retort. "And why do people climb mountains?"

"Because they're there."

Not the greatest show of confidence, but she decided to take what she could get, before Crompton decided not to trust her. "All right," she said, glancing around the barren living room for a seat. There weren't any, just the futon, which was too small for the two of them. She compromised by sitting on the floor, wincing slightly as she sank down on the bare wood.

"Are you all right?"

He didn't miss a thing. She'd have to be extra careful around this man, for more reasons than one. "Just a little stiff from yesterday. I'm not used to being tossed on a floor and jumped on."

Again that faint glint of humor in his dark eyes. "It has its advantages."

She wasn't going to let him wow her. "Not if you're the one on the bottom," she shot back.

He shrugged, moving those gorgeous, bony shoulders of his, and she wondered what he'd say if she asked him to put on a shirt. Maybe he could even slick that long mane of hair back, find himself some ballpoint pens and a pocket protector. Hitch his jeans halfway up to his armpits, or better yet, find something polyester to wear.

It would be a major mistake to let him guess what kind of effect he was having on her. She tossed her hair back, meeting his gaze defiantly. "Who do you think sabotaged your lab?" she said. "And do you think they meant to hurt you, as well?"

"I never said I thought my lab was sabotaged."

"Give me a break, Crompton," she snapped. "You aren't the only person around here with a brain, even if yours is as oversized as your ego."

"All right. For argument's sake let's say someone set a bomb in my lab. You're the obvious suspect, but for now we're going to assume you had nothing to do with it. You simply happened to be in the wrong place at the wrong time."

"That's a matter of opinion," she said. "It's going to make great copy."

"I'm sure it will. When I let you write it."

"*Let* me write it?" she echoed, incensed. "I'd like to see you try to stop me, buster. There is such a thing as free speech, and a free press, and—"

"And if you want me to cooperate and tell you everything I know, then you'll have to cooperate with me," he interrupted smoothly. "I don't want anything going public until I'm sure it's safe."

"And you get to decide?"

"Take it or leave it."

He was maddening. He also held all the cards, and Suzanna knew it. Much as she wanted to tell him off, throw his conditions back in that too-handsome face, she had too much sense. The truth about what was going on at Beebe, rife as it was with industrial sabotage, would give her career the kind of boost most people only fantasized about. Add to that what Uncle Vinnie had referred to as America's secret weapon, and she had a story that would push her to the top of her profession.

"I'll take it," she said firmly. "On one condition."

"What's that?"

"You keep me with you. You can call me your research assistant, your significant other, your sister or your housekeeper. I don't care. You just make sure I'm in on things."

"My research assistants are working on their Ph.D.'s."

"I already have mine. Stanford, 1988, in physics," she said succinctly, hoping he'd be impressed.

He wasn't. "I don't have a sister, and I don't need a housekeeper."

She glanced around the pristine confines of his apartment with transparent contempt. "You certainly don't."

"So I suppose that makes you my mistress."

She blushed. It was the curse of her pale, freckled complexion, an inheritance from her Danish mother. "No," she said flatly.

"Think I'm going to take advantage, Molloy?" he said. "Use it as an excuse to grope you?"

She remembered Henry Osborn, and she shivered. "I know scientists," she said. "You spend so much time in the lab your hormones go awry, and it wouldn't matter if I looked like a truck driver in drag. How about your cousin from out of town?"

He shook his head. "Santa Cristina is a small town, Molloy. You're too well-known. If you won't pose as my mistress, how about a date? We can still be in the courting stage, not the falling-all-over-each-other stage."

"You *have* been locked in your lab too long," she observed coolly. "Mistresses, courting. You must have read historical romances in your childhood."

Again that small, devastating smile. "I've read my share."

She didn't believe him for a moment. "In this day and age, courtship, if it exists at all, consists of sharing lab tests before people do the deed," she said primly.

"Had a lot of experience, have you?"

"More than you've had," she shot back, ignoring the fact that she hadn't gone to bed with anyone since her short-lived, very unsatisfactory engagement three years earlier.

"You want to compare conquests?"

"You're not adding me to your list," she warned him.

"I wasn't aware that I was asking."

She wanted to hit him. "Just in case you were considering it," she said stonily.

"I'm forewarned," he said, still with that annoying trace of amusement. "Okay, so we're not supposed to be lovers. How about friends?"

She could be just as cynical. "That might be even harder to believe."

She startled him into laughing out loud. "Why don't we let them draw their own conclusions?"

"What if someone asks?"

"I'm entirely capable of refusing to answer rude questions. I imagine you could do so, as well. You don't strike me as the most cooperative person I've ever met." He rose from the futon, his movements smooth and graceful as he walked to the window, and she watched, unwillingly, the play of muscles beneath his skin.

"Aren't you cold?" she demanded, unable to stand it any longer.

He glanced over his shoulder at her. "No," he said. "Are you?"

"As a matter of fact, this room is downright chilly."

His dark eyes took on an abstract look. "Interesting," he said. "I was thinking of opening a window."

"How about turning on the heat instead?"

He'd turned back to stare out the window, and something obviously caught his eye. Unable to resist, she rose and joined him, keeping her shoulder away from his as she glanced down at the neat little landscaped yard that adjoined the parking lot.

"What's so interesting?" she demanded, wishing she hadn't moved quite so close, unwilling to betray her discomfort by moving away. One thing was sure—he *was* quite warm. She could feel the heat of his body through the inches of space between them, through her layers of clothing.

"That car down there. I don't remember seeing it before."

"You've memorized all the cars that park here?" she said, disbelieving.

He glanced down at her, and the sensation was unnerving. His gaze was as heated as all that bare skin, which was far too close to hers. "I have that kind of mind," he said. "It doesn't require any effort on my part."

"Maybe there's a new tenant."

"No. Two men were sitting in it, staring up at this building. This window."

"Where are they now?"

"They're over there talking to the security guard. I wonder…"

His voice trailed off as Suzanna leaned forward to get a better look at the two men. She felt her arm brush against his, and she controlled her nervous start. She didn't know what was wrong with her. Men didn't make her nervous. Particularly men like Daniel Crompton, no matter how unexpectedly gorgeous he was turning out to be.

She concentrated on the two men. They were almost ridiculously anonymous, with their dark suits and their bland, middle-aged, middle-class faces. And Daniel was absolutely right—they were in deep conversation with the security guard, and all three of the men were staring directly at their window.

"They've got an out-of-state license plate," she said quietly. "Either that, or it's some sort of official one. I can't quite read it from this distance."

He tilted his head to stare at the gray sedan, focusing intently, and then rubbed his nose absently. "I think it's got Oregon plates," he said after a moment, moving closer, his arm resting against hers. "I can just make them out.…" He twitched his elegant nose, staring at the back of the sedan.

The explosion shattered the morning quiet. The shock of it knocked Suzanna back against Daniel, and his hands came up to catch her, holding her against his hot, hard chest for a breathless moment.

She couldn't move. He was burning up, so hot his hands burned through the soft cotton jersey of her T-shirt, so hot that the smooth skin of his chest scorched her back, so hot that she melted against him, wanting to sink into that heat, lose herself in the glorious warmth of him. And then the glow of the fire down below pulled her out of her momentary weakness, and she jerked herself away, uneasily aware of the fact she hadn't wanted to move at all.

If the touch of her body against his had disturbed him even a fraction as much as it had disturbed her, he didn't show it. He simply leaned past her, looking out the window, a cool, caluclating expression on his face.

"Must be another car bomb," he murmured.

"*Another* car bomb?" Suzanna shrieked, thoroughly rattled. "What are you talking about?"

"The same thing happened when I was walking home this morning. A car exploded." He didn't seem unduly concerned by it all.

"And you think it's a coincidence?" she demanded.

"No." He looked down at her, and there was an unreadable expression in his dark, fire-lit eyes. "I think someone's trying to kill me."

It was such a melodramatic statement, said in such a matter-of-fact tone, but Suzanna could hardly argue with it. Not with the testimony of her own eyes.

"Maybe I don't want to hang around, after all," she said uneasily.

"And miss your chance at the scoop of the century?" he murmured. "Think of the fame and fortune."

"I can't enjoy fame and fortune if I'm caught in the crossfire." She wasn't seriously thinking of wimping out. She'd never been a coward in her life, and she wasn't about to start now. Tempting as the thought might be, she wasn't quite ready to turn her back on Daniel Crompton, if for no other reason than her insatiable curiosity.

"You think you can protect yourself?" he asked idly, moving away from the window as the resulting chaos of the fire lost his interest.

"Do you think you can protect me?"

"You're probably safer with me, even though it makes things more difficult, as far as I'm concerned." He shrugged. "It's up to you, of course. It makes no difference to me."

The thought rankled. Another man would want to protect her, but then, she'd never been one who needed protection. Still, the man might at least show a trace of concern for her well-being.

"You aren't getting rid of me that easily, Crompton," she said. "I didn't like getting bathed in green slime any more than you did. I'd kind of like to find out who was behind it."

He didn't move for a moment. "Then let's go," he said finally.

He'd managed to startle her. "Go where?"

"To the scene of the crime, of course. If we want answers, Beebe is the place to find them."

At least he'd have to put on a shirt. She viewed that prospect with definite mixed feelings. "I don't suppose you have anything to eat in this place? I'm starving."

"There's some vegamin in the refrigerator."

"What's that? It sounds like bug spray."

He'd disappeared into the bedroom, and she resisted the impulse to tiptoe after him and watch him get dressed. "It's a nutritional drink," he said. "Gives you all the nutrients, and you don't have to bother with food."

"Bother with food?" she echoed, aghast. "Food is one of life's greatest pleasures."

"It's a waste of time," he said, reappearing in the bedroom door. He was buttoning a chambray shirt over his lean, muscled chest, and he'd shoved his feet into a worn pair of high tops. "As a matter of fact, I've been told it tastes like bug spray."

"I think I'll pass. There's a fast-food place on the way. I need coffee."

"I don't suppose you have a car."

"It's out at Beebe."

"So is mine. I guess we run."

"Run?" Suzanna echoed, horrified. "Are you crazy? Nothing short of life or death would make me run. You must be some sort of health fanatic."

"Not particularly. Running enlarges the arteries, which is always beneficial."

"My arteries are just fine," she said firmly. "Let's call a taxi."

"We could walk."

"Taxi," she repeated. "And we'll have him stop on the way."

DANIEL HAD NEVER REALIZED how good he'd be at manipulation. The very stubborn and surprisingly luscious Suzanna Molloy had done exactly as he wanted her to, with only the slightest bit of subtle prodding. There was no way he was going to let her out of his sight, but he knew perfectly well she'd fight that unless she thought it was her idea.

It was simple enough to dangle his cooperation in front of those myopic brown eyes. The fact of the matter was, he was intent on keeping her with him, for a number of reasons. For one thing, she'd been in the same explosion he'd been in, an explosion that seemed to raise his body temperature and give him the uncanny ability to disappear. He didn't know what else he could do, but he suspected his strange side effects weren't at an end. He wanted to see if she was similarly affected.

There was always the chance she was behind that explosion in the lab, though he doubted it. He laid the blame squarely at Henry Osborn's door, and he hadn't missed Suzanna's squirm of discomfort when he brought up his name. Something had happened between them, and Daniel intended to find out what. He also meant to find out who his enemies were, and who were his friends.

And then, of course, there was the little matter of sheer, unbridled lust. Ms. Suzanna Molloy happened to have the uncanny ability to push all the right buttons. He wasn't used to being at the mercy of his physical nature. He drank vegamin to fuel his body, ran to keep his energy at peak, but in general he kept his appetites under rigid control.

Molloy endangered that control. If he had any sense he'd keep away from her, but he wasn't feeling particularly sensible. He was feeling adventuruous, edgy and hot.

And that heat was directed at Suzanna Molloy.

Chapter Five

A couple of hours later, Daniel was still distracted by the woman. He had to admit it—Suzanna Molloy fascinated him. It was a novel situation. There was little that interested him outside of his work, but he was finding the bundle of contradictions that had picked the lock to his apartment to be downright mesmerizing. Enough so that he was almost ready to ignore the question of who or what was behind the sabotage at Beebe.

However, even if he wanted to ignore it and concentrate on Molloy, he doubted whether she'd have any part of it. She seemed to have her own agenda, and she didn't strike him as the sort who'd let anything get in her way.

Daniel Crompton wasn't the sort of man who followed anything but his own inclination. Fortunately, right now his inclination followed quite closely with Suzanna's. He was more than willing to give in to her wishes, as long as they dovetailed with his.

She sat as far away from him as she could in the back of the cab, a foam cup of coffee in one capable-looking hand, some disgusting breakfast concoction in the other. It smelled like eggs and sausage and grease, and she was eating it with obvious relish. He'd given her the approximate cholesterol count when she'd first unwrapped it, but her succinct reply had managed to shock him into silence, even as it amused him. Clearly Ms. Molloy fancied herself one tough lady, from the tips of her black leather running shoes to the top of her silky straight hair. Too bad that the faintly yearning expression in her wonderful eyes betrayed her. Too bad her mouth was deliciously vulnerable when it wasn't curled in hostility.

She didn't like him, he knew that much. But he was also quite certain he could change her mind, if he set himself to do so. The question was, why was he even considering such a thing?

He leaned back in the corner of the cab, inhaling the aroma of coffee and grease and old cigarettes, and he smiled faintly. His behavior was completely uncharacteristic, a fact which disturbed him only slightly. He'd become too predictable in the last few years. He was more than ready to change his ways, and Suzanna Molloy offered him the perfect means to do just that.

"Why are you looking at me like that?" she demanded, delicately licking the grease off her fingers like an elegant cat.

"Like what?"

"You're smirking at me," she said. "I don't trust men who smirk."

She had a trace of shining grease on the side of her mouth. He felt the sudden, irrational urge to kiss her there, to taste it. How very odd. "I'm not smirking," he said with an attempt at severity. "I'm simply smiling. You amuse me."

"You're easily amused." As the taxi approached the front entrance to Beebe Control Systems International, she leaned forward and squinted through her wire-rimmed glasses. "Where's my car?" she demanded suspiciously.

The parking lot was practically empty, which was to be expected on a Saturday morning. For some reason the researchers at Beebe weren't encouraged to work on week-ends. "Where did you leave it?" He leaned forward and handed a ten-dollar bill to the long-suffering driver.

"Not far away from that ridiculous car," she said, clambering out of the taxi and staring around her in dismay. It was only a little after nine, and Daniel could see the faint mist rising from the surrounding fields. It was a cool morning, and he still felt hot.

"Which ridiculous car?" he asked evenly. "You mean the Ferrari?"

"Is that what it is? I wouldn't have thought anyone working here could afford such a thing. I can't imagine spending that much on something to drive you to work."

"I can."

She turned to look at him, an arrested expression on her face. "That's your car?"

"It is. I happen to like craftsmanship."

He was half expecting another snotty comment from her. Instead, she merely looked at him, considering. "Isn't it a little small for you? You must have to drive lying down."

"I can do any number of things lying down," he said, keeping his face a perfect blank.

Suspicion darkened her wonderful eyes for a moment, then she clearly dismissed it, unable to believe he would be indulging in even the faintest innuendo. Obviously she didn't think him capable of suggestive remarks. He was capable of a great deal more than that, when so moved, and Suzanna Molloy moved him, more than anyone in his recent memory.

"I want to know where my car is," she said.

"Osborn probably had it towed."

"I'll kill him."

"Bloodthirsty, aren't you? What kind of car did you have? Some yuppie-mobile?"

"Not likely. It's an old wreck that barely runs."

"Then stop whining. If Osborn killed it he'll have to replace it, and Beebe seems to have unlimited money. You play your cards right and you might end up with a Ferrari yourself.''

He watched with fascination as she rubbed a surreptitious hand across her breast. He would have been more than happy to do the same, a fact which still surprised him. The heat was rising in his body, and he reached up and unfastened another button of his chambray shirt.

"I don't want a Ferrari, and I'm not the kind of reporter who takes bribes, Dr. Crompton,'' she said severely. "I want my own car, and I'm not whining.''

"Glad to hear it. I'm going in to check on the lab. If you want to keep harping, feel free to stay here. That, or you can come with me.''

She was torn, he could see it. He irritated the hell out of her, though he expected that wasn't a difficult task. Anyone who wore a shirt that said Eat Quiche and Die had to have an attitude problem.

That was something that didn't bother him in the slightest. He was generally considered to be socially impaired, though he felt his own particular brand of charm was underrated. He had yet to exert it on Suzanna, and he couldn't help but wonder what her reaction might be. She'd probably offer him quiche.

"I'm coming with you,'' she said. "We can worry about my car later.''

"I knew you were a sensible woman.''

NOW WHY DIDN'T SHE LIKE the idea of Daniel Crompton considering her a sensible woman?

The fact that he respected her brain, not her body, was a blessing, wasn't it?

Even if she happened to find him distractingly attractive.

His blue shirt was unbuttoned halfway down his chest, a fact which irritated her. Who did he think he was—some lounge lizard? All he needed was a couple of gold chains to complete the look.

Except that he was far too lean and mean to be a lounge lizard. That bristling intelligence shone in his dark, mesmerizing eyes, twisted his cynical mouth, and his quick, decisive energy wouldn't know the meaning of the word *lounge.*

She just wished he'd button up his damned shirt.

Just as she wished she had a sweater. She'd been cold since she left the hospital, and she should have asked the man for something warmer to wear. Only the fact that she didn't want to wrap herself in any of his clothing had stopped her. He disturbed her, and she wasn't quite sure why. To be sure, he was annoyingly handsome. Condescending, impatient, brilliant, arrogant. There were any number of reasons why she didn't particularly like him.

What she couldn't figure out was why he managed to get to her. She was used to brilliant men, impatient men, and God knows the vast majority of them tended to be arrogant and condescending. It made no sense that she reacted so strongly to Daniel Crompton, and had since she'd first seen him, at a Beebe press conference months ago. If it hadn't been for Uncle Vinnie's inside tip, she would have been more than happy to keep her distance from the man. She didn't like feeling vulnerable.

She could feel the heat emanating from his body. Strange, that. It was a cool day, and yet he was walking around, half-undressed, warmth radiating from his skin, and he wasn't even sweating. She might almost have thought he had a fever, except the man seemed disgustingly healthy.

Maybe he knew the effect he had on her, the irrational attraction that was putting her in such a toweringly bad mood. She wouldn't put it past him. She had only one way to defend herself. Keep as bristly as possible. She might find the man luscious, but that didn't mean she had to betray herself.

She followed Crompton into the anonymous white building, keeping her head down. Even on a Saturday morning with an empty parking lot, the security desk was well manned. She didn't recognize the uniformed guard. Yesterday it had been an elderly man. Today it looked like a Green Beret.

Crompton didn't even bother to slow his headlong pace. He put one of those strong, elegant hands under Suzanna's elbow, and she almost screamed, biting down on her lip to stop her shriek. His flesh was burning hot against her own chilled skin, and it took all her self-control not to jerk away from him.

"Dr. Crompton," the guard growled. "No visitors are allowed on the premises today."

Daniel kept moving. "This isn't a visitor."

"I'm sorry, sir, but she doesn't have security clearance—"

They were already at the elevator. "Of course she does," Crompton snapped. "Do you think I'd bring someone in who'd compromise my work? What kind of fool do you think I am?"

The Green Beret was made of sterner stuff, and he didn't quail in the face of Crompton's biting contempt. "Sir, I'm going to have to ask you to come back while I get clearance for your friend...."

The elevator door swished open. "You get clearance," Daniel said. "We'll stop on our way back." He hauled Suzanna into the elevator, punched the buttons, and a moment later the doors closed and the tiny box began to rise.

Suzanna did not like enclosed spaces. She'd used the stairs yesterday, ostensibly because she was less likely to be caught, but really because she never trusted elevators. The cage began to rise smoothly, and then it jerked to a halt, throwing Suzanna back against the smooth metal walls.

"Damn," Crompton muttered.

Suzanna managed a strained smile, hoping she could fool him. "What happened?"

"I'd think it was obvious. The security guard stopped the elevator."

"Between floors?" She couldn't keep the hollow note out of her voice.

Daniel was busy pushing the various floor buttons, all to no avail. "Not for long. He'll probably try to bring us back down."

Thank God, Suzanna thought devoutly.

"However, I intend to stop him." He shoved open the metal door above the buttons and reached in, coming out with a handful of multicolor wires.

"What do you think you're doing?" They'd already started to descend once more, something she could only view with relief.

"I'm stopping him." He yanked, hard, and the elevator stopped once more. The lights flickered, and then the tiny cage was plunged into claustrophobic darkness.

She thought she did scream then, though in the tiny airless cubicle it came out as nothing more than a helpless whimper. It was pitch-black, airless, smothering, and the heat was suddenly intolerable, an inferno, emanating from Daniel Crompton's dangerously beautiful body.

"Suzanna." His voice was deep, cool and infinitely patient, and she realized distantly that it wasn't the first time he'd said her name. She had backed up against the walls of the elevator, but even the coolness of the metal against her splayed hands couldn't calm her.

"The emergency light," she managed to choke out.

"Doesn't seem to be working." Again that cool, soothing tone. "Are you afraid of the dark?"

It was so cold in there, cold and hot at the same time, like burning ice. She pushed herself harder against the unyielding walls, wishing she could just disappear. "No," she said, trying to sound hostile, knowing that she sounded scared.

He'd crossed the vast, dead space of the pitch-black elevator, and he was standing close, very close. For the first time she didn't find it threatening. The danger from the suffocating darkness was far worse than the danger from one distractingly attractive man.

"Claustrophobic?" he murmured again, coaxing, soothing.

"No," she said, furious that her voice wavered. "I j-j-just don't l-l-l-like elevators."

The touch of his hand on her arm was tentative, gentle, accustoming her to his presence rather than grabbing her out of the darkness like a fiend from hell. She could feel the heat in his fingers, and even in the darkness she could see them—long, elegant, stained with compounds, marked with nicks and scars from long-ago experiments. She wanted those hands on her, holding her against the smothering darkness. She needed those hands on her.

When he pulled her into his arms she didn't even pretend to resist, just closed off her brain, with all its doubts and anger, all its warnings. She sank against Daniel Crompton's fiery body, absorbing the heat, and shut her eyes, as his hand cupped the back of her head and pushed her face against his shoulder, gently, protectively.

A tiny mutinous part of her cried out that she didn't need protecting. But that part was quickly silenced, as she absorbed his heat, his strength and his comfort. As her panicked heartbeat began to slow, the icy chill of fear left her, and she was able to breathe once more.

He seemed to know moments before she did that she needed to pull away. When he released her, the darkness slammed about her once more, but this time she could cope. She took a deep breath, willing the panic to retreat.

"Better now?" His voice was infinitely pragmatic, as if holding her in his arms was a commonplace occurrence.

"Fine," she said, wishing she could have put a little more edge into her voice. Though she suspected, even in the darkness, that she couldn't fool him. "Can we get the hell out of here?"

"Certainly." She heard a rustling in the darkness, a muffled, shifting noise that made her want to scream. A moment later a square of pale light appeared in the ceiling, and she could see Crompton's vague outline.

"You first," he said. "Unless you're afraid of heights, as well."

"I'm not afraid of anything," she shot back, an obvious lie. "What do you mean, me first?"

"If you want to get out of this elevator, there's only one way, and that's up."

"I'm not about to—"

"It's up," he said ruthlessly, "or stay here for what will probably be another two hours. And you'll do it alone. I'm out of here."

"You know what I like about you, Dr. Crompton?" she asked in a silken voice that almost masked her panic.

"No, what?"

"Absolutely nothing."

As a matter of fact, she wasn't particularly crazy about heights. She was even less fond of climbing upward through a narrow, constricted tube, above an object that might suddenly start moving and end up squashing her against the ceiling of the building like a fat bug.

But she wasn't about to spend a minute longer in that elevator than she had to. Particularly not alone.

"Get me out of here, Crompton," she muttered, moving toward him, perversely glad that the darkness hid the expression on her face.

"Up you go," he said, putting his big, hot hands on her waist and hoisting her upward with a total effortlessness that just managed to get through her fear enough to astonish her. She reached out instinctively as he pushed her through the opening, his hands sliding down her hips to cup her rear before she managed to grab hold of something and scramble out of his way.

A moment later he'd vaulted up beside her, and in the improved light she could see his eyes gleaming in the shadows. "That was easy enough."

"Too easy, Crompton. I weigh a hundred and thirty-seven pounds."

"That's not my fault, Molloy. You eat too much grease."

It would be a waste of time to hit him. She could at least wait until he'd gotten her out of this place. "I mean you don't seem the slightest bit strained."

"I'm used to lifting weights."

The hell with waiting, she *was* going to hit him. "We're not talking about a male-dominated distortion of aesthetics, Dr. Crompton," she said icily. "We're talking about—"

"Why are we wasting our time talking? I thought you wanted to get out of here."

"I do."

"Then stop complaining about your weight and follow me."

She spent a moment fondly contemplating his immediate demise, when light began to stream into the elevator shaft. It took her a moment to realize he'd reached over his head and was prying open the doors to the next floor.

Well, maybe she wouldn't kill him after all. Just hurt him very badly.

"Climb up," he offered.

"I'll need a hand."

"The doors will close again."

"I can pry them open. I may not lift weights, but I'm far from a weak woman."

"I never made the mistake of assuming you were weak. Nevertheless, you wouldn't be able to open them yourself. Climb up."

"But how...?"

"Use my body," he said blandly.

The suggestion was startling, until she realized what he meant. "I don't know..."

"Listen, I want to get out of here as much as you do, and I'd like to do it before they get someone in here who can override the system and make this thing start up again. Now move your butt, Molloy, or I'll move it for you."

She'd hurt him with a great deal of pain, she thought fondly, reaching out to touch him. He was hot, something which didn't surprise her. The odd thing was, his clothes were cool to the touch.

She could feel the tension in his muscles. It was an unnerving experience, but as far as she could see, she really had no choice. "All right," she said in a tight little voice. "How do you expect me to do this?"

"Grab hold of my shoulders and start climbing."

He hadn't tied his hair back, and it brushed against her fingers as she settled them on his shoulders, the cool chambray beneath her hands. He was holding very still, keeping the doors open, his arms directly overhead. "I don't think this is going to work," she said, biting her lip.

"Think how much fun you're going to have, stomping all over me. Use your feet, Molloy."

She braced one sneakered foot against his leg, her fingers digging into the bunched-up shoulder muscles, and tried to hoist herself up. Her knee slammed into his stomach, her foot came perilously close to his groin, and the feel of his iron-hard body beneath hers was incredibly distracting.

He was wearing a wide leather belt, and she managed to rest her foot against it, pushing herself upward. Her stomach was face level, and she could feel the warmth of his breath against the zipper of her jeans. Her foot slipped, and she fell against him, his face buried in her crotch.

It didn't take his muffled laughter to send her flying upward through the pried-open doors, belly-flopping onto the carpet. She scrambled out of the way, rolling over in time to see him follow her, just as the door slammed shut behind him.

The power was out in the hall, as well, but the midday sun managed to send squares of light into the corridor, and Suzanna sank back, drinking in the diffuse brightness of the day and the blessed feel of the floor beneath her. "Was that, by any chance, a pass, Molloy?" he inquired.

"Go to hell, Dr. Crompton," she said, pulling herself upright. He was standing there in the shadowed hallway, tall, superior, a gleam of mocking humor in his dark eyes. Now was the time to kill him.

"Let's get moving," he said, reaching out a hand. "We probably won't have much time before Beebe's private army arrives."

She looked up at him. His shirt had come unbuttoned, pulled out of his jeans, and she remembered the feel of his skin beneath her clutching hands. "Maybe I'll wait to kill you," she muttered, putting her hand in his outstretched one.

His was much larger. It closed around hers, warm and strong, and he pulled her to her feet.

"That might be wise," he murmured. "Not much farther, Nancy Drew. Come on."

And he left her to race after him down the hallway, once she'd gotten over her initial shock.

Chapter Six

This situation was getting more and more interesting, Daniel thought, moving down the darkened hallway at a brisk pace. Despite his ongoing fascination with his research project, he found he'd gotten into a rut recently. Certainly the last twenty-four hours had provided enough novelty to keep him entertained for the next twenty-four years.

He was immensely strong. It had taken very little effort to pry open those pneumatic doors, very little to send Suzanna's well-rounded figure up and over the portal and into the hall. Levering himself after her had also been surprisingly simple. He wished he had a moment to experiment further, but he wasn't about to do that with an audience. He wanted to keep Suzanna with him, but he wasn't quite ready to share what was going on with his body.

Fortunately she seemed willing to accompany him, though he didn't have any illusions about her motives. She wanted the truth. She wanted a story, a scoop, and she'd betray him in a flash if she had to. He had no intention of giving her the chance.

He opened the fire door to the staircase. "Think you can handle this?" he asked. "The emergency lights are out here, as well."

"When you pull the plug you don't settle for halfway measures, do you?" she said. "I can do it." She moved past him, into the enveloping darkness of the hallway, and as her body brushed by he could smell the faint trace of soap that clung to her. It was surprisingly erotic.

He let the door swing shut behind him, following her up the stairs in the inky darkness. He could see her quite clearly, hear her struggle to control her nervous breathing as she climbed, slowly, steadily, her hand clutching the metal stair rail.

"You're there, aren't you?" she called out, her voice betraying only a trace of her nerves.

"Right behind you," he said, wondering why she couldn't see him when he could see her quite clearly.

She'd paused, and she was staring in his direction in the darkness, but her own gaze was unfocused. "Your eyes..." she said.

Instinctively he closed his lids. "What about them?"

"Nothing," she mumbled. "Must have been my imagination." He heard her turn away and continue to mount the stairs, and he waited a moment before he followed her. What had she seen in his eyes?

The third floor smelled of smoke and chemicals. The hallway was deserted, though at the far end he could see the rubble that had once been his doorway. A yellow tape stretched in front of it, though Daniel doubted that there'd been a police investigation.

Suzanna's color was decidedly pale, though she looked happier to be out of the darkness. "How much time do you think we've got?"

"Probably not enough," he said, moving past her. "I just want to take a quick look around, see if I can find out what kind of device they used, and then we're out of here."

"Device? You sound pretty certain it was sabotage."

He glanced at her, one part of his mind taking in the way the T-shirt clung to her breasts and remembering the feel of her body as she'd scrambled up him, the rest being coldly analytical. "I don't make mistakes," he said simply.

"Never?"

He paused long enough to consider it. "Not that I can remember."

The lab was a shambles. It stank of chemicals, of smoke, of fire extinguisher foam and wet, charred wood and melted plastic. Most of the green slime had been washed away by the fire hoses, but a little pool of the stuff remained under one of the workbenches, and he squatted down, staring at it for a long time before he scooped some up in a plastic dish he'd brought along for the purpose.

"Why are you doing that?" Suzanna was leaning over his shoulder, close enough to touch him. "Do you think that stuff caused the explosion?"

"No." He rose, coming up beside her, near enough to touch her if he wanted to. He wanted to. "I think it's a by-product of what I was working on, combined with whatever was used to start the fire. It's mutated into something that I intend to identify." He tucked the plastic dish in his hip pocket. "Did you get any of the stuff on you?"

"Just a little. You took a bath in it."

"So I did," he murmured. "I wonder—" He stopped. "They're coming."

"I don't hear anything."

"Don't you? They're coming up the north stairwell—about two flights down. I'd say we have about one minute at the most."

"You can't hear them that far away!" she snapped, but he could see the definite alarm in her beautiful brown eyes.

"Trust me," he muttered, taking her hand in his and starting out of the ruined lab at a run.

For once she didn't argue. She simply followed him, no questions asked, as he dodged debris, racing down the deserted hallway on silent feet.

He darted into Buchanan's lab, slamming the door behind them and closing them in shadowy darkness. Buchanan had left several months ago, and the lab had sat empty since then, despite Daniel's best efforts to co-opt it for his own uses. Not that it was as large as Daniel's lab, but it came equipped with a back staircase, leading directly to the roof.

"Where are we going?" Suzanna finally demanded, breathless. "Why are we running? You don't think we're in any real danger, do you?"

He thought there was a good chance that they were in a great deal of danger, but he wasn't about to explain it to a nosy reporter. "I don't know. I just want to get out of here. Call me paranoid."

"You're paranoid."

He turned to look at her. "You want to wait around for them to come find you?"

"I have a T-shirt that says Just Because You're Paranoid Doesn't Mean They Aren't Out To Get You," she replied.

"Good girl," he muttered, moving toward the door at the back of the lab.

"Don't call me a girl," she snapped, moving past him and reaching for the metal doorknob. Of course it didn't budge, and she yanked harder, muttering under her breath. "I don't suppose you have a key for this?"

"No."

"Then we're stuck." She turned and glared at him, her wheat-blond hair tumbling into her eyes. "That's a safety door—reinforced steel. Unless you can pick locks, there's no way we're going to get past it. Brute force just won't cut it this time."

"I wonder," he said, half to himself, moving past her, ignoring the impractical urge to touch her. He took hold of the shiny steel knob, noting the lock. And then he turned it, crushing the tumblers when they tried to resist, pulling open the door with no effort whatsoever.

She stared at him for a moment, then back at the door latch. The metal workings had been pulverized by some massive force. "How did you do that?" she gasped.

"Shoddy workmanship," he replied. "You first. Three flights up, and if the door's locked up there, we'll open it."

Her parting glance was wary, before she vanished into the shadowy staircase. Daniel watched her for a moment, appreciating the curve of her rear in the faded jeans, before he turned to look at the door. His strength was quite impressive. He really needed to get out of here, away from witnesses, and experiment further. There had to be a limit to it, and he needed to find that limit. He didn't want to accidently injure someone.

He stepped into the narrow staircase, pulling the damaged door shut behind him, hoping it would escape detection, at least for the time being. He could hear Suzanna moving upward, her sneakered feet cautious. She was nervous again, the darkness of the passageway getting to her, and he told himself he ought to catch up with her, hold her hand, even put his arm around her. Just to reassure her, he told himself virtuously. Hell, given his unpredictable strength, he could carry her the rest of the way and barely notice the burden. He rather liked that idea.

There was an odd, sickly sweet smell in the stairwell, not unlike rancid meat and rotted fruit. The higher he climbed, the stronger the stench, and he wondered what Suzanna was doing, why he could no longer hear her tentative footsteps, her nervous breathing, why she wasn't complaining.

He found her on the landing just before the final flight of stairs to the roof. She wasn't alone.

She was standing utterly motionless. The skylight overhead illuminated the area, but Daniel doubted she was grateful for the light. It shone down on the corpse of Robert Jackson.

"Is he dead?" Suzanna's voice came out as no more than a whisper.

Daniel stepped farther, intellectually gratified at having

identified the stench. "Most definitely," he said. "Don't you see the bullet hole in his—"

"Please!" Suzanna begged in a strangled voice.

"Why don't you go on up ahead? I'll be right with you."

"What are you going to do?"

"Search his body. You want to help?"

She disappeared up the final flight of stairs with a quiet shriek of protest. When he reached her side a few moments later, she was leaning against the locked fire door, her hand over her mouth, her eyes wide behind the wire-rimmed glasses.

"Are you going to throw up?" He was unalarmed at the notion, simply curious.

"No." She took a deep, shuddering breath. "Can we get out of here? This door is locked, as well, and I've checked. It's very solidly put together."

"You'd be surprised." He tempered his strength this time, turning the knob just enough to break the lock, not enough to pulverize it. He opened the door for her, pushing her through into the fresh air before she could look too closely.

He started across the deserted rooftop at a fast pace. "Come on," he said. "If our luck holds, we'll be out of here before they realize it."

"And if it doesn't?"

"We might end up like Jackson back there."

Wrong words. She swayed for a moment, and her pale face looked even chalkier. He started back, ready to catch her if she fell, but she managed to straighten her back and square her shoulders. "Not if I have anything to say about it," she muttered.

"Good girl."

"Stop saying that. I'm not a girl."

"Argue with me once we're out of here," he said. "In the meantime, get your delectable butt in gear."

SUZANNA WOULDN'T HAVE thought Daniel Crompton was the sort of man who noticed butts, delectable or otherwise. No one had ever referred to that part of her anatomy in such flattering terms, and she concentrated on that, rather than the vision, the smell, of the dead man in the stairwell, as she followed Crompton over the side of the building and down a metal fire ladder to a deserted parking lot.

Or almost deserted. There was a Jaguar parked there, sleek, forest green and Suzanna's dream car, and she stared at it for a moment when she reached the ground, a wave of covetousness sweeping over her.

"If we're going to steal a car, I opt for that one," she said.

Crompton looked at her. The man was inhuman. He seemed to accept decaying corpses as nothing more than an intellectual exercise, he didn't recognize such a thing as a locked door, and she was beginning to get the feeling that there was something very different about Dr. Daniel Crompton. That first stretch of hallway had been eerie enough. Trapped in the suffocating darkness, she'd turned back, looking for some kind of companionship, and had found only a pair of eyes glowing in the darkness.

It had to have been her imagination. In the inky darkness she could barely see his silhouette, and that odd shining had disappeared in a moment.

Still, she'd tried both of those steel doors. While she'd never pretended to be a superwoman, she had a certain amount of strength, and those doors were locked tight. Yet Crompton had opened them with no visible effort whatsoever.

"Who says we're stealing a car?"

"I don't know where mine is, and they'll be watching yours," she pointed out. "It doesn't take someone with your exalted IQ to figure out that much."

"That Jaguar belongs to Henry Osborn, and he's formidable enough without us taking his precious car. We're taking the Ford over there.''

Suzanna followed his gaze. It was a boring enough vehicle, two door, late model, indiscriminate color. They'd probably blend in well enough, if that was their wish. "I'd still rather have the Jag," she said, trotting along behind him.

Of course the car was locked. She stood at the passenger door, throwing him a mocking glance. "Are you going to rip the door off the hinges this time?" she murmured.

"It might be easier to simply unlock it," he said, pulling a set of keys from his pocket and doing so. She slid into the front seat beside him, rolling down her window to let some of the suffocatingly stale air out, as Crompton started the car and pulled out of the parking lot at an impressive speed. Even with the wind blowing through the open window it was too hot. It took her a moment to remember she was keeping company with a human furnace.

"If this isn't your car, whose is it? How'd you happen to get the keys?" she demanded, fastening the seat belt around her.

"I don't think you want to know."

Horror swept over her. "It isn't!"

Daniel shrugged. "Jackson isn't going to need it anymore. It was simple enough to find his keys."

She looked down at the set hanging from the ignition. The key ring had a shamrock hanging from it. It certainly hadn't provided much luck for the late Jackson. "You're sick," she said, sinking back against the seat.

"Just practical. Speaking of which, I think we'd better get out of town for a while."

"Why?"

"Because this isn't just a case of industrial sabotage or attempted murder. Someone actually managed to kill Jackson, and whoever it was used a fair amount of detail and imagination. I don't think they're going to stop there. Where do you live?''

"Why?''

"I thought you might want to pick up some clothes. Assuming they're not watching your place.''

"What makes you think I'm going with you?''

"Molloy, you've got it made. You're in on a murder. Think of the bidding wars on your movie rights.''

"Sorry, Crompton, you haven't got hero potential,'' she snapped, ignoring the fact that he was better-looking than almost any actor she could think of.

"Who says I'm not the villain?''

That managed to silence her. It was a startling thought. She'd gone along with him, arguing, but trusting, putting her life in his hands. Together they'd found Jackson's body, and yet Daniel had looked at it as if it were nothing more than a lab experiment gone awry.

Could he have killed him? Did he find out that Jackson had tried to sabotage his lab, and shoot him in a rage? She glanced over at his profile. His long hair blew in the wind, away from his strong-featured face. He looked cool, remote, incapable of human emotion. If he ever wanted to kill someone, he was smart enough to get away with it.

"43 West Peacock.''

He glanced over at her. "I beg your pardon?''

"You asked where I lived. It's 43 West Peacock. Just off of High Street.''

"Does that mean you're coming with me?''

"As you pointed out, it's the scoop of the century. I'm going to be your shadow.''

His mouth curved in a faint, mocking smile. "You might find that harder than you think.''

"I can rise to the challenge. Do you know where we're going?''

"Somewhere I can think. You don't talk all the time, do you?''

"Depends on my mood."

"God help me," he muttered. But for some reason he didn't look the slightest bit distressed.

As far as they could tell, no one was watching the old Victorian-style house where she rented her apartment. Crompton stayed in the car while she ran inside and filled an old duffel bag with a dozen T-shirts, all the clean underwear she could find and enough toiletries to keep her human. She yanked her clothes off, throwing them in the trash, and quickly pulled on a new T-shirt and jeans. It was ridiculous, but she felt as if the smell of that long-dead corpse was clinging to her. The sooner she could take a long hot shower, the better.

Daniel was waiting for her in the sedan, his long fingers drumming on the steering wheel. "You're fast," he said approvingly. "You even managed to change your clothes."

"I try not to waste time."

"Nice T-shirt," he said, pulling out into the late afternoon traffic.

She glanced down at the one she'd grabbed. So Many Men, So Few Bullets, it read, in black ink on a red background. She thought back to Jackson and shivered.

He headed out onto the highway, moving north into the mountains. She sank back against the cushions, closing her eyes in sudden exhaustion. She must have drifted off, for the next thing she knew, they were parked outside of a very seedy-looking motel, somewhere in the middle of nowhere, and the digital clock on the dashboard read 5:40.

"Where are we?" she asked with a yawn.

"On the back side of beyond," he said. "I've got us a room for the night. I've been driving around, doubling back, and I don't think they're likely to find us. We're Mr. and Mrs. Smith."

"How original. We're sharing a room?"

She might almost have wished he'd responded with a leer. Instead he simply looked surprised. "I thought the intention of this was to keep each other alive. We can't do that if you're in another room.''

''Don't worry, Dr. Crompton,'' she said wearily. ''I'm not accusing you of having lustful designs on my fair body.''

He didn't even blink. A token protest wouldn't have done her ego any harm, but Daniel wasn't adept in the art of social lies. He simply stared at her for a moment. ''Do you want me to?'' he asked bluntly.

It was getting dark. A fortunate thing, since her damnably fair skin heated up at his artless question. ''No,'' she said flatly.

He nodded. ''I see,'' he said. Something about his tone of voice wasn't particularly reassuring, but before she could identify what it was that bothered her, he'd climbed out of the car and headed for the door of their room.

She grabbed her duffel bag and followed him, telling herself she was glad the big oaf was totally lacking in chauvinistic manners. ''Room number thirteen,'' she noted, stepping inside. ''Just our luck.''

''What's wrong with number thirteen?''

She didn't bother enlightening him—she was too busy surveying the room in dismay.

At least there were two beds. The place was decorated in early American tacky, from the orange quilted bedspreads to the Naugahyde furniture. She checked beyond, to the tiny square of bathroom with its stall shower, and sighed. ''All the comforts of home,'' she said. ''I wonder where Norman Bates is.''

''Who's Norman Bates?''

''Didn't you ever see *Psycho?*''

''No.''

She shook her head again. ''For a brilliant man, Dr. Crompton, you're amazingly ignorant.''

If he heard her, he ignored the remark and busily closed

the curtains against the gathering darkness. "It's hot in here," he said in a low voice.

Oddly enough, a chill swept over Suzanna's body. "I'm going to take a shower," she said, dumping her duffel bag on the bed nearest the bathroom and rummaging through it.

He had a strained look to him, almost haunted. "Go right ahead."

She paused in the bathroom doorway. "Are you all right?"

"Fine. Take your shower. Then we can see about finding something to eat."

There was something wrong. The room was almost suffocating, and heat emanated from the man at the window. He refused to look at her, and she shrugged. "It's almost six now," she said. "I'll be ready to go out at six-thirty."

"Fine," he said in a muffled voice. "Take your shower."

HE WAITED UNTIL THE DOOR shut behind her. The pain was lancing through his body—intense, sweeping shafts of agony. He heard the water running, the sound of it hitting her body as she stepped beneath the spray, and then he let go, sinking down on the bed as the shivering swept over him. He closed his eyes for a moment, then opened them again. He stared down at his legs, but they were vague, out of focus, and he knew it had happened again.

Once more he was invisible. And he didn't know how in hell he was going to explain that to Suzanna Molloy.

Chapter Seven

Daniel Crompton had been properly reared, the only child of elderly, intellectual parents. His mother had very strict rules of propriety, and even as a toddler he'd been expected to behave as a gentleman. At the advanced age of thirty-four he knew perfectly well that he ought to leave the room and return when he was once more visible.

He wasn't going to.

"I'm going out," he called through the closed bathroom door. "I'll be back in a couple of hours." He heard her sputtered protests as he walked heavily to the front door, opened it, and closed it quite loudly. And then he moved, his sneakered feet silent, to the very corner of the room and sat down gingerly on the bed.

"Crompton, don't you dare leave me!" Suzanna shrieked, sticking her head out of the bathroom door. Her hair was wet, she didn't have her glasses on, and her brown eyes focussed myopically around the confined space, moving past the spot where he sat patiently, not lingering. "Damn the man," she muttered, moving back into the bathroom, leaving the door ajar.

He wondered idly whether he could get up, move across the room and peer inside the bathroom door without her hearing him. He'd never had any voyeuristic tendencies— even when he was a hormone-crazed teenager he'd been more interested in the anatomical anomalies of the center-folds than their unlikely charms.

But he found he had a sudden urge to see what Suzanna Molloy looked like under her T-shirt. Whether she was curved and soft, sleek and muscled, or a combination of the two. Oddly enough, it didn't really matter to him. For some reason he wanted her—whether she was plump or lean. It was her brown eyes, her stubborn mouth, her wary nature that turned him on. It made no sense, but then, little had in the last twenty-four hours.

He'd just risen when she came back out of the bathroom, and he had to bite back the groan of disappointment. She was already partly dressed, wearing a plain white pair of panties and a T-shirt that read When God Made Man She Was Only Kidding. Her hair was combed back from her freshly scrubbed face, and she was wearing her glasses once more. He froze, afraid to give away his presence, and looked at her.

Come to think of it, maybe he wasn't disappointed. She had long legs, beautiful legs, not Barbie doll legs but the kind that could wrap around a man. She hadn't bothered with a bra, and the T-shirt clung to her wet body, her wet breasts, and he watched her, wishing he could see her nipples, cursing because the room was too warm.

She had an elegant grace when she thought no one was watching her, and she crossed to the door to put the chain up. "Where is that man?" she muttered underneath her breath, peering out the window. Of course, there was no sign of him, and he watched, wondering what else she was going to say.

She moved over to the mirror that hung above the cheap pine dresser. It should have reflected his own body, as well, but it didn't. He stood there, seeing what she was seeing, judging what she was judging.

"All right," she said out loud, pulling her hair back

away from her face. "So you're no great beauty. No one ever said you were."

He was tempted to disagree, but he wisely kept his peace, wanting to hear more. "And just because the great Dr. Daniel Crompton happens to be unfairly blessed with more than his fair share of looks, it hasn't got a thing to do with you. At least I don't have to look at him for a while. Pretty is as pretty does, and the man is overbearing, cold-blooded and arrogant."

He wondered about that. It seemed a fairly accurate assessment. He did tend to be overbearing—otherwise he wasted too much time trying not to tread on the tender feelings of utter fools. Arrogant...perhaps. He knew what he wanted, what he was interested in and what bored him. What interested him right now was Suzanna Molloy. Not to mention the strange things that kept happening to his body. But oddly enough, he found his oblivious roommate a higher priority.

As for his being cold-blooded, that seemed to have changed recently, in more ways than one. He was hot, burning up, with a kind of dry heat that could set something on fire. And he was even hotter when he looked at her.

Even if he was invisible, his body was capable of reacting humanly enough. Staring at her breasts in the mirror, he found he was getting aroused. That was odd, as well. He usually got turned on when he had a naked, willing woman in his bed. His erections, his lovemaking, as well as everything else, were always ruthlessly efficient.

Not tonight, however. He shifted his jeans, deciding he might be better off sitting down on the bed. He lowered himself slowly, silently, gingerly, then realized with sudden horror that the reflection of the orange quilted bedspread suddenly wrinkled.

Suzanna froze. She whipped around, staring at the spot where he sat motionless on the bed, and for such a fierce young woman she looked scared spitless.

"Daniel?" she managed to croak.

He didn't say a word. If he could just hold himself still, she'd probably decide she'd imagined it. Except that the quilt was bunched up beneath him, and if she tried to straighten it, she'd run right into him.

"You're here, aren't you?" She moved toward him, and he had to admire her courage in the face of her controlled panic. "I don't know how, but you're here, in the room. I can feel you watching me. Say something, damn it!"

Still he kept silent. She'd be better off not knowing. There was no guarantee he could keep her from Osborn, Armstead and their nasty crew, and if they found out what had happened to him, things would go from bad to worse.

It was more than obvious what Beebe Control Systems International wanted from him, and he'd been a fool to blind himself to their machinations. People didn't kill for patents and copyrights, they didn't sabotage labs and risk killing their major researcher, unless they decided they had what they needed.

What they needed was something they could use to control the world, and they thought he had it. They thought he was the one man who'd finally created cold fusion. And they weren't going to use it to solve the world's energy crisis. They were going to use it for weapons.

When the stakes were that high, the lives of two little people didn't mean a hill of beans. He'd heard that line somewhere—he couldn't remember where—but it seemed to fit. The less Suzanna Molloy knew, the better.

But the problem was, she looked as if she was about to cry, and he knew she wasn't the sort of woman who cried easily or often. The thought of her tears didn't distress him any more than the possibility of her throwing up after she found Jackson's body. He wasn't the kind of man who fell apart at the sight of a woman's tears.

But for some reason he didn't want to see her cry.

"I'm going crazy," she whispered to herself in sudden

panic. "I've got to get out of here." She dived for her duffel bag, dragging out a pair of jeans, and it took all his self-control not to leap for her, to try to stop her. He was counting on her to calm herself down, so he wouldn't have to reveal himself, when the utilitarian black phone beside the bed shrilled.

It startled her into a quiet scream; it startled him into moving. He saw the shift of the mattress in the mirror, but Suzanna was too busy staring at the phone.

She started toward it, and he knew he had to stop her. It might very well be only the desk clerk, but he doubted it. They'd been found already.

Her hand was on the receiver, hesitating, when he finally spoke.

"Don't answer it," he said.

He couldn't see her face now, just her straight back, the tension in her shoulders. And then she moved her hand, turned and stared at the empty beds. "Where are you?" she asked with remarkable calm.

He rose. She was still staring at the disarranged bed—she didn't know he was coming closer, close enough to touch her, close enough to pull her into his arms.

He resisted the impulse, but just barely. She'd been through enough, and he was about to put her through more. "Right here," he said softly.

And Suzanna Molloy, tough and fearless, collapsed in a dead faint at his feet.

IT GAVE HIM A CHANCE to experiment. He knelt down beside her, sliding his arms under her limp body, and lifted her up. He might have been lifting a cloud of silk, and yet he knew by looking that Suzanna Molloy was a solidly built young lady. She smelled of shampoo and soap and toothpaste, clean and fresh and unbearably erotic, and he wondered just how conscienceless he was becoming. She was out cold, and he was sorely tempted to—

Her eyes fluttered open. He was carrying her toward the bed, and he could feel her muscles stiffen in his arms, and knew she was about to scream. He couldn't blame her. As far as she could see, she was floating through the air.

He dropped her down on the bed, abruptly enough to surprise the scream out of her. She stared up at him, or at least, in his general direction, and the look of absolute horror on her face was far from flattering.

"I thought you were glad you didn't have to look at me," he said.

She jumped, startled. "Where are you?"

"Standing right in front of you." He wanted to touch her again, but he wasn't sure whether she could handle it or not. Her nerves seemed to be on the ragged edge, and while he didn't usually waste time worrying about other people's needs, in this case it seemed to matter.

"What happened to you?"

He wandered over to the window, glancing out into the night. "I don't know," he said honestly. "It has something to do with the lab accident. The green slime, I suppose. It certainly wasn't anything I was working on."

Her head moved, her eyes following the direction of his voice. "This isn't the first time it's happened?"

He smiled. She was sharp—he liked that about her. Almost as much as he liked her long legs and her breasts and her feisty tongue. "It happened this morning. Six o'clock this morning, to be exact. It lasted exactly two hours, and at eight o'clock I was visible again."

"You were there when I broke into your apartment."

"Yes."

"You were watching me. God, I bumped into you!" she said, remembering.

"Yes," he said again.

"You weren't going to tell me?" Her temper was returning, the color rising in her pale cheeks. "Were you just going to sit there and watch me undress, you pervert?"

"Hardly a pervert. An interest in an unclothed female body of certain attractions isn't the slightest bit abnormal."

"Certain attractions?" she echoed, reacting just as he'd expected.

"Besides, I'm not certain how much I can trust you. Who's to say you won't go to the *National Enquirer* and sell your story?"

"They wouldn't believe me," she said flatly. "Even tabloids have some standards. What else?"

"What do you mean by that?"

"There's more than being invisible. You broke those doors at Beebe, didn't you? And what about the elevator door?"

"I seem to be fairly strong," he allowed.

"How strong? Arnold Schwarzenegger strong? The Incredible Hulk strong? Godzilla strong?"

"I'm not sure. I'm still finding out exactly what's going on," he said, turning to stare at her. She still wasn't wearing a bra, a fact which had temporarily escaped her. The jeans she'd pulled on were a tighter fit than the ones she'd worn earlier, and they encased her long legs. He sighed.

"What do you want from me?" she asked quietly.

"What makes you think I want anything from you?"

"Don't try to trick me, Dr. Crompton. You may have an IQ of 512, but that doesn't mean the rest of us are idiots. You brought me along for a reason. What is it?"

He considered it—and her—for a long moment. "You want the truth?"

She nodded, pushing her damp hair away from her face. "It's usually for the best."

He moved back, across the room, stopping in front of her. "There are a number of reasons."

She jumped when he spoke, startled. "Can't you stay put?" she demanded wtih some asperity. "I can't see you, you know."

"You'll have to get used to me sneaking up on you."

"Charming," she snapped. "Why did you bring me along?"

He decided to be efficient. "Number one," he said, counting on unseen fingers, "I wasn't sure which side you were on. Your arrival at Beebe was, to say the least, suspicious. I thought you might have been behind the lab explosion, and it would be better to have you in sight."

"I wish I could say the same for you," she muttered. "What else?"

"Number two," he said, "you were slimed as well as I was, though you didn't get as thorough a coating. I wanted to see whether you were affected, as well. Number three, I need someone to help me observe the changes in my body, document them. They might prove debilitating, even fatal. I'll need someone I can count on to record them. You're a scientific reporter—I can trust you to keep track of what's happening to me."

"Is that all?" She didn't look particularly gratified at the trust he'd shown her, but then, he wasn't expecting gratitude.

"There are other considerations," he said in his most offhand voice. "I wasn't sure if you already knew what was happening to me, and I didn't want you telling anyone about it. We're better off keeping it a secret, at least for now."

"And?"

"And what?"

"Any other reason?"

None apart from overwhelming animal lust, he thought to himself, smiling wryly. He didn't think Suzanna was ready to hear that. "Isn't that enough?"

"Who says I want to be your dogsbody?" she demanded.

"You've got one of the major qualifications," he said smoothly. "Your nature."

To his surprise, her face creased in reluctant amusement.

"Are you by any chance calling me a bitch, Dr. Crompton?" she asked. "You must admit, I have plenty of reason to be irritable."

"Aren't you always this way?"

"You bring out the worst in me." She pulled her legs up underneath her, and he could see she was beginning to lose her wariness. He wondered if she'd lose it enough to let him touch her. He doubted it.

"I wouldn't get too comfortable if I were you," he said.

She stiffened. "What do you mean?"

"I don't know who was calling here, but I don't like it. I think we'd better leave. And you're going to have to drive."

She cocked her head. "I suppose I am. I suppose I'm going to have to carry the bags, as well?"

He nodded, then realized she couldn't see. "I think being invisible will have its advantages."

"How long is it going to last?"

"A reasonably educated guess would say two hours. That's how long it lasted this morning. I disappeared at 6:00 a.m., reappeared at eight. I disappeared at 6:00 p.m. tonight, so I imagine..." He glanced down at his arm, but the watch attached to his wrist was just as blurred and out of focus as the rest of him.

She seemed to guess what his problem was. "It's seven-fifteen. If you're right, that would give you another forty-five minutes." She rose, and if the hand that pushed her damp hair away from her face trembled slightly, she ignored it. "You're right, let's get out of here. I don't suppose you have any idea where we can go?"

"Keep heading in the same general direction. I had a destination in mind."

"You feel like sharing it?"

"Not particularly. That way you won't know anything if we get separated."

"Charming," she said, slipping her feet into her sneakers. "They can torture me, but I won't be able to tell them anything."

"You've been reading too many bad books. Nobody's going to torture anyone."

"It didn't look as if your friend Jackson had too good a time," she snapped. And then she closed her eyes, suddenly looking vulnerable. "I shouldn't have said that."

"Why not? It's true. For what it's worth, Jackson didn't deserve what happened to him, but he wasn't an innocent victim, either. He was somebody's spy, probably Osborn's, and I wouldn't be surprised if he set the device that almost killed the both of us."

"Nevertheless, he was a human being, and he didn't deserve to die like that," she said sternly, grabbing her duffel bag and reaching for his bag, too.

"Working on your sainthood, Molloy? It'll take more than that to convince me."

She opened the door, patiently waiting for him. "I don't need to convince you, Dr. Crompton. You weren't blessed with many human qualities to begin with, and what little you had seems to have disappeared with the rest of you." She smiled sweetly. "It's just a shame you didn't lose your voice, as well."

He couldn't very well argue with her. The door was open, the light overhead illuminating her dark blond hair, illuminating the supposedly empty room. He had no choice but to follow her. He couldn't even close the door behind him. Not with the desk clerk staring out, insatiably curious.

"Are you going to take care of the doors?" he demanded, as she settled into the driver's seat with seeming ease.

"Damn," she said, scooting back out to slam the motel door, then moving around to open the passenger door for him. He knew she was coming, and he deliberately didn't move, letting her barrel into him, catching her arms in his strong hands, letting her chest rest against his.

He'd unbuttoned his shirt against the incessant heat of his body, and her breasts through the thin cotton jersey were hard, pebbled, and he knew damned well it wasn't from the cold. She jerked away, rattled, and he was just as glad she couldn't see his face. She'd already warned him she didn't like it when he smirked, and he had little doubt he had a full-fledged smirk across his face.

"Tell me when you're in," she said between her teeth. "I wouldn't want to slam the door on your foot."

He climbed in quickly, knowing she'd probably be tempted to do just that. "All set."

She muttered something beneath her breath, slammed the door and returned to the driver's seat. The desk clerk was still watching, and Daniel had no doubt he'd made note of the license plate number. The powers that be were already on their trail, and Daniel wasn't quite ready to deal with them. Not until he had a better idea of the limits and extents of his new body.

He turned back, glancing at the dark sedan parked two doors down from their room. That car hadn't been there before. He didn't like the looks of it—the smoked windows, the heavy steel. That car's presence wasn't a coincidence.

The desk clerk had picked up the telephone. "Get a move on, Molloy," Daniel said.

She didn't wast her time arguing. Putting Jackson's car in gear, she took off, taking the corner at a dangerous speed, racing out into the night.

Daniel looked back. The door to the adjoining room opened, and he could see someone in a uniform that looked suspiciously familiar. Cole Slaughter. He glanced back at the sedan, trying to gauge whether it was powerful enough to catch up with them.

He stared at it, blinked and scrunched his nose absently.

The explosion sent Jackson's car skidding across the pavement. Suzanna swore as she tried to regain control, spinning the steering wheel and pumping the brakes desperately. They were heading sideways for a streetlight, and at their speed Daniel doubted they'd be able to avoid it.

But at the last minute she pulled out of the spin, straightened the wheels and took off into the night.

Leaving the anonymous sedan engulfed in flames.

Chapter Eight

"Oh, no." The voice beside her was hushed, literally disembodied, and yet distractingly solid. When Suzanna slammed her foot down on the accelerator, the car shot forward and she continued driving, hunched forward over the steering wheel like a bat out of hell.

An apt figure of speech. The flames shot into the sky behind them, sending ghoulish shadows across the road ahead. Suzanna yanked the wheel, turned into an alleyway and sped onward, away from the sight, the sound, the smell of the burning automobile.

She waited until they were out on the highway, away from the small town with its orange sky. "Was anyone in the car?" she asked quietly.

She didn't dare glance at the empty seat beside her. If she thought about it she'd be completely freaked out. Better to just be pragmatic about the whole thing. So the man beside her was invisible. Stranger things had been known to happen. She wasn't sure what, but they must have.

"I don't think so," the voice said after a moment's silence.

She couldn't resist. She glanced over at the empty seat, then swerved. "Do you have to wear your seat belt?" she demanded, thoroughly rattled.

The shoulder harness hung suspended in midair, the lap

belt buckled across an invisible lap. "Habit," the voice said, and she heard the click of the seat belt releasing.

"Forget it. Do it up," she said, staring ahead of her. "I imagine you could get hurt if I managed to crash this sucker, and right now I'm feeling disturbed enough to do just that."

"Then slow down."

"Back seat driver," she muttered, nevertheless doing as he suggested. "What happened with that car? Was it another bomb?"

Silence for a moment. "Sorry, I was shaking my head. I don't think it was a bomb, any more than the other two were." He paused. "I think *I* did it."

"This is definitely weird," she muttered under her breath, not daring to look in his direction. "So how do you think you did it?"

"I don't know. Then again, I don't know how I got invisible, or how strong I am, or anything else. I'm learning as I go along. All I know is cars have exploded after I've stared at them."

"But every car you look at doesn't explode."

"No. There has to be more to it than that." She heard the faint creak of the seat, and she could only guess that he was shifting around, trying to get more comfortable. "We need to get away from everybody, so I can experiment."

"I don't know that anyone's going to be volunteering their car for the sake of science," she pointed out.

"This one will do nicely. The sooner we get rid of it the better."

"And how do you intend to replace it?"

Silence again. "Just drive," he muttered. "Head towards the mountains. Route 2A."

"Do you know where we're going?"

"Yes."

She waited for more clarification, but there was utter silence. She'd never realized how much she relied upon body language and facial expressions to read people. "All right," she said finally. "Mind if I turn on the radio? Sitting next to you gives me the creeps."

She startled him into laughing. It was a very sexy laugh, but then, she'd already known that about him. For an arrogant, starchy scientist, Dr. Daniel Crompton was extremely sexy. At least, as far as she was concerned, and she should have known better. That wry amusement in his voice traveled down her spine to lodge somewhere low in her belly, and she wanted to squirm.

"Go right ahead," he said. "I'll try not to be intrusive."

"That shouldn't be too much of a challenge," she shot back.

The radio didn't improve matters. Whoever was programming the music on the only station that came in clearly must have had an overload of hormones. The playlist was a hardheaded woman's nightmare. Chris Isaak was doing his werewolf impersonation on "Wicked Game," his voice sinuous and insinuating. That was followed by Marvin Gaye and "Sexual Healing," which had Suzanna shifting in the bucket seat and wishing to God she could see what Crompton's reaction to all this was.

The final song was Bruce Springsteen's "Fire." At that point Suzanna leaned over and turned the music off, thoroughly shaken. An unseen hand brushed hers, and the music came on again, slowly rocking, entirely suggestive.

"I want to hear it," he said.

"I don't."

"Tough. The irony is irresistible."

"Buy the CD then."

"I own it."

She turned to stare at him in surprise, seeing only her reflection in the passenger window. She turned back, cursing under her breath. "I saw your apartment, Dr. Crompton. You don't even own a CD player, and the only disk I saw was Neil Diamond's *Greatest Hits*. You live like a monk, and I can't say much for your taste in music."

Again that damnably sexy chuckle. "If you choose to believe that, go right ahead, Molloy."

"You're beginning to piss me off. Are you going to stay invisible, or will I be able to see you long enough to hit you?" she demanded.

"I have no idea. I changed back at eight this morning. Maybe in two minutes I'll be visible again."

She glanced at the digital clock on the dashboard. Seven fifty-eight. Bruce was finishing up, and Suzanna felt uncomfortably warm. Not that she wasn't used to it. From the first moment she'd been around Daniel Crompton she'd felt her temperature rise, and it wasn't just the furnacelike heat that emanated from his skin, seen and unseen. She had to face it, the man made her hot.

The radio station took pity on her, launching into a spiel for the kind of car she'd never be able to afford and wouldn't have wanted, anyway, and the seconds ticked away. "One minute to go," his disembodied voice murmured.

Then came an ad for laxatives, and Suzanna felt herself cool off. Until, God help her, a sultry male voice started discussing condoms.

The clock clicked to 8:00 p.m. Dr. Daniel Crompton remained invisible.

"So much for that theory," Suzanna said, hoping to drown out the conversation on latex sensitivity.

"Damn," he muttered. "I don't think I like the thought of remaining invisible."

She had a sudden, horrifying thought. "Are you wearing anything?"

She didn't have to see his grin to know it was there. "Interesting question, Molloy. What were you imagining?"

"How come I can't see your clothes? You aren't wearing

the stuff that got dowsed with the slime, I know. Did you...I don't want to know."

She thought she'd already been unnerved enough, but the notion that he might be sitting next to her in the cozy front seat of the compact car, that long, elegant body of his undressed, was enough to make her want to drive off the road. Especially with the condom ad now over and Wilson Pickett coming on with "In the Midnight Hour."

"Don't panic, Molloy. Whatever I put on—or in—my body seems to disappear. If I just *hold* it, it seems to float through space. I'm still dressed."

"It could prove embarrassing if you were to suddenly rematerialize," she said in her coolest voice.

"For whom? You or me? Besides, I'm completely material now. You just can't see me. Much as you—damn." His voice suddenly sharpened, and there was no missing the thread of pain.

Suzanna slammed on the brakes, staring at the empty passenger seat. "What's wrong? Don't just sit there, Daniel, say something! Are you hurt? Are you..."

Before she could finish her sentence she saw the outline, vague, indistinct, slowly coming into focus. She'd forgotten how tall he was, and how he would crowd into the tiny seat of a compact car. She'd forgotten how long his legs were, too. He had an arm across his flat stomach, and as his face came into view there was no missing the expression of pain.

"Damn," he muttered again, closing his eyes.

"It hurts, Daniel?" she asked softly.

"Every time."

"How much?"

His eyes flew open, and he glared at her. "Enough to make your sadistic little soul happy, Molloy." He glanced down at his body. "I take it I'm visible again?"

"Can't you tell?"

"Not for certain. I look just a bit out of focus." He slid down in the seat with a weary sigh. "Three past eight."

"Maybe you'll stay invisible for longer and longer," she suggested. Having him beside her, suddenly visible, should have been reassuring. Instead, she found herself even more edgy.

"More likely the clocks aren't synchroized," he drawled.

"Why six to eight o'clock?"

"Why invisible?" he countered. "God only knows. Keep driving, Molloy. The sooner we get to my place, the sooner I can start working on some answers."

"Is that where we're going?"

"I have a cabin in the mountains," he said reluctantly. He rolled down the window, staring out into the night. "Fortunately no one knows about it. I keep it very private, and there's no way the people at Beebe can find us there."

"You think we'll be safe?"

"Maybe for a day or two. Then they'll find us, and who knows what'll happen."

"Oh, don't try to comfort me with reassuring lies," she said bitterly. "Just tell it like it is."

He glanced at her, and she found herself wishing that wry, clever smile was still invisible. It had far too potent an effect on her. "Are you worried, Molloy? I thought you were too tough to let a little thing like a megalomaniac megacorporation intent on murder get you upset."

"All in a day's work, Dr. Crompton," she shot back.

"You called me Daniel before."

"A slip of the tongue. I thought you were dying."

He nodded, amusement in his dark eyes. "I liked it," he said. "I'll let you know when I'm dying again."

SUZANNA MOLLOY WAS quite a woman. Whether Daniel wanted to admit it or not, there was no getting around the fact that she was tougher, smarter and far more determined than any woman he'd ever met. It wasn't that she met the challenge of having her companion literally disappear on her that was so impressive. It was the fact that it obviously scared her, scared her spitless, and yet she still managed to deal with it. Bravery without imagination was worthless. Resolution when you knew the consequences was far more honorable.

On top of that, she was the sexiest thing he'd ever seen. She still wasn't wearing a bra, a fact he'd been able to appreciate as he sat beside her, invisible. He would watch her long legs as she shifted gears, the play of her arms as she cornered, the soft swell of her breasts beneath the T-shirt. He could watch as her nipples hardened in response to the undeniably erotic music.

He was half tempted to see whether he could get away with touching her, but he didn't dare. Not this time. She was walking a tightrope of reaction. If he happened to brush against those luscious breasts, she'd probably scream and wreck the car.

He'd give her time. Not that that was a commodity they were particularly blessed with, but by the time they reached his cabin, out in the back of beyond, they'd probably have at least twenty-four hours of peace. Twenty-four hours for him to find some sort of answer as to what had happened to him.

And twenty-four hours to get her in bed.

He'd never set out to seduce a woman before. It was just one more novel experience, and he wondered idly whether the green slime had affected his libido, as well.

He didn't think so. He'd reacted to her in the moments in his lab, before the world and his life had exploded. Much as he would have liked to chalk it up to the aftereffects of the accident, he didn't think he could count on it. At best, having his life knocked sideways may have simply changed his priorities a bit. Before whoever had killed Jackson managed to catch up with them, he wanted to make sure he'd had a chance to see whether Suzanna ever stopped snarling long enough to purr.

"How are we doing for gas?" He kept his voice low, but she jumped, anyway.

"We'll need some."

"There's a truck stop up ahead. I've only stopped there once before, so people aren't likely to recognize me. We can get something to drink, maybe some food. It's going to be a long night."

"How far are we traveling?"

"You don't need to know. Suffice it to say we're not taking the most direct route. We'll be there by dawn."

"I'm not driving all night!" she protested.

"I am. I don't usually bother with much sleep. You can try to get some rest."

"For some reason, I don't feel particularly sleepy," she said with mock innocence.

He had the rash desire to lean forward and kiss her soft, cynical mouth. He would, but not now. "You've lived too staid a life, Molloy," he said calmly. "You're not used to life in the fast lane."

"In the fast lane on a back road?" she muttered.

"Maybe. There's the truck stop."

"Why is there a truck stop on a back road?"

"Beats me. You want to ask them?"

"No. I want a bathroom, I want a Diet Coke, and I want something to eat."

"They can provide all three."

He filled the tank while Suzanna disappeared inside the Quonset hut building. Jackson's credit card was lying in the glove compartment, and he used it without compunction. Jackson was beyond worrying about unpaid bills, and the good folks at Beebe might be a little slower in tracing it. At least it might slow them down a bit.

By the time he'd pulled up under the glare of the streetlights and gone in to find Suzanna, his sense of uneasiness was increasing. She was sitting at a booth, a huge greasy hamburger and french fries piled in front of her. He slid in opposite her, only to find the same noxious mass deposited in front of him.

"I'm not hungry," he told the slatternly waitress.

"You got a problem with the food, sonny?" the woman demanded, beefy arms akimbo.

"We're having a fight," Suzanna interrupted promptly, sliding the bottle of catsup across the table toward him. He caught it automatically. "Eat up, honey. I promise I won't bug you about Junior's report card."

He stared at her blankly, but apparently the waitress was satisfied. "Eat up," she said, in what was meant more as a threat than a suggestion, and disappeared back into the kitchen with a stately waddle.

"I don't eat meat," he said.

"Why not? Moral objections? Given that you're considered America's secret weapon, I find that just a tiny bit hypocritical," she said, picking up a french fry and popping it into her mouth.

"Where did you hear that?" he asked in a very quiet voice.

"My Uncle Vinnie. He knows everything."

"And what else did he tell you about me?"

She tore her attention away from her mound of french fries when she felt the sudden tension in the air. He'd already learned, however, that she wasn't easily intimidated. "He told me you were so brilliant they couldn't even measure your IQ. That no one knows what you've been working on, but it's big. Very big. Something that could change the future of the world. I don't like things like that, Dr. Crompton. I don't like the thought of one man having that much power."

"I don't."

"All right. I don't like the thought of one man having that much knowledge or that much ability. Someone could control you. Everybody has some vulnerability. All they have to do is find yours, and you're putty in their hands.''

"I doubt it," he said, stretching out in the booth and taking the mug of coffee in his hands. It felt cool to the touch. "I don't tend to have recognizable weaknesses," he said, staring at one of the first weaknesses he'd ever noticed. "And why do you think we're running? If Osborn, Armstead or their goons catch up with us, I'm not sure what would happen. You'd think they'd want to keep me going, but they may have gotten some misleading information. They may think they have everything they need from me."

"Do they?" she asked, forgetting about her french fries for the moment.

"No."

To his surprise she didn't ask him any more. She simply nodded, leaned back and concentrated on her food with a dedication that was single-minded and erotic.

He stared down at his own plate. Nothing short of starvation could get him to touch the hamburger, but the potatoes were smelling surprisingly good, and he needed something to cut the taste of the reheated coffee. "Tell me about Uncle Vinnie," he said, starting in on the fries.

"Nothing to tell. He's not really my uncle, he's my college roommate's uncle. He looks out for me."

"I'm a fairly obscure person. How would he have heard of me?"

She shrugged, managing an innocent smile. "Beats me."

His hand shot out and caught her wrist. He did it gently, afraid of his ability to hurt her, but there was no escape, and a flash of pure rage appeared in her warm brown eyes as she tried to jerk away. "Don't lie to me, Suzanna," he said quietly. "I've got top security clearance, and if someone has heard of me, it's someone who shouldn't have. Who and what is Uncle Vinnie?"

"You're hurting me."

"Answer me."

"He's just someone who looks out for me." He increased the pressure on her wrist, just slightly, and her face paled. She was lying to him, and he couldn't afford to let her do that. His life depended on it, perhaps hers as well, if he hadn't been wrong in trusting her. But he couldn't let her keep anything back.

"Who is he?" he asked one more time.

She wanted to keep resisting, he could see that. He could read the struggle, the furious acceptance. "His name is Vincenzo Dartaglia. He's retired from the restaurant business and he has certain contacts—"

"He's organized crime," Daniel corrected flatly. "What has he got to do with Beebe?"

"Nothing. He's just heard things, that's all. He warned me…" She took a deep, shaky breath.

"Warned you about what?"

"To keep away from you."

He stared at her for a long moment. "He was right," he said, releasing her wrist. "But you didn't listen."

"I'm not in the habit of listening to good advice," she said. She didn't rub her wrist, but he knew she wanted to. "He heard rumors about something going on at Beebe, and I decided to investigate. Obviously I got more than I bargained for."

"Obviously," he said quietly.

"I've learned one thing, though. You and Henry Osborn have a great deal in common."

He held himself very still. "What's that?"

"You both like hurting people when you want something."

"Osborn hurt you?"

She smiled at him. It was a cool, brittle upturning of her generous mouth, and he almost thought he could see the faint sheen of tears behind the glasses, in the depths of her defiant brown eyes. But Suzanna Molloy wasn't the kind of woman who'd ever cry. Who'd ever let a man like him make her cry.

"I'm tougher than that," she said. "He tried." She pushed her plate away. "I'll meet you at the car."

"Are you going to run away?"

She rose, and he noticed for the first time that she'd somehow found the time to put on a bra. It was the least he deserved as punishment. "No," she said. "I have a stake in this as well as you do. But, Crompton..." she leaned forward, smelling like flowers and french fries, utterly delicious.

"Yes?"

"You put your hands on me again and I'll cut your liver out."

He watched her saunter out into the parking lot, knowing his weren't the only appreciative male eyes marking her course. He could almost smile at her threat. Almost—if he weren't so thoroughly disgusted with himself.

He told himself he'd had no choice. And it didn't matter. He'd never hurt a weaker, more vulnerable human being in his life. And the fact that he wanted her—needed her—made him even sicker.

Her wrist had been delicate beneath his encircling fingers, the bones and skin vulnerable. He thought about what he'd done to the locked door at Beebe, and he wanted to throw up.

What had Osborn done to her? He already had a score to settle with the man—Suzanna had just upped the ante. And it was only coincidental that when he smashed his fist into Osborn's fat, smiling face, he'd be aiming at his own, as well.

He'd hurt her, and he'd had no choice. And the damnable thing was, he might have to do it again.

Chapter Nine

Suzanna had already taken the passenger seat, fastened the belt around her and closed her eyes by the time Daniel joined her. Her wrist throbbed, and she wondered whether he'd actually hurt her, or if it was simply the heat from his skin. She didn't care. He'd used force on her, something she wouldn't easily forgive. So what if he was drop-dead gorgeous in a remote sort of way. She didn't need gorgeous. She needed tenderness, gentleness and decent behavior.

She turned her face toward the window, away from him, to hide the reluctant smile that curved her mouth. One of her worst problems, she'd learned long ago, was that she saw herself far too clearly. Life would be a great deal easier if she had some illusions about her own sweetness and gentleness. She'd left a number of her favorite T-shirts behind, including the one that read 51% Sweetheart—49% Bitch—Don't push it!'' She wished she was wearing it right now. It might remind her who she wanted to be when she grew up.

"You must be used to subservient females," she muttered.

"If I am, you're a refreshing change."

She bit her lip again, hoping he wouldn't notice. But Crompton was a damnably observant man.

"You couldn't be smiling, could you?" he asked in an astonished voice as he started down the two-lane highway.

She gave up, turning back to him. "What can I say? Life's too bizarre to be taken seriously."

He stared at her for a long moment, at the last minute turning his attention back to his driving before they ended up in a ditch. He drove in complete, utter silence for another five minutes, long enough for Suzanna to regret her remark, long enough for her to begin to drift off to sleep.

"I'm sorry I had to hurt you."

His voice was quiet, so low she should have missed it. He'd pitched it that way deliberately, and she knew he wasn't the sort of man who apologized. No more than he was the sort of man who made a habit of bullying people. He did what he had to do, and pity any poor creature who got in his way.

But she wasn't a poor creature; she could stand up to him. "Just don't do it again," she muttered.

She wasn't expecting it. He reached over and picked up her hand as it lay loosely in her lap. Her muscles tightened as she started to pull away, and his own grip grew stronger. She wasn't sure how a tug-of-war would end, but suddenly she didn't care. She let her hand lie in his for a moment, watching in fascination as he brought it to his mouth.

His lips were burning hot and dry as they pressed against the side of her wrist, where he'd crunched her bones together. The heat was like an electric current, shafting through her, and she turned, looking at him, wanting to move closer to that source of heat and strength.

But if he saw her reaction, he pretended he didn't. He set her hand back in her lap and kept his face turned into the night. "Get some sleep," he said. "We've got a long way to go."

She turned her face away again, uncertain what she wanted to say or do. She closed her eyes, feigning sleep, and within moments illusion became reality, as he drove through the endless darkness, the quiet drone of the car's engine lulling her to sleep.

She woke up several times during the night, turned to look at him, then drifted off again. The man wasn't human, she decided sleepily. No man could be so single-minded, so impervious to physical needs and discomfort. She slept again, dreaming erotic dreams—that his long, elegant hand skimmed her cheek, brushed against her breast, caught her hand in his once more and put it in his lap. And she didn't pull away in maidenly horror. He was hot for her, ready for her, as he drove through the night, and her hand on him was a kind of claiming.

When she finally surfaced from sleep, it was light outside. The radio was on, playing softly, something old and bluesy, and Suzanna shifted in her seat, a sleepy smile on her face.

And then she screamed.

"Damn!" he cursed, and the car swerved off the road, coming to a stop halfway up an embankment. "You scared the hell out of me. Did you have to scream?"

"Did you have to disappear again?" she shot back, furious, hoping he wouldn't notice that her hands were trembling.

"It wasn't up to me," his disembodied voice said, as the gearshift lever was put back into reverse, the steering wheel turned, and as the car started down the postdawn road again. "And I was right—this clock is three minutes fast."

She glanced down at the digital clock. It was almost seven. At least she'd missed close to an hour of Daniel's unnerving appearance. Or lack thereof. "Shouldn't I be driving?"

"The road's deserted. There aren't many people living out this way. If anyone looks too closely, they'll just assume this is a British import with the steering wheel on the opposite side."

"That's pretty farfetched."

"This entire situation is farfetched, but it's damnably real," Daniel replied. "We're not too far from my place now, and with luck we won't be passing anyone. Just let me concentrate on the driving, and we'll be there by eight."

"Just as well," she muttered. "I'd have a hard time following you otherwise."

Suzanna wasn't sure what she'd been expecting when they arrived at their mysterious, final destination almost an hour later. He'd called it a cabin in the woods, and she'd expected something rustic, with no amenities, just a reclaimed hunter's camp.

Either that, or another square box, as soulless and modern and characterless as Daniel's apartment.

The reality was astonishing.

Her companion stopped the car at the foot of a narrow, winding path, unfastening the seat belt and taking the keys. "We're here," his voice announced.

"Where?" she demanded, looking around her at the empty clearing, the tall, dark trees all around. They hadn't passed even a shack since she'd been awake, and she'd yet to see any sign of a building. "I'm not in the mood for a tent or a cave, Dr. Crompton."

She felt the air brush by her, warning her, and then his hand on her chin, cupping it, tilting her face upward, until she spotted the house.

It perched halfway up a cliff, and was made of glass and stone and wood, like some sort of new-age tree house. If he hadn't moved her head she would have missed it. As it was, the house blended in perfectly with the surroundings. "How do we get there?"

"We walk."

"I was afraid of that." She didn't bother to keep the mournful tone from her voice. He was still cupping her chin, and she could feel his long fingers against her jaw, delicate, strong, ridiculously erotic to her confused mind. And hot. "You can let go of me," she said caustically.

He did, quite promptly, and she had no idea whether there was any reluctance in him. One moment he was touching her, in what felt uncannily like a caress, in another he was gone.

The door opened and closed, and she could only assume he'd climbed out. She followed, grabbing her duffel bag as she went, unnerved to see his own canvas bag floating in the air. "I wonder," she said deliberately.

The canvas bag ahead of her stopped moving. "Wonder what?"

"If you took a cold shower, would the water sizzle?"

She heard him laugh, that damnably, sexy laugh. "I have no need of a cold shower, Molloy."

Depressing thought. "No, I suppose you don't," she said grimly, wondering if one would help her irrational state of longing.

"It wouldn't do any good," he added cryptically.

For a moment she considered his words. Would his body temperature withstand an icy bath? Or would his libido?

As far as she knew, the man didn't have a libido. And she had suddenly developed far too much of one. It must have come from having squashed it down for so long, she thought. She'd ignored any little trace of attraction she'd felt for the men she'd met during the last few years, and that squashed, downtrodden sexuality had decided to assert itself at the most damnably inconvenient of times.

She could fight it. She was tough. And fortunately Daniel Crompton had no sexual interest in her whatsoever. Right?

"Lead the way," she said wearily. "Unless you'd rather wait until you're visible again."

"What time is it?"

"You're wearing a watch."

"I can't see it."

"Oh." She glanced at her own. "Ten of eight."

"I don't want to wait. Move away from the car."

"Why?"

"A little experiment. Come over here."

She moved in the direction of his voice, trying to quell the uneasy feeling that washed over her. She walked to the edge of the narrow, snaking path that led up the cliff and stopped by the duffel bag that had recently floated through the air. "Is this far enough?" she asked in a deceptively even voice, bracing for the feel of his hands on her.

"Far enough." His voice was abstracted. She stood there, unmoving, listening to the wind rush through the tall pines overhead, bringing the scent of fall and resin to her nostrils. Nothing happened.

"Damn," Crompton muttered. "I can't do it."

"Can't do what?"

"Can't make the car explode. I was certain..."

The force of the explosion knocked her down. Where Jackson's little car had once stood, a fireball erupted, shooting flames into the sky. Suzanna lay on the ground, watching in horror, the heat enveloping her. She tried to rise, but something pushed her back down into the dirt, something unseen.

"Stay down," he ordered, but there was no panic in his voice. Merely a distant, sort of fascinated sound.

She did as he told her. Not that she had much choice. A hand rested between her shoulder blades, keeping her pressed to the earth, as the remnants of the automobile flamed furiously, burning out of control, and black smoke billowed toward the sky.

She closed her eyes for a moment and shuddered. When she opened them, the first thing she saw was his thigh. He was sitting cross-legged beside her, staring at the inferno, his hand still holding her down.

"It must be after eight o'clock," she muttered, struggling to sit up.

He released her, casting a cursory glance over her doubtless rumpled figure. "I figured it was. The cramps weren't quite as bad this time. Maybe I'm getting used to it."

"How did you do it?"

He nodded in the direction of the burning car. "You mean *that?* I'm not quite sure. I concentrated on it, but nothing happened. I think my nose itched, and I may have blinked a few times. I'll have to try to isolate it a little better. Find out whether it only works on cars, what causes the explosion, whether I can make other things—"

"I don't know if there'll be any more cars to spare," she said, her voice caustic. "How are we going to get out of here now that you've incinerated our only form of transportation?"

He had the grace to look momentarily abashed. "We couldn't go in Jackson's car, anyway. They'd be looking for it."

"You don't think anyone's going to notice the little bonfire we just had?"

"Not likely. We're in a very remote spot." He rose, and she looked up, way up the length of his jean-clad legs. God, it was a sin to be as good-looking as he was, she thought wearily.

"Let's hope so." She struggled to her feet, ready to slap away any helping hands. He didn't offer. He was already starting up the narrow winding path into the woods, and she had no choice but to follow.

She paused at the edge of the clearing, taking one last look at the charred remains of Jackson's car. Whatever had torched it had burned so hotly that even the frame had collapsed into the smoldering embers. It no longer even looked as if a car had been sitting there. The smoke had dissipated into the clear blue sky, and only the lingering smell remained. That and the blackened circle of earth.

She shivered again, despite the lingering warmth. And, hoisting her bag to her shoulder, she started after Daniel.

The woods were dark, overgrown, the path steep and slippery from early morning dew. Daniel forged onward, making no effort to wait for her, and Suzanna struggled to keep up, cursing underneath her breath. She'd just about given up hope of ever reaching the top, when Daniel stopped short, and she barreled into him, absorbing the solidity of his warm body, catching herself on his arms for a moment before she released him.

"Doesn't look like anyone's been here," he said in a meditative voice, still not moving out of her way.

She craned her neck around him, taking in their destination. It was like nothing she'd ever seen. A bizarre, crazy quilt of a cabin, it seemed cobbled together of wood and glass, iron and tile, a mishmash of found objects and odd humor. The door looked as if it belonged to an English castle, the windows on either side were crescents set in the thick walls, the roof was the greeny metallic of old copper. It looked like the Seven Dwarfs' cottage on drugs, and Suzanna stared at it, enchanted.

"This is yours?" she breathed, rapidly adjusting her opinion of the staid Dr. Daniel Crompton, as she'd had to so frequently in the last forty-eight hours.

"This is mine." His voice was neutral, exhibiting neither pride nor embarrassment.

"Where did you find it? Did you trade some crazed old hippie for it?"

He finally moved out of the way, advancing down the ornately patterned brick walkway and reaching up over the vastly high door to fetch a key. "No." He opened the door, standing aside with one of the first shows of gallantry she'd seen him exhibit, and ushered her in.

She fell in love. It was an extraordinary place, full of magic and mystery. The walls were of stained wood and covered with tapestries, quilted hangings, romantic watercolors and tempestuous oils. There were books everywhere—in cases lining every spare inch of wall, piled on the floor, underneath tables. The furniture itself was a blissful mismatch—a Danish modern oak table with three baronial-style chairs. A wide, overstuffed sofa covered in rumpled English cotton, a brass-and-steel table shaped like an elephant. It was a traditional decorator's nightmare. It was wonderful.

She turned back to glance at Daniel's oblique face. "Obviously you haven't owned this place for long," she said, touching a rubbed green velvet cushion with loving fingers.

"Why do you say that?" He closed the door behind them, and the light filtered in from the crescent windows, meeting the blaze of light from the window on the far wall, with its expansive view overlooking the forest below.

"Because you haven't had a chance to sanitize it yet." She picked up a book, caressed it and put it down again. It was, of all things, a Georgette Heyer regency. "You forget, I saw your apartment. If you had the chance, you'd strip this place bare and paint everything white."

"Why do you think I own this place?" It was a simple question, and she considered it.

"You probably bought it because it was so remote. You're not the most sociable of creatures, and you probably liked the fact that people would have a hard time bothering you here. Do you have a telephone?"

"No."

"Electricity? A television? Radio?"

"There's a generator, but no outside source of communication."

She nodded. She wanted to kick off her shoes and collapse into the huge, overstuffed sofa, taking the Heyer book with her. She restrained herself, but just barely. "You see. It proves my point. You own this place because you're an antisocial curmudgeon."

"If you say so." He moved ahead of her, opening up the windows, letting in the fresh forest breeze. There was still a tang of fire lingering in the air, a fact which brought their circumstances home all too sharply. "I'm not sure what there is for food. I don't tend to bother with it, but there'll be enough vitamin drink for both of us."

"Be still, my heart," Suzanna said. "Where do I sleep?"

For a moment there was silence, long enough that she turned to glance at him. "Like the five-thousand-pound gorilla, anywhere you please," he said lightly. "There's a loft upstairs with a bed, and there's the sofa. Take your pick."

"Where are you sleeping?"

Again that charged silence. And then he shrugged. "I told you, I don't sleep much." He dropped down onto the huge sofa, stretching his long legs out in front of him.

"I do," she said flatly. "And I need some coffee. You don't mind if I explore?"

"Mi casa es su casa," he said, sliding down on the sofa and closing his eyes for a moment. She stared at him. For a man who didn't sleep much, he looked unutterably weary. He was used to life in a laboratory, not spending his time invisible, setting things on fire, running for his life and finding dead bodies. He probably wasn't used to having anyone else around, either. All things considered, she was probably lucky he hadn't set her on fire in a fit of pique.

She searched for the kitchen first. It was a small alcove off the living room, with open shelves filled with an odd assortment of staples—dried beans, brown rice and something that looked suspiciously like granola filled an assortment of mason jars. She found instant coffee and creamer, a tiny gas stove and a sink that after a moment or two of rusty shrieks gushed out clear mountain water.

She made a quick inventory. He was right, there wasn't much. Cans of soup, lots of them, thank heavens. Crackers, powdered milk, even powdered eggs. Could someone make a powdered-egg omelet? She had a feeling she was a long ways from her last quarter-pounder and fries.

She found a hand-thrown mug and filled it with the coffee. She'd always hated instant, but that morning, in that mysterious, enchanted little house, it tasted better than any cup made from freshly ground beans she'd ever had.

She took the step up into the living room to tell Crompton just that, only to find him stretched out on the sofa, sound asleep. He'd unbuttoned his shirt, and even from halfway across the room she could feel the heat in his body.

He'd damned well better not spontaneously combust, she thought grimly, staring at him. Apart from the fact that it would be a waste of a gorgeous male, she didn't want to have to deal with it. Though it seemed as if this particular gorgeous male was already going to waste.

There was a workroom off to the left of the living room, and for once Daniel's passion for order seemed to rule. Books lined the walls, stacked haphazardly, but the work surfaces were bare and pristine. More Georgette Heyer. And science fiction, hardcovers, paperbacks, even a stack of comics. It was all very strange.

The walls were far from bare. They bore painted murals with strange, mythic images. There was nothing obviously sexual about them, and yet their sensuality seemed to reach out and entwine itself around her loins. How could the man concentrate in a room like this?

It had the same glorious view of the valley below. She opened the window, letting in the fresh cool breeze, and peered out, looking for any sign of habitation. There was none as far as she could tell. Daniel was right, they were remote and safe. At least for now.

It took her a while to find the narrow stairs up into the loft. It was a small room, with a king-size mattress at an angle on the floor. Light flooded in—a greeny, forest light—and the windows were covered with a filmy white cloth that looked like spiderwebs. The dresser was black-laquered Chinese, the rug was a kilim, the bed piled with antique quilts and laced pillows. Who had lived here, and why had they given it up to an ascetic grouch like Daniel Crompton?

When she came back down the stairs she paused, looking at the man sleeping so peacefully. His long black hair had come undone from the strip of material he'd used to tie it back, and it flowed around him. In repose he looked different. She would have thought he'd look younger, more vulnerable, but nothing could be farther from the truth. In sleep he looked every year of the thirty-four she knew him to be, and the elegant features of his handsome face looked intimidating. She moved closer, vaguely wondering how deeply he slept. She could feel the heat emanating from him as she approached.

He'd unbuttoned his shirt, and she could see his smooth, sleekly muscled chest beneath the denim shirt. She reached out a hand, to touch his forehead, to see if she could gauge his temperature, when his eyes flew open to meet hers.

"Look but don't touch," he said in an unbearably quiet voice.

She was mesmerized, by the darkness in his eyes, by the stillness in his face.

"Why?" she whispered.

"Because if you touch me, I'll take you. And I don't think you're ready for that."

The words shocked her into momentary silence. And then she fought back. "You're really arrogant, you know that, Dr. Crompton?"

He smiled then. A slow, devastatingly sexy smile that would have melted her bones if they weren't locked stiff with fury. "I know," he said. "And you're still not ready."

Chapter Ten

He couldn't have meant it. Suzanna leaned against the wooden counter in the tiny kitchen, staring into her mug of instant soup. Daniel Crompton was hardly the type to talk about taking her, like some romance hero bent on forced seduction. He was doing it to mock her.

But for once there had been no mockery in his dark, still eyes. They had been deadly serious, and she'd stumbled back from him, away from his heat, his intensity, away from temptation that was both a threat and a promise.

He'd risen from the overstuffed sofa, stretched, and he'd looked like a different man than the hidebound Dr. Crompton. His muscles moved sinuously beneath his skin, and he looked real, and dangerous, and far too human.

And Suzanna had run. She could hear him moving around in the living room, but she kept still, unwilling to face him for the moment as she concentrated on the watery soup. She was feeling warm herself, not uncomfortably so, and there was a faint tingling in her hands. Probably stress and exhaustion, she told herself. That would explain her idiot attraction to a man like Crompton, as well. Momentary insanity, caused by not enough sleep.

"Did you find something to eat?"

He stood in the doorway, filled it, and she wished she could tell him to button up his shirt again. She couldn't—

the heat from his body filled the small kitchen, bathing her. "There's not much. What about you?" She was proud of the even tone of her voice.

"I can make my vitamin drink." He didn't move into the room, a fact for which she could only be grateful. It was a small kitchen. With him there beside her, it would be unbearably cramped. Dangerously so.

"You need something else. Aren't you human? Don't you have any physical needs?"

Wrong question. He just looked at her for a moment, and the temperature in the kitchen shot up another couple of notches. "There should be food in the freezer," he said. "I stocked it before I left last time, but I don't usually bother with it."

"You have a freezer?"

"A gas one. In the shed."

She managed a jaunty smile, hoping to cut the tension in the room. "Maybe I won't starve to death after all. The only thing that would make life complete is a bath."

"To the right of the living room."

"There's a bathroom, as well?"

"It's positively sybaritic."

She had to wait till he moved from the doorway. She trailed along behind him, through the living room, past a narrow door she hadn't noticed, then stopped short. "God," she breathed, "it's heaven."

The bathroom was larger than the kitchen. There was a stall shower made of azure tiles, a huge whirlpool tub encased in redwood, a stained-glass skylight letting in filtered rays. "The hot water's gas-fired, as well. You can sit in the tub for hours."

"Daniel, I love you," she muttered, brushing past his hot body. She turned around, a beatific smile on her face. "Who did you buy this place from? It's the most wonderful house I've ever seen in my life."

"I bought the land from a friend of mine. I own about

four hundred acres, he owns the rest. That's why I figure we're relatively safe here. The surrounding forest is private land.''

She had a sudden, unnerving thought. ''You bought the land?''

''About five years ago.''

''Then how did this house get here?'' She didn't want to hear the answer. It would set all her preconceived notions awry.

''I built it.''

''How did you get workmen out here, plumbers, electricians…?''

''No,'' he corrected her. ''I built it. Myself.'' He was watching her, gauging her reaction. ''When it comes right down to it, construction, plumbing and the like is very mathematical. And I've always had a certain aptitude for math.''

She just stared at him. She'd fallen in love with this strange, unexpected little house. That it was the creation of a man she already found far too disturbing to her senses, that it reflected his heart and soul and mind, was something she wasn't ready to accept.

''Enjoy your bath,'' he said, turning and leaving her there.

She heard the music as she lay in the tub, the cool, herb-scented water flowing around her. Somewhere in that outer room he had a stereo, and the music filled the place. Another anomaly. She would have thought he'd like free-form modern jazz, something arrhythmic, atonal, entirely intellectual.

Instead, it was the unmistakable sound of Lyle Lovett, singing something plaintive and soulful. Any man who listened to Lyle Lovett couldn't be all bad.

She didn't want to come out. She didn't want to look into his eyes again and see that cool, detached interest. He was far too tempting as it was.

When she emerged from the tub, she'd be calm, matter-of-fact, impervious to her own irrational streak. She'd make them something for dinner, and if things went as scheduled, she'd watch him disappear promptly at 6:00 p.m. She'd have an easier time with him if she didn't have to look at him, didn't have to keep her gaze from his thin, surprisingly erotic mouth. Didn't have to ignore his eyes, the set of his shoulders, the long, long legs and muscled torso.

Together they could figure out what they were going to do next. She certainly couldn't stay out here indefinitely, even if no one could find them. She'd go crazy.

Except that part of her wanted to drift. To lie in this cool tub of water, to float through this patchwork quilt of a house, to smell the piney air and breathe in the sunshine. She couldn't rid herself of the notion that she'd come home. And she wasn't ready to leave it quite yet.

When she finally rose from the tub, her body was still too warm. She combed her wet hair, slathered some cream on her skin and pulled on the clean clothes she'd brought with her. She surveyed her T-shirt with approval. It read If We Can Send One Man to the Moon, Why Can't We Send Them All? Perhaps Daniel would get the message. She only wished he would.

DANIEL MOVED ONTO the narrow balcony that hung out over the valley, and drank in the cool air. He let his shirt flap around him in the breeze as he leaned forward, gripping the railing. He couldn't imagine ever being cold again. Oddly enough, he wasn't particularly uncomfortable. It was a dry kind of heat, burning inside him, filling him with an edgy energy.

Suzanna was wandering around his house, a cup of instant coffee in her hand, a wary expression on her face. He didn't blame her. She didn't know what to make of him. She'd decided he had to be kidding when he told her he wanted her, and she'd pulled away from him, keeping her distance, treating it all as a joke.

It didn't feel like a joke. He wasn't used to wanting anything as badly as he wanted Suzanna Molloy. Right now it was all he could do to stand out in the afternoon light and concentrate on his erratic powers.

She'd spent an hour in his sybaritic bathroom, and when she'd emerged, fresh-faced, dressed in another defiant T-shirt, looking at him out of wary brown eyes as if he were a polar bear who'd wandered into town, it had taken all his concentration not to grab her.

He didn't consider for a moment that she might be wary of his freakish new powers. Molloy was made of sterner stuff than that. She was afraid of her own reaction to him. Something which pleased him enormously.

He heard her appear behind him on the narrow balcony. "What are you doing out here?" she asked quietly.

"A little scientific experimentation. I want to see whether I can set anything on fire."

She moved past him and leaned out over the railing. He allowed himself the luxury of admiring the lush curve of her hips in the faded denim. "Do you think that's wise?" she said. "I don't think a forest fire would solve anything."

"You're right. But from what I've observed so far, the heat is so strong, and so concentrated, that whatever catches on fire simply disintegrates before the blaze has a chance to spread. I want to see if I'm right."

"And if you're wrong?"

"Science is a far riskier business than most people realize. If you don't take chances, you never learn anything. See that tower through the trees? It's an old metal watchtower, from back in World War Two. It has no earthly use."

"So you're going to put it out of its misery?"

"I'm going to try." He leaned forward, concentrating on

the wire structure, trying to remember how he'd managed to detonate the car. He stared, and nothing happened.

"Maybe it only works when you're invisible," she suggested after a long wait.

"No. Remember the parking lot outside my condo."

"What makes you think you're responsible?"

"An educated guess." He tried blinking a few times, but nothing happened. His nose itched, and he scrunched it.

There was no sound from that distance. Just yellow-white flames rocketing into the sky where the observation tower had once stood.

"Damn," Suzanna said softly.

At least he'd been right about one thing—nothing else caught. Within moments the fire was simply a gray plume of smoke, billowing skyward.

She turned to look at him. "Can you do anything besides metal?"

"I don't know. Pick something."

She peered over the balcony, then pointed to a clearly dead, huge white pine that lay in the midst of fallen trees. "Try that one."

The speed of it shocked him. He looked, he blinked, he scrunched, and the tree burst into flames. They watched in tense silence to see whether the fire would spread to the others, fallen timber, but it simply flamed out at the underside of the tree, leaving nothing but ash and charred fragments.

"Pretty neat trick, Dr. Crompton," Suzanna said in a cool voice. "Got any other little talents?"

He looked at her. She was trying to look blasé, but he could see the worry in her brown eyes behind the wire-rimmed glasses, see the faint anxiety in her soft mouth.

"I don't know," he said. "But I'm going to find out." His eyes narrowed. "You sure you're feeling all right?"

He knew it was cool out on the balcony. He didn't feel

it, with his elevated body heat, but neither did she. She seemed perfectly comfortable wearing only a T-shirt.

"I'm feeling fine. Why shouldn't I be?"

"You got dowsed with the slime, as well. I can't figure out why you haven't been affected."

"Lucky me."

"Do me a favor. Pick an object, stare at it for a moment, blink and scrunch your nose."

"Why?"

"Indulge me."

"I feel like something out of 'Bewitched,'" she muttered, leaning forward. "That tree down there. To the left of what used to be the observation tower." She did as he'd ordered, concentrating. Nothing happened.

"Try it again."

"Trust me, Daniel, I don't have your ability to turn inanimate objects into cinders," she snapped. "You're the superman around here."

"I wish I could be sure."

"Of what?"

"Any number of things. That I was the only one affected. That it was only inanimate things."

She stared at him. "What do you mean?"

"Who's to say I can't incinerate another human being?"

He'd hoped saying it out loud would take some of the horror out of the notion. It only made it worse. He pushed away from the railing.

"I'll be in the lab, working on the slime. Maybe I can break it down enough to find some answers."

"An antidote?"

"If need be. Right now I think we're going to need all the advantages we can muster. I don't think the people at Beebe are going to forget about us."

"What makes you think they know I came with you?"

"They know," he said. And he walked away from her. While he could still make himself do it.

SHE DIDN'T MEAN to fall asleep. She was just going to lie down for a while on the surprisingly comfortable mattress upstairs, just close her eyes and feel the cool air across her skin. When she awoke, it was pitch-dark, and she could only hope it was after eight and she'd missed Daniel's disappearance. She fumbled around for her glasses, then turned on the light beside the bed.

Her scream echoed through the eccentric little house. She heard Daniel, the pounding of his footsteps up the narrow flight of stairs, and while she'd managed to quiet her screams, she couldn't catch her breath. She felt her hands and face grow numb as she gasped for air, and the darkness was all around her, and she was going to die, she knew it, the green slime had simply taken longer to get to her, but it was going to kill her—

Hard hands caught her arms, shaking her. "Stop it," he said. "You're hyperventilating. Snap out of it!"

She bit back her choked protest. Some distant part of her brain told her that he'd be perfectly capable of slapping her if he thought she needed it. She took a deep, shuddering breath, trying to force her panic down.

"Good girl," he murmured, pulling her into his arms, against the fiery heat of his chest. He was wearing a T-shirt—she could feel the soft cotton beneath her clutching fingers, and beneath that the solid bone and muscle. It calmed her, as nothing else would.

"Don't call me *girl*," she muttered, burying her face against his shoulder.

She could feel his smile. "Yes, ma'am. What happened? You're not the type of *woman* who has hysterics."

She pulled away reluctantly, staring up at him through her glasses. "I'm blind," she said simply.

For a moment he didn't move. "What do you mean by that? It's after eight—even I can see my reflection in the mirror."

"I told you, I'm blind. I turned on the light and everything's a complete blur."

"Blurred is better than blind," he said flatly. "Can you see some things better than others? When I'm invisible my body looks blurred to me, but everything else is in focus."

"I'm not invisible," she snapped.

"I know." He sounded just as rattled, which surprised her. "Just answer the question. Is everything fuzzy?"

"Yes."

She could see his outline as he sat on the mattress, watching her. "Describe it. In detail."

"It's the slime, I know it. I've been feeling hot all afternoon. Not a sweaty kind of heat, just a dry, tingling kind of warmth." She shivered. "When I lay down a few hours ago I could see perfectly. Now it feels as if my glasses are coated with Vaseline."

For a moment he didn't move. "Interesting," he murmured. And reaching out, he plucked her glasses off her face.

Everything focused, with a swiftness that was completely disorienting. She stared at him in the half-light, shocked. "This is impossible," she said in a hushed voice.

"Is it?"

"I've worn glasses since I was in the third grade. I can't see a thing without them."

"You can now."

She took her glasses from him and held them up. "Oh, my God," she said quietly.

"Welcome to the world of miracles," he drawled. He reached out and put his hand along the side of her neck in what felt alarmingly like a caress. She tried to jerk away, then stilled.

"That's better. I'm only trying to check your pulse," he said.

"Most people use the wrist."

"The carotid artery is a better indicator. Your pulse is racing."

"I've had a shock," she said, stubbornly ignoring the fact that his hand, straying inside the neck of her T-shirt, was doubtless responsible for at least part of her condition.

"Your skin is warm. Not as warm as mine, but warmer than it was," he observed in a detached voice. "Let me listen to your heart." He moved to press his head against her breasts, but this time she'd had enough. She jumped off the bed and skittered away from him.

"My heart's just fine, thank you," she said.

"I wonder why it took so long for it to affect you," Daniel murmured, suddenly analytical. "It's been more than forty-eight hours since the lab explosion, and I started being affected almost immediately."

"Probably because I didn't take a bath in the stuff," she said crossly. "You got the full brunt of it. I only had a little on my hands."

He looked at her, an arrested expression on his face. "I keep forgetting you have a mind."

"Do you really?" she said acidly. "I guess it's my blond bimbo looks."

"No," he said frankly. "But you *are* distracting."

She wasn't sure how she wanted to respond to that, so she avoided it, getting back to more important matters. "Did you learn anything about the slime?"

"Not yet. You can't rush these things."

"I thought we didn't have much time."

She was trying to rile him. She failed. "You have a point. I'm going back to work." He rose, and she got a good look at the T-shirt he was wearing. "Eat right, exercise, die anyway," it said. Hardly reassuring.

"What about dinner?"

"I'll make myself a vitamin drink."

"No, you won't. I'll make us something."

A wry smile curved his mouth. "You're feeling domestic, Molloy? I wouldn't have thought it of you."

"I'm feeling hungry," she corrected him. "And you need solid food, not vitamin drink. I want you to be in top physical condition."

His smile widened. "Any particular reason?"

"I'd like us to survive."

He touched her again. A brief, tender caress on the side of her face, a whisper of a stroke before he dropped his hand again. "We will, Molloy. I promise you."

She made him pasta, with every kind of vegetable she could find thrown into the sauce. He barely noticed her when she brought a tray into the lab, which was no longer the spotless operating room it had once seemed. Paraphernalia was strewn over the counters, and she shoved a pile of papers out of the way and dumped the tray down.

"Eat," she said.

"Eventually." He didn't move from the microscope.

"Eat," she repeated firmly. "I'm going to stay here and bug you until you do."

He lifted his head, focusing on her as if he'd forgotten her very existence until now. He probably had, she thought wryly.

He glanced at the overfilled plate and sniffed warily. "What's in it?"

"Broccoli, egg, green peppers, onions, mushrooms, pea pods and cheese."

"No beef?"

"There is no beef. Not unless I go out and rustle a cow myself," she said grumpily.

"Good." He hunched one hip onto a stool and took a forkful. He ate half the plate, slowly, methodically, and then looked up at her with dawning surprise. "It's good," he said.

"Of course it's good. I know how to cook. You just don't know how to eat," she grumbled.

He didn't take offense. "Good point," he said, rededicating himself to his dinner. He finished it, ate the garlic bread and then looked up hopefully. "Dessert?"

"I thought you didn't care about food."

"You're having an insidious effect on me." He rose, moving toward her, and it was all she could do not to back away from him. She'd been feeling warmer, but his heat still far outstripped hers. "Dessert?"

"I'll bring it in," she said in a resigned voice. "What about coffee? Or are you going to insist on some god-awful herb tea?"

"Coffee," he muttered, considering it. "With caffeine. Lots of it." He turned and went back to the microscope, dismissing her presence.

She was half tempted to take the tray and slam it over his head. Who did he think she was—his maid?

Then again, she didn't necessarily want his presence. As long as he was immured in his lab she could ignore him. Or, at least, make a damned good stab at it.

He didn't look up when she brought the coffee and brownies in, and she left. He probably wouldn't notice cold coffee, she thought, stuffing her fourth brownie into her mouth. She stepped out onto the balcony, letting the cool air rush over her. The moon was bright overhead, almost full, and she could see a ring of frost around it. It was a cold night. And she could barely feel a chill.

She thought about the man behind the closed door, his erratic powers and the uncanny effect he had on her. She was in trouble—in very deep trouble—since the moment she'd first snuck into Beebe headquarters in search of the elusive Dr. Crompton.

The sooner this whole mess was resolved, the better for her heart and mind.

Because she was realizing, despite her best efforts, she'd done more than fall in love with the man's house. She'd begun falling in love with the man himself, and there was no future for a girl reporter and America's secret weapon. Particularly when he turned into a down-side version of a superhero.

Chapter Eleven

Daniel rubbed a weary hand across his eyes. He was getting nowhere. Each time he thought he was on the verge of isolating the components of the slime, the solution escaped him. He'd been working for hours, stopping only long enough to wander into the darkened kitchen and get himself more brownies and coffee. He'd eaten half a pan of the brownies—he'd never realized he had a sweet tooth. He hadn't paid much attention to the coffee, but at least it had kept him going.

Until now. He glanced at his watch. It was quarter past five in the morning. He had forty-five minutes before he vanished again. He had a hard time working when he was invisible. The blurred outline of his hands distracted him as he worked at the microscope, and he'd jabbed himself in the eye more than once when he'd miscalculated.

Suzanna had disappeared hours ago, and he could only assume she was in the loft, asleep. Lying there, probably wearing nothing more than a T-shirt, her warm body soft and relaxed in sleep. He wondered what would happen if he kissed her. Closing the lab door silently behind him, he started upstairs to find out.

He stopped halfway up the narrow flight and turned, instinct calling to him. The door was open to the narrow balcony, and he could see her out there, bathed in moonlight, hands clutching the railing. And he realized with shock that there was a light snow falling.

He was wrong about the T-shirt. She was wearing a short, silky kind of nightgown, the kind he'd seen in a Victoria's Secret catalog he'd once perused, for scientific purposes, of course. It clung to her curves in a caress, and he wanted to follow those lush curves with his hand.

He came out on the balcony behind her. "It's snowing."

She didn't turn. She must have known he was there. Snow was drifting down onto her bare shoulders, lingering for a moment, then melting. "I had a dream about the man we found in the stairwell."

"Jackson," Daniel supplied. He moved closer, trying to warm her with his heat. She was cold, he could see it in the faint blue color to her soft lips, he could see it in the hardness of her nipples against the silk. He wanted her nipples hard. But he wanted to be the one who made them that way, with his mouth.

"It was an awful way to die."

"I'm not sure if there are any good ways."

She turned and looked at him, sorrow in her healed eyes. "Who do you think killed him? And why? Was it the same person who tried to blow up your lab?"

"I think Jackson was responsible for that. And I don't know why he was killed. Maybe he knew too much. Maybe he was trying to double-cross them. Maybe he'd just outlived his usefulness."

"It sounds like a James Bond novel."

He shrugged, moving closer. She was shivering; he was hot. She'd made a joke about a cold shower sizzling on his skin. He was surprised the snow didn't disappear in a cloud of vapor when it landed on his arms. "It's not a novel," he said. "Unfortunately it's real."

"Yes," she said, "it's real." Suddenly she rubbed her arms. "I'm cold," she added, surprised.

"Let me warm you." He pulled her into his arms, and

after a momentary resistance she let him. The tremors that racked her body increased, and he scooped her up effortlessly, carrying her back into the living room and sliding the door shut behind him.

"Damn," he muttered beneath his breath. "I didn't get the heat going."

"That's all right," she murmured sleepily. "You're very warm."

He glanced down at her. He was more than warm, he was hot—for her. "All right," he said, moving to the huge old sofa, sinking down and bringing her with him. She was still shaking from the cold, and perhaps something else as well, and if he were a decent, honorable man he'd set her down and find her a quilt, wrap her up and leave her be.

He didn't feel the slightest bit decent, or honorable. He sat back, cradled her against him and caught her chin in his hand.

She stared at him out of those newly focused eyes, wary, waiting. But she didn't move when he put his mouth against hers, slowly, deliberately, his lips on hers. Her mouth was cold, and he warmed it. Her lips were dry, and he moistened them. He pressed his thumb against her jaw gently, and her mouth opened beneath his, so that he could taste her, and he heard a quiet little sigh, a moan of pleasure that could have come from her, or from him.

Her body warmed, softened, flowed against his. She lay curled in his lap, her hands clutching his shoulders, as he kissed her, kissed her until he was ready to go up in smoke, breathless, mindless, crazy with the heat and the need. She was soft and sleepy against him, and her tongue met his, shyly, with a touch of eagerness that just about destroyed him. He broke away, trailing slow, hungry kisses down the slender column of her neck, and she arched against him as his hand closed down over one breast.

It fitted his hand perfectly. Cool through the silky material, it warmed, swelled against him, and he wanted to taste her there, too.

There were buttons, damnable tiny pearl buttons down the front of the nightgown. He ignored them, sliding the thin straps down over her arms, baring her small, perfect breasts. And then he froze.

"Did I do that to you?" he demanded, pulling away.

The mood was shattered. Her eyes, dreamily half-closed, now shot open. Color flooded her face, and she yanked the nightgown up, backing away from him on the wide sofa. "Do what?" she managed to choke out.

"The bruises. On your breast."

She tugged the gown around her, a wasted effort, given the skimpiness of the thing. "No."

"Then who did?" A sudden, daunting thought entered his mind. He'd never for one moment considered that she might be involved with someone. The livid bruises on her breast might have been gladly received, the by-product of a little rough sex.

"Go away," she said, curling up in a little ball, turning her face away from him, into the sofa cushion.

He put his hand on her shoulder, felt her coolness, and he turned her, careful to temper his strength, refusing to let her hide from him. "Who did it?"

He could see by the expression in her eyes that it had come from no demanding lover. "Osborn," she said finally. "In the hospital room, when I was pretending to be unconscious."

The fury that swept over him was so strong, so powerful that he thought he might explode with the force and heat of it. He wanted to smash his fist into Osborn's fat, unctuous face. He wanted to storm and rage and kill.

The emotions startled him. He wasn't used to them, to the need for revenge, the fierce protectiveness, any more than he was used to the overwhelming lust he felt for the woman curled up in the sofa, her face hidden from him. Combined with an odd, soul-shattering tenderness.

He took a step away from the sofa, trying to govern his anger. "There are advantages to this," he managed to say in a deceptively cool voice.

She lifted her head to look at him, startled. Her cheeks were still flame red, but her mouth was soft, slightly swollen from his kisses, and he wished to God he wasn't still hard. That he could simply walk away from her, concentrating on his anger.

"What do you mean?" Her voice was quiet, wary.

He leaned against a bookcase. "I'll get a chance to see whether I can turn a man to cinders as quickly as I can a car."

She thought he was kidding. She managed a weak chuckle. "If Osborn holds still long enough for you to experiment."

"I'll make sure he does."

Something in his grim tone penetrated her self-consciousness, and she looked at him. "No, Daniel. I won't let you kill another human being. You're too civilized. It would end up destroying you."

"I'm not nearly as civilized as you think. I never have been. You've made any number of assumptions about me, and most of them have been wrong."

She glanced around her. "I was wrong about the house," she admitted. "But I'm not wrong about you. By nature you're cold, methodical, controlled. You're not a man ruled by his passions...."

He'd hauled her from the sofa before she had time to finish, pulling her up tight against him, her breasts pressed against his chest, her hips against his unmistakable erection. "If you think I'm cold, Suzanna," he said in a quiet, dangerous voice, "then you're forgetting what my hands feel like when they touch you. If you think I'm methodical or controlled, then you haven't been paying attention. And if you think I'm not ruled by my passions..." He kissed her then, hard, his hand threading through her hair to hold her head still, his mouth wet and hungry on hers, giving her no chance to evade him.

She didn't want to. With a little whimper of passion, she threaded her arms around his neck, arching into his embrace. He lifted her against him, and her long legs wrapped around him. Together they tumbled back onto the sofa, and her hands were sliding up under his T-shirt, cool, arousing, as her mouth answered his, and he was ready—

The first cramp hit him with the force of a blow to the stomach. He fell back, away from her, as if he'd been shocked. He willed the damned pain to stop; but it didn't— it washed over him, and he knew what was happening, and there wasn't a thing he could do to stop it. He shuddered, and there was a flash of bone-chilling cold sweeping over him, and his jaw locked in a grimace of pain before he shut his eyes, trying to ride that pain.

When he opened them again, Suzanna was across the room, white-faced. He looked down and saw the too-familair fuzzy outline.

He'd vanished again.

SUZANNA WANTED TO SCREAM and cry. She felt buffeted by emotions, feelings she hadn't experienced in years, if ever. Her body was hot, aroused, exquisitely sensitive, her mouth tender. And the damned man had the gall to disappear.

She had no idea where he was. Her own heart was beating too wildly, her own breath coming too rapidly, for her to hear his. She whirled around, heading for the stairs, stalking.

An unseen hand caught her wrist, halting her abruptly. She could feel the tensile strength in his fingers, and she remembered how easily those fingers had turned the metal lock to powder back at Beebe headquarters. He could do the same to her bones.

But he wouldn't. Despite the danger she had seen in his eyes, despite his insistence that he was far from civilized, she knew he wouldn't hurt her. "Let go of me, Daniel," she said in a very quiet voice.

His fingers encircled her wrist, his thumb stroking the pale, blue-veined pulse. She could see the movement of her skin beneath his touch, but she couldn't see his hand.

And then he let her go. She sensed him moving across the room, away from her, but he had a gift for silence, something that was particularly frustrating. "I'm going to go for a walk." His voice came from over by the door. "I'll be back at eight."

"You don't need to go," she found herself saying.

"Yes, I do." There was no missing the suppressed violence in his voice. The door slammed behind him, and she was alone, bitterly alone in the cold house.

She missed him. Missed the heat of his body, the strength in his arms. Missed his mouth. She'd been ready to let him strip off her clothes and take her, right there and then, on that overstuffed sofa that was almost as wide as a bed. While she should be thanking her lucky stars that fate had intervened, she found instead that she was merely shaking with frustrated reaction.

She took a fast shower, a hot one, to warm her chilled skin. It wasn't until she was pulling on a T-shirt that the obvious hit her.

Daniel Crompton wanted her. Wanted her quite badly, possibly as much as she wanted him. There was no disguising the passion in his mouth, the tension in his hands, the state of his arousal.

She sat down on the mattress, stunned. She could come up with all sorts of reasons why this realization should be disastrous. It was probably just a case of abstinence making the heart grow fonder. He probably had a bevy of willing females, back in Santa Cristina.

Maybe it was the danger that had caused his libido to react, making him reach for the nearest, the only female. Maybe he was the kind of man who simply had to make a pass at every woman.

Or maybe, just maybe, he was as drawn to her as she was to him. For whatever mysterious reason, no matter how impractical it might seem, there was something between them, something dark and dangerous, something bright and triumphant, something that went beyond petty misunderstandings or even the fate of the world.

She moved to the window, looking out into the morning light. It was cool and overcast, and she could see the blackened leaves that had been hit by the heavy frost. How long would he be gone? And what was he planning to do when he came back? Pretend it never happened?

Or finish what he started?

And she didn't know which possibility frightened her more.

IN THE END, it didn't matter. Daniel didn't return at eight o'clock. By nine o'clock Suzanna began to worry. By eleven she was furious. By twelve she was terrified. By one she went in search of him.

There was a light rain falling, more of a mist than an actual cloudburst. She followed the path, deeper into the woods, all the time fighting the questions that hurtled themselves at her head. What if he'd stayed invisible this time? What if Osborn and his crew had caught him? What if he'd decided he'd do better on his own, and he'd abandoned her?

She kept climbing, as the rain started soaking into her T-shirt, chilling her to the bone. She couldn't stand to go back to that cabin alone, not knowing what had happened to him.

In the distance she thought she caught a faint whiff of smoke, and she felt a sudden foreboding. She began to hurry, scrambling her way upward as the path steepened, sliding in the mud and scraping her arm, grabbing hold of old roots to haul herself up toward the ridge. When she finally reached the clearing, she paused, momentarily stunned by the glory of the view.

And then she was equally stunned by the sight of Daniel, sitting cross-legged on the wet ground, completely visible. He didn't seem aware of her approach. He was busy staring at a row of several piles of refuse, brush and twigs and the like, and as she watched he set each one aflame.

Suzanna scrambled to her feet, seething. He glanced at her over his shoulder, then turned back to his little experiment, dismissing her as easily as he'd dismissed her this morning.

She walked over to him and stood directly behind him, wondering how she could hurt him. She was looking around, trying to find something to hit him with, when he leaned back against her legs, his head against her thighs, the warmth shooting through her like an electric current.

She reached down. His long black hair hung wet and loose on his shoulders, and she sifted her fingers through the silky length. And yanked, as hard as she could.

He let out a truly satisfying shriek of pain, leaping away from her. He ended up crouched on the ground, staring at her, shock and affronted dignity warring for control.

"What the hell did you do that for?" he demanded. "That hurt."

"You've been gone for hours," she said coolly. "I was afraid something had happened to you."

"Something did happen to me. A crazy woman tried to pull my hair out." He glared at her. "I don't understand what your problem is. I told you I was going for a walk."

"You left the house at six o'clock this morning. That

was more than seven hours ago. I was afraid you might have fallen off a cliff.''

''It probably wouldn't have hurt as much,'' he said, rubbing his scalp. ''As a matter of fact, I was working. I tend to forget about time when I'm involved in something.''

''Do tell,'' she said acidly. ''And what have you discovered?''

To her increased discomfort he suddenly smiled at her. ''Any number of things. I found I could regulate the area in which I direct the flames, and the intensity, as well. I can scorch something, or turn it to ashes. It's all a matter of control. I also checked the limits of my strength. I could push over that tree over there,'' he nodded in the direction of a good-sized pine tree that lay on its side in the mud, its roots brutally exposed, ''but I couldn't lift it. My vision is the same—no x-ray capabilities, and I'm not—'' he glared at her again ''—impervious to pain. I don't think I quite qualify as a superman. My major talent seems to be reducing things to cinders.''

''Okay, you can be Cinderman,'' she said. ''It has a nice ring. I bet the *National Enquirer* will love it.''

''Don't even think it.''

She was finding an even more satisfying revenge than yanking at his hair. ''They pay quite well, I hear. Especially if you've got something unique, and you, my dear Daniel, are definitely tabloid material. It's too bad we can't throw in a Cinderman diet and tryst with Princess Di, but even so, I imagine we can drum up a fair amount of interest. I could even put my story out for auction. I could be set for life.''

She'd gone too far. The tension in his shoulders relaxed slightly, and he rose slowly and gracefully, the rain beating down around them on the high plateau overlooking the forest.

''You may not *have* a life,'' he said. ''Not if Osborn and his pals have their way.''

"Why? Why should they want to kill you, and me, as well? Why did they murder that man in the stairwell? And don't give me that James Bond crap again. I want to know exactly what is going on."

He considered it for a moment, watching her, and she half held her breath, waiting for another lie, another denial. Instead he came toward her, taking her hand in his and leading her back toward the steep path.

"I want answers," she said, trying to hold back.

She might just as well have tried to stop a raging bull. Daniel kept moving, and his grip on Suzanna never loosened, so that she was forced along after him, skidding a bit in the mud.

"You'll get your answers," he said, starting down the steepest part. "But first I need a hot shower, some coffee and something to eat."

"You can make your vitamin drink."

He glanced back at her, and there was that damnable, seductive sweetess in his smile. "I think I've developed a taste for brownies," he said. "Among other things. Come along, Suzanna."

Following him down the narrow, winding path gave her plenty of time to think of revenge. Never once did he let go of her hand; even when she slid and skidded into him, he absorbed the blow with calm determination. She could always push him off the balcony, she thought. Or maybe get him to try his incendiary powers on a propane tank.

The house loomed up out of the mist, sooner than she would have thought. "Wait a minute," he said, finally releasing her hand, not noticing that she did her best to snatch it to her in affronted dignity. "Stay put."

He advanced on the house silently, doing a swift surveillance. He disappeared behind it, then came back. "I don't think anyone's been here," he said.

"If you thought someone might show up, why did you leave me here alone?" she demanded.

"Oh, I knew you were more than a match for any of Armstead's little army who might happen to show up. You could pull their hair," he said cheerfully.

The balcony, she thought, fuming, brushing past him as she entered the house.

It was damp and chilly inside, and Suzanna shivered. "I'm going to change my clothes."

The moment he closed the door behind him the temperature rose, as if someone had just turned on the heat. "Some coffee would be nice, to go with the brownies," he said.

She just looked at him. "Learn to cook."

Lord, the man shouldn't have a smile like that! Just when he was already driving her crazy. "You can teach me," he said.

"Daniel…" she called after him.

He paused, looking back at her. "What?"

She didn't know what she wanted. Him to touch her, him to kiss her, him to disappear back into his lab or the ether or wherever so he wouldn't be so infuriating, so distracting, so irresistible.

"Don't take all the hot water," she said.

You could take a shower with me, his mind said, so clearly that she thought she heard his voice speak the words.

"All right," he agreed after a moment.

She watched him go, shaken. It had been her imagination. The result of God knew what kind of stress. She couldn't have heard his thoughts—it simply wasn't possible.

But it wasn't possible that her twenty-year nearsightedness had suddenly been cured, and it wasn't possible that Daniel Crompton could set things on fire and turn invisible from six to eight every morning and evening and have superhuman strength. Nevertheless that was exactly what had happened so far.

And now she could read his mind. It was a gift she could have done without, and if it were up to her she'd shut it off.

But it wasn't necessarily up to her, any more than Daniel could control whether he turned invisible or not. She could only hope he'd figure out an antidote to the green goop fast. Before she developed any more unnerving talents.

Chapter Twelve

Suzanna stripped off her rain-sodden clothes, pulled on fresh ones and sat cross-legged on the futon mattress. She didn't want to look at Crompton, didn't want to give herself the opportunity to read his mind. Too much had happened in the last forty-eight hours or so, and she wasn't quite ready to deal with all the ramifications. She didn't want to be able to look into Crompton's cool, dark eyes and see what he thought of her. There were some things better left unknown.

There were piles of books and newspapers in the bedroom as well as every other square inch of the house, and she grabbed for the first thing she could reach. To her amazement she found it was a book on the Spanish riding school in Austria, an odd choice, but in keeping with the catholic nature of his library. He seemed to have a book on almost every subject, and his interests were absurdly varied. She'd seen science fiction, books on car mechanics, financial guides, what seemed to be the complete works of Georgette Heyer and Jane Austen, the history of costume, mixed in with books on scientific subjects so arcane that even she, with her Ph.D., was appalled.

She'd never been particularly interested in horses, but as she heard Daniel leave that absurdly luxurious bathroom she opened the book and immersed herself in the text, determined not to let an errant thought, either hers or his, stray into her consciousness.

"I saved enough hot water for you." His voice floated over the balcony of the loft bedroom.

She didn't answer, concentrating instead on the fine points of dressage. Until she heard his voice at the bottom of the stairs.

"Suzanna?"

She didn't want him coming up there. She didn't want to be in the same small area, looking at him, remembering what had happened in the predawn, remembering the feel and the touch and the taste of him. "I'm fine," she called back. "I'll take a shower in a little while."

Silence, and she held her breath, staring fixedly at the words as they swam in front of her. "I'll be in the lab then," he said. "I'm not likely to surface until you come and get me."

"Fine," she said airily.

Come and get me, his mind echoed in hers, and she pushed her face closer to the book, trying to push his thoughts away. A moment later the door to the lab closed, and she breathed a sigh of relief, rolling onto her back, the book forgotten at her side.

There was a roof window above and the autumn dusk was already settling around the funny little cabin. She could see the massive pines overhead, swaying in the wind. Despite her dry clothes, she was still chilled, and she pulled the duvet around her, turning her face into the pillow, closing her eyes, closing her mind, shutting out the doubts and fears that had been plaguing her. She never thought she was the kind of woman who had doubts and fears. She was tough; she met challenges head-on.

But these recent challenges were too much for her. She wanted peace, she wanted comfort, Lord, she wanted someone to take care of her! An extremely odd notion, when she'd learned through her life that the only person she could rely on was herself.

She wanted to rely on Daniel Crompton. She wanted to know that she didn't have to watch her back, that he'd be watching for her. Just as she could watch out for him, as well.

She wanted a partnership, true love, happy ever after, all that stupid, preprogrammed, fairy-tale stuff that she'd resisted all her life. And she wanted it with Daniel Crompton.

She could hear him moving about in the lab. If she held herself very still, she could hear his thoughts bubbling around in his brilliant mind. He wasn't thinking about her, he was thinking about the green slime. A reassuring, disappointing realization, Suzanna thought with a wry grin.

And pulling the duvet over her head, she fell asleep.

FOR THE FIRST TIME in his life, Daniel was having trouble concentrating. As he hunched over the microscope, adjusting the field, he kept thinking about Suzanna. About the magnificent rage in her warm brown eyes, no longer fettered by glasses, the force in her hands as she'd yanked on his hair, the fury that had vibrated through her tall, gorgeous body.

He had looked at her out on that rain-swept ridge, at the rage and frustration in her face, and known that she loved him. He was still reeling from that knowledge.

She was fighting it—he knew that full well. She didn't want to fall in love, and he couldn't blame her. From what he'd observed, it was messy and inconvenient, distracting even the most disciplined mind from more important matters. Look what it was doing to him.

He lifted his head, stunned at the realization. Hell and damnation, he was not going to fall in love with Suzanna Molloy. She was beautiful, brilliant, cantankerous and an intrusion into his well-ordered life.

Except that his life had been far from well-ordered recently. Having his lab blown up, being covered with green slime, turning into—what had she called him? Cinderman?—had all been far from conventional. Falling in love would be the coup de grace, and he had every intention of fighting it tooth and nail.

That didn't mean he didn't revel in the fact that the mighty Suzanna Molloy had fallen. And he had every intention of taking advantage of that fact, as soon as she'd hold still enough for him to get her in bed.

He might even marry her. He'd never considered marriage, but having spent forty-eight hours with the cranky Ms. Molloy, he could see it would definitely have its advantages. He'd discovered an absolute craving for brownies. And for Suzanna Molloy.

He wondered idly how much convincing she was going to need. She was very, very bright—that was part of what drew him to her. He could simply state the obvious advantages of a union, and if she were as sensible as she was intelligent, she'd agree.

In his experience, women were seldom sensible. Even the best and the brightest of them, and Suzanna fitted or even transcended that category. She might be just as likely to throw his well-planned suggestion in his face.

He leaned back, staring out into the darkening sky. Maybe he'd simply have to seduce her into complying. It had certain appeal. If it hadn't been for the damned clock, he would already have accomplished just that, and there'd be no more arguments about who was going to sleep where.

Or maybe, just maybe, he was better off keeping his distance. Suzanna affected him as no other woman had. Enough so that he was sitting over his microscope, staring out into the twilight like a lovesick calf instead of working. He needed to concentrate. He needed to stop thinking about Suzanna. And the surest way to do that was either to get rid of her or to sleep with her.

If he was truly sensible he'd opt for the former.

But then, good sense had never been his forte. He'd spent his life following his intellect, his instinct, his inclination. And while this time those three things had parted company, he was going to go with instinct and inclination. He was going to make love to Suzanna Molloy so thoroughly that he wouldn't even need to think about her for days.

And then maybe he could solve the riddle of the mutated green slime, and just what it had done to him.

Six o'clock came with damnable regularity, one of the few constants in a world gone awry. He sat back when the first cramp hit him, cursing under his breath, tensing against the pain. It rippled through him, cold and blinding, and then he was gone.

He rose, furious with himself for wasting so much time when he could have been working. Of the hours since they'd been back at the house, he'd spent the vast majority dreaming about Suzanna's legs, wrapped around his back. And while there was nothing he wanted more than to go in search of her, to see just how limber those long, beautiful legs were, now wasn't the time to do it. Even if she couldn't see him, she could feel his touch, and he didn't think she was ready to do it with the Invisible Man.

What he needed was more brownies. He stepped out into the living room as quietly as he could, closing the door behind him. There was no sound from Suzanna, and he glanced up at the loft. A light was burning against the encroaching darkness, but he could hear the evenness of her breathing, the quiet steadiness of her heartbeat. She was asleep.

The brownies were gone. He considered heading upstairs after her, then changed his mind. Instead he threw himself down on the sofa, propping his head on his arms. He listened to the steady thump of her heartbeat, concentrating on it, feeling his own heart beat in rhythm with it. He let himself drift, then slide into the sleep he'd been resisting.

HE WOKE WITH A START, the darkness all around him, and then he heard the sound of the shower.

He lay on the sofa, imagining her in there, water sluicing down over her skin. He wanted to go in and lick the water off her.

Instead he waited for her, listening.

For once fate was kind to him. The door opened, and Suzanna stepped out, her eyes searching the living room warily. She was wearing nothing but a towel. A towel that was definitely too skimpy for her tall, wonderful body, and she clutched it to her like a lifeline as she tiptoed across the room, heading for the stairs. And then she stopped, startled, like a doe caught in the headlights of an oncoming car.

"Damn it, are you in here, Crompton?" she demanded furiously.

"Guilty."

Her face swiveled toward the sofa and the sound of his voice. "Close your eyes."

"You trust me?" The thought amused him.

"Enough to close your eyes if you say you have."

"I've closed my eyes," he said promptly, honestly.

The tension in her body lessened slightly, and she scampered across the room, towel trailing behind her, and raced up the stairs to the loft, and out of sight.

"Thank you for being a gentleman." Her stiff voice floated over the edge of the balcony.

"My pleasure," he murmured. "But to be perfectly fair, I ought to tell you I can see through my eyelids."

The book came sailing over the balcony, landing dangerously close to his head. He rolled out of the way in time, and he found himself grinning like an idiot. It was just as well she couldn't see him. She'd probably slap the smirk off his face.

"You know, Molloy, you're going to give Armstead's and Osborn's goons a run for their money when they show up here," he drawled. "You just need to improve your aim."

She leaned over the balcony, glaring. The T-shirt she'd pulled on read I Love My Attitude Problem, and her wet hair hung down like something out of a fairy tale. "At least I'll be able to see what I'm aiming at," she snapped back. And then there was a sudden, stunned expression on her face. "What makes you think they'll find us?"

"They will. It may take them a while, but they have resources at their disposal that effectively destroy any secrets we might hope to have. They're going to find us, Suzanna. And they're going to try to kill us."

Her face was already pale, but even in the shadowy light he could see the ashen color increase. "Why would they destroy America's secret weapon? Don't they have a use for you any more?"

"They've got two problems. One, they know that I'm not going to work for them any longer. As long as they left me alone, gave me plenty of money, then I was reasonably content. They would have gotten their hands on whatever I discovered in the long run, so they may as well foot the bill and let me work in comfort. And two, they don't realize that they don't have complete documentation of my work. If they did, they wouldn't risk harming even a hair on my head."

"What is it?"

He was getting a crick in his neck, staring up at her. "What is what?" he asked testily.

"What are you working on?"

"You've been trying to find that out ever since you snuck into my lab. I'm really not interested in playing Romeo and Juliet. Come down from your perch and I'll tell you."

She looked wary. "I'm not sure if I believe you."

"What have I got to lose? We may both be dead tomorrow. You might at least know what you're dying for."

"I have no intention of dying," she said, coming down the stairs, keeping her face averted from his general direction.

"Just as well," he said. "I have no intention of letting you get killed." At least, not if I can help it, he added to himself.

She paused at the bottom of the stairs, her head cocked to one side, as if she were listening. "And what if you can't help it?"

Her echoing of his thoughts unnerved him for a moment. "You forget," he said in a passable drawl. "I'm Cinderman. Able to leap tall buildings in a single bound. Faster than a speeding bullet, more powerful than a locomotive..."

"Not that I noticed," she said, edging her way over to the sofa. "You're strong, but I haven't noticed you being particularly fast. As for being able to leap tall buildings..."

"Don't be so literal." He started to move closer, slowly, silently, not wanting to scare her away. He wanted to be near her. To look at her, the high cheekbones, warm brown eyes, the erotic, touching vulnerability in her wide mouth. He wanted to see whether she was wearing a bra or not, he...

She crossed her arms across her chest, glaring at him. "You're still avoiding my questions, Crompton. What are you working on?"

He wasn't about to tell her it was something even more powerful than cold fusion. She wouldn't believe him, and the more she knew, the greater her danger. If she understood the details of bi-level molecular transfer, she'd be—

"You're crazy," she gasped. "There's no such thing as bi-level molecular transfer."

He gave up trying to sneak up on her. He crossed the room in three swift, noisy strides, clamping his hands down on her shoulders and swiveling her around to face him. Not that she could see him. Which was just as well. He'd probably only scare her if she could read his expression. "What did you say?"

There was no way she could miss the quiet menace in his voice but as usual, she didn't let it cow her. "I said, there's no such thing as bi-level molecular transfer. You know as I do that it's a fairy tale, a mad scientist's fantasy. The sort of thing that kept Merlin busy. It doesn't exist."

"It does."

He'd managed to shock her into silence. It was only temporary, of course. "Even you aren't that smart, Crompton," she said weakly, but he could see she believed.

"Why do you think they call me America's secret weapon? I've developed something so powerful, so legendary, that the world as we know it would be changed forever if it gets out."

"What do you mean, *if* it gets out?"

"The good folks at Beebe don't even realize what they've got under their nose. They think it's cold fusion, and they're willing to kill for it."

"Bi-level molecular transfer would make cold fusion seem as archaic as an A-bomb. But what about the practical applications? Surely you can't have gotten that far?" She still seemed stunned by the magnitude of his discovery. As she should be. He released her arms, and she sank down on the sofa.

"What good would it be without practical applications? Proven theory is all fine and good, but you have to be able to make it work."

"And you can make it work," she said in a hollow voice. "Exactly who are the folks at Beebe? You said they would have gotten their hands on it sooner or later, so you decided to work for them. Who are they? They're not organized crime, or Uncle Vinnie would know. Are they CIA? The government? What in God's name is Beebe Control Systems International?"

He considered walking away. She wouldn't be able to

find him, make him answer questions he'd never answered before. Even if she could see him, she wouldn't be able to do that.

But the damnable thing was, he wanted to tell her. For the first time in his life, he wanted to talk to someone about the convoluted world he'd been living in.

"Beebe stands for BB. Big Brother. And that's exactly who supports and owns Beebe. You're wrong about organized crime. The board of BBCSI is composed of some of the most powerful people in the country. They've got Mafia, they've got four-star generals. FBI, CIA, the far right. All the most power-hungry, paranoid groups that make up this country's power elite."

"I thought the cold war was over."

"You thought wrong. At least, it's not over as far as these people are concerned. They're convinced the Russians are just biding their time, stockpiling weapons. They think the sooner they can nuke the Middle East out of existence, the better. They're looking for some nice clean way to gain control over the world, and then they can make their own rules."

"And you went along with that?" she demanded, obviously horrified.

He shrugged, but of course she couldn't see that. "I didn't pay much attention to who was paying the bills. The same kind of people are in charge, whether you work for the government or academia. You just learn to keep your secrets."

"Have they got yours?"

She could be a liar, he thought coolly, dispassionately. She could be a plant, a practiced actress hired by Osborn and his crew to ferret out his secrets. If he told her the truth, trusted her, he could be signing not only his death warrant, but the fate of the world, as well.

"I'm not a liar," she said. "You can trust me."

He considered it for a moment. And then deliberately

made the first step. "They only have half of them. Jackson was copying my research during the last few months—I had a safety lock on the system that recorded every time security was breached, and who did it. But I kept a great deal of my research separately, with me."

"Where?"

He smiled, a wintry smile that she couldn't see. "On a CD disk. It looks like an audio disk instead of something for the computer. The only way you could tell it was a ROM disk was if you tried to play it on the stereo."

"Would it destroy the disk if you did that?"

"Why? Are you thinking of going back to my apartment and finding the rest of my research? The boys at Beebe are very eager to get their hands on it. You could be a very rich young woman, set for life. If they didn't decide to kill you, as well."

"Stuff it, Cinderman," Suzanna snapped. "I don't deserve that. And it's not necessarily the smartest thing you've ever done. It's got to be that Neil Diamond CD. Anyone with any brains would wonder what you'd be doing with something like that. Someone could break into your apartment, take it, and you'd be up a nasty creek without a paddle and they'd have the power to change the world, and probably not for the better."

"Not really."

She peered through the gathering darkness, but there was no way she could see him. He held very still, keeping his breathing quiet, not wanting to give away his presence. "What do you mean by that?"

"I mean there's a crucial piece of the puzzle missing, both from my research in the computers back at Beebe and from the CD ROM."

"And where is that piece of the puzzle?"

"In my brain."

"Don't be ridiculous," she shot back. "You can't rely on memory for something that important."

"I can. I have a photographic memory. You'd be amazed at the stuff I have crammed into my brain."

She rose, staring in the direction of his voice, and he wondered coolly whether now was the moment of truth. Whether she would tell him who and what she really was, and what she wanted from him. Had he been wrong to trust her?

"Damn you," she said in a low, furious voice. "How dare you?"

"How dare I what?" He was momentarily astonished.

"How dare you question who and what I am?" she said, stalking toward him. "I've let you drag me to the back end of beyond, do your disappearing act, lie to me, then treat me like you trust me, when all the time you've been standing there thinking I'm some kind of penny ante Mata Hari, out to steal your secrets and then cut your throat. If I could only see you, I'd be more than happy to…"

· She walked right into him, and his hands came up to capture hers. Before he could think about what he was doing, he did what he'd been wanting to do. He pulled her into his arms and put his mouth on hers, silencing her.

She didn't fight, even though he could feel the rage and resistance in her body. She stood there in the circle of his arms, letting him kiss her, and she felt cool and still against his heat.

Her lack of response should have been a deterrent. It only increased his determination. He used his tongue, sliding along her lower lip, and she opened her mouth for him, reluctantly, and her arms moved up around his waist as she softened against him, absorbing his warmth, absorbing his need, until she was suddenly kissing him back. Her hands clutched at him tightly, and her heart was pounding fiercely against his.

He reached up and cupped her face, his fingers sliding into her shower-damp hair, and he pulled her away and stared down at her. "One question, Molloy," he said in a raspy voice, only slightly breathless.

She closed her eyes and became very still, waiting. "What is it?"

"How long have you been able to read my mind?"

Chapter Thirteen

Suzanna tore herself away from him. Her lips were hot, burning, from the feel of his mouth against hers. Her skin was on fire, itchy, and yet she only wanted the feel of his body against hers. Only the touch of his flesh would soothe her.

She turned her back on him, staring out into the gathering darkness. "I hate trying to talk to you when I can't see you."

"How long have you been able to read my mind?" The question came again, inexorable, and she knew there was no escaping it. She wasn't quite sure why she wanted to.

"I can't read your mind," she said. "I can hear thoughts. And it's only been since we came back from the ridge." She turned and looked back at the empty space where she assumed he was standing. "I don't like it."

"I can't say I'm any too crazy about it, either," he drawled. "What am I thinking about now?"

"If I could find you I'd slap you," she said. "You're thinking about my breasts again."

"That might just be a logical guess. Try again."

She closed her eyes for a moment, opening her mind. And then she shook her head. "It doesn't work."

"What do you mean?"

"I mean I don't seem to be able to control it. Errant

thoughts filter through, when I least expect it, but if I try to reach out for your mind, I just get a blank. Let's face it, Mr. Spock I'm not. There's no Vulcan mind-meld for me.''

"Maybe if you touched me.''

"No, thank you,'' she said sharply. "It unnerves me enough as it is.'' She ran a hand through her damp hair, taking a deep breath. "What time is it?''

"I don't know. I can't see my watch.''

She was cold. It seemed at times that the only way she would ever get warm was to be near him. And yet that was a danger far greater than anything she'd imagined so far. Freezing to death was a dreamy, painless way to go. Death by fire was terrifying.

And yet, like a moth, she was drawn to the flame. The heat of her possible destruction beckoned to her, and she didn't know how much longer she was going to be able to resist.

She heard his swift, pained intake of breath, and for a moment she didn't realize what it signified. He rematerialized slowly, fuzzily at first, and she forced herself to watch him.

"Is it getting worse?'' she asked quietly.

He leaned back against the wall, taking deep breaths. His rumpled white shirt was unbuttoned, hanging loose around him. She'd felt that skin against her when he kissed her, wondered what he'd been wearing. Now she could see it, see his lean, muscled chest, the faded, tight jeans that clung to his long legs, his bare feet on the polished wood floor. His hair was tied back, his face looked severe, remote, and she wanted to cross the room and taste his mouth again, now that she could see it.

"Eight o'clock on the dot,'' he said, glancing at the thin gold watch he wore on one tanned wrist. He looked up at her, and there was a dark, haunted expression in his eyes. "I'm getting tired of this.''

"Superpowers aren't all they're cracked up to be?'' she

said, deliberately keeping her distance, when she felt the pull, as strongly as a magnet on a piece of steel.

"What do you think, oh swami mind reader?" he countered.

"I like being able to see without my glasses."

He shrugged. "I imagine I could come in handy on a camping trip, if someone forgot the matches."

"I'd do well on television game shows."

"I could get a job moving pianos for a living."

She smiled. She couldn't help it. She didn't want to, but somehow the ludicrousness of the situation got to her. "We make a ridiculous pair," she said wryly.

The silence, the heat in the room, was palpable. "I wouldn't say that," he said. "Come here, Suzanna."

The wariness in her body flared into a moment of outright panic. It had been leading to this for a long time. Longer ago than the moment he'd come back to his lab and found her there. It had started with their very first confrontation, at one of Beebe's unctuous public relations efforts. She'd clashed with him then, and she thought he'd dismissed her with his typical scientific arrogance. She knew otherwise now. He remembered that first clash. He was remembering it now.

"Don't," she said, trying to shut it off.

"Come here, Suzanna."

It was her choice. It always had been. She stood by the balcony, and the chill of the autumn night radiated through the glass door, sinking into her bones. It was cold and dark and lonely there. And safe, but was it a safety worth the price?

She looked at him, trying to gauge how much he wanted her, and the longing was so strong, so fiery, it warmed her from across the room. I burn for you, his mind said, his eyes dark and haunted. And the choice was made.

She walked across the room slowly, her eyes never leaving his. She felt strange, disoriented, vulnerable when she stopped in front of him, for the first time allowing herself to just look at him in the stillness.

She was a tall woman, five feet nine in her bare feet, but he was far taller, six feet plus several inches. He still shouldn't have been intimidating. He wasn't bulky and bloated like a bodybuilder—his frame had the sleek, well-muscled grace of a long-distance runner. And he was hot, so very, very hot. And she'd been cold for so long.

He made no move to touch her. "Why do I frighten you, Molloy?" he asked, his voice low, enticing.

"What makes you think you do?"

His smile was slight, self-deprecatory. "Maybe I can read minds, as well."

It was a horrifying thought, one she dismissed almost immediately. If he knew even a fraction of the confused, downright lustful thoughts that had invaded her mind, he wouldn't be standing there, watching her, not touching her. If he could read her mind he'd have her down on the hardwood floor, her clothes scattered around them.

"You don't frighten me," she said.

"Don't lie." It was softly spoken, edged in steel.

"I'll do anything I please."

Again that faint, taunting smile. "Go right ahead," he murmured. "I dare you." And there was a glimmer of devilry in his dark eyes.

She was a tough woman. Not the sort to back down from a challenge. And Lord, the man was challenge personified. He was wrong—it wasn't him she was afraid of. It was herself, her reaction to him. Her undeniable vulnerability, when she'd spent so much time fighting any sign of weakness.

She tried to read his thoughts, but all she came up with was a frustrating blank. There was no safety net. The next move was up to her. Entirely.

She lifted her hands and touched him. She rested her

fingertips against his shoulders for a moment, feeling him through the soft white cotton of his shirt.

The heat was a palpable thing, running through her fingertips, down her veins, burning like a glass of neat whiskey on a frosty afternoon. She broke the contact, stepping back, and she felt his cry of denial. But he didn't move, didn't say a word. He just waited. For her.

She wondered how long his patience would last. Not much longer than hers. She took a step back, toward him, and she knew that this time she wouldn't run.

"I don't want..." she began, then stopped.

"Don't want what? This?"

She shook her head. "I don't want to need you."

"Can you stop?"

"No." She reached up and put her hand against his mouth, and his lips were warm, burning. She wanted that mouth on her body.

He kissed her hand, gently. He reached out and took her other hand, bringing it slowly toward him, giving her plenty of chance to pull back. He placed it on his chest, over his heart, against his skin.

She could feel the beat of his pulse, heavy, sensual, slightly fast against her hand. Outside, the rain had begun once more, but inside they were safe and warm and dry.

She crossed the final step, coming up against his larger, hotter body, trapping their clasped hands between them. She moved her hand away from his lips and slid her fingers through his long dark hair, looking for answers in his dark, fathomless eyes.

But the answers weren't there to see, and she could either run or trust. And she'd decided she wasn't going to run.

He leaned down and kissed her then, very gently, a wordless reassurance that it was going to be all right. And she realized that, conscious decision or not, she trusted him. With her life. With her body. With her soul.

With her love.

She opened her mouth beneath his, deliberately inviting him. And then there was no gentle wooing. The heat that had been slumbering in his body flared up, and his mouth slanted across hers, drinking deep.

She could hear his thoughts then, a jumble of them, rioting through both their minds—dark, erotic, untamed, so fierce and so explicit in their demands that Suzanna felt her own response ignite. He slid his hands under her T-shirt, cupping her bare breasts, and she arched against him, needing his touch, needing his heat, needing his mouth.

He pulled the T-shirt over her head and sent it sailing across the room, and she was standing within his arms, wearing nothing but her jeans. She was no longer cold, she was burning up, and she wanted more, and more, and more.

He bent down and scooped her up effortlessly, holding her tight against him. You don't have to be tough all the time, his mind said, and she melted back against him, giving up the struggle for independence. He was right—she didn't have to fight anymore.

He took her over to the wide couch, lowering her down, following her, and she pushed the white shirt from his shoulders, her hands lingering, touching, learning him.

There were no words, no whispered assurances, no tiny jokes to set her at ease. In utter, absorbed silence he unfastened her jeans and pulled them down her legs, tossing them away. In silence he touched her, his long fingers sliding between her legs, coaxing them apart, and he leaned forward and put his mouth on her breast.

The sensation was fierce, burning, exquisite, and she heard her breathless cry of longing as she arched back against the soft cushions of the huge sofa. Her entire life centered between her legs and in her breast, and he was drawing the life from her, setting her on fire.

He moved his mouth to her other breast, suckling deeply, and she felt hot tears of longing and confusion fill her eyes, as she reached down for him, not sure of what she wanted, only certain that she did.

Her breast felt damp and cool when he moved his mouth away, trailing hot, biting kisses down her torso.

And then he put his mouth between her legs, unexpectedly soon, and she put her hands on his shoulders, unsure. He simply covered her hands with his, the heat of them soothing her doubts, and she let herself slip, slide into a dark and wonderful place, full of brazen images and unspoken desires, lost, whirling in a kind of mad splendor that sharpened into a blinding clarity as she climaxed against his mouth.

She was only vaguely aware of him moving up and over her, shucking his jeans, kneeling between her trembling legs. She waited, watching as he protected her, wanting to reach out and touch him, to do it for him, still too shaky and shy to move. And then he was pressing against her, sliding deep, filling her with one sure thrust, and he was so burning hot that she was burning with him, pushing her body against his, her long legs right around his hips, wanting more, wanting all of him, everything he was willing to give, resenting anything that came between them, even the thin barrier of latex.

His hands cupped her hips, pulling her more tightly against him. His mouth crushed hers, and she heard him, the words, sifting through his mind, love and lust and longing, striving for an end that was only a beginning. She clutched at him, shivering, building, shattering once more as she felt him explode in her arms, a white hot flame of passion that seemed to last an eternity.

When she opened her eyes, she found him collapsed on top of her, his long hair in her face, his heart still pounding furiously against her. He was heavy, and she didn't mind for even a moment.

She felt better than she had in her entire life. Her body was hot, nerveless, completely sated, her mind at ease. And her heart—her heart was full of an indescribable feeling that had a very simple definition.

And that was *love*.

She heard the word shift through his mind, unconsciously before it was pushed away in sudden fear. If she asked him for those words, he might give them to her, but it was no good asking. Those words had to be freely given, out of his need, not hers.

He lifted his head and looked at her, and she could feel his doubt. But she couldn't sense where that doubt had come from.

"Are you all right?" he asked, his voice barely more than a whisper.

He was worried he might have hurt her, that much was clear. She couldn't resist. There was no way she could stop the wide, smug grin that curved her mouth, any more than she could stop the warmth that filled her inside. "I'll survive," she said.

He stared at her for a long moment. And then he smiled too, a slow, sensuous grin that temporarily banished the shadows that lingered around them. He put his mouth against hers, offering a slow, lingering kiss. He was still deep inside her, and he was growing hard again, and she was growing damp and hot, and her hands slid around him as she kissed him back, losing herself in the sheer heaven of his mouth.

When he finally pulled away from her, she let him go reluctantly. "No," she said.

He paused, staring down at her. "No?" he echoed.

"No, you can't use a condom twice. At least, I don't think so," she added truthfully.

"I forgot you could read my mind."

"Not all the time."

"What else have I been thinking?"

She found, to her amazement, that she could blush. Lying

beneath him in the shadowy living room, his aroused body still tight within hers, she could blush.

"I guess that's answer enough." He pulled away, slowly, reluctantly. "I'll be back." There was an old quilt over the arm of the sofa, and he tossed it around her naked body. "Don't go anywhere."

She snuggled down in the cushions, closing her eyes with a sigh. Odd, that temporary resentment of the protection he'd used. She was smart enough, mature enough to understand the necessity of it. But for the first time in her life she'd felt like a lovesick fool, wanting everything from her lover, willing to risk an unplanned pregnancy and worse in her need to be close to him.

He came back to her. She heard an odd sound, and looked up to see him drop a pile of red foil packets on the floor beside the couch before he knelt down beside her. "Second thoughts?" he asked. "Regrets?"

"Should I have?" she answered, trying to read his thoughts. But they were shuttered, impossible to detect.

He simply shook his head. "No," he said. "This has been a long time coming." He brushed her hair away from her face, then frowned. "You were crying."

"I suppose so."

"Did I hurt you? I'm not certain of my strength. You should have said something—"

She stopped his mouth, sitting up and letting the cover drop to her waist, putting her lips against his. She let her mouth rest gently against his, touching, tasting, her tongue sliding against his firm lips, letting his mouth open against hers so she could kiss him fully. When she pulled back, she managed a shaky smile. "I always cry when I'm happy," she said.

"And you were happy?"

"Very."

"How are you right now?"

"I could be happier."

His smile was slow, sensual, as he picked up her hand in his, his thumb stroking the back of it. "I have a few ideas," he murmured, and he put her hand on him, the silky strength of him, already hard for her.

Her fingers wrapped around him, gently, learning him, her fingertips soft and questing. "I have a few of my own, Dr. Crompton," she replied.

"I'm sure you do, Molloy," he said as his breath caught in reaction. "I imagine you can be extremely inventive."

"Try me."

"I have every intention of doing just that." And pulling the cover away from her, he pulled her body up against his, heat against heat, and his mouth covered hers.

THE RAIN STOPPED. The sky was still cloudy, and Suzanna rolled onto her back, looking out the roof window into the gathering dawn. She was still mostly asleep, her body floating in some wonderful daze of exhausted pleasure. She wondered where Daniel was. And then she knew.

She reached over and touched him. He was closer than she'd realized, but she didn't waken him. Or, at least, she could only assume she didn't. He made a snoring sort of grunt, and she felt the futon shift beneath them, and then she was wrapped in his arms once more, her cheek pressed up against his chest. A chest she couldn't see.

More's the pity, she thought idly, reaching her hand up to gently stroke his arm. He had a truly beautiful chest. She'd always thought she liked lots of hair on a man. He had very little, just bone and muscle and golden skin.

He'd carried her upstairs at one point during the night, and she couldn't be quite sure when. She'd been clinging to him, legs wrapped around his waist, and he'd been buried deep inside her as he mounted the stairs. They'd collapsed at the top, finishing there on the bare wood, and just managed to crawl to the bed. At some point they'd even ended up in the hot tub together, before collapsing into a deep, exhausted sleep.

She pressed her face against him, inhaling the scent of his skin, the lingering smell of the soap they'd used with erotic abandon. Outside, the world was a dark, threatening place. Inside, in this magical little house, everything was just wonderful.

She could smell a faint trace of gasoline. An odd scent, one she hadn't noticed before, and she wondered if it had anything to do with Daniel's peculiar powers. Was he somehow able to project something inflammable?

Her body had tensed, and he was awake beside her, his arms tightening around her. "What's wrong?" His voice was sleepy, just becoming alert.

"I thought I smelled gas. I wasn't sure...."

"I smell it, too," he said, and she found herself released. "Someone's here."

He was already off the bed, and she had the eerie sensation of watching clothes float through the air as he grabbed them, then watched them disappear as he pulled them over his body. "Stay put," he ordered. "I'm going to check on things."

"The hell I will," she said, sitting up.

An invisible hand shoved her back against the pillows. "Don't be an idiot, Molloy. If someone's out there, they won't see me. They sure as hell will see you. Use your brain for once."

"You mean, as opposed to last night," she countered, stung.

She couldn't see him, but she could hear his thoughts. Feel his cool, angry withdrawal. "That's your decision," he said finally. "You can occupy your time figuring it out. But if you try to follow me, I swear I'll punch you."

"I always wanted an abusive lover."

"Suzanna..."

"Go away, Daniel. I'll be a good little girl and stay put."

She could feel his reluctant smile. "I thought no one was supposed to call you *girl*."

She found she could smile, as well, despite her bad mood. "So I'm feeling a little girlish today. Go out and save the world, Cinderman. The little woman will be waiting with a hot meal."

She felt the air rush beside her, and then he kissed her, hard. She closed her eyes—it was too disorienting, being kissed by an invisible man. His kisses were shattering enough. She reached up to clutch his shoulders, but he slipped away from her.

"I knew I could count on you."

She leaned back on the mattress, unable to watch him leave. The bottom sheet was pulled halfway off, the duvet was on the floor, and she reached and pulled it over her. It was already cooler without him in the room. The temperature had dropped, and her inner warmth had turned to ice.

He was enjoying himself, damn it. She felt the excitement blazing through him as he went in search of the intruder. He was looking forward to this, a superhero confronting evil. She wanted to slap him. She wanted to clutch him and tell him to be careful, for God's sake. She wanted to lie in bed with the covers over her head and pray for him to return safely.

She heard the door open, the footsteps in the big room below, and she rose from the bed, leaning over the balcony with the duvet clutched around her, ready to offer him a provocative invitation. The words died in her throat as she recognized the man beneath her, wandering through Daniel's precious house, his elegant, cruel hands rifling through the papers and books that littered the place.

He didn't look up, didn't realize she stood there, watching him in bemused horror. "Where the hell are you, Crompton?" he muttered under his breath, slamming open the door to the lab.

No answer, of course, and no sign of him. Suzanna wondered if he was in the house, or if he was outside, looking for their intruder.

And would he realize the man inside was a far cry from the civilized businessman he appeared to be?

Looking down at Henry Osborn's pale, pink head, she could only hope so.

Chapter Fourteen

Suzanna backed away from the balcony as silently as she could. Her clothes lay scattered on the living room floor beneath her, but she was able to rifle through her duffel bag and come up with another pair of jeans and a T-shirt. She'd just pulled it over her head when she felt the eyes on her, and she knew they weren't Daniel's unseen eyes.

She turned, slowly, taking a deep breath to control her sudden panic. He was standing there, blocking the narrow stairway, and he looked impeccable, unruffled, despite the smell of gasoline that clung to him.

"We've been looking for you, Ms. Molloy," he said in a charming, genial voice. "You know, I didn't believe Daniel when he told me you two had something going, but I guess I was wrong. You certainly have a well-screwed look."

She barely blinked at his deliberate crudeness. "What are you doing here, Mr. Osborn?"

"You were awake two nights ago, weren't you?" He took a step closer, a small, sadistic smile on his face. "I thought you might be, even though you managed to hide it. Maybe you have a taste for pain."

"Not particularly." She sounded very cool, something she could congratulate herself on. Of course, she felt more than cool. She felt chilled to the bone.

"Don't make this difficult, Ms. Molloy. Where is he?"

"Where is who?"

He closed his eyes, sighing in genteel exasperation. "I don't mind doing my own dirty work, you know," he confided. "It's been years since I've been in the trenches, but an old soldier never loses his touch. If for no other reason, this latest debacle has been instructive. But I don't care to prolong it any further. I have people who want answers, and I intend to provide them. Where is Dr. Crompton?"

"Didn't you see him when you came in?"

"No."

"We heard you," she said in a dulcet voice. "He went in search of you. I wouldn't be surprised if you walked right past him and didn't see him."

"Not likely," he said with a snort. "I'm going to want you to come downstairs, Ms. Molloy. Very slowly and carefully—no sudden moves or shouts for help."

"Why should I?"

"Because I have a gun. I know how to use it. I'm actually quite good with it," he said in a calm, measured voice. "I think I would start by shooting you in the throat. That way you wouldn't be able to call for assistance."

She hadn't even noticed the gun in his hand. It was small, black and undoubtedly capable of doing all he said and more. She put an involuntary hand up to her throat, and his smile widened.

"Come along, Ms. Molloy. Let's go downstairs and wait for Dr. Crompton to return."

"What if he's left?" she asked, moving slowly, carefully ahead of him, down the narrow flight of stairs. "What if he's gone for help?"

"Where could he go? There's no one around for miles. If it weren't for my contacts, we would never have found this place."

"We?" She took a brief, surreptitious glance around the living room. It was cold down there, icy, and she knew that

Daniel must still be outside. The smell of the gasoline was even stronger downstairs, and there was no way she could dismiss her sense of impending doom.

"Surely you must realize by now that Beebe has limitless resources. The finest minds, the greatest talents of this country, have lent themselves to Beebe, and I can say quite truthfully that there's no stopping us."

"No stopping you from what?"

Osborn smiled like a rat. "Have a seat while we wait for the good doctor."

He gestured with the gun, and Suzanna didn't make the mistake of thinking she had any choice in the matter. She took the seat he pointed at, putting her hands in her lap and trying to still her panic. "No stopping you from what?" she asked again.

"Our noble cause. Our patriotic duty. We're not fools, Ms. Molloy, even if Washington seems to be overrun these days with bleeding-heart liberals. Those who ignore their history are doomed to repeat it. If we're fools enough to seek isolation, to let those third-world countries fend for themselves, then we're asking for the collapse of the United States as a world power."

"I didn't know we were letting them fend for themselves," she began, watching warily as Osborn drew a thin nylon cord out of his perfectly tailored pocket.

"The hell with economic help or economic sanctions. Blackmail won't get us what we want," he said, tucking the gun in his pocket and advancing on her, the nylon cord extended. "Arms. Weapons. That's the only power these people will understand."

"How does Dr. Crompton fit into that?" She tensed herself. She could fight back. He wasn't any taller than she was, and he was a great deal older. She had a chance against him, as long as he put that gun away.

"He's brilliant. Quite our most valuable asset. We assumed he was working on cold fusion, and if he'd managed to perfect it we would have been in the catbird seat."

"Then why were you trying to kill him?"

Osborn looked disgruntled. "We were fed the wrong information. That fool Jackson said he'd perfected it, that he was only a liability. If Crompton suffered from a fatal lab accident, there'd be no one to interfere with our plans for cold fusion."

"Wouldn't that be killing the goose that laid the golden egg?" she asked, and in the far recesses of her mind she heard Crompton's disgruntled reaction to being called a goose.

"We wouldn't have needed him any longer. He's not the only brilliant scientist in the world. With his research, we could have hired other, more practical men, and gone on to develop a power base such as the world has never seen."

"But things went wrong."

Osborn grimaced. "Thank God. Once Jackson had time to put all the research together, we knew we were in trouble. Whatever Crompton was working on, it had nothing to do with cold fusion. It didn't resemble anything anyone could recognize."

"So why don't you kill him?"

"I'm not a fool, Ms. Molloy. I didn't get where I am today by ignoring potential. He's America's secret weapon. Whatever that amazing brain has come up with will be worth billions. Trillions. The entire national debt. I'm taking him back with me, if I can."

"And if you can't?"

He smiled. "Then sooner or later someone will be able to take his research and make sense of it."

"What are you going to do with me?"

"Why, nothing at all, my dear. Just tie you up so you won't interfere. I promise I won't tie you so tightly that you won't be able to loosen your bonds within a couple of hours."

She shook her head. "What makes you the executioner, Mr. Osborn? I would have thought that duty would be left for underlings. Or do you have a taste for killing?"

"My dear girl," he said in his unctuous voice, "I don't usually waste my time with enforcement duties. But this has partly been my responsibility, letting things get out of hand like this, and I want to make sure things are handled right from now on. Besides, I have a certain talent." He was standing close enough that she could smell his cologne, mixed with the scent of gasoline. It was very elegant, expensive cologne. Her father had used it, as well. "Put your hands at your sides, my dear, and I promise I won't tie them too tightly."

She looked up at him. Where was Crompton? "That answers one question," she said, keeping her hands folded in her lap, her muscles coiled to spring.

"What's that?"

"You're not planning on putting that rope around my wrists. You're planning on strangling me with it."

She'd managed to shock him out of his slimy equanimity. "My dear girl," he protested, moving closer, the nylon rope stretched tight between his two soft white hands.

"I can read your mind," she said savagely. "And don't call me *girl!*"

He lunged for her then, but she was too fast for him, ducking and rolling out of the chair, onto the hard wood floor. "Daniel!" she screamed as Osborn fell on top of her, the rope snaking around her throat.

She grabbed at it with her hands, but the man was murderously strong, brutally efficient. His knee pressed into her back as he wrapped the rope twice around her neck.

Time stood still. Years ago she'd read an article about a woman who'd almost been strangled to death by a maniac. She'd been saved, but the loss of oxygen to her brain had left her in a wheelchair, her nerves and muscles useless. Suzanna clawed at the rope, trying to scream again, but it was too tight. No sound came out, and she knew she was going to die. Better that than to be left a living corpse. But she hadn't been able to tell Daniel she loved him, she loved him...

The weight disappeared from her back with shocking speed, the tension slackened from the rope around her throat, and she yanked it away, coughing and choking, barely aware of her surroundings. And then she heard Osborn babbling.

She sat up, dazed. The man who'd tried to strangle her lay spread-eagled on the floor, a look of glazed horror on his face. "What's going on here?" he gasped.

"I'm going to kill you, Osborn." Daniel's voice came from thin air, cool, unyielding, deadly.

Osborn stared around him, trying to see the source of that voice. "Where are you, Crompton?" he demanded, getting back some of his bluster. "You know I wasn't really going to hurt the girl. I was just trying to scare her."

"Don't call her *girl*," Daniel said in a tight, lethal voice. "Thirty seconds more and she would have passed out. Another minute and she would have suffered permanent brain damage. But you weren't going to hurt her, were you, Hank?" His voice was savage as he called the dignified old man by his totally inappropriate nickname. "Any more than you were going to hurt her when you mauled her in the hospital. Where did you get your training, Osborn? You're too young to be a Nazi, even if you have the personality for it."

Osborn sat up, his equilibrium momentarily back in place. "It's some kind of remote speaker, isn't it?" he said with renewed self-confidence. "And just so you don't underestimate me, I should tell you I got my training with the best. The CIA taught me everything I know. Now where are you, Crompton, and how did you manage to throw me? Was it some sort of electric shock?" He brushed a speck of dust off his rumpled jacket.

An invisible hand punched him in his shoulder, knocking him backward. "It's a shock, all right," Daniel said. "Suzanna, I want you to get out of here."

She'd managed to pull herself together, just barely. Her throat was on fire, and the smell of gasoline was growing even stronger. "I won't let you kill him, Daniel," she said.

"You can't stop me."

"Daniel, if you kill him, you'll become just like him."

"Do you think I give a damn? I don't spend my life worrying about petty notions of morality. He hurt you, he was going to kill you—"

"Daniel…"

"Get out of here."

Osborn lay back on the rug. "Don't leave me," he croaked. "I don't know what's going on here, but don't leave me alone."

"The problem is, Osborn, that you're not alone," Daniel said in a silken voice, close enough to him that Osborn must have felt his breath on his face.

Osborn jumped a mile, scuttling backward till he came up against the wall. "Is this what you've been working on? Some kind of invisible ray?"

"It's the side effect of that little lab explosion you and Jackson manufactured for me," he said. "Just one of the benefits of hazardous work. By the way, did you kill Jackson, or was it Armstead's little army?"

Osborn's color was ghastly. He stared straight ahead, like a blind man. "It's hot here," he choked, loosening his tie.

"It was you, wasn't it? You've got a taste for such things. I'm sure Armstead didn't tell you to come and kill Suzanna. You just decided to show a little initiative."

"I don't take orders from Armstead."

"Oh, but you do. You're an errand boy, Osborn. A figurehead for Big Brother, doing what they tell you, taking your punishment like a man. Are you ready to die?"

"Daniel!" Suzanna shrieked in protest.

Osborn lurched to his feet, throwing himself toward the sound of Daniel's voice, arms outstretched to topple him. He connected with nothing and went down hard.

He lay there, panting, and when he tried to rise, something in the middle of his back shoved him downward again. Suzanna could only suppose it was Daniel's foot.

"I'm not the only one who's going to die," he wheezed, his face twisted and malevolent. "You're going with me, and your girlfriend, as well."

"Who have you got waiting for us, Osborn?" Daniel's voice was silky with menace. "One of Armstead's mercenaries?"

"I don't need anyone. This place is set to blow, and I'm the only one who can stop it. Get off me, and this whole conversation will be academic." Osborn tried to get up, but the invisible foot stayed planted in the center of his back.

"How long?"

Osborn's pale face had a grimace of triumph. "Let me up," he said again. "Or the girlfriend goes up with us."

"Bastard," Daniel muttered, but Suzanna could sense him move away from the prone man. It shouldn't have come as a surprise when unseen hands wrapped around her arms and hauled her to her feet. "Get out of here, Suzanna. Get down the hill as fast as you can, and keep your eyes open for any of his little buddies."

"Not without you," she said in a raw, rasping voice.

"I'll be right behind you."

"How will I know that?" she said stubbornly. Henry Osborn had managed to climb to his feet, and he stood there, swaying, his perfect white hair mussed, his elegantly groomed face a mask of violent rage.

"You'll have to trust me." Daniel's hands were strong, unyielding, as they pushed her toward the door.

She was still fighting him, even knowing that she was a dangerous distraction. "Are you going to kill him?" she demanded in a hoarse whisper.

She heard his long-suffering sigh, and she could just imagine the expression on his face. She put out her hand and touched him, connecting with his cheek, brushing against his mouth in a last caress.

"He deserves it," he muttered. "If I weren't such a sentimental fool, I'd throw him over the balcony."

For me, she wanted to ask, but was afraid to.

For you, he thought, and she heard it, even though he wouldn't say the words aloud. And she smiled up at him. "I'll wait for you at the bottom of the path." Then she was gone.

"She's not going to get very far, Crompton," Osborn said in a casual voice. He'd straightened his silk tie, and his pale pink hands weren't even shaking.

Daniel turned from his spot by the door. He knew what Osborn had in mind. As long as he could engage him in conversation, he could pinpoint his location. Daniel had no intention of giving him that edge.

"Haven't you realized by now just how far-reaching Beebe is? You scientists, with your dreams and your heads in the clouds…you don't have any idea what real power is all about. Beebe is about power. There's no place she'll be safe. Even if you lied to her, and I don't make it down this hillside, Armstead and his men will be waiting. If she doesn't go back to Santa Cristina, they'll still find her. It may take a while, but those men are dedicated. Sooner or later they'll run her to ground, and they'll wipe her existence off the face of the earth."

Daniel moved slowly, silently toward the sliding doors leading onto the narrow balcony. He'd have to pass Osborn to get out there, and while he knew he could manage to accomplish that without making any noise, he was afraid his body heat would give him away.

But he had to get out of there. Osborn assumed he hadn't noticed the innocuous little box tucked into a corner of the deck, or the almost transparent wires leading away from it.

He'd underestimated his opponent, a fatal mistake. Daniel wasn't a man who missed anything, and he'd noticed that box instantly. He had to get rid of it, or the whole house that he'd built with his bare hands would be a pile of cinders. And he'd probably be in the ashes, as well.

Osborn took a step, blocking the center of the door. "I'm afraid not, Crompton. You've become too great a liability, despite your undeniable gifts. I'm afraid your usefulness is at an end. It's a pity, too. For a man with your intellect, you could have had anything you wanted. You always struck me as such a ruthless, practical man. You've changed."

Daniel was standing directly in front of him. "Yes," he said finally.

Osborn jumped, but recovered himself with impressive speed. "You've become practically human," he observed. "What in God's name happened to you? Don't tell me you've been fool enough to fall in love with that girl?"

"Don't call her a girl," Daniel said absently.

"Is that it? Has true love made an idiot out of you?"

"Not exactly," Daniel drawled. "It was more likely a case of green slime."

He heard the change. The quiet, merciless little hum of the box on the porch suddenly went into a high-pitched squeal, so painful that Daniel held his ears for a moment. Osborn didn't move, obviously deaf to the sound.

He didn't have any time to waste. "Out of my way," he snarled, shoving at him. He'd forgotten Osborn's training. Those deceptively soft hands shot out and caught him, and Osborn managed to pull him off balance, before Daniel loosened himself and tossed the man away.

Unfortunately he tossed him toward the glass doors. Osborn went crashing through, landing in a heap on top of the incendiary device. For a moment Daniel didn't move, hoping to God Osborn was knocked unconscious, hoping that for once Suzanna had listened to him and made her way down the hill, hoping that there was some way out of this mess that had blown up out of nowhere.

Osborn rose, the box in his hand. "I always wanted to die for my country," he said, a fanatic light gleaming in his eye. "Crompton," he murmured, "you're toast."

Instinct took over. Daniel hadn't realized he could move so fast. He could hear the metal contacts click together just as he leapt over the balcony. The force of the blast sent him head over heels, and then he was falling, falling, over and over, through the tall pines, down the steep cliff to the rocky ledge below. The flames were behind him, shooting into the sky, black and inky, and he knew Osborn was dead. As he would be, once he hit the ground.

He could hear her scream of disbelieving horror. And then everything went black, as the granite ledge rushed up to meet him, and his last thought was a faint regret that he'd never told Suzanna he was in love with her. And now it was too late.

SUZANNA SANK TO HER KNEES in the mud. "No," she moaned. "No, no, no." But there was no answer to her strangled cries. Just the crackle of the blazing house as the fire consumed it, and the cry of the wind in the trees overhead.

"Daniel," she whispered, but there was no answer. She scrambled to her feet, clawing her way back up to where the house had stood. The heat was suffocating, the smoke choking, the house caving in on itself. "Daniel," she screamed in her raw voice, but there was no answer. In that tiny clearing that had once held a magic cottage and now held only a blazing inferno, there was no one left alive to hear her.

Chapter Fifteen

Suzanna had no idea how long she knelt in the clearing, blasted by the heat of the burning building, or what made her struggle to her feet. She moved back down the narrow trail like a robot, her mind a deliberate blank. She had only one thought. Daniel was dead, and she had to run—away from the men who killed him, and away from the knowledge of his death. She needed to run as far and as fast as she could, find some place to crawl into. And then maybe she could mourn.

The Jaguar sat parked at the bottom of the hill, directly over the spot where Jackson's sedan had been incinerated. Daniel would have liked to have made ashes of that car, as well, with Osborn inside. She wondered whether he'd started the fire. If he had, it would have been an accident. Despite the ruthlessness in his voice, he wouldn't have murdered Osborn in cold blood. And he wouldn't have destroyed his beautiful house.

Osborn must have rigged something, determined to destroy them all. And she had escaped.

It was no comfort, none at all. She stared at the hunter-green luxury car and wondered what kind of luck she'd have hot-wiring the thing. She opened the passenger door, expecting the blare of antitheft devices. Instead she got a discreet little buzz, so quiet and well-bred that it took her a dazed moment to realize that Osborn had left the keys in the ignition.

She slid into the driver's seat and slammed the door behind her. It was blisteringly hot in the car, oddly so, considering the early morning hour. She jerked the seat forward and turned the key, half expecting the car to explode. It started with a throaty purr, and she tore back down the narrow, rutted dirt road with a complete disregard for the elegant car she drove.

She punched on the air-conditioning. Her hands were trembling, her mind a careful blank. All she wanted to do was drive, and keep on driving, as far away from her conscious thoughts as she could go.

For a moment she closed her eyes, trying to hear Daniel's thoughts, to find out for sure if he was really dead. Nothing answered her, not even the breath of an emotion. Daniel Crompton was gone, wiped out, incinerated from the face of this earth. Cinderman was cinders.

She heard the faint moan of anguish, and she shoved a fist in her mouth to quiet it. She couldn't let go now. She had to get away, as fast as she possibly could. She just had to wait until she found a place to hide.

It was still unbearably hot. The heat was coming from the empty back seat, and she wondered whether the heating system in the car was malfunctioning, sending warmth out the back ducts. She couldn't afford to spend the time checking. She cranked the air-conditioning higher, shoved her bare foot down on the accelerator and kept going, pulling out onto the narrow paved road with a skid of tires.

The blessed numbness lasted less than an hour. It lasted until she happened to glance at the digital clock on the leather-and-wood dashboard, in time to see that it was now only eight o'clock. The conflagration at the cabin had happened in a deathly short period of time. It was the hour for Daniel to regain his visibility. But Daniel was gone—there was no more body to appear.

The first sob took her by surprise, shaking her body. The second one was even worse, tearing her apart, and out of sheer self-preservation she slowed her manic speed, as the tears streamed down her face and her body was racked with sobs. "I can't stand it," she wept, pounding the steering wheel. "He can't be dead." She glanced in the rearview mirror, to make sure no one was pulling up behind her as she crept along the road, her body shaking with misery.

In the rearview mirror appeared the disheveled face of Daniel Crompton. "I'm not," he said blandly.

Suzanna promptly ran into a tree.

What little self-control she'd still owned disappeared as the car stalled out, and she buried her face in her hands. She heard the rear door open, heard her own driver's door open, but when he put his hands on her she lost it completely, screaming at him, beating at him, fury and pain and relief exploding from her in a wild rage.

He was so strong. He simply pulled her into his arms, out of the car, held her flailing fists with one hand, tucking her against him as he sank down on the grass. And then she began to weep, great ugly sobs that tore her apart.

He said nothing. His body was strong and so hot that it spread warmth through her suddenly chilled flesh. His hand was soothing her tangled hair.

She had no idea how long her crying fit lasted. The spasms that racked her body slowed, then stumbled to a halt, and she was simply lying in his arms, weak, wasted, the tears finally gone.

"I hate you," she said in a small, pained voice.

"Why?" It was an eminently logical question, what she'd expect from him. Even as his hands were stroking her, soothing her.

"Because you let me think you were dead. You somehow managed to sneak away and hide in the back of the car, and you never said a word...."

"I didn't sneak away," he said. "I jumped over the balcony when Osborn detonated the device he'd rigged."

She lifted her head. Her face was wet with tears, and he smoothed them away with his deft thumbs. "You couldn't have," she said. "It was a sheer drop, onto granite. You'd be dead."

He shrugged. "Interesting, isn't it? I blacked out, but I'm most assuredly not dead. I feel kind of stiff and sore, but apart from that I'm in one piece. I managed to crawl to Henry's car, but I'm afraid I passed out in the back seat. I wasn't in any shape to say anything."

She looked at him in awe. "Does that mean you're invulnerable, as well? You can't die?"

The idea didn't seem to please him. "I have no idea. Obviously I can survive a fall like that. We'll simply have to find someplace where I can experiment a bit more. Damn," he said abruptly.

"What?"

"The specimen I was working on. It's gone."

"So is the house," she said mournfully. She'd loved that house.

He shrugged. "Houses can be rebuilt. I don't know how I'll ever find more green slime. Unless Beebe has some squirreled away. I want an antidote, and I'm not going to come up with one if I can't figure out what it was in the first place."

She managed a watery smile. "You mean you don't want to be Cinderman after all?"

"Not particularly. What about you?" he asked, pushing her hair away from her tear-damp face. "You want to spend the rest of your life doing a mind-reading act?"

"No," she said, just looking at him, at the face she'd never expected to see again. "But I do like going without my glasses."

He managed a wry grin. "Maybe we'll let you keep your powers. You feel ready to continue on?"

For a moment she didn't move. "Where are we going?"

"Back to Santa Cristina. They're not going to let us be, Molloy. We can't keep running. I've got to go back and face them."

"What about me?"

"I'll take you someplace safe, if we can think of it."

She shook her head. "I'm staying with you." She ought to tell him. She'd almost lost him once—now was the time to tell him.

But she couldn't. He sat there looking at her, cool and composed, despite the streak of dirt on his face and the twigs and leaves in his long hair. He wasn't the kind of man she could easily say "I love you" to. He'd probably ask her to define it scientifically.

She smiled wryly. "Any objections?" she added.

"Would you listen to them?"

"Nope."

"Then I'll save my breath. Let's get moving. I want to be off the road by six o'clock."

She climbed off him reluctantly, wondering if she was imagining the way his hands clung to her for a moment before releasing her. Wondering if he'd thought of her when he vaulted over the balcony to what should have been a certain death below.

"Do you want to tell me what happened back there?" she asked. "Did you start the fire?"

He looked bleak for a moment. "No," he said. "To both questions. I'll drive."

She could have argued, but in truth, her knees were weak, her hands were trembling, and all she wanted to do was crawl into the soft leather seat of the Jaguar and look at him. "All right," she said.

He threw her a mocking glance. "Docile all of a sudden, are we? What happened to the tough creature who ate male chauvinist pigs for breakfast?"

She glanced down at the T-shirt she'd grabbed in the

darkness: The Truth Shall Set You Free, But First It Will
Piss You Off. Apt enough for today. "She's tired," Suzanna said wearily. "I'll be more than ready to go ten
rounds when we get back to California."

"I'll be looking forward to it."

DANIEL DECIDED he didn't like Jaguars. Or, at least, he
didn't like this particular one. Not that it didn't have plenty
of power, a smooth ride and a decent radio. It even came
equipped with a CD player, but since the late Henry Osborn's taste in music had tended toward marching bands
and motivational tapes, he made do with the FM.

But it had a soft, leathery bucket seat, and Suzanna lay
curled up, miles away in her own soft, leathery bucket seat.
And he wanted her curled up next to him, with her head in
his lap, her blond hair spread over his thighs.

It had been quite a night. So active that he should have
used up his sexual energy for the next six months. He'd
certainly used up his supply of condoms.

So it made no sense that the very sight of her, the sound
of her soft breathing, the scent of her, would be driving
him crazy with lust.

And that's all it was, he told himself self-righteously.
That's all he believed in. Chemistry, animal attraction. For
some reason he and the cantankerous Suzanna Molloy
made a perfect match. It wouldn't last, of course. But it
certainly was far stronger than anything he'd felt in his
entire life.

He suspected it was the same for her. For a moment he
wished he had her uncanny ability to read other people's
thoughts. He would have liked to know what went on behind those warm, wary brown eyes when she looked at him.
She hadn't come to bed with him like a woman who was
used to that sort of thing. She'd been hesitant, shy, disarm-
ingly so. Out of bed she was a tiger—in his arms she was
surprisingly unsure.

He was used to sexual athletes. Wonderwomen, who knew what they wanted and how to achieve it with the minimum of fuss. Suzanna had been uncertain, and he'd had to woo her, each time breaking down her resistance.

He wondered whether he was going to have to woo her when they got back to Santa Cristina. Or whether he'd be able to stop her in the first lonely place he found and take her standing up, her legs wrapped around his hips, her nails digging into his back.

He adjusted his jeans, shifting in the seat, and glanced over at her. She was asleep, and he could see the pale mauve shadows beneath her eyes. She needed to be left alone, to recoup her strength and self-assurance. The past twenty-four hours had thrown her off balance, from lying on her back beneath him to watching the house explode into flames, thinking he was inside.

He had never stopped to consider what it might mean to her. He'd never thought that someone might care so much if he met a fiery end. His own elderly parents would most likely accept it as they accepted everything. With calm, measured practicality. His parents weren't much for emotion, only intellect, and now that they were in their late seventies they seemed absolute strangers to any kind of feeling. They'd mourn, of course, but probably more for the waste of potential than for their only son.

But Suzanna hadn't accepted his supposed loss with equanimity, or even a sentimental tear or two. She'd been shattered, and that rage of emotion, of raw feeling, frightened him as little else could. He didn't want to mean that much to anyone.

He glanced over at her. He could still see the salty traces of the tears that had run down her pale face. He didn't want her to love him. It complicated things, it made him uneasy, unsure, and at a time when he needed to concentrate all his energies, all his intellect, on stopping Beebe.

He turned his face away, staring out into the bright midday light as he drove south toward California and fate. He didn't believe in love, and he didn't have time for it. He'd have to make that abundantly clear to Suzanna Molloy. What they had together was a certain argumentative compatibility and a powerful sexual communication. It didn't have to be cloaked in hearts and flowers. It wasn't love.

She shifted next to him, and he started guiltily. "Did you know," she said, her voice cool and clear, "that I could hear some of Osborn's thoughts?"

"Interesting," he replied.

"Not as clearly as yours, though. Only a thought or two filtered through from him. Whereas with you I tend to hear far too much." It was a warning, gently spoken.

"Suzanna," he said, suddenly feeling like the lowest creature of all creation.

"You might turn the radio up," she said quietly. "That might drown some of it out."

He leaned forward and did so, and the annoying sound of rap music filled the elegant car. It was probably the first time in its short history the car had been subjected to such an indignity. He deliberately envisioned her, naked, lying beneath him, legs spread and waiting, and he glanced over to see her reaction.

No telltale blush. No reaction whatsoever. "That's better," she murmured, closing her eyes again.

"We need to talk."

"Not now," she said, turning her back on him. He could see the straight line of her spine beneath her T-shirt. It looked strong, it looked angry, it looked vulnerable.

He'd give her time. And deliberately he concentrated on the antiestablishment, kill-the-Man rhetoric on the radio. For once it was something he could identify with.

He drove steadily through the day. The only time Suzanna emerged from the cocoon she'd spun about herself was when he stopped at a fast-food restaurant. Even the sight of a hamburger and french fries couldn't bring back the light in her eyes, but at least she managed to eat an indecent amount. She said nothing about his choice of salad and milk shake, and he missed her razzing him. But he had the good sense to give her time and space. He simply looked at his salad and calculated how many grams of fat were in the dressing, shielding his thoughts from her.

It was just after five when he pulled the car to a stop. It was getting dark already, the autumn light fading quickly, and he killed the motor, waiting for Suzanna to emerge from her daylong retreat.

"Where are we?" she asked, looking around sleepily.

"About ten miles from Beebe, if you take back roads and go across country a bit."

"Lord," she moaned. "Don't tell me you're still trying to get me to walk?"

"No. There's an old place back in the woods here. I was thinking of buying it. We can hide out here for a while, at least until after eight."

She looked at him curiously. "Why don't you want to go there until eight? Aren't you wasting any possible advantage you might have?"

"No." He'd figured it all out while she slept. If he went in while he was invisible, he would simply be leaving Suzanna as the only available target. He already knew he wouldn't be able to get her to stay behind, short of binding and gagging her, and he didn't think she'd let him get away with that.

She smiled wryly. "Thanks."

"For what?"

"For your chivalry."

He slammed his hand against the steering wheel. "You know what it's like, having a voyeur peering at my every thought?"

"Hey, I don't like it, either," she snapped back, her tentative smile vanishing. "And it's not your every thought. It's just the occasional one."

"It's still too damned many."

"I agree."

Silence, heated, angry, filling the car. "Let's get out of here," he said finally. "I don't know whether anyone noticed us as we got nearer Santa Cristina. It's a distinctive car."

She accepted the peace offering, for what it was, unfastening the seat belt and sliding out of the front seat. "Lead on, MacDuff. Let's just hope we can find some food at this place."

"I wouldn't count on it. Besides, you ate an indecent amount at the burger place."

"Most people eat more than once every twenty-four hours," she said in a deceptively tranquil voice.

He bit back his instinctive retort. The driveway of the old house was overgrown, neglected for the last few years as the old lady owner of the house had grown older and less observant. With the approaching dusk and the hunter green of the car, it would most likely escape detection, unless someone was looking for it at that particular place, which wasn't at all likely. As of Thursday afternoon, the old house had been on the market for more than six months, and he was the only one who'd shown the slightest bit of interest.

She said nothing as he led her up the winding driveway to the front door. He wasn't sure what he expected from her. She looked up at the deserted house with a bleak expression on her face, and he would have given anything for the momentary ability to read her thoughts.

"Stay here," he said. "I'll go around and let you in."

"You have a key?"

He didn't bother lying to her. "I know the easiest way to break in."

If he expected an argument, he didn't get one. She waited there, patient, quiet, until he opened the front door and drew her into the dusty little hallway.

"The power's still on," he said. "There's a television, if you're so inclined, and some of the furniture is still here, the worthless stuff. According to the real estate agent the antiques were already sold to—"

"You're babbling," Suzanna said, moving past him. "It's very nice."

He shut his mouth. "Yes," he said briefly. She was obviously having a monumental case of sulks because he wouldn't tell her he was in love with her, and it wasn't fair, just because he didn't believe in such things...

"Would you stop it!" she snapped, her temper frayed.

"Stop what?"

"Stop obsessing about not being in love with me! Did I ask you to? Have I been throwing myself at you, declaring my undying devotion, insisting on promises and vows of eternal love? Have I?" she demanded furiously.

"No."

"Then why do you keep fussing about it? I don't expect you to love me. I'm certain you're entirely incapable of it. We're good in bed, right? What was that lovely phrase you thought of—a certain argumentative compatibility? Why don't we just strip off our clothes and do it and stop arguing about imaginary things like being in love."

She looked magnificent, standing there in the dusky shadows, her breasts rising and falling beneath the T-shirt. She looked like the answer to his every dream and more.

"I need a copy of that T-shirt," he said abruptly.

He'd manage to startle her. "What T-shirt?"

"The one you wore when I saw you for the first time. At the press conference, last summer. Denial Is Not Just a River in Egypt."

She just stared at him for a moment. "You remember that?"

"I remember everything about you."

"What are you trying to tell me?"

"Nothing I'm ready to say right now." He moved away

from her, coward that he was, and she let him go. "We'll wait here until after eight o'clock. I'm not sure what we'll do till then...."

But she was gone. He heard her footsteps on the bare wood floors, and he wondered if she was running away from him. He'd have to go after her—it wasn't safe. And if he went after her, he might say what he didn't mean, didn't believe in, wasn't ready for...

"Hell and damnation," he muttered. His brain must have melted under the assault of green slime.

He went into the hallway, following her. She'd gone up the sharply angled staircase—he could hear her in the distance, his oddly acute hearing tuned in to her breathing. He heard the creak of a bed, the rustle of clothing, and he started after her.

The cramp hit him halfway up the second flight, sharp and hard, and he cursed, something brief and obscene, sagging against the wall, waiting for the pain to pass, waiting for his body to fade into nothingness. He didn't hear her come, but he looked up and she was standing there at the top of the stairs, looking down at him as he held his stomach.

"It must be almost six," she said.

He shut his eyes for a moment. "I'll go for a walk," he said. "As soon as this stops..."

She came up beside him and put her arm through his, tugging him gently upward. "Stop fighting, Daniel."

"What do you mean?"

"You need to rest. Stop fighting the pain, stop fighting me. Come and lie down. I'll wake you up when it's eight. It'll be easy enough to tell," she added with a wry smile.

He looked at her. He was already beginning to fade, and he could see from the determined expression on her face that she wasn't going to let that bother her. She tugged, and he went. She was right—he needed to stop fighting.

"That's right," she murmured soothingly. "Just give it

up for a couple of hours." She pulled him into the bedroom at the top of the stairs, and by the time he was through the door he was invisible. "On the bed," she ordered.

It was most likely a horribly uncomfortable old bed. Even the old lady's heirs hadn't wanted it. It was a sagging double bed, with a concave mattress covered by faded ticking, and a plain barred iron headboard that looked as if it belonged in a reformatory. It looked like heaven.

"Just an hour," he agreed, sinking down on it and closing his eyes in relief. "Wake me at seven, and we'll talk."

"I don't want to talk to you, Daniel," she said. "I don't think I'm going to like anything you have to say. Go to sleep," she said firmly.

He opened his eyes for a moment. She was standing at the foot of the bed, her eyes shadowed. "What are you going to do?"

"Wake you when it's eight o'clock," she said gently. And she turned and left the room.

He had never felt so alone in his life. The narrow double bed was huge. He wanted to call after her, to tell her—

The words stopped. She didn't want to hear them. In his mind, in his voice.

And for once, she was right. He needed to sleep. He'd just about exhausted every last ounce of his reserves.

He'd wake himself up at seven. And then he'd make her listen.

Chapter Sixteen

Suzanna leaned forward and clicked off the black-and-white television set. Mistake number one was turning it on in the first place. She'd done so just in time to hear about the unfortunate demise of Henry Osborn, Daniel Crompton and his unnamed female companion in a fire of suspicious origin, up in an uninhabited tract of woodland in eastern Oregon.

Uncle Vinnie would be frantic. Not to mention Daniel's elderly parents. The phones were disconnected, and for a brief moment she considered taking the car and driving to the nearest pay phone, just long enough to set Uncle Vinnie's mind at ease.

And then she remembered what car they had. She hadn't looked, but if Henry Osborn's car didn't come equipped with a cellular phone, she'd turn invisible herself.

It was after seven when she came back from the car. It had taken her ages to figure out how to work the damned thing, and then Uncle Vinnie had asked all sorts of questions that she hadn't been prepared to answer. She'd finally ended up hanging up on him, after she'd gotten his promise to track down Daniel's parents and inform them that their son was very much alive. It was the least she could do. She remembered how it felt, twelve hours ago, when she'd knelt in the dirt and mourned his death. She couldn't let that happen to another human being, not without just cause.

The house was still and silent when she came back in, closing the door behind her. She was cold—she only had her T-shirt and jeans and bare feet, and the night air was brisk. She looked around for some kind of heat, then realized the most potent form of it was upstairs, asleep. All she had to do was go up to that bedroom and sit in the chair, and Daniel's inner blaze would warm her chilled bones.

She left the lights off as she went upstairs. The shadows had their customary, unnerving effect, but she decided to play it safe. Despite the fact that the house was deep within the woods, someone might come looking. Now that Uncle Vinnie knew she was somewhere near by, he might be foolish enough to mount a rescue attempt. She didn't want to involve him any more than she had to.

There was a full moon rising beyond the dusty, multi-paned window, and it shone on the empty bed. Except that it wasn't empty at all. She stood in the doorway, and she could hear his breathing, feel the heat emanating from his flesh. It was hot in the room, wonderfully warm.

And then she noticed the clothes on the floor. His jeans and T-shirt lay in a haphazard pile, which could mean one of two things. Either he'd changed his clothes—and she knew all their extra clothes had burned with the house—or he was lying on the bed, wearing nothing but his hot, smooth skin.

The old springs creaked in the night, and she knew he was awake. "Just as well you can't see me," he murmured, his voice low and beguiling.

"Why?"

"You'd blush."

She could feel color suffuse her face. "I have pale skin," she protested.

She could feel his silence. Feel his longing. Feel him burning for her. As she burned for him.

"Denial is not just a river in Egypt," he murmured, and unbelieving she heard the next words, the ones she'd longed for, in his mind.

She couldn't see him, so she simply closed her eyes. And reaching down, she pulled her T-shirt over her head and sent it sailing onto the floor, where it landed beside his.

The jeans came next. She was wearing plain white cotton bikini panties, and she stripped those off, as well, so that she was standing in the moonlit darkness, naked, vulnerable.

She knew he watched her—she could feel his eyes on her body like a caress, running down her long legs, up over her stomach, cupping her breasts. She tilted her head back, reveling in the heat of his gaze, and her shoulder-length hair trailed down her back. When she looked at the bed again there was a faint, possessive smile on her face.

"You're an idiot, Dr. Crompton," she said, moving toward the sagging mattress.

"Why do you say that, Molloy?" He sounded merely curious, but the husky note in his voice betrayed his reaction to her as surely as the sight of him would have.

She stopped beside the bed, feeling the luscious heat wash over her. "Because you're afraid of the best thing that ever happened to you."

"I don't..." he began, but she leaned down, unerringly, putting her hand against his unseen mouth.

"Shut up, Daniel," she said kindly. "I'll take care of things." And she put her mouth where her hand had been.

His mouth was hot, damp, open for her. She threaded her hands through his long hair, and she could feel the stubble of his beard. He hadn't shaved all day—Osborn had woken them out of an exhausted sleep, and they'd been running so long that she hadn't even noticed.

She liked the roughness of his cheeks. She drew her

mouth away and rubbed her face against his unseen one, still feeling his beard against her tender skin. She was kneeling on the bed beside him, and she felt his hands slide around her waist, hot against her cool skin, and she leaned against him, absorbing the feel of him, the warmth of him, the strength of him.

He tried to tug her down beside him, beneath him, but she held back. "Not this time," she murmured.

"What do you mean?"

"I mean that I've never had the chance to make love to an invisible man in my life. It seems likely that you're going to be spending a lot of time in that condition, and I intend to be spending a lot of time with you. I'd better get used to it."

She let her hands trail down the sides of his face, exploring the feel of him, and let them rest on his bare shoulders.

She let her eyes drift closed. She'd never realized how intensely erotic it could be, touching without seeing. She learned him, the shape and texture of him, as she'd never learned a man before. With only her other senses available, with taste and touch and smell, she had to concentrate on the slightest clues. The pebbled hardness of his flat male nipples, the faint, rasping sound of his breath as she trailed her mouth across his stomach, the tension in his skin, his hands, as he forced himself to let her discover him. When he lay back on the bare mattress, she heard the shift of the springs beneath him. She slid her hands up, to discover he'd wrapped his own strong hands around the iron bedstead. She could feel the pressure, the strength in them, and she smiled, opening her eyes to stare down into nothingness.

"You're showing wonderful restraint," she murmured approvingly, leaning forward to brush a kiss against his mouth. She missed her target, landing instead on his chin, but he moved, swiftly, unerringly, his mouth meeting hers, and she could taste his hunger, taste his need.

"Stay like that," she whispered, learning him with her mouth, letting her lips taste and nibble their way down his smooth, hot chest, past his stomach and the faint roughness of hair. She put her hands around him, gently, and he groaned, and she heard the creak of the springs as he arched beneath her.

He was huge, and hard, and damp for her. He didn't need to say a word—she knew what he wanted, she could hear his desperate longing in his mind, and it matched her own. She leaned down and put her mouth on him, taking him deep inside, her hands clutching his hips.

He didn't touch her, and she knew why. If he touched her, he'd take over, and he knew she needed to do this. Needed to take control, to learn him, without fear of the consequences. She needed to do just what she wanted, and she needed him to lie back and let her.

He was shaking. She could feel the trembling in his body, and it matched her own. She wanted him this way, she wanted him every way there was, but she could hear his protest. And then he spoke, his voice raw and strained in the empty darkness.

"Not without you," he said, and she knew he loved her.

Reluctantly she pulled away, and she could feel his silent cry of pain. And then she slid up, over him, and as she slowly sank down she could feel the iron-hard tension in every muscle in his body, as he controlled his need to surge into her.

He waited until she'd taken him fully. Waited until she leaned forward, her breasts against his hot chest, her hands sliding up his outstretched arms to cover his hands as they clutched the iron railing. He waited while she moved, awkwardly at first, unsure, and then suddenly she was fluid, light and darkness, heat and desire, taking him, owning him, and he was trembling, shaking apart beneath her, and she was trembling, shaking apart, and then the world exploded. She screamed, unable to stop herself, and she was lost, as he finally began to move, thrusting up into her, taking her, filling her with his heat, his seed, his life.

She didn't want to open her eyes. She could still feel his heart pounding beneath hers, feel the strangled rasp of his breathing as it stirred her hair, still feel him within her body. His hands loosened their fierce hold of the iron bedstead and turned beneath hers, clasping hers, and she wanted to weep at the beauty of it. If she opened her eyes reality would intrude. For now, there were only the two of them, alone in the universe.

SHE MUST HAVE DOZED. She awoke with the room in pitch-blackness, the moon gone behind dark, scudding clouds. Unseen hands were turning her, tucking her next to a fiery body, and she breathed a sigh of pure contentment as his hands pulled her closer.

He leaned forward, his mouth brushing her ear, and she waited for his words of love. "Where are you in your menstrual cycle?" he asked endearingly.

She shoved at him. "Do you have to be quite so practical?"

"So sue me. I'm a scientist."

"Not, however, a biologist," she pointed out, glad the darkness hid the blush she knew suffused her face.

"I had a fair amount of pre-med. I didn't use any protection. I'm no longer worried about other side-effects, but an unplanned pregnancy is still a concern."

"What other side-effects?" she asked warily.

"I've been exposed to something quite extraordinary, something that's changed my body chemistry. It didn't seem a wise idea to introduce any fluids into your body without checking."

"How romantic," she murmured sarcastically. "What makes you think it's all right now?"

"I checked."

"How'd you manage that?"

She didn't have to see him to recognize the wicked grin in his voice. "I just needed to check a sample under the microscope. Easy enough to procure one. I just closed my eyes and thought of you."

She didn't know whether to hit him or kiss him. He was absolutely the most damnable, frustrating, erotic, endearing man on the face of the planet. Even if she was unable to see him for too much of the time.

She let herself relax against him, sliding into his warmth. "They think we're dead, you know. It was on the television news."

He didn't seem surprised. "I heard it on the car radio while you slept."

"I called Uncle Vinnie and asked him to let your parents know you were all right...."

"You did what?"

He pulled away from her, sitting up in the darkness, and there was no missing the anger in his unseen body, any more than she could miss the faint red glow in his eyes.

She stared in his direction, fascinated. "I can see your eyes glowing," she murmured.

"The hell with my eyes! Why did you call him?"

"Don't get into such a swivet. You may not care what people think, but I wasn't about to have them holding a memorial service for me. I have people who love me. I figure even you do, though it's hard to imagine. I expect your parents might experience a pang or two if they thought their only child had burned up in a forest fire." Her voice was caustic.

"They would have survived a couple of days thinking that. They're pragmatic people."

"No one's pragmatic enough to accept the loss of their child."

"Maybe. But did you stop and think about what your little good deed for the day might have done?"

"They couldn't trace the call, if that's what you're worried about. I used Osborn's cellular phone—there's no way they could tap it.''

''You'd be surprised at what they can do. But they wouldn't have to tap Osborn's phone. They just have to tap the phones of people you'd be likely to call. My parents would have been first on the list. Hell and damnation!''

''I didn't even talk to them. I just told Vinnie to call, and I didn't give him any specific information, apart from telling him we were still alive and Osborn was dead. We'll be perfectly safe.''

''I'm not worried about us. I'm worried about my parents. About your damned Uncle Vinnie, for that matter. If they know we care enough to be in touch with them, they'll use them for bargaining chips. And I don't think they're about to let anybody walk away from this mess.''

''Oh, God,'' Suzanna murmured. ''Daniel, I'm sorry.''

There was a stunned silence. ''And here I thought supersensitive hearing was part of my metamorphosis. Suzanna Molloy is not a girl to say she's sorry.''

''Don't call me *girl*,'' she said miserably in token protest.

She felt his hand reach up under her hair and stroke her face gently. ''They'll be all right, Molloy. We'll get the bad guys. I'm not about to let them get away with this.''

''But there are so many of them,'' she said.

''Yeah, but you forget. I'm Cinderman, crusader for truth and justice. With my faithful companion, Suzanna the mind-reading swami, beside me, there's no way the armies of evil will triumph.''

''This isn't a comic book, Daniel,'' she said sternly.

''Life's a comic book, Molloy. The sooner you realize that, the better off you'll be.''

She stared up at him. The moon had reappeared from behind the clouds, and she could see his outline in the darkness. ''It must be after eight,'' she said.

''It is. I changed back while you were sleeping.'' He

reached over and turned on the light, and she closed her eyes against the brightness. "We've got to get moving, swami," he muttered. "We don't have any time to waste."

She scrambled for her clothes on the far side of the bed, yanking her T-shirt over her head in belated embarrassment. It had been easy enough to be a wanton in the dark, with no visible witness. The memory of what they'd done was suddenly overwhelming.

Daniel was standing in the middle of the room, motionless, staring past her. He'd pulled on his jeans, and there was a bemused expression on his face.

"What are you staring at?" she demanded.

"The bed."

She didn't know what she'd expected. She was almost afraid to look. When she turned to follow his gaze, she was momentarily breathless.

The sturdy iron bedstead had been bent like an old wire coat hanger.

She remembered her hands on his in the darkness, clutching those heavy iron bars. "Goodness," she said quietly.

"Or as Mae West once said, 'Goodness has nothing to do with it,'" he replied. "Get your clothes on, Suzanna. You're far too distracting that way, and we have work to do."

She was tempted to point out just how distracting he was, then thought better of it. "Where are we going?"

"To get the bad guys, Suzanna. Before they get us."

IF HE'D HAD THE CHOICE, Daniel thought, he would have clipped Ms. Suzanna Molloy on the chin and left her safely tied up back at the deserted old house. But he didn't have the choice. She knew half the things he was thinking—there'd be no way he could sneak up on her without her guessing. And he had no guarantee she'd be any safer back there. At least, with him, she had supernatural powers on her side. For some reason he didn't think twenty-twenty vision and the ability to read certain thoughts were going to be enough to protect her from people like Armstead and his crew of disenchanted ex-Green Berets.

There was never any doubt in his mind where he'd find Armstead. He'd be at Beebe, waiting for him to come in. They understood each other in ways far more direct than Suzanna's swami act. They were too much alike. Megalomaniacs, with only one purpose. For Armstead, it was the control of the world with his own particular agenda. For Daniel, it was the quest for knowledge.

Except that he had another purpose, one that had sneaked up on him when he wasn't looking. Another interest, one he was as passionately devoted to as he was to bi-level molecular transfer. And that was Suzanna Molloy.

One thing was certain—if they were going to stay together, he was going to have to figure out a way to shield his thoughts from her. He didn't fancy spending the rest of his life with a mental voyeur in his bed.

But he didn't fancy spending the rest of his life without her, either.

There'd be time enough for dealing with that later. Assuming there was a later. For now he had to concentrate on bringing Armstead and his army of creeps down. There was simply too damned much at stake.

The huge white headquarters of Beebe Control Systems International looked deserted when he drove Osborn's Jaguar into the empty parking lot, but Daniel wasn't fooled for a moment. They were there, behind those darkened windows, waiting for him. He only hoped Cinderman was ready for them.

Suzanna slid out of the car and came to stand beside him. He'd parked in front of the entrance, taking a cool sip of defiance in leaving the front tires on the handicapped accessible walkway that had never seen anyone in a wheelchair. There was a cool breeze, one that he barely felt with his heated skin, but it blew Suzanna's hair back against his shoulder, and he caught the faint trace of her shampoo. He wanted to stop right then and there, drag her back to the Jaguar and push her down onto the back seat.

He simply took her hand, running his thumb over her long, strong fingers. "I can't persuade you to run away and hide, can I?" he asked, almost absently.

"No."

He glanced down at her. "I have a funny feeling about tonight."

He saw the flicker of sheer panic in her eyes, saw her swiftly control it. "Funny like what?"

"Funny like I'm not going to walk out of there alive."

She didn't make a sound, but he could hear the sudden panicked lurch of her heart. "In that case, it doesn't really matter whether I come with you or not," she observed in a deceptive drawl. "You don't have any funny feelings that I'm not going to make it, do you?"

"No."

"Then I'll come with you," she said firmly. "Two against an army is better than one."

"I don't want you doing anything foolish."

"Like what?"

"Like making any dramatic gestures to save me if things get out of control. I want you to promise me."

"Promise you what?"

"That you'll do as I say. That you'll trust my judgment."

She turned and stared at him, and he thought he could see the faint glimmer of tears in her perfect eyes. "Are you crazy, Daniel? Me, trust your judgment? Give me a good reason."

"Because I don't want you to die, too."

She was silent. And then she rallied, as he knew she would, and he found it in him to grin. "Why not?" she demanded.

"Read my mind," he whispered, leaning down and brushing his lips against hers.

He felt the shock that went through her, the yearning. And then he set her away, staring up at the monstrous edifice that housed Armstead and his goons and the fruits of his own work for the last five years. The secrets to bi-level molecular transfer.

"No," she said, following his gaze. "You can't do it."

He didn't bother denying it. "Why not? Just a stare, a blink, a scrunch of my nose and this place will be a pile of cinders. Those are the bad guys inside, Molloy. Tell me why I should give them a chance to get us first."

"Because we're the good guys."

He considered it for a moment. "The problem with you, Molloy," he drawled, "is that you're usually right. Come on."

She held back, just for a moment. "How are we going to get in?"

"I expect they've unlocked the door for us. There'll be a welcoming party. Are you sure you don't want to run while you still have the chance?"

"Do you?"

"Not on your life."

"Then I'm coming with you."

Chapter Seventeen

"We expected you earlier, Dr. Crompton." The man stepped out of the shadows in the cavernous, deserted hallway, and Daniel didn't need any light to identify him.

"I try not to be predictable, Cole," he said easily. "I don't think you met Suzanna when we were here earlier. Suzanna, this is General Armstead's favorite gofer. Cole Slaughter."

"Great name," Suzanna muttered, glancing at Slaughter's camouflage fatigues and blunt, brutal face.

He didn't even register her presence. "General Armstead is awaiting your presence, sir," he said, the essence of military politeness.

"I'm sure he is," Daniel drawled. "Are you going to escort us, or shall we find him ourselves?"

"He wasn't expecting Ms. Molloy."

"If you know her last name, then you must have had a fairly good idea she'd be with me. She stays with me, Slaughter. Got that?"

"Yes, sir. If you'll follow me." He turned, leading the way through the shadowy hallway, and Daniel reached out his hand for Suzanna's, wondering if she'd take it, or if she'd be determined to prove how tough she still was.

A moment later her hand was tucked into his, holding tightly. He could feel the chill in her flesh—magnified because he was so hot. He wished there was some way to keep her out of this mess, but she was already in it up to her ears. His best chance of keeping her safe was keeping her with him, no matter what they ended up confronting.

"There you are." General Armstead rose from his thronelike seat at the end of the huge walnut table. He'd taken up residence in the boardroom, and he looked like a squat, evil spider. He was wearing a combat uniform not unlike Slaughter's—an odd choice for a retired soldier. But then, the truth was, Armstead was far from retired.

"Sorry to keep you waiting," Daniel murmured, still holding Suzanna's hand tightly. "Where are the rest of your little soldier boys? Surely you don't think you can rule the world with an army of one Robocop?"

Slaughter made a growling noise in the back of his throat, but he didn't move. He remained standing to one side, awaiting orders.

Armstead took a step toward them, a genial expression on his face. "But I don't need an army, son. It's better to keep your team down to the bare minimum—less fuss, less danger of betrayal. Slaughter here has been with me since Nam. He was just a boy then—fifteen—but big for his age. He already had a real gift back then. One he's honed."

"I can imagine," Daniel said dryly.

"By the way, where's Osborn? I sent him to get you. That, or dispose of you. Am I to assume, since you arrived here in his car, that he didn't make it back from Oregon?"

"You can assume all you like. At least *part* of that news story you fed the press was correct."

"Dear me," Armstead said, not the slightest bit disturbed. "Slaughter, I'll let you be the one to console his wife. The woman's a bit too hungry for me."

"Yes, sir," said Slaughter, sounding more and more like a robot.

"And now, my dear Dr. Crompton, I'm afraid we've wasted far too much time playing games. You know what

I want. Beebe has paid for it, paid you extravagant sums of money, along with footing your research. It's time for the results.''

''What if I told you I didn't have any results? That it had all been a waste?''

''I wouldn't believe you,'' Armstead said simply. ''I'd be willing to bet you all that money you have squirreled away in some Swiss bank account that you possess the secret that could rule the universe. And I want that secret, Daniel. I have no intention of waiting any longer. This whole organization has already been compromised. With Osborn dead, we'll be facing some unpleasant questions. I'll find a good use for your research, my boy. After all, I paid for it.''

''You and your rich, paranoid cronies.'' Daniel shrugged. ''You stole my notes. You know as much as I do.''

''Ah, yes, those notes. Very cryptic of you. We almost overlooked that disk when we searched your apartment. Fortunately Slaughter pointed out that you were hardly the man to own a Neil Diamond CD. And there wasn't even a stereo in your condo.''

Daniel glanced over at the enigmatic Slaughter. ''All this, and brains too, Cole? Will wonders never cease.''

Again that low, warning growl. ''I wouldn't, if I were you, Crompton,'' Armstead said gently. ''Major Slaughter doesn't possess much of a sense of humor. And he's experienced enough to know who to take it out on. I don't think you'd enjoy seeing what a man with Slaughter's talent would do with Ms. Molloy.''

Daniel's hand tightened automatically around Suzanna's, and it was sheer force of will that kept him from imagining exactly what kind of things Slaughter might do. Suzanna was entirely capable of reading his thoughts, and if she wasn't terrified already, it would send her over the edge.

''So tell me what you want, Armstead,'' Daniel said with

deceptive calm. "You have my notes. Surely Beebe can afford to pay a competent scientist to decipher them, to replicate my experiments."

"We've already had a competent scientist do just that. Unfortunately, Dr. Jackson showed an unfortunate level of greed. That's the problem with working within an organization. You're only as strong as your weakest link. That's why I decided to take Slaughter and Osborn on as partners in our own little enterprise, and not worry about the rest of Beebe's infrastructure. You can never be sure of anyone's limits. I would have had Jackson join us, too, if he hadn't proven so acquisitive."

"Is that why you killed him?"

"Actually, Slaughter and Osborn did the honors. Slaughter finished him up, but not before he had Jackson explain exactly what bi-level molecular transfer is."

Daniel didn't even blink. "And what does he think it is?"

"Alchemy." It was a little more than a groan from Slaughter, but not much.

Daniel managed a wintry smile. "That's succinct."

"I want the formula," Armstead said.

"You have it."

"You know as well as I do that it's missing one crucial piece. I want to know where that is."

"Someplace where you'll never find it," Daniel replied.

"Son," Armstead said heavily, "don't make me do this."

"I'm not your son," Daniel said. "And I'm not one of your damned Robocops. You're not getting it out of me—you'll have to kill me first."

Armstead simply shook his grizzled gray head. "I'm afraid, dear boy," he murmured, "that's hardly a threat. We were going to kill you, anyway. We'll just start with Ms. Molloy. And it will be very, very painful. Slaughter."

"Keep your hands off her," Crompton snarled, enraged,

but he didn't move fast enough. Slaughter had already spun her away, and if Daniel had made the mistake of holding on, her wrist would have been crushed.

Suzanna didn't say a word. She just looked at him, silent, horrified, and Slaughter pulled her back against his uniformed body, a slender, professional-looking knife at the delicate column of her throat.

"I think we're at a standoff," Armstead announced pleasantly. "Do you feel like being more cooperative, Dr. Crompton? Or do you want to see how much blood it will take to soak through that offensive T-shirt? Where is the missing piece of information?"

He didn't hesitate any longer. "In my brain. And if you don't get away from her, right now, you're never going to find out the answer."

"Dear me," the general murmured. "That's quite unfortunate. I wonder, Slaughter, whether we ought to call his bluff?"

"You needn't worry, sir. I can finish with this one and then get what you want out of the doctor," Slaughter said confidently, and the knife glittered in the low light like the caress of a silver-fingered butcher. "He's not going to be able to stand up to me."

"You'd be surprised, Slaughter," Armstead said, leaning back against the table. "The good doctor has had a surprising amount of training. As a matter of fact, I was one of the ones who approved it, back before I retired. With an asset like his mind, we didn't want to take any risks. He'd be harder to crack than you think. Let the girl go."

"Don't," Suzanna said, her voice strangled against the pressure of the knife, "call me *girl*." And she slammed her elbow backward into Slaughter's unprotected belly.

He doubled over in shock, and she kicked back, directly into his groin. In a few seconds he was writhing on the floor, shrieking with pain, the knife skittering across the thick carpeted floor.

She leapt for Daniel, but Armstead's voice stopped her. "Don't move," he said. He had a gun trained on her, and it was a very large, very nasty-looking one.

"Not again," she said wearily. "Aren't you men tired of playing spies?"

Armstead's smile was a travesty. "I'm going to shoot you in the knee, Ms. Molloy. If Dr. Crompton doesn't start talking, I'll shoot you in the other knee. And then I'll work my way upward. This gun has eight bullets, and they're large ones. I can do a great deal of damage, cause a great deal of pain. I do, however, promise that the final one will go in your brain."

"Kind of you," she said faintly. She glanced at Daniel. "I think you should know, Daniel, that he's really going to do it. You have no choice."

He accepted the message as gospel. There was no way out—Suzanna had heard Armstead's thoughts and knew just how bad they were. If he didn't stop him, the one way he could, then Suzanna would be dead.

Armstead cocked the gun and pointed it, not at Suzanna's knee, but directly toward her belly. Slaughter was already struggling upward, and Daniel had less than a second to decide.

He didn't decide. He acted. Armstead fired the gun, Daniel shoved Suzanna to the floor, and in the millisecond before Armstead could fire again, he was a human torch.

He didn't even have time to scream.

Suzanna was in his arms, her face hidden against his chest, before the ash and cinder collapsed in a heap on the floor, the charcoaled remains of General Jack Armstead.

"Oh, my God," Slaughter moaned in horror. He'd managed to struggle to his feet, but his color was still white from pain and shock. "I'm outta here," he muttered. And he took off at a dead run, before Daniel could move.

"Let's get out of here," he said, keeping her face turned away from what little was left of Armstead. He steered her out the door, and she went, shaking slightly, quiet, as docile as he'd ever seen her.

By the time they reached the front lobby there was no sign of Slaughter, and Daniel had no doubt he was gone for good. "Damn," he said, and Suzanna raised her head, following his gaze.

Bright white headlights were spearing their way across the darkened parking lot, pulling to a stop inches away from the abandoned Jaguar. She could see the shape of the familiar white Cadillac, and she knew with crushing certainty just who had arrived to rescue her.

"It's Uncle Vinnie," she said, watching as he approached the front entrance, flanked by Guido and Vito, his two huge nephews who were probably no more his nephews that she was his niece.

Daniel released her. "Go talk to him," he said smoothly. "Get him away from here."

She started to move, then halted, turning back to stare at him. "What about you?"

"I have to see to a few things."

"You're not going after Slaughter, are you?"

"No. He's lost Armstead, and he has to live with his own panic. That's the worst punishment for a killing machine like him. He's ruined."

"Then what are you going back for?"

"I have to make sure the research is destroyed. I don't want any trace of bi-level molecular transfer left."

"Why?" she protested. "After all your work…"

"It's too dangerous. There are too many men like Osborn and Armstead. Men who wouldn't think of using me, of using you to get to me. You won't be safe—hell, the world won't be safe—until it's gone."

She didn't move. Guido was holding the door for Uncle Vinnie, but she didn't even glance their way. "You can't," she said. "You can't get rid of all of it. Part of it's in your brain. You can't…"

"Yes," he said, very gently. "I can. Take her with you, Uncle Vinnie. Don't let her back in this place."

"No!" Suzanna shrieked, but Vinnie was quick to move. Vito caught her up in his burly arms, and she was no match for him. He carried her out of the building, Guido following, as she screamed and cried, shouting curses at his head.

Vinnie looked up at Daniel. "You must be Dr. Crompton," he said.

"And you're Uncle Vinnie."

Vinnie smiled faintly. "She loves you."

"I know. You'll see to her, won't you? This won't be easy for her."

"You have no choice?" he asked delicately.

Daniel simply shook his head, a cynical smile on his face. "I'm America's secret weapon, remember? No one knows better than me that there's no choice. As long as the information in my brain survives, she won't be safe. And I can think of only one way to get rid of this place, and my memory. It won't take long."

Vinnie's eyes were huge and sad. "I'll go to her."

Daniel watched him turn and head toward the door. In the distance he could see Suzanna still struggling as the nephews tried to strong-arm her into the waiting Cadillac. "Tell her—" he said, and then stopped himself.

"Tell her what?" Vinnie asked.

Daniel shook his head. "Never mind. She'll know."

SHE COULD NO LONGER scream. Her voice was gone, silenced. She could no longer cry. Her tears had dried up. She could only sit there, trapped in the back seat of Vinnie's Cadillac, and shake.

"I'm sorry it had to be this way," Vinnie said from the front seat as Guido started the car. Vito sat beside her, his hamlike hand a manacle across her wrist, but she was beyond struggling. She accepted defeat, and loss, and despair.

She looked up, and a shaft of flame shot through the

roof, spearing toward the sky. Another followed, a bright white fireball, and within seconds the huge building was in flames.

Guido stopped the car, staring in amazement at the conflagration, and even Vinnie was awed. "What in God's name did he do?" he gasped.

Suzanna watched, dry-eyed, empty-hearted. And then she heard him. Heard the words, clear and true, through the heat and smoke of the fiery inferno. *I love you, Molloy.*

She could make a sound after all. It was a low, keening whimper, like an animal in pain, as she felt her heart torn out and incinerated. They sat in the car and watched as the building collapsed in a pile of blazing ash.

"That couldn't have happened," Vinnie muttered. "Things can't burn that quickly. A bomb, maybe, but the fire should have lasted...."

Guido was murmuring, and it took Suzanna a moment to realize it was the Latin prayers he'd learned in his youth, as he stared up at the remnants of the huge building with superstitious horror.

"We have to get out of here. The fire department's gonna show up, and we don't want to be here when they start asking their questions," Vinnie announced, his voice still shaken. "Get moving, Guido."

Guido just stared, unable to move. Vito was equally shocked, craning his neck to peer out the window, releasing his grip on Suzanna. She stared out the smoked window, into the conflagration.

And then she saw movement.

"Stop the car," she screamed, her voice a raw travesty.

"Keep driving," Vinnie ordered. "I can hear the sirens already."

Guido kept driving. Suzanna twisted the door handle and rolled out, moving too fast for Vito to stop her.

She hit the ground running, racing across the deserted parking lot toward the glowing remains of the huge building. Osborn's Jaguar had disappeared in the flames, and nothing was left standing of Daniel's funeral pyre.

And then she saw movement again. She heard the fire-engine sirens and saw the reflection of the flashing lights in the distance as they raced toward the ruins, but she ignored them, focusing instead on the smoldering debris. The white Cadillac started to drive off, leaving her in the pre-dawn darkness.

The charred remains shifted, moving once more, and the shadow grew. She stood there alone, sobbing, as his shape took form, and Daniel Crompton walked out of the fire, and into her arms.

The Cadillac screeched up beside them, the door opened, and Vinnie pulled them in. "For God's sake, let's go," he yelled, and this time Guido drove as he'd been trained to do, out of sight before the first fire engine pulled up to the charred remains of Beebe Control Systems International.

Vito kept out of her way as she held Daniel tightly in her arms. His eyes were closed, his breathing hoarse, and she clutched him, murmuring over and over again, soothing words, crazy words, telling him she hated him, she'd kill him, she loved him, she'd kill him.

He smiled against her face, not opening his eyes, and her tears washed some of the soot from his face. "Hush," he said finally, pulling her tight against him. "It's over."

"No, it's not," she wept in a raw voice, rocking him back and forth. "It will never be over. I hate you, I hate you..."

"It's over," he said again, and she pressed her face against his cool skin, trembling.

"Where do you want me to drive, Uncle Vinnie?" Guido asked. "You want to go home now?"

"What time is it?" Vinnie asked absently.

"A little after seven. We could stop for breakfast at Mama Lucia's. A nice omelet, some *cafe latte*. We can bring some out for the doc and Ms. Molloy."

Suzanna held herself very still. "What time did you say it was?"

"After seven. It's been a long night, *cara,*" Vinnie murmured. "But it's morning now. A new day. A new beginning." The car pulled up in front of a cheery-looking trattoria on the outskirts of Santa Cristina. "You want anything to eat?"

"She always does," Daniel murmured faintly. "Just bring her out something with cholesterol."

"And you, my boy?"

"Something hot. I've got a chill."

She waited until they were alone in the back seat. "Your skin is cool," she said.

"And I feel weak as a kitten," he added. "And best of all, I can't remember what I've been working on for the past two years."

"What do you mean?"

"Just that. My notes were wiped out in the fire, and I can't even begin to remember where I started. I guess I'll have to find something new to work on. Maybe cold fusion."

She held herself very still. "Sure, try something easy for a change."

He smiled up at her, then shifted until he lay with his head in her lap. "You'd better marry me," he said, closing his eyes again.

"Another one of your romantic overtures, Dr. Crompton?"

"Just trying to tell you what to do, Molloy. I need help rebuilding the place in Oregon. Though this time maybe we'll make it a little larger. I want a bigger lab if I'm going to work there full-time, and you'll probably want an office of your own."

"Not to mention a better kitchen. And a television, and a satellite dish. And while you're at it, why don't you tell me what I'm supposed to do out there at the back of beyond?'' she demanded in the raw travesty that once was her voice.

He eyed her. ''I thought you liked it there. Don't you have any ideas?''

''A number of them. I think I'll write science fiction. I take it money isn't a problem?''

''The late Beebe Control Systems International paid me huge amounts of their ill-gotten gains. We'll be more than comfortable.''

''Then I think I'll write a series of novels about the Invisible Man.''

He groaned, reached up, pulled her head down and kissed her. His mouth was cool and delicious. ''I love you,'' he said.

''I know. I heard.''

He kissed her again, a little more lingering, a little deeper. ''It's gone, you know. Everything vanished in that inferno. Cinderman died in the fire.''

''Do you mind?''

''Not at all. Though it's going to give you an unfair advantage.''

''Hey, I'll need all the advantages I can get to keep up with you and whatever little geniuses you happen to beget.'' She looked down at him, love in her eyes, in her heart, in her ruined voice.

''We'll have to make the place even bigger.''

''We'll have time.''

He looked up at her, for a moment sweetly vulnerable. ''I really did forget everything,'' he murmured.

''Of course you did,'' she said, looking into his mind, understanding him very well. ''And you're going to have lots of fun playing with that green slime you brought out of the fire.''

He stared at her for a moment, and then a wry smile lit his face. ''I'm never going to be able to lie to you.''

"Accept it. I'm your destiny, Cinderman, your ball and chain. There's no way you'll escape me."

"Dear girl," he said faintly, "I wouldn't think of it."

"Don't," she said, "call me *girl*." And she leaned down to kiss him again, as his hand twined in her hair, and there was no more need for words.

Epilogue

The house perched on the edge of the cliff was a magical house, filled with light and laughter, love and warmth. Suzanna sat barefoot in the garden, hands folded neatly on her pregnant belly, wearing a T-shirt that read She Who Rocks the Cradle Rules the World—Watch Out! She watched the twins argue amicably enough, used to it by now. Albert Einstein Molloy Crompton had decided that Charles Dickens was a sexist pig, albeit a good storyteller, but he much preferred Jane Austen and Georgette Heyer, like his father. His sister, Marie Curie Molloy Crompton, insisted that he ought to be paying more attention to the writings of his namesake than to stories, even if their mother made a fairly good living writing them.

They were both five years old.

She smiled fondly. This was an old battle, without any particular rancor, and it had been going on since they were three. "Where's your father, Marie?" she asked, feeling the baby kick. At least there was only one this time. Two, even with Daniel's fascinated assistance, was a little more challenge than she felt like facing again.

"Can't you listen for him?" Albert asked, used to her odd powers.

"He's keeping me out," Suzanna said. "Singing those stupid songs so I can't eavesdrop."

"He says you're a voyeur," Marie said cheerfully.

"I'm just curious— Oh, my God!" The explosion rocked the ground, glass shattered, and a billow of pure white smoke shot out the broken window of the lab. She struggled awkwardly to her feet, holding her belly, and ran toward the house.

She barreled straight into something, and strong arms reached out to catch her.

"You'll never guess what I've discovered," Daniel's disembodied voice announced with disgusting cheer.

Marielle Brandt and Simon Sebriskie were both misfits, but they fit *together* perfectly.

Cry for the Moon

Chapter One

Marielle Brandt stared up, way up at the building in front of her. Her five-year-old daughter Emily was gripping her challis skirt, her eighteen-month-old son Christopher was slipping off her hip. There was a cool Chicago breeze blowing around them, whipping off Lake Michigan and whistling through the autumn leaves that still clung to the trees. It would look even worse, Marielle decided gloomily, when the trees were bare.

The mansion in front of her was a crenellated, fenestrated old horror, tucked behind rusting iron fencing, set on grounds that seemed better suited to a jungle than a residential neighborhood in the heart of one of America's great cities. The gabled, multileveled roof was patched and stained, several of the diamond-paned windows on the five and a half floors were cracked or missing with rags stuffed in the holes, the stone walls were crumbling, the wooden trim peeling, the front porch sagging dangerously. Some of the steps were broken, limbs were down from the huge oak trees surrounding the place, and the whole building reeked of neglect and decay.

"I tried to warn you," Liam O'Donnell said primly, setting down the diaper bag he'd grudgingly carried on the cracked sidewalk. "You would have been better off staying in New York. Farnum's Castle is fit for nothing but a wrecking ball. I may not be your family attorney, but I've told you more than once my advice is to take that very generous offer and stay where you belong.''

"I don't belong in New York," Marielle said calmly, allowing herself a brief glance away from the monstrosity in front of her to the fussy, elderly attorney who'd met her at O'Hare Airport. "Neither do my children. Farnum's Castle will do just fine. It can't be in as bad shape as it looks," she added on a more hopeful note, shifting Christopher's clinging body.

"Oh, can't it?" O'Donnell said. "Allow me to give you a tour of your new apartment building, Mrs. Brandt."

"Ms.," she corrected absently, still staring, still fighting the sinking feeling that was rumbling in her empty stomach. She'd been too nervous to eat, and she was paying for it now.

If she'd wanted to offend O'Donnell further she couldn't have chosen a better way. "You've only been widowed for six months!" he said, aghast.

But she didn't want to turn her one, albeit grudging ally in the unknown city of Chicago into more of an enemy than he already was. "Call me Marielle," she said somewhat desperately.

Liam O'Donnell stooped down and picked up the brightly colored box of Pampers and the diaper bag. "This way, Mrs. Brandt."

Marielle allowed herself a brief sigh. The lawyer had been disapproving from the start, pressuring her from a thousand miles away to sell the building to some anonymous conglomerate that probably wanted the place for a parking garage. If she'd had any sense she would have done so, but for once she'd grown stubborn. She didn't want to take anyone's advice, particularly any man's advice. For the first time in eight years her life was her own, whether she liked it or not, and it was up to her to make the decisions, up to her to make do with the hand fate had dealt her.

She took one more look at Farnum's Castle as she reached down to detach Emily's hand from her skirt and hold it tightly in her own. "What do you think, kiddo?"

Emily was a child of few words, particularly in the last six months since Greg had died. "It's okay," she said quietly, clinging close.

Marielle nodded. "It's an apartment building," she said brightly, following O'Donnell's prissy figure through the iron gate and up the uneven sidewalk. "Not much like Yorktown Towers, is it? And we won't just be living here, we'll be taking care of the place, just like Mr. Sanchez did in New York. But maybe there'll be some kids your age here."

"Maybe," Emily said, her voice not promising, and for the hundredth time Marielle felt the rush of anger and grief that she kept hoping she'd put behind her. Damn Greg. Damn him for dying like that, a thirty-three-year-old man dead of a heart attack. It was absurd, totally unexpected that a vigorous man such as Greg could suddenly be gone. Almost as absurd as the fact that the brilliant, workaholic husband she'd lived with since she was twenty years old had left her with a mountain of bills and just about no assets. He'd even cashed in his life insurance in the debt-plagued months before his death, and she'd never had the faintest idea they were in financial trouble. By the time the dust had settled and the debts were cleared, all she had left between herself and destitution was a crumbling old apartment building in Chicago and a very small bank balance.

"We're going to have a great time," Marielle said, climbing gingerly over the broken steps. "Mr. O'Donnell said we get half of the fourth floor. You and Christopher will share a room at first, but later, when we fix the place up a bit, you can have a room of your own. Won't that be wonderful?"

"Sure."

"Mr. O'Donnell had some of the furniture taken out of storage for us." She hated the falsely jolly note in her voice almost as much as she hated her daughter's quiet misery. "We'll have to make do with it for now, but after we start collecting a few of the back rents owed we might be able to buy you some new furniture. Maybe a bunk bed. You've always wanted one."

"Sure," said Emily.

"Sure," echoed Marielle, bouncing Christopher on her hip as she stepped inside the gloomy hallway.

The place was dark and deserted in the middle of the afternoon. The soot-encrusted windows let in only minimal light, and the dark-stained woodwork added to the atmosphere of dreariness and decay. Marielle managed to swallow the large lump in the back of her throat as she followed O'Donnell's natty little figure down the hall, past the wide, curving, decidedly dangerous looking staircase. Emily's hand was gripping tightly, Christopher was starting to slide off her hip, and all Marielle wanted to do was cry.

O'Donnell was standing inside a small closet that on closer inspection turned out to be an elevator. He was tapping one well-polished shoe, and she could just make out his disgruntled glare in the cramped space. "Get in, Mrs. Brandt. I assure you that at least the elevator works. A bill from the repair company arrived at our office. It's with the papers I have for you."

"It's a little small," she said, cramming herself and her two children into the coffinlike space along with O'Donnell, the diaper bag and the giant box of Pampers. The door shut, and an ominous vibration began to shake the *faux* wooden walls. There was a great creaking noise that seemed to come from the very bowels of the building, and then, with a jerk that flung Marielle back against the lawyer, the elevator started upward.

Marielle didn't like small, confined places. She took

deep, calming breaths, but it didn't feel as if there was enough air in the tiny elevator. Christopher uttered an amiable protest as her arm tightened around him; she could feel her heart racing.

Marielle didn't like the dark much, either. As the elevator slowly creaked and jerked its way to the upper floors, the dim light bulb overhead flickered and went out. Marielle opened her mouth to scream, but the light came on just as she took a deep breath, and she let it out in a relieved *whoosh*. They shuddered to a halt, the light went off again, but at least the door slid open, revealing a hallway some six inches above the level of the elevator floor.

"After you, Mrs. Brandt," O'Donnell said testily. Of course he didn't have much choice in the matter, she thought, scrambling up into the hallway with more relieved haste than dignity. She'd been blocking the only escape route.

The fourth-floor hallway was a bit brighter than the main floor, and a great deal colder. The bottom half of the hall window was out completely, letting in sunshine and a vast amount of cold air. The oppressive wooden paneling had given way to wainscoting and wallpaper, but the fuchsia cabbage roses were only a slight improvement on the gloom downstairs. If she looked too closely the watermarks marring the pattern looked like nasty little worms crawling over the bright pink petals.

"What pretty flowers," she announced brightly, primarily for the benefit of her silent daughter.

O'Donnell's snort was his only comment as he pushed past her and pulled out a set of keys worthy of a Gothic chatelaine. The door opened with a sepulchral creak and Marielle stepped inside, hoping for the best, expecting the worst.

She got the latter. The windows were intact but filthy, the walls painted olive green, the floor was covered with torn gold carpeting, and the furniture, culled from stuff stored in one of the empty apartments, resembled something out of *The Bride of Frankenstein*. There were a couple of very uncomfortable-looking baronial chairs, an old sofa, a chest that resembled a medieval sarcophagus and a Formica-topped table. One bedroom contained a portable crib with bars missing and a foldout cot, the other a dynasty-founding bed carved with salacious gargoyles and leering satyrs.

If O'Donnell was waiting for her to cry he'd have a long wait, she decided, letting Christopher down to inspect his new home as she finished her tour. "This will be fine," she said brightly. "It's lucky there was enough furniture to tide us over until we can afford to buy some."

"And when will that be?" O'Donnell stood by the door, clearly in a hurry to leave. "I understood that Farnum's Castle was all your husband left you."

She wanted to point out to him that it wasn't any of his business, but she was, as always, unerringly polite in the face of hostility. "There's got to be some income from this place. Rents...."

"The upkeep, such as it is, far exceeds any rent you might manage to collect from the bunch of weirdos and deadbeats who inhabit this building. I told you that in the first place and you didn't choose to believe me. Now that you've seen it for yourself, I'm sure you realize that anyone in his right mind who could afford rent would live somewhere else. The best thing that could be done would be to evict everyone and tear down the monstrosity."

Her politeness was beginning to slip. "Well," she said with just the trace of an edge to her voice, "I like it here. It has...character."

O'Donnell snorted. "Among other things. As far as I know the offer is still open for the place, but I can't guarantee that situation will last forever. Try it out for a while, if you must. But don't expect my office to be on twenty-four-hour call for every little emergency."

"I wouldn't think of it." She looked about her. "I think we'll be just fine."

O'Donnell just shook his silver-maned head. "I give you two weeks, tops, before you and your children are on a plane back to New York."

She considered explaining to him that she didn't have the airfare to spare—or the credit and she had no place to live even if she could get back to New York. A year ago she could have stayed with one of her friends in the bland new apartment building on New York's Upper East Side, but during the past few months they'd all gone their separate ways. Her parents lived in a very small condo near Orlando, and there simply wasn't room for herself and the two little ones for any length of time. And she wasn't going to ask for money, not unless her children's welfare truly was at stake.

She had yet to be convinced of that. She had her health, lots of energy and enthusiasm, and while her financial skills were a little shaky, all it would take was a little determination to get this place back to making a profit. She didn't need to be rich—she'd led the life of an upscale yuppie mother in New York and hadn't been happy. She just needed enough money to keep the three of them together while she decided what she wanted to do with her life. Managing a run-down apartment building would enable her to keep the kids with her while she sorted out her future. Then she'd sell Farnum's Castle to developers, move somewhere warm with a school system that didn't go on strike every other year, and never look back.

If Liam O'Donnell had shown her an ounce of sympathy, she would have explained all this. But from the start he had lectured her, wrinkling his patrician nose in utter fastidiousness, so she merely took his limp, unoffered hand in hers and shook it. "Thank you for your help. We'll try not to bother you again."

"I'll let you know if the offer is withdrawn," he said,

removing his hand from her grasp. He moved into the hallway, pausing for maximum effect. "Perhaps I should mention one thing. I didn't think it pertinent, because I don't believe in such things, but you might be interested."

Christopher was climbing onto a kitchen chair, and Emily was wandering through the apartment like a lost soul, looking, Marielle suspected, for a television set. "Yes?" she said politely, thinking she probably didn't want to hear O'Donnell's parting salvo.

Her instincts were right. She didn't. "According to your rather bizarre tenants, not to mention the previous owners," O'Donnell said in his prissy little voice, "Farnum's Castle is haunted."

Marielle just stared at him. "By whom?" The question was just as absurd as O'Donnell's statement, but he took it seriously.

"Old Vittorio Farnum, of course. One of the most ruthless gangsters in Chicago's history before he found religion. They say he wanders the hallways."

"He'd better not wander my hallways," Marielle said. "I'll call the cops. I imagine he didn't like them when he was alive any more than his ghost will like them now."

"For that you'll have to get to a telephone. And the only phone in the place is upstairs in Simon Zebriskie's apartment."

"No telephone?" she asked faintly.

"No telephone. Good afternoon, Mrs. Brandt. I'll look forward to your acceptance of that offer."

He shut the door quietly behind him. Marielle stared at the peeling paint, the flimsy lock, the thin, cracked wood that wouldn't stand up to a strong breeze or a ghost, much less anyone more dangerous who happened to come in from the mean streets of Chicago to make a little mischief.

She felt a shiver race across her body, even though the apartment wasn't really cold. Another shiver followed, and the burning behind her eyes and in the back of her throat presaged another bout of impotent tears—one that would leave her exhausted, frighten the children and do no one any good.

She could wait to cry, wait until the children were asleep and she was alone in that Gothic horror of a bed. For now she had to somehow get the three of them settled, track down something for dinner and worry about ghosts later.

The knock on her door was so soft, so tentative that at first Marielle didn't hear it. When she finally answered it she didn't know what to expect—Vittorio Farnum's unearthly shade or the prosaic figure of the delivery van driver with the piles of luggage O'Donnell had refused to transport.

It was something in between. Standing in her doorway was a tiny old woman, with wild, flyaway white hair, dark, mischievous eyes, a wrinkled face and a nose and chin so pointed they almost met. Voluminous black clothing covered her sturdy little body, but by her side, instead of the expected black cat, stood a tall, dark-haired girl in her late teens and at an advanced stage of pregnancy.

"Welcome to Farnum's Castle," the apparition announced cheerfully, dragging her reluctant companion into the apartment before Marielle could recover from her amazement. "We're your neighbors. We live in the first-floor apartment on the right. I'm Esmerelda deCarlo and this is Julie. She's going to have a baby." This was announced in a breathless wheeze as her ancient face creased in an engaging smile. "And you have children!" she said, advancing on the fascinated Emily. "How delightful! Julie is wonderful with children, and it will do her good to practice. Not that she's planning to keep the baby. Some nice couple will get the fruit of her labor, but still, someday she'll have one of her own and I know she'll be a wonderful mother. Won't you, dear?"

"Esmy," Julie said in a soft, hesitant voice, her beautiful

brown eyes watching Marielle suspiciously. "I don't know that we should barge in like this...."

"Of course we should," Esmerelda said, scooping up Christopher's chubby little form and seating herself on one of the uncomfortable chairs. She held out an arm and to Marielle's amazement Emily went, tucking her slender body against the old woman's voluminous garments. "How can she go down and get her luggage if we don't watch them for her? She can't very well cart them back and forth along with all those suitcases and boxes, can she?"

"My luggage is here?" Marielle cut to the heart of the matter.

"The man dumped it in the front hall. Guess he didn't want a tip," Julie announced. "We'll watch the kids for you while you bring it up. That is, if you trust us." Her eyes were bright with a belligerent suspicion, daring Marielle to voice her concern.

But Marielle could see beyond the anger to the vulnerability beneath. Besides, Esmerelda was right—she did need help. She'd simply have to take chances and learn to trust. And her instincts, infallible as usual, told her that her children would be safe.

"I'd really appreciate it," she said. "It shouldn't take long...."

"Are you kidding?" Julie said, her tight, defensive stance relaxing slightly. "If you can get the elevator working it'll take you four trips at least. If you try to carry it all up the stairs it'll take you longer. Maybe you should get what you need and wait for Simon to come home."

"That's a good idea. Simon will take care of it," Esmerelda said, rocking Christopher. "Simon takes care of all of us."

That was the last thing Marielle needed or wanted—a man to take care of her. O'Donnell had said every tenant in Farnum's Castle was an eccentric—she could just picture the mysterious Simon with the only telephone in the place.

Some interfering old patriarch perhaps, or maybe a computer nerd. "I'll get it," she said, casting a doubtful eye on Emily. But Emily seemed perfectly at home nestled next to Esmerelda, so Marielle decided to take her chance while she could.

She ran down the stairs rather than deal with the claustrophobic elevator more than she had to. By the time she'd wrestled two suitcases and a box into the closetlike lift she was too out of breath to be nervous. She had just pushed the fourth-floor button when a hand shot out and caught the closing door, and a tall figure stepped into the cramped area.

She barely had time to see him before the door shut and the light began to flicker. The elevator began jerking upward, the groans and creaks of the machinery precluding conversation. Marielle held her breath, trying to still her heartbeat, telling herself she wouldn't suffocate, the elevator would stop, her unwanted passenger would get out, and she'd end up on the fourth floor with her possessions and her children and her safety intact.

The elevator stopped all right. Halfway between the third and fourth floors it shuddered to a halt. Then the lights went off, plunging them into darkness.

I won't scream, she told herself. *It's all right, it's just another tenant in here with me, not Farnum's ghost. He'll probably even know how to get the elevator going again.*

A deep, sepulchral voice slid through the darkness. "I was stuck in here three hours last time this happened," he said, his rich, eerie voice as chilling as his words. "How are you at screaming for help?"

Chapter Two

Marielle was frozen in a mindless, gibbering panic. Forcing herself to take a deep breath, she inquired of her faceless companion with deceptive calm, "Why should I scream for help?"

His cynical laugh was as funereal as his voice had been. "Because we could use some help getting out of this tomb," he said.

Marielle could feel the panic clawing at her as the darkness pressed around her in thick, smothering folds. The creature trapped with her was just one more threat, someone else to steal the oxygen that was rapidly disappearing. She struggled for breath, but there was none to be had. She pressed her back against the walls of the elevator, hoping to make herself smaller, but it did no good. Her heart was pounding so loudly it throbbed through the tiny space, and all she could think of was her children left abandoned to the mercies of two strange women while she suffocated in this airless box, stuck between floors until she rotted....

"That's all I need," her companion announced to the walls. "A claustrophobic female on the edge of hysteria. For God's sake, calm down! Just breathe slowly and I'll get a light on."

She tried to listen to his words, to take slow breaths, but the fear was still beating at her. She needed light, yet she was afraid. The tall shadow in front of her had a voice like death—what if he had a face to match? What if she'd somehow stumbled into the twilight zone?

The shadow in front of her raised his fist and she flinched, pressing against the wall, waiting for him to strike her. Instead he gave the wall two sharp blows. The overhead light flickered dimly and then stayed on, illuminating the tiny space, illuminating her companion.

He was only a man, after all, not some harbinger of death. He was quite tall, but she'd known that even in the shadows, and he had the kind of rangy body that never put on weight. His hair was straight and dark, streaked with gray, and it brushed the collar of his freshly ironed blue chambray work shirt. His face was long, narrow and clever looking, with high cheekbones, slightly tilted eyes of a disturbing pale gray, and a wide, thin-lipped mouth that Marielle assumed some women would find sexy. He was looking down at her with a combination of irritation and compassion that she found deeply unsettling, and she tried to make herself even smaller. He reached out a hand to her, and she flinched again.

"Don't touch me," she managed to say in a tight, panic-stricken voice.

His hand had dropped the moment he'd seen her reaction. "Lady, I wouldn't think of it," he replied in that deep voice of his. "This elevator is crowded enough as it is without you screaming the house down. I suppose these are your things?"

She managed a nervous nod, half mesmerized by the voice.

He sighed wearily. "You're moving in, aren't you? Fourth floor, right? Esmerelda waved at me from the window, so I assumed someone was fool enough to rent one of the empty apartments. I'm just above you on the top floor. My name is Simon Zebriskie, and I can tell you right now you don't belong here." He didn't hold out his hand, just stood there, as far from her as he could manage in that tiny space, and Marielle felt a bit more of her panic melt away, to be replaced by a very real irritation with his unwelcoming attitude. If the rest of the tenants were like him, it was no wonder she had empty apartments.

"Marielle Brandt," she said, her voice still shaky. "And apart from this horrible elevator I happen to like it here. What makes you think I don't belong?"

"Maybe someone will fix it for good," he replied, his strange, tilted eyes staring at her with no emotion whatsoever. "But I wouldn't count on it. Farnum's Castle is a perfect place for people down on their luck, but the modern conveniences have a habit of breaking down at the most inconvenient of times. You don't look like you're used to inconveniences."

"You mean I don't look down on my luck?" She straightened her back, forgetting for a moment that she was going to suffocate.

"Not particularly. At least, not until one looks into those blue eyes of yours and sees beyond the princess."

By then she'd completely forgotten her panic. "I look like a princess who's down on her luck?" she demanded, half astounded, half outraged.

Simon Zebriskie smiled reluctantly, his wide mouth curving. He had big, strong white teeth and for a moment Marielle was reminded of the big bad wolf. "Exactly," he said. "Now that your panic attack is over, you want to help me get out of this damned elevator? Your suitcase is digging into my shins."

Marielle just looked at him for a moment. "I don't know if I like you."

"You probably don't," he said easily. "Once you get to know me you'll be absolutely certain of it."

"Who says I'm going to get to know you?"

"If you're going to stay here you will. For one thing, I've got the only telephone in the place, and even if you had the money, the phone company always makes excuses not to come here. So does everyone else, for that matter. For another thing, I'm the only one who can keep old man O'Donnell off your back when you can't meet the rent.'' Simon was deftly twisting the control panel plate off its moorings as he talked, exposing a complex mass of multicolored wires.

''Who says I can't meet the rent? Even a princess who's down on her luck has some assets. And the rent's not very high.''

''Maybe not for you,'' he said, pulling out the wires and detaching a purple one. ''But any rent at all is too much for most of the people here. They can just manage to pay the utilities and that's that. It's a good thing the newest owner is some New York socialite who couldn't care less about the money. These people would be in big trouble if they had to cough up the rent.''

The narrow door began to open, with the slow, jerky movements that characterized everything about the elevator. They were smack-dab between floors, and Marielle could see curious faces staring at her feet, while she got a wonderful view of a pair of skinny ankles wrapped in woolen support stockings.

''Is that you, Simon?'' a British voice demanded from the upper floor. The ankles and legs attached to them dropped to the floor, and another old lady peered at them. This one was the complete opposite of Esmerelda deCarlo. Even folded sideways Marielle could see that she was very tall, very skinny and very aristocratic. Her clothes were wispy gray draperies, and her milky blue eyes were suspicious.

''It's me and your new neighbor. Marielle Brandt, this is Granita Dunkirk. She has the other first-floor apartment next to Esmerelda and Julie.''

''That charlatan,'' Granita sniffed. ''If you ever need any advice, my dear Mrs. Brandt, any connection with the spirit world, come to me. Esmerelda likes to think she has certain gifts, but we know the poor thing only deludes herself. On the other hand, I…''

"Mrs. Brandt?" Simon echoed, and Marielle couldn't miss the added edge to it.

"She has two of the most adorable children, Simon," Granita added with real enthusiasm. "Of course Esmerelda was her usual pushy self, forcing her way in, but I got a chance to visit with them, and they are the most precious things. It's so nice to have some children in the old place at last."

"I'm a widow," Marielle said, wondering why she felt the need to explain to this thoroughly cantankerous man.

"And we're sorry for your loss," Granita continued cheerfully, peering at her from the ceiling level of the elevator. "So young for such a tragedy. But he's not really gone, you know, dear, he's just on the other side. Any time you want to talk to him, to seek some comfort, we could try a little séance. I have much greater success talking to those who've passed over than Esmerelda has, no matter what she tells you. Maybe we could try it tonight after you get settled."

"Granita," Simon said, his deep voice firm and calm. "I think you should wait until Marielle asks you. Right now what she needs is to get out of this elevator and back to her children. Why don't you move out of the way while I give her a boost up?"

"Of course, of course. You know I only wanted to help, Simon. Sometimes I can be almost as tactless as Esmerelda," she said in a worried little voice, scrambling out of the way.

"Sometimes," Simon agreed with far more gentleness than he'd shown her, Marielle thought indignantly. "Granita and Esmerelda, in case you haven't figured it out yet, are our resident psychics. They do séances, palmistry, tarot reading and all sorts of useful things."

"Really?" Marielle said faintly, looking up at the cheerful old woman and wondering what the other one was doing to her babies.

Once again Simon seemed to know what she was thinking. "Your children are fine," he said in an undertone that was surprisingly reassuring. "Esmerelda's perfectly harmless, and Julie's great with kids."

She looked up at him suspiciously. "Are you sure those two are the only psychics around here?" she demanded.

"Lady, your face is absolutely transparent. Don't ever play poker." He peered up to the fourth-floor landing. "If I were a psychic I'd know what the hell you were doing in a place like this, with children, no less. While you don't look old enough to have much common sense, it doesn't take much to realize this isn't the place for someone like you. So why are you here?"

Marielle just looked at him for a moment, stubbornly reluctant to tell him anything. "Ask Granita," she said instead. "Maybe her crystal ball will tell you." She began climbing over her luggage and boxes to the elevator door.

Simon held out his hand and she took it, noting absently that it was strong and warm, the kind of hand you could trust. She scrambled up onto the upper floor, and that same hand reached behind her rump and gave her an enthusiastic shove. She was out before she had a chance to protest, but she didn't know whether to glare at him or thank him.

He was busy handing up her suitcases through the narrow opening, so she decided the impolite assist had been innocently meant. He followed her boxes with an agility that made her wish she was a little more limber, and walked behind her down the hall, carrying the things she and Granita couldn't manage.

If she'd expected tears or at least excitement upon her return, she got nothing more than a pleased smile from both her children. "You don't have to worry about dinner, Marielle. Fritzie's bringing a casserole up in another hour,"

Julie announced from her position on the floor beside Christopher. "Hey, Simon."

"Hey, Julie," Simon replied, his deep voice several degrees warmer. "So Fritzie's part of the welcome wagon? At least you'll be well fed. He's a great cook."

"Fritzie?" Marielle echoed. "What does he do for a living, exorcism?"

"You've already heard about the ghost of old Vittorio roaming the halls, have you?" Simon said. "Don't tell me you're scared of ghosts—you'll be in deep trouble living here. Not that Vittorio's been too active in recent years. He's just rumor—none of us have been lucky enough to see him since old Jesse passed away, and he used to see spacemen in the laundry and angels in the trees. No, Fritzie's a witch."

"A witch?" Marielle echoed faintly, knowing she was in over her head.

"A warlock," Granita corrected primly.

"Oh, God," Marielle moaned, carrying the suitcases into her bedroom.

Simon was right behind her again, dumping the boxes and giving her ornate bed no more than a raised eyebrow. "Then there are the Meltirks living two flights below you, and I'd as soon not know the details of their religion. It does seem to involve animals and odd-smelling fires, but they're basically harmless. They're from Baluchistan and don't speak a word of English, but Esmerelda manages to communicate with them quite well. If you manage to stand it here more than a couple of weeks and the animals get too noisy I'll do something about it."

"Sounds like you're the landlord around here," she said, looking up at him. Her earlier nervousness had faded, and once more her instincts had taken over. Despite his lack of welcome, Simon Zebriskie was no threat to her or her children. At least, not in any way she could think of.

"There is no landlord. We look after ourselves."

''So that explains everybody's otherworldly connections but yours. How do you earn your living, digging graves?''

He laughed, a short, reluctant sound. ''I'm just a working stiff, if you'll pardon the expression. I work at a radio station here in town.''

''Doing what?''

''Midnight to 6 a.m.,'' he said, watching her. ''Better known as the graveyard shift.''

''I give up. Maybe I should move back to New York.''

''That's the smartest thing you've said so far. Why did you come here?''

A direct question, and this time she couldn't very well refuse to answer. ''Let's just say that New York socialites sometimes need money, too.''

If she expected his distrust and withdrawal to increase, she was disappointed. He merely nodded. ''That explains it. The new owner.''

''Exactly.''

''And I suppose you're going to want people to pay their rents?''

''It's customary.''

Simon shook his head. ''You're living in a dreamworld, Marielle Brandt. You'll soon find out that nothing about Farnum's Castle is customary. Half these people would be on the streets if they had to come up with the kind of money it costs to live in Chicago. That, or they'd be institutionalized, and that's no life for gentle, harmless creatures like Esmerelda and Granita.''

''Do you pay rent?''

''As a matter of fact, I do. I send old man O'Donnell a hefty amount every month, just like clockwork. And the government pays for the Meltirks.''

''The government?''

''Someone the government didn't like invaded Baluchistan. Mrs. Meltirk happens to be part of the ruling family, so someone like the CIA got them out and stashed them here until they can return.''

Marielle just stared at him. ''In Farnum's Castle?''

Simon shrugged. ''Baluchistan isn't one of your more strategic countries. Besides, this looks like Shangri-la to the Meltirks. Anything with flush toilets has to be an improvement.''

''How many Meltirks are there?''

''We lost count. Eight or nine. Three grandparents, two parents, assorted children, and her royal highness is pregnant again,'' Simon drawled. ''Anyway, at least you're assured of the rent on two of the apartments. And Fritzie usually comes up with something. He's an antique dealer on the side, so he has another income.''

''Will I get enough to live on?''

If she was expecting some sympathy she didn't get it. ''I doubt it,'' he said. ''Don't you have any money?''

''Do you think I'd be here if I did?'' Marielle countered.

He shook his head. ''I don't think the rents you're going to collect will even keep this place functioning, much less leave anything to cover your own expenses. Go back home.''

''I have no home to go back to,'' she said, hating to expose herself to his unsympathetic eyes. ''I'll have to sell,'' she added with a trace of desperation. She'd only been in the place a couple of hours, she'd been trapped in an elevator and bombarded with crazies, not the least of which was the cynical loony with the tomblike voice, yet she didn't want to leave Farnum's Castle. Not yet. Just a few months to pull herself together was all she asked for!

''Hey, not so fast!'' Simon protested, finally jarred out of his remote disapproval. ''Maybe some of us can come up with more money. Anything's possible. If we have to put up with having you here I suppose we can survive.''

She looked at him for a long, thoughtful moment. ''You're wrong,'' she said finally. ''I do like you.''

He shrugged. "I already told you, I don't think much of your common sense."

The bedroom was very small. There was room for the huge bed and not much else, and suddenly it seemed as if they were standing very close together. She was a bit above average height, but felt dwarfed by Simon's tall, wiry figure. For some obscure reason the effect was disturbing in a way she couldn't understand, and she felt a sudden warmth starting between her shoulders and moving downward.

She could see his eyes widen in surprised recognition. And then it vanished as quickly as it had appeared, and he was cool, distant, backing from the tiny room.

"Come on, Julie," he said, moving rapidly away from Marielle. "There are a few more boxes downstairs. Help me with the elevator while I get them and then we'll let Marielle have some time to get herself settled."

"Marielle likes company," Esmerelda announced.

"No one likes company all the time," Simon replied, pausing long enough to look at Emily, who was returning his gaze quite fearlessly. He opened his mouth to say something, then clearly thought better of it. "We'll be back." And he practically ran from the room, Julie sauntering along behind him.

"What's gotten into Simon?" Esmerelda demanded.

"If you were more in touch with your spirit guides you'd know," Granita sniffed.

Emily turned to her mother, and for the first time in months the shadows were gone from her clear blue eyes. "I like it here," she announced.

And Marielle decided then and there that nothing, not poverty, not lucrative offers, not Simon Zebriskie, not even the shade of old Vittorio himself would get her out of Farnum's Castle until she was ready to go. "So do I, darling," she said firmly. "So do I."

HALF AN HOUR LATER Simon Zebriskie shut the flimsy door of his fifth-floor apartment and leaned against it, muttering a heartfelt curse. Just his luck—another lost soul, this time equipped with children.

It never failed—every time life got to a point where things were tolerable, peaceful, even pleasant, something came along to disrupt the status quo. He'd just been thinking how easy things had become, and then Marielle Brandt had to show up. And he had to start feeling things he should know better than to feel.

How long had it been since he'd had that kind of school-boy reaction? He would have thought that at the age of forty-two he'd be past such adolescent urges. But he'd stood there in that ridiculous little bedroom and looked down into those soulful blue eyes of hers and he'd almost lost it completely.

It didn't matter if she was a widow with two children; she was still nothing more than a baby herself. He'd be surprised if she was even in her mid-twenties, which made him maybe twenty years older than she was and a dirty old man into the bargain. On top of that, she looked about twelve, fifteen tops.

It wasn't just the age difference. He'd already failed at marriage and wasn't the sort of man to take that kind of failure lightly. He'd accepted the fact that he didn't have a talent for marriage, and rather than let some other woman down he planned to spend the next forty-two years steering clear of it. And Marielle Brandt, with her innocent eyes and her two babies, needed marriage.

But still, he thought, pushing away from the door and heading toward the kitchen, she had to be the prettiest woman he'd seen in as long as he could remember. The women he ran into were attractive, beautiful, striking, plain, but none of them were just simply pretty the way Marielle Brandt was. With her heart-shaped face, shoulder-length blond hair, shy smile and innocent eyes she was every adolescent's dream. Her body was small in the right places, deliciously rounded in others.

Did senility strike at age forty-two? he wondered, opening his nearly empty refrigerator and reaching for a Heineken. Maybe it was another midlife crisis. Except he didn't feel as if he was in the midst of a crisis—he still wanted his easy, solitary life. And he certainly didn't want Marielle Brandt and her children disrupting it.

He was overreacting and knew it. At his age he could recognize physical attraction when he felt it, but it didn't mean he had to act on it. He'd have to be in his eighties, not his forties, not to realize Marielle Brandt was a very attractive young lady. Certainly he was old enough to look without touching, particularly when someone was so patently off-limits.

Heading back into the living room, he switched on the FM before sinking onto the comfortable old sofa that his ex-wife had never been able to make him give up. Miles Van Cortland's too-mellow voice filled the room, and Simon snorted as a John Denver love song came on the air. "Annie's Song." Trust Miles to find the sweetest music the station owned. He must have another hangover.

Miles would leave all that soft, sweet, romantic music all over the place, and he'd have to put it away so he could get out stuff with a harder edge. The way he was feeling right now, he'd have to use every ounce of his determination to keep from playing some syrupy love songs himself.

She was too young, he was too old, she was too innocent, he was too jaded, he told himself, moving from the couch and flicking off the radio. And if she expected the tenants of Farnum's Castle to support her she wasn't going to be here very long, thank God. All he had to do was make himself scarce and wait it out. And continue to be as unfriendly as he could manage.

He could hear the soft murmur of voices beneath him, the quiet thump of people moving around, and once more he pictured her, her controlled panic in the broken elevator, the widening of her big blue eyes when she finally saw him in the bedroom. And he knew, deep in his heart, that she was as scared of him as he was of her.

She'd leave, he'd be safe from temptation. All he had to do was wait.

Chapter Three

Blessed peace and quiet settled around Marielle like a warm blanket. It was ten-thirty at night, her visitors had left ages ago, and the children were asleep, Emily on the foldaway cot and Christopher in the portable crib in the bedroom next to Marielle's. Fritzie, the infamous warlock, had turned out to be a very sweet middle-aged man who resembled Winnie the Pooh more than something out of *The Exorcist*. And his Peruvian chicken casserole had been so delicious that even Emily hadn't balked.

Granita and Esmerelda had spent the evening squabbling, over their professions, over Marielle's future love life, over the children, but it hadn't taken Marielle long to realize that beneath the bickering was a real devotion between the two old women, and she felt more than a pang of guilt at the thought that her presence threatened their security. She didn't want to threaten anyone, she thought, sinking onto a hard little chair in the now-empty living room. She just needed enough money to survive. If Granita and Esmerelda couldn't afford to pay their rent, maybe they could qualify for some sort of government assistance. She could even help them fill out the myriad of forms most bureaucracies required.

It would work out. For all its inconveniences and shady history she'd already grown attached to Farnum's Castle.

All she needed was enough energy and just a little bit of money and she could make a go of it. Tomorrow she'd call O'Donnell's office and see what sort of income the building brought in. She had a couple of thousand in savings, enough to make it through perhaps a month or two if she was very careful, and maybe even allow a little bit for repairs on the place. At the very least she needed a telephone of her own.

She sighed, looking around her at the bare walls, the bricked-up fireplace, the peeling paint and cracked windows, and suddenly felt very alone. Her friends were miles away, scattered over the country, and there was no one she could talk to, no one she could turn to for comfort and encouragement. Jaime was off in New Orleans, living, as far as Marielle understood it, with a witch doctor. Abbie was in California and Suzanne was where she'd always wanted to be, somewhere on the road. There was no one left in the old building in New York any more—her life there had vanished. But right then she would have given anything for a familiar voice.

If she had a phone she could always call her parents. It would have been worth putting up with her mother's non-stop helpful suggestions, none of which Marielle planned on following, just to hear from someone who'd known her for more than five hours. But she couldn't feel comfortable leaving the sleeping children to wander around looking for Simon Zebriskie's telephone.

She slumped in her chair. There was no coffee in the house, no food besides the leftover casserole, and she was no longer in the mood for black olives and onions. She'd have to borrow something from the ladies downstairs for breakfast before she attempted dragging both kids out to the grocery store. She could only hope they'd have something reasonably normal like toast. She wouldn't put it past the witchlike Esmerelda to breakfast on bat wings in milk.

She smiled to herself at the thought. The wind was whipping around the building, sliding through cracks and crevices in the old windows. There was heat from some source, though it wasn't particularly effective, and with a sudden sinking feeling Marielle realized that as owner and manager of this place she was responsible for heat. She could only pray it continued to work properly until she was able to orient herself better, or else that Chicago had a particularly balmy autumn.

Branches were tapping against the window, ghostly fingers rapping at her peace of mind, she thought. Then she realized someone was tapping at her door.

Her first thought was Simon, and the instinctive rush of pleasure surprised her enough to effectively wipe that emotion away before she could think about it. She wasn't ready to be vulnerable again—she'd spent too much of her life in reflecting someone else's, rather than being her own person. And if she were going to get involved with someone again she'd certainly have enough sense to choose someone with at least a trace of charm, a speck of warmth for someone other than old women and pregnant teenagers. Still, there was something about his eyes....

She ran nervous hands through her tangled blond hair before answering the door. Julie's stolid gaze met hers. "You expecting someone in particular?" she inquired.

"Not a soul," Marielle said.

"Esmerelda thought you might want to use the phone, let your family know you were settled in all right. I can stay with the kids while you go upstairs."

"I couldn't ask you to do that," Marielle protested.

"You aren't asking," Julie said flatly. "I'm here, sounds like your kids are asleep, and I brought a book." She held up a slightly tattered-looking romance. "Go ahead and call if you want."

"I haven't asked Simon...."

"He's probably gone by now. Besides, the phone's in the hall where anyone can use it. You won't be bothering anyone.'' She tapped her foot with all the impatience of youth. ''You wanna call someone or not?''

Marielle didn't hesitate any longer. ''Thank you, Julie. I appreciate it.''

''No problem.'' Julie pushed past her, her shape making her slightly unwieldy as she headed for the chair. ''Take your time.''

The light bulb in the hall was dangerously dim as Marielle started up the final winding flight of stairs. Replacing a light bulb was one thing she could certainly manage to do, she thought, holding on to the railing as she went. Someone could fall and break his leg, and then she'd really be up a creek without a paddle. No one ever hurt themselves in a public building nowadays without suing, and she'd be lucky if the price offered for Farnum's Castle equalled damages awarded.

God, she was being gloomy tonight, she thought as she reached the top-floor landing. She needed Abbie's brisk common sense to help clear away her obnoxious self-pity. She only hoped she'd be able to track her down somewhere in the heart of Wheeler, California.

There was a comfortable chair sitting in the hallway, better than anything in her threadbare apartment, and the telephone even had an adjustment for the hard of hearing. Marielle stared at it a moment before dialing. More of Simon's charity work. The man was an enigma.

No answer at Abbie's father's home. No answer at her apartment in Yorktown Towers, either, but that had been a long shot anyway. It was too late to call her parents, and her younger sister was on a retreat in some Buddhist commune in northern Vermont. There was no one she could turn to.

She set the receiver down quietly, sat back in the chair and closed her eyes, trying to blink away the sting of tears. And then her eyes shot open again as the door to Simon Zebriskie's apartment opened.

He looked as surprised to see her as she was to see him, and fully as uncomfortable. She couldn't figure out why— at least he hadn't been crying.

"I was using the telephone," she said. "I hope you don't mind. Julie said you'd probably be gone by now...."

"Anytime," he said. In the dimly lit hallway he seemed almost sinister, with his clear gray eyes in shadow and his eerie, deep voice. He was still wearing the chambray work shirt and faded jeans, and his boots had seen better days.

Maybe he hadn't seen she was crying. Maybe if she sat there in the shadows and waited until he was gone he'd think she was waiting for another phone call and...

"You've been crying," he said.

So much for that thought. "Just feeling sorry for myself," she said brightly, rubbing away the dampness from her face. "I don't usually give in to it."

He moved closer, standing over her. "Everybody has the right to feel sorry for themselves sometime," he said slowly. "Even I indulge in a little self-pity every now and then."

She wished she could see him in the darkness, but the shadows were too deep, he was too tall, and she didn't trust herself to stand up. They would have been close, dangerously close, and there were things going on that she didn't understand, didn't want to understand.

And then he backed away, suddenly, as if burned. "This won't work," he said, his deep voice very definite.

She didn't move, staring up at him, confused and uncertain and still tingling from an unlikely awareness. "What won't?"

"I'm not going to take on one more lost soul. There are too many in this apartment building as it is, and there isn't room for a vacationing socialite trying to find herself. Go back to New York. Go back to your upscale life and let us deal with our own problems."

She stared at him, a slow-growing anger burning away

the last of her miserable self-pity. "I don't have an upscale life to go back to," she said between her teeth. "I'm a widow, remember? No husband, no apartment, no money. All I have is this damned monstrosity, and somehow or other, I'm going to make the best of it."

"By sitting in my hallway crying?"

"If I had a telephone in my apartment I'd be sitting there. Crying," she added defiantly.

He moved into the light, and she expected his eyes to be cold and gray and angry. They were still gray all right, and the irritation was plain to see. So were the unwilling concern and compassion. Marielle's anger vanished.

"You don't belong here," he said more gently. "Surely you can see that as well as I can?"

"Whether you believe it or not, I have no choice in the matter. I'm here and I'm going to make it." She wished she could summon up a glare, but his sudden compassion stripped away her righteous indignation.

"And nothing I say will change your mind?"

"Nothing." This time she could glare, but it was a poor excuse for anger.

"Great," he said wearily. "You want to do me one more favor?"

"Sure thing."

He put his hand under her chin, turning her bemused face up to his. "Don't cry any more," he said gruffly. "You shouldn't have to cry."

She didn't say a word, just looked up into those pale gray eyes. And then, before she realized what was happening, his head moved down, his mouth lingering just above hers for a long, breathless minute. She shut her eyes, waiting, but he moved no closer. And then he was gone.

"Damn," he muttered, practically falling down the wide, curving stairs in his haste to get away from her. "I'm not going to do that."

She leaned over the bannister, watching him go, prey to

reactions and emotions she couldn't begin to understand. She rubbed her eyes, taking a deep, calming breath. It was no wonder she was confused. The uncertainty of the last few days and months had taken its toll. Add to that the last few sleepless nights, and it was a wonder she could function at all.

One thing was certain—she didn't understand Simon Zebriskie. With his bristling anger, his sudden kindness, he was an enigma. An unsettling one.

Maybe after a decent night's sleep this would begin to make some sense. Maybe that odd, irrational awareness would resolve itself into something she understood and could cope with. For now all she could do was head back to her apartment and try to put everything out of her mind. Particularly the mystery that was Simon Zebriskie.

IT WAS A COLD, WINDY NIGHT as Simon drove his '72 Mustang down Michigan Avenue toward the elegant old building that housed WAKS, and a chilly rain had begun to fall. The old oil furnace at Farnum's Castle usually chose nights like this to conk out, and he could only hope it wouldn't run true to form. Marielle wouldn't know how to deal with it, and old people like Esmy and Granita couldn't afford to be without their heat.

Marielle probably thought he was a coldhearted bastard and a half. It couldn't be helped. He didn't need any dilettantes distracting him from the people who really needed his help. He didn't need an impossibly attractive young woman making him forget all the things he had to remember, making him think he could have... God, what was that awful word nowadays? A relationship? There were no relationships in his future, not with the likes of Marielle Brandt.

He'd handled her well, he thought, with more hope than self-assurance. Until he'd almost kissed her he'd done very well, trying to get rid of her. Now she probably thought he was crazy.

That was the least of his worries. In his forty-two years on earth plenty of people had thought he was off the wall, and plenty would continue to think so. No one would ever understand why he'd given up a job at the biggest station in Chicago, with a salary in the six figures, for the nighttime shift on a small independent station that had trouble making ends meet. Of course, WAKS wouldn't have as much trouble if Miles Van Cortland, the program director and station manager, didn't insist on paying himself such a hefty salary.

And people didn't understand why Simon stayed on at Farnum's Castle when he could definitely afford some nice bland condo on Lake Shore Drive. He didn't bother to explain. It was something in his past, and it was nobody's business but his. He'd learned long ago to accept the fact that he was out of step with yuppie society.

Which was where Marielle Brandt belonged, he thought gloomily. In some nice, elegant place with nice, elegant people. She wasn't the sort to be scrambling for a living, game though she was. She hadn't wanted him to see her crying, and with his unfriendly attitude he'd done his best to make her cry some more.

But she hadn't cried. She'd straightened her shoulders and glared at him, and he had to admire her pluck. Maybe she wouldn't be another drain on his increasingly limited reserve. Maybe she wouldn't even prove a distraction, a temptation. Maybe he could think of her with the same impartial concern that he thought of all the others in the building. And maybe not, he thought gloomily. Maybe not.

MARIELLE SLOWLY MADE HER WAY back down the flight of stairs to her fourth-floor apartment, her brow wrinkled in thought. Simon Zebriskie had to be the oddest of all the extremely odd people living in Farnum's Castle. An extremely attractive sort of odd, she had to admit, despite his gruff manner. If she didn't know better she would have thought he was attracted to her. For a moment it had almost seemed as if he was going to kiss her. It had to be her overwrought imagination, of course. Why would a man who was clearly intent on getting rid of her want to kiss her?

It was a good thing he wasn't interested. The last thing she wanted was another relationship so soon after Greg. Not that her marriage had been so tumultuously wonderful—in fact, quite the opposite. Greg had been a workaholic, a man with an overwhelming personality who was seldom home, and when he was, spent most of his time issuing orders. They'd met in college, when she'd been young and stupid enough to be attracted to his masterful ways. In the last years of their marriage they'd been little more than bedmates, and after Christopher had been born, not even that. He'd been on the verge of moving out, the separation in the hands of the lawyers when he'd died. She was still coping with the nagging guilt and regret, with grief for Greg's lost youth, for the failure of a marriage that had seemed to hold so much promise, for the loss of her children's father. For the loss of her illusions.

No, there'd been nothing so marvelous about married life that she was tempted to repeat the experiment, at least not for now. She wouldn't marry a man for security—it would be doomed to failure. She wouldn't marry a man to provide a stepfather for the children—he could turn around and be just as uninterested as their real father had been. And she certainly wouldn't marry a man for the sake of sex. She knew only too well what a farce and a sham that was. Making love was a messy, disappointing business. She liked the kissing ahead of time, the holding afterward, but as far as she could see the central act was vastly overrated.

No, celibacy suited her just fine for now. In a few years, if she wanted some companionship, she might be willing to pay the price. But right now she needed to prove to herself that she didn't need anyone else telling her what to do, laying claim to her time and her body.

"Did I hear Simon in the hall?" Julie questioned, looking up from her book as Marielle reentered the unlocked apartment.

"He hadn't left yet." She knew her cheeks were still slightly red from her peculiar encounter, and Julie's flat brown eyes were far too observant. "He's a funny guy."

"Simon's the best there is," Julie said, bristling. "He's just a little grumpy sometimes. He likes his privacy."

"I didn't say he wasn't a wonderful human being," Marielle said mildly. "I just said he was peculiar. I can't get over the feeling that I know him from somewhere."

Julie said nothing, shutting her book with dignified deliberation and heaving her bulk from the chair. "The kids are still sound asleep. If you need anything, just run down and get me." She paused by the door. "When are you going to tell the others who you are?"

"I beg your pardon?"

"I saw you arrive with old man O'Donnell. You own this rattrap, don't you?" Her eyes were accusing.

There was no point in lying. "Yes."

"You planning to evict Esmy and Granita?"

"No."

Julie relaxed a little. "What about me? I don't pay any rent either."

"I'm not going to evict anyone, whether they pay rent or not," Marielle said wearily. "I just want to make a home for me and my children."

"We help each other around here. We take care of each other. We can take care of you, too."

"I don't want anyone to take care of me...."

"All right, next time you can forget your damn phone call."

"I didn't mean to sound ungrateful."

"Forget it," Julie said grudgingly. "You've got nice kids. You're not too bad yourself. As long as you're not planning to hurt anyone it's okay with me."

Once again Marielle had to swallow the smile that threatened to spill over. Julie was very jealous of her dignity, and she wouldn't appreciate Marielle's reluctant amusement.

"Thank you," she said gravely.

"Tell you what," Julie said. "Anytime you need babysitting, you come to me. It's the least I can do."

Marielle stared at her for a long moment. How could she turn this tough, vulnerable teenager out on the street? How could she evict two harmless old ladies? At least the Meltirks and Simon paid rent. Maybe they could all get by.

"I'd appreciate that," Marielle said, knowing that any polite demurrals would be taken as a dire insult. "Maybe you could stay with them while I buy some food tomorrow?"

"Sure," Julie said. "Just come and get me."

Marielle shut the door behind her. The locks didn't work, but that didn't surprise her. At least if no one paid rent no one could expect her to do much maintenance.

Of course, she thought half an hour later, she'd have to put up with minimal hot water, sporadic heat, drafty windows and flickering electricity herself. Maybe tomorrow she'd better include a bookstore in her shopping trip. She was going to need a self-help manual on home repair or freeze to death in her apartment.

She hadn't unpacked any sheets, so she had no choice but to wrap herself up in an afghan and curl up on the old mattress. The gargoyles overhead would be bound to give her nightmares, and the wind whistling through the eaves of the old building sounded unpleasantly ghostlike. At least the children were sleeping soundly.

She had brought a small portable radio. She turned it on and was randomly flicking the dial when she stopped, mesmerized by a familiar voice. It was Simon's voice, deep and sepulchral, coming through the tiny box on the floor beside the bed.

"It's twelve thirty-three in the morning," he said, his voice melting over her like warm honey, "and here's something I should have enough sense not to play." And coming over the airwaves, in all its sensual sweetness, was John Denver singing "Annie's Song."

Chapter Four

Marielle's eyes shot open. She'd fallen asleep with the meagerly watted light bulb still shining, and in the early morning glow it cast strange shadows over the gargoyles adorning her bed. She was still fully dressed in jeans and a cotton T-shirt, and she was soaked with sweat, her heart pounding, adrenaline shooting through her body.

Her first thought was the children. Within seconds she was off the bed and into the other room, but her panic had been groundless. They were both sound asleep, Christopher with his diapered rump in the air, Emily sprawled sideways across the folding cot.

Marielle stepped back into the hallway, leaning against the wall to catch her breath. And then she heard it again, the sound that must have awakened her in the first place.

It was a hollow, scraping noise, quiet enough, eerily so, and it seemed to emanate from the walls. Marielle took another deep breath, placing her palms against the plaster, and was rewarded with the barest hint of a vibration. Moving along the corridor she followed the noise into her own room, over to the bricked-up fireplace.

There was no question as to where the sound was coming from. Marielle pressed her ear against the brick, holding her breath to listen. Somewhere below her in the chimney that presumably ran the full height of the house, someone was scratching and tapping.

She moved away, climbing back onto the bare mattress and pulling the threadbare quilt around her. The gargoyles and satyrs above her leered down, and she found herself keeping her back to them, leaning against the headboard and staring fixedly at the old fireplace.

"Squirrels," she said out loud, the sound of her voice in the silent apartment drowning the scratching noises. "Or mice," she added, less pleased with that possibility. "Or rats," she had to be honest enough to admit. "Maybe I'd prefer ghosts."

The scratching stopped abruptly. Whoever, whatever it was had abandoned its efforts, maybe scared off by the sound of her voice. Marielle scrunched down on the bed, wrapping the quilt more tightly around her, and waited for the sound to resume.

Silence closed around her like a thick, velvet cloak. In her sleepy mind she tried to reconstruct the layout of Farnum's Castle. There were two apartments on each floor. The first floor held Granita's and Esmerelda's apartments, the Meltirks and Fritzie lived on the second, and the entire floor below her was empty, as was the second apartment on her floor. Simon Zebriskie commandeered the entire floor and a half above her, but that wasn't bothering her at the moment. It was the empty apartment beneath her where the trouble was located.

A sensible, committed landlord would go downstairs immediately and investigate. But just then the most sensible thing in the world was to stay right where she was, away from mysterious noises and things that went bump in the night. If she did go roaming around like some Gothic heroine she'd deserve to be committed.

She huddled down further on the lumpy mattress. She could hear a steady thumping, but this time she knew it was only her heart. Whoever, whatever had been in the chimney was gone, leaving her to reclaim what sleep she could.

She peered out the curtainless windows, but the Chicago night was artificially bright, so she couldn't tell if it was anywhere near dawn. Her watch was in what passed for a kitchen, and the clock radio she'd listened to earlier still flashed 12:00 with monotonous regularity. She reached out to turn it on, then pulled her hand back. The last thing she needed, alone and nervous in the middle of the night, was Simon Zebriskie's deep voice comforting her. She didn't need to know what time it was—the kids would wake up at seven o'clock on the dot. Or, God help her, six o'clock Central Time. She'd better grab what sleep she could, and forget about harmless creatures resting in her chimney.

She shut her eyes, allowing a weary sigh to escape her. Sleep, blessed sleep. And as she began to drift off, the scratching and tapping began once more.

WHEN MARIELLE FINALLY WOKE UP again, three pairs of eyes were staring at her. Christopher was on the floor, dressed in a disposable diaper, a T-shirt and a big grin, Emily was sitting beside him, her Pound Puppies nightshirt smeared with what looked like strawberry jam, and in the doorway stood Esmerelda, her raisin-dark eyes both wary and reproachful.

"Julie told me who you were," she said, her voice quavering slightly. "Are you going to kick us out?"

Marielle shook her head slightly, more to clear the fogs of sleep away than as an expression of negation. Christopher raced over to her, his gap-toothed grin endearing, and Emily plopped onto the bed beside her, swinging her long legs. "I'm not going to kick anyone out," Marielle said, pulling Christopher onto the bed as well. She wished there was some way she could skirt the issue rather than make an outright promise. But the fear in Esmerelda's dark eyes and the bravado in Julie's made polite nothings useless.

"You haven't seen your electric bill yet," Simon's deep voice called from the living room. "You shouldn't make promises you can't keep."

"Good heavens, is the entire apartment building visiting me this morning?" Marielle demanded, pushing back her covers and climbing from the bed, hoisting Christopher onto her hip.

"Fritzie's gone on a buying trip," Granita announced, appearing in the doorway, her tall, skinny body draped once again in gray. "And the Meltirks probably aren't even aware you're here. Come on out and have some coffee. Fortunately Simon brought enough for all of us."

"Oh, he did, did he?" Marielle muttered, wishing she could at least look in a mirror, knowing the results would only depress her.

"And he brought me Froot Loops," Emily said, her voice rich with satisfaction.

Simon was sitting by the window reading the paper, a Styrofoam cup of coffee beside him. The look he cast her was far from welcoming, a fact that managed to spark some irritation in Marielle's tired brain. After all, it was her apartment.

"Finish your cereal, Emily Brandt," Julie admonished, taking Christopher from Marielle's arms and handing her a cup of black coffee. "And then we'll go out and find the park. Your ma's got a lot to accomplish today, and she doesn't need us underfoot."

Marielle waited for Emily's tears and an attack of clinging. Instead Emily climbed back onto the chair, tucked her plastic spoon into her cup of cereal and announced with a beatific smile, "I like Froot Loops."

"You've got a slave for life," Marielle told Simon, sinking to the ratty carpet and taking a sip of coffee. It was absolutely awful—watery and bitter—but at least it contained a good dose of caffeine, so she swallowed half the cup, shuddering.

Simon looked down at her, his light gray eyes distant and unreadable. It was as though the odd conversation in his hallway last night had never happened. "I can always do with more groupies," he said, folding the paper and setting it down. "How'd you sleep?"

"Fine except for the ghosts," she said, draining the coffee.

"Ghosts?" Granita murmured, suddenly alert. "You were blessed with a visitation?"

"I wouldn't call it blessed and I wouldn't call it a visitation," Marielle replied, stretching her legs in front of her. "I'm sure it was just squirrels."

"In the chimney?" Esmerelda questioned.

Marielle had thought her nerves from the night before were gone, but Esmerelda's bright question brought them back. "As a matter of fact, yes. Has there been a problem with them before?"

Esmerelda opened her mouth to speak, but Simon was ahead of her. "Julie, why don't you get the children dressed for outdoors? I'm sure Emily would like the carousel in the park, and you could stop for an ice-cream cone on the way there."

"She's already had too much sugar," Marielle protested, but with her customary efficiency Julie had already whisked the children from the room. Marielle stared after them, wishing that just once she might accomplish something as simple as getting the two of them dressed without arguments and discussions and a wrestling match from her younger child. Julie made it look so damned easy.

"I wasn't going to say anything, Simon," Esmerelda said plaintively. "I wouldn't want to scare the children."

"Of course you wouldn't, Esmy," he said with more patience than he had showed Marielle. "But sometimes accidents happen, and people say things they shouldn't."

"Say what?" Marielle demanded, incensed. "Don't tell me old Vittorio's ghost haunts the chimneys?"

"Not exactly," Granita said. "Though something definitely does."

"Rumor has it," Esmerelda said delicately, "that old Vittorio might have disposed of one of his enemies."

Marielle just stared at her. "I would have thought he'd disposed of a great many of his enemies. He was a Prohibition era gangster, wasn't he?"

"No, my dear. I mean one particular victim. In the... chimney."

Marielle could feel her face turn pale and the nasty coffee churn in her stomach. "You're kidding."

"It's just a rumor," Simon said, unmoved by her horror. "Probably started by my boss. I sincerely doubt it's true."

"Yes, but you can't ignore what he says. Miles Van Cortland is an expert on Chicago in that time period," Esmy insisted. "You know how he's always poking around here when he comes to see you."

"Miles isn't an expert on anything," Simon grumbled. "Except on being charming."

"He is that," Esmerelda said soulfully. "You'll have to meet him, Marielle. The most delightful man. And he's a bachelor," she added significantly. "All he needs is the right woman and he'll be more than ready to settle down."

"I'm not looking for a new husband," Marielle replied absently, turning her attention to weightier matters. "You don't mean there's really a dead body stuffed in the chimney?"

"Of course not," Esmy soothed. "We would have felt the vibrations. It's probably just squirrels looking for a nice warm place to spend the winter."

"They won't find it here unless she does something about the boiler," Simon muttered.

"The furnace?" Marielle echoed in a strained voice.

"It's on its last legs," he announced with an air of satisfaction.

"And the electric bill?"

"I believe it's up to four figures."

Marielle slumped to the floor with a strangled moan, but Simon reached down, caught her hand, pulled her up again—and instantly released her. It was a good hand, she thought. Warm and strong and capable.

"You're in over your head," he said. "You should get out while the getting is good."

"I can deal with it. All I need is another cup of that horrible coffee and I can deal with anything."

"Hey!" Simon protested, insulted. "At least it's better than instant."

"Maybe," said Marielle.

"What do you mean, you don't want a new husband?" Esmerelda demanded, still working on that statement. "Of course you do. You don't want to have to struggle for a living yourself, and your children need a father."

"My children will do just fine without a father."

"If you don't like Miles I can think of several other possibilities," Granita said, not to be outdone. "There's Mr. McFarlane who runs the dry cleaning establishment down the street, if you like them mature. Or there's Mr. Davies from the State Department who comes to check on the Meltirks. I don't think he's married, and he's young and quite presentable, besides having a decent job. Or there's that nice young man from the tax assessors' office who was here last month, or..."

"Tax assessor?" Marielle asked faintly.

"Or there's Simon!" Esmerelda broke in on a note of triumph, casting a fond glance at both of them.

"Esmy!" Simon said in a dangerous voice. "Don't you think it's up to Marielle to find a new husband? When she's ready?"

"But Simon," Esmy said, fluttering her crepey eyelids at him soulfully, "some people are so diffident! Here Marielle thinks she doesn't even want a new husband, when I'm certain nothing would make her happier. If you don't want her I have no doubt I could find any number of suitable men...."

"Don't!" Marielle protested in a strangled tone.

"What makes you think you're the only one capable of matchmaking?" Granita broke in huffily. "I'll have you know there are some remarkably successful marriages that have been a direct result of my machinations. And I don't know that we should rule out Simon entirely...."

"Ladies!" Simon thundered, his deep, rich voice rattling the windows. "Stop meddling! You seem to forget that Marielle has been widowed for only a short while. Don't you think you ought to respect her grief?"

"She doesn't seem to be grieving," Esmy pointed out with damning practicality. "But you're right, Simon. We've been too precipitate. Come along, Granita. We have plans to make."

The two old ladies, one tall and elegant, the other short and round, stalked from the apartment, leaving Marielle alone with Simon Zebriskie.

She swiveled around on the tattered carpet, looking up at him quite fearlessly. "I don't think they're going to drop it," she said gloomily.

He watched her out of hooded gray eyes, and his mouth wasn't smiling. "They seldom do. The two of them are like a dog with a bone—they won't let go of something that takes their fancy. Be prepared to have a whole crew of suitable prospects paraded in front of you."

"Just what I need," she sighed.

"Maybe it is."

"I beg your pardon?"

Simon shrugged. "Maybe Esmy and Granita are right. Maybe the best thing you can do is find a new husband to take care of you."

"I don't want anyone taking care of me." Her tone was fierce. "I have no intention of getting involved with anyone for a long, long time."

"Did you love him that much?" he asked, as if he couldn't keep his curiosity at bay any longer.

"Whom?" Marielle was honestly mystified.

"Your late husband?"

The last thing she should do was confide in Simon Zebriskie, but for some reason she couldn't help herself. "No," she said. "We weren't going to stay married."

He still didn't move. "You hated him so much that you don't want to try again?"

"No. Frankly, it just doesn't seem worth the trouble. True love and marriage are vastly overrated commodities. I can do without."

Simon rose, towering over her, and she once more felt that strange flutter, a pleasant sort of apprehension in the pit of her stomach. "What about making love?" he said with what sounded like no more than casual curiosity. "Are you going to do without that, too?"

Marielle couldn't believe she was having this conversation with a total stranger. But since she'd started, she might as well make her position clear. "The most overrated commodity of all," she said firmly.

He stared at her for a long moment. "If you say so. Let's go see if there are any goblins downstairs."

"Sounds promising." She moved to the hallway. "Julie, could you watch the kids while I go see the third-floor apartment? It should only take a few minutes."

"Go right ahead. I thought I might take them to the park. That is, if it's all right." Julie was looking defensive again, but Marielle had already learned to read her.

Marielle's smile didn't waver. "Wonderful," she said, squashing her doubts. "I'll be here when you get back."

Simon didn't say a word until they were standing in the third-floor apartment and Marielle was trying to sort through ten pounds of keys. "She's a good kid, you know. You don't need to worry."

"All mothers worry. If I didn't trust her I wouldn't let

them go. I'm just going to worry anyway. Do you mind?'' The third key worked, and she reached for the tarnished brass doorknob.

"It's a waste of time,'' he said, leaning against the wall. Some of his open combativeness had vanished, Marielle recognized with gratitude, not bothering to try to figure out why.

"But it's my time I'm wasting,'' she said, tossing her hair over one shoulder. "Let's see if there are any ghosts in here.'' She pushed the door open, and a wave of cold air washed over them.

Whether it was another broken window or the notorious chill that accompanied supernatural occurrences Marielle had no way of knowing. But foolhardy or not, she was glad Simon Zebriskie was one pace behind her as she stepped into the deserted apartment and faced the demon from last night.

Chapter Five

He was getting in deeper and deeper, Simon thought, looking around the deserted apartment and out the cracked, grimy windows, in fact anywhere but at the slender female figure beside him. Why couldn't he trust his first instincts—to keep as far away from her as possible? The more he was around her, the more he was drawn in.

It was probably just part of his paternalistic feeling toward the people in Farnum's Castle. Marielle was simply another lost soul who needed his help while she served her time in the decrepit old place. But looking at her, the slender, defiant back, the tangle of blond hair, the long legs, he knew his feelings weren't the slightest bit paternal. And he ought to be up in his apartment, letting her fend for herself.

"God, it's cold in here," Marielle said, moving over to the window and wrapping her arms about her slender body. "Why isn't anyone in this apartment? It looks in better shape than the one I'm in."

"The pipes broke last winter," he said, following her and peering into the overgrown yard that surrounded the old place. "The plumber capped them off, but that was it. No one thought it was worth the trouble to fix them."

"Who was taking care of the building? Didn't you have a superintendent, a landlord or something?"

"We had one. He spent all his time in the basement

doing drugs and watching soap operas. Life in the big city isn't pretty.''

''I lived in New York,'' Marielle said absently. ''I'm not used to hearts and flowers.''

''Where in New York? I can't see you anywhere but the Upper East Side.''

She grinned ruefully. ''Guilty. Did you live in New York?''

''At one point in my checkered past.''

''Were you always a disc jockey?''

He grimaced. ''I did other things.''

''Like what?''

''Nosy, aren't you? I thought we were down here looking for ghosts.''

She looked around, wrinkling her nose. ''The place looks empty to me. What did you do?''

''Why do you want to know?'' He was stalling, knowing that sooner or later he'd have to tell her.

''Because you look familiar. I can't get over the feeling I know you from somewhere, but I can't place it.'' She seemed to have forgotten all about skeletons and ghosts in the chimneys. ''Who are you?''

''Did your parents let you watch television when you were a kid?''

''Of course. What's that got to do with anything?''

''What about horror movies? Maybe when you were about ten years old?''

She stared up at him in dawning realization. ''Simon Zee,'' she said, her voice awed. ''You used to dress up like a cross between a vampire and Frankenstein and introduce old horror movies. Was that really you?''

''Throwing spaghetti and calling it veins? Yes, that was me.''

''But that was so long ago,'' she said artlessly, then blushed.

He hadn't seen a woman blush in more than a decade. "I told you, I'm an old man and you're a child."

"You're full of…spaghetti," she amended, staring up at him in disbelief. "I can hardly recognize you."

"I wore lots of makeup. Not to mention the fact that almost twenty years have passed since I used to do that."

"What did you do after you were Simon Zee?"

"If you'd like I'll drop my résumé off at your apartment," he snapped.

"I'm just curious."

"You're too curious."

She waited, saying nothing, and finally he sighed. "After the horror movies I hosted a dance show on cable. If you think the old movies were scary, you should have seen disco at its height. From there it was a logical step to FM radio." He moved away from the window. "Enough? Or would you like references?"

"How come you're so touchy about your past?"

"You want to tell me more about your sex life with your husband?" The moment the words were out of his mouth he regretted them. He wasn't used to hurting people; all he wanted was to stay in his nice, safe shell. The expression on Marielle's face was like a knife thrust to his heart.

But he wouldn't apologize. To say he was sorry would be to let down boundaries he needed to keep firmly in place. "Which chimney do you think the sounds were coming from?"

"There's more than one?" she inquired, after only a moment's hesitation.

"There are four or five. Not to mention seventeen fireplaces. If Vittorio stashed a victim in one of them, it's going to take a while to pinpoint which one."

"You don't really think he did?" she asked.

There it was again—that absurdly vulnerable streak in her that brought forth all sorts of unwelcome feelings. "It's highly unlikely. Despite all you've heard about Santa Claus, people can't fit into chimneys.''

"If they're in one piece," Marielle added gloomily.

Simon grimaced. "With that kind of imagination it's no wonder you hear noises at night."

"You've got to admit it's a possibility."

"I don't have to admit anything. Let's check out the fireplaces and get out of here. It's too damned cold."

"Ghosts are supposed to make places unnaturally cold," she said, rubbing her bare arms beneath the threadbare T-shirt.

Her arms were too skinny, he thought, watching her, but even the bagginess of the oversize shirt didn't disguise her curves.

"Broken windows do an even better job." He squatted beside the boarded-up fireplace, poking at it. "Seems intact."

"It wouldn't have been from that chimney. I heard it in my bedroom—if there's a fireplace directly below it..."

"Are you sure it wasn't the effect of that horrific bed you were sleeping in? I think that was part of Vittorio's stuff that no one would take."

"I'm not that gullible. I just..." She stopped dead still in the bedroom doorway so that it took all Simon's balance not to careen into her.

"No, I guess you're not." With his superior height he could easily see over her shoulder into the room, where a pile of bricks littered the stained and pitted wooden flooring. The window wasn't broken, but it was wide open to the chilly autumn air, and the metal fire escape swung gently in the breeze, clanging against the outside wall.

She looked over her shoulder at him, and once again he could see her eyes widen in surprised reaction to his closeness. He knew he should back away but held his ground. She didn't seem capable of moving farther into the room. "Do we want to look?" she whispered.

"At what?" He kept his deep voice at a normal level, trying to break the eerie atmosphere.

"To see if there's anyone in the chimney. Or part of anyone," she added, with a shiver not attributable to the cold air.

"Sure thing." He pushed past her into the room and squatted by the fireplace. Someone had done a fairly effective job of pulling out the old bricks and mortar that had been blocking it. He peered up into the chimney, saw that bits of twigs and shredded newspapers still clung to the inside, then backed out.

"No skeletons, no corpses, no miscellaneous body parts," he said, standing up and brushing his hands against his jeans. "Want to take a look?"

"I'll take your word for it." She still hadn't moved from the doorway. "Who do you think did this?"

"Not the ghost of old Vittorio." He went over and shut the window. "He doesn't need to use fire escapes."

"Then who?"

He shrugged. "I expect those old rumors are circulating again. Every few years we have incidents of vandalism, and then people forget all about it."

"Forget all about what?"

"Vittorio Farnum was one of the meanest, nastiest, dirtiest SOBs to ever set up shop in Chicago. In his heyday he could make Al Capone look like a choirboy. But then he found religion, gave up his wicked ways, and died in bed at the ripe old age of seventy."

"Not my bed, I hope," Marielle said devoutly.

"I wouldn't count on it." He was clearly unwilling to give her any comfort.

Marielle shivered. "Go on."

"So the old guy left most of his money to the church. But there was a huge portion missing. And Vittorio had always said his treasure was in his castle, where even the fires of hell couldn't reach it. Maybe someone took the story literally and thought he'd stashed the loot in the fire-place.''

Marielle moaned, slumping against the wall. "That's all I need. Treasure hunters vandalizing the place.''

"I think," said Simon, "that's the least of your problems.''

She raised her head. "Why do you say that?''

"I shut the window and it's still getting colder. The boiler must have conked out again.''

For a moment he thought she might cry. He didn't know what he'd do if she did. If he put his arms around her to comfort her he might not be able to maintain his gruff, avuncular attitude. But he couldn't just let her stand there and weep.

He'd underestimated her. She stiffened her back and sighed. "Okay," she said. "You want to show me the boiler?''

THE DAY, MARIELLE THOUGHT later, had gone from bad to worse. If being ripped from a sound sleep after a restless night wasn't bad enough, the strange things going on in Farnum's Castle added to the strain. To top it all off the boiler proved to be just as mysterious and on its last legs as she'd suspected it would be, the price of replacement mentioned by the repairman would just about empty her savings account, and that still left the four-figure electric bill looming over her.

Still, there had been compensations, she thought as she leaned against the wall, stretching out her legs on the threadbare carpet and taking a deep sip of coffee. For one thing, the expensive repairman *had* come promptly, and he had managed to coax a modicum of heat out of the antique machinery. And Christopher and Emily had had a wonderful day, going to the park with Julie, eating their fill in Esmerelda's tiny kitchen, and were now sleeping soundly in their cozy little bedroom.

She'd met the Meltirks, or at least been introduced to her serene highness and her consort. Her highness was in the middle stages of pregnancy, a few months behind Julie, and her communication consisted of smiles and nods and an incomprehensible babble that only Esmerelda seemed to understand. Marielle thought she could hear livestock in the distance, behind the closed door of their apartment, and the smoky smell was a cross between incense and burned cabbage, but who was she to quibble with people who paid rent? She'd smiled and nodded too, hoping to God the Meltirks were careful with their fires.

And in the stack of bills forwarded from her old apartment in Yorktown Towers, there'd been a postcard from Suzanne. Marielle had looked at it and laughed, her first genuine laugh of the day. On the front of the postcard was a cowboy, complete with chaps, lariat, oversize Stetson and pointy-toed boots. The postmark was Laramie, Wyoming, and on the back was a message in Suzanne's typically brief style.

"Would you believe I've fallen in love with a cowboy? Not with the guy on the postcard—Billy's cuter. We're living together in a house in Laramie, of all the remote places. I'm going to college and I'm very, very happy. Mouse married the cop I told you about and sends her love. With my luck I'm going to be a grandmother before I'm forty. Take care, Suzanne."

Marielle allowed herself a full five minutes to miss her, to miss her other friends who had been closer than her spacey sister had ever been. Suzanne with her funny, wise-cracking nature, finally in love. And Jaime engaged to a doctor, settling down in her hometown of New Orleans. Happy endings for both of them. She still didn't know what was going on with Abbie, and could only hope the same luck held for her. If her three best friends could find happiness, maybe there was still hope for herself.

Surprisingly enough, one of the day's compensations had

been Simon. For all his odd manner and his gruff, cynical nature, she'd begun to understand him. Or at least to make her peace with him. She still didn't quite understand what a man with his background would be doing living in a decaying hovel like Farnum's Castle, babysitting a lot of people who were, to put it politely, not enjoying the fruits of the burgeoning economy. Right now she was surrounded by the weirdest people she'd ever known in her fairly sheltered life, and surprisingly enough, she was enjoying it. Most of all she was enjoying Simon, Simon of the dour outlook and gentle charm with the old ladies. She could have done with some gentle charm herself, but apparently he didn't have enough to go around.

At least they seemed to have settled into some sort of truce. It was reassuring to know he was up there within shrieking distance if whoever vandalized the fireplace in the apartment beneath her decided to go one floor higher.

"Damn," she said out loud, sitting up and pulling her legs under her. "Why did I have to think of that?" She cast an anxious glance at the window, but all was darkness and gloom beyond the newly washed glass.

She ought to go to bed. The kids had been asleep since eight, it was now half past ten and Marielle was exhausted. Once she'd dealt with the furnace and the highway robber who called himself a repairman, she'd tackled the apartment, stripping off decades of grime and filth from the walls, the windows, the floors. Aesthetically it wasn't much improvement, but at least she knew that if she leaned against the wall now she wouldn't stick to it, and that was some consolation. She hadn't even minded the distinctly chilly shower she'd indulged in once the kids had gone to bed. She'd managed to unpack sheets for everyone and a few kitchen utensils, but heaven only knew where the hair dryer was. She shivered slightly as her damp hair drifted in the breeze wafting from the tightly closed window. How much would storm windows cost? Maybe she could at least dig up enough money for insulated curtains. And it was only October.

She didn't bother to get up when she heard the knock at the door. It could be no one but Julie, who'd promised to check back and see if she needed any last-minute help. Back in New York Marielle wouldn't have been caught dead answering the door in wet hair, no makeup, sweat-pants and a stretched-out T-shirt with Virginia Woolf's faded visage plastered across her chest. But things had changed, Marielle had changed, and she had no standards to live up to but her own.

"Come in, Julie," she called lazily, stretching out on her stomach on the carpet. It was still slightly damp, but at least no longer had things crawling in it, and anything was more comfortable than the sturdy wooden chairs that had to date back to old Vittorio himself, probably in his peni-tential days.

The door with the broken lock opened, but instead of Julie she got a perfect view of a man's beautiful leather shoes. She didn't for one moment suspect they could be-long to Simon—he was clearly a devotee of running shoes and Frye boots, and besides, the man wearing these shoes had small, neat feet. She looked up past perfectly tailored legs and a thick knit sweater that had to have come from Ireland to the handsomest face she'd ever seen. Mesmer-ized, she sat up, her mouth hanging open as her disbeliev-ing eyes took in the vision in front of her.

He had thick blond hair, tumbling rakishly across his high forehead. He had beautifully sculptured lips, curling back in a smile that exposed straight white teeth. He had a short, perfect nose, a golden tan and blue eyes shining with intelligence and humor. Marielle simply stared, not even noticing Simon's taller figure directly behind the glorious apparition.

"What on earth have you been doing?" Simon de-manded, striding into the apartment with his companion.

"I cleaned the place," she said.

Simon looked around him. "I guess it's an improvement. Are you just going to roll around the floor like Little Egypt or would you like to meet Miles?"

"Simon, your social graces leave a great deal to be desired," Prince Charming murmured in a voice as thick and rich as imported honey. He crossed the room and reached out a bronzed hand to the benumbed Marielle, pulling her gently to her feet. "You'd never guess that he really knows how to behave, would you?"

Marielle shook her head. Simon snorted, moving past her to the kitchen area and peering inside her aging refrigerator. Finding nothing more exciting than Diet Pepsi and milk, he shut it again. "This is Miles Van Cortland," he said, his tone offhand, his gray eyes alert. "You remember, the one Esmerelda said you should marry?"

"He is a beast, isn't he?" Marielle had by this time recovered her equilibrium, and she gave the gorgeous Mr. Van Cortland a friendly smile.

"He's just trying to protect his turf," Miles said. "Never mind that he's insulting his boss."

"You're his boss?" Marielle echoed, walking past him into the kitchen. She pulled Simon out of the open refrigerator which, after an afternoon's defrosting, was already building up a new coating of ice, and firmly shut the door.

"He is," Simon rumbled, looking down at her. "He's also an expert on old Chicago architecture, not to mention certain legends surrounding the gangsters in the twenties and thirties. I thought maybe he could tell you a bit about Farnum's Castle. I never paid much attention to details, but Miles can be downright compulsive. Can't you, Miles?"

"I wouldn't put it that way, Simon," he protested politely. "Just because I happen to like trivia…"

"Whatever," Simon said airily. "Tell Marielle what you know about the castle, make a date with her for later, and then let's get to the studio."

Miles smiled faintly. "Simon asked me to stop by on my way to the studio to meet an absolutely beautiful young widow, but I think he's forgotten he wanted to set us up. Are you sure you haven't got designs on her yourself, old man?"

"I haven't," Simon said flatly, adding, "young man." He pushed away from the counter, moving past Marielle without another glance. "I'll meet you downstairs in fifteen minutes." And without another word he was gone.

"My, my," Miles said, sinking gracefully into one of the uncomfortable chairs. "I seem to have tweaked the lion's tail. I've never known Simon to be so touchy."

"Really? I thought he was always that grumpy," Marielle said, staring after the tightly shut door, no longer interested in the refugee from *Gentleman's Quarterly* ensconced in her living room. Just when she was thinking she was beginning to understand how Simon's mind worked, he did something completely unexpected.

"Not usually," Miles said.

Marielle was still staring at the door when she realized an uncomfortable silence had fallen over the room. She turned back to her guest, once more the perfect hostess. "I'm sorry. My mind's been wandering. Did you say something?"

"I said, you don't really want me here, do you?"

Marielle stared at him for a long moment. "I'd have to be mad not to," she said bluntly, secretly appalled at her own outspokenness. For years she'd been the model of discretion; now suddenly she seemed to have no sense of polite behavior.

Miles Van Cortland grinned in appreciation. "Clearly you weren't expecting visitors. But despite Simon's heavy-handed matchmaking, which was clearly intended to do more harm than good, I would love to take you out to dinner sometime. I think we'd do better without his disapproving ghost hanging over us."

"I think it's Vittorio's ghost that worries Simon."

"No, it isn't. Simon doesn't believe in him."

"Do you?" she questioned.

The humor was suddenly, chillingly gone from Miles Van Cortland's beautiful blue eyes. "I don't want to," he said seriously.

Tiny tendrils of fear were beginning to creep up Marielle's scantily covered backbone, and she wished she could fling open the door and call for Simon to come and take Miles away before he could scare her further. But Simon was probably out of earshot and might not pay any attention even if she yelled. "You're scaring me," she said in her most even voice.

"I wouldn't want to do that. Warn you, perhaps. Things have happened here, things without rational explanation. It wouldn't do to be too smug."

Marielle just stared at him, thinking of the nightmare bed she'd be sleeping in, thinking of the midnight visitor in the deserted apartment beneath her, thinking of what might be hidden in the closed-off chimneys. "I think I'd rather discuss this in the light of day."

"What about lunch, then?"

"I think I'd better say no," Marielle said slowly, knowing she was out of her mind. The best-looking man she'd ever seen was asking her out, and she was telling him no.

"Dinner?"

"Sorry."

"What about a guided tour of your new domicile, complete with architectural history? With Simon along for moral support? Though I assure you I'm not the slightest bit dangerous. I haven't thrown myself on an unwilling female in at least ten days."

She laughed. All those beautiful features and humor, too. She was out of her mind. "I'd like that. If you have the time."

"I have the time." He rose, and Marielle realized he was

exactly Greg's height, a few inches taller than her own five foot seven. "What about Saturday for the grand tour? Neither Simon nor I work and we'd have plenty of time."

"That would be terrific."

He looked at her, his eyes slightly troubled. "In the meantime, would you do me a favor?"

"If I can."

He smiled, a rueful, self-deprecating smile. "I know this sounds crazy," he said, "and if you're feeling nervous I know you won't want me to go into details. Whether you believe in the supernatural or not, please, for your own sake, keep away from the fireplaces."

Marielle, her throat choked with creeping nervousness, could do nothing more than nod.

Chapter Six

Another miserable, disrupted night, Marielle thought with a groan, pulling herself out of bed and shivering in the cool morning air. It was six-thirty, the children were still asleep, but she didn't want to risk awakening to an audience of half the tenants two days in a row. She wasn't going to get any more sleep, no matter how desperately she needed it, and the best thing she could do was brew herself a pot of strong, dark coffee, throw on some clothes and prepare to face the day—and the myriad of problems Farnum's Castle would no doubt present.

It wasn't that she'd stayed awake listening for the eerie *tap-tap, scrape-scrape* that had never come. It wasn't that she'd been tormented by the suspicion that evil old Vittorio had breathed his last in the very bed she was lying in. Nor was she worried someone would break into her apartment if she allowed herself some desperately needed sleep.

She'd tossed and turned, dozed and then been jarred awake, for the simple reason that she couldn't get Simon Zebriskie off her mind. She was oddly attracted to him, though she knew she shouldn't be, and it was only the knowledge that it was impossible and the last thing Simon wanted that made her even entertain some fleeting, wistful thoughts. As far as she could tell, Simon was just as strange as the rest of the odd people holed up in Farnum's Castle; his eccentricities were just a little better hidden.

What she should do, she thought, pulling on clean clothes and a thick sweatshirt, was to keep her distance from him. But that left her essentially alone and friendless in the huge city of Chicago, and she didn't fancy prissy old Liam O'Donnell would offer much help. Whether Simon paid lip service to polite conventions or not, she knew she could count on him. And faced with the overwhelming problems and complexities of her new life, she needed some sort of help. Or at least a reluctant shoulder to cry on.

The children were still soundly, blissfully asleep. It was icy cold in the hallway outside their bedroom, with a sharp wind whistling through the predawn apartment. Marielle paused with her hand on the light switch. The artificial Chicago light barely penetrated the tree-filled grounds and thick, crumbling walls of Farnum's Castle, but even in the murky darkness she could tell something wasn't right.

"You've got two choices," she informed herself out loud. "Both rotten. One, the furnace conked out again. Two, your window's open, which means someone got in here last night while you were sleeping. Take your poison." And she flicked on the light switch.

Parenthood was a strange and wondrous thing, she thought absently, not moving. When panic and horror made you want to scream at the top of your lungs, some inner guard clamped down, keeping you silent, keeping you from terrifying your children when caught up in your own fright. She stared at the rubbled pile of bricks and mortar on her once-clean carpet, stared at the open window letting in a chill morning breeze, and let the stray shiver of unadulterated panic wash over her silent body.

She was still standing there, frozen in time and space, when she heard the footsteps on the creaking wooden stairs. Someone was moving stealthily, trying not to be heard. For a moment Marielle was torn between the desperate desire to rush into the children's room and make a last stand against the creature of the night stalking her, and the equally strong desire to face whatever person or persons were tormenting her.

She didn't allow herself time to hesitate. On silent bare feet she raced across the room and flung open the door to the hallway, prepared to confront chain-wielding hoodlums or the shade of old Vittorio himself. What she saw was a weary-looking Simon, trudging up the stairs, his gray-streaked hair rumpled, his eyes shadowed, a Styrofoam cup of what was no doubt the same hideous coffee in his hand.

He paused, looking at her in surprise. "What's wrong?"

It might have been the relief that it was someone safe and not the creature she'd been fearing. It might have been silliness from lack of sleep, or just something as simple as Simon knowing there was something wrong from the expression on her face in the dimly lit hallway. Whatever the reason, she hurtled across the empty hallway and threw herself into his arms.

The hot coffee went flying, splattering the hallway, splattering both of them, but Marielle was scarcely aware of it, and if Simon noticed he was too busy wrapping his long arms around her, holding her trembling body close against his own.

His jacket still held the cold from outside. He smelled of coffee and night air and clean male flesh, and he was strong and solid against her. For a long moment she closed her eyes and breathed in the smell and strength and comfort of him, allowing herself a few short moments of weakness.

And then she pushed away, just as his arms began to tighten, as his hands began to move. He let her go with unflattering haste, and she had no trouble reading his expression. It contained both relief and regret, and the relief was by far the stronger emotion.

"I repeat," he said, his deep voice unemotional as he brushed at his coffee-stained clothes. "What's wrong?"

She should have had more sense, but for some reason she couldn't resist touching him again. And he didn't seem to be able to pull back. She took his hand in both of hers and pulled him into the apartment without a word.

He stood surveying the mess, his expression inscrutable. Pulling off his venerable denim jacket and covering his hands with the material, he crossed to the window and closed it. The cessation of the cold draft was an immediate relief, and the knocking and clanging of the old radiator assured her that for now the furnace was still working.

"Did you hear anything?" Simon demanded.

"Not a sound," Marielle said. "And I was awake half the night listening for it."

Simon stared at the fireplace for a long, thoughtful moment. "This time we call the police. Stay put while I go get Julie to watch the kids."

Marielle had no intention of moving. Much as she wanted to clear away the debris, to clear away any sign of her privacy being violated, she knew better than to do so. Even Simon had had the immediate good sense not to mess with possible fingerprints.

She listened to his footsteps descending the stairs. He was no longer making any attempt to be quiet, and in retrospect she realized he'd been trying not to wake her when he'd been creeping up the stairs. The tantalizing aroma of coffee was strong in the morning air, and it took her a moment to trace it to the wet stains across her chest.

She stumbled to the kitchen area, flicked on the light and began making coffee with numb ease. Probably she shouldn't even do that—the intruder might have left fingerprints in her kitchen, but right then caffeine was even more important than catching the vandal. By the time Simon returned with a sleepy-eyed Julie she was already inhaling the perfectly brewed coffee.

"You shouldn't have touched anything," Simon said, accepting a mug.

"If I didn't have coffee I would have died, and then it wouldn't have made any difference if they caught the person who did this," she said flatly. She could see the coffee stains across his chambray work shirt, and she suspected they were a mirror image of the ones across her chest. After all, the coffee had been plastered between them during that too-brief embrace in the hallway, and it only made sense they'd be matching inkblots. If she looked at the splotchy stain with her eyes half closed she could imagine all sorts of things, none of them particularly healthy for her peace of mind.

"There's milk in the refrigerator," Simon informed Julie, ignoring Marielle as he drained half the mug of steaming coffee without flinching. "Drink some, and then you can have coffee."

Marielle waited for Julie to take offense, but all the young girl did was stick out her tongue at him. "I prefer Diet Pepsi."

"Bellywash," Simon sneered. "After you drink some milk. Marielle and I won't be gone too long."

"Take your time," Julie said with an airy wave, moving into the kitchen and peering into the refrigerator. "If the kids wake up I'll take 'em down to Esmy's to watch cartoons."

Marielle considered protesting, then swallowed her objections. So what if her kids had eaten more sugar and watched more TV in the last forty-eight hours than they had in their entire lives? The two of them were thriving, showing more life than they had in the six months since Greg had died, and she could just make them brush their teeth six times a day. As for television, it would take more than a little black box to put a dent in Emily's fevered imagination.

She refilled her mug of coffee before she followed

Simon's rangy figure out the door. On a day that had begun as inauspiciously as this one, she was going to need all the caffeine she could get. She wondered briefly what her friend Jaime would say if she could see her now. Jaime had always had the ridiculous notion that Marielle could deal with anything, and do it with calm good humor. Right now Marielle felt like flinging herself onto the winding stairs and weeping in frustration and worry. But she wasn't going to let Simon see her anxiety, just as she had never let Jaime see it. Coping was second nature to her, and there were times that came in awfully handy, times like these. But she wished to hell there was some point when she could just give way and howl and let someone else cope, for a change.

Simon ignored the telephone in the hallway, opening his apartment door and gesturing for her to enter. Marielle stopped, staring suspiciously. "You don't lock your apartment?"

"Who would I keep out? Esmy?"

"Maybe whoever trashed my apartment and the one beneath me," she suggested, still not moving.

"I hate to point this out, but locked doors didn't do any good in either case. Besides, I always lose my keys."

"Aren't we going to use the telephone?" she stalled.

"We're going to use the one in my apartment. That way if someone comes up to use the telephone they won't overhear something that will put them in a panic."

"I thought you put the telephone in the hall because you couldn't stand having one in the apartment?"

He stood in the doorway for a long moment. "So I lied. The people in the apartment building need a telephone, and no one else can afford one. I tried to get the phone company to put it on the first floor so it would be easier to reach, but they were, as usual, obstructionist. If there's one thing I've kept from the sixties it's a strong distrust of the phone company." He tilted his head to one side, staring at her through hooded eyes. "Are you going to stand there in the hallway asking more questions or are we going to call the police?"

"We'll call the police."

His apartment wasn't at all what she would have expected, but when she thought about it she realized it was exactly right for him. While she might have thought he'd live in austere, Eastern simplicity or modular, streamlined yuppie heaven, the jumbled, cluttered, homey feel to the place attested to a man who knew what he wanted. At least one apartment in the decrepit old building had recently been painted, and the old horror movie posters on the white walls were an oddly cheerful splash of color. The furniture was old and comfortable, the bookcases were piled haphazardly with books and magazines, the Oriental rug had the pattern almost walked off it. And it was warm, blissfully, gloriously warm.

"How come you've got the only apartment with decent heat in it?" she demanded, sinking onto the old sofa and wrapping herself in its sprawling comfort. She let out a surreptitious sigh, setting her coffee on the cluttered table in front of her. There were times when she'd thought she'd die for a bed as comfortable as this tattered old couch.

He had an odd expression on his face as he stood by the window, watching her nestle into his sofa, one she couldn't begin to read and didn't have the energy to try. "That's one of the problems of old-fashioned steam heat. There's one thermostat, all the heat rises, and the people on the top floors roast while the people lower down freeze. Esmy and Granita need the heat a hell of a lot more than I do, but they don't need a five-floor climb. So we all live with it."

"Will the new boiler even things out? Assuming I can even dig up the money for it." She stretched out her long legs on the cushions, surveying her dusty bare feet for a moment. When she'd gotten dressed that morning she hadn't expected to be leaving the apartment so soon, and it was the first time she'd realized she was barefoot.

He was watching her feet, too. "I don't know. It couldn't hurt."

"I don't want to spend that much money on something that has only a vague chance of helping."

"Do you have any alternative?"

Marielle shut her eyes for a pained moment. "Let's not talk about it now. Do you want to call the police or shall I?"

"Oh, you can definitely do the honors. I'm not crazy about the police, either."

"Along with the phone company," she said. "What sort of life of crime did you lead?"

Simon's smile was wintry. "Let's just say they wouldn't let me on the supreme court."

Marielle sat up abruptly. "I hope this was all part of your sordid past?"

"It's none of your damned business," he said, leaning against the wall, his shoulder resting against Colin Clive as Dr. Frankenstein. "But yes, it's all part of my distant past. Sins, however, have a habit of backfiring on the sinner."

"Yes, they do," she said. "Do you have any other sins waiting to catch up with you?"

He pushed away from the wall. "Maybe," he said, his deep voice giving nothing away. "The telephone's beside the couch. But don't expect a whole lot of help from the cops. They've been here too many times checking out treasure hunters to get too excited about the latest rash of breaking and entering."

"Even though I and my children were asleep in the same apartment?" Marielle demanded, incensed.

"They didn't bother you, did they? Didn't even wake you up. I don't think Chicago's finest are going to break their hearts over it. There's too much real crime going on."

Marielle crossed her legs under her. "I think you must be the most cynical man I know."

"Maybe. But if I were you I wouldn't take Miles Van Cortland at face value, either. Beneath that golden yuppie charm lurks the heart of a shark. Are you going to go out with him?"

"Why don't you ask Miles?"

"He wouldn't tell me. Are you?"

"Why do you want to know?"

Simon shrugged. "I went to all that trouble to matchmake for you; I'd like to know if I was successful."

Marielle reached for the phone. "You got just what you wanted, Simon," she said obscurely, dialing 911.

Simon glared at her. "I'm very happy for both of you. Let me know when the big date is and I'll make sure Julie can baby-sit."

"I can take care of my own baby-sitters, thank you," she said in a tranquil voice that was calculated to drive him crazy. "Julie and I have an understanding."

"Great," growled Simon. "Terrific." And he stomped into another room, presumably the kitchen, and began banging pots and pans around with great enthusiasm.

She found him a few minutes later, staring disconsolately into a mug of black coffee. The jar of instant sat out on the counter, and Marielle gave it a passing grimace. "You were right," she said, hoisting herself onto the spotless butcher-block counter and swinging her legs. "The police weren't very excited about the whole thing. They promised they'd send someone over later today, but I don't think we're going to get the full attention of the Chicago police department."

"I warned you," Simon said.

"Want to say 'I told you so' just to make things even pleasanter?" she suggested sweetly.

A small smile tugged at the corner of his mouth. If she'd been into mouths she knew she'd find his mouth particularly attractive. It was lucky she didn't care about such things, or Simon Zebriskie might be extremely distracting.

"I told you so," he said.

"Wretch. And don't even bother to offer me instant coffee. I'd rather drink Drano."

"I don't think I have any."

"What I don't understand," she said, looking around her at the spotless little room, "is why you keep your kitchen so neat? I've never in my life known a man to have such a clean kitchen."

"Sexist," he said mildly, pouring the rest of his coffee into the sink. "I don't think you want to know why my kitchen is so clean."

Marielle just stared at him. "Why?" she asked in a doomed voice.

"Cockroaches."

"Oh, God!" she moaned. "I thought that was one thing I left behind in New York."

"I didn't think cockroaches lived in the Upper East Side. I thought they were confined to the West Side and the Village."

"Sometimes," Marielle said, "they get forged papers and cross Central Park at night where they take over nice new apartment buildings like Yorktown Towers and drive fastidious housekeepers crazy."

"Are you a fastidious housekeeper?" Simon asked with real curiosity.

"I am when someone's holding a gun to my head. Be it a demanding husband or an army of cockroaches. I thought I could relax my standards a bit here."

"Be my guest. That way my cockroaches will always know where they can find a good meal."

"Damn," she said, shaking her head. "A dying boiler, a huge electric bill, poverty-stricken tenants, vandals, and now cockroaches. What else can possibly go wrong?"

"You haven't talked to the tax assessor yet."

She glared at him. "You know," she said in a conversational tone, "you're so nice to Julie and the old ladies. Don't you think you might consider being nice to me, too?"

He shook his head. "Can't do it. I have a very limited supply of kindness for my fellow man, and they use it all up. You'll have to make do with what's left. Besides, you're not in need like the rest of them."

"Not in need of kindness?" Her voice came out just the tiniest bit rough. For some totally bizarre reason she felt like crying, she who never cried, she who was calm and capable and good-humored and always in control. "Don't you think everyone needs a little kindness?"

If she didn't know better she would have thought that was guilt shadowing his gray eyes. "Sure," he said. "But maybe being kind to you would prove dangerous to my peace of mind. You'll have to count on Miles for kindness."

"I don't think that's a very good idea," she said. "I don't think I'd trust Miles not to be out for number one."

"Would you trust me?" The moment the words were out of his mouth it was clear he regretted them, but Marielle answered before he could call them back.

"Yes," she said. "I'd trust you." He wasn't very far away, less than a foot from where her legs hung over the counter. His eyes had a fine network of lines fanning out from them, and she wondered if those lines came from smiling, if there was someone he smiled with, laughed with, joked with. For some odd reason she wanted to reach out and smooth the frown away from his narrow, clever face, to push the thick, straight hair from his high forehead....

She jumped back, shocked at her wayward thoughts. There was a strange light in his eyes, and for a moment she wondered if he'd read her mind. But the moment passed.

"I don't know if you should," he said, and she stared at him blankly. "Trust me, that is."

"I don't think I'm going to get much help from the police," she said, deliberately changing the subject to one more prosaic. "Are you telling me you won't help, either?"

"I'll tell you what." He moved closer so that his hipbone was millimeters away from her knee. "I'll help you find out who's breaking into the apartments, I'll help you get things sorted out with the electric company, the tax assessor and the heating contractor. I'll help you get everything under control," he said, "and then you can leave."

"Why should I want to leave?"

"You do, don't you? You don't want to spend your life in this ramshackle old building with a bunch of crazies. You want to live someplace clean and warm and sunny. Like New Mexico."

Marielle stared at him for a long moment. For a moment she hated him, hated herself for being that transparent. But her anger would have been a waste of time, and she prided herself on being levelheaded and practical. "How am I going to do that?"

"I'm not sure. But I'm going to do everything I can to help you, starting with finding out who's been haunting Farnum's Castle. If worse comes to worst we'll find someone who'll buy you out, someone who won't tear down the place and turn it into a high rise or a parking lot. We'll find an answer," he said, "and you'll find your freedom."

"You'd be going to a lot of effort to get rid of me," she said evenly.

He didn't even blink. "I consider it a worthy investment of my time."

"I accept it. I'm not in the position to turn down anyone's help." She started to scoot down from the high counter, and almost instinctively his hands went around her.

Then he stopped, so that she was halfway off the counter, his long, strong fingers wrapped around her waist, his eyes

level with hers, his mouth level with hers—and dangerously, enticingly close. For a moment neither of them
moved, and the silence grew and stretched in the small,
spotless kitchen. And then she deliberately broke the moment, pushing away from him, landing on the floor, moving
from the room with undignified haste.

"Will you come down when the police show up?" she
asked, tugging down her sweatshirt, keeping her eyes on
her toes.

"Just send Julie up."

"What if you're asleep?"

"I'll wake up."

"Okay," she said, looking at the faded carpet in the
living room, looking at the bottom of the apartment door.
"See you."

"If you don't lift your head you're going to bump into
the wall," he drawled.

She did lift her head at that, staring at him defiantly.
"New Mexico," she said sharply, "will be a definite improvement."

"Keep remembering that," he said. "And I'll keep reminding you."

Chapter Seven

Simon was dead wrong, Marielle thought hours later as she hurried along the sidewalk, ducking her head into the wind as she headed for the closest thing to a supermarket this side of Evanston. The police had been blessedly, wonderfully helpful, so much so that she was practically dancing down the street. In a fit of good humor she'd even promised the kids Alpha-Bits, telling herself that if they weren't nutritional at least they were educational, and she had every intention of buying *TV Guide*. Simon had sent down an old thirteen-inch color television, insisting that he had no need for it, and the children were in seventh heaven, absorbed in *Sesame Street* while she dealt with the late-arriving police.

And now she was on her own in the early evening streets of Chicago. The area around Farnum's Castle was genteelly run-down—an old residential area becoming gracefully seedy, not unlike the tenants of her decrepit apartment building. Not that she'd call Simon gracefully seedy, she thought with a smile. She could think of a thousand adjectives, words like cynical, nonconformist, gruff, bad-tempered, charming, protective, attractive....

Not that she was attracted to him, mind you. She had too much common sense for that. Eight years of married life had been enough, enough to hold her for at least eight years of single life. She wasn't going to let herself in for more disappointment if she could help it, and she was too levelheaded to fall into any romantic traps. Not that Simon would set one for her. He had no intention of getting involved with her, thank heaven. All he wanted to do was get her out of there, and she'd accept his help quite happily.

Traffic was light that time of night—rush hour had ended early and midweek wasn't prime shopping time. The crisp autumn air had just enough bite to be invigorating, Marielle knew her kids were safe and sound with Julie watching them, and she'd had her first bit of good news concerning the old wreck she'd inherited. She couldn't wait to tell Simon, to have her own chance to say "I told you so."

She was spending much too much time thinking about Simon, she thought absently. She was almost more interested in his reaction to her good news than the import of that stroke of luck itself.

Simon had been true to his word, coming downstairs when Officers Toody and Muldoon had arrived. While he'd gone off with the tall, skinny Toody, Marielle had been left with the rubicund Muldoon—the cheery Muldoon who, along with his wife and three children had a brother-in-law crammed into his small suburban house, a brother-in-law who was a licensed plumber and electrician. Licensed, that is, in the faraway hills of New Hampshire, not in the union-dominated heart of Chicago. On top of that, the young man was no longer interested in practicing such noble arts—instead he wished to find himself by writing hard-boiled detective novels. There not being a vast market for unwritten novels, Dennis McMurtry was sponging off his long-suffering brother-in-law and fast wearing out his welcome.

And blessed Officer Muldoon, upon viewing the empty apartment with the broken water pipes, had suggested a trade. A free apartment in exchange for Dennis McMurtry's precious talents.

"What makes you think he'll go for it?" Marielle had asked, not daring to believe her luck.

"He'll go for it," Muldoon had said grimly. "Have you ever shared a bedroom with a five-year-old and a seven-year-old? Mind you, he's great with them. But the man's ready for a place of his own. I'll have him call you the moment I get home."

"I don't have a telephone."

"I'll have him appear on your doorstep the moment I can get him out of the house," Muldoon promised with a streak of ruthlessness. And Marielle had not the slightest doubt that he would.

She'd still have to pay for supplies, pipes and fittings and wiring and the like. But at least, if this worked out, she wouldn't be saddled with a hundred dollars an hour or whatever plumbers and electricians cost nowadays. Once Dennis turned into the next Elmore Leonard and moved to Lake Shore Drive she'd have a usable apartment to rent. And chances were a plumber-electrician even knew about boilers and heating systems. Things were definitely looking up.

She wasn't quite so sanguine half an hour later as she struggled back up the sidewalk, cursing her own stupidity. She'd lived in a city long enough to know you couldn't buy too much at a grocery store if you had to carry it all yourself, but remembering her empty refrigerator and enticed by the rows of food, she'd simply forgotten. The Diet Pepsi alone weighed at least five pounds, the Alpha-Bits kept slipping out of the bag, the gallon of milk that would last her not much more than a day weighed a ton, and the Ben and Jerry's Ice Cream was melting, pressed as it was to her breast. To top it all off, some lowlife in a beaten up old Mustang was slowing down as she did her best to hurry along, clutching the bags that seemed determined to take a suicide leap to the cracked sidewalk.

Marielle kept her head averted, knowing with a sinking

heart that the unseen driver was rolling down his window, bracing herself for some obscene proposition or at least a sexist comment. The streets were relatively empty and she allowed herself a tiny tendril of fear. Would the unknown people of Chicago help a woman in trouble, or were they just as apathetic as New Yorkers?

The driver leaned his head out of the window. "Don't you know better than to buy too much at one time?" Simon's deep voice demanded. "You could at least have asked me to drive you."

Marielle stopped dead still, and the bag with the Pepsi slid to the ground with a clang. "I didn't realize you had a car," she said. Then her eyes surveyed the battered old wreck. "I'm still not sure you do," she added dubiously.

"Beggars can't be choosers. Do you want a ride back to the apartment or not?"

"I want a ride back to the apartment." She slipped into the cracked leather seat, dumping her groceries at her feet. "Why in heaven's name do you drive such a rattletrap? I thought you were some lowlife about to come on to me."

"I drive it because it runs," he said, pulling into the nonexistent traffic and heading toward Farnum's Castle. "And what makes you think I'm not a lowlife?"

Are you coming on to me? she couldn't help but wonder, then quickly wiped the thought from her docile mind as she settled back in the bucket seat. The dashboard was cracked and so was the windshield, the engine had clearly seen better days, and she knew if she looked behind her there'd be a trail of greasy black smoke. The radio was turned so low it was almost inaudible, and without thinking she reached forward to turn it up.

His hand shot out and caught hers. "I'm not in the mood to listen to Miles Van Cortland," he grumbled.

"Why not?"

"All he plays is stuff calculated to put you to sleep. Soft, easy-listening garbage that's been proven to melt your brain.''

Marielle laughed. "What do you play?''

"Anything I damned well please. That's one of the reasons I work at WAKS. There's no playlist, no restriction. I can play Erma Franklin singing 'Piece of my Heart', and I can play yuppie muzak like George Winston. I can play Miles Davis and Otis Redding and Queen Ida and even Reba MacEntire if I'm in the mood.''

"I heard you playing John Denver a couple of nights ago,'' she said. "The one about 'You fill up my senses.'''

"A momentary aberration. I'm over it. Why didn't you ask me to drive you to the store?'' he asked abruptly.

Marielle shrugged. "Several reasons. Number one, I didn't know you had a car—such as it is,'' she added mischievously. "Number two, I'm already asking a lot from you. I didn't want to wear out my welcome.''

"I told you, I'm willing,'' he said, turning onto the rutted driveway and speeding past the old house to a tumbledown three-stall garage behind it.

"I hadn't even realized this was here,'' she marveled as she climbed out of the car.

"If you decided to evict the old ladies it could be a strong selling point, if you want to rent to yuppies.'' There was no mistaking the disapproval in his voice.

"I've got a better idea,'' she returned sweetly. "Why not make Esmerelda and Granita sleep out here? We'll get a little straw, maybe even throw in a sleeping bag or two....''

"Okay, okay. I realize you're not going to kick them out.''

"You, on the other hand, are more than expendable. And you could always sleep in your car.''

"I'm six feet three inches tall, Marielle. I don't fit in a Mustang. A Cadillac, maybe.''

"Then it's a shame your tastes don't run to Cadillacs." She struggled toward the house with her two bags clasped to her chest, but Simon blocked her way.

"Are you going to give me one of those bags?"

"No."

"All right." Without any warning he reached out to take one, his hand slipping down between the bag and her chest, sliding against her breast before he pulled the groceries away. He grinned at her shocked expression. "It's best not to thwart me," he said. "I don't put too much stock in polite conventions when I want my own way."

A bra, a camisole, a turtleneck, a flannel shirt and a sweatshirt lay between him and his momentary, supposedly inadvertent caress. So why was her flesh tingling? "Do that again," she said in a strangled voice, "and I'll break your arm."

"You and who else?" he taunted, clearly enjoying her temper.

There was a full moon that night, and a strong breeze sent the leaves scudding from the trees, lifted the mane of hair from the back of her neck, tumbled his gray-streaked hair into his too discerning eyes. It was all cool and crisp and strangely beautiful, and Marielle let out her pent-up breath and her anger with a sigh. "You're going to drive me crazy, Simon," she said, shaking her head.

"Not me. Maybe your midnight intruder, but not me. Are we going in, or are we going to stand out here like something out of *Wuthering Heights*?"

"We are going in."

"Good," he said. "Then you can tell me who the hell Dennis McMurtry is."

Marielle merely smiled mysteriously. "Is he here?"

"He is. With three suitcases and a typewriter. He says he's a writer and he's come to live with you."

"Well," she said, scuffling through the leaves as she

headed for the front of the house, "that's true. I don't suppose there's a back entrance to the castle, is there?"

"Don't change the subject. The back porch is boarded up—it's unsafe. We almost lost a meter reader there a couple of years ago. How long have you known McMurtry? I didn't realize you were involved with someone. I wouldn't have bothered to set you up with Miles if I'd known."

Marielle stopped for a moment to smile back at him. "I'm not going to tell you a thing, Simon," she said. "So stop asking."

"Why aren't you going to tell me a thing?" They'd reached the front door by then, and Simon blocked the door, clutching her battered bag of groceries and glowering at her in the unnatural light.

"Because it drives you crazy." She ducked under his arm and went inside, not even considering the death trap of an elevator. Simon wasn't far behind her, and she could sense his disapproval spreading over her like a vast dark cloud. That disapproval was oddly like jealousy. For a man who said he was determined to both match her up with someone and get her out of the state, it seemed a pretty strange emotion. But then Simon Zebriskie, like most of the people in the building, was slightly, delightfully strange.

It took Marielle one look at Dennis McMurtry to realize what was bugging Simon. As she dealt with two small figures hurtling themselves at her in an excess of delight, she glanced up and saw her new tenant. And she saw the light shining in Julie's eyes when her young friend thought no one was looking.

Not that Dennis had anywhere near Miles Van Cortland's phenomenal good looks. He appeared to be in his late twenties, with curly auburn hair, a pugnacious tilt to his jaw, frankly freckled skin and a pair of merry brown eyes. But he was young and strong and handsome, and even if Marielle had not the faintest interest in such things, Simon didn't know that.

"You must be Mrs. Brandt," Dennis said artlessly, coming up and shaking her hand with boyish enthusiasm.

"Marielle," she corrected. "This is another one of the tenants, Simon Zebriskie."

"Simon Zee!" Dennis said, dropping her hand and grabbing Simon's with even more delight. "Man, I used to watch you when I was a kid. Used to scare the bejesus out of me when you'd throw cauliflowers around and call them brains."

"What happened to that fun-loving creature?" Marielle murmured plaintively.

"And I listen to you on the radio whenever I'm up late. What're you doing on such a chicken-feed radio station like WAKS, anyway?"

"Yes, I wondered that myself," Marielle said, enjoying Simon's discomfiture. Clearly he wasn't used to hero worship, but he was having a hard time disliking such an obvious fan.

"Penance," said Simon obscurely. "If you didn't know Marielle, how come you're moving in with her?"

"I'm not. I'm moving into an empty apartment so I can finish my novel."

"A writer," Simon said in a resigned voice. "I don't suppose you have any money?"

"Not a cent," Dennis said cheerfully.

"And you're not planning to pay rent?"

"Not a cent."

Simon nodded as if his worst fears were confirmed. "Not that we aren't thrilled to have you, Dennis," he said, his voice deep and slow, "but none of the empty apartments are habitable. If they were, I'd think Marielle would rather have someone with a little more wherewithal...."

"Shut up, Simon," Marielle said sweetly. "Dennis is Officer Muldoon's brother-in-law."

"I see. So we get special police protection by giving you shelter?"

"I imagine Francis will have a vested interest in keeping this place safe and keeping me out of his hair," Dennis agreed. "But I think Marielle was more taken with the fact that I hold licenses as both a plumber and electrician. The licenses are only good in New Hampshire, but I don't imagine my lovely landlord cares about that. And I've even had some experience with your type of heating system. I took the liberty of checking it out on my way up here. I'm a firm believer in staying warm."

"So am I," said Marielle, taking in Simon's reaction with absolute delight. It was even better than saying "I told you so."

"By the way, if I were you I'd keep that basement locked. The whole place is wide open to whoever might wander in off the street. If you're having trouble with breaking and entering you ought to at least use a few locks. It might discourage some of the less dedicated criminal element in our fair city."

"You're an expert on that, too?" Simon grumbled.

Dennis grinned. "Didn't like me calling her lovely, did you? Message received, over and out. But I've picked up a few pointers from Muldoon. And locking doors is only common sense."

"I don't have any claim on Marielle." Simon was instantly defensive. "You can call her anything you please."

"Sure thing, man," Dennis said. "Hands off."

"Listen...." Simon's voice was definitely warning, and Marielle decided it was time to intervene. Julie was still practically hiding in the kitchen, watching Dennis McMurtry out of absurdly vulnerable old-young eyes. Hiding, Marielle realized, behind the chest-high partition.

Sorrow and sympathy knifed through her, and she wished with all her heart that there was some way to spare Julie, to shield her from the hurts that seemed to be hanging over her like a dark rain cloud. But there was no way she could, and no way Julie could spend the next two or three weeks hiding behind partitions whenever an attractive man turned up.

"Why don't you take Dennis down and show him the apartment, Julie?" she suggested.

"Hey, that would be great," Dennis said. "We were having a good time talking, waiting for you. Your folks live here, Julie?"

"I'm on my own," she said with her usual defiance, moving slowly from behind the barrier.

Dennis didn't even blink, and Marielle's initial positive response positively blossomed. "I know what you mean," he said. "I left home when I was seventeen. Joined the navy and saw the world when I was too young and dumb to know any better." He continued chattering in an amiable voice as he followed Julie's cumbersome figure out the door. "See you tomorrow, landlady," he shot back over his shoulder.

"Tomorrow, Dennis." The door shut behind them, leaving her alone with Simon. "He wasn't coming on to her, was he?" she added, a sudden worry assailing her.

"I doubt it. He's nothing more than a great friendly puppy dog. The only one he'd be coming on to is you."

Marielle shook her head. "Trust me, Simon. He's not interested."

"That's good," he growled.

"Is it?"

"Yup. I'd hate to have my matchmaking for Miles go down the tubes."

"That would be a tragedy," she said in her iciest tone.

Her obvious hostility seemed to cheer Simon. "In the meantime, maybe I'll check out the basement and lock everything I can. The boy's right—it doesn't hurt to take a few precautions, even if your midnight caller has been coming in through the windows."

"Dennis has to be thirty if he's a day."

"Dennis," Simon said, "is young enough to be my son."

"Go away, Simon."

"I'm going. You going to call Dennis if old Vittorio's ghost comes visiting?"

"You'll be gone, won't you?"

"Not tonight. Even the graveyard shift gets a few nights off every now and then."

"Then I'm going to call you," she said. "Unless you have some objections."

"No objections. I promised to help, didn't I?"

Marielle stared at him for a long, breathless moment. "Do you always keep your promises?"

He didn't even need to think about it. "No," he said, and there was an odd note of pain in his voice. "But I'll keep that one. Good night, Marielle. Have a peaceful night."

"If Vittorio will let me," Marielle said. "Good night, Simon." And she stood there a long time without moving as she listened to the sound his footsteps down the hallway outside her door.

Chapter Eight

Marielle slid between the chilly sheets, deliberately averting her gaze from the gargoyles overhead, prepared to enjoy her first decent night of sleep since she'd packed up the kids and moved to Chicago. There were no guarantees, of course, but her instincts told her that there'd be no midnight visitors, no ghostly tappings, no open windows and trashed fireplaces.

Maybe it was the knowledge that Simon would be home tonight, right above her, well within screaming distance. And Dennis would be underneath, Dennis who looked strong and brave and had a cop for a brother-in-law. Marielle felt safer than she had in a long, long time, and she was fully prepared to enjoy the effect by sleeping soundly through the night.

She could hear the rumble of voices in the apartment beneath her—Julie and Dennis must still be talking. She was a fool to worry about Julie's well-being. The girl was far more levelheaded than most women twice her age. She might have made a mistake once, but Marielle knew for certain she wasn't about to repeat that mistake. And Simon was right—Dennis certainly didn't seem the type to take advantage.

No, they'd be fine, she assured herself, sinking into the soft mattress. Julie needed all the friends she could get in her current predicament, and Dennis was nothing if not friendly. Things were finally beginning to improve.

Three hours later she wasn't so sure. The bright full moon shone directly in her window, into her eyes. She lay there, jarred out of sleep, cursing the moonlight and wondering which of her sheets she could turn into curtains, when the sound came again. Someone in her apartment was crying.

Adrenalin shot through her body, as it had in similar situations since the day her first child had been born. Within seconds she was out of bed and in the next room. Christopher slept as soundly as he always did—nothing short of a nuclear war could wake him. But Emily lay in her cot, eyes shut, face contorted in grief, tears pouring down her face.

"Oh, baby," Marielle murmured, bending over the precariously unsteady little bed and scooping Emily into her arms. Her little body was hot, damp and tense, the tears rolled down her pale face, and she huddled against her mother for nameless comfort. Marielle realized with sudden shock that her daughter was still soundly, deeply asleep.

Her own form of despair washed over Marielle. In the six months since Greg had died Emily had been as quietly in control as her mother, and Marielle had hoped her instincts were wrong, hoped that beneath Emily's quiet, calm demeanor there didn't lurk a ravaged heart. Clearly her hope had been vain. When sleep came and ripped away her five-year-old daughter's defenses, grief took over, and she wept against her mother's chest with all the hopelessness of a child who has lost her father.

They sat that way for a long time, Emily weeping in her mother's lap, Marielle murmuring meaningless, soothing phrases as she smoothed the tumbled hair away from her daughter's sleeping, tear-streaked face. Gradually the tears abated, the tense little body relaxed into a deeper sleep, and with a great, shuddering sigh Emily released Marielle's flannel nightgown from her tight fists.

Slowly, carefully Marielle settled her back into the folding cot. Emily's breathing was deep and peaceful once more; the pain that had surfaced through her sleep had for the moment left her. But Marielle's pain had just begun.

She left the children's door ajar as she tiptoed into the hall, hugging herself in the cool night air. And then she heard the crying again. This time from her living room.

LATE-NIGHT TELEVISION STANK, Simon thought, pressing the remote control that was one of his few concessions to the video age. The nineteen-inch screen went blank, and only the overhead light from the kitchen illuminated the sprawling apartment.

He was stretched out on the overstuffed sofa, dressed in baggy gray sweatpants and an old black T-shirt, hot as always. If Dennis really could even out the heating system in Farnum's Castle he'd be a friend for life, despite the overwhelming cheeriness of the man. Simon sincerely doubted he could deal with that engaging grin first thing in the morning, but with luck their hours would be very different and he'd only have to put up with Dennis's overwhelming bonhomie when he'd already spent part of his day dealing with the other petty annoyances of life in the nineteen-eighties.

Of course, Simon thought, flipping onto his stomach, maybe Marielle liked that good-natured boyish charm. If Dennis could just abandon his literary pretensions, get his Illinois license and join a union, the guy would make more than enough to support the Brandt family in decent style. Maybe he should forget about Miles and see what he could do about matchmaking for his newest neighbors.

No, that wasn't an option. He couldn't see Marielle in the midst of middle-class suburbia, married to a plumber. Actually he couldn't see her married to an elitist sleaze like

Miles, either. Maybe he should give up matchmaking altogether and concentrate his energies on simply getting her out of Chicago. The longer she stayed the more tempting she was, and he was too old and too smart to give in to temptation. Wasn't he?

It was after three in the morning. Instead of lying on the couch thinking about the woman beneath him, he should go to bed and try to get some sleep. That was the problem with working nights—he never could sleep on his day off. If he were a reasonable person he'd take one of the jobs offered him at the bigger stations in town. Jobs that offered benefits, a much higher salary and whatever hours he chose. Jobs that offered fame and fortune. Jobs that he simply wouldn't allow himself to take.

Penance, he'd told Dennis earlier, knowing there was too much going on for anyone to take him up on it. And in the dark of night, with the bright full moon shining in and the wind whipping the leaves off the trees, he knew he hadn't completed his atonement. Old Vittorio would have approved, he thought with a mirthless grin. The old scoundrel had spent the last fifteen years of his wicked life atoning for his sins. Maybe there was something about Farnum's Castle that brought out the penitential in all of them.

He couldn't see Marielle donning sackcloth and ashes. He probably didn't have to worry about fixing her up with anyone. A few more months of widowhood and she'd get tired of a cloistered existence. She'd go out and find someone on her own. It was up to him to remind her she'd have an easier time of it in New Mexico.

Why did life have to get so complicated? Twenty years ago he couldn't have cared less about scruples and penance; twenty years ago he would have taken the best-paying job he could find, have gotten Marielle Brandt into bed as fast as he could, and dropped both when something better came along. Nowadays he thought about consequences and debts and honor and fairness, not money and lust. Well, he amended, not so much about lust.

If only he at least had the satisfaction of knowing he was a better person for it. But the truth was that he'd been much more self-satisfied at twenty-two than he was now. Nowadays he saw himself clearly, too clearly. And if that clarity of vision meant his life was a little less comfortable than it could have been, then that was his choice.

He pushed himself off the sofa, heading through the dim, moonlit apartment for his bedroom. Maybe if he pulled the curtains he'd be able to sleep. Maybe if he could just think about something pleasant, like *Night of the Living Dead*, he wouldn't have to think about Marielle Brandt. But maybe nothing in this world or the next was going to keep him from fantasizing, as hopeless as he knew it was.

MARIELLE HESITATED for only a moment. It didn't matter who was crying in her living room. Whether it was some petty criminal regretting his vandalism, the ghost of one of Vittorio's victims or one of her hapless tenants, her course was clear. Someone was in pain, in need of comfort, and Marielle was too much of a mother to ignore that need.

She didn't turn on the living-room light, but there was no need. The moonlight pouring in the windows illuminated Julie's bulky figure huddled on the sofa, and the muffled sobs and groans sent a sudden panic through Marielle.

She rushed to her side, sinking onto the cushions and drawing the girl's trembling body into her arms. "Julie," she whispered, hugging her tightly. "Is it the baby? Is the baby coming early?"

Julie lifted her tear-streaked face, trying to swallow her choking sobs. "No," she said in a hushed, raspy voice. "The baby's fine."

"Then what is it? Did someone hurt you? Did Dennis...?" She finally allowed her doubts to surface.

"Dennis didn't do anything," Julie said, fiercely defensive. "He's good and kind."

"Then what is it?"

"I just wish," Julie said on a choked sob, "that I'd met him some other time." And her strangled weeping began again in earnest.

Marielle held her tight, brushing the tangled hair away from her brow, murmuring soothing, meaningless words, the same words she'd just murmured to her daughter. She could come up with no answers, no easy solutions, either for Emily or for Julie. Greg was dead, and all a child's misery or a mother's wanting couldn't bring him back. Julie was eighteen, alone and eight and a half months pregnant, and nothing but time would change that. All Marielle could do was comfort the wounded and curse her own helplessness.

Finally Julie's tears slowed to a halt. "Tissue," she mumbled, and Marielle released her to go in search of a box. Then she sat down beside her again, waiting while Julie blew her nose, wiped her face and pulled her courage back around her.

"Feeling better?" Marielle murmured.

Julie's shy, embarrassed smile was a revelation. "Yes, thank you. I'm sorry I had to bother you like that, but Esmy sleeps very lightly, and I don't like her to know when things get too much for me sometimes. She takes things so to heart, you know."

"What about you? Don't you take things to heart?"

Julie tossed back her tangled length of dark hair. "I'm tough," she said, and Marielle had no doubt about that one. "I've had to be, growing up around here."

"Julie, where are your parents? Where is your family? Shouldn't they be with you at a time like this?"

Bleakness shuttered Julie's features. "Not if you ask them. My ma's dead, my old man's ashamed of me, and his girlfriend was glad of an excuse to kick me out. I wouldn't go back there if they crawled on their hands and knees; I wouldn't go back there if they paid me. If you kick me out I'll work the streets before I'll..."

"No one's going to kick you out, Julie," Marielle said firmly. "We're your family now."

Julie managed a watery grin. "It didn't take you long to figure that out. How long have you been here—two days?"

"Three." *And I'd kill for a decent night's sleep,* Marielle added to herself.

"Do you mind if I spend the rest of the night here? I told Esmy you thought you might need some help."

"Sure. But I don't have a bed...."

"I like the floor. My back's been killing me, and the only place I can get comfortable is on something hard. Trust me, I'll be fine."

"Okay," Marielle said. "As a matter of fact, I did want to use the telephone...."

"Don't worry; I'll keep an ear out for the kids. They trust me; I don't think they'd mind if they woke up and found me here."

"No, I don't think they would. Thank you, Julie."

"No problem."

Marielle looked down at the tough, determined woman-child in front of her. "No problem," she echoed.

She grabbed the first thing she could find, an old black shawl, and wrapped it around her flannel nightgown. She didn't bother with slippers—it grew progressively warmer as one headed up the last flight of stairs, and she knew she'd be quite comfortable curled up in the chair outside Simon's apartment. She was suddenly in a desperate hurry to get out of her apartment, away from witnesses, away from her own overwhelming need to be strong and nurturing.

"Emily's been awake once," she said, pausing at the door, surprised to feel the tightness in her own throat. "She shouldn't wake up again, but come and get me if she does. I'll be in the hallway...."

"She'll be fine," Julie said. "Take your time."

It was cold in the hallway, as it always was. For one brief moment Marielle considered ghosts, considered whether she ought to be roaming Farnum's Castle in the middle of the night with no more protection than a pair of powerful lungs. She could have at least taken a rolling pin from the kitchen. Except that in her unorganized kitchen there were no rolling pins. There was nothing more lethal than a paring knife and a pizza cutter.

Simon would be sound asleep, she thought as she ran swiftly, silently up the stairs. She could hide out in that comfortable chair and do what she'd needed to do for the past hour, for the past week, for the past year. She'd cry.

There was no one she could turn to, no one's shoulder she could cry on. Somewhere downstairs in one of the unpacked boxes was her address book with Jaime's new phone number. But Jaime would have been the last person Marielle would have chosen to call. Jaime thought Marielle was strong and wise and brave, in control of everything, the perfect earth mother, everything her own glamorous mother hadn't been. It would probably do her some good to find out Marielle had feet of clay.

But at that moment Marielle had no interest in anyone else's well-being. She was burned-out, incapable of taking care of one more lost soul. For an hour or two, alone in Simon's hallway, she was going to think of nothing but herself.

She didn't even have Suzanne's phone number. Not that Suzanne would have been much help in her current predicament—she wasn't the nurturing type, either. She'd offer Marielle a few wisecracks to cheer her up, suggest she take up smoking, and probably offer to send her daughter Mouse back to baby-sit.

Of all her friends Abbie was the warmest, the most likely

to give her a sympathetic ear and a shoulder to cry on. Abbie was the one person she could track down, and with the time difference it wouldn't even be that late a phone call.

But she wouldn't call Abbie. Much as she needed help, she couldn't ask for it. She was a fine one to mourn her daughter's defenses when her own were so firmly in place. Once she started to let her vulnerability show there'd be no stopping it. She'd be weeping all over Chicago, and Emily was feeling insecure enough without a waterworks for a mother.

She curled up in the comfortable chair, leaned back and willed the tears to come. Nothing happened. Her eyes still burned, her throat felt tight and miserable, her chest throbbed, but everything was still locked up tight inside. She thought about Emily's miserable expression. She thought about Greg's funeral, the look of blame on his mother's face. Sara Brandt had known they were about to separate. Without question she blamed that stress for her son's unexpected heart attack, ignoring the fact that he'd lived with an undiagnosed heart defect for his entire thirty-three years.

She remembered the phone call, the shock, the disbelief, the pain of knowing someone she'd once loved dearly was gone. But still she sat alone in Simon's hallway, dry-eyed.

She thought of Julie crying for the moon, for all the lost chances, for young men like Dennis, for the baby she was too wise not to relinquish.

And she thought of her four-figure electricity bill and her very tiny savings account.

Not a tear. The fist around her heart tightened, clamping down until she was gasping for breath. But still the relief of tears was beyond her.

It was sort of like sex, she thought distantly, huddling deeper into the chair and wrapping the shawl around her body. The only person she'd ever made love with was

Greg, and during the last few years that hadn't been very often. But even in the rush of youth it hadn't been very exciting, though there had been times when it seemed as if there was something else, something just out of reach, something absolutely wonderful that she couldn't quite accomplish.

Her feelings at the moment were almost identical. She was wrapped in a tight little ball of misery, not even certain if the tears she sought would bring her any release at all.

There were advantages in having no one to turn to. She had no witnesses, could sit here all night if she had a mind to, and no one would have to know. She could tell Julie she fell asleep in the chair, waiting for someone to return her call. And if Julie didn't believe her she was too much of a good person to say so.

She took a few tentative, deep breaths, hoping to ease the iron band around her chest. It released its grip a few centimeters, and Marielle drew in a deeper breath, struggling for the calm that was her second choice, since an orgy of weeping seemed to be denied her.

Her usual calm self-control was within her grasp now. A few more moments and she'd be fine, able to return to her apartment and her surprisingly comfortable bed, able to tend to Julie and Emily if they should need her again during the long predawn hours. It wasn't even four o'clock yet— hours to go before the autumn sun rose over the city. If she were lucky she'd still manage another few hours of sleep.

She took another deep breath, willing the tension to leave her, willing calm to return, when without warning the door to Simon's apartment was flung open and a dark, menacing form loomed over her like a vengeful ghost.

And Marielle, looking up into Simon's dark, distant face, burst into tears.

Chapter Nine

"Damn," said Simon. "I thought I told you not to cry."
But his tone of voice belied the harsh words, and before
she even realized what he was doing he'd scooped her up
in his arms and carried her into his darkened apartment, the
shawl trailing on the floor behind them.

If Simon's appearance had broken through her blocked
tears, his touch destroyed the dam entirely. She let loose a
torrent of weeping, burying her face against his shoulder
and releasing all the pent-up misery and despair that had
been so well battened down. For a few short moments all
her responsibilities vanished, for a few short moments there
was someone else to shoulder them for her. She was hardly
aware of him sinking onto the huge old sofa; all she knew
was the warmth and comfort of his arms around her.

He didn't utter the soothing phrases she specialized in.
He didn't push her damp hair away from her tear-soaked
face, didn't rub her shoulders or pat her back or murmur,
"It's all right." He was just there, a solid, dependable presence, there as no one had been for her since she'd grown
up and had to be everybody else's mother. He was there,
and the sensation was such a delightful relief that she cried
even harder, her hands clinging to him, to the soft, stretchy
cotton of his T-shirt, to the hard, muscled flesh beneath.

At that point he did say something, but Marielle couldn't

quite hear it beyond her tears. It might have been her name,
it might have been a strangled protest, perhaps even encouragement. She wasn't paying much attention, being too
busily awash in an absolute riot of misery. She knew he
was lying back on the couch, knew he was taking her with
him, stretching her out beside him, tucking her against his
body and holding her, but all these things were part of the
dream state she seemed to be in, a dream state brought
about by overwhelming emotion and not enough sleep.

She couldn't see—the room was too dark and she was
blinded by tears. She could smell, though, the faint, soapy
smell of him, the lingering traces of whatever he'd had for
dinner, the pleasantly musty scent of the old sofa. And she
could feel him, the oddly comforting textures, the juxta-
position of soft and hard, the softness of his T-shirt and
sweatpants, the hardness of bone and muscle beneath the
garments.

Abruptly her tears vanished, swallowed in sudden surprise. Her eyes flew open, and the room was brighter than
she'd realized. Moonlight was shining in, flooding Simon's
face as he leaned over her, mere inches away, his breath
smelling of brandy and toothpaste, his eyes absolutely
opaque as he stared into hers.

Her flannel nightgown had somehow ridden up her legs,
her bare thighs were pressed against him, but the overheated air of his apartment was only partially responsible
for the flush that suffused her body, for the flaming color
in her face and the burning ache in the pit of her stomach.
The tightness was back in her chest, but it was a different
kind of tightness, an odd sort of yearning she couldn't and
wouldn't understand.

"Let go of me," she said, her voice a hushed command
in the still room.

"Yes," said Simon, not moving.

"We can't do this."

"No," he agreed.

"Simon." Her voice held a very definite note of warning.

"Yes," he said. Then, "No." And then he dipped his head, blotting out the moonlight, and his mouth caught hers.

Unbelievably, it had been years since she'd been kissed. Possibly not since the night Christopher had been conceived, and she wasn't even sure of that. And she'd never been kissed the way Simon was kissing her, all urgency gone now, slowly, thoroughly, his mouth touching and teasing and tasting, nudging away her panic until she had no choice but to soften her mouth, to part her lips for him, to let him take possession with a sudden sly ferocity that left her trembling beneath him.

Somehow he'd managed to maneuver her into the corner of the couch, and his long, hard body was stretched over hers, pressing her against the frayed upholstery. One of his arms was still around her, holding her against him, the other hand was cupping her chin, keeping her face still for his leisurely, totally devastating kiss.

She could do no more than accept that kiss passively, willingly, too overwhelmed to do anything else. Her own hands were up, an ineffectual barrier pressing against his chest, pushing him away, but her fingers were kneading the soft material over his hard chest like the paws of a cat in heat. She even sounded like one, she thought dismally, listening to the tiny whimper of denial and desire that was swallowed up by Simon's hungry mouth.

But she didn't want the kiss to end. She wanted to drown in it, to lose herself in the mesmerizing power of his clever, hungry mouth on hers, just as she'd lost herself in his warmth and comfort moments before. She was still ready to relinquish all responsibility, just for a little while, even though that distant, conscious part of her knew better. But right now she didn't care; he was in control, not she, and nothing mattered but the nagging, worrisome, overwhelming pleasure he was coaxing from her with nothing more than his mouth laying claim to hers.

And then he pulled his mouth away abruptly, laying his head beside her own. She could hear his rasping breath in her ear, feel the tension trembling in the body covering hers, and she could feel her own intense response, her own labored breathing.

"Damn," he muttered hoarsely, his voice not much more than a whisper in her ear. "We weren't going to do that."

Marielle swallowed the protest that rose to her sensitized lips. "Let me up," she said, suddenly desperate.

"Please." Simon's voice was strangled. "I won't touch you again. But just stay put for a minute. Please."

She stayed where she was. The body pressed so closely against hers felt tense and almost feverish. She could practically feel the nerves jumping underneath his skin, and each deep, shaky breath he took pressed against her breasts beneath the flannel nightgown.

Then he moved, slipping away from her off the couch, and was halfway across the room before she even knew what had happened. Her hands were reaching out for him, and she quickly drew them back, wrapping her arms around her suddenly chilled body. The overheated top floor no longer felt so warm without Simon's body heat.

He was silhouetted in the moonlight. His face, his expression were hidden in the shadows, but she could see the faint gleam of his eyes watching her, could see the telltale rise and fall of his chest as he slowly brought himself back under total and rigid control.

She was a woman who could understand and respect self-control, but Simon's self-possession was curiously wounding. She lay on the couch without moving, her flannel nightgown still halfway up her thighs, and waited for him to say something.

It wasn't what she expected. Leaning forward, he turned on a light, flooding the room with an unwelcome brightness. "Do you want to go into the bedroom with me?" he asked bluntly, his face absolutely emotionless. "Or do you want to go back to your apartment?"

"I want," she said carefully, "to slap your face."

"Why? I didn't do anything you didn't want me to do. What I want to know is, do you want me to do more?"

She sat up slowly, pulling down her nightgown around her ankles, pulling up her knees to her chest, reaching for the shawl and wrapping it around her. "Go away, Simon."

"This is my apartment, remember? I actually pay rent on it."

"Then I'll go." Her feet had barely touched the floor before he'd crossed the room and shoved her back with ungentle hands. "You'll stay put," he snapped. And then he stopped himself. "Sorry," he said. "Let's start all over again. What were you doing in my hallway trying not to cry?"

"You've got it all wrong." She watched him warily as he sank back onto the large sofa, a nice safe distance away from her. "I was sitting there trying to cry and getting nowhere. At least until you showed up."

"Always glad to be of service. I scare babies and make people cry," Simon growled. "Why did you want to cry?"

"Everybody else was. Why not me?" She decided not to look at him. Looking at him reminded her of what they'd been doing just a short while ago, and thinking about that had the strange effect of making her want to do it again, irrational as such a wish might be.

"Who else was crying, Marielle?"

"Emily. Crying for her father. And Julie, crying for things she couldn't change."

Simon nodded, leaning back against the high-backed sofa with a weary sigh. "Which did you want to cry for? Your dead husband? Or were you crying for the moon?"

"Definitely the moon," she said. "Greg and I were in the midst of separating when he had his heart attack. That doesn't mean I didn't mourn him or greatly regret his death. But I'd already let go of him, said goodbye to him.''

"So what were you crying for?" he persisted.

"It's none of your business."

"If it's none of my business, why did you come up here for comfort?"

"I didn't. I came up to the hallway because it was the only place I thought I could be alone."

"Why?" he pushed.

He'd pushed too hard. "Damn it!" Marielle said, turning to him. "I needed to stop being everybody's mother for a few minutes, okay? Responsible for my children, for Julie, for this whole decaying apartment building and all the indigent people living here. For a few minutes I only wanted to think about myself. Is that a crime?"

"No," he said. "Come here."

"I thought we decided this wasn't a good idea."

Simon reached out and caught her arm, tugging—no, hauling—her across the couch. "I'm not going to make another pass at you," he said, tucking her against him, wrapping his arms around her. "You just need a little comfort on a cold night. I'm giving it."

"You're just as bad as I am." She sniffed. "You took on all these old people before I ever did. Now you seem to be taking on me and my family as well."

"It's just temporary." His deep, rich voice rumbled in his chest. Marielle gave in to the sleepy temptation of rubbing her face against the soft, stretchy cotton of his T-shirt, nuzzling against the warm, hard flesh beneath. "We'll get this old place in decent shape so that you and the children can go off and live somewhere warm and sunny and just cash the rent checks while someone else takes care of the dirty work."

She was so tired, the room was so warm, and the body beside her was so comforting. "What if we don't want to live somewhere warm and sunny?'' she murmured sleepily. ''What if I like cold, windy cities and derelict buildings?''

He didn't bother to answer, and she didn't bother to notice. She was, astonishingly, trustingly, sound asleep.

ANOTHER LOST SOUL to add to his collection, Simon thought with a stifled yawn, careful not to jar her sleeping body. He was going to be hard-pressed to keep up his feelings of animosity at this rate. As long as he could view her as a dilettante, someone who didn't really need to be here, someone who was playing at being self-supporting before she gave up and cashed in her trust fund, then he could keep those treacherous feelings at bay.

But it was damned hard to distance himself from a warm, clinging body leaning so trustingly against his, to distance himself from the sleeping, endearingly pretty face that still bore traces of tears. Her lips were slightly swollen, and he wanted to crane his neck and kiss her again to see if he could make them respond.

He needed to remind himself that she was just like Esmy and Granita, like Julie and the Meltirks. Nothing more, nothing less. If he viewed her as one more responsibility, like the others, then maybe he wouldn't be so damned tempted.

But she wasn't like the others; that was the problem. It wasn't that she was young and pretty—Julie was young and pretty too, despite the advanced pregnancy. And it wasn't that she needed him—they all needed him. And it wasn't that she was trying to make a go of it. All the residents of Farnum's Castle were trying, in their own ways, to make a life for themselves and those around them.

It was the fact that she was taking responsibility, not just for herself and her family but for the others, just as he had. Right now she might be a little burned-out by it all, but he already knew that by tomorrow she'd be facing things once again. He hated to admit it, but Dennis McMurtry was a brilliant addition to their extended household. He'd never thought of bartering living space for plumbing and electrical expertise. Not that it would have been his place to do it, but Farnum's Castle had been ignored for so long that he pretty much did what he pleased. Fritzie was there because of him. So, for that matter, was Granita.

Sweet, elegant Granita with the noble carriage and the British accent and the impeccable manners had been just this side of becoming a bag lady. The residence she'd lived in had been closed down by the city, she had no family, no money, and her only possessions were stuffed into an old suitcase that was held together by rope. She hadn't eaten or slept in days, and she'd been sitting in the Pan Am terminal at O'Hare Airport, dodging the security guards. He'd brought her back with him, settled her in with Esmerelda, and time had taken care of the rest.

Esmy and Granita's relationship particularly amused him. They had a great deal of fun squabbling, arguing over everything from how to cook meat loaf to whether God was a woman. Esmy's interest in the occult had always been marginal until Granita had shown up, but it had been one-upmanship from then on.

The only real fight they'd ever had had been over Julie, and it had been severe enough to make Granita move across the hall into a recently vacated apartment. Granita thought Julie should try to patch things up with her father and stepmother, while Esmerelda was convinced she should turn her back on them, just as they had turned their backs on her. It had been a bitter fight, with the two old ladies not exchanging a word for over two weeks, but in the end it was Julie who'd had the final say. Her father had cleared out her room, thrown her belongings into the street, and told the parish priest she'd died in a car accident in California. She'd had no choice and no desire but to accept the situation.

Simon had been paying for Julie's prenatal care. Maybe

that was part of his sensitivity about age. The one time he'd gone with Julie the nurse had given him a condemning, disgusted look, one that despite his complete innocence, made him feel like the worst sort of lecher. It didn't matter that Marielle was more than ten years older than Julie—he still felt like a dirty old man.

Not enough that he'd wake her up and send her back downstairs, however. Julie was there with the children, and Marielle needed a few hours of sleep. He had complete faith in Julie's ability to deal with Christopher and Emily. She'd be a wonderful mother—it was a damned shame she couldn't keep her own child.

Marielle stirred, sighing, and the warmth of her breath brushed his bare arm, stirring the hairs. Simon let himself settle back and she went with him, still sound asleep. Despite what she said, she must miss her husband, Simon thought. Otherwise she wouldn't sleep so peacefully and well with a strange body wrapped around her.

Of course, just because she had been in the middle of a separation that didn't mean she wasn't involved with someone else, he reminded himself, then dismissed the idea as soon as it came. For one thing, Marielle simply wasn't that kind of person.

For another, her response to his kiss fitted exactly with what she'd said yesterday afternoon. She'd said sex was the most overrated commodity of all. If that was how she usually responded to a kiss, it was no wonder she thought the whole thing was a big fuss over nothing.

Of course, he could be kidding himself. It could be *his* kiss she was so passive about. Except that he could feel the stirring tendrils of response deep within her, in the clinging of her fists to his T-shirt, in the restlessness of her hips beneath his, in the dazed expression in her clear blue eyes when he'd moved away.

It was more than obvious that someone hadn't done it right. And the temptation to show her just how delicious, how exhilarating, how overwhelming it could be was just one more barb in his lacerated soul. He had to keep his hands off, damn it. Someone else would show her, sooner or later. Someone would take the time and care that were needed to make her realize that sex, when it was done right, when it was done with love, simply couldn't be overrated.

But he didn't have the love, the time or the caring to spare. And when he thought about it clearly he knew that he didn't deserve Marielle Brandt or her two children, any more than he deserved a more upscale job. Penance, he reminded himself again, breathing in the faint, flowery scent that lingered in Marielle's hair and sent a sharp fist to his gut. He wondered if there'd be a time when he'd ever feel as if he'd paid enough. And if he'd ever trust anyone enough to tell them exactly what he did.

Actually, it was a particularly nasty kind of slow torture to be wrapped around Marielle Brandt and to know he couldn't touch her again, shouldn't have her no matter how much his body, mind, and yes, his very soul were beginning to ache for her. So maybe it was okay to let her sleep like that, to endure the torment for just a little bit longer. All in the name of penance, he reminded himself.

The full moon had disappeared, and the sky was beginning to lighten with the first streakings of dawn. He wished he hadn't turned on that damned light that kept shining in his eyes, but he wasn't about to get up and do anything about it. He was going to sit there and watch the sun come up and breathe in the enticing scent of Marielle's perfume. In a few hours he'd be his usual irascible self. For now he was going to have a brief indulgence, a moment or two to pretend the past never happened. And resting his stubbled cheek lightly on Marielle's blond head, he drifted into sleep.

It seemed like moments later when his eyes flew open. The room was flooded with daylight, Marielle was standing a few feet away, her eyes panicked, her body in its ridiculous granny nightgown tense with fear. A terrified scream still echoed in his sleep-drugged consciousness, and he wondered if that scream had come from her when she awoke and realized where she was.

And then it came again, a loud, terrified shriek, floating up the flights of stairs and in through the open door of his apartment. "Granita," he identified the voice, leaping to his feet. But Marielle was already out the door, racing in the direction of that frightened voice.

Chapter Ten

Julie was standing in the doorway of Marielle's apartment, panic and indecision on her face. "What's wrong? I thought I heard Granita...."

"Stay put," Marielle ordered, not stopping her headlong pace down the angular flights of stairs. "Watch the children. We'll find out what's happened."

"But..."

"Stay put." Simon's voice behind her repeated the order. He'd caught up with her between the fourth and third floors, passed her at the Meltirks' apartment and raced on ahead to the first, to Granita and Esmerelda's apartments. Half a dozen Meltirks were roaming the hall in various stages of undress, the most alarming of which was her serene highness, with a purple velvet nightgown flowing around her impressive bulk and a head full of pink plastic curlers. Since her highness always wore a turban the curlers might have seemed a bit redundant, but Marielle didn't have time to ponder the matter as she caught her foot on an uneven stair tread, began to tumble, and barely caught herself on the wide bannister.

Granita was stretched out on the sofa in her overstuffed apartment, with Esmerelda bustling around, fanning her erstwhile competitor's ashen face, clucking and muttering in counterpoint to Granita's intermittent moans. Dennis was already there, already being marvelously efficient, pouring a glass of ice water down Granita's throat, chafing her long, bony hands.

Marielle paused inside the apartment long enough to take in the scene. She would have thought Simon might not be too pleased at having Dennis take over as dispenser of aid to the needy, but he seemed surprisingly unaffected, even going to give Dennis a nod of approval that was free of the underlying hostility of the night before.

"Simon," Granita moaned piteously—a bit too piteously, Marielle thought—and held out a shaking hand. Simon sat down on the couch beside her, still dressed in his old gray sweatpants and black T-shirt. His feet were bare, as were hers, and she suddenly realized that she was even more scantily dressed than the others, enveloped as she was in the flannel nightie.

She could feel her face turn a bright crimson, and could only be thankful all eyes were on Granita and not on her own miserably guilty countenance. But if she'd been where she should have been, fast asleep, alone in her own bed, she would have been dressed just the same, and she doubted she would have had the sense to grab her bathrobe before she responded to Granita's shrill scream. As a matter of fact, she hadn't even unpacked her bathrobe yet.

The shawl, however, was still lying on Simon's floor. And Julie would know she'd been coming down at dawn from the fifth-floor apartment, and not her own bed.

Where Marielle Brandt spent the night turned out to be the least of her worries, however, when Granita could finally be persuaded to gasp out what had happened. With Simon beside her, holding one hand, and Dennis still patting the other, she managed to pull herself together enough to enjoy the attention, and Esmerelda emitted a disparaging sniff.

"I don't sleep well," Granita said by way of preamble. "I'm usually up by half past four, and this morning was no different. I feed the cat, make myself a pot of tea, and write a few letters. Then I meditate for a bit...."

"Get on with it, Granita." Esmerelda spoke the words everyone else wanted to but was far too polite to utter. "What happened?"

"The cat was outside. I could see her from my bedroom window, and I knew without a doubt that she'd been in when I went to bed last night. When I went to let her in I heard a noise from the dining room. You know I hardly use it, only for an occasional reading or a séance. Not that it isn't a nice enough room, even though it is a bit drafty despite the bricked-up fireplace, and I'm lucky to have the space...."

"Granita!" Esmy shrieked. "Get to the point. What was in the dining room?"

While Granita's distress was clearly very real, she couldn't resist the melodrama of the moment. Her long, horsey face quivered, her faded blue eyes widened, and her voice grew low and hushed. "Vittorio Farnum."

"No!" Simon said instantly.

"Who?" Dennis asked at the same time.

"Oh, God," murmured Marielle.

"Damn," declared Esmy. "You have all the luck."

Granita allowed herself a small, satisfied smirk before she resumed her tragic queen pose. "You wouldn't call having your apartment vandalized a stroke of luck," she informed her friend with great dignity.

"Oh, wouldn't I? By old Vittorio himself? Guess again, Granita." Esmy was beside herself with envy.

"Granita," Simon said, and his deep, sepulchral voice was firm but gentle. "Tell us exactly what happened. What made you think it was Vittorio?"

"How do you even know what Vittorio looks like?" Marielle couldn't keep from asking.

She should have kept her mouth shut. Everyone turned to stare at her from the tips of her bare feet to the top of her tangled hair, and she could feel the color flood her pale complexion, the curse of a Scandinavian mother. Even Simon seemed momentarily distracted by her appearance.

"Why shouldn't I know what Vittorio looks like?" Granita said loftily. "Don't I look at him every night before I go to sleep?"

Marielle couldn't bring herself to question that statement—she didn't know if she wanted to hear the answer. Esmerelda must have seen her expression, for she sniffed audibly.

"It's not as mysterious as it sounds," she said flatly, doing her best to deflate Granita's pretensions. "The old phony found a portrait of Vittorio in the basement and before anyone knew what was happening she'd hung it in her bedroom."

"Old phony?" Granita shrieked, sitting bolt upright and forgetting that she was supposed to be recovering from shock. "If anyone's a charlatan around here…"

"You still haven't told me what happened," Simon interrupted the squabble with the long-suffering air of someone who'd intervened many times. "You heard a noise in the dining room and what?"

"I went in, of course. I thought it might be one of my spirit guides." Granita fixed Esmerelda with a warning glare, but the other woman was momentarily silent. "The light wasn't very good, and at first I thought it might be rats or squirrels or something. It was just a sort of scrabbling sound."

"Like I heard the night before," Marielle said gloomily.

"But when I looked in I saw someone kneeling by the fireplace in an almost prayerful position. He was dark all over, like a fiend from hell…."

"I thought you didn't believe in hell," Esmy said.

"Be quiet, Esmy," Simon said, concentrating on Granita. "What happened then?"

"Well, of course I uttered a little mantra for self-protection. And then the creature turned and looked at me, and his features were all dark and blurry. But even so I could recognize Vittorio. I was so startled I must have screamed. He ran, and I kept screaming until you all ran in here."

"Old fool," Esmy sniffed. "You should have welcomed him. How can we ever expect anyone to cross over if people spend their time shrieking? Think of the things he could have told us about the afterlife. Think of the knowledge lost by your silly hysterics! There are times, Granita..."

"Ladies," Dennis interrupted with his engaging grin. "I would give anything to see a portrait of that old mobster. I've heard stories about him, and my brother-in-law filled me in on some of the history of the house, but I've never actually seen a ghost, even a portrait of someone before he became a ghost, if you know what I mean."

"Certainly," Granita said, rising with somewhat unsteady dignity. "I'd be more than happy to show you. Though you must realize the bed isn't made."

"He's not interested in an old maid's bed," snapped Esmerelda, trailing along behind them. "He just wants to see Vittorio."

"I didn't say you could come along." Granita stopped at the doorway.

"Try and stop me." Esmerelda was nothing if not persistent.

"I wouldn't lower myself. Come if you must." Granita swept through the doorway, then paused once more, tossing a brief phrase over her shoulder as a sort of afterthought. "And who says I'm an old maid?"

Marielle found Simon's dark gray eyes watching her with a certain solemnity. For all practical purposes they were alone once more—the sound of the two old ladies arguing, with Dennis's gentle comments interspersed, floated out from the bedroom, and the Meltirks milling around in the hallway couldn't understand a word of English. Simon could say anything he wanted to her.

"We'd better check the fireplace," he said, rising, ignoring the question in her eyes. "I expect it's the same people who broke into your place the night before."

"I suppose so." She didn't move, and neither did he. "Uh, Simon…"

"Yes."

An unhelpful response if ever she heard one, Marielle thought, standing her ground. "About last night."

"Yes." If she didn't know better she'd think there was a faint light of amusement in those steely gray eyes. But Simon Zebriskie wasn't someone who was easily amused, and while her discomfiture might be enough to tickle his morbid sense of humor, she decided to give him the benefit of the doubt.

"I must have fallen asleep." It sounded pretty lame when it came out, but without his cooperation this conversation was doomed to failure anyway, she thought.

"Yes."

"Why didn't you wake me up?" She lobbed the ball neatly back into his court.

"I must have fallen asleep myself."

Damn. There was no way she could keep skirting the issue. The Meltirks were growing more restive; the prince consort, a portly young man in a puce sweat suit, was peering in the door and describing the situation in voluble detail to his royal wife, and Marielle had a distinct suspicion that she could hear a goat in the apartment above.

"I'm sorry I ended up crying on your shoulder," she said, trying to sound rueful, ending up sounding stiff and uncomfortable. "I was just looking for a place to be alone for a while so I could feel properly sorry for myself, and your hallway seemed to be the perfect spot, complete with a comfortable chair for crying in. I wouldn't have come up if I'd thought I'd wake you. I won't do it again."

"Won't feel sorry for yourself or won't come upstairs again?" Simon countered, crossing the room and standing much too close to her. The prince consort had edged into the room, too, so that he was only a few inches behind her, listening to their conversation with avid interest. Simon ignored him, something Marielle had a harder time doing. "A little self-pity is a healthy thing every now and then, as long as it's not carried to extremes."

"Last night was extreme." The prince was breathing down her neck. Marielle turned to give him a discouraging smile, but the poor man panicked when she tried to meet his gaze, scampering from the room like a frightened rabbit. The noise in the corridor increased, then all the Meltirks vanished into their second-floor apartment, and the sound of the goat blended with the unmistakable noise and odor of chickens before the door slammed shut.

"Maybe," continued Simon, not the slightest bit distracted by their neighbors. "Or maybe it was a normal reaction that was long overdue."

"Normal or not, it won't happen again." The words came out in not much more than a whisper. No one could see them now, the conversation in Granita's bedroom was lively and loud, and Marielle wished, for some reason she couldn't begin to fathom, that Simon would touch her.

Simon did no such thing. Nor did he give her the denial she wanted to hear. Her own words had been half wishful thinking, half a challenge. Either way, Simon seemed to have lost interest.

"Let's check out the fireplace," was all he said, turning from her and moving silently across the room. And letting out her breath in a soundless, pent-up sigh, Marielle followed him.

The rubble-strewn fireplace here didn't look much different from those in the other two vandalized apartments. Someone, or something, Marielle thought with an effort to be fair to the supernatural elements, had chipped away at the mortar, removed some of the bricks and pulled away some of the twigs and dead leaves that had fallen down the chimney. Whether that someone or -thing had found anything of value or use she couldn't tell. She moved closer, planning to lean over Simon's kneeling figure, when she stepped on something sharp and let out a yelp of pain, falling against him and knocking him into the rubble.

She lay there on the floor of Granita's apartment, sprawled on top of him, for a long, silent moment. He was looking up at her, and for a brief second she thought she saw a flare of pure, physical desire of such intensity that it frightened her. As soon as she saw it it was gone, leaving her wondering if she'd only imagined it, if it had been the result of paranoid nightmares. Or wishful thinking.

"I thought we weren't going to do this," his deep voice drawled, his expression now carefully masked.

She still didn't move. If she were fool enough to fall in love again, she could fall in love with that wonderful voice of his. And the lean, wiry body beneath hers wasn't too bad, either. Not to mention his ridiculously sexy mouth. And his eyes, which could be absurdly kind.

She rolled off him, scrambling to her feet and limping slightly as she hurried to get away from insane temptation. "We're not," she said. She contemplated reaching out a hand to help him up, then thought better of it. Simon didn't need her help for anything.

Slowly he sat up, brushing the rubble from his black T-shirt. He stayed that way for a moment, resting his arms on his drawn-up knees, watching her, and this time there was no mistaking the expression in his eyes. "If you say so. I wouldn't count on it, if I were you."

"Simon..."

"Just go," he grumbled. "Or come back upstairs with me."

Marielle went.

Dennis raised an eyebrow at her when she practically ran into the tiny bedroom, but didn't say a word.

"There you are, my dear," Granita greeted her. "What do you think of the old rascal?"

For a moment Marielle thought she meant Simon, and she could feel herself flush. And then she followed the direction of Granita's gesture to the very bad oil painting that was hanging over another, still-untouched and bricked-up fireplace.

Vittorio Farnum was a surprisingly handsome man, apparently in his mid-fifties. He had a hawklike nose, a wide-lipped, sensual mouth, and piercing brown eyes set under heavy, beetled brows. He was painted wearing, of all things, a monk's robe, with a heavy jeweled cross resting against his barrel chest and a tattered-looking Bible in one long-fingered hand. The technique was lousy—Vittorio's eyes surely couldn't have been two such disparate sizes, and the color was muddy and drab, leaving Vittorio's skin tone more a pea green than a Mediterranean olive.

He also looked hauntingly familiar.

Marielle stared up at him, squinting her eyes, tilting her head to the right and then to the left. "Where have I seen him before?" she murmured, then mentally slapped herself when she realized she'd spoken the words out loud.

"You've seen him before?" Granita pounced on the statement. "I didn't realize you'd actually had a visitation. This is most exciting. Esmy, did you hear…?"

"I heard," Esmy said, looking at Marielle thoughtfully. "When did you see him, dear?"

"I have no idea." She was acutely aware that Simon had now come into the tiny room and was standing much too close to her. So close that she could see the fine grains of plaster dust clinging to his bare forearm. "I certainly haven't seen any ghosts lately," she added in a more forceful tone.

"I think we have to do it," Granita said mysteriously.

"I'm afraid you're right, dear," Esmy agreed. "Tonight?"

"Tonight," said Granita, fastening her pale blue eyes on the others. "You'll all participate, of course."

"Of course," said Dennis.

"Yes," said Simon in a resigned tone.

"Participate in what?" Marielle questioned.

Granita looked up, way up into old Vittorio's dark brown eyes. "A séance," she said. "If you haven't seen Vittorio Farnum before, you'll see him tonight."

And Marielle, following Granita's gaze, shivered, moving an unconscious, instinctive step back toward Simon. "No, thanks," she said hastily. "I'll pass on this one."

"No, you won't." Simon's hands reached up and caught her arms, holding her in place in front of him. "If I have to put up with it, so do you," he added in a muttered undertone.

"Simon understands these things." Granita smiled at him. "We need everyone's cooperation for the powers to be in tune."

"You don't need a skeptic at the table," Marielle said.

"Nonsense. No one could be more cynical than Simon, and he's never interfered with the vibrations. If anything, his attitude has helped matters. Maybe," Granita said in a soulful hush, "we'll actually be able to talk to Vittorio." She smiled, a beatific grin. "Wouldn't that be absolutely splendid?"

Marielle didn't have the heart to raise any more objections. At least it could do no harm. "Splendid," she echoed gloomily. And she stepped away from Simon's enticing, imprisoning hands.

THE CHILDREN WERE EATING Cap'n Crunch cereal and watching *Muppet Babies*, a safe enough occupation, when Marielle finally returned from Granita's apartment. They greeted their mother's early morning return with their usual enthusiasm, and there was no trace of last night's tears on Emily's rosy face.

Julie looked equally sanguine, both about Marielle's unexplained absence during the long hours of the night and about the séance. "They're harmless," she said carelessly. "Miss Granita shakes and moans a bit, and Esmy tries to outdo her, but it's all in their heads. The most that's ever happened was when Miss Granita keeled over in a dead faint, and Esmy passed out on top of her. Of course, Esmy was faking and Miss Granita had forgotten to eat for two days, but the whole thing was very exciting."

"I still don't like the idea," Marielle mumbled into her own bowl of Cap'n Crunch. She knew better than to eat such empty calories, but she'd always had a sneaking fondness for the old Cap'n, and this morning she needed all the comfort she could find, even if it was in a box of presweetened cereal.

"Don't worry. I'll watch the children for you. I bet you find it entertaining."

"How about if I watch the children and you go? At this rate they've hardly seen me in the last few days." Marielle could see that the moment the words were out of her mouth she'd deeply offended Julie, and she quickly hurried to undo the harm she'd caused. "I don't want to take advantage of you, Julie."

"I don't mind. It's something to do, and you've got real special kids. I...like them," she said with her usual diffidence.

Marielle swallowed a smile. "They like you."

"Besides, Esmy says my pregnancy upsets the vibrations, so she wouldn't let me be around, anyway. If I know them they're counting on having you there. It's not often they get someone new to perform for."

"Two people," Marielle said wryly. "Dennis promised to go, too."

At the mention of Dennis's name Julie's face went carefully blank. "He should find it interesting."

Marielle's brain finally began working. "As a matter of fact, you might want to go down and check what happened to Granita's fireplace," she said with a diffidence that matched Julie's.

She didn't have to be a psychic to read Julie's mind. The younger girl opened her mouth to ask Marielle if Dennis was still down there, and then shut it again, afraid to know.

She should know better than to matchmake, Marielle thought, particularly in Julie's tangled circumstances. Look at how infuriating Simon's heavy-handed machinations were. But then Simon had a hidden agenda. Marielle simply wanted Julie to be happy.

"Go on down," she said again. "You never know what you might find down there."

And Julie, with a last, indecisive frown, went, leaving Marielle to wonder if she'd made a very big mistake.

Chapter Eleven

It was after nine that evening when Marielle knocked on Granita's scarred wooden door. She did so with great misgivings. She was dressed in an old black evening gown that had been unearthed from heaven only knew where. It smelled of mothballs and old perfume, and it had been worn by someone with a great deal more height and girth than Marielle was blessed with. The wispy black folds dragged along the floor, obscuring her practical Nikes, the sleeves drooped over her knuckles, and the low-cut, lacy neckline gaped over Marielle's less than abundant charms. Simon had returned her black shawl, and Marielle had it firmly wrapped around her overexposed figure, but she couldn't help feeling like a Halloween character.

She wished she hadn't had to join in this preposterous séance. The last thing on earth she wanted to do was spend the evening around a table with two eccentric old women trying to call forth ghosts. At best she figured she'd be heartily bored. At worst, if the séance actually worked and Vittorio showed up, she'd be scared witless, probably pack up the kids and run straight back to…

She didn't know where she could run to. There was no one in New York, and she wasn't in the habit of turning to other people for help. People usually turned to her, even her own parents. She was always so calm, so stable, so peacefully maternal that no one ever considered the fact that there were times when she needed to be mothered herself.

And she wasn't ready to leave Chicago, to leave Farnum's Castle, even if it did turn into something out of *Ghostbusters*. Her need to stay had something to do with the tenuous, gradually increasing feeling of self-sufficiency. It had something to do with the weird, wonderful people inhabiting the place. And it had something to do with the man who lived above her. What, she wasn't quite sure. She just knew she didn't want to risk never seeing Simon Zebriskie again.

The Meltirks had been uncharacteristically quiet when she'd passed their apartment on the way down. As usual the strange, smoky smells were issuing forth, and Marielle had no idea whether it was a ceremonial fire or simply Baluchistani cooking. She wasn't sure if she wanted to find out, particularly if the latter proved to be the case and she was forced to partake of something that smelled like that. She paused for a moment outside their door, but there were no voices, no sounds of animals. Maybe she'd imagined the goat and the chickens. Or maybe they were dinner.

She wasn't too keen on the smells coming from Granita's apartment, either, and for a moment she wondered whether she could get away with sneaking back upstairs and pretending to be sick. But no sooner had that delightfully devious thought entered her mind than the door swung open, revealing Granita in all her Stygian splendor.

She was draped in black from her veiled head to her large, flat feet. She was even wearing black support stockings, Marielle noticed. Music—if you could call it that— was issuing from the candle-lit living room. A small cassette recorder was putting out strange, atonal sounds, and the incense burning on the table smelled like rotting watermelon.

"Perfect." Granita's brisk, no-nonsense British accent was at odds with the theatrical setting. "You look perfect."

"She looks like the bride of Dracula," Simon drawled. "Where did you get that outfit?"

With a grimace Marielle picked up her trailing black skirt. "Don't you like it? Granita said it would be just the thing to summon Vittorio."

"I would say so," Miles Van Cortland said, stepping into view, his handsome face wreathed in an appreciative grin, his blue eyes oddly assessing. "That dress was worn by Vittorio's wife just before she died. I've seen old photographs of it. Where in the world did you find it?"

Marielle dropped the skirt with a startled screech. "You didn't tell me that!" she exclaimed accusingly, wishing there were some way she could get the clinging folds off her.

"I didn't know that," Granita replied calmly. "Miles is the great expert on Farnum's Castle, not me. That's one of the reasons I invited him to join us."

"Besides, she didn't die in the dress," he said, his beautifully sculpted mouth curving in a smile. "She died of pneumonia a few months after she wore it. And she never looked half as beautiful as you do in it."

Marielle's initial distaste began to fade, particularly when she noticed the absolutely ominous expression on Simon's face. "Not the bride of Dracula?" she murmured.

"Simon never had any taste in women. Look at his ex-wife."

"Ex-wife?" Marielle echoed, clutching the shawl around her more tightly. The room was warm, too warm, but there was no way she was going to let her modesty shield fall. "I didn't realize Simon was married."

"Simon is getting damned tired of this," Simon said, his gray eyes flinty. "Can we get on with it?"

"In good time, dear, in good time," Esmy soothed, bustling into the room in the same black garb as Granita. Even

Simon was in black—a black T-shirt again, though not the one she'd pulled out of shape with her hungry, clinging hands. And black jeans. She'd better not start looking at his jeans, she told herself.

"We're not all here yet," Granita intoned, sinking gracefully into her chair. The requisite round table was covered with something that resembled a gypsy shawl, and the crystal ball sat squarely in the middle.

Where in the world did people find crystal balls nowadays? Marielle wondered, pulling the shawl still more tightly around her and ignoring the flush of heat that was climbing her cheekbones. Since she couldn't be tactless enough to ask that question, she went for another. "What happened to your wife?"

"I drowned her in the bathtub," Simon snapped.

Miles, his black wool suit impeccably tailored, moved up beside her and cupped her elbow with his strong, smooth hand. "Don't pay any attention to the man. It was a very civilized divorce. He was married to a career woman who wanted someone a little more ambitious. Didn't Sharon try to pay you alimony?"

"You're treading on thin ice, Miles. It's only because of Granita and Esmy that I don't use the language I'm longing to," Simon snapped.

"Oh, go right ahead, dear," Esmy said with an airy wave. "Granita and I are used to it. We deplore it, of course, but there are times when a good solid cuss word is so satisfying."

Simon smiled faintly. "I agree. However, I think Marielle's a bit more sheltered."

Marielle could feel the heat rise to her face, and she squirmed beneath her smothering shawl. "I'm not as sheltered as you'd think," she said, knowing it was a lie. She was probably even more innocent than Simon suspected. She moved away, sitting down at the table across from

Granita, and pressed a faintly trembling hand to her cool, damp forehead.

"I wish to heavens the furnace would work right," she said. "It's miserably hot in here."

Esmy leaned over her, clucking sympathetically. "It's not really that bad, you know. It's better than being icy cold."

Before she realized what was happening, Simon's long fingers reached down and plucked off the hot woolen shawl. "If you're hot you don't need...this." The words trailed away as he realized how remarkably indecent Mrs. Farnum's black ball dress actually was. "My, my," he said. "I didn't realize old Vittorio had been married to such a temptress."

"I think she had a little more to hold it up," Marielle said, striving for an air of unconcern.

Miles sank down beside her, flashing that beautiful smile, his observant blue eyes never dropping below her chin. "She wasn't nearly as gorgeous as you are."

Simon sat down on her other side, and Marielle thought she could hear his teeth grinding in rage. "I'm so glad my matchmaking worked out," he snarled, his attempt at an affable smile failing miserably.

"Sorry to disappoint you, Simon," Miles said. "The lady keeps turning me down."

The expression of outrage, relief and confusion on Simon's long, narrow face was too much for Marielle. Quickly she ducked her head, biting her lip.

"You lied to me," Simon said, his deep voice accusing.

She looked up at him, trying to keep her expression innocent, then spoiled it all by giggling. "No, I didn't. I said you got what you wanted. You didn't really want me going out with Miles, and I didn't want to go out with him."

"Could we change the subject?" Miles requested in a pained voice. "I'm really not used to being considered so dispensable."

Marielle smiled at him, and Miles smiled back. "It's nothing personal. I'm not interested in getting involved with anyone at all. Simon knows that, but he won't listen."

"I could change your mind, you know," Miles said gently.

She looked at him, arrested by the soft promise in his voice. She looked at his wickedly handsome face, his beautiful mouth and aloof blue eyes, and shook her head. "No," she said, just as gently, just as sure, "you couldn't." If Simon couldn't, no one could, she thought. And Simon couldn't.

"It doesn't seem as if I'm going to get a chance to try." There was still the hint of a question in Miles's voice.

"The lady said no," Simon rumbled, clearly forgetting he was supposed to be in favor of the match.

"Message received, over and out."

"Am I too late?" Dennis appeared in the doorway, dressed in the requisite black, his red hair and open, friendly expression at odds with the funereal clothing. He looked around the room, his eyes fastened on Marielle's neckline and he let out a long, appreciative whistle. "If Vittorio won't come back from the grave for Marielle then nothing'll get him," he said, taking a seat beside Granita.

Marielle looked over her shoulder for her protective shawl, but Simon had tossed it out of reach. She could feel the blush reach her exposed chest, and there was nothing she could do but sit there while everyone stared at her exposed collarbones.

"Anyone else?" Simon asked, his voice impatient. "I'm due at the station by eleven-thirty, and I don't know if my boss will understand if I'm late."

"Jackie can always work a little over if you don't get back in time," Miles said, and a trace of malicious humor lit his eyes. "She'll just put on that thirty-minute song by Musclebound and take a nap."

"No!" Simon said, his voice strangled. "I'll be there on time."

"I wish I knew what you had against Musclebound," Miles said plaintively. "Their last album went platinum, they've been around for years and years, and you steadfastly refuse to play any of their records. It doesn't make sense."

"It does to me," Simon said stubbornly. "Just ancient history."

Marielle looked from the man on her right to the one on her left. Simon looked hostile, defensive and completely furious. Miles, on the other hand, looked almost smug. Not for one moment did Marielle believe that Miles didn't know what was behind Simon's attitude, despite his disclaimers.

She was still feeling hot, uncomfortable and short of breath. The kids had already fallen asleep by the time she'd put on her costume and trailed her way downstairs, and she wished she could be lying up there too, even in Vittorio's nasty carved bed, and Julie be down here in her place.

The final participant in the séance appeared at the door, and for a moment Marielle thought it was Julie. But her serene highness, Mrs. Meltirk wasn't as far advanced in her current pregnancy as Julie was, despite her imposing bulk, and she moved majestically into the room, nodding at her neighbors with her usual dignity. As she seated herself beside Dennis, Marielle caught the faint, unmistakable odor of goat, and her dizziness increased.

"Now we're ready," Granita announced with an air of satisfaction.

Marielle looked around the table. There were seven of them—Dennis, Granita, Esmerelda and Mrs. Meltirk on one side, Simon, Miles and herself on the other.

Miles was sitting too close; she could swear there was no need for him to hover over her like that. Simon was sitting too close. His jeans-clad leg wasn't touching her thigh, but she knew it was close, enticingly close. For some twisted reason she moved closer to Miles. She had no interest in Miles—he held no threat. She wasn't interested in Simon either, she reminded herself. She just didn't trust her own incomprehensible reaction to his nearness, she thought, wishing there were a little more air in the overheated room, wishing Granita had better taste in incense.

"I thought Julie's pregnancy interfered with the vibrations," she said somewhat desperately, looking for a final escape. "What about her highness?"

"Julie is an adolescent," Esmy explained. "Adolescent girls are full of undisciplined energies, pregnant or not. We couldn't risk upsetting the spirits...."

"She's eighteen," Dennis announced flatly. "And she's more mature than most thirty-year-olds I've met."

Everyone turned to look at him, surprise, calculation and hope among the predominant emotions. Dennis accepted their interest with equanimity—and with just a trace of defiance.

"Okay," said Simon, his slow, deliberate tone almost comical. "Shall we get on with this?"

Granita nodded her head. "If you would all just hold hands, we may begin."

And Marielle, fighting the wave of dizziness, lifted her black silk arms to the men on either side. Miles's clasp was cool and dry, light and just faintly possessive. Clearly he didn't like to give up easily, and whether he really wanted her or not, he didn't take no for an answer.

Simon's hand was much larger, warm and strong and pulsing with energy. Her hand disappeared within his grasp, and her left side felt warm, safe, tucked into him. Her right side was cold and lonely, despite Miles's encroaching thigh.

Maybe she was coming down with flu, she thought desperately. Maybe she should have remembered to eat something in the last two days besides sugary cereal. And maybe this time she was going to outdo Esmy and Granita and be the first to pass out.

The grip on her left side, Simon's side, tightened momentarily. She turned and looked at him out of slightly hazy eyes. For all his determined cynicism he seemed surprisingly kind, watching her out of worried gray eyes.

"Are you okay?" he whispered, and his voice seemed to rumble along her backbone.

She summoned up her best, falsest smile. "Just fine," she whispered, turning her attention to Granita, ignoring the strange sensation of someone touching, stroking her hair. She could see the hands on the table. It had to be her imagination.

The old woman's face had taken on a pale glow, and her milky blue eyes were shining with excitement. "If everyone is ready," she said in her schoolmarm voice. There were no more whispers. "Then let us begin."

And in a low throaty growl she began to moan.

GRANITA WAS RUNNING pretty true to form, Simon thought as he sat poker-faced in the uncomfortable folding chair. The moans, the incantations, the shaking of the table were all standard. The only difference tonight was the woman beside him, her cold, damp hand trembling in his.

And then there was Miles on the other side, breathing down that absurd excuse for a dress. If Simon had seen the dress that Granita had given Marielle he would have put a stop to it before Miles could run his lascivious eyes over her. He'd been half tempted to wrap the shawl back around her like a mummy, but had resisted the impulse. The other half of him couldn't stand to cover up such a delectable expanse of flesh, particularly when she blushed so charmingly. And it was nowhere near indecent, just slightly, irresistibly daring.

Nevertheless, tomorrow morning he was going to get that dress away from her and hide it. She shouldn't be allowed out in public in it—it was too tempting. If it were up to him he'd keep it around for her to wear when no one else was around. No one but himself.

But it wasn't up to him—it was none of his business. The only thing he could do was get rid of the damned thing, so she didn't get into any more trouble she couldn't handle, he told himself with a shade of self-righteousness he knew was absurd.

Miles wasn't paying any more attention to Granita's mumbo jumbo than he was, which was surprising, considering this was the first time he'd been invited. Simon had been at least vaguely interested the first couple of times he'd been forced to sit through one of these. But Miles seemed far more interested in peering down Marielle's dress, something that Simon would have found extremely annoying if it hadn't been for Marielle's discomfort. She had the good sense to see Miles for the lecherous fribble that he was. So instead of wanting to strangle Miles, Simon decided he'd be satisfied with bashing his perfect teeth in.

That crack about the rock group Musclebound was another thing, Simon thought morosely. It had to have been a coincidence, an unfortunate slip of the tongue. There was no way Miles could know anything about that whole sordid, damnable period in his life.

Except that Simon didn't believe in coincidences. And Miles had an uncanny ability to know things that no one else could possibly know, and he took absolute delight in using that knowledge for his own advantage.

Maybe he'd been hiding his head in the sand too long. Maybe it was time to have it out with his manipulative boss, find out what he really knew and what, for that matter, he thought about it. Not that Miles's opinion meant anything. Miles was such a manipulative sleaze he'd probably have more respect for Simon if he knew how low he'd sunk in the past.

Granita's moans increased and Mrs. Meltirk began to

moan in counterpoint. Her highness always enjoyed these evenings, even though she understood not a single word. Esmy was making her own unique little gruntlike whimpers, and Dennis was following all this with complete, sober fascination. But then, Dennis had delusions of being a writer. He probably thought all this would be fascinating in a book. Little did he know how boring it would swiftly grow to be.

Simon moved his head a fraction of an inch so he could see Marielle's profile. She was very pale, her thick blond hair hanging down around her face, and her eyes had a haunted look. Not enough sleep, he told himself with a forced lack of sympathy.

Though actually she'd slept quite well in his arms, once they'd finally decided that that was all they were going to do. She was a surprisingly restful woman in certain ways; the way her body molded so sweetly to his, the way she looked after her children, the staunch way she'd been accepting the harsh blows that fate had dealt her.

On the other hand, she was surprisingly disruptive. He knew without any doubt that he was going to have a hell of a time stretching out on that old couch without missing her body. Even his bed wouldn't be safe. She'd never been in the bedroom, yet he knew when he tried to sleep he'd be imagining her there with him.

Even in the broad daylight or the dark of night, when he was busiest doing other things totally unconnected with her, the memory of her face, the way she tilted her head, that troubled, lonely expression in her eyes would sneak up and hit him, and he'd find himself mooning over her like a teenager whose hormones had run amok.

She seemed to have that effect on a lot of people, Miles included. It was a good thing Dennis was immune, or he'd be going even crazier than he was already. But Dennis seemed to have his eye on Julie, unlikely as that might seem. Maybe there was a chance for a happy ending after all. At least for them.

But not for himself. He turned his gaze back to Marielle, allowing himself the dangerous luxury of lowering his gaze to her scantily covered breasts. He could remember how she felt against his hands; now he could almost see what he'd touched. Sometime, just once before he died, he'd like the chance to see and touch at the same time.

If Granita was worried about adolescent hormones wreaking havoc with the vibrations around the table, she hadn't reckoned with his own libido and Marielle's effect on it. He pulled his mind back, trying to think chaste, depressing thoughts, but all he could see was Marielle's soft, sweet mouth.

Her hand definitely felt cool in his, almost cold. And her face was too pale, with sweat beading her high forehead. He was almost ready to say something, to stop the séance, when there was a loud crashing of glass as one of the windows in the living room caved in, bringing in huge gusts of wind that immediately extinguished all the candles.

"Don't break the circle!" Granita shouted in a hoarse, strained voice.

Indeed, most of them were too stunned to move. In the darkness of the old living room came an unearthly light, a grayish-green glow, centered in the broken window. And in the center of that glow, beady brows, hooked nose and all, shimmered the shadowy, shifting planes of Vittorio Farnum's cruel face.

The first scream came from beside him as Marielle's icy cold hand slipped from his as she slumped over the table in an undeniable faint. The second came floating at least three stories down from the top of the building. And it could only have come from Julie.

Chapter Twelve

Simon caught Marielle as she tumbled sideways toward him, her body limp in its flowing black silk. The hideous apparition in the broken window had vanished, the room was pitch-black, and it was several seconds before someone had the sense to stumble towards the light switch.

Dennis was already out the door, racing up the flights of stairs. They could hear the faint sounds of children crying, and Simon rose, cradling Marielle against him, desperately torn. He needed to find out what had happened, but he had to make sure Marielle was all right before he went.

Esmy came up beside him. "Put her down on the sofa, Simon," she said, her raspy little voice efficient. "We'll take care of her while you make sure the children are safe."

"But..."

"Go ahead, Simon," Miles said, moving with his usual grace and taking one of Marielle's lifeless hands in his own. "You'll do better grappling with whatever demons of the night are up there. I'll keep watch down here. I think our visitations have departed for now."

Simon's lip curled. "Coward."

Miles's smile was very pure. "Absolutely."

Simon allowed himself one last, worried glance at Marielle's pale figure before he ran after Dennis, taking the steps three at a time. The tableau that met his eyes on the fourth floor was both worse and better than he'd imagined.

Another window was broken, letting in blasts of cold air. The door to Marielle's apartment was splintered and hanging from one weak-looking hinge, but Simon suspected the mayhem had been caused by Dennis in his zeal to get to the source of that bloodcurdling shriek, not by whatever midnight intruder had ventured forth.

Julie was sitting on the couch, trying, not very successfully, to hold two wailing children in her almost nonexistent lap. Dennis was doing his best to help, sitting beside her and dabbing at the scratch on her forehead, and the children seemed equally frightened, although neither of them looked as if they'd been hurt.

Without thinking, Simon held out his arms to the miserable children. And to his amazement they both ran to him, Christopher clinging to one knee with fierce abandon, wailing in relief, Emily flinging herself against his chest and hanging on like a monkey.

He collapsed in an uncomfortable chair, taking the children with him, and his big hands were soothing, reassuring as he eyed Julie's sorry appearance. "What happened?"

"I was watching TV, and the kids were asleep," she said, her voice still shaky. She didn't seem to notice that Dennis had his arm around her shoulder, that his expression was an odd mixture of concern, anger and fierce protectiveness. "I thought I heard a noise in the chimney. It sounded as if it was coming from upstairs."

Simon's reaction was short, intense and not suitable for the ears of a five-year-old and an eighteen-month-old. "And you weren't smart enough to stay put?" he demanded, worry making him angry.

"Leave her alone!" Dennis fired back. "All she did was open the door. Some damned mugger was creeping down from your place. She screamed, he hit her, the children woke up and he got away."

"Damn," Simon said more mildly, remembering the children's ears. "Are you all right? Should we take you to the hospital?"

"I'm more frightened than hurt." Surreptitiously she was pressing a hand to her swollen stomach, and Simon had a sudden, horrifying fear.

"You're not going into labor, are you?" he demanded.

"Don't worry, Simon, I've got three weeks to go. He's just kicking." She patted her stomach with a wistful fondness, unaware that Dennis was watching her, lifting his own hand to touch her swollen belly, pulling it back before she even realized what he'd almost done. He stood up abruptly, his eyes met Simon's, and a rueful acknowledgment passed between them.

"I'm calling my brother-in-law," he said shortly. "And then I'll drive Julie to the emergency room. Anyone this close to term shouldn't take chances."

"You aren't by any chance an obstetrician as well as being a plumber and an electrician?" Simon drawled.

Dennis's grin was self-deprecating. "Nope. But I did serve a stint as a medic when I was in the navy. I've been in a few delivery rooms. When it comes right down to it, it's all plumbing."

"Thanks a lot," Julie grumbled.

"On a much grander scale," Dennis said quickly, not missing the offended tone of voice. "Let me call Francis, and then we'll head out."

Simon listened to all this with decidedly mixed feelings. On the one hand he wanted to protest, to tell this young upstart that Julie and everyone else in Farnum's Castle were his responsibility, and if anyone was going to drive her to the hospital it would be himself.

On the other hand, Julie looked at Dennis as if the sun rose and set in his eyes and she'd much prefer having him by her side. And Simon's reasons for taking care of the lost souls at the castle were supposed to be for their sake, not his.

"Anyone know what he did to my apartment?" he asked instead.

"I think we should wait till Francis gets here to check. There might be fingerprints, evidence."

"If you're going to call anyone," Simon said evenly, "you're going to have to go upstairs. And if anyone's going upstairs it's going to be me."

"Me too," Emily said, clinging tightly.

"Me too," said Christopher, chewing on Simon's knee.

Simon looked at Dennis. "You call," he said wearily. "I'd better go down and see how Marielle is."

"What's wrong with Marielle?" Julie demanded, rising stiffly on unsteady feet.

"She fainted at the séance. I didn't have time to see if she was all right...." To his complete and utter horror Emily began to cry again, loud, piercing wails, and Christopher immediately joined in. "Oh, lord, I forgot," he muttered over Emily's loud demands for her mother. "Listen, your mother's fine. She just got a little dizzy. We'll go down and see her, right now. Okay? Okay?"

On the second okay the screeching stopped, Emily nodded her head, managing a semblance of her usual beatific smile, and Christopher uttered a watery chuckle as Simon rose, hoisting his small, wiggling body into his arms.

They felt surprisingly good to him, those two small packages of humanity leaning against him so trustingly. He'd never thought he wanted children, but then he'd never thought he wouldn't. Somehow during his long, misspent life the subject just hadn't come up. But there was something about them, the clean, fresh smell of them, the sweet faces, even the tempestuous tears, that was insidiously touching. If he didn't watch his step he'd find himself seduced just as thoroughly by Marielle's children as he was by their mother.

Marielle was sitting up on the sofa when they reached the bottom floor, and some of her color had returned to her pale cheeks. And her pale cleavage, Simon couldn't help but notice, mentally slapping himself. He set down the children, watching as they catapulted themselves across the room and into Marielle's arms.

He waited until the noise level abated somewhat before filling them in on what happened upstairs. Granita nodded, still so pleased with her visitation from Vittorio that she couldn't really concentrate on the simultaneous break-in. Esmy looked more thoughtful, but said nothing, and Marielle, her blue eyes horrified, kept her mouth shut as she cuddled her children.

It was up to Miles to respond. "This place sounds like a booby trap," he said with his usual lazy charm. "I think you should all get out of here before something even worse happens."

"And where do you suggest we go, Miles?" Simon demanded. "You going to put us up at the expensive penthouse on Lake Shore Drive?"

"It may have escaped your notice, but you live in a penthouse too, Simon. Of course, a haunted penthouse in Farnum's Castle is a far cry from my apartment. I wouldn't be caught dead spending another night here, after all you've been going through. When I think of that apparition in the window..." He shuddered, and Simon almost believed him. Almost. "Surely there are city agencies that can help find places for most of you. And Simon, I know that even with the pittance I pay you, you can afford a better place."

"Where do you suggest we go?" Marielle demanded, her faint voice slightly tart.

Miles smiled his glorious smile at her, and Simon controlled the urge to kick him out the broken window. "Now I think I might be able to find room for you."

"And my kids?"

"They must have grandparents somewhere," he suggested hopefully. "Aunts and uncles?"

"Forget it, Miles," she said, dismissing him as completely as Simon could have hoped. "We're staying."

"Well, I hate to be so trite, but don't say I didn't warn you," he practically purred.

Enough was enough, Simon thought. "Dennis is taking Julie to the emergency room," he said, moving into the room. "Do you want to have them take a look at you, too?"

Marielle looked up, startled. "What's wrong with Julie?"

"Just a bump on her head. She's fine, but Dennis thought they'd better check her out, anyway. What about you?"

She shook her head. "I've been pushing myself too hard. A good night's sleep will take care of it."

"And a few decent meals," Julie said from the doorway. "Cap'n Crunch is not enough to keep any grown woman on her feet."

"It has added vitamins," Marielle defended it faintly. "You look terrible, Julie."

"So do you."

Dennis cleared his throat, barely swallowing his grin. "Francis and his partner will be right over. He said to keep off the top floor."

"I'll keep out of the entire house," Miles said. "And if the rest of you had any sense you'd do the same. I presume you aren't going to make it into work tonight, Simon?"

"Not if you can find someone to take my place." Simon knew perfectly well he'd have no trouble finding a replacement. Miles kept a lengthy list of would-be disc jockeys who'd pay him for the chance to fill in. "Just so long as they know the rules."

Miles emitted a long-suffering sigh. "No playing Musclebound on your shift," he repeated wearily. "Someday, Simon, you'll explain that to me."

"Someday, Miles," Simon returned with utter calm, "you'll admit you know more than you have any right to know."

"And someday," Miles said, "you'll learn not to underestimate me, Simon. I always know more than I have any right to know. I'll get someone to cover for you. Let me know what happens, will you? And if you need any help finding places for people to live, I know a few people with influence. You can count on me for help."

"We'll be just fine," Marielle said, and there was no missing the defiance in her voice. Miles only smiled.

Simon waited until he heard the front door close, waited until the sound of Miles's footsteps was swallowed up by the night before he turned he spoke. "I hate to admit it," he said slowly, "but Miles is right. It's dangerous here, and you'll all be better off someplace else."

"Where would we go?" Granita demanded, some of her delight vanishing. "I don't want to go back to some wretched home—I don't think I could bear it. I don't think any ghosts are going to hurt me."

"You're going to get pneumonia from that broken window," he pointed out.

"Nonsense. I know perfectly well that you'll fix it, as you've fixed things before."

"No, he won't," Marielle said, pulling herself upright and reaching for the shawl. Simon watched with great regret as she proceeded to envelope herself in its voluminous folds. "I own the building. I'll do the repairs. Just give me a few moments to change my clothes and…"

"And who'll stay with the kids?" Simon countered. "Not to mention that someone, probably Dennis, smashed your door down. That should be repaired before the night's out, too. Face it, Marielle, we're all going to have to pitch in. I'll board up Granita's window—there's some old plywood in the basement that will probably cover it. I also have every intention of going over the frame with a fine-toothed comb. Much as I hate to disappoint you all, I don't think that was Vittorio Farnum peering in at us. He wouldn't have needed to break a window to do it. It was a trick of some sort, and I intend to find out how it was done and who did it."

"It wasn't a trick!" Granita insisted. "Couldn't you feel the vibrations, the hunger in the air?"

The only hunger in the air had been his, for Marielle, but he decided not to mention that in front of the assembled group. "If it wasn't a trick it won't do any harm to check, now will it?"

"You could offend the spirits," Esmy said. "It might make them feel unwelcome, drive them away."

"Good." Marielle lifted her head, brushing the thick tangle of blond hair away from her face. "I hate to break this to you, but the spirits aren't welcome here, and I'd like nothing better than for them to get as far away as possible."

"You don't realize what a golden opportunity you're throwing away," Esmy said earnestly. "You saw him as well as we did. You couldn't have any doubt who it was."

"It was an apparition that looked uncannily like Vittorio Farnum," she agreed. "Like Simon, I'm just not sure it wasn't a carefully manufactured one."

"But who would do such a thing?" Granita demanded. "And why?"

"Don't be a ninny," Esmy snapped. "The treasure, of course."

"And we could have asked Vittorio himself!" Granita moaned. "If only you hadn't fainted, my dear. I know you couldn't help it, but next time if you could try to control your dizziness…"

"Next time?" Marielle echoed faintly.

"Dare we try for tomorrow night?" Esmy suggested. "No, perhaps we ought to wait a bit. The moon will be new next Monday—perhaps that will be auspicious."

"Why not do it Halloween?" Marielle said, fully as sarcastic as Simon could be. "It's only a couple of days away...."

"Perfect!" breathed Granita, taking her absurd suggestion seriously. "We'll count on your assistance."

Before Marielle could speak Simon interrupted. If he had his way there would be no need for another séance on Halloween. He had every intention of finding out what in hell was going on around there well before then. "In the meantime," he said, his deep voice immediately gaining their attention, "I don't think anyone should be staying alone. There's definitely something peculiar going on around here, and I want people to double up. Granita, do you want to move in with Esmy or the other way around?"

The two old women glared at each for a long, combative moment. "I suppose she might as well move back in with me," Esmy said grudgingly. "After all, my windows are intact."

"Graciously put, but I prefer to remain here," Granita sniffed. "You have Julie to keep you company, and I, for one, am not afraid of Vittorio."

"Granita." Simon didn't need to say another word—just her name was warning enough.

"Oh, very well. But that doesn't account for the others. What about Marielle?"

"We'll put Julie in with Marielle—that way there'll always be someone to stay with the kids, and there'll be Dennis below and me above. No ghost in his right mind would go near the Meltirks.... Where is her highness, by the way?"

Marielle laughed wryly. "According to Esmy she thanked us all for an entertaining evening and went home to bed. I gather ghosts are a common occurrence in Baluchistan."

"Maybe the Meltirks are responsible for the sudden increase in supernatural visitations," Esmy suggested. "All the spirits want is a welcome."

"There's no welcome here," Marielle said. Christopher was sitting in her lap, his curly golden head drooping against her shawl-covered chest, and Emily's yawn seemed about to split her face in two.

"Let me help you get these kids back to bed," Simon said. "Granita, you move in with Esmy for tonight. I'll board up the window, but I'm not sure how quickly I can get to it. I imagine Officer Muldoon will want to talk with all of you, so don't go to bed quite yet." He reached down and hoisted the sleeping Emily into his arms. She rested her head quite comfortably on his shoulder, and he extended a hand to help Marielle to her feet.

She was staring up at him, openmouthed in amazement. "What magic spell did you use?" she questioned softly, adjusting her own eighteen-month-old burden on her shoulder. "She doesn't like strangers."

"I'm not a stranger."

She didn't move, apparently oblivious to the avid old ladies watching and listening to every word, every nuance. "No," she said finally, "I guess you're not."

If she could ignore the audience so could he. "And unlike her mother," he said, "she has excellent taste in men."

The smile started slowly, that delicious smile that tilted the corners of her blue eyes and wrinkled her short nose. "Oh, I didn't do so badly last night."

There was a pleasantly shocked intake of breath, but Simon's attention was all on Marielle's first, tentative flirtation. "You don't listen to warnings, do you?" he murmured.

"I'm willing to take a few chances. Aren't you?"

"No," he said flatly.

"Liar," she said, laughing up at him, her color and humor restored.

"My dear," said Granita, "I had no idea something like this was going on. Why didn't you tell us?"

"Nothing's going on, Granita." Simon was suddenly all business. "And nothing will."

Granita ignored him. "What do you think, Esmerelda? A Christmas wedding?"

"Don't be a ridiculous old woman," Esmy snapped, fully contemptuous.

"I knew I could count on you to be sensible," Simon said approvingly.

"They'll be married by Thanksgiving," Esmy announced.

"Let's get out of here," Simon said, giving up. "The kids need their sleep and you need to get out of that contraption you're wearing."

By this time Marielle had gotten a little cocky, probably from the aftermath of fear as much as anything. "Oh, I decided I rather liked it. It's fun to watch people's eyes bulge out of their heads."

Just for a moment he considered mentioning what else happened to bulge at the sight of that ridiculous dress, but the present company was too young and too old and altogether too innocent to hear such a thing. "Come along, earth mother," he grumbled. "Any chance you'd be willing to trust the elevator?"

"I'd be more likely to fly up there on my broomstick."

"That's the spirit," said Esmy. "Now you're fitting in to Farnum's Castle."

"She doesn't need a broomstick," Simon drawled, starting out the door and trusting she'd follow.

She did, trudging up the stairs after him, only slightly out of breath as they climbed flight after flight. "I'll try to get Muldoon to wait till tomorrow to talk to you," he said, pausing between the third and fourth floors. "But I can't promise."

"I don't think I'm going to be able to sleep tonight, anyway. If you could just keep him at bay until after the children are settled again, that would be relief enough."

"I can do that." He followed her into the apartment, past the splintered door and into the children's bedroom. Emily was already asleep in his arms, her heavy breathing and angelic expression leaving no doubt. He set her down very carefully, but she did nothing more than curl up, hand under her chin, breathing a deep, heartbreaking sigh.

Marielle turned from the Porta-crib, an odd expression on her face. "You do that quite well," she whispered. "You must have lots of practice."

He felt his mouth curve in a faint smile. "First time," he murmured back. "I must be a natural."

A sudden, strained silence filled the room. It was too enticing, the warm, sexy woman in front of him, the sweetly sleeping children, the whole domestic life that he'd learned he wasn't cut out for. Standing there in the shadows Marielle no longer looked fifteen, she looked like a woman. Like a woman he wanted quite desperately to kiss.

"I'll keep Muldoon away," he said, backing out the door, as big a coward as Miles Van Cortland ever was. And before she could say another word he was gone.

Chapter Thirteen

Marielle rubbed the woolen shawl over her suddenly chilled arms. She followed Simon's fleeing figure out of the children's bedroom, flicking off the light as she went. A blast of cold air rushed from the hallway through her apartment, and she surveyed her splintered door with a resigned shake of the head. She could only hope they were able to rout Vittorio's ghost or his present-day counterparts before winter set in. It was cold enough in October—December in Chicago with broken windows didn't bear thinking about.

For a moment she wondered why she hadn't confided in Simon. The eerie sensation during the séance still lingered in the back of her mind. Someone had touched her, someone had placed a gentle, almost loving hand on her back at a time when she could plainly see everyone's hands. The first time she'd ignored it, the second was when the ghostly image of Vittorio had appeared in the smashed window.

But she knew why she hadn't told Simon, or anyone else. For one thing, she didn't want to feed their fantasies. For another, she didn't want them to scoff. And lastly, and perhaps most importantly, she didn't want to think about it, even for the length of time it would take to tell someone. She would dismiss it from her mind as the figment of her imagination she knew it was.

Marielle had no idea whether Simon had headed upstairs

or back down to Granita's apartment, and she decided she was better off not knowing. She closed the door as best she could, setting it into the splintered frame, and sank onto the sofa that wasn't even remotely as comfortable as Simon's ancient, overstuffed couch. She should do something about the broken window in the hallway, but the police would probably prefer her to wait. So wait she would, curled up on the sofa, wondering why she felt abandoned and bereft.

Maybe she should start thinking seriously about New Mexico. While the offer for Farnum's Castle hadn't been particularly overwhelming, it would at least provide her future with a decent start. If she were at all reasonable she'd think about getting out before things got any worse, before someone else got hurt. Before her children got hurt.

The very thought sent a shiver of horror racing through her body. Did she have any right to take chances when the welfare of her babies was at stake? It was one thing to hold out against superstition and coercion, another to endanger everything that was most important to her. Maybe she had no business doing anything but taking the children and running.

There was, of course, another alternative. She'd promised her parents that the children would come visit them in their safe, comfortable condo not twenty miles from Disney World. Greg's parents were only another hour away—she could send the children down, do her duty to the grandparents, and keep her children safe at the same time. They could have their week visiting their adored grandparents, and she could have a week to get to the bottom of the haunting of Farnum's Castle.

There was only one major flaw in the plan. She didn't want to let them go. They were everything to her, her reason for living, her reason for most of the myriad decisions, good and bad, that she made nowadays. They were all she had, and she couldn't bear the thought of sending them away.

But she couldn't stand the alternatives, either. She couldn't go with them, give up on Farnum's Castle and its hapless inhabitants. And she couldn't keep them here and put them in danger.

They'd survive the separation probably much better than she would. While she sat around moping they'd be having the time of their lives, cosseted by doting relatives. And within a week they'd be able to return to a safe environment.

If they couldn't find out what was going on at Farnum's Castle and put a stop to it in that week, then her choice was clear. She'd take the offer Liam O'Donnell's client had made, take it and run, and to hell with Granita and Esmerelda and Fritzie and Julie. Simon could take over once more.

But that wasn't going to happen. They'd find out who was vandalizing the apartments, who was appearing as the shade of Vittorio Farnum. And since she was about to ask a favor of her parents, she might as well go ahead and accept some of the money her well-to-do in-laws kept trying to force on her. Guilt money or not, she might as well take advantage of it.

She heard the modified rumble of footsteps and voices as the police arrived and climbed the endless flights to Simon's apartment. She sat there watching the ceiling as she listened to them move from room to room, their voices a muffled soporific, and slowly her head began to nod. It was after eleven, she was still dressed in that ridiculous, ill-fitting, immodest dress, and she needed her sleep. It was too late to call her parents now—tomorrow would be soon enough. Soon enough to make the plane reservations, to deal with the thought of being without Emily and Christopher.

She could barely summon up the energy to crawl into

the bedroom. She'd never fainted before in her life, and if she wasn't intimately aware of how little she'd eaten, how little she'd slept and what time of the month it was, she'd be worried. She always felt a little wrung out when her period was over, and this time was no different. And she couldn't control her insomnia, not with burglars and ghosts popping in and out of windows at any time of night. But she could remember to eat properly, particularly when her children's well-being might depend on it.

She managed to slide out of the dress, leaving it in a graceful heap of silk on the wooden floor beside her bed. The gargoyles were shadowed in darkness, and she told herself that they wouldn't be leering tonight. Even carved satyrs would have pity on a woman on the edge of collapse. She did collapse, onto the too-soft mattress, too tired to climb between the sheets. If the police needed to talk to her tonight it would be up to them to wake her. Right then she didn't think Vittorio Farnum and all the fiends of hell could rouse her from the deep sleep her body was craving.

She surfaced for a few brief moments when she heard her battered door fall open, but the whispering voices belonged to Julie and Dennis, and she sank back into sleep. At one point a shadow moved through her room, picking up the discarded silk dress, pulling the heavy quilt over her body, brushing her hair away from her sleeping face. She was tempted to wake up and confront the intruder, but her instincts, even while she was sleeping, told her she was safe. It was probably just Julie, restless in her advancing pregnancy.

The touch on her face was so light that she could scarcely feel it, but there was gentleness and affection in that feathery caress. She knew without opening her eyes that it was the same hand that had touched her during the séance, and that it meant her no harm. Marielle settled deeper into sleep.

SHE'D HALF HOPED her parents wouldn't be able to take the kids, that some desperately important tennis tournament or bridge play-off would be keeping them too busy. She should have known better. Her mother jumped at the possibility of a visit like a starving woman at a feast, and instead of complaining that Marielle couldn't accompany the children, she seemed to be particularly delighted to have them all to herself.

"Now don't you worry about a thing, Marielle. A little bit of sunshine and doting grandparents is just what they need. Are you sure a week is long enough? Why don't I make the plane reservations for ten days apart? That would give us a little extra time...."

"One week, Mother," Marielle said in the tone of voice her mother always obeyed. "If things haven't improved around here by then, I'll come down and join you. There must be someplace I can stash a sleeping bag."

"Of course, darling. I do wish I could call you—this telephone situation is impossible. We'll pick up the tab for the airfare, of course. I'll make the plane reservations, then wait to hear from you. We'll do it tomorrow if there's space on any of the flights."

"Tomorrow?" Marielle gasped. "So soon?"

"It sounds as if the sooner they're out of there the better. Listen darling, if you can't trust your own mother, whom can you trust?"

Whom indeed? Marielle thought, replacing the receiver. From her seat in Simon's hallway she could see directly into his apartment. It was a disaster—books and papers strewn everywhere, posters torn off the wall, their glass frames smashed, the previously sealed-off fireplace a mass of rubble. She was half tempted to go in and start cleaning it up, but resisted the impulse. For one thing, it was none of her business. For another, she had enough to keep her busy without taking on new projects. If she knew her mother the children would be flying out some time tomor-

row—Virginia Watson could be as ruthlessly efficient as a
general in pursuit of what she wanted, and she wanted Marielle's children.

In the meantime she should be preparing the kids for
their imminent departure, trying to get their clothes packed,
to find what kind of laundry services the old building
boasted. She probably didn't want to know. It would doubtless turn out to be one more thing that needed to be repaired.

Of course, she was forgetting her live-in plumber. And
if he was feeling too caught up in Julie's welfare she could
always remind him that Julie had laundry, too. She didn't
really expect to have any problem getting Dennis to work,
though. He seemed more than willing to help out.

The coffee would be ready by now—she needed to head
back downstairs to the apartment and see what she could
do about her splintered door. But there was one last thing
she needed to check in Simon's deserted apartment.

He'd gone out early that morning—she'd heard the
creaking and jerking of the elevator while she was struggling to find something a little more nutritious than Cap'n
Crunch. Julie was still sound asleep on the living-room
couch, the bandage on her forehead partially obscured by
her hair, and the children were still snoring faintly, well
past the time for *Sesame Street*. She'd crept upstairs barefoot, dressed in old jeans and a sweater, calling her parents
before she could change her mind, instinctively knowing it
would be hours before Simon would return, hours that
would give her enough time to figure out how she was
going to deal with him.

She suspected even weeks wouldn't be enough. She
wasn't going to be able to deal with him until she learned
to handle her own, incomprehensible reaction to him.

But she'd face that later. Right now she wanted to know
one thing and one thing only. Had the vandal trashed

Simon's celestially comfortable sofa in his orgy of destruction?

She tiptoed in, knowing there was no need for silence, being silent anyway. The place really was a shambles—it looked more as if a poltergeist had been at work than a thief. Most of the destruction looked wanton—flour and ground coffee strewn over the floors, furniture upended, obscene, incomprehensible messages scrawled on the bare white walls. She stared around her in shocked dismay.

"They did a thorough job, didn't they?" Simon spoke from directly behind her.

With a great effort Marielle controlled the start of surprise that his sudden reappearance engendered. "Who are Musclebound?" she asked instead, looking at the name written in what seemed to be blood, but which on closer examination smelled like ketchup.

Simon's short bark of laughter was far from amused. "Weren't you listening to Miles's sniping comments last night?" he asked, moving into the room and picking up some of the scattered papers. "They're a rock group, a very successful one, as a matter of fact. And I don't play their records."

"I know that. I mean, I've heard of the group. I wondered why the name is painted on your walls. Why don't you play their records?"

Simon kept his back to her. His graying black hair touched his collar, and she had the sudden, inexplicable urge to brush it back. Instead she knelt on the floor, scooping up papers, her eyes still watching his averted profile.

"Why don't you ask Miles?" he muttered, dumping a pile on the desk and leaning down for more.

"I don't think he knows." She sat back on her heels, the papers resting in her hands. "And I don't want him to tell me. I want you to."

He turned and looked at her then, and she was shocked at the dark pain in his eyes, the cynical twist of his mouth.

"You really want to know?" he asked. "Then maybe I'll tell you. You won't like it, but then it's a sordid enough little story."

Marielle's heart twisted a little. "I can survive sordid details."

"Can you? It's no great tragedy, of course. Human greed, human venality, human weakness are all pretty standard for people in the modern world. I used to think I was invulnerable but I learned the hard way that I wasn't." Bitterness and self-loathing made his deep, beautiful voice raw and ugly, and he turned away from her, moving to the window to look out over the overgrown yard.

She sat without moving for a long moment. "So what did you do, Simon?" she asked gently. "Take a bribe from a record company?"

"Fairly obvious, isn't it?" He still wouldn't look at her. "Payola's a nasty crime. People lose their jobs, lose their licenses, lose their freedom if the courts so choose. If they happen to get caught. I didn't get caught."

She rose silently, leaving the papers scattered around her. "They paid you money to play Musclebound? I would have thought a group that successful wouldn't need to resort to payola."

"That's the incredibly stupid thing about it. If they'd just gone about it through normal channels they would have been as big a hit as they are now. But they took the sleazy way."

"And brought you down with it." Her voice was very gentle. "How long ago was this?"

"Nine years ago. I was at a big station in New York, and I was greedy. I thought it was all right to take a generous gift from the sales rep. No, scratch that. I knew it wasn't all right. I just decided to do it anyway. Everyone else was doing it, I needed the money, and I said yes. And I played Musclebound every hour for a week."

"But you stopped, didn't you? Isn't that something?"

He still kept his back to her. "Half the disc jockeys at the station got caught. Some ended up with their licenses suspended, one ended up with a six-month sentence. The station lost its license, and I was out of a job. But no one realized I'd had my hand in the cookie jar, too. I had too noble a reputation. So I never got caught. I moved back to Chicago, worked for a while at a big station, and then quit. I took a job with Miles's two-bit station, and I've been here ever since."

"Penance," Marielle said softly. "You said something about penance a few days ago. Is that what you're doing here?"

"Among other things." He turned then, leaning against the wall and looking at her. "So where's the Mary Sunshine absolution? Aren't you going to tell me I'm making a big fuss over nothing, that I've punished myself long enough? Come on, Marielle, tell me what a fool I'm being over a minor indiscretion."

She crossed the last few feet to stand directly in front of him. Inches away, her bare toes touching his well-worn running shoes. "You betrayed your principles. That's not a minor indiscretion. You don't need me to forgive you. You need to forgive yourself."

He looked down at her, his mouth curved in a mocking smile. "What if I don't think I'm worth forgiving?"

"Then that would be another major mistake on your part," she said. On impulse she reached up, pressing her cool lips against his. There was no response, though she could feel a faint tremor ripple through his body, and she drew back.

"You want to kiss the boo-boo and make it better? I'm not one of your children, Marielle."

"I can't help it if you act like a five-year-old." She reached up again without thinking, and pressed her mouth against his, increasing the pressure this time. She was shocked to feel his mouth open beneath hers, and she put her hands on his shoulders to brace herself. Suddenly she decided to shock him in return, to prove to him that she wasn't the skittish little coward he seemed to think her. Reaching out with the tip of her tongue she touched the firm contours of his lips, teasing the edge of his teeth, exploring, very gently, very shyly.

She was unprepared for the intensity of his reaction. He'd been standing there completely passively, hands at his sides, when a strangled groan caught at the back of his throat and he pulled her into his arms, his tongue meeting hers. He picked her up and turned her in his arms, pressing her against the graffiti-covered wall of the apartment as his tongue took up where hers had left off.

She didn't know people kissed like that. She didn't want it to stop; she wanted him to pick her up and carry her over to the sofa before she could start thinking again. Maybe a little disappointment in the end would be worth it, if the beginning was as astonishingly delightful as this.

And then he moved away, mere inches, his hands pressed against the wall on either side of her, imprisoning her. His breath was coming in strangled rasps, as was hers. They looked into each other's eyes for a long, startled moment.

"Why do we always end up doing this?" Marielle asked when she got her breathing back under control. "We can't be alone for more than five minutes before this starts."

The smile that curved his mouth was very small, but it was free from the bitterness that had twisted it moments before. "Maybe it's too big to fight."

"Nothing's too big to fight," Marielle said fiercely.

Simon simply stood there for another moment, then dropped his arms. "What are you doing here?" he asked, moving away and scooping up more of the scattered papers.

She couldn't very well tell him she'd wanted to see if the couch was still in one piece. It would prove she was far too interested in it and in what had almost happened on it two nights ago. "I was looking for you," she said, knowing deep down that it was the truth. "The children are going to visit my parents in Florida."

She tossed out the statement, determined not to show him how torn she felt, but she underestimated his sensitivity. "How do you feel about that?" he asked, dropping the papers once more.

"At this rate we're never going to get your apartment cleaned up," she joked, avoiding his question.

"To hell with the apartment. How do you feel about sending the children away?"

"Who says I'm sending them away?"

"Of course you are. It's a very wise idea, given that things have escalated around here in the last few days. If you want them to be safe you should send them away. You should go yourself."

She knew that was coming. "I'm not going."

He grinned then, a fully fledged, resigned grin. "I know that, too. I just thought I'd suggest it. What are you going to do while they're gone?"

She smiled faintly. "It's really quite simple. I'm going to make this place safe for all of us, the children included. With your help, or without it."

"Oh, with my help," he said promptly. "And how are you planning to perform this enormous feat?"

"It's quite obvious, really," she said. "We'll just find Vittorio's treasure before anyone else does."

Chapter Fourteen

She heard no groan of protest. "It sounds logical," Simon admitted. "If the treasure turns up, then no one would have any need to search for it. Assuming, of course, that the treasure actually exists and isn't part of some Chicago folklore."

"It exists," Marielle said flatly.

"What makes you so certain?"

"Someone's going to a great deal of trouble to get us all out of here. Night after night they're breaking in and trashing the apartments. They're setting up elaborate phony ghosts to scare us and they're absolutely relentless in their determination to find Vittorio's treasure. No one would go to all that trouble on the basis of folklore."

Simon dumped a pile of papers on the bleached oak table, then scooped up more. "A reasonable enough assumption. But what if you're wrong? What if the ghosts aren't phony? What if the break-ins are the responsibility of one of Vittorio's long-dead victims, come to wreak havoc on his old enemy?"

"You actually used to watch those old movies, didn't you?" Marielle said admiringly. "This isn't the night of the living dead, Simon. This is Chicago at the end of the nineteen-eighties. If the ghost of an old gangster were going to rise up and cause trouble don't you think he would have done so long ago?''

"Maybe something set him off. Maybe all the pregnant women in the building... You're not pregnant, are you?''

The question took her by surprise. "Of course not!'' she snapped. "Not that it's any of your business.''

He shrugged. "Women don't usually faint unless they're pregnant.''

"They do when they're confronted by a ghost.''

"I thought you didn't believe in ghosts,'' he shot back.

"I don't know what I believe in. I just think the trouble at Farnum's Castle is more likely caused by greedy humans than otherworldly visitors. You can't seriously believe that Vittorio or one of his victims trashed your apartment.''

"No. But I can always hope.''

He was baiting her, and she'd been much too quick to rise to the provocation. "You're just as sick as Granita and Esmy,'' she said with a weary sigh. "I'd just as soon be spared the ghosts. Give me a Chicago thug any day.''

"That's precisely what Vittorio was,'' he pointed out.

She floundered, searching for a suitable response, then gave up and stuck out her tongue at him. "Why are you giving me a hard time?'' she demanded, suddenly much more cheerful than she'd been half an hour ago. "I know perfectly well that you're even more skeptical about ghosts than I am.''

"It keeps you on your toes,'' he replied, unrepentant.

"Why are you pushing the idea of a ghost? Is it simply to drive me out of here, or did you find something last night when you boarded up Granita's window?''

"What makes you think that?'' Simon's narrow, clever face was completely blank, but Marielle was beginning to see behind the facade.

"You did find something!'' she said. "What was it? Ectoplasm?''

"Ectoplasm?'' Simon echoed in disgust. "Where's your

skepticism when we need it? I found traces of fluorescent paint, piano wire, nails embedded in the window frame. All sorts of nice little bits of fakery. Even more interesting— it was all gone this morning when the police checked.''

''A setup,'' Marielle breathed, pleased. ''And we know there have to be at least two of them. One was upstairs trashing your apartment while the other was lurking outside Granita's windows. I don't suppose there were any nice muddy footprints?''

''Life isn't that convenient. At least we know our hideous apparition of last night was caused by flesh and blood and not ectoplasm.''

''So why were you trying to convince me it was a ghost?''

''To see if I could persuade you to leave with the children.''

It was absurd, the tiny little dart of pain that shafted through her. She'd always known he wanted her gone. ''I'm not leaving, Simon,'' she said evenly.

''I know.'' His tone was resigned. ''Are you sure I can't talk you into going with them? You wouldn't want the kids to travel alone, would you? Why don't you take a nice, safe, warm vacation while the rest of us sort this out?''

''Why don't you...?'' She swallowed the retort. ''Never mind. And you haven't had the dubious pleasure of meeting my mother. I have no doubt she'll fly up to meet the children and accompany them back. If I know her she won't even leave O'Hare.''

''So what are you worried about? Wasn't she a decent mother? It sounds like she'll be a perfectly doting, overprotective grandmother.''

''Who says I'm worried?''

He laughed, a short, cynical laugh. ''I may not know your mother, but after five days I know exactly what's going on in that devious little brain of yours. You're sick at the thought of sending the children away, but you're too levelheaded to put them at risk. That doesn't mean you still won't be miserable while they're gone. Which is exactly why you should go with them.''

"Simon…" Her voice held a definite warning.

"I know, you're not leaving," he said wearily. "Where do we start looking for this famous treasure? There are at least seventeen fireplaces in the building and our friendly housebreaker has only trashed half a dozen. Want to start with them, or do you prefer to be more subtle? Maybe checking out the basement?''

"What I need to do is get the kids' things packed. If I know my mother she's going to have them on a plane in less than twenty-four hours.''

"That sounds like a good idea. I need some sleep if I'm going to manage to work tonight. Let me grab a few hours and then we'll start.''

She was halfway across the littered room, looking at him, feeling strange, unaccountable emotions churning inside her. Maybe he was right. Maybe getting out of Farnum's Castle, out of Chicago, away from Simon Zebriskie was the smartest thing she could possibly do. After all, she didn't want anything from him, despite her seemingly irresistible urge to kiss him at the oddest moments.

No, ghosts and burglars and criminal treasure hunters weren't going to drive her away from the new home she was trying to make for her children. Nor was her inexplicable attraction to Simon Zebriskie. "A few hours," she said briskly. "We can start in the empty apartment beside mine.''

"It's not empty. That's where all the old furniture is stored.''

"Even better. We'll start by going through Vittorio's possessions and see if he left any clues. Maybe we should take down that old portrait.''

"It'll be over Granita's dead body. Go away and let me

sleep, Marielle,'' he said drowsily. "Even better, come sleep with me.''

"I'll see you later,'' she said, ignoring the crazy little stirring inside her and hurrying out the door before she could even begin to contemplate temptation.

"Later,'' he agreed, his deep voice following her into the hallway and down the stairs.

He must be getting punchy, he thought, watching her go. Another minute and he would have grabbed her. The odd thing was, he didn't think she'd have put up much of a fight if he had pulled her over to the couch and proceeded to finish what they'd started far too many times.

Despite her belief in the uselessness of sex, she certainly responded every time he was fool enough to touch her. Her response astonished her as much as it should have surprised him. But he knew better than she just how good sex could be, and he suspected that even he didn't know the half of it. He was experienced enough to recognize mutual attraction, even if Marielle chose to hide from it. He was also experienced enough to know that his attraction to Marielle was stronger than anything he'd felt in years. If ever.

It was too late—he knew it as well as he knew his own body. Even if he could manage the impossible and send her away, the damage had been done. He was probably a fool to fight it.

He crossed the room and shut the door behind her, leaning his head against the frame for a moment. He couldn't believe he'd told her about the payola. The ugly deed that had flayed him raw for nine years, his own nasty little guilt that weighed down upon him, never letting him free, had been a secret from absolutely everyone.

For some reason he felt curiously weightless. Maybe that old chestnut about confession being good for the soul had an element of truth. He'd told Marielle the worst about himself, and she hadn't flinched, hadn't shied away in horror. As a matter of fact, she'd responded by planting a very brave kiss on his lips. With a little time, a little tutelage, she could be quite astonishing....

Cancel that thought, he ordered himself sternly, throwing his weary body onto the welcoming sofa. They weren't going to have the time. He was going to keep on fighting it with every breath in his body. At least until the children were safely in Florida, he added honestly. And then, maybe he'd just see what happened when Marielle had no other responsibilities. Maybe her curiosity might overcome her doubts. And maybe there'd be no escaping the inevitable for either of them.

On that troubling, optimistic note he fell sound asleep in the midst of his littered apartment.

IF SHE'D EXPECTED, secretly hoped for a little reluctance, a little misery from her children when she informed them of their imminent departure, then Marielle was doomed to disappointment. While Emily managed a cursory interest in her mother's whereabouts during their upcoming vacation, her concentration quickly shifted to Disney World, and for the rest of the day her piping little voice could be heard informing a sanguine Christopher about the treats in store for them.

Even Julie seemed dangerously cheerful, despite the lump on her forehead. She'd checked out fine at the emergency room; the baby was fine, everything was fine. The usually reserved girl was whistling as she bustled around the kitchen, fixing the biggest breakfast Marielle had ever seen and forcing her to eat it, scrambled eggs, bacon, muffins, coffee and all. The food had its expected effect and Marielle had begun to relax, when a peremptory knock sounded at the damaged door.

In response the door caved inward, ripping off the remaining hinge and exposing Liam O'Donnell, as prissy and as neatly put together as ever, glowering in the entrance to her apartment.

Marielle's good mood vanished instantly. In her experience lawyers never came bearing good news. Slowly she began to rise, reluctant to hear whatever he had come to say, when Julie moved her pregnant bulk in front of her.

"Were you looking for me?" Julie's belligerence was back with full force, and this time Marielle couldn't blame her. O'Donnell could bring out the belligerence in anyone.

"As a matter of fact, I was." O'Donnell stepped over the broken door and into the room, unasked, ignoring Marielle. "I heard you went to the emergency room last night. I was concerned for your health."

"You were concerned for your commission from my baby's adoptive parents," Julie said bitterly. "Don't worry, the baby's safe. You'll get your ten thousand dollars."

"You know perfectly well we're not talking about that kind of money," O'Donnell said, his wrinkled little mouth pursed in disapproval. "I'm doing this out of the goodness of my heart, trying to help out a girl in trouble and a couple who's desperate for a child."

"I didn't think you had a heart," Marielle broke in cheerfully. "What's the money going to cover?"

"I'm charging a pittance to cover court costs." He glared at Marielle's interested expression. "Is there somewhere we can talk in private?"

"We can talk in front of Marielle. She's my friend," Julie said staunchly, dropping onto the sofa beside her.

"Have you met the adoptive parents?" Marielle questioned, tucking her feet beneath her and preparing to stay.

"I don't consider that wise," O'Donnell said stiffly.

"I don't think he's decided who's going to get my baby," Julie said, her voice low and miserable.

"It shouldn't be up to him, Julie," Marielle said, much to O'Donnell's outrage. "It's up to you. And if you want to meet them before you relinquish the baby, then insist on it. You're not doing anyone any favors if you give up this baby without making absolutely sure it's what you want to do.''

"I don't have any choice in the matter. I don't have the money to support the baby, I don't even have my high school diploma yet, and a baby needs two parents.''

"Mine only have one.''

"That wasn't up to you. I chose to carry this baby, and I'm not going to weaken now. It's going to go to the best, happiest family I can find.''

"I wouldn't trust Liam O'Donnell to know the best and happiest,'' Marielle said frankly. "I think he'll go for the most money. Don't you?''

"That's it!'' Liam slammed down his briefcase, advancing on Marielle like a slender, infuriated rabbit. "You will kindly cease to slander me in front of my client! You have no basis for that kind of remark, no basis at all.''

"You're right,'' Marielle admitted. "Just pure instinct.'' She turned her back on him. "Julie, I think you should look into an agency. They'd be sure to screen prospective parents carefully, they'd provide counseling for you and even help you look into alternatives if you decide to keep the baby.''

Julie's face contorted in anguish. "I can't keep the baby,'' she said, her voice rippling with pain. "I've gone over and over it in my mind. There's no way I can do it.''

Marielle opened her mouth to protest, then shut it again. There was nothing she could say that wouldn't make things even worse than they already were. It wasn't up to her to help Julie keep the baby. But she'd never forgive herself if she didn't do everything she could to make sure Julie made a choice that she could live with for the rest of her life.

"I'm clearly wasting my time here,'' the elderly lawyer sniffed. "I'd like you to come into my office so we can begin the preliminary paperwork, Julie. I'll send a car for you tomorrow morning. Say around ten?''

"I'm not ready to do that,'' Julie said.

"Really, my dear, we both know this is best for the baby. And I'm a very busy man. I can't wait till the last minute and then drop everything for a charity case."

"I bet the only charity that benefits from this is the Liam O'Donnell Mercedes fund," Marielle snapped. "Don't push her. If the paperwork is too much for you, I'm sure we can find a state agency that'll be more than happy to handle the matter. If Julie decides that's what she wants to do."

She could practically see the smoke coming out of his ears. With a noticeable effort he controlled his rage. "Very well. Let me know when you feel like dealing with it, Julie. But don't take too long. You want your child to grow up with every advantage, don't you? My clients are from a much higher level of society than any you'd find through a public agency. Who knows, if you go through the state your child might be adopted by truck drivers." He shuddered delicately.

"My grandfather was a truck driver," Julie said fiercely. "And you couldn't have asked for a better father."

"I don't seem to be able to say anything right," O'Donnell said stiffly. "I'll wait for you to get in touch. And Mrs. Brandt?"

Now it was her turn. "Yes?" Marielle managed a tight smile.

His answering smile was as sour as a lemon. "You've had another offer on this monstrosity. The client has gone up another five thousand, but he says that's the limit, and if you don't respond within forty-eight hours the offer will be withdrawn. I suggest you take it. I know the bidder's reputation, and this isn't an idle bluff."

She could take off with her children tomorrow and never have to think again about the motley crew she'd be leaving behind. She wouldn't have to worry about courting disaster and disappointment and eventual heartbreak with Simon

Zebriskie. She'd be safe, free and reasonably solvent. She must be out of her mind.

"I don't need forty-eight hours, Mr. O'Donnell. The answer is no."

Wasn't there some sort of fairy-tale figure who went into such a rage that he vanished in a puff of smoke? She half expected to see Liam O'Donnell do just that. But he was made of sterner stuff. After one last stare of loathing at the two young women, he turned on his heel, stomping on the broken door and moving into the hallway.

"I hope he takes the elevator and gets stuck," Marielle said with a muffled giggle.

She couldn't coax an answering smile from Julie's mournful face. "I don't. That'd just mean he'd be around longer."

"You're right. The sooner he's out of the building the happier I'll be. Julie…"

"Don't start in on me," the other girl said, pushing herself up from the couch. "I've got to go now. I'll be back, okay? I just need a little space."

"Julie…" She didn't know what to say. "I'm so sorry."

"Yeah," said Julie, her mouth curved in bitterness. "So am I."

Marielle stretched out on the couch, listening to Julie's footsteps on the stairs. She could only hope she wasn't trying to catch up with Liam O'Donnell. That evil man was trying to rip her off; Marielle just knew it. He probably had half a dozen desperate couples on the line and was planning to sell Julie's baby to the highest bidder.

Marielle's sense of motherhood was outraged. Children were precious, not a commodity to be bought and sold by a weasel like Liam O'Donnell. She'd been willing to give the lawyer the benefit of the doubt, but no longer. Any man who'd be willing to manipulate people in this sort of situation deserved nothing. He'd get his profit, from Julie and the desperate people he was bartering with, and leave misery in his wake.

It was a damned shame. Julie was so good with children, a natural. Young as she was, she still deserved to have one of her own, one to fuss over and love. It just wasn't fair.

At first she thought Julie's footsteps had simply moved out of earshot. The muffled sound of voices might have come from someone's radio. And then she recognized the sound of Dennis's baritone, raised in frustration, and a hopeful smile wreathed her face.

Dennis was her one hope—Dennis of the plumbing and heating expertise, a practical knight-errant if ever she saw one. She'd watched the way he looked at Julie and the way Julie looked back, both of them unaware of the other's interest. It wouldn't be the most auspicious way to start a marriage, but she could think of worse ones.

She heard the tinny thump of Dennis's door. The voices more muffled now, were directly beneath her. Better and better. If Julie could turn to Dennis in her hour of need, it wouldn't take him too long to come up with a solution. All Marielle could do was lie there on her sofa and cross her fingers, hoping for a happy ending. And try not to think of the couch she'd rather be on.

It was a losing battle. She was getting more and more preoccupied with things that shouldn't matter in the least. Simon Zebriskie, Simon's couch, Simon's hands. She needed a dose of common sense, and she was going to make one last attempt at finding it.

She pushed herself off the sofa. She needed to talk to someone levelheaded, needed that very badly. So she rounded up the children and made the trek up the curving flight of stairs to Simon's hallway telephone, cursing the phone company once more. Christopher and Emily were uncharacteristically docile, sitting at her feet with paper and crayons while she once more dialed Abbie's California phone number.

She had little hope she'd be able to reach her old friend. Every time she'd tried in the past she'd either come up with a busy signal or no answer at all.

Abbie was the practical one, devoid of romantic sentiment. She was the only woman Marielle had ever known who'd had the sense of self-preservation to terminate a hopeless relationship. Surely she'd be able to help Marielle come to her senses!

She listened with only half a mind as the phone rang, so preoccupied that she almost didn't respond when Abbie's familiar voice answered the phone.

"Marielle, I've been thinking about you!" she cried when Marielle finally identified herself. "Why don't you have a telephone?"

"It's too complicated. Let's just say I'm working on it."

"How are the children? Do they like Chicago?"

Marielle laughed, happier than she'd been in days, wrapped in the familiar warmth of her old friend. "They've discovered they like sugared cereal and nonstop television. I'm sending them to stay with my mother for a week or two. Things are really in an upheaval around here." It was the perfect opening, and Abbie dutifully prodded her.

"What's been going on?"

For some reason Marielle wasn't quite ready to confess. She didn't know what there was to confess—that she was getting irrationally absorbed in a man who wasn't interested in her, that she was dealing with vandals and ghosts and hidden treasure? It all seemed so unbelievable, so instead she stalled. "Did you hear from Suzanne?"

"About her cowboy? Sure did. Who would have thought a big-city sophisticate like Suzanne would be happy in the wild west?"

"And little Mouse is married," Marielle added. "Not to mention Jaime."

"Not to mention me."

"What?" Marielle shrieked. "I don't believe it!"

"Believe it," Abbie said. "The mighty have fallen, and fallen hard. We're not rushing into anything, mind you. But I don't have any doubts about it. T. J. is The One."

"He feels the same way?"

"Absolutely. You should see us, Marielle. We're so much in love it would amaze you."

"Nothing would amaze me," Marielle said, swallowing the unexpected lump in her throat. "You deserve every happiness."

"I still can't quite believe it," Abbie said with a little laugh. "But tell me what's been happening with you. I know your voice too well. Something's on your mind."

"Not a thing except your happiness," Marielle lied. Now was not the time to burden Abbie with her confusion and anxiety. "Am I invited to the wedding?"

"Of course. It probably won't be till spring, but you'll be the first to know." There was a pause. "Are you sure something isn't wrong?"

"Not a thing," she said staunchly. "I just wanted to make sure everything was going well with you. I'll be in touch."

"Wait. I wanted to talk with you. I still..."

"The kids are about to fall off the landing," Marielle said desperately, and her two quiet children looked up at her in surprise. "I'll call you back the minute I have a chance."

"Marielle..."

"Give my best to T. J. Tell him he'd better treat you right." Her voice was getting a little rough around the edges.

"Marielle, wait..."

"Goodbye, Abbie, lots of love." And she set the telephone back on its cradle.

Emily and Christopher were looking up at her out of solemn eyes. She couldn't just sit there and burst into tears. Besides, she was happy for her friends, truly, delightfully happy. It just had the unfortunate side effect of making her feel even lonelier and more bereft.

"Let's go back to the apartment," she said brightly. "If you guys are going to Disney World we'd better get you packed."

And with gentle hands she herded her small brood back downstairs, putting her momentary lapse into self-pity out of her mind.

Chapter Fifteen

"Ms. Brandt, Her Serene Highness the Crown Princess of Baluchistan requests your presence."

Marielle just stared at the neatly dressed young bureaucrat at her door. She'd been stretched out, half asleep, half awake while the children were enraptured by *Sesame Street*, when a shadow had appeared at her door. She'd blinked sleepily, only to realize it wasn't Simon, after all.

She sat up, setting her bare feet on the floor and running a careless hand through her blond hair. She felt sleepy, messy and completely comfortable, a fact that secretly amazed her. Being properly turned out at all times had been part of her job description as Greg's upscale young wife. Now that she was on her own she could wear what she wanted to wear, do what she wanted to do, and if young men in gray suits showed up at her broken door, then they were running the risk of seeing Ms. Marielle Brandt at less than her most stylish.

"I beg your pardon," she said belatedly.

"Sorry." The young man stepped gingerly around the door and held out his wallet with an official-looking identification card in it. "I'm John Davies, with the State Department. I'm responsible for the Meltirks, and her highness asked me to have you visit her."

Just what she needed, Marielle thought wearily. "Do you have any idea what she wants?"

"I never know what her highness wants," Davies said mournfully. "I've tried to move them to better quarters, but they adamantly refuse. I beg your pardon—you own this building, don't you?"

Marielle smiled. If John Davies was going to have a future as a diplomat, he was going to have to watch his tongue. "I wouldn't live here either if I didn't have to," she said, even though that wasn't strictly true. "I'll have to wait till my baby-sitter gets back. Do you think she's in any particular hurry?"

"The Baluchistanis don't know the meaning of the word hurry," Davies assured her. "Life goes on at an almost sedentary pace. I think the only reason the revolution succeeded was because the ruling family was too lazy to argue. Any time this afternoon will be fine. Mrs. deCarlo has offered to translate, though her highness has a way of being understood if she wants to. Or I could always come back."

It took a moment for Marielle to realize what was going on. John Davies was standing there, smiling an ingenuous smile, and she knew quite definitely that he wouldn't have offered to come back for one of the old ladies or for Simon. "I...er..."

"And if your baby-sitter was still around we could go out to dinner and discuss the Meltirks. I'm sure they can't be the easiest tenants, what with their refusal to learn English and those ceremonial fires going all the time. I could fill you in on all sorts of Baluchistani background. Their religious ceremonies, their moral standards. Maybe we could even go dancing afterward."

"And you could show me Baluchistani folk dances," she suggested wryly, a slow grin lighting her face. It was nice to be appreciated by a man, even in her current dishabille, even if she had no interest in him whatsoever. It was nice to suddenly feel free and wanted.

John Davies grinned back. "I could. Or we could try something a little slower, where you get to hold on to your partner."

"Sounds peachy," Simon grumbled from the doorway. "You want me to baby-sit?"

John Davies's handsome face turned bright red. He looked like a little boy whose hand was caught in a cookie jar. "Hi, Simon," he mumbled.

"John." Simon's voice was deep and disapproving, and it was all Marielle could do to stifle a giggle. Simon was acting like an overprotective father, John like a guilty teenager. If he was going to go any further in the State Department he was going to have to learn to control his blushes too, she thought critically. And Simon needed to realize that his own feelings for her weren't in the slightest bit paternal, for all his patriarchal air.

"That's sweet of you to offer, Simon," she said. "But I was about to refuse John's invitation. The children are leaving tomorrow morning and I want to spend all the time I can with them. I'm sure Esmy will manage to translate just fine for me."

"Your children are leaving?" John's expression brightened considerably. "What about Saturday or even...?"

"No," said Simon.

"No?" echoed John Davies.

"No," said Marielle, regretfully. "But I do appreciate the invitation."

"Oh," said John Davies. "Oh." He looked from Simon's glowering expression to Marielle's impish one. "I guess I've been obtuse. I didn't mean to trespass." He backed from the room, tripping over the fallen door, steering clear of Simon's menacing figure, disappearing down the hallway as fast as his neatly shod feet could carry him.

"He's not real big on diplomacy, is he?" Marielle questioned lightly.

"John's okay. He's just young." Simon moved into the

room and picked up the fallen door, leaning it against the wall. "I didn't mean to scare him off."

"Didn't you?" Marielle was frankly, cheerfully skeptical. "You sure did a good job of it."

Simon opened his mouth to protest, then shut it with a snap as Julie appeared in the doorway. Her large brown eyes were still puffy and red-rimmed, but her expression was calmer, almost hopeful. Apparently Dennis had managed to work wonders. And Marielle felt her own hopes rise.

"I'm feeling much better," she announced, forestalling Marielle's question. "Esmy's waiting down at the Meltirks. Why don't you go ahead and I'll watch the kids?"

"I'll start going through the old furniture next door," Simon offered, and if Marielle hadn't known better she would have thought there was an apology in his voice. "That's where most of your horrific furniture came from, and there's tons more. Maybe Vittorio left a clue in a dresser drawer."

"And maybe the moon's made of green cheese," Marielle countered. "I don't suppose anyone knows what the princess wants of me, do they?"

"Maybe they want you to participate in one of their animal sacrifices," Simon drawled.

Marielle stared at him in dawning horror. "They don't really?" she demanded, aghast.

"Probably not. All I know is animals go in there and they never come out." He dropped his voice so that it was low and sepulchral, and she suddenly remembered Simon Zee and the horror movies.

"Don't give me the creeps," she said, shuddering.

Simon smiled blandly, pleased with himself. "Go ask her highness. I'll be in the next apartment rummaging through old sarcophagi."

"Cut it out!"

"Halloween's in two days," he said, unabashed. "Are you sure you wouldn't rather be in Florida?"

"Go to hell!"

She could still hear him laughing when she reached the Meltirks' apartment two flights down. The prince consort, this time wearing a Mickey Mouse T-shirt and silver lamé running shorts, answered the door, ushering her in with a spate of words that sounded embarrassingly fulsome. Apparently her serene highness felt the same, for she cut off his greeting with a short, admonitory word.

The room was smoky, redolent of strange herbs. Her highness was sitting in state in front of the grimy, diamond-paned windows, her purple turban slightly askew, her eyes watery from the ceremonial fire that smoked and burned in front of her in a brass brazier. There were no smoke detectors around, the fire hazard was probably enormous, and they would probably all die in their beds before the week was out, but Marielle was beyond worrying about such things. She sank down onto the cushion offered her, smiled at Esmy and waited.

"Her highness bids you welcome," Esmy said formally. "She wishes you peace and long life and a good strong man to give you many more children."

Marielle choked, swallowing the sound in a polite cough. "Tell her I wish her the same."

"Her highness says she hates to add to your troubles," Esmy continued after translating, "but she has gathered it is customary for there to be hot water in American apartments. She would like there to be some in hers."

"No hot water?" Marielle echoed.

"Apparently not. I already mentioned it to Dennis and he said he could take care of it very easily."

"Thank God. Did you tell her highness?"

"I will now. I know she'd rather hear it coming from you. She doesn't think too highly of the male of the species.

She comes from a matriarchal society and considers males to be of only limited use.''

"In the procreation of many children, I gather?''

"Exactly.'' She translated to Mrs. Meltirk, who nodded, a regal smile wreathing her full, unpainted lips. She began to speak then, long and earnestly, the rich vowels and consonants of her native language rolling over Marielle, wrapping her in a cocoon of words. Marielle swayed slightly, unaccountably sleepy. Maybe it was the combination of the long, mellifluous speech and the heady smoke, she reflected.

Her highness finally stopped speaking. With great effort Marielle roused herself and looked to Esmy for a translation. Esmy merely smiled, shrugging her plump shoulders. "She says she's glad you are here, and you should not let the wicked men scare you. The spirits mean you no harm; you should not be frightened of what you cannot see. You should take the one who is offered, even if he's not sure, and have babies.''

"Do you have any idea what she's talking about?''

"Not the foggiest. I've learned it's better not to ask. In the Baluchistani religion members of the ruling family are considered to be oracles. Actually you've been given quite an honor. I'll express your gratitude.

"Do that. And if there's any way you could find out what she meant...'' The words trailed off as a goat raced into the room, followed closely by a knife-wielding senior member of the Meltirk family.

"No!'' Marielle shrieked, jumping from her cushion. Since the goat looked marginally less nasty than the butcher knife she grabbed the animal, catching the ungrateful beast around his shaggy neck.

A shocked silence filled the apartment, broken only by the hiss of the fire and the noise of the outraged goat as it struggled in Marielle's grasp.

"Marielle, you shouldn't interfere....'' Esmy began.

"They can't sacrifice this animal," she said fiercely, rising to her feet and keeping a fierce grip on the goat's long, curly hair. "I'll put up with just about anything, with ghosts in the chimneys, apparitions in the windows, ceremonial fires, no plumbing and overdue electric bills, but I will not put up with animal sacrifice." She started toward the door, dragging the goat with her. The Meltirks were too stunned to move.

"I don't think you realize..." Esmy began again, but Marielle had already fumbled with the doorknob and was in the hall.

"Express my regrets to her highness," Marielle said. "I don't care if I cause an international incident. There will be no killing of animals here."

Her highness spoke then, in long, sibilant tones, her expression infinitely sad. Standing in the hallway, Marielle kept her grip on the goat, waiting for the translation.

Esmy shook her head. "Her serene highness wishes you well, and if you wish the goat you may have it with her blessing. He was going to provide their dinner for the next few days, but if you prefer, they'll eat the chickens."

"Good God!" Marielle groaned, wondering whether she dared stage a raid and rescue a bunch of noisy, smelly chickens.

"Her highness feels she must warn you, however," Esmy continued, looking decidedly unhappy with the message she had to impart, "that the gods will curse you if you don't get rid of the evil that haunts this building."

Marielle looked down at her sneaker-clad feet. The goat had just deposited a dozen olivelike pellets all over the floor. "The gods," she said glumly, "have already done so." And turning away, she led the goat down the stairs.

"YOU PUT THE GOAT in the garage?" Simon demanded, incensed. "He'll probably eat my car!"

"If I remember correctly, your car deserves to be eaten,"

Marielle said, perching on a carved mahogany table that wobbled slightly beneath her and munching an apple she'd grabbed from her apartment across the hallway.

Simon allowed himself a brief moment to admire her long legs before returning to his perusal of the ancient walnut chest of drawers. She was growing steadily more distracting, and his own behavior was surprising him. He'd always considered himself a reasonable, if somewhat bad-tempered sort of person, but his reaction to John Davies and to Miles had bordered on the violent. He'd actually wanted to take Davies and throw his little yuppie body out the window.

God, why couldn't she get out of here? With her long legs, and with her strong white teeth crunching into the apple, she was driving him absolutely crazy. You wouldn't think he was a mature man in his forties, old enough to know better. And you wouldn't think she was a mere child in her late twenties, young enough to be his...sister.

"I don't think they were actually going to sacrifice him," she added. "I think the animals were simply there as food."

"Still sounds pretty bad to me," Simon murmured, pushing and pulling at the various panels of the drawer, looking for a secret compartment.

"To me, too," Marielle allowed. "Still, I imagine we're being a little picky. After all, isn't Chicago hog butcher to the world or something like that? And the Meltirks are merely following their traditions. After all, we all eat meat—why should we be so squeamish about how that meat gets to the table? At least the Meltirks aren't hypocrites."

"Take the goat back to them, then."

Marielle's forehead wrinkled in thought, and Simon found himself wanting to cross the room and kiss every line. He dived back into the drawer with renewed vigor.

"I can't do that," she said. "But maybe we could see if they could work something out with the stockyards."

"Sort of like cutting your own Christmas trees?" Simon said with a laugh. "Maybe that's where you can find enough money to support this place. Start a Slaughter Your Supper franchise. It should go over big with the NRA."

"Aging hippie," Marielle said without rancor. "I'm just trying to be open-minded about the whole thing. I want to respect their customs."

"I think their customs include multiple husbands for the ruling family. What do you think of that?"

"One is more than enough," she said, finishing her apple and looking around for a place to put the core.

"That's what I think. By the way, I haven't found anything."

"Nothing?" She sat there, swinging her legs, the apple core forgotten. "I was sure we'd find something. A secret compartment, a hidden drawer."

"Oh, I found plenty of those," Simon said, closing the last drawer and skirting the mountain of furniture to reach Marielle's side. "There just wasn't anything in them."

"Might you have overlooked something?"

"You're welcome to go over everything again," he said gruffly.

"I trust you." Her sigh was resigned. "Anything worth looking at in my place?"

"There might be a secret compartment in your bed. There were lots of them in the other carved furniture."

"What if there is something hidden that's too small to see. A microdot, or something?"

"Marielle, my sweet, they didn't have microdots in the nineteen-thirties."

"Who says the place is being trashed for Vittorio's treasure?" she countered brightly. "Maybe the Meltirks are Russian spies who've hidden secret information all over the place."

"And the goat is their go-between? Give me a break, Ms. Brandt. Let's check out your god-awful bed and have done with it."

"I suppose you're right," she sighed, hopping down from the table in one graceful movement. "But it sure would make things a little more interesting. Modern spies are easier to catch than ghosts."

"Says who? I'd prefer the shade of old Vittorio to a modern KGB agent any day. I just don't happen to think we're dealing with either."

"What do you think we're dealing with?" she asked, crossing the hallway into her open apartment.

"Someone very greedy, very devious and very manipulative," he said, then stopped for a minute, struck by an unpleasant thought. He knew someone who fitted that description to a *T*, someone he never would have suspected of being involved in the haunting of Farnum's Castle. It made no sense whatsoever, but the more he thought of it the more likely it seemed.

"Why are you looking like that?" Marielle demanded, suddenly alert.

"Like what?"

"Like you just swallowed a salamander?"

"Nasty thought. I just had an unpleasant suspicion as to who might be behind this."

"Who?" she breathed, her eyes lighting up.

"I have no intention of telling you. For one thing, I have no proof, no real motive, only a gut instinct. For another, I could be dead wrong and I'm not about to slander someone on a mere guess."

"Wrong, Simon. You're going to tell me," she said fiercely.

He just looked at her. She was comical rather than threatening, with her blond hair a tangled mess around her pretty face, no makeup and her clothes comfortable rather than stylish. He liked her a lot better than when she'd shown up looking like a Lake Shore Drive matron. Hell, every second he liked her a lot better, to a point where it was getting downright dangerous to his peaceful way of life.

"Or what?" he couldn't keep himself from taunting.

She glared at him. "Or else."

"Tell you what. Let me check out a few things, ask a few questions, and I'll tell you tomorrow."

"On Halloween? How fitting," she said icily. "What if your suspect decides to murder me in the meantime?"

"I don't think the villain I have in mind really wants to hurt anyone."

"And you're willing to stake my safety on it?"

"Sure," he said cheerfully. "After all, you're the one who refuses to go to Florida. You're up to facing a little danger."

"Simon," she said, "you're the one who's in danger now."

"Marielle," he returned, amused by her threat, "let's go check out your bed."

She opened her mouth in outrage, ready to blister him, then shut it again as she realized the prosaic meaning of his words. She sighed, suddenly deflated. "Yes," she agreed. "Let's go find the bed." Simon almost wished she were still fighting him.

She tried to bring the children along for protection, but Emily would have none of it, and Christopher, as always, followed in his older sister's footsteps. "I'm telling Julie about Disney World," Emily announced with great dignity. "She's never been there."

"Neither have you," her mother pointed out.

"No, but Grandma has told me all about it," the child explained, as if to an idiot. "And I've watched a lot of TV."

"So you have, dear heart," Marielle said, and Simon could hear the resignation and guilt in her voice. "Come in and keep us company if you get bored."

"Yes, ma'am," said Emily, dismissing her mother.

She'd made her bed, he noticed when he walked into the tiny room. She had flannel sheets on the huge thing, blue with tiny white flowers. She had four pillows on the bed, too many for one person. She'd hung a poster on the wall, one of Monet's water lilies, and he stared at it for a long moment.

He should pay attention to such things, he reminded himself. While his walls held *Night of the Living Dead* and *Invasion of the Body Snatchers*, she had romantic paintings. It was as plain as the walls in front of him that they had no future together.

Slipping off her sneakers, Marielle climbed onto the high bed and clambered toward the huge, ornately carved headboard. "You check the bottom," she said, reaching up, her hair tumbling down her back.

He considered running back to his apartment. He considered his better judgment, said to hell with it, and climbed onto the soft high bed with her.

Upon closer examination the carvings on the bed had a distinctly salacious air. The nymphs and satyrs cavorted in a far from innocent manner, and he doubted Marielle would appreciate what the carved goats were busy doing. He pushed and pulled, poked and prodded, but nothing moved.

"No luck," he said, turning and walking toward the head of the bed. The mattress shifted beneath his weight, throwing Marielle off balance so that she landed against his chest. She clung for a minute, her eyes wide, her lips soft and parted, and he felt that all too familiar tightening in his gut.

Someone groaned, probably himself, as he dropped his head to meet hers. All he could think of was the blue sheets with the white flowers, her mouth and that half-stunned, half-expectant expression in her blue eyes.

Then she pushed him away, hard, as she scrambled off the bed, backing up against the wall. "What in heaven's name is wrong with me?" she asked, speaking more to herself than to him. "My children are in the next room, you don't even want me—you just want to get me out of Chicago, and I don't even like making love. What is happening to me?"

He stood there in the middle of her flowered sheets. "The same thing that's happening to me," he said glumly. "And who says I don't want you?" Without another word he climbed down off the bed and walked past her, out of the bedroom and out of the apartment.

Chapter Sixteen

Marielle's mother was usually the most flutter-brained, inefficient, charmingly helpless creature on earth—except when it came to something she wanted, and she wanted a few weeks of her grandchildren. The plane reservations for Orlando were set for nine o'clock the next morning. Virginia Watson was planning to fly out at six and be there waiting at O'Hare for Emily and Christopher, and she'd already taken care of diapers, a crib, food and toys.

Marielle had no choice but to let herself be swept up in her mother's uncustomary whirlwind, squashing her own indecision and regrets. She had no doubt about her parents' ability to take care of the children—they were born to be grandparents. Doting, responsible, strict only when absolutely necessary, they would provide the perfect cocoon of love and safety for the few days the children had to be away. If things went well, if they were able to clear up the mystery of Farnum's Castle early, Marielle had no doubt Emily would put up a loud and long protest at being ripped away from the wonders of Disney World before her time was up.

They took a taxi out to O'Hare, damning the expense. She knew Simon would be more than happy to drive them, but she deliberately lied about the time of the plane. She wasn't quite sure exactly why. For one thing, she wasn't ready for her inquisitive mother to meet him. Virginia Watson possessed a sixth sense when it came to men, and she'd scent a romance where absolutely none existed.

And none did exist, Marielle told herself stubbornly. They'd shared a few kisses, a certain odd camaraderie, but that was where it ended. And she didn't need her mother jumping to the same embarrassing conclusions Granita had. The expression on Simon's face had been more than instructive, and his speedy escape from her bed and the apartment imprinted the message on her brain, a message he'd already given her over and over again. He wasn't going to get involved with her, he wasn't going to get married again.

She wasn't going to get involved with him, either, she reminded herself sternly. Her brain knew that full well, but her body and emotions seemed to be lagging behind in understanding. With the children gone she'd simply have to be more alert.

She also hadn't wanted Simon along as a witness to her relinquishing her children, even for a few short days. She made it through the departure, greeting her mother with bustling good cheer, hugging and kissing the children, remaining calm even when Emily's last-minute doubts surfaced and she burst into excited tears as Virginia led the children through the security gate. The last Marielle saw of them, Christopher was waving at her over her mother's impeccably tailored shoulder, and Emily was giving her one final forlorn glance as she clung tightly to her grandmother's hand.

Marielle kept waving, a bright, encouraging grin on her face. She waited until they turned a corner and disappeared from sight, and then promptly burst into her own tears.

She'd brought her sunglasses and a huge wad of tissues, just in case. She cried from the security gate to the sidewalk, she cried on the diesel-smelling bus that had the nerve to call itself a limousine, she cried from the center of the Loop all the way out to the residential neighborhood that held Farnum's Castle. And she cried for the last three blocks, finishing her last tissue as she reached the rusty iron gate of the monstrosity she'd inherited.

She stopped for a moment, looking up, way up at its seedy grandeur. It was only half past ten in the morning and the day, the whole empty, childless day lay before her. What she needed, she told herself, walking up her cracked, uneven sidewalk, was a shower, a nap and a new lease on life. The sooner she found out what was going on, the sooner her babies would be back.

Another yuppie bureaucrat was waiting for her in the downstairs hall. She closed the door behind her, shutting out the chilly October wind, and peered through the gloom at the visitor. Another State Department employee looking after the Meltirks? she wondered. Or more trouble? With her recent spate of luck it could only be the latter.

"Mrs. Brandt?" he queried, peering back at her.

She looked at him uneasily, expecting a summons. But his hands were loose at his side, and he held no incriminating papers in them. Besides, who would want to issue her a summons? She hadn't done anything wrong other than inheriting this decaying monstrosity.

"Yes," she admitted, wondering if she was making a very grave mistake, wondering if she was going to get her shower and nap.

"I'm from the tax assessor's office. I've been in touch with Mr. O'Donnell at Parker and Stearns, and he informed me you were no longer a client."

Marielle looked at him for a long, sickening moment. "Do I need a lawyer?" she asked. Her voice felt rusty from tension and an hour and a half of crying, but she kept her face very calm.

Her newest bureaucrat didn't crack a smile. "It might be useful. Taxes haven't been paid on this building since 1984."

"Really? I don't know when my husband acquired it...."

"Nineteen eighty-four," he replied. "And as his wife, you're liable."

"All right," she said faintly. "What's the damage?"

"Twelve thousand dollars, not including late fees, interest or the last two years."

"Twelve thousand dollars?" she shrieked, and the sound echoed up the stairwell. "On this dump?"

"Chicago real estate is worth a great deal, Mrs. Brandt. Even though the building is in compromised shape, the land beneath it is extremely valuable. Speaking of the condition of the building, I believe an inspector will be visiting you early next month. In a rental property there are codes that must be followed, and this building seems, even to my inexperienced eye, to fall well short of those standards."

Marielle allowed herself the luxury of a quiet moan. She would have burst into tears and embarrassed the dickens out of the tax man, but she was all cried out. All she could do was lean against the cracked paneling and stare at him wordlessly.

"You have thirty days, Mrs. Brandt," he said, taking her limp hand and pressing into it the paper she'd thought hadn't existed. "Let us know if we can assist you in any way." *Yes, you can call off your wolves,* Marielle thought dizzily. She was barely aware of the front door closing behind him, or the steady, almost mincing tread of well-shod feet from the floors above.

"I warned you."

Marielle lifted her beaten head to look into Liam O'Donnell's chilly eyes. She said nothing, knowing that screaming in rage at the man would get her nowhere.

But O'Donnell didn't need any encouragement. "You should have taken that offer when I presented it. This is too much for a woman to handle. If you'd had any sense at all you would have listened to me, accepted the very generous offer and gone straight back to New York."

She didn't trust the man. Not one inch, not one centimeter. For all his dapper appearance, his seemingly impeccable lineage and respected reputation, he seemed to be just this side of sleazy. "And now it's too late?" she queried.

It might have been the shadowy darkness of the ill-lit hall, her red-rimmed eyes might have blurred her vision, or it might have been sheer imagination. But an expression of triumph and avarice swept over O'Donnell's features before he could control it.

"I don't know," he said, and Marielle knew he lied. "I have a fair amount of influence. If you'd agree to the offer right now, today, I might be able to work something out. The tax liability is a problem, of course, and the indigent misfits living here are another, but with my powers of persuasion I imagine that I could get that offer repeated. I can't promise anything—you may have to settle for less than the original offer, but I'm sure it would be more than generous." He practically rubbed his dry little hands together. "Shall I get in touch with my client?"

For a brief moment, a mere millisecond, she was tempted. She was at low ebb, emotionally, physically, depleted by tears and sleeplessness and uncertainty. She looked into O'Donnell's papery white face, and from the distance she could hear the sound of someone crying.

She panicked, then realized with mingled regret and relief that it couldn't be her children. They were somewhere over Florida by now, not even thinking of her.

"Why are you here?" she asked instead, knowing the answer lay behind the muffled sound of crying that was floating down the stairs.

"That's privileged information," he informed her primly. "Between my client and me."

Julie, she thought. He'd been badgering Julie again. The rotten, money-grubbing, heartless bastard.

"Well," he prodded, clearly impatient. "What shall I tell my client?"

"You can tell him," she said, very calmly, "to go to hell. And you, Liam O'Donnell, can go with him."

How could she have thought his eyes were colorless? Now they were dark with a sudden flash of rage, and it took all Marielle's considerable strength of mind not to step back a pace.

"You'll regret this," he said very quietly.

"Maybe. But in the meantime I'd like you to get off my property. Now."

He drew himself up to his full height, a few inches shorter than Marielle's five feet seven, and positively bristled with fury. Without another word he pushed past her and out into the chilly autumn morning.

He left the door wide open to the brisk wind, and she was glad he had. The stiff breeze swept through the hall, bringing a few dead leaves with it, sweeping out the presence of the evil old man. She only wished it could sweep out the ghost of the other evil old man as thoroughly.

"Well done," said Simon, standing in the open door of the elevator.

"Thanks for coming to my rescue," she said sarcastically.

"You were doing just fine without my interference," he drawled. "I would have assisted him out the door if need be, but you managed to rout him quite effectively. We'll have to tell Julie you got rid of the old creep. It might cheer her up."

"Where is she?" Marielle headed for the stairs, but Simon slid a restraining arm around her waist, pulling her back.

"Dennis is taking care of her. They're better off alone." He looked down at her, still keeping his arm around her. "I must say you're a more successful matchmaker than I was. You lied about going out with Miles. You weren't the slightest bit interested in him, were you?"

"Nope."

"Why not? He's young, attractive, charming. A bit overextended financially, but then so are most people. I would have thought you'd make a perfect pair."

She looked up at him. "You thought wrong. I'm not interested in coupling in any sense of the word."

He looked down at his arm encircling her, their bodies resting against each other, her complete acceptance of the situation. "Okay," he said easily. "I'll believe you." And he released her, leaving her suddenly bereft in the wind-swept hallway. "Are you ready?"

"Ready for what?" she asked warily.

"The park."

"I beg your pardon?"

"You've spent the last six days cooped up in this old building. You need to get out and enjoy yourself, and I've been elected to the job of seeing that you do."

"Who elected you?"

He grinned then, the smile lighting his usual dark expression. "I did. Come on, kid. You need sunshine and distraction. We'll go to the zoo and feed the baboons, we'll go to the planetarium and you can watch the star show and realize how insignificant you are."

"Just the thing to cheer me up," she said grumpily. "I was going to go upstairs and go to bed."

"Well, we could do that," he allowed, "but I thought you figured it was a waste of time."

"Alone," she said, trying to keep from smiling.

"Sorry. You're not allowed to be alone today. It's too easy to feel depressed when you're alone. If you're lucky I'll introduce you to my favorite orangutan. He does have embarrassing habits, but he's an ape after my own heart."

"I'll go," she said, unable to resist him in his unexpectedly lighthearted mood.

"Now?"

"Now," she agreed.

"Good. Then you can tell me why you didn't let me drive you and kids to the airport this morning."

Her defenses were still down. *An hour and a half of public crying will do that to you,* she thought. "I didn't want you to meet my mother," she said frankly. "My mother has too vivid an imagination."

He raised an eyebrow. "You think I'd scare her?"

"I think you'd raise her hopes in a direction where they shouldn't be raised."

"I can't believe she'd think I was a suitable replacement."

"Then you haven't met my mother. She'd fall at your feet," Marielle said bitterly.

"Wouldn't she think I was robbing the cradle? Not to mention the fact that I've been divorced?" His tone of voice was distant, as if he were no more than vaguely interested.

"Not my mother. She'd figure you'd learned from your mistakes and would be even better husband material than a bachelor." They weren't talking about her mother anymore, and both of them knew it.

"What about the age difference?"

"I've always been mature for my age. Besides, my father's seventeen years older than my mother and they've always been divinely happy. I'm sure she'd be fool enough to think history could repeat itself."

"A foolish thought, indeed." His voice was low, abstracted, his eyes watching her lips.

"My mother's not very practical."

"It's a lucky thing that we are."

"Yes," said Marielle huskily. "Very lucky." And she lifted her face, waiting for him to kiss her.

He didn't. Instead he moved away, heading for the open door and the brisk autumn morning. "Let's go feed some baboons."

Why should she feel rejected? Why should she feel de-

pressed and unwanted when he was taking her to see baboons? Plastering a bright smile on her face, she followed
him out into the bright sunshine. And this time her sunglasses didn't cover tears but a very measuring, uncertain
expression.

TOO LATE, TOO LATE, TOO LATE. The worn tires of the Mustang whirred out the refrain that echoed in his brain as he
drove through the rain-slick late night streets of downtown
Chicago. He couldn't even excuse himself on the grounds
that he hadn't known what was happening.

He'd known from the very beginning. He'd taken one
look at Marielle Brandt and known that he'd have to be
very careful. And knowing that, he'd gone into it full tilt,
paying no attention to the warning signals.

He pressed down harder on the accelerator and the
venerable old car leaped ahead, jerkily, he had to admit,
but with still a semblance of its old power. To give himself
his due, he hadn't realized quite how dangerous she was,
for the simple reason that in his forty-two years he'd never
felt like this before. Not for Sharon, his hardheaded former
wife who was only out for corporate advancement, not for
the women who'd come and gone before and after his brief
marriage. He'd loved them as best he could, but in retrospect his feelings for them seemed very shallow. Nothing
compared to the intense, tangled web of emotion that
wrapped around him when he looked at Marielle Brandt.

The park had been one of his dumbest ideas. Watching
her toss her head back and laugh at the orangutan's obscene
behavior, he'd felt a curious piercing in his heart. Scuffling
through the fallen leaves, not touching, they'd walked for
miles through Grant Park, talking, laughing at times, at others in a silence so peaceful and natural that it gave him the
creeps to remember. It wasn't fair that she'd be perfect for
him. Not when it was impossible.

He didn't really have to go in tonight. He wasn't scheduled to work, but he didn't think he'd last the night without going crazy thinking about her one floor beneath, no children to interrupt, no responsibilities to demand her attention. If only she hadn't spent the night in his arms, if only she hadn't kissed him yesterday morning, if only, if only…

The fine mist was coming down at a steady rate, and there was a nasty bite in the air. He had to admit he felt a lot more secure with Dennis in the house. For one thing, he could count on the heat lasting through the night. During the cold snap last winter he'd gone crazy imagining the old ladies freezing to death in their apartments, unable to do anything about the temperamental furnace.

And he was glad Dennis was there for protection. Now that he was reasonably certain Dennis was only interested in Julie and not his winsome landlady, he could accept his tenancy with absolute pleasure.

God, what a fool he was being! What an addled, jealous idiot he was! Without any warning whatsoever he pulled a U-turn, disregarding the sparse traffic and heading back to Farnum's Castle. This had gone on long enough. Ignoring the problem was useless—he spent all his spare time thinking about her. It was time to confront it head-on.

When he slid into the old garage, he nearly hit the damned goat. The animal lifted its ugly head to glare at him, then went back to munching on the bicycle someone, probably Dennis, had been fool enough to leave there. He cursed the animal, pulled up his denim jacket and headed for the house through the freezing drizzle.

MARIELLE WAITED UNTIL she heard Simon leave. The thinness of the walls and her hastily repaired door were mixed blessings. The door opened and closed again, if one was very careful, but it did little to shut out the various noises from the hallways, and it would provide absolutely no protection if whoever, whatever had been tormenting them chose to repeat his efforts.

Not that even a solid steel door would provide any protection from ghosts, she reminded herself with a touch of asperity. And mortal felons could always get in through the windows. *Let's face it,* she told herself, she wasn't safe no matter what she did, so all she could do was wait for their next visitation.

But her mind wasn't on visitations, not right now. She'd wasted her day strolling through the sprawling lakeside park with Simon Zebriskie. As always she'd allowed him to tempt her from her duty, and her lack of progress today meant her children would be away twenty-four hours longer. And it meant that she was even more tied to Simon, when all she wanted was freedom.

How could such a cynical, gruff, sarcastic man be so persuasive, so—she might as well admit it—seductive? How could she let herself be drawn to him when she didn't want any man? And how could she have forgotten her children for most of the sunny afternoon, letting herself enjoy Simon's dry wit and the wonderfully prosaic pleasures of the zoo and the planetarium?

She couldn't forget them now. Alone in her apartment, with a cold rain splattering the windows, all she could think about was the empty cot, the empty crib. Would they be missing her? Would her mother remember that Christopher could only sleep with his tattered Pooh Bear, that Emily liked one story and three songs before she'd settle down?

If anyone had cried more than Marielle that day it had been Julie. Her eyes were red and swollen when Marielle returned from a ridiculously filling dinner at an Italian restaurant over on Wacker Drive, and every now and then she'd let loose with another strangled sob. Marielle had greeted her departure for a visit with Esmerelda with relief, but once she was alone the quiet closed in, the loneliness settling around her like a velvet shroud.

Simon's disappearing footsteps had been the final straw. She'd held her breath, waiting for his knock on her door, but he hadn't even hesitated. Clearly he'd been able to put her out of his mind far more successfully than she'd been able to dismiss him. A blessing, she assured herself, wrapping her arms around her chilled body. Someone needed to be sensible, and it was becoming increasingly clear that it wasn't going to be her.

The first creak didn't alarm her. It was an old building—creaks and groans were to be expected. The second she also dismissed as part of the settling process, even though a mansion of some sixty-odd years ought to have settled by now. But there was no ignoring the eerie, translucent light emanating from the chimney, or the muffled, barely discernible moans that floated on the howling wind.

The scratching began again, but there was no one anywhere near the chimney. The lights flickered and dimmed, and she heard a crash in her bedroom, followed by another, louder one and a low-pitched whining that sounded like a slow-motion scream.

The door fell off the hinges as she yanked it open and dashed into the hallway. She tripped, sliding down the last five steps, and began pounding on Dennis's door. There was no answer, and she realized with frustration that he must be gone. She raced barefoot down the next flight, ignoring the Meltirks' tightly shut door, and on down the next, terror beating at her heart, panic strangling her lungs, running, running, smack into the immovable strength of a monster.

She screamed at the top of her lungs. The sound vibrated through the entire mansion and the monster shook her hard, choking off her second hysterical shriek.

"What the hell is going on?" it demanded in a voice from the tomb. And in the shadowy darkness, Marielle stared into Simon's smokey-gray eyes and didn't know whether she'd at last found safety. Or another kind of danger, even more devastating. At that moment she no longer cared.

Chapter Seventeen

They were standing on the second-floor landing. Marielle hadn't yet gotten around to replacing the light bulbs, and if the tax assessor had his way she wouldn't have the money to upgrade from twenty-five watts to one hundred. She took a deep, shuddering breath, dimly aware of Simon's fingers digging into her arms, glad of the discomfort. He was solid, flesh and blood—and there.

"There...there was something in m-m-m-my room." She'd never stammered before in her life, but she realized her teeth were chattering, both in panic and from the cold. Farnum's Castle wasn't warm enough to race around barefoot, but what with the banshees wailing in her chimney she hadn't had time to look for her shoes before she ran out.

"What?" Simon's tone was wonderfully down-to-earth, despite the sepulchral depth of his voice.

"Th-th-the ghost," she managed to say. "Crashing around in my bedroom, pounding at the chimney, wailing and howling...."

He shook her again, not as hard this time. "Did you see anything?"

"I just told you. There was crashing and pounding and wailing and I couldn't find anyone. Dennis and Julie..."

"Dennis is in the basement working on the blasted furnace. Julie's handing him tools. Seems like the ghost was all sound and fury. You didn't actually see Vittorio materialize before your eyes, did you?"

Marielle was slowly growing calmer. "No," she said. "I didn't."

Simon nodded. His hands were still holding her upper arms, but now the grip was gentler, almost caressing. "Let's go and check it out. Come on." He tugged her away from the stairs.

She pulled back. "My apartment is upstairs."

"We're taking the elevator."

"The hell we are! Nothing short of the devil himself is going to get me in that traveling coffin."

He laughed then, an unaffected bark of humor. "I've been called worse." And he pulled her down the darkened hallway to the tiny little elevator.

"You're not getting me in there," she warned him.

"I'm not climbing five flights of stairs," he answered, shoving her into the compartment and pulling the door shut behind them. He punched a few buttons, the dim light flickered, and the boxlike structure jerked and shuddered, inching upward.

Marielle had backed into a corner and stood rigid, her fists clenched at her sides. "I'm not in the mood for this, Simon. I don't need to risk entombment after the day I've had."

They were moving awfully slowly. Despite her distrust of the elevator she hadn't thought it was this bad. "You didn't have a rotten day," Simon said, bridging the narrow distance, his tall, lean body hovering over her in the shadows. "You had a rotten morning and a miserable evening, but the rest of the day was just fine."

She should have felt even more claustrophobic with him looming over her like that. Instead she felt light, liberated, full of an odd sort of anticipation, and her fear of enclosed spaces, particularly of faulty elevators, vanished. "You're right,'' she said, her voice low. ''I liked the park and the planetarium.''

''What about the company?'' His knees were touching her, his breath was ruffling her hair, and all she wanted was to lean forward and rest her head against his chest. *Danger, danger,* she warned herself, still fighting.

''The company was acceptable.'' Her qualification would have been fine if it hadn't come out in a husky murmur just as his head dipped toward hers.

His mouth touched hers, gently, softly, a mere taste. She lifted her head but he'd already moved on, feathering kisses across her cheekbones, her nose, her eyelids. She could feel her heart shuddering and pounding, her clenched fists trembling as the elevator moved up, up, and Simon's mouth moved down, down. She pressed her fists against the walls of the elevator, anything to keep from touching him. She was wearing an oversize flannel shirt with a silk camisole beneath it, and Simon had somehow managed to unfasten the buttons without touching her skin. He kissed her collarbones, the soft swell of her breast, her fluttering heartbeat, and finally she could stand it no longer.

Marielle pushed herself away from the wall and into his arms, sliding her hands around his waist and holding on tight. ''This is stupid,'' she murmured against his shoulder. ''It's a waste of time. It'll only lead to disappointment and embarrassment.''

''Mmm-hmm,'' he murmured in agreement, nuzzling her ear beneath the tangled sheaf of hair.

''It'll destroy our friendship,'' she said desperately, clinging tighter. She'd always had sensitive ears.

''We aren't friends,'' Simon said, kissing her neck. ''We're two people spending too much energy trying not to be lovers.''

She moaned in reluctant pleasure. She'd always had a sensitive neck, but somehow Greg had never found the right spot. Simon had, the very first time. She made one final protest. "We shouldn't do this," she said, pulling his shirt from his jeans and sliding her hands up his back, along the warm, smoothly-muscled skin.

"You're right," he said, his mouth moving along her jawline. She'd always had a sensitive jawline, too. The light overhead flickered and went out, the elevator shuddered to a stop and the door slid open, revealing the fifth-floor hallway a few inches above the elevator floor. Simon's hallway, she thought. Simon's apartment. Simon's bed.

He pulled away, a few inches, enough to give her breathing space. "Do you want to go back to your apartment?" The question was patient, but Marielle could feel the tension running through his tall body, could recognize it as the same tension that was thrumming through hers.

"What about the ghost?"

"He'll be back." He didn't push her, didn't kiss her. He simply stood there in the shadows, waiting for her to make up her mind.

She shut her eyes, misery and indecision sweeping over her. "Simon, I'm not good at this sort of thing. I don't enjoy it much. You'll be just as disappointed as I am."

If she expected him to persuade her she was disappointed. He didn't say a word, but just stood there, enticingly close—still waiting for her to make up her mind.

"Simon," she said weakly, "don't do this to me. Don't make me decide. If I had any brains at all I'd go back downstairs right now."

"Your problem, Marielle," he said gently, cupping her face in his large, strong hands, "is that you've got too many brains. And you spend too much time worrying and fussing about others, and not enough just taking for yourself. I'll make the decision for you, absolve you of responsibility. I'm going to take you into my apartment and make love to you, and if you're miserably embarrassed and disappointed it won't be anybody's fault but mine. You warned me and I didn't listen. Okay?"

She looked up at him, her heart in her throat, hammering, choking her. "Okay," she whispered.

He kissed her then, setting his mouth on hers, warm and wet and open, and she responded, shakily at first, then with growing delight. His hands released her face, sliding down her body, cupping her breasts through the thin silk camisole, her open shirt hanging loose around her. She wanted to get closer to him, pushing her breasts against his hands, vaguely aware that despite the heat between them her nipples had hardened under his touch.

He pulled away, looking down at her, his breath coming in labored rasps that matched her own. "You don't like that, do you?" he whispered. "You probably won't like this, either." And he leaned down and put his mouth where his hand had been, on her taut nipple, drawing her into his mouth, suckling her through the whisper-thin silk.

She heard the moan, knew it had to be her own, but it sounded distant, foreign. He moved to the second breast, and she could feel the dampness of the silk against her hot skin, the burning and aching between her thighs. She reached up and caught his head, meaning to pull him away, meaning to stop the torment that was burning her alive, but instead she threaded her fingers through his thick, straight hair and held him against her.

Marielle could feel his hard, hot hands beneath her camisole, on her flat stomach. She braced herself, expecting them to move upward toward her breasts, but instead the button of her jeans was deftly unsnapped, the zipper drawn down, and he was pushing down the jeans over her narrow hips, out of his way. Then he slid his hand inside her bikini panties toward the hot, damp core of her, and she tried to jerk away, releasing his hair and pushing against his shoulders in sudden confusion.

Simon paid no attention to her protests. He kissed her, his mouth covering hers and sealing her objections as his long, deft fingers stroked and caressed her. Now she was clutching his arms, fingers digging into his hard-muscled flesh. She wanted to beg him to stop—except that she didn't want him to stop. She wanted him to keep on, keep on forever, his hand between her legs invading her, arousing her, taking her from blind innocence to someplace dark and dangerous and overwhelming.

Marielle tore her mouth away from his. "No!" she choked. "No, stop! I can't stand it! I can't..."

"Yes, you can." He was relentless, and for just a moment she fought him, pushing against him. Then the first wave hit, a jolt of sheer, agonizing pleasure shooting through her with the power of an electrical charge. She went rigid in his arms, shock and reaction keeping her still for a moment. Then her body convulsed against him as wave after endless wave of response twisted her into a helpless rag doll.

Simon picked her up in his arms, leaving her jeans in a heap on the elevator floor as he carried her into the hallway, kicking open his unlocked door and moving through the darkened apartment with the sureness of the night creature he was. He didn't bother to turn on the bedroom light, and the street light shining in was filtered by the steady rain. He set her down on the bed, and she lay there silent and trembling as he stripped off her flannel shirt and camisole, tossed her panties onto the floor and proceeded to strip off his own clothes.

Marielle had a brief, shocked realization that he'd seduced and undressed her in the elevator. That he'd done more than that in what was essentially a public place. Then his hard, hot body covered hers, and she was beyond rational thought.

"I finally found a way to keep you quiet," he murmured in her ear, a note of laughter in his voice. "I should have done that days ago." He took her arms and pulled them around his neck, then kissed her, long and hard and deep.

She had thought herself too weary to respond. But her

mouth opened beneath his, her tongue reached out and her skin softened beneath his touch.

She had thought her body too unbearably sensitized to stand any more. But he moved slowly, carefully, arousing her all over again, and when his mouth found her breasts she arched against him; when his hand slid down beneath her thighs she let him part them, shivering in anticipation.

Simon took her hand and placed it on him, on the hard, smooth length of him. He was big, more so than she'd expected, and damp, and she realized he wanted her very badly. She let her fingers trail across the silk and steel of him, wanting more, yet afraid of it.

He groaned, pushing against her hand, showing her what he wanted, where he wanted pressure, where he wanted softness. She wanted to kiss him, she wanted his mouth on hers, and she tugged at him. He moved then, kneeling between her legs, hot and hard against her, and she tensed, not knowing what to expect.

"Now is not the time to be frightened," Simon whispered in her ear, nibbling on her sensitive lobe, but she could feel the tension running through him, the trembling in his arms as he held himself in check. "I'd like to make this last longer, but I don't know if you can take much more this time. And I don't know if I can."

She shut her eyes, still tense, still waiting. But he made no move at all, despite the power vibrating in his arms, despite the need covering his body with a fine film of sweat.

"Look at me, Marielle." There was a hoarse note of pleading in his voice, one she couldn't resist. Her eyes shot open. "Say something, Marielle. Anything."

"I thought you liked me quiet." It didn't sound like her voice. It was raw with need and wonder and emotion.

He still didn't move. "Not that quiet. Say something, Marielle. Say you want me."

A ghost of a smile twisted her mouth. "Of course I want you. I've never in my life wanted anyone the way I want you. I never thought I'd want anyone the way I want you. I want you, I need you, I...'' His mouth silenced the last, dangerous statement that might have slipped out, and his body pushed into hers, settling deep.

She could feel the tremors shivering through her, the unexpected little shimmers of response that she thought she'd already used up. Simon's big hands cupped her hips, holding her still for his driving invasion, and she wrapped her legs around him, pulling him closer. This time was for him, she thought. This time her joy would be in giving, in holding him and taking his body and his pleasure into her, in savoring his delight.

But Simon had other ideas. She could feel her own tension begin to build once more, feel her own body covered with sweat, feel the inexplicable wanting taking over once again. She kissed him, short, hurried kisses that he responded to in kind, and she could feel his strong, undulating body grow even more taut. She waited in uncertainty, in anticipation, expecting nothing but his pleasure. Then he reached between their bodies and touched her.

She exploded, arching in a delight so intense it was almost unbearable. She could feel Simon all around her, tense in her arms as his body went rigid with his climax, and through the maelstrom of darkness and confusion all she could do was cling to him, for safety, for comfort, for love, as she shattered into a thousand fragments.

A long time later he pulled away. He'd grown heavy, but she hadn't minded. She didn't want to look at him, didn't want to say anything; she simply wanted to hide her head against his shoulder and never move again. He rolled onto his side, taking her with him, and his hand brushed against her face, coming away wet with her tears. His own breathing had settled down to a reasonable facsimile of normal, and if his heartbeat was still a bit too fast it was nothing compared to hers.

She tried to duck her head, to bury it against his chest,

and he let her, cradling her, still gently stroking her. It struck her that Simon was a kind man. Despite his gruff nature and deep-rooted cynicism, there was a streak of gentle caring about him that was easy to miss. And she had the sudden, unnerving fear that the last hour had simply been another demonstration of his kindness.

"Listen," he said, his voice a low growl, "we'll get better with practice."

She couldn't help herself. At his words she raised her head and looked at him incredulously. "If we get any better," she said, her voice heavy with emotion, "I'll be dead before I'm thirty."

He laughed then, and she realized with amazement that he hadn't been quite sure of her reaction. It suddenly made him much more human, and she settled back against him with a pleasant sigh. "I wish you were thirty," he murmured. "Or thirty-five."

I wish you were in love with me, she thought. *The way I am with you. The way I have been for days and days on end.* "Give me time," she said, keeping her thoughts to herself. "I'll be there sooner or later."

He could have said something then, but didn't. He simply pulled up the cover around them, wrapped her tighter in his arms and went to sleep, his hands gentle and possessive even in his dreams. And Marielle had no choice but to do the same. Tomorrow would be soon enough to deal with the overwhelming turn her life had taken. For now she needed a few hours of rest. Tomorrow she'd face everything.

HE'D MADE SOME STUPID MISTAKES in his life, Simon thought, shifting carefully so he wouldn't disturb Marielle. Up to and including both his marriage, his idiotic acceptance of payola and his obsessive forms of penance ever since. But falling in love with Marielle Brandt had to take the cake.

He hadn't meant to do it. Hadn't even realized things were getting quite so intense. Granted, he felt hollow and empty when he went for most of a day without seeing her. He knew it required an almost inhuman effort on his part not to touch her. He knew he was drawn to her as he'd never been drawn to anyone in his life.

But he hadn't realized it was going to be the *Big L.*

He'd been so damned sure of himself, so smug. He could take her to bed, show her how pleasurable it really could be, and then walk away. He'd shown her, all right. But he'd shown himself, too, that what he'd just expected to be good sex had turned out to be something much, much more—something he'd never experienced before in his long, misspent life.

He looked at the woman sleeping so peacefully in his arms, a trace of dried tears on her soft cheeks, and a reluctant grin twisted his mouth. She hadn't known what had hit her last night. If his ego had ever needed boosting, her shocked, shivering reaction had done just that. She had clung to him as if he were life itself, and he had relished it.

So what was he going to do now? Nothing had changed—she was still too young and innocent for him. If he had any decency at all he'd back off, give her time to find someone more her type.

The children wouldn't be a drawback—they were great kids. Tough, adaptable, loving—any man would be lucky to get them along with their generous, warmhearted mother.

But he didn't want some suitable man to become their stepfather. He wanted Marielle himself and he wanted her children. Hell, he even wanted to have children with her— children who would be theirs.

But the best thing he could do was put an end to it, now, before it was too late. He could manage to dredge up one more noble act from his weary old soul. He could set her free to find the kind of life she should have.

And that was exactly what he was going to do, he told himself, cupping the soft swell of her breast as the sun began to rise over the Chicago skyline. She made a low, sexy noise in the back of her throat and moved closer, rubbing against him like a sleepy kitten. Tomorrow.

Chapter Eighteen

When Marielle opened her eyes for the second time that morning the first thing she saw was Bela Lugosi leering down at her, a cape covering half of his face. She swallowed the scream that was instinctive, huddled under the covers, then realized it was just one more of Simon's old movie posters. If she had anything to say about it, it would have to go.

She looked around her, resting her chin on her drawn-up knees. She had no idea whether she'd have anything to say about it or not. Simon had never expressed any interest in a permanent relationship—on the contrary, he'd repeatedly told her to go away. Maybe last night had changed things—maybe not.

She was alone in the bedroom. It was an overcast, cloudy day outside. Fitting for Halloween, she thought. The room was part of one of the castle's turrets—it was octagonal, with windows on every other wall. The bed was large and rumpled, the covers tossed every which way. On one side of the bed there was a digital clock and a pile of books. There were a few scattered pieces of her clothing on the other side.

She reached for her flannel shirt, remembering with dismay that her jeans were probably still riding up and down in that lousy elevator. But no one in the building ever used it except Simon. They all had too much sense.

If she'd just kept off the elevator last night she probably wouldn't be where she was now, a flush of remembered pleasure covering her body, a tangle of doubt and worry assailing her brain. What was going to happen next?

It took all her courage to climb out of bed and retrieve her fallen pieces of clothing from where they lay. At the last minute she stole a pair of Simon's old jeans, rolling up the legs, closing the too loose waistband with a pin. Taking a deep breath, she stepped hesitantly into the living room.

Simon was nowhere around. The front door of the apartment was open, the elevator door was closed, and the smell of coffee brought forth Marielle's first sigh of relief.

She was half tempted to beat a hasty retreat to her own apartment, a pilfered cup of coffee in her hand. But she knew she'd be putting off the inevitable. She'd wait, long enough to drink her coffee, long enough to see if his departure was temporary—or if he'd fled the city, the state and the country in an effort to get away from her.

The coffee was wretched, but at least it was brewed, not instant. That was another thing in Simon Zebriskie's life that needed to be taken in hand. His coffee, his choice of artwork, his mornings, his evenings…

Marielle sighed, setting down the half-drunk cup of coffee and staring about her. He'd cleaned up most of the mess left by the vandals, but the walls were still a mess, and nothing short of a new paint job would take care of that. Maybe a shade with a touch of warmth to it to soften the lofty spaces.

She was in deep trouble. One night of sex and she was redecorating his apartment and reorienting his life! She'd better get back to her own apartment and her own life before she let her fantasies get out of hand. He hadn't said a word about love.

He hadn't even said a word about going steady, she reminded herself wryly. She took one more drink of the bitter coffee, left the cup in the kitchen sink and headed for the door, wanting only to escape. As luck would have it, Simon chose that moment to reappear, her jeans slung over his arm.

If she hadn't known what to expect, Simon's expression wouldn't have helped her out. He looked distant, unapproachable, as if last night had never happened—but Marielle happened to know damned well that it had happened. That closely shaven chin of his had scratched her last night—she still had the rash to prove it. His hands... She looked away from them, away from him to some point over his shoulder in the hallway.

"I thought you might want your clothes," Simon said, his voice diffident. "I see you found something to wear."

"I hope you don't mind," she said politely.

"Not at all." He was equally courteous.

"I helped myself to a cup of coffee. It was horrible."

She didn't have to look to know he didn't crack a smile. "I don't mind it," was all he said.

"I'd better go." She waited for him to move closer, to say something, anything.

"That's probably a good idea."

Five words. Five cruel, nasty little words, spoken so politely as they knifed through her heart. She looked at him then, at his distant, emotionless face, at the mouth that had kissed her senseless. "You win," Marielle said quietly.

"I beg your pardon?"

"I'll leave Chicago." She was trying to force a response from him. She didn't get the one she wanted.

He laughed. Granted, there wasn't much humor in it, but the sound was like a razor on her soul. "You take things too seriously, Marielle. That's the problem with youth—everything's so earth-shattering. You don't have to leave Chicago if you don't want to. I always thought you'd be happier somewhere else, but that's up to you. You certainly don't have to leave on account of last night.''

So much for redecorating his apartment and teaching him how to make coffee. If he could be distant, so could she. "You're right," she said briskly, moving toward the door. "I happen to like it here. Actually, I'm very grateful to you. Now that I know sex can be enjoyable, my best bet would be to find someone a little younger, someone with a little more youthful energy."

She'd really wanted to wound him.

Instead he laughed again, and this time the sound was less strained. "I didn't know you could fight back," he murmured, his tone oddly admiring.

It took every ounce of self-possession in her to walk past him without edging out of the way. Simon could have reached out and touched her, but of course he did no such thing. He simply watched her, his gray eyes hooded, his face expressionless.

She closed the door behind her, quietly, carefully, resisting the impulse to slam it. He'd simply condemn her as childish if she gave in to that overwhelming temptation. She heard something behind the door, a word; it could have meant anything. It shouldn't have given her a speck of hope, it should have hardened her heart. It had been a very solid, very heartfelt "Damn!" and it proved that no matter how hard he tried to convince her otherwise, he was far from unmoved.

She headed for the stairs, studiously ignoring the elevator. If she wanted to she could consider that "Damn!" a good sign. Or merely proof that his comfortable life had been disturbed. The less she thought about it the better. The less she saw of him the better. All she needed was a shower, and she'd feel free to face the world....

She heard the crash five flights below. She heard the cry, a piteous, weak thing, barely able to float up all those flights. She raced to the bannister, peering over and down,

down. Lying in the middle of the first floor, the broken railing on top of her, was a huddled pile of dark clothing that could only be Esmy.

"Simon!" Marielle shrieked, dismissing her lingering problems as the minor inconveniences they were. "Come quickly!" And she stumbled down the stairs, still barefoot.

Simon passed her outside the Meltirks' apartment. Her highness was silhouetted in the doorway, a worried expression on her usually phlegmatic countenance, but Marielle couldn't take the time to try to communicate with the other woman. She kept running, holding up Simon's oversize pants with one hand.

He'd already managed to get the broken bannister off Esmy's plump body by the time Marielle reached them. Esmy's face was unnaturally pale, and she was moaning softly. Granita was pacing around, wringing her long hands, cursing Vittorio Farnum and his haunted house in loud, irritating tones. Julie was kneeling on one side of Esmy, Simon on the other, both holding her hands.

Simon looked up at her, through her for a moment, and she told herself it didn't hurt, it didn't matter. Then he focused on her. "Call an ambulance," he ordered. "I think she's broken something."

THE DAY REFLECTED HER MOOD, Marielle thought, tidying her already neat apartment, wandering to the window to look out over the rain-swept streets of Chicago, then back to the definitely sparse furniture. A coat of paint, a few posters, she thought, looking about her. Or a one-way ticket to Florida.

"You okay?" Dennis poked his head in the open door. He had a streak of grease on his cheekbone and a box of tools in his hand. He looked wonderfully normal, and Marielle could have hugged him.

"Fine. I'm just worried about Esmy."

"Now you know there's nothing to be worried about.

Julie called from the hospital and said it was nothing more than a simple fracture. Given her age they want to keep her overnight for observation, but by tomorrow or the next day at the latest she'll be back.''

"I don't know if she should come back. This place is dangerous.''

"Feeling guilty, are you?'' he said shrewdly, leaning against the doorframe. "You shouldn't, you know. Esmy's lived here for the past six years. This is her home.''

"But things have escalated since I came here. I can't rid myself of the feeling that maybe this place is haunted, after all.'' She shivered slightly, wrapping her arms around her body. "This wouldn't have happened if I'd managed to keep the place in decent repair.''

"Maybe,'' Dennis said. "But I don't think it was a ghost who sawed through that bannister. And keeping up on repairs wouldn't have much effect on a deliberate act of sabotage.''

"What?''

"You heard me. Someone booby-trapped that bannister. Nobody uses the elevator in this place—they all take the stairs. Whoever sawed through the bannister knew he wouldn't have to wait long for someone to take a tumble.''

"That could have been murder!'' Marielle breathed, horrified.

"Not likely. It was the lower section of the stairs—not one of the upper floors. It was unfortunate that one of the old ladies fell—their bones are more fragile.''

"What if it had been Julie?'' she couldn't help but ask.

Dennis's face darkened, and Marielle was very glad he was on her side. "It didn't happen,'' he said finally, releasing his pent-up breath. "As a matter of fact, I wanted to talk to you about Julie. Indirectly, that is.''

"Okay. Indirectly, what do you have to say?''

"I was thinking of applying for my Illinois licenses. I don't know if I'd qualify as both plumber and electrician—

their standards may be more rigid than New Hampshire, but I stand a good chance of making at least one. I could make a pretty good living if I wanted to. Plumbers and electricians are hard to find, especially good ones. No one wants to work anymore—they all want to be lawyers.''

Marielle smiled uneasily at his joke. She wasn't quite sure where this was leading. ''Does that mean you don't want to do any more work on this building?'' If that was the case, she was going to call a taxi to O'Hare and take the first plane to Florida. She couldn't stand another setback.

''Not at all. I'd have plenty of time to keep up with things around here.''

''But what about your writing? I thought you wanted to be another Elmore Leonard?''

He shrugged. ''I've got time. Hell, I'm only twenty-seven, I'm strong and I've got a lot of energy. I can do anything I want, if I work hard enough.''

''That sounds fine.''

''I thought I might do a little bit of work on my apartment. That is, if you're going to let me stay on there.''

''Of course.'' She was still mystified as to the eventual destination of this rambling conversation.

''Would you consider giving me a lease? I could promise a certain amount of hours of work per week, with an eye on paying rent after a while.''

''Certainly. Don't you trust me?''

He looked shocked. ''Of course, Marielle. I just thought it might be nice to have a bit of security in our lives.''

''Our lives?'' Marielle echoed. Maybe today wouldn't be such a total disaster, after all.

''I...er...thought I might turn one of the rooms into a nursery. Fix up a changing table, bring in a rocking chair, that sort of thing,'' he said self-consciously.

For all Simon's insistence on her extreme youth, Marielle

suddenly felt very old when faced with such naive enthusiasm. "That sounds very nice. Does Julie know?"

"I thought I'd better talk with you first. I didn't want to promise her anything I couldn't follow through on."

"Very wise. I think she's had enough promises broken. I'll give you a lease," she said. "In writing, notarized, the whole nine yards. I don't think Liam O'Donnell will serve as my lawyer, but I imagine Simon knows someone." Her voice was admirably cool when she said his name.

"That little sleaze," Dennis said bitterly, and for a moment Marielle was about to protest. Simon was a cold-hearted bastard, but not a little worm. Then she realized he meant O'Donnell. "He tried to get Julie to sign papers relinquishing the baby before it was even born. It's lucky he's been making himself scarce—I would have thrown him down the stairs myself."

"He does give the legal profession a lousy name," Marielle agreed. "When are you going to talk to Julie?"

"As soon as she gets back from the hospital. Granita's planning on spending the night there with Esmy, so there's no need for Julie to stay."

"Am I correct in assuming this offer is more than room and board?" she questioned gently.

Dennis drew himself up to his full five feet eleven inches, deeply affronted. "What kind of man do you think I am?" he demanded. "I want her to be my wife."

"Just wanted to make sure your intentions were honorable," she replied, feeling older by the minute. "Let me know what happens."

"You'll be invited to the celebration."

THE WIND HAD PICKED UP, lashing the rain against the windowpanes. It grew dark early, and by the time Marielle remembered it was Halloween it was too late to go out and buy candy for the trick or treaters. Still, it would be a foolhardy child indeed who'd brave the haunted premises of

Farnum's Castle for something as mundane as a Hershey bar. She made herself a pot of decent coffee, curled up on her sofa and began to drink it, waiting for Julie to come home.

She wasn't waiting for Simon, she reminded herself. She had nothing to say to Simon, nothing that wasn't insulting. It didn't matter that her body was experiencing strange, mournful twinges, that her lips felt stung and swollen, that her skin still tingled in errant memory. She was alone and determined to enjoy herself, despite the mess her life was in.

Esmy was fine, Julie had assured her. The children were having a ball, her mother had said. Simon had returned from the hospital only to disappear more than an hour ago, the sound of the elevator signaling his departure. She couldn't care less where he'd gone, she told herself. He probably wouldn't even be back that night. He'd been neglecting his work recently. As far as she could tell no one at the radio station cared whether Simon showed up or not, but sooner or later he was going to have to put his job ahead of Farnum's Castle.

Unless part of his penance was to get himself fired from his two-bit job. She wouldn't put it past him—anyone with the need to punish himself like Simon was capable of anything. Maybe going to bed with her last night had been just as self-destructive for him.

She tried beating herself with that miserable theory, then rejected it despite its morose appeal. Simon had wanted her, wanted her enough for it to overcome his better judgment. It was too bad that the good judgment had reappeared the next morning.

It was going to be a nasty night. She wasn't going to risk calling anyone else on the off-chance that Simon might return and find her camped on his doorstep. She wouldn't be able to bear it if he touched her. On the other hand, she wouldn't be able to bear it if he didn't, if he walked past her and shut the door.

She'd better get used to the idea of being alone. Granita and Esmy would be at the hospital, Simon would be at work, Fritzie was still in northern Wisconsin on an antique-buying trip, and there was no question at all that Julie and Dennis would be wrapped up in each other. She would definitely be a fifth wheel where they were concerned.

That left the Meltirks, and she couldn't quite envision herself cozying up to her serene highness and the ceremonial fire. The best thing she could do on such a rainy, lonely night was forget the coffee, pour herself a glass of wine, indulge herself with something tasty for dinner, and dress up for no one but herself.

It was a crazy impulse that made Marielle pick up the black ball dress. This time she used safety pins to keep it reasonably chaste, dispensing with the woolen shawl. She put on black lace stockings and ridiculously high heels, very red lipstick and very black mascara, and swept up her blond hair in a haphazard, decorative knot, held in place by an ornate black comb that had been unearthed along with the dress. She sprayed herself with so much perfume that she choked, surveyed her wavy reflection in the unsilvering glass of the dresser mirror, and held up her wineglass in a toast that wasn't nearly as self-pitying as she'd expected it to be.

"Here's looking at you, kid," she murmured. Her mysterious reflection smiled back, a little mournful, a little smug, and then she wandered into the deserted living room, her long skirts trailing, in search of something a little more lively than Lean Cuisine for dinner.

Marielle didn't hear the elevator, didn't hear his footsteps on the stairs. His silhouette blocked out the dim hall light, and she wished vaguely she'd done something about the door, something to keep him out. She kept her back to the open doorway, waiting for him to say something.

"Good heavens!" was what he came out with. She turned, and dropped her wineglass in shock.

"Good heavens!" she echoed, staring at the apparition in front of her.

It wasn't Simon Zebriskie standing in her doorway, watching her. It was Simon Zee in full regalia. In his rough jeans and work shirts he always seemed very tall; in charcoal-gray, tattered evening dress he looked mammoth. The usual gray streaks in his dark hair were augmented by sheer white, and the black-circled eyes, dead white complexion and thin, hungry mouth were something out of a nightmare.

Except that she'd seen him like that countless times, years ago on television. And the effect, while eerie, was having another, inexplicable impact on her disordered senses.

"Why are you dressed like that?" Simon demanded, seemingly unaware of his own bizarre appearance.

"Presumably for the same reason you are. It's Halloween."

"This—" he gestured with a disparaging, white-gloved hand "—is part of my job. I have to show up at a couple of Halloween parties as part of a PR thing. What's your excuse?"

"Cocktail parties for your radio station's clients? I don't believe you."

"You don't have to. That's not what I said. I just said parties."

"Where?"

He shrugged. "Where do you think a noble character like me would go? To the children's hospital on Wacker Drive, among other places."

Maybe it was the two glasses of wine, or the roller coaster of emotion she'd been riding; maybe it was just time to take a chance and stop being so damned serious. Marielle lifted her flowing black chiffon skirts, just high enough to expose black lace ankles and spiky black shoes, and sauntered across the room toward a wary-looking Simon. "Saint Simon," she murmured, her voice low and throaty when she reached him, "am I another one of your charity cases?" And before she could think better of it she reached up and pressed her red-painted lips on his, her heady perfume enveloping them both.

His hands were on her waist, pulling her close, and she realized with surprise and triumph that he was hard against her. She swayed toward him, longing for him with a bittersweet ache that threatened to choke her. His mouth opened beneath hers, and suddenly he was kissing her with a fierce passion that should have frightened her. It only made her exultant, and she pressed herself against him, her hips, her breasts, her mouth, wanting to be absorbed into his very pores, wanting to merge and cling and blend with him so that there might be no telling where Simon ended and Marielle began. His mouth left hers, trailing kisses across her cheekbones, her nose, her chin, and his hands were just the tiniest bit rough as they pushed at her dress, sliding it down to her waist so that he could feel her breasts warm and soft against him.

She wanted to touch his skin, too, and she pulled the dress shirt from his pants, sliding her hands around his waist, along his heated flesh. She was about to rip at the tarnished shirt studs when he lifted his head, looking down at her, his dark-rimmed eyes suddenly intent as he said the very last thing she expected him to say.

"Do you smell smoke?"

Chapter Nineteen

Billowing black smoke was pouring from the basement doorway, thick and acrid. By the time Marielle had managed to dump her dangerous shoes and follow Simon he'd disappeared into the cellar. She stood uncertainly at the top of the basement stairs, when Dennis appeared out of the murk, coughing, choking, his face streaked with soot. In his arms he carried an ashen-faced Julie.

Simon was right behind him, striding to the front door and opening it. The nasty smoke was sucked out into the rainy night, and Simon stood in the doorway, taking in deep breaths of the cold night air. "Fire's out," he said, turning back to face Marielle.

Dennis had already maneuvered Julie into the narrow elevator. Even for Julie's sake Marielle wasn't about to join them, but she stood in the doorway, her eyes anxious.

"Is she all right?" Simon came up behind her, a solid, reassuring presence.

Julie managed a weak smile. "I just breathed in a little too much smoke."

"Don't you think we should take you to the hospital?" Dennis inquired, with the air of someone who had asked the question half a dozen times already.

"I'm okay, Dennis," she assured him but her face was pale beneath the smoky grime, and there were beads of sweat on her brow. "I just want to lie down for a few minutes. I promise, if I'm feeling worse I'll go to the emergency room."

Simon pulled Marielle out of the doorway, shutting it so that Dennis could activate the elevator. She listened to it begin its laborious journey upward, her face creased with misgivings. "What if they get stuck in there?" she demanded.

Without a word Simon pulled her into his arms. He smelled of smoke and rain and warm male flesh, and she leaned against him, shivering in sudden reaction. "It's all right, Marielle," he said, his voice a deep rumble beneath her ear. "The fire was very small, contained in an old metal barrel. Julie had it out before we even got there, and there's no chance of it spreading."

"Who started it?" she mumbled against his chest, keeping her eyes closed. "Why was Julie in the basement in the first place? What the hell is going on here?"

"I don't have the answers to those questions. I can make a few educated guesses, but guesses don't help anyone. Let's go make sure Julie's all right."

Marielle lifted her head to look up at him. "Dennis is going to ask her to marry him," she said.

He raised an eyebrow. If she thought he'd react in any way relevant to their own tangled situation, she was in for a disappointment. "Then he'd better hurry."

Marielle didn't have to ask what he meant. "You think she's in labor."

"You know more about such things. What do you think?" he countered.

"She certainly has all the signs of it," Marielle said gloomily. "And if she is, I'm not going to be much help."

"Why not? You've been through this before. Twice."

"I was knocked out. I had both of the children by caesarean, and my doctor didn't believe in mothers being awake during the delivery. Neither did my husband, and at the time I wasn't into arguing.''

"Oh, that's just great!" he said bitterly. "I guess there's nothing we can do but check to make sure our suspicions are correct, and then call the hospital.''

He still had his arms around her, a fact she realized with belated embarrassment. She stepped back and he let her go, too readily. The elevator had returned like a stately old lady to the ground floor, and the door opened.

Simon's expression was quizzical, but she could see the glint of humor behind his dark-rimmed eyes. "I'll walk, thank you," she said, turning her back on him and heading for the stairs.

"I'll ride—" his voice floated behind her "—I've gotten rather fond of the elevator.''

It was a good thing he couldn't see her face, see the bright red color mounting her cheeks. She kept her backbone stiff beneath the trailing black material, moving with great dignity until she heard the elevator start to move once more. Then she picked up her skirts and ran up the three flights of stairs to Dennis's apartment, arriving moments before the elevator stopped.

She had just enough time to smooth back her tumbled hair and take a deep breath before the door opened. She moved past Simon.

"I never said the elevator was faster, Marielle," he said under his breath. "Just more fun.''

Dennis answered the door. He'd washed the smoke and grime from his face and was in the midst of rolling down his shirt sleeves. He greeted them with faint surprise. "What's up?"

"How's Julie?"

"Fine, I think. She wanted to lie down for a while. She's probably asleep.''

"I don't think so," Marielle said, moving past him into the apartment. He'd already been working on it—the cracked window panes had been replaced, the trashed fireplace cleaned out. She headed down the hallway, the two men trailing after her, and peered into the first bedroom.

The room was dark. Julie was lying on a mattress on the floor, unmoving, but Marielle knew she wasn't asleep.

She reached for the light switch, flooding the room with light. Julie quickly covered her eyes from the glare, but Marielle ignored the gesture, kneeling down beside her and taking her hand.

"How long, Julie?" she asked quietly.

Julie looked up at her, suddenly very young and very frightened. "A few hours. I thought it might be false labor. I thought if I just got home I'd be all right."

"Damn it, Julie, why didn't you stay at the hospital? I would have come down!" Dennis exploded.

"Don't yell at her," Marielle said quietly. "She didn't want O'Donnell to find her. Isn't that it?"

Julie nodded, miserable, and then her face creased in a spasm of pain as another contraction hit her.

"He won't get the baby," Dennis said, dropping to the other side of the mattress and taking her hand from Marielle's grip. "We'll get you to the hospital, get this baby born, and then we'll get married. Okay?"

Julie looked up at him through wondering, pain-glazed eyes. "Okay," she managed to croak.

"Better call the hospital, Simon," Marielle said, her voice raw with suppressed emotion. "This baby wants to be born."

He was already gone. Marielle rose, giving herself a tiny shake. "She'll be all right for now. Just hold her hand when the contractions come. I'll go find her suitcase. She's going to want her own things at the hospital. By the time I get it the ambulance should be here."

Dennis nodded, barely noticing her, all his attention on Julie's pale, sweating face. "Hurry," he said, more a prayer than an order. "Hurry."

Julie's things were all over the old building. Marielle found a pitifully beautiful assortment of tiny, handmade baby clothes in the back bedroom of Esmy's apartment and a handful of clean, mended clothes that could only have belonged to a prepregnant Julie in a box under the bed. From her own apartment she took her best Austrian flannel nightgown, the one with buttons down the front, in case Julie wanted to breast-feed. She packed everything in one of her suitcases, throwing in the warm woolen shawl that was part of her Halloween costume. She found she was crying as she packed.

Babies did that to her every time. She loved babies, loved the magic of childbirth and everything about it. Another precious child was coming into the world, and it was coming into the world with a father and mother to love it and care for it. What more could anyone ask?

She was just leaving her apartment when she met Simon coming down the stairs. She only needed a swift glance at his expression to know things weren't going well. "What's wrong?" she demanded. "Won't an ambulance come to this part of town?"

"The telephone's out."

"That doesn't make sense. The lights are still working. Did you remember to pay your bill?"

"Yes," he said irritably. "And the phone's not broken. The line's been cut."

Marielle swallowed the retort that had risen to her lips. "The line's been cut?" she repeated in a sick voice. "And someone set a fire in the basement? What next?"

"Vampires, most likely," he snapped. "Go tell Dennis to get her ready. I'll bring the car around to the front."

"You think that'll be safe? If someone tampered with the phone lines, they could have messed with your car. The garage doesn't even have a door, much less a lock."

"It has a killer goat tied up there to scare anyone away. God, Marielle, I don't know," he said, running a harassed hand through his long, streaked hair. Some of the white came off on his hand. "But the alternative isn't terrific, either. I'm not ready to deliver Julie's baby. Are you?"

"Get the car."

By the time Marielle reached Dennis's door her legs were shaking. It seemed as if she'd done nothing but run up and down five flights of stairs since she'd moved into Farnum's Castle.

Dennis was in the hallway outside the bedroom, looking for her. "I don't know if we have time to wait for an ambulance," he greeted her, his face pale. "I don't know much about these things, but the pains are coming almost nonstop."

"Simon's gone to get the car. The phone's not working." She didn't see any need to add to his worries by telling him why the phone was out of order.

"Did someone cut the wire?" At her reluctant nod he swore. "We've all got to get out of here. I don't think Simon can keep you and a horde of unintelligible Meltirks safe from whatever wants to get into this place."

"Don't worry about us. Worry about Julie and the baby."

"What do you mean by that?" he demanded, his voice hoarse. "Is something wrong?"

"Nothing's wrong. She just needs your attention right now. The rest of us can take care of ourselves." A groan from the mattress caught their attention, and she gave him a little shove. "Go see how she's doing. I'll see what's keeping Simon."

Down more flights of stairs, she thought, her muscles shrieking a protest. If she kept this up she should qualify for the New York Marathon. Or whatever Chicago equivalent there was.

She met Simon one flight down, in front of the Meltirks' closed door. He was soaked with rain, and the expression in his eyes was far from reassuring.

"The damned goat ate my tires."

"What?" Marielle's shriek echoed through the hallway. The Meltirks' door opened, and her serene highness appeared, draped in fuchsia.

She greeted them in her own incomprehensible language, and over her shoulder Marielle saw the wizened features of Mrs. Meltirk's mother. Or mother-in-law, she wasn't quite sure.

"I'm sorry, your highness, but Esmy isn't here, and no one else can translate. We've got an emergency."

Mrs. Meltirk just looked at Marielle, her heavy features placid.

"Julie's gone into labor," Marielle continued, her voice desperate with worry and the frustration of explaining to someone who didn't understand a word she was saying. "The phone's dead, so we can't call an ambulance, and Simon's car is broken so we can't drive her to the hospital."

Slowly, ponderously her serene highness, the crown princess of Baluchistan, nodded. "There is no need for hospitals," she said in slow, perfect English. "My mother is a midwife. I myself have brought many children into the world. Julie will be fine."

Marielle stared at her openmouthed. "You speak English?"

Her highness shrugged her massive shoulders, gesturing to her mother to follow her as she moved out into the hallway with all the majesty of an ocean liner.

They moved up the stairs, a curious procession, Marielle not sure whether she ought to cry in relief or laugh at the ridiculousness of it all. "Why haven't you spoken before?" she asked as they plodded their way into Dennis's apartment.

"It didn't suit me," the princess replied with her customary dignity. "If your government knew I spoke English, they would have asked me all sorts of exhausting questions and wanted me to make inflammatory statements about the wild young men who overran my country. If I were to make such statements there would be no chance of my returning to my country without further bloodshed. Very few people outside of Baluchistan speak my language—so very few people were able to disturb us. It was working very well."

She turned to her mother, issuing a long, involved statement. Her mother nodded, sketched a tiny bow and moved to Julie's side, muttering under her breath and shooing Dennis away.

"My mother says things are going well. It won't be long. And," she added, "it will be a girl." The heiress to the monarchy of a matriarchal society smiled. "That is good."

"I just want the baby born safely," Dennis muttered, looking askance at the Baluchistani contingent.

"My mother has never lost a baby or a mother in all her years," said her highness. "A father, perhaps." And she began to wheeze, a low, rumbling sound that Marielle finally identified as a laugh.

The old lady was speaking to Julie, a litany of long, cooing sounds that must have been incomprehensible, but nevertheless seemed to soothe her.

"Damn," Dennis said, sitting back on his heels beside the mattress. "I'd wanted us to be married before the baby is born. It's too late for that now, but I'd hoped..."

"Why is it too late?" her highness inquired. She'd settled her impressive bulk on the only chair in the room, prepared to await the outcome in relative comfort.

"There's no priest," Dennis pointed out, half distracted, as Julie moaned. "Not to mention no marriage license, no blood tests, no banns posted. We can't even manage a civil ceremony."

"I can marry you," her highness announced.

"Really?" Marielle demanded in a moment of curiosity.

"Of course. It would be perfectly legal in Baluchistan,

and this country would be forced to accept it. Your government does not say no to me," she added simply.

"Fine," said Dennis. "But this isn't Baluchistan. This is Chicago."

Her highness smiled. "Dear child," she corrected him, "wherever I am *is* Baluchistan. Do you wish to be married or not?"

He hesitated for only a second, then capitulated. "What harm can it do? How do we do it?"

"Take her hand, young man." And leaning back, Mrs. Meltirk began to intone.

The Baluchistani marriage ceremony was a long-winded one. Julie's labor was short—for a while it was a horse race as to which would finish first.

But even her indolent majesty had a sense of the importance of matters. Three minutes before Esmerelda Granita McMurtry arrived in the world, red-faced and screaming, Dennis and Julie were pronounced husband and wife. Or the Baluchistani equivalent thereof.

Marielle looked across the room at Simon. They'd both been banished to the living room as unnecessary either to birth or to marriage, and they'd spent the last half hour alternatively pacing and staring.

They both ran to the bedroom door and peered inside. "Everything is fine," her highness announced, heaving her bulk out of the spindly chair. "You can take them both to the hospital if you like. There is no need, but Americans like to be reassured."

Indeed, there didn't seem to be the slightest need at all. The newest Esmy was tiny, perfectly formed, and now that the indignity of birth had passed, was sleeping peacefully in her mother's arms. The new parents stared down at the little scrap of humanity with expressions of awe and wonder. Marielle backed out of the room and into the bathroom and burst into tears.

Simon followed her, shutting the door behind them, shutting the two of them in. He pulled her into his arms, holding her tight, and she bawled loudly against his absurd evening clothes.

Someone pounded on the door. Simon ignored it for a moment, then reluctantly released her, opening the door to see Francis Muldoon's beefy red face. "So suddenly I've got a sister-in-law and a niece," he announced. "I didn't realize Dennis had it in him. The boy can work fast when he has a mind to."

Marielle managed a watery smile. "That he can. What are you doing here?"

"Got a call that a prowler was seen outside the building. Combine that with the phone being on the blink and we thought it might behoove us to check the old place out. Did you have a fire?"

"Just a small one. Julie put it out."

"Arson?" Muldoon was suddenly all business, no longer the proud new uncle.

"Presumably," Simon said.

"We've radioed for an ambulance. Once we get them settled we'll call in backup and go over this place with a fine-toothed comb. We'll start with the grounds and work our way inward. They're making a mockery of the Chicago police department," Officer Muldoon said severely. "And we don't like that." He moved away, back to the delivery room, and Marielle could hear the low rumble of voices.

Simon was gazing down at her, a peculiar expression on his face. "You look," he said wryly, "as bad as I do." He turned her shoulders gently to the mirror.

Her makeup had run down her face in long black streaks. Sometime during the last few hours she'd bitten off her bright red lipstick, and her hair had fallen around her shoulders. "I'd better do something about this," she murmured self-consciously, pushing at her hair.

"Not on my account. You look like a perfect lady vampire.'' His voice was very gentle, almost loving. A trick, she thought. Wishful thinking on her part.

"I'd better go," she said again, pulling away. He let her go. Was she imagining his reluctance? she wondered.

"I'll make sure they get off to the hospital," he said. "And then I'll come up to your apartment."

"Why?"

"We have to talk."

"We already talked," she said stubbornly, refusing to meet his eyes.

His hand caught her chin, turning her face up to his. "Maybe things have changed."

"Maybe they haven't."

"It's Halloween, Marielle. Time for a little trick or treat," he murmured, brushing his lips against hers, his hand holding her face still when she would have turned her head away.

She couldn't help it. Her lips clung to his, almost of their own volition. He didn't deepen the kiss, keeping it gentle and sweet, and when he lifted his head she found she was smiling.

"Give me half an hour," he said. "And then I'll be up. Will you talk to me?"

"I can't keep you out. My door's still broken."

"You could keep me out. If you wanted to. Do you?"

She really didn't want to be pinned down, but Simon was insisting. "Yes," she breathed. "No. I mean, I'll wait for you."

He smiled then, a sweet, loving smile that lit the darkness of his gray eyes. "I'll be there," he said.

And she still didn't know whether he was about to break her heart.

Chapter Twenty

Farnum's Castle felt oddly empty as Marielle wearily climbed the last flights of stairs to her fourth-floor apartment. She could only be glad of the sensation. The Meltirks were once again snug in their second-floor suite and she realized the sense of being unobserved, unthreatened.

She looked out her apartment window to the grounds surrounding the old building, out toward the street. The ambulance was there, its lights flashing in a lazy circle, and she could see the outline of Muldoon's police car. Simon's tall, spare figure was silhouetted in the street light as he looked back toward the house. She didn't know whether he could see her, mooning after him from her tower window, and she didn't care. Crying for the moon, that was what she was doing. Moping around for something that was forever out of reach. Maybe Simon was right; maybe she was just a child believing in happy endings and true love.

She was crying again. She pulled herself away from the window and headed into the bathroom. Icy-cold water did wonders for her self-pity, even if it couldn't help her red-rimmed eyes. The streaked black makeup washed off on her white facecloth, leaving her pale and weary-looking, her hair in witch locks around her face. She would make a perfect bride for Dracula, she thought with distant amusement. Bloodless, lifeless, soulless.

In a last trace of defiance she repainted her mouth, twisted her hair back up and slipped on her high heels. Simon said he wanted to talk, so she planned to face him with most of her defences intact. She held out very little hope for the outcome of their conversation. He'd probably tell her again to leave, she'd start crying, and it would all end miserably.

Or maybe, just maybe, there might be a happy ending for her, too. Miracles did happen.

Dangerous as it might be, she headed for the bottle of wine in her refrigerator. Dutch courage or not, after such an evening, such a day, such a week, she was in need of a little support. She was taking her first, tentative sip of the icy-cold chardonnay when she heard the noise.

If her apartment door weren't still splintered off its hinges she wouldn't have heard anything. If her children had been around, with the TV incessantly blaring, no one would have ever been the wiser. If Dennis had still been in residence and not on his way to the hospital with his brand-new wife and baby, she might have just assumed it was he making noises downstairs.

But no one was within three floors of her apartment but the quiet Meltirks. Simon and the police were combing the grounds before they searched the house, and there was no one on the floor below. No one.

She set down the glass on the stained and scratched Formica and headed for the door. Her high-heeled sandals made a clicking noise, so she slipped them off again. Her black silk stockings were already shredded, so it didn't matter if they took one more interminable trip down the stairs.

Dennis had left his door open, lights still illuminating the rain-swept night. She poked her head in, listening, but there was nothing. She turned, looking at the door of the one apartment in her dubious inheritance she'd yet to visit.

It might be the ghost of Vittorio Farnum, cozily ensconced in his own residence. Or it might be nothing at all—another empty apartment in a building with too many empty apartments. Or it might be someone evil—someone so obsessed with finding Vittorio's fortune that he no longer cared whom he hurt.

She crossed the hallway, pressing her ear against the door. There was no mistaking the noises from within. The hollow chink of bricks, noisy, yet muffled breathing, even an occasional curse.

She should have raced down the next three flights of stairs. But she'd had enough of stairs to last her for at least twenty-four hours. Besides, if she left, there was a good chance that when the police and Simon returned the intruder would be gone—perhaps even taking with him the long-lost treasure.

She put her hand on the tarnished brass doorknob. It turned easily, silently beneath her fingertips. Once more she hesitated. Their villain had yet to do any real, deliberate harm. The fire had been set in a metal barrel—there'd been almost no chance of it spreading. And if anyone other than an elderly lady had fallen through the bannister, he or she would have escaped with a few bruises.

No, she wouldn't be dealing with a murderer. If she just kept her wits about her she could find out who was behind the sabotage. And suddenly that need to know overcame any concern for her own safety. Pushing the door open, she stepped into the last empty apartment.

Only it wasn't empty. There were rugs on the floor. The same kind of cast-off furniture that furnished her own apartment, which was stored in abundance directly above this apartment, could be seen from the long narrow hallway. A dim light was burning in the living room, and Marielle moved slowly, quietly, leaving the door open behind her.

A dark figure was kneeling in front of the fireplace. Bricks and rubble were strewn all over the faded Oriental carpet, books were tossed this way and that. The figure in front of the fireplace had a stocking pulled over his head, gloves on his hands, and he was staring at the fireplace and cursing.

She must have made a noise, though she thought she'd been completely silent. He turned swiftly, staring up at her, and through the distorting mesh of the stocking her intruder looked uncannily like the portrait of Vittorio Farnum still hanging in Granita's bedroom. But she had already guessed who it was.

"Find anything interesting, Miles?" she questioned coolly.

He didn't move, his body coiled in tension, and for a moment Marielle wondered whether she'd misread his basic cowardice, whether he'd rush her, hurt her.

Then he reached up and pulled the panty hose off his head, revealing his beautiful blond hair standing straight up. He'd used something to darken his face and eyebrows beneath the mask, otherwise she never would have noticed the resemblance.

"I found my grandfather's treasure," he said with a bitter laugh. "A bunch of lousy Bibles. Trust the old skinflint of a fanatic. There's nothing so dangerous as a convert."

Marielle looked down at the books on the floor. They looked very old, heavy, with leather bindings. "I suppose they were a treasure to him."

"They're not to me," he said, sitting back on his heels. "Do you realize what I've gone through to get these?"

"Yes," Marielle said gently. "I do."

His mouth twisted in a wry smile. "Yes, I suppose you do. And I think I'd better get the hell out of here before Simon gets back. I have no intention of having my teeth kicked in." He rose, lithe and graceful as always, completely at ease even in this bizarre situation. "No one will be able to prove a thing, you realize. It'll be your word against mine, and I happen to have a lawyer safe in my pocket. A very devious, successful lawyer who isn't above resorting to a little financial incentive for the proper witnesses. Not to mentionn that he has a certain talent for hiring muggers and setting up fake ghosts. He's a very clever man.''

''Liam O'Donnell.''

''Exactly. And if that doesn't work, the station owner happens to have a brother who's a very influential judge. Plus a daughter who's deeply enamored of me. I have no doubt whatsoever that I could work something out in that area. Of course, you could always promise not to say anything.'' He smiled at her, that warm, charming smile that had doubtless melted harder female hearts than hers.

Marielle was both aghast and amused at his gall. ''Why in the world should I do that?''

''Well, now that the 'treasure'—'' he kicked a Bible with his black sneaker ''—is found, there'll be no more reason to break into this old mausoleum in the middle of the night. No need to drive you out, to try to get you to sell to me. As a matter of fact, I've gotten off quite lucky. If you'd taken me up on my offer I would have been out a considerable sum of money, with absolutely nothing to show for it but a pile of worthless old books.''

''I don't think you're going to get off so lightly, Miles. I have every intention of seeing you're prosecuted to the full extent of the law,'' she said very calmly.

He just looked at her for a long moment. ''Then I guess I'd better get the hell out of here,'' he said abruptly, diving past her and down the narrow hallway. He hadn't heard what she'd heard—the sound of someone climbing the stairs.

It was over in a matter of seconds, with shouts, curses and the splintering of wood. It must have been a trick of the light, or of her confused and weary mind. For a split second Marielle thought she saw two of Miles, the second one older, darker, dressed in a monk's robe. And then they were both gone, and Miles lay in an untidy heap two flights down, his leg twisted beneath him, his face white with pain.

Another sawn-through bannister pressed down on him while Francis Muldoon, ignoring his groans, proceeded to read him his rights.

Simon was only a few feet away from her. "What the hell are you doing down here?" he demanded, his voice hoarse with strain and worry.

"I heard a noise and decided to check it out," she replied.

She'd never seen him angry before, really angry. He didn't raise his voice much above a hoarse shout, and didn't leave her any space to break in. He merely explained in loud, definite tones why she should never, ever risk her safety in such a foolhardy way.

"Don't you realize, you fool woman," he rasped, "that there are people who love you, people who depend on you in this life, people who wouldn't survive if something happened to you!"

Muldoon had already yanked a sweating, grunting Miles out to the police car, disdaining the use of an ambulance for this particular felon. They were alone on the stairway, and if Marielle noticed the Meltirks' door had opened a crack, she ignored it.

"Such as?" she prodded.

"Such as your children. Such as the people in this building," he shot back.

"Not good enough, Simon," she said, very sure of herself for the first time in months, in years. "Who else loves me and needs me?"

He glared at her. "First you scare the hell out of me, then you make me say it," he grumbled, not as loudly.

The Meltirks' door opened a little wider, and Marielle could see the shadow of her serene highness's turban silhouetted against the wall.

"I'm waiting."

"All right, damn it. I love you. I need you. And if you ever do something as stupid as walking in on a criminal in the midst of a crime I will strangle you. Do you understand?''

She smiled at him, feeling as if her face would split in delight. ''Is that it?''

''Isn't it enough?''

She would have liked a proposal. She would have liked him to look a little happier about the whole thing. ''I'll take what I can get,'' she said, moving to the top of the stairs. He was standing two steps down; her eyes were even with his, her mouth was even with his. ''So what's next?''

His eyes were smoldering, no longer with fear and rage but with an intensity that made her knees weak. ''Next, I get out of this wet evening suit. I'm freezing to death.''

''What about me?''

''You could always get out of that dry evening gown and warm me up,'' he suggested, almost diffidently.

She went into his arms, plastering herself against his wet body, pressing her mouth on his. ''Sounds wonderful,'' she murmured. ''Are you going to carry me upstairs like Rhett Butler?''

''I'm going to make love to you right here on the stairs if you don't get moving,'' he growled. And Marielle had no doubt whatsoever that he meant it.

IT WAS THREE IN THE MORNING before they made it back downstairs to the third-floor apartment. Marielle was wrapped in Simon's little-used red chamois bathrobe, Simon was wearing tattered gray sweatpants and a T-shirt. The heating system, thanks to Dennis's recent ministrations, was deliciously efficient, and the chill that always seemed to linger at the back of Marielle's senses had disappeared.

Simon knelt down in front of the fireplace in the third-floor suite, picking up one of the heavy, leather-covered Bibles in careful hands. ''This is Vittorio Farnum's famous treasure? This is what fifty years of fuss have been about?'' he asked.

"That was Miles's reaction. Total disgust," Marielle said, pulling the long robe around her as she sank to her knees beside him.

"The problem with Miles," Simon said in a meditative voice, leafing through the first Bible, "is that he seldom looks beyond the surface. He's all flash and no substance. He wouldn't know a treasure if it came up and bit him."

Marielle looked at him in surprise. "Is there something hidden in the pages?"

"Like hundred-dollar bills in Deuteronomy? No, my sweet. You're just as prosaic as Miles. Take a look at this." He held out the first Bible for her perusal.

"It's in German."

"Very old German. Unless I miss my guess, this is from some time in the late fifteen hundreds or early sixteen hundreds. From Martin Luther's Germany."

"Religious sentiment aside, are you telling me this Bible is worth something?"

"If it's just any Bible from that time period it would be worth a great deal. If it's the *Ein' feste Burg* Bible, it's priceless." He set it down very, very carefully, and picked up another.

Marielle eyed it warily. "What's that one—the Dead Sea Scrolls?"

"Looks like it's French, but not any French I can read. I couldn't even begin to make a guess on these, but I expect they're all extraordinarily valuable."

"Who owns them?"

Simon grinned at her. "Practical as ever. I expect you do. Unless they're stolen property and the statute of limitations hasn't yet run out, or something equally unlikely. When one buys real estate one usually buys everything involved. This was part of the interior of Farnum's Castle, therefore it was part of the purchase and belongs to the present owner. I doubt Vittorio's newfound grandson has the slightest claim.''

"Did you ever have the faintest idea?'' she questioned him, momentarily distracted. "Miles did seem to know an awful lot about the place.''

Simon shrugged. "His father was Swedish. Until he darkened his face the resemblance was almost impossible to notice. And his mother had done everything to live down the connection. As far as I was concerned, he was just a Chicago aristocrat dabbling in city history.''

"He's not going to be dabbling in much besides jail for the next few years.''

"Don't count on it,'' Simon drawled. "He's going to get off with a slapped wrist. He'll throw himself on Abigail Harbison's mercy, she'll take him, and her father will pull enough strings to get him off.''

"Damn.''

"Look at it this way—he'll be in a cast for months, he's got a mild concussion, and he's going to have to marry someone he has absolutely no interest in, someone who's going to keep him firmly in line. Miles isn't in for smooth sailing by any account.''

"I suppose that'll have to do,'' Marielle said mournfully. "I still would have liked some revenge, for Esmy's broken ankle if for nothing else.''

"Esmy'll forgive him. You may as well, too.'' He sat back on his heels, watching her out of hooded eyes. "So what are you going to do about these Bibles? You could live quite a comfortable life on the proceeds of these. Travel, buy a house someplace warm and safe where it never rains.'' As if to punctuate his statement the rain increased, pounding against the windows.

"Still trying to get rid of me?'' she inquired, resigned. She reached out and touched the French Bible. "This should take care of the back taxes. Sounds like the German

Bible will provide a new elevator, a bannister, a few years' electric bills and even a new boiler.''

"And then some."

"And the others—" she gestured to the half dozen other books lying scattered amid the rubble "—should cover any contingency that might come up for a good long time."

"It should." He had retreated again behind that distant, unreadable expression. "I've been married," he said abruptly.

"So have I," she said. "Want to try again?"

If she'd hoped to shock him she failed. "Marielle, we haven't known each other for very long. I'm fourteen years older than you. I've been a loser when it comes to marriage...."

"I've heard all this a dozen times, Simon," she said, feeling very calm. "I know that beneath your gruff cynicism is the kindest man I've ever met. Also the sexiest. And I'm not going to give that up without a fight. Come on, Simon. Marry me for my newfound wealth. Take me out of pity. Just take me."

He reached a hand behind her neck and pulled her, not ungently, into his lap. "You're crazy, you know that? You're asking for trouble."

She twined both arms around his neck, smiling up at him. "I hope you like kids," she said, broaching the one subject they'd never tackled.

"I love kids. Particularly yours."

"Want to have more? Seeing little Esmy born has given me a wicked case of the baby blues."

"Woman, are you never satisfied!" Simon said, rolling his eyes heavenward.

"Now you know better than anyone that that's not true," Marielle purred, sliding her hand under his loose T-shirt. "So how about it? Are you ready to take a child bride of twenty-eight?"

He looked down at her, his mobile mouth twisted in a grin. "How can I resist such an offer? And she's rich, too."

"And cute into the bargain," she added, snuggling closer.

"Not to mention that I'm in love with her," Simon murmured.

"Let's not get too mushy, or she might have to start telling you how much she loves you, and then this would deteriorate into the kind of saccharine scene that would turn an old cynic like you green."

He kissed her, a full gentle kiss on her smiling mouth. "Don't worry," he said. "I'll turn you into a cynic before I'm done."

"Maybe," she said. "But I bet I turn you into an optimist instead."

"I doubt it."

"Try me," she suggested.

And for the fourth time that day, he did.

Epilogue

It was a Thanksgiving wedding. The children had returned from Florida, and Simon didn't believe in long engagements. They were married in the recently converted first-floor suite. Granita and Esmerelda were peacefully sharing an apartment once more, and Esmy was getting quite mobile in her cast, given the aid of the brand-new, smooth-running elevator. She had no trouble zipping upstairs to check on her namesake and the newlyweds at the most inopportune moments.

Granita's old apartment was to be a community room, and that was where the wedding was held, with the smells of freshly sawn pine and new paint blending with the scent of flowers.

Little Esmy came out with her first smile as she sat in her father's lap, her mother watching her with indulgent eyes. Christopher and Emily were proud observers and Marielle's bridesmaids, Abbie, Suzanne and Jaime, had flown in from all parts of the country. They were all jammed into the only empty apartment left in the rapidly improving building, and the four of them had been up half the night, laughing and talking and crying.

Jaime was glowing with an ease and self-assurance Marielle had never seen before. She'd finally come to terms with her overwhelming mother, and she couldn't mention

Quaid, her new husband, without going all soft and sentimental.

Suzanne, on the other hand, was still her usual sharp-tongued self. She'd left her darling Billy behind in Wyoming. Apparently he divided his time between Suzanne's house in the city and his ranch, and he'd been ignoring his duties too long. Besides, Suzanne said, she wanted to enjoy being around her old friends without having to consider anyone else. And yes, Mouse was well on her way to making her a grandmother, damn it.

But of all her friends Abbie was the most changed. She suddenly seemed years younger, as if a huge burden had been lifted from her shoulders. Marielle had never realized how very solemn Abbie could be, until she saw her free.

She imagined she must look just the same—silly and happy and young, with tears and giggles and salacious gossip ringing in her ears. It was the last time they'd be like this, she thought. Reality would set in again for all of them, but for now, for this Thanksgiving wedding weekend, they could all be the best, the closest of friends, and the memory of it would last through years of infrequent letters and phone calls.

A good portion of Chicago showed up for the ceremony and the huge Thanksgiving dinner afterward. Even Miles had the gall to appear, debonair as ever in a walking cast, his possessive fiancée and future father-in-law along as protection.

It was all Marielle could do to summon a polite smile, and when Miles tried to kiss her she ducked, giving him the faintest, most surreptitious kick in the cast she could manage.

He managed to smother a groan as he hobbled away. Then unfortunately, she was faced with the task of offering good wishes to the next bride-to-be.

Simon was right; Abigail Harbison wasn't Miles's type. She was built along sturdy lines, with a wide, generous mouth, shrewd eyes behind her wire-rimmed glasses, and had a no-nonsense air that could have been intimidating.

"Don't look at me like that," Abigail said under her breath in a cheerful voice. "I know what I'm doing. I understand Miles far too well. That's what scares the hell out of him."

Marielle blinked. "I wish you every happiness."

"I expect we'll have a harder time than you and Simon," Abigail admitted frankly. "That's why I'm glad he's in a cast. It's easier to keep him in line." And moving on, she enveloped Simon in an exuberant bear hug.

"Poor Miles," Marielle murmured to Simon a few moments later. "You're right—he's going to be much more restrained than he would have been in prison."

"She'll be the making of him," Simon replied.

She looked up at her new husband, laughing. "I told you I'd turn you into an optimist," she said. "I just didn't think it would be this quick."

He dropped a kiss on her upturned mouth. "Wait till I start the day shift at the new station. Then you'll find out just how cynical I can be."

"But at least I get you all night long. That should cheer you up."

"It does," said Simon. "Enormously. As long as we've finished with visitations and nocturnal visitors."

"Vittorio's gone for good," she replied.

He raised an eyebrow. "Vittorio hasn't been here in almost fifty years."

"If you say so, dear." She smiled sweetly, remembering the gentle touch of a hand, the scene on the landing and Miles's convenient fall.

"Marielle, don't tell me you ever really believed in ghosts," Simon begged.

Marielle looked over his shoulder to the portrait of wicked old Vittorio, still hanging in state over the newly refurbished fireplace. His evil old eyes seemed to wink at her.

"Never for a moment, darling," she promised. And smiling up at Vittorio, she winked back.

The moment he met Sally MacArthur,
P.I. Jack Diamond knew he was in for trouble.
And Sally was more than willing to give it to him....

Chasing Trouble

Chapter One

Sarah "Sally" Gallimard MacArthur had been in sleazier, scrungier, dirtier places in her life, but not many. And usually not on her own accord. This seedy office building in the worst part of the Tenderloin District of San Francisco should have been condemned years ago. The green-painted hallways were littered with trash, the offices seemed to be rented by one-room venues with names like Novelty Toys and Rubber, Inc., and that faint scuffling overhead had to come from little rodent feet. The windows were so dirt-engrimed that nobody could see out into the decaying city street, and the whole place reeked of grime, sweat and despair.

Sally absolutely loved it.

Even at eleven o'clock on a hot September morning, the place was dark and dank. The halls were deserted—their usual denizens had probably slunk out into the daylight, blinking. It took her longer than she expected to find the third-floor office, but it was worth the trouble. It was perfect.

The rippled glass door was cracked, a jagged lightning streak through the stenciled name. James Diamond, Private Investigator. She took a deep breath of pure pleasure. Sam Spade himself would have been at home there. For the first time in days—weeks, maybe—her luck had taken a turn for the better. She'd been right to go with her instincts. When the chips were down, those instincts came through for her every time. With a brisk knock, she turned the door handle and stepped into the office.

"What can I do for you?" The man stepping out from the inner office was somewhat of a disappointment, but then, she couldn't expect everything to be like an old movie. He was too clean-cut, for one thing. He looked more like a seminary student than an ex-cop turned private detective, with his neat polyester suit, his short hair, his phony smile and his wary eyes.

"I need a private detective," she announced. "I've got this little problem that I need some help with."

He reached out and took her hand in his own soft ones. "There, there. Why don't you come into my office and tell me all about it? I'm sure I can help you deal with whatever it is."

"I'm not so sure about that," she said doubtfully. Private eyes shouldn't have soft hands, should they? There was certainly a lecherous expression in his slightly bloodshot eyes, and that was reasonable enough, but still…

"Get out of here." The voice was rough, hostile, coming up behind her, and she jumped in panic, ready to run. Instead, however, the seminary student turned a bright red and began slinking toward the door.

"I didn't mean any harm," he muttered. "Just trying to be helpful."

"The day I need your help, Frankie, is the day they put me under. Take your pal with you."

"Not my pal, Diamond. I think she's a client. Better not be too rash. You need all the work you can get." With that, the seminary student disappeared out the office door, slamming it behind him, widening the crack that speared through James Diamond's name.

It took all Sally's self-control to hide her smile of pure pleasure when she saw him. This was what she'd been hoping for. This man was unshaven, his dark hair needed cutting quite badly, his suit was rumpled, as if he'd slept in it, and his expression was sour and unfriendly. If his face was a little too handsome beneath the day's growth of heavy beard, if his body was a little too tall and lean to be quite right, she was willing to overlook those deficiencies. This was her down-and-out detective, like something out of Raymond Chandler. This was her savior.

"You a client or one of Frankie's girls?" Diamond asked, eyeing her up and down as he lit a cigarette. His hands shook slightly, but they didn't look soft. Not soft at all.

"One of Frankie's girls? You mean he's a...?"

"That's right." He blew the smoke in her direction. "Although he calls himself a 'talent manager.' I guess that's as good a job title as anything. All right, you weren't here to see him. That means you must be here to see me." He glanced at her again. "You from the IRS? The telephone company? Pacific Gas?"

She'd really tried to dress down. She should have known a private investigator would see through her pathetic attempts. Even with a cheap dress and bargain-basement shoes she couldn't disguise a two-hundred-dollar haircut. Though why a down-and-out detective should recognize Antonio's best work was a question in itself.

"You heard Frankie. I'm a client."

"Oh, yeah?" He didn't sound promising. "Well, I don't do drug buys for spoiled rich girls, and I don't make blackmail drops. You can't be in the midst of a divorce—you look too cheerful for that—and you look too clean for kinky sex, so that rules out just about everything."

"I want you to find my sister."

For a moment, he didn't move. "Your sister's into drugs and kinky sex?" he asked finally, as if the question bored him.

"Not that I know of."

"Then what's the problem?"

"Do you suppose we could go in and sit down?" she asked, choking slightly as another stream of cigarette smoke made a beeline for her. "I think better sitting down."

"I think better standing up."

"Frankie said you were in need of clients, and looking around me, I can believe it. Don't you think you ought to make an effort to get me to hire you instead of trying to chase me away?"

"No," said James Diamond, moving past her into the inner office. She followed him before he could shut the door in her face, almost choking on the thick, stale air in the room. It reeked of old cigarettes and whiskey. Perfectly in keeping with what she wanted, but it was hard to breathe in there.

"Mind if I open a window?" Without waiting for an answer, she headed for one grime-coated one and began tugging. It couldn't have been painted shut—there'd been no fresh coat of paint on these windows since the Korean War, but it was proving almost as stubborn as the man she'd come to hire.

"I mind," he said, dropping down into a chair behind the cluttered desk and tipping back, putting his feet on top of a pile of papers. That was one thing she didn't like. He was wearing sneakers. Sam Spade wouldn't wear sneakers.

Sally gave one more shove, the window jammed upward and the glass shattered. "Oops," she said.

Diamond didn't move. "Why don't you go away before you destroy my office?"

"It would take more than me to destroy this place," she announced, looking around her. There was one other chair, something that looked like Mission Oak. Pretrendy mission oak, just something found at a junk store and dumped there. James Diamond was clearly the kind of man who'd sell it in an instant if he had any idea of its value.

The sofa was sagging Naugahyde, one that had obviously provided its owner with more than one good night's sleep. Sally wondered for a moment whether it had had other, more energetic uses. No, rampant sexuality wasn't part of this particular fantasy. The hard-boiled detective wasn't someone who tumbled clients on his office couch. Even if he did have sinfully beautiful blue eyes.

"Tell me what you want and then leave," Diamond said in a world-weary voice, lighting another cigarette from the end of his old one before stubbing it out.

"Do you always smoke so much?" Sally questioned artlessly, sliding onto the top of his desk beside his large, sneakered feet, dumping half the papers on the floor at the same time. "It's no wonder your voice sounds like gravel and your office smells like toxic waste. If you keep this up, you'll die young."

He just stared at her, as if he couldn't quite believe her gall. She'd seen that expression often enough—she didn't let it slow her down. "It's too late," he said. "I've already missed dying young by at least five years. You, however, might make it under the deadline if you don't tell me what you're doing here."

She let her long legs swing back and forth under his patently uninterested gaze. She had wonderful legs—long and shapely, and she was wearing a skirt made for the express purpose of exposing most of their length. Private eyes were supposed to be fascinated by legs, but Diamond didn't seem to care. Maybe she should have unbuttoned another button or two on her dress.

"Why don't you want to take me on as a client?" she asked instead.

He let out a long-suffering sigh, tipping back farther to stare at her out of those sinful eyes. He should have been wearing a fedora, but then, no one wore a fedora in the 1990s, more's the pity. Maybe if she bought one, stomped on it a bit to give it some character and then gave it to him, he might be persuaded to wear it.

"You're trouble, lady. From the tips of your brand-new shoes to the top of your up-scale haircut, you're the kind of client I do my best to steer clear of."

She glanced around the seedy office meaningfully. "Obviously. I pay very well."

"And I have scruples. Standards. I know those things might be foreign to someone like you, but I don't break the law for anyone."

"How do you earn a living?"

He hesitated, but it was clear she wasn't moving from her perch on top of his old desk, and short of throwing her out the window she'd already broken, he wasn't going to get rid of her. He had enough sense to know that. "Divorces," he said finally.

"Pretty sleazy."

"Hey, it's a living. So why don't you tell me what you want from me, and I'll steer you in the direction of someone who can help you."

"What makes you think you can't help me?" She swung her legs back and forth and was pleased to notice his eyes followed the movement of her long legs.

"Instincts. You learn to trust 'em when you get to my age."

"Ah, yes, your advanced age. That's the second time you've mentioned it. You're thirty-eight years old. I hardly think that qualifies you for a wheelchair."

She'd gone too far this time. He sat forward with a snap, and his formerly impassive face looked downright dangerous. For the first time, Sally wondered whether she was as much in control as she'd thought.

"How do you know I'm thirty-eight?" Diamond demanded.

"Simple. I had you investigated once I decided I wanted to hire you."

He sat back, momentarily stunned. "You had me investigated? Why the hell would you hire investigators to investigate an investigator? For that matter, why didn't you use those investigators to investigate whatever the hell it is you want investigated?"

"You're confusing me."

"Good. You've done nothing but confuse me since you waltzed in my door."

"Maybe you're easily confused," she pointed out. "I didn't mean that I had someone investigate you. I mean I checked with the licensing bureau to see whether you were someone reputable before I contacted you."

He seemed to believe her; at least he didn't call her an outright liar. "And why did I have the honor of being chosen for your problem? I don't advertise on buses or park benches. I don't do much to drum up business."

"But you are in the Yellow Pages."

He just looked at her. "The Yellow Pages," he echoed faintly. "There are over two hundred private investigators listed in the Bay Area directory. Why me?"

"Isn't it obvious?" she said cheerfully.

"Not to me."

"Your name. It just sounds like a private eye's." She gave him a beatific smile. "The moment I saw your name in the Yellow Pages I knew you were the one for the job. I mean, how could I hire someone like Edwin Bunce or Liebowitz, Inc., when there's someone with a name like James Diamond?"

He shook his head. "Trouble," he muttered under his breath, stubbing out his cigarette without lighting another one. "Just plain trouble. Why don't you tell me about your sister so I can get rid of you once and for all?"

"It's not going to be so easy." She swung off his desk, deciding he'd had enough time to appreciate her legs. She figured the rest of her wasn't really his style, even though her looks were something she usually took for granted. A hard-boiled P.I. like Diamond wouldn't be attracted to porcelain skin, silky black hair and blue eyes, and he wouldn't like her slightly voluptuous body. He'd like reed-slim women with platinum hair. "I already told you, I need you to find my sister."

"And what's happened to your sister, and why can't the police help you, and what the hell are you doing?"

"Making coffee," she said cheerfully, not quite sure how to handle the electric kettle. "And I haven't gone to the police."

"Why not?"

"It's a family matter. My sister—actually she's my half sister, Lucy. My mother went through three husbands and unfortunately, Lucy's father was the only one without money. Anyway, Lucy got involved with an unsavory character and took off with something she shouldn't have taken. I need to get her back, return the item before it's missed and get rid of her boyfriend. It's really quite simple."

He stared at her, clearly fascinated despite himself. "Simple," he muttered. "You expect me to kill this boyfriend?"

She smiled at him. "I don't suppose you'd consider it? It would certainly solve most of our problems."

"I would not."

She dished out some lumpy instant coffee into two disposable cups. "I didn't think so. We'll have to figure some other way around it. Did you know fish choke on plastic foam? It's one of the worst ecological disasters…"

"I don't give a rat's behind about the ecology," Diamond said flatly.

That stopped her cold. "You don't?"

"Nope. I'll be dead and gone by the time the ozone layer disappears, and I'm certainly not going to have any family to leave behind, so who gives a damn?"

"You're not going to have any friends to leave behind, either, if this is your usual attitude," Sally said sternly.

"Since I won't be here, it won't matter."

"God, you're cynical. I love it."

"I beg your pardon?"

"Never mind." Sally poured boiling water from the kettle and then set it back with an ominous crack that didn't bode well for its future use, handing Diamond one of the polluting cups. "Drink your coffee, and I'll give you the details about my sister."

He stared down at his cup, at the nuggets of crystallized coffee still floating in the foam on top. "I need milk and sugar."

"Don't be ridiculous, a man like you would drink it black," she said flatly, dropping onto the aging sofa. It was surprisingly comfortable despite the deep sag in the middle.

"A man like me drinks it with milk and sugar."

She didn't bother arguing. She'd already checked the supplies. The sugar bowl had ants in it; the coffee creamer had hardened into a lump. Let him deal with it. "Lucy's been gone for five days. I figure we have maybe another five days to find her without the manure hitting the fan."

"What happens in five days?"

"My father comes back from Asia, finds his prize Chinese figurine missing and raises holy hell. He's a stern man—it wouldn't matter if my sister was the culprit. It wouldn't matter if I were the culprit. He has a Biblical sense of justice, and Lucy would end up behind bars before she could blink. Lucy wouldn't be able to survive."

"You'd be surprised at how many people survive prison," Diamond said, taking a sip of his black coffee. He probably knew all too well the condition of his cream and sugar and had only been trying to bait her.

"Not Lucy. She's not like me. She's flighty, impractical, a little silly."

"Not like you," he murmured wryly. "I bet she talks too much, too."

Sally nodded. "A regular chatterbox. As a matter of fact,

I'm surprised Vinnie can put up with her. I used to drive him crazy—'' Her own runaway tongue had tripped her up again.

''You used to be involved with your sister's unsavory character?''

Sally considered lying, something she was quite adept at, but saw no point in it. She only lied when she thought she could get away with it or if she was bored. As long as she was in James Diamond's cynical company, she wasn't the slightest bit bored. ''I was engaged to him. Until I realized he was more interested in my father's collection than in me, and then I dumped him. Next thing I knew, Lucy had stars in her eyes and the figurine was missing. And then Lucy and Vinnie were gone, Father was on his way home and I had no choice but save the bacon.''

''In five days,'' Diamond said faintly. ''I don't suppose you have any idea where they went?''

She drew herself up straight. ''Of course I do. I don't expect the impossible. I have a very good idea exactly where they went. I'm just not sure how to find it.''

''But you're going to share your information with me.''

''Even better. I'm going with you.''

''No, you're not. If I take this job, I'll do it alone.''

''Don't be ridiculous, you wouldn't be able talk Lucy into coming home and throwing herself on Father's mercy. You'll be too busy dealing with Vinnie. Did I happen to mention that Vinnie has connections?''

''What kind of connections?''

''Organized crime. That's another reason why I picked you. You used to work for the police force. You must have dealt with thousands of gangsters.''

''Thousands,'' Diamond agreed faintly.

''So you'll know exactly what to do to get rid of him, even if you won't kill him. I'll talk Lucy into coming back home, and everything will be absolutely wonderful.''

''Except for one thing.'' He pulled out his crumpled pack

of cigarettes and lit another one, blowing the smoke in Sally's direction.

She gave a meaningful little cough. "And what's that?"

"I'm not taking the case."

She stared at him nonplussed. This was a lot harder than she'd ever expected. Humphrey Bogart didn't turn down cases, particularly when Lauren Bacall showed up and swung her long legs in front of him. Of course, Sally was no Lauren Bacall. And James Diamond was too young and too pretty, even beneath that stubble, to be the great Bogie. But he was a start, if he just wouldn't be so damned stubborn.

"Why not?" she asked.

He didn't hesitate. He didn't strike her as someone who hesitated in this life. "Because you're lying to me."

"I am not—" she began hotly.

"Then you're not telling me the entire truth. And I don't walk into situations blindfolded, lady. Speaking of which, what's your name?"

"My name?" she asked blankly, her mind working at a feverish pace. She'd hoped to get a commitment from him without having to go into all the sordid details. She'd hoped she could manage to rescue Lucy without having to tell him much at all. If he really wasn't going to take the case, and she didn't believe that for a minute, then it would be better if he didn't know who she was.

"Your name, lady," he said, pushing back from the desk and standing up. He was too tall for Sam Spade or Philip Marlowe, but he looked suitably seedy in that rumpled suit and unshaven, too-handsome face.

"Bridget O'Shaunessy," she said promptly, not bothering to rise from her seat on his sagging couch. If he wanted to get rid of her, he was going to have to throw her out. "I'm a costs analyst at Wells Fargo." She didn't actually know what that was, but it sounded properly impressive.

James Diamond had skirted his desk and strode over to

her. "Bridget O'Shaunessy, is it?" he said. "Which branch of Wells Fargo?"

Sally blinked at him. "The downtown one," she said.

He reached down, caught her hand in his and hauled her upward. "Sure, lady. But my name's James Diamond, not Sam Spade, and I don't believe a word you're saying. Now take your pretty little upscale butt—" he pushed her toward the door "—and go away before I have to get real hostile."

She held back as much as she could, but he was strong and not possessed of any gentlemanly scruples about using that strength to get rid of unwanted visitors. "But what about my sister?" she demanded.

"Go back to the Yellow Pages. Maybe you'll find a listing for Philip Marlowe." And with that, he shoved her out the front door, slamming it behind her.

She stood there for a moment, disheveled, rumpled, as she listened to the sound of the door being locked. For a moment, she considered bashing her purse through the cracked smoked glass window, then thought better of it. She'd lost the first skirmish, but she had no doubt whatsoever that she'd get him to do what she wanted. People were seldom able to hold out against her once she made up her mind, and she'd made up her mind about James Diamond. She only hoped she could convince him in time.

BRIDGET O'SHAUNESSY, James thought, leaning back in his chair and lighting another cigarette. Who the hell did she think she was kidding? If there was a private investigator alive who hadn't seen *The Maltese Falcon* he'd eat his hat, if he wore one. She'd probably escaped from some lunatic asylum. Her connection with reality was extremely iffy, and he'd be surprised if she even had a sister.

Still, she did have absolutely wonderful legs. Just the kind he liked, long and shapely, the kind that could wrap around— No, he'd better not start thinking like that. His infallible instincts had taken one look at that dizzy female and decreed that she was nothing but trouble. If there was one thing he'd learned during the last tough years, it was that it was better to trust his instincts than his hormones.

She was right about one thing, though. He had a definite lack of clients, and he had an overdue rent bill, gas bill, electric bill, and the IRS was getting edgy. Maybe he shouldn't have been so quick to turn down her offer. Her clothes might have been department store, but her hair and the way she held herself projected big money. He could baby-sit her for a couple of days and have enough to at least crawl out of the hole he'd managed to dig for himself the past few months.

She was too pretty, though, with that silky black hair and porcelain skin. Her mouth looked tempting, if it stopped talking long enough, and her eyes were absolutely wonderful. It was no wonder he didn't want to get anywhere near her.

Still, it might be an interesting game to find out who she really was and where she came from. It wasn't as if he had anything else to do on this damnably hot morning but recover from his hangover. He could make a little bet with himself. If he knew who she was by five o'clock, he'd consider himself still in fighting trim. If it took longer than that, then his skills were in poor shape and he'd better give up his passing acquaintance with the whiskey bottle.

He knew that already. But maybe Miss Bridget O'Shaunessy would be able to distract him enough to forget about it. Maybe once he found out exactly who she was, he'd reconsider her offer. After all, what else did he have to do?

If only she weren't so damned pretty.

Chapter Two

James Michael Diamond was everything a private investigator should be. He'd grown up in a boisterous Irish Catholic family in Boston, had got a scholarship to Berkeley and had stayed in the area ever since. He'd taken his degree with him into the police force, hoping to do some good, but it hadn't taken long for his ideals to be knocked out of him. The police force in the 1970s didn't take kindly to Berkeley graduates, and he'd had the stuffing pounded out of him a number of times before he learned to keep his mouth shut.

Fifteen years in the department had been more than enough. Enough to make him so damned cynical he wouldn't trust the Pope himself. Enough to make James so burned out that it was only a question of when, not if, he was going to explode. After Kaz died, it was only a matter of time and choice. Whether he'd go back to law school, get his degree and try to change the world for the better and make a pack of money. Or whether he'd go into business as a private investigator, slide deeper into the human cesspool he'd been wading in and manage to scrape by each month.

It had been no contest. The world wasn't worth saving, and James didn't give a damn about the things money could buy. What he could do, and do damned well, was find the truth behind lies. Find the people who were missing, find out who was cheating whom, find the dirt, find the filth, find the lies. Why give up a God-given talent, he'd decided with his usual cynicism. It wasn't as if he had anyone to answer to. His wife had decamped seven years ago with their joint savings account, and once he'd satisfied his curiosity and discovered where she'd gone, he hadn't thought about her since. She was happily remarried with two kids, and he didn't give a damn.

Kaz was a different matter, as James's ex-wife had known. They'd been partners for years, and when Kaz died, a part of James had died, too.

It would have been better all around if someone had shot Kaz. The survivors' benefits would have been a lot better than a simple pension for Marge and the kids. And James would have had a purpose in life, a villain he could go after, hunt down and wipe out.

Instead, he could just think about something as irrationally stupid as a strep infection that moved so fast, his best friend was dead in three days from his first sniffle. And all James could do was crawl into a bottle and hide there for a while.

By the time he crawled out, James was feeling decades older than his thirty-eight years, and the sleazy environs of Hubbard Street felt like home. Besides, that was the kind of neighborhood in which most of his business originated or ended, so he might as well make himself comfortable, he thought. He'd got his drinking under control again, except for the occasional bad night, and if he smoked too much, there was no one around to complain.

Unless someone like his recent visitor made the mistake of bothering him. He didn't trust the yuppie types—they wouldn't seek out someone in his part of town if they didn't want something sneaky pulled. He'd assumed the fictitious Bridget wanted something like that done, but now he wasn't so sure. She was just flaky enough to have gone for his name in the Yellow Pages. He didn't think anyone read Dashiel Hammett or Raymond Chandler anymore, but maybe his recent visitor was offbeat enough to do so.

Maybe it was his hangover. Maybe it was just his skills getting rusty. He told himself if he didn't discover who and what the so-called Bridget O'Shaunessy was by five o'clock, he'd take the job. At quarter past seven that night, he was driving his decrepit little Volkswagen Beetle up the winding driveway of the MacArthur mansion, cursing under his breath.

WHEN SALLY CRASH-LANDED her Alfa Romeo in front of her father's imposing mansion, she was out of her car in a bound, kicking her shoes off in the marble front hall and racing toward the kitchen at her usual breakneck speed. She seldom walked when she could run, drove when she could race, was quiet when she could talk. Energy bristled out of her like a jagged aura, and the vast, echoing emptiness of her father's house was enough to drive her crazy.

Jenkins was in the kitchen, his proper butler's coat off and his sleeves rolled up as he polished the silver that no one ever used. He didn't bother to look up. He'd been with the family since before Sally was born, and he knew that any noise would have to come from his rambunctious mistress.

"Any word?" she demanded breathlessly.

"None, miss. Were you expecting any?" Jenkins was concentrating on the coffee urn, but Sally wasn't fooled. He was just as worried as she was. The two of them had watched over Lucy since their mutual mother had dropped her off in San Francisco on one of her round-the-world jaunts and then simply failed to reappear. Together, they'd brought Lucy up, covered up for her minor peccadilloes and rescued her from her major ones. This latest mess, however, seemed to be proving beyond even their abilities.

"One can always hope." Sally plopped herself down on

the stool next to Jenkins and took the heavy silver creamer and a polishing cloth. "Things didn't go too well with James Diamond."

"I can't imagine why you wanted to hire him. Wouldn't we be better off with Blackheart, Inc. or one of the bigger agencies?"

"The bigger agencies would tip Father off, and you know it. Besides, I know James Diamond is the man to help us. You wouldn't believe his office, Jenkins. It's like something out of an old 1930s movie. And he fits the part, or almost. If only he were a little bit older. And if he didn't wear sneakers," she added truthfully, staring at her reflection in the silver.

"I don't suppose that matters if he won't take the case. Who are you going to ask?"

"He's going to take the case, Jenkins. I simply haven't managed to talk him into it yet."

Jenkins looked up from the urn and his expression was severe. "We don't have much time, miss."

"I know, Jenkins, I know. I have to figure how to plan my next attack on the surly Mr. Diamond." She set the creamer down and reached for the sugar bowl. "Don't worry, you old darling, there's no reason why anyone has to find out the truth."

"If you say so," he said gloomily. "I wish I had your faith."

Sally grinned at him. "Frankly, so do I."

Jenkins turned his head at the sound of the electronic beep from the security system, and with a sigh, he went to the bank of sinks to wash his hands. "Someone just drove in."

Sally slipped off her stool, dumping the polishing cloth onto the floor. "I'll check and see who it is."

"Your father didn't spend a fortune on security systems without reason, Miss Sally. Don't be foolish enough to open the door without checking the security monitor."

She grinned. "I promise." She heard Jenkins's disapproving sniff as she headed back out into the hallway, bypassing her discarded shoes without a glance, secure in the fact that Jenkins knew well enough not to try to stop her. Besides, the entire place was absolutely riddled with security devices and cameras. He'd be watching any visitor, wanted or otherwise, in any place in the house, short of her bathroom or bedroom. And there'd be no one she'd be taking upstairs to her bedroom. Particularly not James Diamond.

She knew it was Diamond even before she opened the wide front door without even glancing at the video screen discreetly placed behind a curtain. She stood framed in the doorway, frowning slightly as his beatup VW pulled up the winding drive.

She waited as he unfolded his long body from the small car and started up the wide, marble steps. "You don't look surprised to see me," he said in that low, sexy rumble of a voice.

"You're a private detective. You wouldn't be worth hiring if you couldn't see through a simple alias and find me."

"Simple is right. You think I never saw *The Maltese Falcon?*"

She let her gaze slide down his length. He was wearing the same clothes he'd been wearing before—a dark rumpled suit, a flamboyant tie that was pulled loose and those damned sneakers. Still no fedora, but not bad. "You've seen *The Maltese Falcon,*" she acknowledged. "You couldn't be this close by accident."

"This close to what?"

"To the quintessential hard-boiled detective," she said. "I've already explained it to you—that's why I hired you. I just wish I could figure out what kind of car you should be driving. That Beetle won't do."

"You haven't hired me—I haven't said I'll take the case. And what do you mean by that crack about my car? I'll drive what I can afford, and that means a 1974 Super Beetle with the bottom rusting out.''

"Of course I've hired you," Sally said, serenely self-confident. "Why else would you have gone to the trouble of finding out who I am and coming to the house? A nice black Packard would be the perfect car if this were fifty years ago, but…''

"No, it wouldn't. The Packard was a luxury car. No self-respecting private detective would be driving one. Philip Marlowe drove a Chrysler.''

Her mouth dropped open. "Diamond, I'm in love with you," she breathed, starting toward him. "Any man who understands Philip Marlowe—''

He put up a restraining arm. "Keep your distance, Miss MacArthur. I didn't come out here to fulfill your kinky sexual fantasies.''

Those words stopped her more effectively than his outstretched arm. Lauren Bacall would have slapped Humphrey Bogart, but then, Bogie would have slapped her back. So would James Diamond. Sally settled for glaring at him. "They're not kinky, and they're not sexual. If anything, I tend to romanticize things a bit, but you're not here to fill my bed. You're here to find my sister.''

"Wrong. I'm here to tell you I'm still not taking the job.''

Her momentary anger vanished in the sheer enjoyment of the situation, the bantering. Sally leaned back against the door frame, stretching one long leg across the other. She saw his gaze drawn to that bit of byplay and watched him quickly look away, over her shoulder. So he wasn't as immune to her long legs as she'd thought. There was definitely some hope in the situation.

"Any particular reason why you came all the way out here to tell me that? You already said as much before you kicked me out of your office. Didn't you think I got the message?''

"I think nothing short of a brick wall falling on you would make you get the message."

She glanced around her. "The walls around this place are in no danger of tumbling down, more's the pity. I'm sorry I overestimated your abilities, Diamond. I should have realized this would be too difficult—"

"Don't give me that crap. I won't fall for it. I could find your sister in twenty-four hours if I had a mind to do so."

"Then why don't you? You surely aren't overloaded with work, and I can pay you extremely well. You wouldn't be breaking any laws, you'd be doing everyone a favor, and you'd end up with your rent paid up and money besides. You could even buy a better pair of shoes."

"What makes you think my rent's not paid up?"

If she told him how much she knew about it, she'd have blown her last chance. "Lucky guess," she said. "Philip Marlowe was always behind on his rent."

"I'm not Philip Marlowe," Diamond snapped.

"No, you're not. He wouldn't refuse to help a lady in distress," she shot back.

"Is that how you see yourself? Someone in need of being rescued?"

"No. I need help, plain and simple, and I'm smart enough to ask for it, and to ask for it from someone who knows what he's doing. I just can't figure out why you're not smart enough to take the job."

He hesitated and she knew she had him. Had known it, as a matter of fact, since he drove up the winding driveway to her father's house, but now all that was left was preserving his dignity. She was willing to do that, as long as he'd do what she wanted.

"You can buy me a cup of coffee," he said finally, "and explain exactly what's going on with your sister and your ex-boyfriend. And maybe I'll consider it."

"But I already told you—"

"I want details. Every last little thing you can think of.

And I'm expensive. Five hundred dollars a day plus expenses, with no satisfaction guaranteed.''

"You forget that I had you checked out before I came calling. You usually charge between two and three hundred a day,'' she said. "Think you can take a rich girl for a ride?''

"Nope. My standard fee is three hundred dollars a day. I'm adding an extra two for the irritation factor.''

"Irritation factor?''

"You annoy the hell out of me, lady,'' he said, and his eyes momentarily strayed to her long legs. "I figure that's worth a substantial bonus. Take it or leave it.''

"Can I talk you into wearing a fedora?''

"I already have a hat.''

"Would you get rid of those fancy running shoes?''

"Nope.'' He lit a cigarette, took a deep drag and blew the smoke in her direction. He used one of those old-fashioned lighters, silver, and the smell of lighter fluid, pungent in the afternoon air, mixed with the smoke of his filtered cigarette.

She sighed. "It's a deal. Come on in and meet Jenkins.''

"I'm already here, miss.'' Jenkins appeared from behind the open door. He'd put his fancy coat back on and had slicked back his thinning white hair. He looked every inch the proper English butler, and Diamond stared at him in astonishment.

"You come from Central Casting too?'' he drawled, moving past Sally's lounging figure into the huge front hallway.

"Mr. Isaiah doesn't approve of people smoking in the house, sir,'' Jenkins said with a faint cough.

"But Mr. Isaiah's not home. And if his ditzy daughter wants my help, she's going to have to put up with my cigarettes. She wanted a hard-boiled detective, and they usually come with a three-pack-a-day habit. Just be thankful I try to keep it to one and a half.''

"Yes, sir," Jenkins said dutifully.

"Would you bring us some coffee into the library, Jenksy? Lots of cream and sugar for our guest—he's a major wuss when it comes to coffee."

"You're treading on thin ice, lady," Diamond muttered.

She smiled up at him, finally secure that she'd got him hooked. "And dig out the ashtrays. We're in for a long siege."

JAMES WANTED TO PLANT the toe of the sneakers his new client disdained into her saucy little butt as Sarah MacArthur led him into a walnut-paneled library that looked like something out of a movie set. He still couldn't understand why he'd come out to her place, why he'd ever allowed himself to be drawn into a conversation with this silly female and why he was finding himself agreeing to take a job that he knew was pure poison.

He didn't like doing irrational things. He was the only thing he counted on in this life, and when even he started acting strange, that was the time to worry. Maybe he was merely enamored of Sarah MacArthur's long legs. She looked like she had a luscious body underneath that baggy dress, but he was smart enough not to get involved with someone like her. Wasn't he? Or maybe he was just so damned burned-out and bored that he didn't mind playing Philip Marlowe for a few days. Especially since he was going to be well paid for the privilege.

"They're somewhere up north," Sarah was saying, flinging herself down onto the leather sofa and ignoring the fact that her skirt had slid halfway up her thigh. Or maybe she knew exactly what she was doing and how he was reacting to it, despite his poker face.

He stared into the cup of coffee Jenkins had provided him with. Fancy, wafer-thin cups, thick cream, probably fresh-ground beans. Now if only he had a shot of Scotch to go in there....

''Up north where?'' he said, taking a drink. It wasn't coffee, it was the best thing he'd ever tasted. Even without the Scotch.

''Vinnie said his uncle used to go fishing at some lake near the Oregon border. Lake Judgment. He always promised to take me up there sometime.''

''I don't suppose you went?''

''Heavens, no. I don't like fishing, I prefer the ocean to lakes, and by that time, I didn't care much for Vinnie, either. The thought of being holed up in some rustic cabin with him was enough to make me break the engagement.''

''How many men have you been engaged to?''

''What's that got to do with my sister?'' she demanded.

''Nothing. I'm just curious.''

''Be curious about my sister. She's never been engaged before in her life. She has a more cavalier attitude about men. Love 'em and leave 'em. That's why I'm so worried about Vinnie. He's a little more old-fashioned. And she's never threatened to marry anyone before.''

''Whereas you've been engaged six times in the last five years?'' She glared at him. James liked her blue eyes, even at their frostiest.

''If you knew, why did you bother asking?''

''How do you define 'love 'em and leave 'em' as opposed to six engagements? I'm asking because of your sister,'' he added quickly, when it looked like she was going to object.

''At least I'm trying to make a commitment.''

She drained her coffee with the same respect he gave the instant slop he was used to. *So much for the difference between the classes,* he thought. ''Not doing too good a job at it, are you?'' He wanted to linger over his own coffee, but she was already pouring herself another cup and he figured he'd better move fast if he didn't want her to hog it all. ''So what makes you think that's where they'd go?

Just because he wanted to take you up there doesn't mean he'd necessarily take your sister.''

She hesitated, a bare second, long enough for James to know that she was about to lie to him. ''Instinct,'' she said with enough promptness to fool most men. ''Besides, it's a place to start. Got any better ideas?''

''Of course, I do. I'm a professional, remember? You can give me a list of Vinnie's friends and acquaintances, his full name and address, his place of business, and I can run a check in a matter of a couple of days.''

''We don't have a couple of days.''

''Why not?''

Again that infinitesimal hesitation, the shift in her wonderful blue eyes that signaled a lie. ''Because my father's due back soon, and if he finds she's gone, and taken his damned sculpture, he's going to be furious. This time, she'll have gone too far, and I want to protect her from the consequences of her behavior.''

''You can't spend your life protecting people. When they make mistakes, they need to pay for them. Otherwise, they'll never learn not to make mistakes.'' His voice was flat, matter-of-fact.

''Life isn't that simple, shamus,'' she said, looking at him over the rim of her coffee cup.

''Shamus?'' he echoed, aghast. ''Give me a break. Listen, lady, I expect you know as well as I do that I'm simply an ex-cop out to make a living the only way I know how.''

''I love it when you talk that way,'' she murmured happily.

He glared at her. ''I'm not Philip Marlowe or Sam Spade or any of your other lurid fantasies. I'm a private investigator. I investigate things that don't necessarily come under the jurisdiction of the local police, and I know how to be discreet and look the other way if need be. If the matter isn't too serious. But I'm not, repeat, *not,* something out of a 1930s novel.''

"I was thinking more of a 1930s movie," she said, totally unrepentant.

"This is the 1990s."

"I'll work on it," she said, and he didn't believe her for one minute. "In the meantime, when can you start?"

"I still haven't said I'm starting."

"Diamond, you're sitting in my father's drawing room drinking Kona coffee and lecturing me about our professional relationship. Of course, you've taken the job. When can we leave for the mountains?"

"We?"

"You'll never find it without me."

"Lady, I work alone."

"Do you always argue this much with your clients?"

"Always," he said gloomily. "That's why I'm months behind on my rent."

"Well, I'm tolerant," she said with a breezy smile. "Let's leave first thing tomorrow morning. I need to get Lucy back before my father shows up. I don't quite know what he'd do if he found she'd taken the falcon."

"The falcon?" he echoed, filled with sudden foreboding. "This sculpture is a falcon?"

"Yup. Made of jade. But don't worry, it didn't come from Malta."

"Thank heaven for small favors. Where did it come from?"

"Tenth-century Manchuria."

"God help us. We're after the Manchurian falcon," he said with a groan.

"And I know you'll do a wonderful job finding it. While I take care of my sister."

"I'm going alone, Ms. MacArthur."

"Call me Sally," she said in dulcet tones. "And we'll see about that.

"We certainly will," James said grimly. Knowing with the unerring instinct that had saved his life more than a dozen times and solved countless unsolvable riddles that Sally MacArthur was going to be breathing down his neck if and when he found her damned jade falcon. If he had any sense at all, he'd drain his second cup of magnificent coffee, get up and walk away without another word, another question, even a moment's hesitation.

He looked at her, at those magnificent blue eyes, her charming, elfin face, her eagerness, and yes, the damned lies lurking behind the charm. And cursing himself for a major sucker, he leaned back against the sofa, lit another cigarette, and said, "Okay, tell me about Vinnie the Viper."

Chapter Three

Sally wasn't sure whether she was relieved or disappointed when James Diamond left her. If she hadn't come up with her contingency plan, on the off chance that he wouldn't take the case, then she would have been perfectly happy sitting there drinking coffee and breathing in the fragrant odor of his filtered cigarettes. That was another little touch she was uncertain about. Of course, any hard-boiled detective would smoke heavily. Diamond smoked Marlboros, but they were low tar and filtered. Bogey wouldn't have been caught smoking anything as wimpy as a filtered cigarette. But then, Bogey had died of lung cancer, hadn't he?

Maybe she'd work on Diamond to forego that little aspect of his persona. He could be hard-boiled without a cigarette dangling out of his mouth, couldn't he? They'd use her car tomorrow. The VW didn't suit his image or his long legs, and she'd simply inform him she didn't allow people to smoke in her car.

She could just imagine what he'd inform her right back. Maybe she'd better concentrate on one thing at a time. He didn't even want her coming with him when he headed up to Vinnie's fishing camp. She could fight the battle of the cigarettes later.

Though there was a good chance that either they wouldn't need to go at all or that it would simply be a

quick jaunt to fetch her sister and the falcon. After all, she
wouldn't be going ahead with her plan tonight if she didn't
think it had a good chance of working. Salvatore Calderini
was a human being, just like everybody else. He must have
a decent side to which she could appeal. Sally had squirmed
her way through the violent *Godfather* movies often enough
to know that family was important to even the most hard-
bitten criminal. She intended to fling herself on Don Salvatore's mercy. And if he resisted, she'd simply try a little
bit of blackmail on her own.

If Diamond had given her half a chance, she would have
told him about her plan. Maybe included him as a little
backup protection. Except that he probably would have insisted on doing it his way, and besides, one of his many
assets was the fact that he looked exactly like what he was.
A tough, down-on-his luck ex-cop turned private detective.
Albeit a too-handsome one. Salvatore Calderini and his
army of henchmen—at least Sally assumed he had an army
of henchmen—would see through Diamond immediately.

No, tonight would, of necessity, be a solo performance.
If Don Salvatore refused to budge, then they'd do it the
hard way. Go in search of Vinnie's rustic little fishing cabin
and break up the romance of the century. Before it turned
into the crime of the century.

It would have been nice if she'd been able to be honest
with someone other than Jenkins, she thought as she
stepped into her room-sized shower and let the tiny needles
of water sluice down over her. If she felt she could trust
Diamond enough to tell him everything. But she knew how
he'd react to the unvarnished truth. He'd make her go to
the police and the FBI, and probably the CIA, and if she
refused, he'd go in her place. She didn't trust all those
alphabet-soup organizations to do the right thing in such a
tangled mess of a situation.

No, for the time being, she'd play her cards very close
to her chest, starting with bearding the old lion in his den,

she thought, pleased with her mixed metaphors. Salvatore Calderini spent his evenings at the Panama Lounge and Supper Club. She knew that from her short tenure as Vinnie's fiancée. She'd even met the old man once, at a family wedding that looked like something out of *The Godfather,* though she doubted he'd remember her.

She did know he had a soft spot for pretty young women, and she had every intention of dressing to the nines. If she couldn't appeal to his heart, maybe she could appeal to his aging vanity. Or if worse came to worst, for her sister's sake and her own culpability in the current situation, maybe she could appeal to his lust.

The turquoise-beaded dress was too tight on her, purchased after she'd just emerged from a bout with Slimfast. That nice ten pounds hadn't stayed off for long, and soon, she was back to her own pleasantly rounded form, but she kept the dress on the off chance that maybe she'd manage to flog the weight off again. She could zip it up, just barely, and it made her breasts plump out over the low neckline. The dress clung so tightly, it made her figure look far more hourglass than it was, and the hem crept up higher than it was supposed to go, exposing another two inches of her long legs. With any luck, Don Salvatore would be drooling.

Of course, there was always the possibility that he'd be as immune to her as James Diamond. No, scratch that. Diamond wasn't immune to her. She'd seen the flicker in his dark blue eyes, the slight twisting of his mobile mouth. He'd noticed her legs, he'd noticed whatever admirable attributes she had. He'd just been tough enough to discard whatever wayward attraction had crept in.

Just as well. She wasn't Lauren Bacall, even though she wore her hair in a page boy and had a husky voice. She was a little too rounded, and much too energetic. Still, it was fun to fantasize. Maybe once they got the mess with Lucy settled, she could talk Diamond into a Fedora and wing tips. She could wear great-aunt Betty's suit, and they could go dancing.

Hell would freeze over first, Sally thought, grabbing her beaded purse and heading out the front door. James Diamond was determined to resist her, and it would be a waste of time trying to break down that resistance. Besides, why should she want to? Apart from the fact that he was sinfully handsome and seemed to fulfill all her deepest fantasies.

She shook her head, pausing beneath the light on the front steps. Tonight wasn't a night to think about fantasies. Tonight was a night to make one last-ditch effort to rescue Lucy from the consequences of her folly. Not to mention the consequences of Sally's folly. She could fantasize when she got safely back in bed.

She ran down the steps, jumped into her Alfa and started the engine. It made its usual brave roar, then settled down into a sensual purr. Maybe she could talk Diamond into using her car, after all. What man in his right mind could resist an Alfa Romeo?

JAMES SANK DOWN LOWER in the sagging front seat of his VW and stubbed out his cigarette as Sally sped past him. That was one hell of a car, he thought with a trace of envy. He hadn't thought much about cars since he was seventeen years old, but a hunter-green, late-model Alfa Romeo was enough to engender most adolescent fantasies.

So, for that matter, was the woman driving it. He'd had a good look at her as she paused beneath the light over the front steps of her father's mansion. That dress would have been banned in Boston. He hadn't realized she was so voluptuous. She'd made certain he'd noticed her legs, but the rest of her had been shrouded in loose-fitting clothes. It was just as well. He'd already had a hard enough time ignoring those legs. If he'd been as aware of the rest of her, there would have been no chance of him seeing through the web of lies she'd spun him.

He wasn't sure if he could tell where the truth ended and the lies started. He expected they were all twisted together, and unraveling them would be one hell of a chore. He already knew her well enough to guess she had something planned for tonight, and he'd simply decided to sit and watch for her.

It had taken her maybe an hour and a quarter to go from upscale debutante to the hot little number who'd just squealed out of the curving driveway. He was going to be disappointed as hell if he found she was simply going out on a date, maybe on the prowl for fiancé number seven.

But he didn't think so. He counted on his instincts—they'd saved his butt more times than he cared to remember, and he trusted them implicitly. Lying Miss Sally was up to no good. Something rash and dangerous, and if he didn't look out for her, she was going to end up in deep trouble. Worse than she already was.

He shook his head in disgust as he sped after her, his VW making its usual chirping noise. If he still had any doubts as to the level of his involvement, he might as well accept the fact that he'd jumped in, hook, line and sinker. She'd asked him to help her find her sister and the jade falcon and bring them both back. She hadn't asked him to play nursemaid and/or bodyguard.

Within a couple of blocks of her destination, he knew where she was going and he cursed, pounding on the steering wheel in impotent fury. It couldn't be coincidence that the Panama Lounge and Supper Club was nearby. The moment she'd mentioned Vinnie the Viper's full name, Vincenzo Calderini, James had been filled with misgivings. Salvatore Calderini was becoming a name to reckon with, an éminence grise of the San Francisco underworld. Word on the street had it that he was involved with the Chinese in a new gambling operation. Not the San Francisco Chinese, but the real thing, a branch of mainland criminals who were eager to rake in some profits from the New World.

Salvatore was doing his best to make that happen, and the San Francisco police were doing their best to stop it. So far, Salvatore had the winning hand.

There was no way James was going to get into the Panama looking like he did. And there was no way he was going to simply go home and ignore the fact that idiotic Miss MacArthur had just walked into a mess of trouble. He was going to have to do something about it, and fast. Before things moved to a point at which even he couldn't fix it.

No one knew San Francisco better than James Diamond. He knew where he could get a dark tie and a pair of size-ten, narrow-width shoes within a few minutes, not to mention an electric razor to shave the stubble he'd been ignoring for several days. Within half an hour of the moment Sally MacArthur had sashayed her beaded hips through the front doors of the Panama Lounge, he was after her, hoping no one would have the misfortune of remembering where and when they might have seen his face before.

He knew half the people working there. It was a busy night and the place was crowded, a faceless blur of high rollers and big spenders mixed in with insensate tourists and a few slumming yuppies. The security people, the bartenders and most of the waiters had police records he could practically recite from memory. At the moment, they were all too busy to notice him. Even if they did, each and every one of them had been arrested often enough that they wouldn't necessarily remember that at least once, they'd been arrested by James Diamond.

He'd been in the Panama before, on a vice bust. They'd cleaned it up a bit, and most people wouldn't know that there was high-stakes gambling going on one floor above the big dining room. But then, he wasn't most people. They'd added a band and a dance floor, probably hoping to drown out the occasional shouts of triumph that sometimes filtered down from a craps game, or the thud of a body hitting the carpeting. He squinted through the smoke, trying to avoid the maître d' bearing down on him. He'd never arrested Tony the Cannon Delmaggio, but that didn't mean James didn't recognize him and know his rap sheet better than he knew his mother's birthday. And there was a damned good chance Tony would know James.

His eyes caught the glitter of blue beading and he focused, suddenly intent. She was at a table in front, on the edge of the dance floor, too near the band. And she wasn't alone.

Even from a distance, James could see the carefully controlled panic in those terrific eyes of hers. He could see the rapid rise and fall of her chest as it tried to squeeze out of the too-small dress. And he wished to hell he hadn't left his gun in the glove compartment of the VW.

"As I live and breathe, if it isn't Detective Diamond," Tony the Cannon said in his ear, an unpleasant smile wreathing his unpleasant face. "To what do we owe the pleasure of your company tonight? And all dressed up? Surely this isn't a social call?"

James turned slowly, giving Tony an icy glare that had quelled many lesser souls. "You're not as up on things as you ought to be, Tony," he said mildly. "You should know I quit the force more than a year and a half ago."

"So I heard. I just don't believe everything everyone tells me."

"Smart man. This time it's the truth. I work on my own."

"Doing what?"

"This and that. Do I have to pass a test to get a table, Tony?"

"I don't know that you're welcome around here." Tony's tuxedo was tailor-made. For some reason, it didn't seem to fit as well as it had a few moments ago. James noticed the perfect manicure on Tony's hands as he tugged at his collar. He didn't trust a man with a manicure. But then, there'd never been any question that he'd trust a jumped up hoodlum like Tony.

"Discrimination, Tony? On what grounds?"

Tony's instant smile exposed two rows of badly discolored teeth. "Don't get me wrong, copper. Of course, we're happy to have you here. We just wondered why you decided to grace us with your presence tonight. And where's your date?"

"Who's 'we,' Tony?"

"The boss. And me."

James nodded. "That's what I thought. As a matter of fact, I'm meeting my date here. I believe she already arrived. Don't do it." His hand shot out, grabbing Tony in a vise-like grip before the man could make a move. "You know as well as I do where she is. But I expect your boss doesn't realize she had any backup. She does, Tony. And you know I can be a mean son of a bitch if you get in my way."

It took a fair amount to scare a hardnose like Tony. James was pleased to recognize that he still had the ability to do so. Tony nodded, swallowing. "You mean the babe in the blue dress."

"I mean the babe in the blue dress," James echoed. "Am I going to have any trouble taking her out of here?"

"No, man. At least, I don't think so. I don't know what's been going on between her and the boss, but if you get her before she puts her foot in her mouth, you should be okay. I won't stop you."

"Even if Salvatore orders you to?"

Tony shrugged, an edgy look in his eyes. "Hey, man, I'm just doing my job."

"I can do my job, too," James said, very softly. "And you know it."

"I know it."

James released him. "Now you be easy, Tony, and let me take care of things. Salvatore will understand that you weren't able to deck me." Tony was approximately four inches shorter than James's own six-foot-two height, and twenty pounds lighter. He was well armed, but he was also a convicted felon. There was no way he'd flash a gun around even a retired police officer unless his life depended on it. James was counting on that.

"Hey, man, I'm cool. Just take the bitch out of here."

James's eyes narrowed. "Lady, Tony. She's a lady."

"Sure, Diamond. Sure thing." He backed away, into a waiter, almost precipitating a crash.

James looked back at the table. Sally looked like a butterfly, pined there by an avid collector. He'd never seen the estimable Salvatore Calderini up close. He was about to get his chance.

THIS, SALLY THOUGHT, was definitely a dumb move. It had all made perfect sense when she'd been planning it. All she had to do was bat her eyelashes and plead prettily, and Salvatore Calderini would be moved to humanity.

A nice enough idea, but she hadn't seen the man sitting next to her up close.

She'd been expecting Marlon Brando, of course. Someone avuncular, faintly sinister but approachable. When Don Salvatore arrived at her table, she'd been momentarily relieved. And then frightened.

He was a small, spare man with thinning white hair combed over his scalp, slightly bulging eyes and a curiously childlike face. Impeccably dressed and groomed, he sat down beside her at the table and listened with utmost courtesy as she outlined her request.

Even to her own ears, it had sounded disconcertingly brash. "Let me understand this," Calderini had said in his eerily soft voice, once she'd finished. "You want me to call Vincenzo home, have him break off his relationship with your sister and relinquish all interest in the falcon. In return for this, you offer absolutely nothing. Was there anything else?''

''I didn't say I'd offer absolutely nothing. I promise I wouldn't mention this unfortunate incident to anyone. Like the police.'' The moment the words were out of her mouth, she realized she'd made a tactical error. Don Salvatore had been amused, perhaps even considering her request. Now that she'd threatened him, she'd sealed her own fate.

''You're trying to blackmail me, Miss MacArthur?'' he asked softly. ''You're a very foolish little girl to think you could do such a thing. I'm afraid I'm going to be forced to teach you a lesson.'' To her horror, he placed his hand on her knee, under the damask-covered table.

She squirmed away, but there wasn't anywhere to go on the banquette seating, and his small hand was like a taloned claw, squeezing into her flesh. ''Such a pretty little thing you are,'' he murmured, ignoring the fact that she was several inches taller and a few ripe pounds heavier than he was. ''I never realized what a looker you are. I don't know why Vinnie prefers your little sister when he could have had an armful like you.''

''I dumped Vinnie.''

Salvatore frowned. ''No one dumps Vinnie. Not unless he wants to be dumped. You're smarter than your sister, that's the problem. Though you haven't shown much sign of it in coming here tonight and threatening me. I think we'll go back to my office.''

''I'm not going anywhere.''

''Of course you are.'' His fingers were massaging her silk-covered leg, and she vainly tried to slap his hand away and pull the hem down at the same time. ''We'll have a little champagne supper and I'll teach you a thing or two about Calderini men.''

''Please...'' Sally hated that frightened little moan. She wasn't used to being frightened.

''There you are.'' If ever there was a deus ex machina,

the man who suddenly appeared at the table was it. James
Diamond wore a dark tie and dark shoes, and he'd even
managed to shave. He looked devastatingly attractive and
very dangerous. It didn't matter how attractive he was at
that moment. To Sally, even Bigfoot would have been gorgeous. "I thought you were going to wait for me."

"I... I..."

Diamond's hand was on her arm, pulling her up from
the banquette and toward him. Salvatore's hand was still
on her leg, and for a moment, Sally wondered dizzily
whether they were going to have a tug of war, yanking her
apart like a rag doll. "Let go of her, Mouse."

Salvatore's face froze into an angry glare and his fingers
still dug into Sally's knee. "Who the hell do you think you
are, coming into my place and assaulting my guests?"

"She's not your guest, she's mine," Diamond snapped.
"This is the last time I'm telling you. Let go of her."

One of the elegantly dressed waiters leaned over and
whispered something in Salvatore Calderini's ear. The old
man's face took on an even more glacial expression, but
the clawlike grip on her knee loosened and Sally scuttled
out from behind the table with indecent haste, half hauled
by Diamond's grip on her bare arm.

She was going to have an interesting set of bruises tomorrow, she thought, tugging uselessly at the bulging neckline and climbing hemline of her stupid beaded dress.

"You should have told me you had protection, little
lady," Salvatore said in a gentle voice. "I would have had
you dumped in a back alley instead of wasting my time
with you."

"I still want to make a deal...." she said breathlessly,
but Diamond was already dragging her away.

"No deal," Salvatore said flatly.

"No deal," Diamond said, just as immovable.

She had one last glance at the old man at the table as
Diamond dragged her through the maze of crowded tables.

Don Salvatore was sitting there, staring after her, a phalanx of dark-suited men behind him. Sally knew that all he had to do was snap his fingers and she and Diamond wouldn't be taking one step farther. A sudden, bone-shaking cold swept over her, and she began to shiver.

Diamond was paying no attention to her sudden reaction. He simply continued dragging her out of the place, not even bothering to look back at the very dangerous bunch of men he was leaving behind.

The night was cool, with a damp fog off the bay hanging thick in the air. She had no idea where her Alfa was, and obviously, Diamond didn't care. He was pulling her down the sidewalk in the direction of his beat-up VW when he noticed her hanging back.

He stopped, turning to stare at her with obvious impatience. "What the hell's your problem now?" he demanded. "If you're worried about your car, don't be. We have more important things to deal with."

She opened her mouth to deny it, but to her horror words refused to form themselves. "I—I—I—" she stammered. She could feel hot, wet tears begin to tumble down her face. She never cried. She certainly wasn't going to cry in front of Sam Spade.

The tears splashed down the front of her cleavage, but she was beyond trying to tug it up. She was shivering, her teeth chattering, and all she wanted to do was curl up in a little ball and howl like a baby.

Diamond took one look at her, let out a long-suffering sigh and scooped her up in his arms. The sheer romantic gallantry of such an act effectively shocked her into a momentary calm, but by the time he'd angled her into the front seat of the Beetle and started down the road, she was shaking and crying again.

The drive back to the MacArthur mansion was endless. He turned the heater on full blast, but it failed to warm her. He handed her a wad of napkins filched from a fast-food restaurant, but they couldn't stem the tears. By the time they pulled up in front of the huge house, Sally was so distraught and so disgusted with herself, she could barely move.

Once more, he scooped her up into his arms, moving up the wide front steps with seeming effortlessness. Jenkins was there, and Sally caught a brief glimpse of his worried face as Diamond sailed past him heading for the long, curving stairs.

"Where's her bedroom?" he demanded, starting up.

"Third door on the right," Jenkins replied. "Shall I bring her anything?"

"A brandy," Diamond said, panting slightly from the exertion. Sally immediately regretted the cheesecake she'd had for lunch, but the anxiety was finally beginning to vanish, and she was starting to enjoy herself tremendously.

He didn't bother to turn on her light when he kicked open the door. He headed straight to the huge, canopy bed, pausing there for a moment with her beaded body still held tight in his arms.

She looked up at him, eyes swimming with tears, her lips damp and trembling and slightly parted.

"What are you looking at me like that for?" he demanded irritably.

"I don't just like detective movies," she said. "I'm also quite partial to *Gone With the Wind*."

She couldn't believe it, the man actually smiled. It was a revelation in his darkly handsome face, and she told herself that if she was really as ditsy as people believed, she would have fallen in love with him at that moment.

"Yeah," he said, "but you're forgetting one thing. I'm Philip Marlowe, not Rhett Butler." And he dropped her onto the bed.

A moment later, he was gone. No good-night kiss, but then, Sally didn't necessarily need one. No man had ever been strong enough or forceful enough to carry her up to bed. It was more than promising. It was downright hopeful. With a blissful sigh, she snuggled down into the bed, wondering what Diamond would look like dressed like Rhett Butler.

Chapter Four

James passed the butler on the stairs as Jenkins headed toward Sally's room with a dark glass of brandy on a silver tray. James scooped up the crystal snifter, drained the brandy and set the glass back down with a snap. "That was for me," he said.

Jenkins's severe face showed just the glimmer of a smile. "Does Miss Sally need anything?"

"Not that I know of. It wouldn't hurt to check." He watched the butler disappear at the top of the stairs. He was in a hell of a bad mood, and he wasn't quite sure why. Part of it had to be the certain knowledge that Sally MacArthur was lying to him. Another was the fact that this simple little time waster was going to be a bit more complicated than he'd first imagined. Earning his five hundred a day wasn't going to be as easy as he'd thought. Not only did he have to deal with the dizzy female upstairs, he also had to run up against a crowd of people who had every reason to hold their own assorted grudges. The Calderini family wasn't as dangerous as some of their East Coast counterparts, but it wouldn't do to underestimate them, either.

There was one other, more basic reason for James's rotten mood, and that was the way Miss Sally MacArthur felt in his arms, the way she looked up at him when he held her over that ridiculous bed. If he'd been a different man, in different circumstances, he wouldn't have left quite so quickly. Hell, he might not have left at all.

It didn't do any good to start thinking that way. He made it a hard and fast rule never to get involved with a client, and he certainly wasn't dumb enough to get involved with someone like Sally MacArthur. Even if her legs were outrageously wonderful, her mouth delicious looking, her body...

"Hell and damnation," he muttered aloud, sprinting down the stairs two at a time in his hurry to get away from temptation. He'd just reached the bottom when the telephone rang.

He was going to ignore it, figuring Sally had to have a phone in her bedroom. If she did, it was either not working or a separate line, for the phone kept up its insistent buzz. James headed for the door, then stopped, turning back and grabbing the phone on a last-minute impulse.

"Yeah?" he barked into it, not wasting time with amenities.

"Is this the MacArthur residence?" a fairly stuffy voice demanded.

"Who wants to know?"

"Isaiah MacArthur, that's who!"

The ogre Sally wanted to protect her sister from. "You were supposed to be in the Far East," Diamond said accusingly.

"I got back early. To whom am I speaking?"

James considered it for a moment. "James Diamond. I'm a friend of your daughter's."

"Which one?"

"Which friend?"

"Which daughter?"

That didn't sound like a man who was too hard on his unwanted stepdaughter. "Sally's friend."

"Oh, God, not another fiancé," Isaiah moaned.

"We're not engaged."

"Not yet," he said in a resigned voice. "But you will be. That girl collects fiancés the way I collect jade. Could I speak to her, please?"

"She's gone to bed."

"What about Jenkins?"

"He's not around."

"Then what are you still doing there?"

"I was on my way out the door," James replied. "You want me to track Jenkins down?"

"Damn it, I need a ride home from the airport. I've got terminal jet lag, twelve pieces of luggage and the worst case of Montezuma's revenge this side of Acapulco."

"No problem. I'll be there in twenty minutes." The decision was automatic. If Sally was going to lie to him, maybe he could ferret out some of the truth from her monster of a father, a man who sounded far more reasonable than she'd suggested.

The other man hesitated. "Are you sure it wouldn't be too much trouble?"

"If you think I'm going to end up being engaged to Sally, I might as well meet my future father-in-law."

"Oh, she never marries 'em. As a matter of fact, I think she gets engaged as a way of ending her relationships. I'll be at Gate 53 in the Pan Am terminal. The sooner you get here, the happier I'll be."

"I'm on my way."

San Francisco airport was relatively empty at a little past midnight. James walked past the sourdough racks and bookstores without even glancing at them, intent on finding Isaiah MacArthur and discovering exactly what Sally was covering up. The old man had sounded bad tempered and fretful, but not the oppressive ogre Sally had described. James had every intention of scoping him out, and if necessary, explaining to him exactly what was happening with his wayward family.

There was only one man waiting at the Pan Am counter,

and James had a moment to survey him and quickly discard any notion of telling him what Sally was up to before he crossed the industrial carpeting.

He was quite old and frail looking. Of course, the digestive problems he'd picked up while traveling would be bound to take their toll, but James realized the man was easily seventy years old and not in the best of health. He glanced up at James as he approached, then looked away, dismissing him.

"Mr. MacArthur?" James said with more courtesy than he usually bothered to exhibit.

The old man looked up again, his faded blue eyes narrowing in disbelief. "You couldn't be my daughter's latest fiancé!"

"I told you, we aren't engaged."

MacArthur's perusal was leisurely. "You're certainly a far cry from the type she usually attracts. She tends to like 'em a bit on the pansy side as far as I'm concerned. How did you two meet?"

James blinked. "At a party." The lie was automatic, instinctive.

"Whose party?"

"Want to wait till we get to the car before you give me the third degree?" James drawled. "Or do I need to past muster before you do me the great honor of allowing me to drive you home at 1:23 in the morning?"

MacArthur cackled. "Yup, you're a far cry from Sally's usual wimps. You might just be the making of her."

"I have no intention of making her."

"Oh, really?" The old man managed to look both exhausted and arch at the same time. "Maybe you're a pansy after all."

James wasn't in the best of moods. For one thing, he needed a drink. For another, he needed a cigarette and there was no smoking in the San Francisco airport. For another, he was feeling tired, restless and edgy. And he couldn't get this old man's feckless daughter out of his mind.

"Old man," he said with specious patience, "I'm going to give you to the count of ten to start out toward the car with me...." His voice trailed off as an airport cart zoomed in their direction, beeping needlessly in the deserted terminal. MacArthur struggled to his feet, swaying slightly, and James told himself he didn't feel the slightest bit guilty as he quickly put a supporting hand beneath his frail arm.

"Want a ride, hotshot?" MacArthur demanded as he settled onto the seat of the cart. "Or are you going to jog along side to show me how macho you are?"

"You're going to give me your claim checks, I'm going to pick up your baggage and meet you at the south entrance," James said in a deceptively calm voice. He glanced at the driver. "That okay with you?"

The driver shrugged, clearly bored. "What else have I got to do?"

James cursed all the way to the baggage claim. MacArthur wasn't kidding; he had twelve pieces of luggage. Four of them were matched leather suitcases. The rest were boxes and bundles wrapped with the excessive string that seemed to characterize the packages of all old men James knew, whether they were multimillionaires like MacArthur or retired cops in Oakland. He loaded everything on a cart, wheeled it out to the VW and used every bit of his ingenuity to squeeze it all in. By the time he got to the south entrance of the Pan Am terminal, more than half an hour had passed and he expected MacArthur to greet him with a tirade.

Instead, MacArthur and the cart driver were smoking cigarettes on the front sidewalk, deep in conversation about the Oakland A's. "Should you be smoking those things?" Diamond demanded as he climbed out of his car.

MacArthur was eyeing the VW with deep misgivings.

"You actually expect me to ride in that thing?" he demanded. "Why didn't you bring the Bentley?"

"Because I thought you needed to see how the other half lives." James helped the old man up, filching the cigarette from him and dropping it in the road.

"Hey, that was the first cigarette I've had in days," MacArthur protested.

"And I'm sure you weren't supposed to have that." James palmed a generous tip to the operator before heading around to the driver's seat.

"Not according to my daughter," MacArthur said with a sniff. "But that's not your problem, is it? The state of my health? If anything, you should hope that I kick the bucket. Then Sally and Lucy will inherit a tidy little piece of change."

"Since Sally never marries her fiancés, I don't think that will matter," James said, heading out of the airport.

"True enough. But you're not her fiancé. I find that a very hopeful sign. Maybe she'll just skip a step and marry you without an engagement."

James shuddered. "I don't think so. What are you leaving to Lucy?"

"Fancy her, do you? Forget it. She's fallen in love with that quasigangster that Sally dropped."

James glanced at the man beside him. "How do you know that?"

"Hell, I know a lot more than my daughters give me credit for. It makes 'em happy to think they're keeping me in the dark, and I want to make them happy."

Interesting, James thought. "I thought Sally was your only child. Isn't she going to inherit the bulk of your estate?"

The old man's eyes glittered in the darkened car. "Lucy's been around so long, I tend to forget I didn't breed her. She and Sally split the pot. There's more than enough for both of them, and neither one is what I'd call a down-to-earth, practical type. They need the cushion of a little money."

This was the judgmental old devil who'd send this unwanted stepdaughter to jail, James thought, wishing Sally MacArthur were there so he could wring her neck. Of course, her neck and a great deal of her chest were exposed in that damned beaded dress, and if he put his hands on her, they probably wouldn't end up in the vicinity of her throat.

He cleared his own throat as he pulled up to the toll booth. "Fond of them, are you?"

"What father wouldn't be?" MacArthur demanded, blinking slightly as James opened the tiny glove compartment and pulled out his stash of tokens.

Too late, he remembered he'd left his gun in there. MacArthur was staring at it as though he'd found a tarantula sitting in front of him, and James shut the little door with a snap.

"I've got a license for it," he said.

"What else have you got a license for?"

"I beg your pardon?" They were heading toward the city, the VW whistling away as it picked up speed.

"I should have known Sally wouldn't have the good sense to pick a real man. You're either a weasel like Vincent, or you're on the other side of the law. Either way, I don't like it."

"I'm not police."

"No, but you were, weren't you?"

James didn't bother to deny it. "You got any reason to avoid the police?"

MacArthur cackled. "Hell, boy, I've broken my share of laws along the way. Show me a rich man who hasn't. But most of my crimes are petty ones. I can't imagine you'd be after me. So I guess it must have something to do with my daughters."

"I'm not a cop," James said again.

"Are you going to tell me who and what you are?"

For a moment, James actually considered it. Client confidentiality was a basic tenet in his business, but he was also a maverick enough to bend the rules when need be. That particular trait had been responsible both for his success in the police department and his ultimate undoing.

But nothing would be accomplished by telling Isaiah MacArthur exactly what was going on. It would make Sally so mad, she'd fire him, and there was no way she could go after her sister on her own. Her precipitate meeting with the senior Calderini that night was proof of it.

And there was no way this elderly, querulous man would be able to help her, much as he doubtless thought he could.

James couldn't toss Sally MacArthur to the wolves known as the Calderini clan. Nor could he abandon this fractious old man or even the unknown but flighty Lucy. At least, not yet.

He'd give it a few days. Five, he thought at random. Five days to track down Vinnie Calderini and his upscale fiancée. Five days to find out where Sally's lies ended and the truth began. Five days to do his best for the MacArthur clan and make enough money to keep Pacific Gas off his back.

"I told you who I am. My name's James Diamond and I'm a friend of your daughter Sally." He used the voice most effective at stopping impertinent questions.

He was dealing with a millionaire, not a two-bit street thug. "What do you do for a living?"

"This and that."

"This and that what?"

James glanced at the fuming old man. "Actually I'm a fortune hunter," he said. "I'm after your daughter for her inheritance."

MacArthur sniffed in patent disbelief. "I'll just have to ask her myself. Not that she'll tell me the truth. That girl tells more stories than Sheherezade. Don't know where she got such an imagination from. Probably her mother.''

''Speaking of which, where is her mother?''

MacArthur snorted. ''You don't need to worry about having to share my fortune. Marietta is out of the running. She's been through so many husbands since she dumped me that she probably doesn't even remember she ever married me. She's off in Europe somewhere—doesn't stay put more than a week at a time. I think the last time the girls heard from her was Christmas 1989.'' The VW pulled to a stop and the old man looked around him in surprise as he recognized his own imposing mansion. ''This little car does pretty good for something that sounds like a cricket and rides like an oversized roller skate. Come in and join me for a drink.''

James preferred to drink alone. He'd taken to sitting in the dark, at his desk, quietly making inroads on a bottle of first-class Scotch. When he had to switch to second-rate, he knew he'd be in trouble. That time was coming closer and closer.

''Not tonight,'' he said, and was surprised to find he regretted his decision. ''I'm making an early start tomorrow.''

''Where are you heading?''

''I was planning to go fishing up near the Oregon border,'' he said, glad he didn't really have to lie. He was going fishing, all right, but for Vinnie Calderini and his hostage.

''I see,'' MacArthur said. ''Sally going with you?''

''Not if I can help it.''

The old man laughed. ''How the hell are you going to find Calderini's fishing camp without her along? Besides, she's like a big, fat, juicy tick. Once she catches hold, she's not likely to let go.''

''Old man, is there anything you don't know?'' James demanded, exasperated.

"Not much." Jenkins was opening the door with solicitous care, and MacArthur gave him a playful jab in the shoulder. "The girls are in trouble, I take it."

"I couldn't say, sir," Jenkins said dolefully, helping him out of the car.

"Won't say, you mean. What do you think of Diamond here?"

Jenkins glanced at him over the rounded top of the Beetle, and James found himself suddenly curious as to the butler's opinion.

"He'll do, sir," Jenkins said briefly.

Faint praise, but MacArthur seemed satisfied. "That's what I thought, Horace. We'll get Sally settled yet."

"Wait just a damned minute..." James said, horrified.

The two elderly men were making their way slowly up the broad front steps. "Just leave the luggage on the porch, sir," Jenkins called over his shoulder, ignoring James's protest. "I'll deal with it later."

"Not all the luggage, fool!" MacArthur protested. "That small box carries the most beautiful jade peregrine I've ever seen. Not as fine a piece as my falcon, but she'll make a good companion piece."

Once more, Jenkins's eyes met James's, and a silent warning was passed. So the old man didn't know quite as much as he thought he did. "I'll leave it in the hall," James said quietly.

JAMES HEADED STRAIGHT for his office. He had more food in the tiny little refrigerator there than he had in his one-bedroom inefficiency apartment near the Embarcadero, and his bottle of Scotch was residing in the bottom drawer of his desk. Besides, he needed to make a few phone calls before he took off toward the Oregon border, and the people he intended to call were the type to work all night and sleep all day.

As far as he knew, the Calderini family didn't go in for

cold-blooded murder, probably for two reasons. Number one, it attracted too much attention. Number two, their position was secure. There were no incipient gang wars. The Calderinis knew how to keep things prosperous and well-ordered, and the various territories in the Bay Area were well-defined. They didn't encroach on the tong districts in Chinatown, and the Chinese gangs left the Calderinis strictly alone.

Which didn't explain the Calderinis' involvement with the mainland Chinese who wanted a piece of San Francisco action. Why were they dealing with the Calderinis, not the tongs? He hadn't paid much attention—it wasn't any of his business anymore, except if a case happened to overlap. Which certainly seemed to be the situation. Isaiah MacArthur collected Oriental jade, Vincent Calderini had run off with a MacArthur daughter and a piece from MacArthur's collection, and there was no reason on this earth why the Calderini family would be interested in jade. Unless they were planning on handing it over to the their new Asian confederates. James couldn't imagine why the mainland Chinese crime lords would be interested, but he'd bet his last ounce of Scotch that they were behind it.

So why wasn't Sally telling him the truth? She'd spun him a bunch of lies and half truths, and the only thing he knew for certain was that Lucy MacArthur, if that was even her last name, and the Manchurian falcon were off somewhere with Vinnie the Viper.

He could hear the distant scuffle of rats as he moved through his darkened office building, and the slightly noisier movements from the two-legged variety that roamed the halls after midnight. Frankie was probably out and about, drumming up trade. He just damned well better not be drumming it up in James's office.

The third floor was relatively quiet, and James wrinkled his nose as he let himself into his stale-smelling office. The air was filled with ancient cigarettes, and in self-defense, he lit a fresh one, inhaling with a grimace. He'd spent so much time running around after his client tonight that he hadn't smoked in hours. Even now, he could still remember the exotic fragrance that had clung to Sally's lush skin. Something rich, far from subtle and frankly erotic.

There'd been nothing erotic about the fear in her eyes when he'd first appeared at the table. Nothing erotic about her obvious panic. He owed old man Calderini something for that. Sooner or later, he'd get the chance to put the fear of God into the head of the Calderini family. He'd take a great deal of pleasure in doing just that.

In the meantime, he needed a stiff shot of whiskey and a few quiet minutes on the telephone. And then just enough sleep on his sagging old couch to make sure he'd be able to head out toward Oregon by first light. Long before Sally MacArthur crawled out of that ridiculous bed with the soft white sheets.

He groaned, picturing her all too vividly lying in those sheets. He'd told her she was trouble from the moment she walked into his office.

He was beginning to realize just how much trouble she really was. And to know that he'd be damned lucky if he got out of this with everything still in working order. Particularly his armor-plated heart.

Chapter Five

Coffee. Rich, delicious coffee wafting under his sleeping nostrils. There was nothing, absolutely nothing, that smelled better than fresh-brewed coffee. Not single-malt Scotch, not fresh-baked bread, not roast turkey on Thanksgiving. Not even that teasing, tantalizingly erotic scent that clung to Sally MacArthur's ripe skin, though that came a close second.

The coffee he was smelling through the rapidly disappearing fogs of sleep had to be the best coffee he ever smelled. Probably because it came accompanied by the tang of Sally's perfume....

His eyes shot open, immediately focusing on long, stockinged legs. She had her back to him, and she was leaning over his desk. For a moment, he allowed himself a brief, lustful appreciation of her wonderful legs and ripe curves. By the time she turned around, a mug of coffee in each hand, he had his own reaction back under control.

"What the hell are you doing here?" he grumbled, giving vent to his irritation and the headache that was plaguing him. Though this time it was more the result of too little sleep than too much Scotch. "And how the hell did you get in? I keep the doors locked. And what the hell...?"

"That's three hells," she said primly, squatting down beside him. The skirt hiked up, exposing even more of her legs, and he almost groaned. "You forgot to lock the door last night, and I'm here to bring you coffee and generally make your day start a little easier. We have a lot to do, and Lake Judgment is at least six hours' drive, most of it on twisty back roads where you can't do more than forty without risking life and limb. I could tell that you didn't have a secretary, so I thought I'd show up here with coffee and doughnuts and see if I couldn't put you in a better mood. You aren't really going to smoke that, are you?"

He'd already lit his first cigarette of the day. He glared at her. "Yeah, I'm really going to smoke that." He took the coffee from her, swallowing half of it in one gulp. It was too hot, a marvel in itself, but he didn't even flinch.

Clearly, Sally decided, now was not the time to fight the battle of the coffin nails. "I checked the weather report, and it's supposed to be rainy up north. I thought we should get an early start, so as soon as you shower and change, we can head out. I brought my car—it's newer and faster and it probably gets better gas mileage, and besides, every man I've ever known has wanted to drive my Alfa, so I decided that you might be more agreeable to having me come along if you could…"

"Shut up!" James roared suddenly, slopping some of the coffee onto his knee and burning himself.

She subsided, staring at him with those huge eyes of hers. "I suppose you're one of those people who wake up grumpy," she said in a subdued little voice.

"I am one of those people who hates being yammered at before I've had at least three cups of coffee." He drained his ceramic mug and held it out to her for more, telling himself he should be feeling guilty. It wasn't his fault that she suddenly looked like a wounded fawn.

She poured more coffee for him from something that looked more like a pitcher than a thermos, and the aroma went a little ways toward improving his mood. Except that he didn't know how he was going to get rid of her while he went in search of her sister.

She handed the mug back to him in hurt silence, but James steeled his diamond-hard heart. "You're not coming with me," he said, knowing he had to get this perfectly clear.

"You'll like the Alfa, Diamond," Sally said, sliding onto his desktop, her pert little rump displacing all his notes. "She's very fast and smooth, even on the bumpiest roads. And she has a terrific sound system—"

"Why do you call it a 'she'?"

"I feel we're soul mates," she said, picking up her own mug of coffee and taking a delicate sip.

"So you've both got great headlights," he grumbled. "I'm driving the VW, and I'm going alone."

"Have some more coffee," she said in an affable tone of voice. "I can wait."

He stubbed out his cigarette and drained the mug. "I hate to tell you this, babe, but my office doesn't come equipped with a shower. I'll have to go home, pack a few things and meet you."

"Just like that?" She took another delicate sip. "I thought I was going to have to convince you for another hour or two."

"Hell, I've been around. I know when it's a losing battle. Listen, it'll take me a couple of hours. Let's say three. I'll come by your place and pick you up."

"No! I mean, I don't think that would be a good idea. My father came home unexpectedly last night, and I don't want to have to answer any questions. Besides, I don't want you two to meet."

"Why not?" So the old man hadn't told her about his ride home from the airport, James thought. Obviously, here was a family that kept secrets.

"Because I don't think he'd like you."

James grinned. Score one for him—the old man had definitely approved. "What makes you think that?" he said. "Don't you think he'd be bowled over by my personable charm?"

Sally snorted. "You have as much charm as a rattlesnake."

"You can find yourself another private investigator."

"Not one who's so close to Philip Marlowe," she said. "Besides, I'm not too fond of charmers. Vinnie the Viper was full of charm."

"Which reminds me, what the hell did you think you were doing, going off to the Panama like that? And how did you get your car back? Last I knew, the parking valet had the keys and you were in the midst of a Victorian swoon all the way back to your father's house."

Sally sat up stiffly, affronted. "You really can be a swine," she informed him. "If you think I wasn't scared—"

"Oh, you were scared, all right. Just not scared enough. How did you get the car?"

"I got a taxi."

James said a few pungent things about the brain power of certain women as he lit another cigarette. "So you went back there alone?"

"I had another set of keys."

"You know you aren't dealing with the Rover Boys. They could have wired your car."

"You mean so they could follow me?" she asked, fascinated.

"No, lady. So they could blow you up."

For a moment, she looked faintly green, and once more, the damnable guilt cropped up in the bottom of James's gut. Maybe he shouldn't have tried to scare her, but damn it, someone had to make her see reason.

She managed to smile. "There's no reason to kill me. I don't know anything that I shouldn't, I don't have anything they want. I may be a nuisance, trying to get my sister and the sculpture back, but they don't kill people simply because they're being a nuisance.''

''You want to bet? I've seen people killed because they belched at the wrong time. You're still living in a fantasy world, kid, and you're going to be a very unhappy young lady if you don't smarten up.''

She slid off the desk, crossing over to him, and her lush hips were at eye level. Some men might find her hips a little too round. Personally, James liked a woman with curves.

''But Diamond,'' she said, squatting down in front of him and reaching out for his loosened tie. ''That's why I hired you. To protect me from the baddies of this world.''

''Then why don't you do as I tell you?'' he said, ignoring the impulse to catch her hands in his. ''Why don't you go home, stay put and let me protect you?''

She hesitated, looking up at him, her hands on his tie. Nice hands, he thought. No gunky rings or bright red polish. Long-fingered, deft-looking, capable hands. He wondered how they'd feel on his body.

''You promise you'll come get me?'' she asked in a low voice, suddenly very serious. She was giving him a chance; she was willing to trust him, just a little.

Which is more than he could say for himself. He wasn't going to trust her farther than an inch. ''I promise,'' he said, and told himself it wasn't guilt eating away at his stomach, it was his hangover.

He wasn't sure if she believed him, but she dropped his tie and rose. ''I'll be waiting for you just outside the gates,'' she said. ''Eleven o'clock?''

He wasn't going anywhere in the vicinity of the MacArthur mansion, but he had to keep up the pretense. ''I told you it would take me three hours....''

''It's quarter to eight.''

''In the morning?'' His voice rose in an indignant shriek.

"You came down here to wake me up at seven in the morning?"

"Or thereabouts. I thought it would be wiser to get my car before everyone was up and about." She smiled brightly. "Besides, you wanted to get an early start, didn't you? This is the best portion of the day."

Diamond glanced out into the smoggy, overcast morning, and something halfway between a growl and a snarl issued from his throat. "I'll meet you at eleven."

THE SLEAZY STREETS OF Diamond's neighborhood were blessedly deserted at that hour of the morning. The half hour or so Sally had spent in his office hadn't made an appreciable difference on the denizens of the area. Apparently, people didn't work nine-to-five jobs around here, which came as no surprise to her. These were night people, including James Diamond. She half expected him to throw his coffee at her when she told him what time it was.

She glanced up at the windows of his third floor office, half hoping he'd be watching her. The filthy glass was blank and empty—apparently she'd been dismissed from his mind as easily as if she were a one-night stand.

She knew perfectly well he'd dismissed her for the next few days. He wasn't going to show up at the gates of her father's house—at least, not until he had her sister and the falcon in tow. If she could count on him to do just that, she would have, she told herself. She'd sit back and twiddle her thumbs. Or she might have.

If her father hadn't come home unexpectedly, throwing all her plans into disarray. Things had been complicated enough; Isaiah's precipitate return had been the final straw. She had been counting on five more days. When Jenkins had woken her from a sound sleep that morning with the dreadful news, she knew she had no choice but to hightail it out of there as fast as she could and leave it to Jenksy to cover for her.

If only she could trust someone, anyone. The only one who knew most of the truth was Jenkins, and he'd be home, baby-sitting her father and keeping him from working himself into a fatal apoplexy. He was going to have at least a minor fit when he went into his library and found his beloved Manchurian falcon missing.

How did things get so complicated? It hadn't really been her fault. Certainly she'd been a fool to be bowled over by Vinnie Calderini's elegant looks and solicitous charm. She'd learned by now that charm was a greatly overrated commodity. It was no wonder she was finding Diamond to be a refreshing change.

But she'd already begun to be uncertain about Vinnie's masterful performance. It had been sheer luck that she'd overheard his conversation with his driver, when they'd discussed how long it was going to take them to retrieve the Manchurian falcon.

No, scratch that. She could lie to everyone else, but she couldn't lie to herself. It hadn't been luck at all. She'd seen him deep in conversation, and she'd deliberately moved closer with the express intention of eavesdropping.

She couldn't remember what she'd expected to hear. Maybe something a little shady—she was more than aware of Vinnie's family connection, and she had expected the mild thrill of hearing about some gambling operation, maybe bookies or something.

Instead, she had found out that the pride and joy of her father's collection, the Manchurian falcon, was the object of the Calderinis' current quest, and that she was simply the means to the end.

She'd listened in growing fury, hugging her arms around her body to keep from shaking apart. It wouldn't have come as such a shock, except that she'd decided she'd been too flighty. That she really ought to make an effort to marry this, the sixth of her fiancés.

Her damaged pride, which was far more battered than

her armored heart, would have been bad enough. Until the other shoe dropped and she remembered that the Manchurian falcon wasn't simply her father's finest sculpture, one treasured and hoarded and loved; it was also stolen, taken from the mainland Chinese during the debacle that engulfed China at the end of the Second World War. And no one outside the family even knew Isaiah owned it.

He kept it locked in a series of vaults, taking it out to gloat over it at odd occasions. He never said much about it, but Sally, who was possessed of an excellent brain despite her flighty tendencies, had been able to put two and two together and come up with a nefarious four.

The fact that the Calderinis knew about the falcon was bad enough. That Vinnie was willing to court her to get it instead of having someone just breaking in and stealing it made things worse. And there was no one she could go to for help. She couldn't very well call the police and tell them she thought the quasigangster she'd been fool enough to become engaged to was going to steal her father's already stolen art treasure.

So she did the only sensible thing. She ran.

She sent a vague letter breaking off her engagement before she took off for Europe. She'd had enough practice dismissing unwanted fiancés, and that part had been particularly easy. Getting her hands on the falcon before she left wasn't much harder—the MacArthurs had a tendency to underestimate each other and it was simple enough to find the various combinations to the vaults and to wheedle the others out of Jenkins.

It was getting the copy made that proved the real difficulty. Unfortunately, the Yellow Pages didn't have a listing for art forgers and the only criminal she knew was Vincent Calderini. She certainly couldn't ask him for help.

She'd finally had the inspiration to head to a local art school, hoping a struggling young student could manage to make a creditable copy. Instead, the teacher had taken the commission, providing a matching Manchurian falcon that was so like the original, it took Sally's breath away.

She'd replaced the real one with the phony, hiding the priceless original inside an empty box at the back of her cluttered closet. And then she'd taken off, content in the knowledge that even if Vinnie didn't take his dismissal well, even if he decided it was time for direct action and had someone try to steal the falcon, they'd end up with the phony one.

Unfortunately, Vinnie still had more tricks up his sleeve. Sally had been sunning herself on the Riviera, smugly content and only faintly bored, when her sister had called, breathless with excitement and not listening to a word of caution. She was getting married. Right away. To Vincent Calderini. And taking a dowry of sorts, one that Isaiah would never miss.

The phone went dead before Sally could start screaming. In the time it took for her to get back to San Francisco, jet lagged and exhausted, Vinnie and Lucy had already had a head start. It was no wonder that the phony Manchurian falcon was missing from its perch behind a series of five locked doors. The only surprise was that Lucy had figured out how to get to it.

Sally had hoped, had truly hoped, that Lucy had found the real falcon and taken that, too. But it was still safely ensconced in the welter of Sally's closet, gleaming in all its malevolent beauty. Sally set it back on its pedestal and wondered how in God's name she was going to be able to get her sister back safely.

If the Calderinis knew they'd been stiffed, Lucy's life wouldn't be worth a plug nickel. Vinnie might not actually be the killer sort—his hands were too soft and his smile was too practiced. But he had access to any number of people who'd do the dirty trick, up to and including his driver. Vinnie had taken Lucy along with the falcon, but Sally couldn't imagine why.

Once he had what he wanted, why had he bothered to take Lucy with him? Why hadn't he simply abandoned her, dumped her as her sister had dumped him? Did he have doubts about the authenticity of the falcon? Was he holding Lucy for ransom?

One thing was clear, it was up to Sally to get her feckless sister back. And there was only one obvious way to do it. She had to trade the real falcon for the phony one and her sister's life.

But she didn't know who could help her. Not the police. Not her father, who'd have a stroke if he realized he was going to lose his precious falcon. Who'd also have a stroke if he knew Lucy was in the hands of a mobster.

Sally needed an outsider to fix things, someone who could get her where she needed to go and then step back and let her negotiate. James Diamond had been that man, but he had an alarming tendency to think he could get Lucy back without Sally's help.

If she told him the whole truth, he might be in a better position to help. But he might also walk away in disgust. And besides, her simple plan of exchanging the real falcon for Lucy had run into a major snag. Someone had stolen the real one.

She'd been a fool to put it back in its original place behind the five locked doors. But she'd assumed Vinnie had gotten what he wanted and that, for now, the falcon would be safe.

It wasn't. Three mornings ago, the day she'd first found Diamond's name in the Yellow Pages, she'd gone to check the falcon and found it missing. She'd stared at the empty pedestal in horror, shrieking for Jenkins. But while his re-action had been equally aghast, there was nothing they could do. There were no clues. No sign of forced entry. Nothing else was missing. A ghost had simply waltzed through the walls of the MacArthur mansion, picked up the real Manchurian falcon and then disappeared.

For an agonizing day, she'd hoped and prayed it had been Lucy and Vinnie going after the real thing. Lucy's breathless late-night phone call had dispelled that particular hope.

She and Vinnie were at Lake Judgment on the California–Oregon border. They were breathlessly happy and hadn't left each other's side in the five days they'd been there. Lucy hoped Isaiah wouldn't mind about the falcon, but Vinnie needed it for a business deal with some Chinese importers, and surely it should have stayed in China in the first place.

Before Sally could come up with questions, objections, warnings, Lucy had rung off, and Sally had cursed her sister's brainless chatter, chatter that even outdistanced her own.

She'd had to admit defeat, then, and her need for help. If Vinnie was planning to hoard the statue just as Isaiah had, it wouldn't have been as great a problem. He might never discover it was a newly minted fake.

If he was presenting it as a goodwill gesture to some Chinese importers, who were probably Chinese gangsters, then someone was going to find out, and find out right quick, that the falcon was a fake. And then Lucy's ersatz honeymoon was going to be over.

Sally had to get to Lake Judgment and confront Vinnie. She had to get Lucy back. Originally, she'd hoped to bring back one of the falcons, it didn't matter which, and hope that Isaiah would never look too closely. That option was now closed to her.

So she had to rescue Lucy any way she could before Vinnie found out he had the phony falcon. And she was going to need James Diamond's help to do that.

Sally eyed her beloved Alfa with a trace of doubt. She'd seen enough movies to know that cars could have bombs set in them, but the Calderinis would have no reason to do that. Still, there had been no sign of Diamond while she was woolgathering on the cracked pavement outside his sleazy office. She knew she'd better get moving if she intended to follow through on her plan.

James Diamond wasn't going to come by the house at eleven o'clock and pick her up. He was going to keep as far away as possible, heading straight to Lake Judgment before she realized what was going on. Her plan was simple. Find an out-of-the-way place near his apartment, wait for him to come out and follow him up north. By the time he realized she was behind him, it would be too late for him to do anything about it.

IT TOOK JAMES less than an hour to shower, scrape a dull razor across his stubble and throw some clothes into a battered, old suitcase. Sometime between three and five in the morning, he'd gotten the information he'd needed from the people who lived by night and slept by day, and he was ready to take off after Vinnie the Viper and his hostage bride without a dark-haired distraction by his side.

He controlled his instinctive shudder as he glanced at the digital clock on his way out the door to the VW. Ninefifteen. He usually wasn't even awake at that hour, much less on the road. Clearly, Sally MacArthur was having a dangerous effect on him. He needed to find her sister and find her fast before he got further entangled with someone who was far too great a distraction.

Such a distraction that he didn't even notice the car tailing him until he reached the outskirts of the city. His instincts told him it couldn't be. He'd convinced her. He'd looked up into her vulnerable, baby blue eyes and sworn he'd come by the MacArthur house and fetch her. And she'd trusted him.

Not far enough. There were a number of hunter green late-model Alfa Romeos around San Francisco, and possibly a fair number of them were driven by young women.

But the creature in the scarf, oversized dark glasses and intense, hunched posture could only be one person.

It would be child's play to lose her now that he'd emerged from his abstraction to notice her. It was possible she could find her own way to Lake Judgment, but he was willing to bet she was the sort of woman who couldn't read a map and who always took at least five wrong turns. If he pulled a few smooth moves, he wouldn't see her till it was all over.

James pressed his foot down on the gas pedal, hard, and his trusty little VW shot forward. He made a sudden, unheralded right turn, zipping forward, but she was still doing her best to keep up with him.

She should have known she'd be no match for one of San Francisco's finest, even with her Alfa pitted against his old rust bucket. He had one last glimpse of her face, pale mouth beneath the dark glasses, before he disappeared around another corner, then another, finally losing her. And it was only then that he realized there was a faint sheen on her face, one that might have come from sweat on this cool autumn day. But more likely came from tears.

He cursed loud and long. He hit the tiny steering wheel with his large hand, called himself every kind of stupid, sentimental name. And then he pulled over to the side of the road and waited for her to catch up.

Chapter Six

The Alfa Romeo pulled up beside him. James had slouched back in the driver's seat, hands draped loosely over the steering wheel, waiting with infinite patience as Sally switched off the engine, pulled off her scarf and sunglasses and opened the door.

He was still half tempted to make a run for it. From what he'd discovered in the small hours of the morning, this little excursion wasn't going to be the piece of cake he'd first envisioned. She might sulk and rage if he left her behind, but at least she'd be safe.

And then he remembered her rash visit to Don Salvatore. And he knew, deep in his heart, that the only way she was going to have any chance of being safe was either by being under lock and key or by his side.

He should have called Jenkins and enlisted his aid. If Isaiah MacArthur hadn't returned home, James would have done just that. Despite his frailty, Jenkins looked like the sort of man who could keep his mistress safely locked up if her life depended on it.

But the arrival of the equally frail Isaiah MacArthur threw a monkey wrench into the plan. He wouldn't sit by and let his daughter be locked in her bedroom, and he didn't look as if he were strong enough to hear the truth. So James really only had one choice. If he shook the Alfa

Romeo and lost Sally somewhere along the backroads on the way to Lake Judgment, she'd probably walk directly into trouble, popping up when he could least afford it. No, she was better off where he could keep an eye on her. If worse came to worst, he'd tie her up himself.

She opened the passenger door and slid into the seat beside him. "Hi there," she said with a bright smile. He could see the shimmer of tears in her sky blue eyes, and he told himself he wasn't a heel. "You sure you want to take this car rather than mine? It's not that I'm particularly worried about the Alfa, mind you. I've locked it, and if by any chance someone steals it, it's well insured. But it certainly goes faster than this old rust bucket."

James looked at her for a moment. Reaching over, he cupped her willful chin in his hand and wiped a stray tear away with his thumb. "You are one major pain in the butt, lady," he said. "Why can't you just do as you're told and stay put?"

"It's not in my job description." She'd become very still the moment he'd touched her, and he could feel the warmth flowing between them, see the startled expression in her eyes, the wariness. He'd been a fool to touch her. A fool not to let her go immediately. A fool to let his fingers linger on the warm, firm skin beneath her chin. "Why did you lie to me?"

He did release her then, turning away. "Because I knew you wouldn't take no for an answer. This would work a lot better as a one-man operation. You may think this is a game, but people like the Calderinis don't know how to play. Everything's life or death with them."

"Don't you think I realize that? If I thought it would all blow over, I'd concoct some lie for my father until Lucy decided to reappear. But I don't think she's going to get the chance to reappear on her own, and I can't sit back and leave her in danger."

"You're good at concocting lies," James said evenly,

starting the VW and pulling onto the highway. "And we're taking this car. I can't afford to have mine stolen, even if you can."

"My lies don't seem to work too well with you."

"Don't let that get you down. I'm an old hand at seeing through lies. Most people would believe you when you told them that your father was a rigid pig who'd send your half sister to jail the moment he heard about his missing statue. Most people would believe you don't know why your sister's in trouble. I'm just not most people."

Sally was silent for a moment, digesting this. "What makes you think my father isn't a rigid pig?"

"Because I happened to pick him up at the airport last night and drive him home. We had a very illuminating time."

"You didn't tell him about Lucy?" she demanded, her panic obvious.

"I have eyes in my head, Ms. MacArthur. For all he's a tough old buzzard, he's also too old and frail to deal with the mess his children have gotten into. And Lucy's his child, or at least he certainly seems to consider her as such. He told me he's leaving her half his estate."

"Why in heaven's name were you discussing his estate?"

"He wanted to make sure I wasn't a fortune hunter."

"Didn't you tell him who you were?"

"No."

She was very wary. "Why not?"

"He was much better off thinking I was about to become fiancé number seven."

She laughed at that, a low, throaty chuckle, and James found he liked her laugh. Even if he wasn't sure he liked the cause of it. "You're a far cry from my fiancés," she said.

"That's what Isaiah told me. He suggested I skip the engagement and elope."

Her blue eyes were bright curious. "And what did you say to that?"

"I asked him if I looked like someone with a history of mental illness. He dropped the subject."

"He lied to me," Sally said, sliding down in the cramped seat and stretching her legs out in front of her. "He told me he had Jenkins drive him home."

"Lying must run in the family."

"I wouldn't call it lying. *Creativity* is a better word."

"Creativity is a crock. You're all a bunch of pathological liars and I'm a fool to become involved with you."

"Then why are you?" she asked, her voice calm and reasonable.

So reasonable that for a moment, James didn't know what to say. He had other ways of making money—he didn't need this aggravation. But he couldn't walk away from her and the convoluted mess she'd created. "Maybe because I know if you're left on your own, you might end up in the bottom of San Francisco Bay."

"The Calderinis—"

"The Calderinis don't tend to go in for cold-blooded murder. But they're in the midst of a major international expansion, and people get a little edgy in times like these."

"I don't see why. The Chinese..." Her voice trailed off uneasily.

"The Chinese?" James said in a silken tone. "What exactly do you know about the Chinese connection?"

"Is that something like the French connection?"

"Don't act innocent with me, you already know that I don't buy it. What do you know about the relationship between the Calderinis and the Chinese? And how do you know about it?"

"Vinnie said something?"

"Nope. Vinnie Calderini knows how to keep his mouth shut, and he certainly wouldn't blab anything to a space cadet like you. Why don't you tell me the truth for a change? If we're going to have any chance of getting your sister back, then you need to be straight with me.''

She didn't like the notion; he could see it. She ducked her head, staring at the hands clasped in her lap. ''I overheard him talking,'' she said in a very low voice.

''That's unlike Vinnie. He wouldn't have a conversation where he could be easily overheard.''

''It wasn't easy. I had to hide in the bushes by his Lincoln while he talked with that so-called chauffeur that takes him everywhere. It started to rain and a spider bit me, and I had to use the bathroom and the damned people wouldn't leave.'' She sounded aggrieved at the very notion.

''Yeah, well, surveillance is like that. Boring and uncomfortable. Why were you crouched in the bushes, eavesdropping?''

''I was curious.''

Diamond swore under his breath, something brief and explicit. ''Why were you curious?''

''I didn't trust Vinnie. He seemed far too interested in my father's jade collection, far too interested in staying home and...'' Her voice trailed off.

''And getting you in bed?'' James supplied, keeping his irrational annoyance down.

She glanced up at him. ''Actually, no. That was what made me suspicious. I usually have to spend the majority of the time fighting off my fiancés. With Vinnie, it was only a token effort. He didn't really want me. And while I don't have delusions that I'm the most seductive woman in the world, I still expect that if someone wants to marry me, he also wants to sleep with me. It's only reasonable.''

''Only reasonable,'' James echoed. ''So how come you don't sleep with them? Your half dozen fiancés?''

''Who says I don't?''

''You just did. You said you spend the majority of your engagements fighting off your fiancés. Why do they need to be fought off?''

"Maybe I'm a tease," she suggested, as if the notion interested her.

"Maybe."

"Or maybe I just want to make sure someone really, really loves me before I go to bed with him."

"Wouldn't they really really love you if they want to marry you?"

"I'm half heir to my father's fortune. It's quite considerable, you know, and Isaiah's not in very good shape. He's also quite old. Within ten years, I'll be a very wealthy woman, and people tend to underestimate my intelligence. A man might think he could marry me and be assured of a comfortable life for as long as he cared to hang around."

"Yeah, but he'd have to stick it out until Isaiah croaked. That would be years of wedded bliss without much remuneration."

She smiled then, a warm, self-deprecating grin that hit him hard below the belt. "I guess most of them have realized that. The prize isn't worth the game."

He glanced at her, at the sweep of midnight hair, the sky blue eyes, the soft, tempting mouth. "I wouldn't say that," he muttered beneath his breath. "So let's get back to the business at hand," he added abruptly, forestalling any reaction she might have had to that statement. "You were crouched in the bushes, listening to Vinnie talk with Alf."

"Alf? How did you know his name?"

"Alfredo Mitchell is one of Salvatore's right-hand men. He usually drives the old man around, but in the past few months, he's been low profile. He's a chauffeur, all right, but he's also an enforcer and one of the Calderinis' nastiest employees."

"I don't suppose when you say nasty that you mean he's rude?" Sally asked in a quavering voice.

"We're not talking rude, here. We're talking lethal. Did he go with Vinnie and your sister?"

"I imagine so."

"Then we're in deeper than I realized," James said. "So are you going to tell me the truth for once? Tell me what they were talking about. Or am I going to stop the car and let you hitchhike back to the Alfa?"

"You wouldn't do that."

"Try me."

She leaned back and James knew from the stubborn set of her mouth that she was going to embark on another string of lies. All of a sudden, he noticed the rearview mirror. Or to be more precise, the huge black car riding up on the almost nonexistent tail of the Beetle.

"Hell and damnation," he said, pushing down hard on the gas pedal. The VW made its usual chirping noise and jolted ahead, maybe pushing from fifty-two miles-an-hour to an even fifty-four.

Sally swiveled around in her seat. "We've got trouble?"

"We've got trouble," James affirmed. "Got your seat belt on?"

"Of course, but why...?" Her question was answered before it was formed. The big black Ford came up and gently kissed the bumper of the VW, sending it shooting forward on the rain-slick road.

"How the hell could they have made us so fast?" James demanded, more of himself than of her.

"You think that's Calderini behind us?"

"More likely a representative. Take off your seat belt."

"Are you out of your mind? Some huge tank is ramming into us, trying to kill us, and you want me to take off my seat belt? I know I'm annoying but this—"

"Take it off!" He'd unfastened his. "We're going to take a little detour, and you need to be ready to open the door, jump out and run like hell."

"Really?"

"Don't panic, just do everything I say and it'll be okay." He glanced over at her, considered putting a reassuring hand over hers, when the expression on her face stopped him.

"This is wonderful!" Sally breathed, excitement shimmering out of her.

"This isn't a game!" he snapped, reaching across for the glove compartment instead of her hand. "The people behind us are going to be shooting real bullets." He pulled out his gun and tucked it in his jacket.

"Bullets?" Sally said, undaunted. "God, Diamond, this is just great."

"When we get where we're going, I'm going to spank you," James muttered furiously, trying to coax more speed out of the poor, aging engine of his car. "Hold on tight." The black Ford hit once more, and with no more warning, James jerked the wheel to the right and the sturdy little car veered off the road and down over the bank toward a ravine at a murderous pace.

"Jump!" he shouted, opening his own door. Sally was looking utterly fearless and ridiculously happy as the car jolted down the side of the hill. "Jump, damn you." And without waiting to see whether she'd follow orders, he leaned over, opened her door and shoved her.

He was out his own door a second later, lying there in the wet grass and mud, the wind knocked out of him, as he listened for the sound of bullets, for Sally's scream of pain, for any number of sounds signaling disaster.

The only sound he heard was the crash and crunch of aging metal as his beloved car collided with several trees before taking one last, graceful dive into the ravine.

He didn't move. He couldn't. Even with his face in the mud and the gun digging into his stomach, he couldn't move, could only gasp for breath like a landed fish and hope to God Sally had survived.

In the distance, he heard the Ford roar away, and he could only hope his pursuers believed the two of them had gone over the cliff with the Beetle.

He heard the scrabble of sliding rocks, and for a moment, he wondered whether he'd made a mistake, whether someone was coming down the hill after them. And then he felt Sally's warm breath in his ear.

"Are you dead, shamus?" she asked. "Or just having a little nap?"

He lifted his head to glare at her. "Why couldn't you have broken a leg?" he demanded. "Even better, both legs? Something to keep you out of my hair for the next six weeks."

She laughed and the sound was a little shaky in the rainy afternoon. "I tried my best. I guess I'm just too flexible. How about you? Did you stab yourself with your gun?"

"They've gone, haven't they?"

"Of course, they have. Do you think I'd be fool enough to move until they left? They must think we went over the side with your poor car."

"My car!" James lifted his head in belated distress. "Is it…?"

"Gone. Looks like a recycled tin can down there on the rocks. Guess we're going to have to use the Alfa."

"Guess again. We're going to take you back to San Francisco and then I'll come out alone in a nice anonymous rental." He pulled himself into a sitting position, groaning loudly as he began to brush the twigs and dirt from his clothes.

"You guess again. I haven't gone through this just to be sent to my room like a good girl."

He turned on her, the strain of the past few minutes freeing his rage. "You're going to do exactly what I—" His words stopped abruptly. "You're hurt."

She managed an undaunted grin. "I told you I tried to break my leg for you. It's just a scrape. Take your hands off me, Diamond."

He ignored her as his fingers gently poked her bleeding

shin. "It's not a scrape, it's a gash. Stop squirming, I want to make sure nothing's broken."

"I wouldn't have been able to scramble over here if it was."

"Don't count on it. I know someone who managed to climb seventy vertical feet and then walk three miles on a leg that was broken in three places. Stress and adrenaline can make you ignore pain."

She was pale in the lightly falling rain, but her eyes were bright and sassy. "That someone was you, wasn't it, Diamond? I don't know what you're being shy about. You're allowed to be macho."

"Give me strength," he muttered under his breath. "Why couldn't you have broken your jaw?"

"And smashed my porcelain beauty?" she countered cheerfully.

He looked at her then for a long, silent moment on the rainy hillside. "No, I suppose I wouldn't want that," he said finally, surging to his feet.

She struggled up after him. "Hey, I was only kidding, Diamond. A great beauty I'm not, and we both know it. We—" She let out a little shriek as he hoisted her over his shoulder like a sack of potatoes. "What the hell do you think you're doing?" she demanded.

"Getting us up the hillside the only way I know how."

"I can walk, damn it!"

"Maybe. But I can carry you faster."

"What are we in such a hurry for? I wasn't aware that salvation lay at the top of this hill."

"The sooner we get back on the highway, the sooner we can hitch a ride back to your car. We're not going to accomplish anything if we don't get moving."

"What if the black sedan comes back?"

"Then we're in deep—"

"I get the picture," Sally said. "Your shoulder is digging into my stomach."

"Trust me, lady, I'm in more discomfort than you are," James grunted. "Just stop wiggling, and we'll both be a lot happier."

"Why will I be happier?"

"Because I won't find it necessary to smack your butt."

"That's the second time you've threatened to spank me, Diamond," she said in a dangerous voice. "That sort of sexist behavior went out centuries ago."

"Can't have it both ways, lady. Either I'm a forties shamus or I'm a New Age kind of guy."

"How about a reasonable human being?"

"You go first," he suggested affably, puffing slightly as he reached the highway. He let her down, trying to ignore the feel of her body as it slid over his. Her leg buckled beneath her and he caught her, but a moment later, she'd pushed him away and was standing shakily on her own two feet. She glared at him, but the slight wobble in her stance wiped out any lingering acrimony.

He caught her arm, ignoring her faint struggle, supporting her. "Come on, lady, just relax and be a damsel in distress. We can fight after we get warm and dry."

She must have been feeling even worse than she looked. She leaned against him, and there was a faint catch in her voice. "How do you expect to manage that?"

"Simple," he said as the sound of a vehicle preceded its arrival. "We just flag down the next car."

Half an hour later, they were thoroughly soaked, the light drizzle having turned into a pouring rain. Twenty-seven vehicles had passed them, sedans and vans and semis and pickups, before one finally stopped. They climbed into the bed of a pickup that had to have held manure or goats or possibly both, and rode the endless miles back to Sally's car in miserable silence.

"We've got a problem, Diamond," Sally said as they watched the truck disappear down the rain-swept road.

"What's that?"

"My keys are in my purse."

He just stared at her. "And your purse...?"

"Is at the bottom of the ravine twenty miles back."

"Great. I don't suppose you keep an extra?"

"In the car. And the car is locked."

"Clever. Make yourself comfortable. This is going to take me a few minutes."

"Can you break into a car?"

"I could break into Fort Knox if I had to at this point. Shut up while I concentrate." He reached into his pocket and pulled out a crumpled pack of cigarettes. He could have used a shot of whiskey to ward off the chill that had seeped into his bones, but his flask had gone over the hillside with her purse.

"Do you really need those things?" Sally asked imprudently as she sank down daintily on the side of the road.

"Yes," he said flatly, concentrating on the locked door.

It took him longer than a few minutes, but eventually, sheer willpower prevailed. If it had taken much longer, he would have ripped the door off with his bare fingers.

"I'll drive," Sally said, rising from her perch in the dirt and starting past him with a noticeable limp.

He caught her arm and deftly steered her to the passenger side. "I'll drive," he corrected, moving back to the driver's side so that he could reach in and unlock her door.

To his numb rage she simply reached out and opened it. "I never lock the passenger side," she said evenly, climbing in.

"And you didn't bother to tell me that?" His voice was very dangerous. He wouldn't get more than ten years for justifiable homicide, would he?

"I forgot."

Diamond slid in beside her and held his hand out for the key. She fished it from under the seat, dropping it into his hand. He was about to let his absolute fury blast forth when she began to shiver, a slight, convulsive movement of her wet shoulders.

He subsided, starting the car with a roar and contenting himself by muttering under his breath. He was reaching into his pocket for another cigarette when Sally's voice forestalled him.

"I'd prefer if you wouldn't smoke in my car," she said faintly.

"If I don't smoke, I'm going to strangle you," James said evenly. "Take your pick."

"I'll choke either way."

"Choose cigarettes," he suggested affably.

She glared at him as he pulled onto the highway. "You know, Diamond, this isn't as much fun as I thought it was going to be. I'm cold and wet, I smell of manure and my leg hurts like hell."

"Welcome to the real world, Sally," he muttered. "Trust me, it's only going to get worse."

"It couldn't."

"It could. The best thing you could do is go back to San Francisco and let me deal with it." He glanced over at her, looking for signs of agreement. She wasn't used to this kind of rough stuff. He knew perfectly well she was going to take her little tail straight back home to Daddy, and he should be damned glad of it.

"Diamond," she said, her voice soft and sweet.

"Yes?"

"Not on your life. You don't get rid of me that easily."

Now why didn't he feel more annoyance? "I should have known," he said with an exaggerated sigh. "You're an albatross, kid."

"And I'm here for the duration. Face it, Diamond. You've got a partner."

"God help us both," James muttered. And wondered why he felt curiously lighthearted.

Chapter Seven

This wasn't going the way she had planned, Sally thought. Forty-five minutes later, the two of them were ensconced in a seedy establishment optimistically called the Sleep-Suite Motel, a hostelry that didn't consist of suites at all, but instead boasted five run-down cabins complete with rusty water, sagging twin beds covered with ripped chenille bedspreads and a black-and-white TV that seemed to get nothing but old episodes of *The Brady Bunch*. Sally had headed straight for the shower, a tin stall that provided a steady stream of flaking paint as well as tepid brown water, but she was beyond caring. The threadbare white towels were designed for midgets, but she still felt marginally more human by the time she stepped back into the room, clean underwear and a silk bathrobe wrapped securely around her still-damp body.

She was alone. She'd left Diamond waiting there, cooling his heels, determined to stake her claim to the shower first. She should have realized he'd decamp.

"Hell and damnation," she muttered, fighting back the absurd emotional weakness that had been plaguing her for the past few days. Lauren Bacall wouldn't cry. She'd simply hitch up her skirts and take off after Bogey if he dared dump her at some flea-bitten motel.

She limped over to the window, peering out into the

pouring rain. It was already getting dark, assisted by the gloomy weather, and her gashed shin bone was throbbing. The Alfa was gone, of course, but then, she'd expected as much. She'd brought her suitcase in with her, but she had no money, credit cards or identification. So she was stuck here with a hunger the size of Pittsburgh and no way to feed it.

She sank down on one noisy-springed bed, sticking her legs out in front of her. He'd left the television on, probably to cover the sound of him absconding in her car, and the Bradys were now in the midst of a Christmas episode. Sally had always hated the Bradys, and right then, she wasn't in the mood for Christmas.

She looked around her for a telephone, coming up empty. Apparently the Sleep-Suite Motel wasn't equipped with such amenities; making a phone call to Jenksy an impossibility. It was just as well. Jenkins would be having his hands full lying to Isaiah, and Isaiah was damnably hard to lie to. Who should know that better than his own daughter, who'd spent most of her twenty-some years trying to con him?

She hadn't trusted Diamond any more than he'd trusted her, she reminded herself, sniffing loudly, so there was absolutely no reason why she should feel bereft, betrayed, shattered, despairing, miserable…

The door to the cabin opened, and James Diamond filled it, soaking wet, glowering at her. "You're going to be the death of me," he announced flatly, dumping a greasy paper bag at the foot of her bed. From that greasy paper bag emitted smells so wonderful that Sally almost did burst into tears.

"What is it?"

"Hot meatball sub with extra garlic. Take it or leave it."

"I'll take it," she said, attacking the bag with a blissful sigh. "What else did you get?"

"First-aid stuff and some clothes for me. There's a general store a few miles down the road that had what I needed.'' He dumped the other bag on the rickety table, pulling out some dark cloth. ''I assume madame has finished with the bath?''

She didn't even mind the cynicism in his voice. She swallowed a huge bite of the meatball sandwich, then glanced up at him. ''I was afraid you'd abandon me. I should have known you wouldn't.''

''You shouldn't have known any such thing. I tried like hell to ditch you. I was twenty miles past the store when my damned conscience took over and I turned back. You're an albatross, lady, and I wish to God you'd never walked into my office that day.''

She took all this with remarkable equanimity. ''Why did you come back?''

''Guilty conscience?'' he suggested.

''You don't strike me as the type to be bothered by something as mundane as a conscience,'' she pointed out, taking another big bite of the sandwich. ''I don't think you suddenly remembered who was paying your salary or succumbed to an unexpected case of lust.''

''Oh, yeah?'' he drawled, pausing by the bathroom door, his expression giving nothing away. ''Then what do you think caused me to be such a monumental sap and come back for you?''

''I think you discovered a belated sense of decency. Honor. You couldn't abandon me to the wolves, no matter how tempted you were. You couldn't just leave me here with no money or credit cards while you went off on an adventure.''

Diamond had a dumbfounded expression on his face as he sank down on the other bed amidst the shriek of rusting springs. ''Give me strength,'' he said in a voice weak enough to suggest he really needed it. ''I'm not abandoning you to the wolves. If I take you with me, I'm transporting you directly into their den. And trust me, it'll be no adventure. People shoot real bullets, and the Calderini family seem to be very edgy nowadays. If you don't believe me, look at your shin. Look at the bruises all over you...." His voice trailed off, as his gaze rested directly on the four long bruises above her knee. "That didn't come from this afternoon," he remarked in a deceptively even tone of voice.

For some reason, she didn't want to tell him. She opened her mouth to spin him a tale that would at least temporarily distract him, and then shut it again.

"You've thought better of lying," he noted. "That's an improvement." He rose from his bed, went to the other paper bag and removed some first-aid supplies. He sat beside her, the bed creaking ominously, and began unscrewing the bottle of iodine. "I assume Calderini did that to you?"

"I bruise very easily," she began, uneasy about the sudden blackness in Diamond's already dark eyes. She pushed up the bright silk sleeve to expose similar bruises on her arm. "You inflicted these."

He regarded them stonily enough, showing none of the guilt she'd hoped for but hadn't really expected. "There's a slight difference. Calderini was trying to hurt you. I was trying to rescue you from the consequences of your short-sighted stupidity."

"It wasn't stupidity, it was—yeaooow!" she shrieked, as he dabbed iodine on her leg with what she considered to be sadistic enthusiasm.

"Trust me, it was stupidity," he growled, setting the iodine down and bandaging her shin with a huge gauze patch. "Got any other wounds you want me to attend to?"

"I don't care much for your bedside manner," she said in a lofty voice.

"Tough. I'm not thrilled about you saying I've got honor and decency." He rose, heading for the bathroom. "I assume I can trust you to stay put while I take a hot shower and get out of these clothes?"

''Assume anything you want,'' she said, turning her face to the Bradys with a set expression.

She waited until she heard the sound of the shower on those tin walls. She heard the thud and bang as Diamond tried to squeeze his tall body into that narrow metal space, and then she was up, throwing her things back into her suitcase. She was getting out of here and now. She wasn't sure where she was going, she wasn't sure how she was going to rescue Lucy, all she knew was that she had to leave.

The rain was coming down in earnest as she dashed outside, dived into the front seat of the car and reached for the keys.

They weren't there.

Of course. They were probably inside, in James Diamond's pants pocket. Which meant she had two choices. She could slink back inside, get back on her creaking bed and pretend she'd never tried to make a break for it. Or she could sneak inside the bathroom with its lockless door and hope Diamond would be too occupied behind that thin, plastic shower curtain to hear her. She certainly had no desire to confront all six foot whatever of James Diamond, soaking wet, naked and furious.

She dragged her suitcase back out of the car and up the broken steps to the cabin. He opened the door for her, reaching out to take the suitcase from her limp hand, and she no longer had any choices.

He wasn't naked, but there was far too much skin showing. He was dressed in a pair of black sweat pants and nothing else, and he was dripping wet from the shower. She didn't need to look at his face to know how furious he was, so she simply pushed past him and limped back to her bed. ''You can't blame a girl for trying,'' she muttered, staring at the Brady Bunch.

He moved closer, blocking her view with his torso. It was a very impressive torso, she had to admit. Hard, well-muscled, tanned, with just enough dark hair to be enticing. She was willing to bet that Philip Marlowe hadn't looked that good without a shirt.

"Where did you think you were going?"

She forced herself to look up at him. Right now, he didn't look much like the hard-boiled detective of her dreams. He looked far too contemporary, normal and extremely male for her peace of mind. Philip Marlowe and Sam Spade were fantasies. The man standing in front of her was much too real. She could smell the faint scent of the soap the motel had grudgingly provided; the water on his warm skin.

She scooted backward on the bed, suddenly feeling very vulnerable. "I wasn't sure. It was clear to me that your heart isn't in this job, so I thought…"

He ran an exasperated hand through his thick, wet hair. "Do me a favor, Sally," he said wearily. "Don't think. I promise not to dump you, even if your life depends on it, if you promise not to take off. I'll trust you if you trust me."

"All right, Diamond. It's a deal. Though it seems to me we already agreed to this before."

"I expect we'll have to renegotiate almost every day," he said with a weary sigh, turning away and dropping onto the bed.

"I expect we will. You aren't going to smoke, are you?"

He'd already lit a cigarette. He glanced over at her, and with cool, deliberate calculation, he blew a stream of smoke directly at her. "Yup. You can sleep in the car if you don't like it."

"The car already smells like cigarettes. Do you know what you're doing to your lungs, Diamond? To the environment? To my lungs, for that matter?"

He glanced at her. Her silk bathrobe, now spotted with rainwater, was gaping open in the front, exposing far too much of her admittedly generous endowments. "Your lungs look just fine to me,'' he drawled, leaning back against the lumpy little pillow.

She ignored the comment just as she ignored her own flattered reaction to it. ''Why are we sitting here? Aren't we going on to Lake Judgment?

''We are.''

''When?''

''Tonight.'' He blew a smoke ring in her direction, damn him.

''Tonight?'' she shrieked. ''But we must be miles from there! It's dark and rainy and nasty outside and—''

''I'll be more than happy to leave you here with the Brady Bunch,'' he said in a silken voice.

Sally looked at the television screen and shuddered. ''No, thank you. If you're going, I'm going too. But...''

''We're exactly nine miles from Lake Judgment. Eleven miles from Vinnie's so-called fishing cabin. It's only a little past five right now. I figure we'll warm up, dry off and head up there in another hour, hour and a half. That meet with your approval, your high-and-mightiness?''

''It sounds as if you've already made the decision. What did you mean by his 'so-called fishing cabin'? What else would it be?''

Diamond smiled obliquely. ''You'll see.''

''Don't you think you ought to warn me?''

''Nope. The less you know, the better.''

''Diamond,'' she said, sitting up on her bed and pulling the silk kimono tightly around her, ''you are the most irritating human being in the entire world.''

He reached over and stubbed out his cigarette in the already dirty ashtray. ''No, I'm not,'' he said, still stretched out on his bed. ''You are.'' He shut his eyes, missing the full splendor of her glare.

''What do you think you're doing?'' she demanded.

''Taking a nap. We're not going anywhere for at least another hour, and I, for one, am tired. Some fool woman woke me up at eight o'clock this morning, and I've had a busy day.''

"You could at least put a shirt on."

He opened his eyes at that, a faint amusement making him suddenly very approachable. "Does all this naked flesh offend you, Miss MacArthur? Tough. My clothes are drying out in the bathroom, and even for your tender sensibilities, I won't put on a wet shirt."

"Don't be ridiculous! You could go around naked for all I care," she scoffed. "I just thought you might be cold."

"Sure you did. Look the other way if I disturb you. That's what I plan to do."

It took a moment for the import of what he was saying to sink in. "What do you mean by that?"

He moved so fast she was too befuddled to move. One moment, he was lying stretched out on his sagging bed, the next, he was sitting on hers, looming over her, too close. Much too close. "I mean, lady, that you bother me. Disturb me. Irritate me. I don't know whether I want to throttle you or make love to you, but I do know that you are driving me absolutely crazy. Why you didn't think to pack a pair of baggy sweats is beyond me, or at least a bulky old bathrobe. Instead, you prance around in that slinky thing and expect me to ignore it. Well, I'm doing my damnedest. But I'd find life a lot easier if you'd either put more clothes on or slide under the covers. Or join me on my bed."

The last suggestion hung between them in the still night air. The Bradys were still in the background, fussing about something, but neither Diamond nor Sally was paying any attention. She wet her lips nervously, wishing she could still the sudden pounding of her heart. "I don't think that would be a good idea," she said in a husky voice.

"I don't, either. As long as we both agree, we should be all right." He still didn't move. She wondered whether it would be such a terrible mistake, after all. She wondered if his mouth would taste of cigarettes. Maybe she ought to kiss him, just a little, so she could find out. "Don't look at me like that," he warned her.

She licked her lips again. "Like what?"

He moved closer, so that his mouth hovered just over hers. "Like you're asking for trouble. I've told you before, I'm not your fantasy lover. I'm not Philip Marlowe, Sam Spade, Rhett Butler or Dirty Harry. I'm a man with too much history and too many problems to mess with a woman like you, and even if you're on the verge of forgetting it, I'm not."

He was so close. "I'm not forgetting it," she whispered. "You are." And she closed her eyes, waiting for him to bridge the last tiny bit of distance and kiss her.

The scream of the protesting springs wasn't any louder than the cry of her protesting heart as he moved away, quickly, without touching her. He dropped back down on his own bed and shut his eyes. Within moments, his breathing had regulated into the deep, even sound of sleep.

She stared at him in mute frustration, then glanced at the pack of cigarettes lying on the table beside him. For a brief, mad moment she could understand the temptation of them. She could picture herself looking like Veronica Lake, puffing away on one of them as she peered up at Bogart through her curtain of hair....

Shut up, Sally, she ordered herself, sliding down on the bed. *Get your head out of the movies for just a few minutes. Long enough to go to sleep like that damned man lying next to you, lying much too close, with much too much skin showing, and try to think about stuff like income taxes and Isaiah's ill health. Or whether Vinnie's realized that the Manchurian falcon isn't the real thing at all. Or whether James Diamond is as devastating to the senses in bed as well as out of it.*

JAMES WAITED UNTIL HE WAS certain she was asleep before he allowed himself to breathe normally. Despite what he'd said to Sally, he'd never been one for catnaps. He'd only had four hours of sleep the night before, but he was used to making do on even less, a holdover from his years in the police department. Stakeouts were incredibly boring, and the night hours were the worst. You couldn't allow yourself to sleep, you couldn't allow yourself to relax your vigilance even for a moment or you, or the person you were watching, could wind up dead.

He felt unnervingly like he used to when he was on a stakeout. Edgy, nerves crawling under his skin, a burning in the pit of his stomach, an achy, restless kind of feeling in his chest. Sort of like male PMS, his partner Kaz used to describe it.

James didn't like that feeling. It had been one of the reasons he'd left the force, along with a heavy-handed push from Internal Affairs. He thought he'd gotten rid of it, but it had come back, in slightly altered form, since Sally MacArthur had sashayed into his life.

He knew what it meant—he was old enough and experienced enough to recognize the signs and listen to his instincts. It meant that there was more trouble with the simple little story than Sally was admitting. It meant the Calderinis had become a great deal more dangerous in the past couple of years, and if he didn't handle things just right, it might all end in disaster.

It also meant one more thing. That restless little edge was more familiar. It meant he couldn't keep his damned mind off Sally MacArthur and her ripe body. He was near to being obsessed with her, and the more he told himself she was a pain, the more he wanted her.

It wasn't just her body, luscious though it was. Bodies could be had, ones just as nice, with an easier personality accompanying it. He'd never had a problem looking for female companionship, and if he preferred it with the minimum of attachments, most women were willing to accept him on those terms.

But there was something about Sally that drove him nuts. Something about the way she sassed him, chased him and lied to him, and thought she could get away with it. The way she wanted to rescue her sister, protect her father, watch over Jenkins and, hell, even protect him, was both exasperating and utterly enchanting. He never thought he'd be the sort to be enchanted by a female.

He climbed out of bed, the noise of *The Brady Bunch* covering the sound of the noisy springs. He moved over to the rickety chair, lit another cigarette and stretched his legs out in front of him.

Damn, he missed his car. He and the little Beetle had been together for longer than he cared to remember, and in one brief moment, it was gone. He should be used to life being like that—he'd seen enough people go in the line of duty to know how uncertain things are. He needed something a little newer, a little bigger, something with more convenience and less personality. He and his bank account had avoided that major purchase, but now it was out of his hands. Maybe Pacific Gas would have to wait another month while he replaced his car.

One thing troubled him, though. In the car were any number of things that would be hard to replace. The license for his gun. A couple of changes of clothing that he couldn't afford to lose. Sally MacArthur's purse, which probably came equipped with a fat wad of bank notes and a raft of plastic.

But the thing that he missed most, at that moment, was the flask in the bottom of the suitcase. The one he hadn't thought he needed but always packed just in case. The one that always left his office full and came back empty.

He would have bought another bottle at the store down the road, but his cash supply was damnably short. He was running low on cigarettes, too, and if he didn't watch it, he was going to end up a damned saint. Sober, cigaretteless and celibate. What a hell of a combination.

He glanced over at Sally MacArthur lying on that concave bed, his eyes lingering on the bruise on her thigh. He was going to get Calderini for that one. He wasn't quite sure how, but that little piece of cruelty wasn't going unavenged. He wasn't going to let a sleaze like Calderini mark his woman and get away with it....

His woman? *Whoa, Diamond, cool down.* Sally MacArthur is no more your woman than Madonna is. She's hired you, you'll drag her around after you, and once you get her sister, you dump her, picking up a fat check in the bargain.

James stubbed out the cigarette, headed into the bathroom and put on his still-damp clothes, shivering slightly in the too-cool motel room. When he came back, Sally was sitting up, blinking dazedly as she struggled out of the mists of sleep. She'd look like that every time she woke up, he couldn't help thinking. What would it be like to wake up with her?

"You got any money?" he demanded abruptly, wiping that particular thought out of his mind. "Besides in your purse? We know that's out of reach."

"No. Unless you can get me to a bank."

"Not tonight. We'll have to make do on my limited funds."

"What are we going to need money for?" She yawned, pushing her silky, black hair away from her face.

"You'll see. By the way, my fees have gone up."

She looked up, startled. "You're already charging me five hundred dollars a day."

"Plus expenses. I figure the loss of my car is a legitimate expense. Those were Calderini's men who drove us off the road. I'll expect you to cover my losses."

She slid her legs over the side of the bed, the silk robe sliding up, exposing most of her gorgeous thighs. "Sure, Diamond. I think I can come up with the seventy-five dollars she was worth."

"I figure replacement value. She was a classic car."

"She was a classic piece of garbage. Don't worry, Diamond. You get my sister back safely and you can have a brand-new Ferrari."

"I'll settle for an Alfa." He lit another cigarette, lounging in the door of the bathroom. "Are you coming with me or staying behind?"

She stood up, a little wobbly, then smiled with deceptive sweetness. "I'm coming with you, Diamond. I figure you're gonna need me for backup."

He blew the smoke out his nostrils, looking like an enraged dragon. "The day I need you for backup is the day I move into a nursing home."

"Diamond," she murmured, moving past him, brushing up against him, her skin smelling like flowers, "I hope you have Medicare."

Chapter Eight

"Why are people out hunting at this hour of the night? In this weather?" Sally demanded, peering through the inky, rain-swept darkness as they drove up the winding road toward Lake Judgment. She could see the shadowy figures wandering around, in groups of two or three, nasty-looking guns over their shoulders, dressed in ill-fitting camouflage hunting gear. "I didn't realize it was hunting season."

"Around here, it's always hunting season," Diamond muttered, taking a sharp right onto a dirt road. One that had obviously seen a surprising amount of traffic, considering how far off the beaten track they were. "You need to follow my lead and keep your mouth shut. For once, just trust me." He pulled up to a dark cabin. There were even more hunters strolling around, and Sally noticed with interest that some of them were wearing sunglasses in the rainy darkness. And they all wore the same shoes. Not hunting boots or even comfortable running shoes. They all wore highly polished dress shoes.

"Those aren't hunters, are they?" she said.

"Not of animals, they aren't. They're Calderini's men."

"Then we're here. At Vinnie's fishing cabin?" She peered through the darkness. "They need all these people to guard Lucy?"

"I don't think Lucy's got anything to do with it. This place usually comes equipped with this much security."

"A fishing cabin?"

"It's not what it appears to be. Come on, princess. Do as I say and maybe we'll get lucky."

"But what is it?" Sally demanded, following him out of the car. "Listen, Diamond, I'll do a lot better if I know what I'm walking into…"

He put his hand under her elbow, his long fingers tightening slightly in warning. "You're walking into a log cabin, darling," he murmured. "Isn't it obvious?"

One of the hunters was stationed at the door, and he laughed as he overheard Diamond's words. "A surprise for the little lady?" he inquired cheerfully, opening the door for them.

"The answer to her dreams," Diamond replied, drawing a reluctant Sally into a room that looked just as it ought to, complete with rough-hewn table, a fire burning in a stone fireplace and mounted heads on the log walls.

"Where are we going?" Sally demanded again.

"Be quiet. We have to look like we know what we're doing or they're not going to let us in there."

"In where? If this is some weird sort of sex club, Diamond, I'm going to—"

"You're the one with the weird sex fantasies, not me," he growled back, halting her as the cupboard on the opposite wall began to open. Noise and heat and light spilled forth from beyond it, and it took Sally a moment to realize just what she was witnessing.

Diamond half assisted, half shoved her through the door, past the elegantly dressed couple who were just leaving, and the door closed behind them, sealing them in.

"It's a gambling casino," Sally gasped.

"Exactly. The Calderinis wouldn't waste their time with something as mundane as a fishing cabin. Word on the street has it that this place has been going strong for more than ten years.''

''If I'd known Vinnie wanted to bring me here, I wouldn't have been so skittish,'' Sally murmured, looking around her with unabashed fascination.

''You like to gamble?'' Diamond's disapproval was obvious.

''Not much. But I was afraid he had other, more personal matters on his mind, and the thought of a secluded weekend with Vinnie the Viper wasn't exactly to my taste. If I'd known it was simply a business trip...''

''An illegal business trip. This isn't Nevada, you know.''

''Why do they bother? I mean, why would someone want to go gamble illegally when Lake Tahoe isn't that far away?''

''Because the odds are better, the stakes are higher and the risk is part of the attraction. If gamblers liked to play it safe, they wouldn't be gambling in the first place.''

She glanced up at him, caught by his bitter tone of voice. ''Do you like to gamble, Diamond?''

''Too much. I drink too much, smoke too much, and I'm a hell of a lot better off if I keep away from all games of chance. Once I start I can't stop.''

''What about women?''

He stared at her, his bitterness vanishing in sudden confusion. ''What do you mean?''

''I mean, do your addictions extend to women? You've managed to leave me alone, but do you tend to...''

''Tend to what?'' He looked back over the oblivious crowd. There had to be at least two hundred people in the huge, noisy room, and the smell of smoke and whiskey and excitement was overpowering in such an enclosed space.

''Tend to sleep with any female who'll hold still long enough?'' she said in a torrent of words.

He turned back to her. ''I've been able to resist you so

far, haven't I? Trust me, lady, if I can resist you, I can resist anyone.''

He couldn't be meaning that the way it sounded, she told herself. ''But, Diamond—''

''We're in trouble,'' he said. ''Follow me.'' And without another word, he began snaking through the intent crowd of brightly dressed people, heading toward the opposite end of the room. Sally followed, resisting the impulse to look back over her shoulder to make sure no one was following them. She didn't need to check—the prickling feeling in the back of her neck told her someone was on their trail, and it wasn't a friendly sort.

Suddenly Diamond disappeared, swallowed up in the crowd. She panicked, dodging to the left, but a small, hard hand clamped down on her shoulder, and a voice breathed a garlicky threat in her ear. ''Keep on walking, Miss Mac-Arthur, and you won't be hurt. Make a fuss, and you'll be very, very sorry.''

The voice was vaguely familiar, but she couldn't quite place it, and the steely strength in that small hand didn't allow her to turn around and look. She had no choice but to nod, allowing that hand to propel her forward through the excited, oblivious crowd.

She was hoping, counting on coming face-to-face with Vinnie. Despite everything that had happened in the past few weeks, despite her miserable failure with Vinnie's formidable father, she still had no doubt that she'd be able to get Vinnie to accede to her wishes. Despite his lineage, despite his leanings toward chicanery and organized crime, he was still a basically decent Yale Law School dropout who, she suspected, had an honest fondness for her sister. If she could just get him alone...

But the room beyond the casino was empty, with nothing but a desk and two chairs. The hand on her shoulder gave her a harsh little shove, and when she turned, she almost wished she didn't recognize the man who'd brought her here.

It was a lucky thing she'd had so much practice with tall tales. She immediately plastered a bright, cheerful smile on her face, pressing a theatrical hand to her heart. "Goodness, you scared me! You're Vinnie's chauffeur, aren't you? Thank heavens! I've been trying to get in touch with him for days now. I really need to see him as soon as possible. He's here, isn't he?" She racked her brain for the man's name, but for a moment, all she could think of was Smurf. Or Garfield. Some cartoony kind of name.

The man didn't even blink. "You brought a friend along to help you find your way?"

Her smile didn't waver. "Yes, and now he's abandoned me, probably for some bimbo in a tight dress." Alf, that was his name! Like the furry alien. "Maybe you could help me find him, Alf. But first, I need to see Vinnie."

"How'd you know my name?"

Sally's smile wavered. "You're Vinnie's driver. I remember you...."

"I was using a different name then. Your buddy Diamond must have tipped you to my real name. And he's not off with a bimbo. Tony the Cannon spotted the two of you, and they're having a little argument out in the back. Him and a couple of the boys."

Sally's smile vanished completely. On the one hand, this sort of discussion was like something straight out of a Bogart movie. On the other hand, if Diamond was in trouble, being hurt, then this was getting a little too real for comfort. "I want to see him," she said, suddenly urgent.

"I thought you wanted to see Vinnie first. Actually, we both know you're looking for your sister, and she ain't here. Neither is Vinnie, for that matter. They left three days ago."

"Left for where?"

Alf shook his head. "If either Vinnie or your sister

wanted to get in touch with you, I think they'd know how to find you. You've been real lucky so far, Miss MacArthur. Luckier than your friend Diamond. The men who gave his car a nudge down the hillside tend to be a little overenthusiastic. And they're the ones who are working him over.''

''They're not going to hurt him?'' she asked in horror.

''Honey, they've already hurt him by this time. A lot. Better you should ask whether they're going to kill him. And I don't think so. At least, not this time.''

''Take me to him!'' There was no pleading. There was pure, old San Francisco patrician demand in her voice. ''Take me to him or I'll start screaming the place down.''

''This room is soundproof,'' Alf pointed out. ''But I'll take you to see him. Maybe it'll teach you a lesson as well. Don't stick your nose where it don't belong. And don't mess with the Calderinis.''

''I'd much prefer not to mess with the Calderinis at this point. I simply want my sister back.''

''She don't want to come.''

''That's for her to say.''

''No way. That's for Vinnie to say, and he says she stays. 'Smatter of fact, maybe I'd better do a little checking. If the boys get a little too rough with Diamond, we may end up with some explaining to do. And you know a little too much.''

To Sally's amazement, Alf left the room, closing the door behind him. She waited for the telltale noise of a lock, but there was nothing but the muffled noise from the casino beyond. She dived for the door, yanking on it, but it held fast. She began kicking at it, but the sound was no more than a muffled thump. Staring around her in frantic haste, she started toward the desk chair, thinking she might try crashing that against the door, when she noticed the business card on the floor.

''Desert Glory,'' it read. A spa for physical and spiritual

fitness in Glory, California. Without thinking, she shoved the card into her pocket just as the door opened again.

Alf reentered, looking a tiny bit ruffled. Someone had managed to connect with his jaw, and he was nursing his knuckles as if they'd run into something. Something like Diamond. "He's a tough son of a bitch, I'll say that for him," Alf muttered. "I'm taking you out to the car. They'll pour him into it when they're finished with him."

"They're not finished yet?" She tried to control her mounting panic.

"I told you, he's a tough guy. If he'd just learn to take a fall, he'd end up with a lot less grief. Damned fool had the nerve to take a lunge at me." He held up his abraded knuckles, staring at them disconsolately. "Come along with me—we'll go out the back. And watch yourself."

The last thing Sally considered herself to be was a physical coward. But for some reason, the notion of sharing whatever Diamond was going through was unappealing, so she shut her mouth, following Alf's short, burly form through the utility tunnels that ran behind the rambling complex.

She stared around her in fascination. "This is amazing," she said, struggling to keep up with him. "It just looks like a log cabin on the outside."

"It's supposed to," Alf said in a bored voice, not bothering to look behind him. "The Calderinis know what they're doing."

"But don't the police guess?"

Alf snorted in genuine amusement. "The police fall into two categories—those who are paid not to notice, and those who can't get enough on us to make a bust. The first group of police make sure the second group stay that way, too. It works out well, and it gives our poor, underpaid men in blue a well needed second source of income."

"This is disgusting," Sally said, her spirits rising. Maybe

not so much Philip Marlowe as Serpico, but still quite nice as fantasies go.

Someone had moved her car. The back utility lot was filled with panel trucks and anonymous-looking sedans, but even in the darkness, Sally could tell that neither Vinnie's Bentley nor his red Mercedes was anywhere in sight. She had no choice but to take Alf's word for it. He was waiting for her by the driver's side of her car, and in the distance, she could see a group of dark figures huddled around something, could hear the sound of thumps and grunts of pain.

"Is that Diamond?" she asked, starting toward the men in sudden urgency, but Alf's meaty hand clamped down once more, propelling her back against the car.

"You just stay here. Don't want to interfere while the boys are working. They know how to judge these things just right, but if you distract them, they might make a few mistakes. Just climb in the car and wait." He opened the driver's door.

"Diamond has the key," she said helplessly, sliding in.

"That's okay. He won't be in any shape to drive. You just wait. I'll see if I can't hurry them up a bit. They tend to be perfectionists, take a lot of pride in their work. But I think we'd all agree that the sooner you two get back to San Francisco, the happier everyone will be."

"Yes," she said, since that seemed to be the called for response.

"You aren't going to make the mistake of keeping on with this?" Alf demanded, suddenly suspicious.

"Of course not," she lied.

"Trust me, Diamond isn't going to be in any shape to do much more than moan for the next two weeks. You take him home and take good care of him, Miss MacArthur. And remind him he's lucky that we didn't decide to teach him an even bigger lesson."

"I'm sure he'll feel very lucky," she muttered. "But I'm taking him to a hospital first."

"I wouldn't do that if I were you. And I'm sure Diamond will tell you the same thing. Lessons like these are supposed to be private." He glanced over his shoulder to the men heading toward the Alfa. They were dragging something between them, and Sally knew with a sick feeling that it was Diamond.

They dumped him into the passenger seat, but even with the brightness of the interior light, she couldn't see how badly he was hurt. She could see the brightness of fresh blood and hear his groan of pain, and she found tears filling her eyes.

One of the men tossed the key toward her before slamming the door, plunging them into darkness. The key fell somewhere around her legs, and as she searched around for it, she heard Diamond's rough breathing change slightly.

"Get the hell out of here," he wheezed, pain making his voice breathy. "Before they change their minds."

"Thank God." She sobbed as her shaking fingers connected with the spare key. "I thought they'd killed you."

"Not a chance. Get moving!"

It took her a moment to get the key into the slot, and the car stalled when she first tried to start it. A moment later, they were off, the back of the car fishtailing as she sped out of the parking lot.

Sally glanced behind her for the telltale signs of pursuit, but the road was black behind her as she tore down the muddy dirt road, skidding slightly on the slick surface. Diamond's body thudded against the side of the car as she swerved to regain control.

His pain-wracked cursing was so poetically graphic that at least some of Sally's panic began to abate. "You can't be dying," she said, easing off the gas pedal a fraction. "You couldn't be so inventive if you were dying."

"Well, I feel like it," he gasped back. "Where are we going?"

"I'm going to find an emergency room—"

"You're going to do no such thing. Calderini's boys aren't as good as they think they are—I've gone through worse beatings than this one and been doing sit-ups the next day. We just need to find a drug store, a liquor store and a motel. Preferably as soon as possible."

"If you insist. I still think you ought to have a doctor look at you. You might have a broken rib, a concussion, a—"

"The rib's only cracked, if that, and they didn't connect with my thick skull," he wheezed. "It'll be a simple job of taping—"

"Your rib's cracked?" she screeched, swerving on the road again."

"For Pete's sake, drive in a straight line!" Diamond gasped, clutching his side as he tried to pull himself upright. "A cracked rib isn't going to kill me—I've had enough so that I know what they feel like."

"But it could poke into your lung, your heart, you could bleed to death—"

"Stop babbling. I thought we already figured out that I don't have a heart, and if it came anywhere near my lungs, it would probably figure I've done them enough damage with my smoking. Speaking of which, I don't suppose you'd light me a cigarette? I really need one." He was trying for a plaintive tone, and it came out reasonably well, given the obvious pain he was in, but Sally refused to be moved.

"A cigarette's the worst thing for you now. You're right, we need to get you taken care of, and if you refuse to see a doctor, we'll have to do it ourselves. What do you want from the drug store?"

"An elastic bandage, ibuprofen, ice pack, morphine if they have it."

"I doubt they'll hand over morphine," she said dryly.

"That's why we go to the liquor store. You get the biggest bottle of mid-priced Scotch we can afford. I need something for anesthesia.'' He glanced over at her. ''They didn't hurt you, did they?''

She wished she could see his face in the darkness. ''No. But they told me Vinnie and Lucy weren't there.''

''They weren't,'' Diamond said on a little gasp of pain. ''They left three days ago for some place in the desert.''

''Then that's simple enough. As soon as you're feeling better, we'll head for the desert.''

''Lady, 'the desert' is an awfully vague destination. We can't just drive across it and expect to find them.''

''No. But I have a clue.''

''God help me, a clue,'' he echoed in an aggrieved tone of voice. ''Now we're beginning to sound like a Charlie Chan mystery.''

''I sort of like the idea of Nancy Drew.''

''I sort of like the idea of getting someplace where I can lie down,'' he snapped. ''You can play out your fantasies while I get quietly drunk.''

Sally grew very quiet at that. She could sense from the unevenness of his breathing that he was in unbearable pain, and she wished she had the force of will to override him and take him to a hospital.

But she found she had to trust him. Trust him to know his own body and the limits he could endure. And there would be a lot of uncomfortable questions, there was no doubt about that. Doctors probably didn't have to report beatings the way they were required to report gunshot wounds, but she and Diamond wouldn't be able to leave the hospital with a few Band-Aids and a handful of pain-killers.

No, Diamond was right, they could take care of it them-selves. If, in the light of whatever motel they ended up in, he looked even worse than she suspected, she could always call an ambulance. He wasn't going to die on her. He wouldn't dare.

The muddy track turned into pavement and from pavement into highway as the rain beat down steadily on the Alfa. The interior of the car was silent, broken only by each painful rasp of James Diamond's breathing. Sally clenched the steering wheel, afraid to floor the gas pedal but just as frightened of getting lost, when the dim lights of a town speared through the darkness.

It wasn't much of a town. There was no drug store, no liquor store. Just a gas station with a mom-and-pop convenience store added on to the back. It seemed more equipped with hunting gear than the necessities of life.

Fortunately, the hunters of the area also appreciated a strong drink at the end of the day, so the liquor department was reasonably well stocked. Sally thought of Diamond, huddled down in the front of the Alfa, and bought the largest bottle of Chivas the meager contents of his wallet could afford. Which looked like something you'd get on an airplane.

By the time the toothless grandmother behind the hand-cranked cash register had totalled up her purchases, Diamond's wallet contained two parking tickets, an expired credit card, and one dollar. The paper bag contained an elastic bandage, the minibottle of Scotch, a bag of taco chips and three cans of diet Coke that cost just slightly more than the Chivas.

The Beddy-Bye Motor Hotel wasn't an improvement over the Sleep-Suite. These cabins came equipped with insect wildlife, the black-and-white television couldn't even offer forth the Bradys. The light bulbs were all twenty-five watters, and the bed was a double. A very small double. It looked even smaller with James Diamond collapsed across it.

Sally shut the door behind her, leaning against it and staring into the shadowy gloom of the motel room. It was going to be a very long night.

Chapter Nine

James had felt better in his life. As a matter of fact, despite his macho assertion, he'd seldom felt worse. His rib hurt like hell, not to mention his face, his stomach, his fists and just about every square inch of his flesh. The last thing he wanted was for Sally MacArthur to see him in this battered, weakened condition. The last thing he wanted was for her to put her hands on him. Particularly when he was in too rough shape to do anything about it.

Maybe if he didn't move he'd fall asleep. Maybe she'd let him be and when he woke up tomorrow morning, he'd be feeling normal again. Scratch that. If he didn't get his rib taped, his cuts washed and cleaned, ice on his wrist and medication in his system, he was going to be feeling even worse than he felt right now, even if that seemed an outright impossibility.

"What do you want first?" Sally asked from halfway across the room. "First aid, ibuprofen or whiskey?"

"Whiskey," he managed to say on a wheeze of pain as he struggled to sit upright. A small hand planted itself in the middle of his aching chest, pushing him back downward again.

"Don't move," Sally said, peering at him through the murky light. "You look like death warmed over. I'll get you your drink while you try to get your jacket off. I'm afraid it's in rather poor shape. Do you want ice and water?''

"I want the bottle," he growled, holding out one hand. For a moment, his mind didn't register when she placed something the size of a perfume bottle in his aching hand. "What the hell is this?"

"Your bottle of Scotch. Chivas Regal, as a matter of fact. I thought you deserved the best after what you went through.''

"I deserve a quart of this stuff. How many bottles did you buy?"

"Just this one," she said cheerfully, pulling a can of something out of the bag and opening it. "That was all we had money for.''

"I'm going to strangle you," he said, hurting too much to even struggle to his feet.

"You can't scare me, Diamond. You're in rough shape and we both know it. I figured drinking too much on top of everything else wasn't going to do you any good.''

"I figured getting drunk on top of everything else was going to do me a hell of a lot of good." He tried to break the seal on the miniature bottle, but his fingers were too numb and swollen to comply and he dropped the ridiculous thimble, listening to it roll under the bed with only faint regret.

"Let's get you cleaned up," Sally said, setting her drink down on the rickety little table. "Then you'll feel better.''

"Unlikely. I don't suppose that's beer you're drinking," he said morosely, staring at the ceiling.

"Are you always this obsessed with drinking?" She sat down on the bed, and the shift of the mattress beneath her weight made his chest scream in agony.

"Not always," he said between clenched teeth. "Listen, you can sing me temperance songs all night long if you just go out and get me a normal-sized bottle.''

"Can't do it." Her hands were fiendishly gentle as they

pushed the torn jacket from his bruised shoulders. "I spent all the money."

"All *my* money?" She'd managed to get the jacket off and dumped it on the floor. Now she was at work on the buttons of his shirt. He didn't know why she bothered—it was ripped up the back and not worth saving. But he let her work on it, for some reason enjoying her ministrations.

"Don't worry, Diamond, we'll put it down to expenses. Including your bottle of Chivas. Now stop bitching for a moment while I get this shirt off." There was a sudden, swift silence in the seedy motel room. "God, Diamond, what did they do to you?" she asked in a quiet little voice.

"You know what they did to me. They beat the hell out of me. Something about teaching me to keep my nose out of their business. It probably looks worse than it feels. Though I'm not sure if that's possible."

"James," Sally said, still in that very quiet voice.

"Yes."

"I'm afraid I'm going to faint." And without another word, she slumped backward on the bed, out cold.

With a grunt, he pulled himself from the bed, limping over to the desilvering mirror that hung at an obvious angle to the sagging double bed. No one could accuse him of being a fantasy hero at this point, that much was certain. His face was battered and bloody, with one eye almost swollen shut. The dark stain across his torso was spreading, and in a few hours, it would probably be a bright purple.

But he was right when he told Sally it looked worse than it felt. He'd been beaten up enough to know what was dangerous and what wasn't. He hurt like hell, but within a couple of days, he was barely going to notice. The cracked rib might twinge a bit, but apart from that, he was going to be more than ready to meet up with Tony the Cannon again. Not to mention the sadistic Alf. As a matter of fact, he was looking forward to it.

The slight movement on the bed signaled Sally's return to consciousness. She sat up, blinking, her face pale.

"It's lucky I didn't get shot," he said, his customary drawl sounding slightly muffled through his battered mouth. "You probably would have puked."

Her head snapped up, color brightening her pale cheeks again, her blue eyes losing their wan look. "You must think I'm a wimp."

"Hell, no. I think you're a civilian. That's why you should have stayed home, safe in that nice big house, and let me take care of things."

"Who would have driven you out of there if I hadn't been with you?" she countered with a trace of her old fire.

"Who's to say they would have recognized me if I'd had a chance to go in there alone?"

She pushed her sheaf of silky, black hair away from her face, and he noticed her hand was trembling. "We're wasting our time with what ifs. Don't you want me to tape that rib?"

"Can you do it without fainting?"

"If you can keep your mouth shut," she said sweetly. "Get on the bed."

He was about to come back with a suggestive response, and then wisely thought better of it. For one thing, she was about to tape his rib, and she'd be in the perfect position to inflict a great deal of pain if he riled her. For another, unless she was going to make do with the floor, they'd be sharing that very narrow double bed, and even in his current battered condition, he was going to have a hard time keeping his mind off her very tempting presence. The less said the better.

He shrugged out of his tattered shirt and moved gingerly to the bed, sinking down with a muffled groan of pain. "Ever taped cracked ribs before?"

"Not in this lifetime." She sat beside him with surprising delicacy as she unwrapped the elastic bandage. "Any special tricks to it?"

"Make it tight."

Her face was very close to his as she began wrapping his torso. She was concentrating, biting down on her lower lip as she wound the bandage around him, and he could smell that flowery scent that always seemed to cling to her. He wished he could lower his arms around her, pull her down onto the bed with him. But even if that wasn't a professionally disastrous idea, it was a physical impossibility. He could hear the faint catch in her breath, hear his own rattled breathing as her silky hair brushed against his stomach.

When she finally fastened the end with those tiny silver clips and pulled back, her face was even more flushed than it had been. "How does that feel?"

"Like hell," he groused.

"I can rewrap—"

"Hands off," he snapped. "You did an okay job. It's just going to hurt for a few days."

Sally nodded, accepting the thanks he hadn't really given. "Lie down and let me take care of the rest of you."

Didn't he wish? Again, he kept his mouth shut, stretching out carefully on one side of the bed.

Her hands were surprisingly gentle as she bathed the cuts on his face. At least the Beddy-Bye Motel had an ice machine, and she must have used every threadbare towel in the place, fashioning ice packs for his wrist and his jaw. She even scrambled under the bed to find the miniature bottle of Scotch, holding it out to him as a peace offering.

He was still half tempted to fling it back at her. But her words still rankled—he *was* more upset about the lack of whiskey than the state of his abused body. If the booze mattered that much, it was more than time to give it up.

"You drink it," he said. "You're probably going to have

a harder time sleeping than I am.'' He closed his eyes, trying to forget how much he wanted a drink.

"You're not going to sleep like that?'' she demanded in a scandalized voice. "With no shirt on?''

"I'd prefer to take off my pants, too, but I figured I ought to spare you such temptation. Are you coming to bed?''

"With you?''

"Honey, I don't see anyplace else to sleep around here. I wouldn't choose the floor if I were you—I saw something moving down there a little while ago.''

"I'm not going to sleep with you.''

"That's your choice. I'm certainly not in any shape to ravish you, even if I were tempted, which I'm not.'' The lie came out quite easily. He didn't expect her to believe that he wasn't tempted, but he felt he ought to at least pretend not to be. "I'm going to have a cigarette and then I'm going to sleep. Preferably through the night. And while I'd prefer to have this bed to myself, I'm enough of a gentleman to be willing to share it, even with a harridan like you.''

"Harridan? What kind of word is that for an ex-cop to use?''

"I went to Berkeley,'' he muttered drowsily, reaching on the bedside table for his cigarettes.

"I forgot.''

He opened his eyes again. "Why did you know? Was that part of your little checkup?''

"I like to know who I'm hiring.''

James's cursing was genial and obscene. "I don't suppose you know where I put my cigarettes?''

"In the car. I'll make a deal with you, Diamond. I'll share the bed with you if you don't smoke.''

He tried to sit up, but it hurt too damned much. He had to content himself with glaring at her. "Lady, I'm doing you a favor by sharing this bed. Don't push me.''

For a moment, she didn't move. A second later, he heard

the door slam and he wondered whether he'd pushed her too far. Whether she was going to abandon him in this run-down motel with nothing but a thimbleful of Scotch. *Stop thinking about the Scotch, damn it!*

A moment later, the door opened again and something landed in the center of his taped chest. Something cold and wet and hard. "Here are your damned cigarettes," she said, crossing the room and turning on the television set. Nothing came on but black-and-white fuzz.

He fumbled with the cigarettes, but his hands were too numb and stiff to manage. She must have been watching because he heard her exasperated sigh and a moment later, she'd grabbed the cigarettes out of his hands and put one in her mouth, lighting it with a certain amount of savoir faire that made her look just a bit too much like a forties movie heroine. She spoiled it with her coughing fit, but when she placed the cigarette between his lips, he could just picture Lauren Bacall and Humphrey Bogart.

He took a deep drag, trying not to cough himself. "I don't know how you can smoke those disgusting things," she remarked. "They taste like an ashtray."

"Reasonable enough." He took another deep drag, regretfully, and then handed it back to her. "That's enough. You can stub it out."

"I'll drown it in the toilet."

"Whatever makes you happy." He shut his eyes again, listening to her move around the motel room. His body ached, and the ibuprofen was burning a hole in his stomach even as it smoothed away the sharp edges of the pain. It was just as well he hadn't washed it down with his customary half a bottle of Scotch.

He didn't know when he fell into a pain-filled sleep. He didn't know what time Sally finally gave in and crawled into bed beside him. He felt the scratchy weight of the blanket draped over him, felt the warmth of a smaller body beside him. For a moment, he wondered how she managed to find that much space to put between them in such a small bed. And then he fell back to sleep again, curiously content.

It took Sally a long time to get up the nerve to get in bed with James Diamond. She felt like a fool for hesitating. As he'd put it so succinctly, he wasn't in any shape to make a pass at her, even if he was so inclined. She still wasn't quite sure whether he was so inclined or not.

On the one hand, she occasionally caught an expression in his dark blue eyes that convinced her that he wasn't the slightest bit immune to her dubious charms. On the other hand, he hadn't done a thing about it, and most of their conversations seemed to degenerate into arguments.

She wasn't about to delude herself in the matter. She knew perfectly well that she was more attracted to James Diamond than she had been to her six fiancés. Put together. She'd always managed to get involved with men who left her essentially untouched. No one threatened her sense of self, her firm belief that life was hers to make what she wanted of it.

Diamond was different. Diamond wasn't a man she could twist around her little finger and then abandon when he made too many demands. Diamond wasn't a charming companion, an easy friend, a handsome partner for silly social gatherings.

Diamond was a man. And if Diamond were to make demands of her, chances are she'd agree, and willingly. If she didn't run away.

But he hadn't made any demands. He hadn't touched her, kissed her, flirted with her, charmed her. He'd threatened her, pushed her, cursed her and possibly saved her life a number of times. If she had any sense at all, she'd realize that the man lying half-naked in the bed wasn't the kind of man she should be attracted to. He wasn't Sam Spade or Philip Marlowe. He was James Diamond, a slightly broken-down ex-cop who probably found her completely unappealing. Maybe.

The room was chilly. She left the light on in the bathroom, a little nervous of the crawly creatures Diamond had mentioned. Diamond had shifted in his sleep, taking up a good two-thirds of the bed, and he shivered slightly. She kicked off her shoes and climbed onto the bed, still dressed in her black pants and turtleneck. The pants were a bit too tight, the turtleneck shirt constricting even if it was made of silk. She knew she'd be a lot more comfortable in her bathrobe. Still, she needed as much protection from James Diamond's exposed flesh as she could muster. He might be in too much pain to experience temptation. She wasn't.

The bed had a concave dip in the middle. She perched herself on the edge, feeling her body slip toward his as if she were steel being drawn to a magnet. She clutched the edge of the bedsprings, holding herself in place, and let out a weary sigh. How a man who smoked cigarettes could smell enticing in the dark of night was a mystery to her. But he did. He was warm and male and near, and she wanted to cross that concave dip and wrap her arms and legs around him. She could just imagine his scream of pain if she did any such thing.

She pulled the blanket up around them, wishing there was more to keep them warm, more than simple body heat. He was warm beside her, an absolute furnace, and for a moment, she allowed her paranoia to run wild. His rib had punctured a lung, he was bleeding internally and infection had set in, spiking a monumental fever, and tomorrow, she'd be in bed with a corpse.

She reached out a hand to touch his forehead, one of the few parts of his face that wasn't battered and bruised. Warm, but not too warm. His cheek was cool from the ice pack, his mouth soft and—

His hand shot out and caught her wrist. "What are you doing, Sally?" His voice was low and sleep dazed.

"I wanted to see whether you had a fever. You felt warm...." She tugged at her hand, but his grip was surprisingly strong.

"I don't. I always run a few degrees warmer than other people. For crying out loud, will you just lie down and go back to sleep?"

"I will if you let me go."

He didn't seem to be aware of the fact that he was still holding on to her. "As a matter of fact, you feel cold."

"I am cold. This place only has one thin blanket, and I don't happen to come equipped with an inner furnace." She should never have admitted it. A moment later, he'd pulled her across the narrow gap that separated them, tucking her against his bandaged chest.

"Don't be ridiculous, Diamond," she muttered, struggling, both against his enveloping arms and her own baser instincts. "You've been hurt, you're in pain, you—"

"I'd be in a hell of a lot better shape if you didn't wiggle so. Stop talking and go to sleep."

His shoulder was warm. Hot, even. Well muscled and smooth, and his arms were strong. How long had it been since she'd slept in a man's arms? Had she ever?

Certainly she hadn't with her six fiancés. She hadn't slept with, made love with or had sex with any of them. She hadn't made love with very many men in this life, and the ones she'd chosen had all been ultimately bad choices. Was she making another bad choice after years of being careful?

She wasn't making love with Diamond, she reminded herself. She was simply sleeping with him. There was a great deal of difference between the two. And yet, when she thought back to the three very different men she'd been involved with before she got into the habit of getting engaged, she knew that sharing this bed with James Diamond was a very great deal more intimate than sharing her body with her overeager boyfriend when she was eighteen, or her lawyer's clerk when she was twenty-one, or Teddy Van Lessing when she was twenty-two.

She ought to run. She'd be safer on the floor with the cockroaches. Safer in the car, risking pneumonia in the cold night air, than lying in the arms of a man she could fall in love with.

She was going to run. In just a few minutes. After she got warm. After she allowed herself a taste of what it could be like. After she flirted with danger, emotional disaster, for a brief moment.

Diamond wouldn't know. He was already asleep again, his arms clasped loosely around her, his breathing steady and even. He wouldn't know the torment she was going through, the temptation and despair. He wouldn't know that she wanted to rip off the rest of the clothes and crawl right inside his skin. He wouldn't know that she wanted to find out if there was any truth to fantasies, to desires that never seemed to be fulfilled. She wanted to know if he was the one, even if she knew he couldn't be.

Just a few more minutes and she'd do what she had to do. Pull away from him, at least to her own side of the bed, or maybe out of the bed all together. Just a few more minutes.

THE LIGHT FILTERING in the uncurtained window was gray, wet and sullen. Sally's eyes fluttered open, and she lay very still, wondering how she could feel so glorious, so brightly optimistic on such a gloomy day.

And then she turned her head to look at the face on the pillow next to hers, the body entwined with hers. One of his long legs was between hers, and his hand was under her loose silk turtleneck, cupping her breast through the thin lace bra.

She went rigid with shock, but her sudden tension failed to waken Diamond. He slept on, peacefully enough, and she noticed he looked even worse in the light of day. More battered and bruised than before. And oddly, curiously dear.

She ought to pull away in outrage, slap his face and declaim "how dare you!" like a proper Victorian virgin. Except that she was neither Victorian nor a virgin, and that had never been her particular fantasy. What would Lauren Bacall do in a situation like this?

She reached out the one hand that wasn't trapped beneath their bodies and she touched his face very gently, a light benediction on his battle scars. His breathing was regular, even, the sleep of exhaustion, she thought, drawing her hand down his arm. And then she placed it over his, over the strong, long-fingered hand that cupped her breast, and she pressed just slightly.

His fingers flexed, automatically. He shifted, murmured something in sleep, and his thigh moved up to the juncture of her own thighs, pressing, arousing. Phrases like "don't wake the sleeping tiger" flitted through her mind. And then her mind went blank when he moved over her, his mouth settling on her unsuspecting one.

Chapter Ten

For a first kiss it was a revelation. A deeply disturbing one. If only she hadn't spent the night wrapped up next to him, absorbing his heat. If only she wasn't half-asleep herself, vulnerable, oddly innocent. If only she wasn't half in love with the man. Maybe three quarters of the way in love.

His mouth was warm, wet on hers, kissing her with a leisureliness that was both insulting and highly erotic. His one hand continued to knead her breast, his other reached up to cup her face, to hold her still for his long, measured assault on her defenseless mouth.

She would have been able to resist an attempt to overwhelm her. Men had tried it often enough, and she had simply shoved them away. She would have been able to resist a polite brushing of his lips against hers. That was usually all she allowed. But she couldn't resist the slow, sensuous nibbling of her lips, the way he drew her lower lip into his mouth and sucked lightly, the way his tongue moved against hers, the way his fingers stroked her breast into pebbled hardness, feeding the fire that was burning in the pit of her stomach.

She slanted her head just slightly, wanting to kiss him back, and she moved her arms around him, her hands greedy on the smooth warm skin of his back as she melted against him, increasing the pressure....

He let out a muffled shriek of pain, releasing her as if she were radioactive waste and rolling onto his back. His curses, punctuated by groans of pain, filled the dawn-lit room. Sally lay on her back, not touching him, trying to control her rapid breathing, her pounding heart, her sweating palms and the twisting ache in the pit of her stomach. She listened to him curse as she fought her own frustration and felt a certain savage satisfaction. She was hurting as much as he was, in a far different way.

She slipped out of the bed, tugging her shirt back down, shifting her clothes back around her and heading for the bathroom. Her reflection in the mirror was a total shock.

She looked wanton. Her black hair was a tousled witch's mass around her pale face. Her lips were swollen, damp. Her eyes were glazed with passion and anger. She looked like a woman interrupted in the act of making love. Which, she supposed, she was.

When she returned to the room, Diamond was sitting up in the bed, a thunderous expression on his face. At least, she assumed it was thunderous. With the bruising, it was hard to tell. He'd pulled his tattered shirt back on and was trying to button it. For a moment, she was tempted to go over and help him, and then she dismissed the notion. For one thing, he was sure to bat her hands away. For another, she didn't trust getting that close to him right now. She was still feeling edgy, unsettled, warm and uneasy. She wasn't about to define her problem, but she had enough sense to know that proximity to James Diamond made it worse.

"How are you feeling?" she asked in a brisk, bright voice, delving into the paper bag and coming up with two lukewarm cans of diet Coke and the bag of taco chips. "No, don't answer that. I'm not crazy about obscenities first thing in the morning. Obviously, you feel like three-week-old garbage. You need some breakfast." She popped open one can and held it out to him.

He glared at her, the effect increased by the truly startling black eye. "You've got to be kidding."

"It's caffeine, Diamond. Don't be picky. Maybe once we hit the road, we can afford to share a cup of coffee from McDonald's. In the meantime, you need something to help you wake up."

"Did you drink that Scotch?" he growled.

For a moment, she was shocked into silence. "You're not serious," she finally managed to say.

He stared at her for a moment. "No, I don't suppose I am," he muttered. "Hand me the damned soda." He drained half of it in one gulp, shuddering, and lit a cigarette.

She opened a soda for herself, ripped open the bag of taco chips and perched on the one rickety chair the motel room boasted. Not for the life of her would she risk getting near that bed again. "So what's next?" she asked.

"Do you always have to be so damned perky in the morning?" he responded.

"Do you have to smoke in the morning?" she countered sweetly.

His answering growl was warning enough. "The way I see it, we have only one obvious choice. We drive back down to San Francisco, where I get new clothes, a new car and a life of my own. You go home, tell your father the truth and wait for your sister to return home."

"That's the obvious choice, is it?"

"It is."

"And you can seriously sit there, in the shape you're in, and say that my sister isn't in any danger?"

"Why would she be in danger? Vinnie has the statue, and he has her. He hasn't made any effort to send her home yet. Presumably, they're both very happy."

"For now," Sally muttered gloomily.

"Why do I have the horrible feeling you're not telling me everything?" he inquired of his cigarette. "Maybe it's the innocent expression in your eyes. Maybe it's the way

I've caught you in lies before. Maybe it's just instinct, but my instincts have saved my hide any number of times and I've learned to listen to them.''

''They didn't save your hide last night.''

''No, they didn't. You want to tell me why the Calderini boys would be so upset that we showed up?''

''They don't want to lose the falcon or Lucy.''

''Why not? I mean, they're not going to lose the falcon unless they want to. You and I aren't much of a threat to that kind of muscle. And I can't see why anyone would want to hold on to your sister if she wanted to leave. What's the point? Vinnie's not a white slaver. Unless she's some sort of hostage,'' he added slowly, stubbing out his cigarette and staring at Sally. ''Is that it?''

She tried to look limpid. Since she wasn't quite sure what limpid looked like, it was a trial and a waste. Diamond wasn't buying it. ''Why should she be a hostage? They have the falcon.''

For a moment, he didn't move. Then he scooted back on the bed somewhat gingerly, nodding. ''So that's it. They don't have the real falcon, do they?''

Sally went from limpid to outraged innocence. ''Why in the world would you think that?''

He nodded, more to himself. ''That's it. Where's the real one?''

''I don't know what you're talking about.''

''The real one, Sally. Stop playing games with me. If the Calderinis discover they've got a phony statue, they're going to be very upset. And they have your sister to get upset with.''

Sally gave up. ''Don't you think I haven't realized that? Why do you supposed I'm so determined to get her back?''

''Where's the real falcon?''

''I don't know what you're talking about.''

She didn't realize he could move so swiftly, given his general condition. He was up off the bed with a fluid grace unmarred by his grunt of pain, towering over her in tightly controlled rage. He caught her chin in his hand, forcing her to look up at him, and she knew without question that she wasn't going to get away with any more prevarication. "Where's the real falcon?" he said again, the words terse and sharp.

"I don't know."

"Explain." He hadn't let go of her chin, but his long fingers were cool against her warm skin, almost caressing.

"When I found out that Vinnie was after me just because he wanted the falcon, I had a copy made. I hid the original in my closet and put the real one in the safe, and then I took off for Europe. I didn't realize he was so determined to get the falcon that he'd go after Lucy. I figured he might have someone break into the place, but I never thought he'd take Lucy, too."

"So where's the real falcon?"

"I don't know!" Sally cried. "When they took the copy, I put the real one back in the safe. A couple of days later, that one was gone, too. Maybe Vinnie came back. I don't know. I can't believe he'd take the real one without saying anything."

"So, you think Vinnie only has the phony. Do you think he knows?"

"I'm afraid he might suspect. Otherwise, everyone wouldn't be so unfriendly when I've tried to get in touch with Lucy."

"Hey, they're an unfriendly bunch." Diamond released her chin, moving back toward the bed and his unfinished can of soda. "Besides, you haven't exactly been discreet. If they didn't suspect something before, your desperate attempts to get in touch with your sister would have to arouse their suspicions."

"Are you blaming me?"

"Damned right. Didn't you realize you can't play games

with people like the Calderinis? They don't come equipped with a sense of humor.''

It took all of Sally's considerable self-possession to keep from losing her temper. On the one hand, she was still feeling shaken, edgy, and the sight of his bruised, bandaged, strong back beneath the tattered shirt wasn't doing much to calm her. On the other hand, she didn't think it would be a good idea to goad him further. Goad him into putting his hands on her again. Despite his hostility, she had the feeling that he wouldn't want to stop any more than she did.

"All right," she said calmly enough. "We're not getting anywhere arguing about it. So I blew it. We need to worry about where we go from here."

"I told you where we go from here. Back to San Francisco. And then, if you ask me real nice, I might head back out on my own and start looking for your sister. If the Calderinis discover they've got the wrong falcon, we're going to have some very angry gentlemen. Particularly since the Chinese contingent are expected in this country sometime within the week."

"The Chinese contingent?"

"You remember. The people you overheard Vinnie discussing with Alf," he said.

"Oh," Sally said, having conveniently forgotten that. "If they're coming within the week, then I don't think we have time to go back to San Francisco, get you a new car and then get back up here. Besides, what do you need a new car for? We can use this one."

"*We* aren't going to use anything. I told you, you're going back home. We don't have any choice—we're broke and your purse is gone."

"I keep extra credit cards in the glove compartment."

"And besides— What did you say?"

"I said, I keep extra credit cards in the glove compartment. Plus bank cards. All we have to do is find the right kind of machine and we can have cash coming out the ears.'' She looked up at him, expecting praise, or at least a pat on the head.

''Why didn't you tell me that yesterday?''

''I forgot. Listen, Diamond, we were forced off the road, I gashed my shin, hitchhiked in a manure truck, then had the dubious pleasure of having someone beat the hell out of you. I'm not used to physical violence, and I find it just a little distracting.''

'' 'Distracting,' '' he echoed faintly. ''What's your credit limit?''

''I don't think that I have one.''

He shook his head, sinking down on the bed again. ''Sally…'' he began.

She moved swiftly, no longer afraid to touch him. She sank down on the floor beside him, taking his battered hands in hers and looking up at him beseechingly. No longer limpid or innocent or like a wounded puppy dog. For once, all her playacting had vanished. ''Don't send me back, Diamond. I can't go back and wait to hear. I have to come with you, don't you understand that? It's my fault Lucy got into this mess. It's my fault they have the phony falcon. I *have* to go with you. I have to.''

He stared down at her. His gaze dropped to the hands clutching his, and seemingly without volition his long thumbs stroked the backs of her hands. ''I'm not sure I can protect you.''

''I can protect myself.''

''Sure, you've given me ample proof of that,'' he scoffed.

''Diamond, please. Don't send me back.''

He was going to kiss her again. He was going to pull her into his arms, up across the bed, and she'd go willingly, gladly. All he had to do was give her a little tug. All he had to do was touch his bruised mouth to hers. All he had to do…

He dropped her hands, rising and pushing past her. "It's your funeral," he said in a carefully noncommittal voice. "If you don't mind the heat, you may as well hang around. You're right—getting a new car will be a major pain. I'd be more inclined to do it after I've got your sister safely back and you're feeling generous."

She didn't believe him for a moment. She wasn't sure why he wasn't sending her back, but it wasn't because he thought he could get more money out of her. Worried as he might be about her safety, he didn't want her to go any more than she wanted to.

"Thank you, Diamond," she said, hiding her sudden burst of happiness. "I promise to behave myself."

He snorted as he pulled on his jacket, grimacing with pain. "That'll be the day. Get your shoes on and let's get out of here. I'm ready to show you how easily I can be bought."

"How easily is that?" She rose, slipping on her sneakers and grabbing her can of diet Coke.

"A decent-sized breakfast ought to do it."

"Cheap," she scoffed. She saw the tiny bottle of Chivas lying on its side next to the bed. "I would have thought it would require at least half a gallon of good Scotch."

"That's if you want me to be nice," he said, his eyes following the direction of her gaze. "You gonna pick up the bottle or leave it as a tip for the chambermaid?"

"Do you think they have chambermaids here?"

"Not likely. If they do, they've probably already had more Scotch than is good for them."

"Do you want me to bring the bottle?"

A wry grin curved the corner of his mouth. "What is this, a morality test? Leave the damned bottle."

"All right," she said, hiding her rush of relief as she followed him out of the door.

"You can buy me a half gallon later," he said over his shoulder.

She stopped short, staring after him. And then, for lack of anything better to do, she stuck her tongue out at his retreating back before following him out into the early-morning air.

A HUGE BREAKFAST ACTUALLY did go a great ways toward improving his mood, James thought a few hours later. A new change of clothes, a carton of cigarettes and Sally being uncharacteristically docile also helped. Particularly since he knew Sally's docility wasn't the sort to last for very long.

He was being a fool and a half for letting her come with him, he knew that. He was counting on the Calderinis' old-world deference to womanhood to protect her to some extent, but even that had its limits. Once the Calderinis found they had the wrong falcon they were going to be infuriated, and James didn't relish either of them being in the way.

But sister Lucy couldn't be thrown to the wolves, either. Sometime during the past twenty-four hours, his last reservations about the case had vanished. Maybe it was when the Calderinis had trashed his car and nearly killed him and Sally for no better reason than they might be inconvenienced. Maybe it was when he'd felt Tony the Cannon's pointed boot in his ribs. Maybe it was when he'd felt Sally MacArthur's soft mouth under his.

Whatever the reason, it was no longer a case he was pursuing with half-hearted reluctance. It was personal. And it was a cause. He wasn't going to back down when things got a little inconvenient or dangerous. He was going to get Lucy extricated from Vinnie's clutches, and if he managed to find the real falcon at the same time, so much the better. In any case, he was going to do the job he was hired to do.

And he wasn't going to go to bed with Sally MacArthur. No matter how tempted he was.

Lord, that woman was exhausting! Her sheer babbling energy was enough to make him want to run for cover. To stop her mouth at all costs. Unfortunately, he kept thinking of the most effective way of stopping that mouth. With his.

He lit a cigarette, glancing over at her as she drove down the highway and tacitly ignoring her glare of disapproval. "I hate to be picky," he drawled, "but where are you going?"

"I'm not sure. I thought we might head toward the mountains."

"Why?"

"We have a vacation home up near Mount Sara. It's about four hours from here. I thought they might have gone there."

James shifted in the seat with a muffled groan that was becoming more reflexive than necessary. "What makes you think that? The word was they'd headed to some place in the desert."

"That's what they want us to think. Anyway, maybe I've been overreacting. Maybe they really did want some time alone together. Obviously, the little fishing cabin at Lake Judgment isn't the place for privacy. Maybe Lucy told him about our place at Mount Sara."

"It's worth a try," he said finally. "Four hours, you say? We could make it by midafternoon. If there's no sign of them, we head back to San Francisco."

"Diamond, you promised…!"

"I didn't say I was going to leave you there. I have some people to talk to, to see if I can get a line on where in the desert Vinnie and your sister might have gone to. Assuming they're not in the mountains."

"Couldn't you just phone them?"

He snorted in amusement. "Not likely. The kind of people I need to see don't have regular addresses or telephones. They like to deliver their information face-to-face and to be paid for it. I'm afraid I can't call in with a credit card."

"Oh." Her hands were gripping the steering wheel. Good hands, he thought, not for the first time: Long fingers,

short, buffed nails, no rings. More capable hands than he
would have expected of her. He hated long fingernails and
too much jewelry on a woman. At least, on a woman who
mattered. He liked women who looked like they could accomplish things with their hands, not just use them to
model jewelry. He wondered if her hands were as capable
as they looked. If they were downright inventive.

"Oh," he echoed, trying to distract himself from the
direction his thoughts kept heading. He should never have
slept with her. That was half the problem. Once you share
a mattress with a woman, breath the same air in your sleep,
then you've got ties. Commitments. And he wasn't interested in either. He didn't have time for either.

"If you think you're going to dump me, Diamond, you
better just disabuse yourself of that notion," she warned
him, some of her old energy reemerging.

"I can't do that—I need your car."

"You could always steal it."

"Good idea. But there's no guarantee you wouldn't call
the cops on me. And there are any number of people on
the SFPD who'd love the chance to pick me up."

"Made a few enemies on the job, Diamond?" she inquired sweetly.

"A few. Must be my charm."

"Why'd you quit the force?" she asked, her clear, blue
eyes concentrating on the horizon. It was a warm, clear,
fall day, the rains of the day before having thankfully vanished.

"I didn't quit. I was encouraged to seek my professional
fulfillment elsewhere."

"You were fired?"

"More like a mutual agreement. My partner had died,
and I'd always been a pain in the butt to anyone in au-
thority. I liked to do things my own way, and the police
department is a bureaucracy just like every part of city government."

Sally smacked the steering wheel. "That's my problem," she said. "I've been wrong about you, Diamond. You're not Philip Marlowe or Sam Spade at all."

He had a sudden, horrified suspicion of what was coming next. "Don't say it, Sally," he warned her. "There's no telling what I'll do...."

But there was no stopping her. "You're Dirty Harry," she said triumphantly. "Come on, Diamond, growl it just once."

"I don't growl things," he growled. "And I don't know what the hell you're talking about."

"Just once, Diamond...."

"Listen, Sally, we've come to a temporary truce. Don't push it."

"Or what?" she asked too damned cheerfully.

He shut his eyes and offered up a silent request for patience. "Or I might tie you up and gag you and dump you in the back seat," he snapped. "Now just be quiet and drive us to Mount Sara. I intend to sleep most of the way there."

"As long as you don't smoke."

"I can't smoke in my sleep," he murmured.

There was silence in the car, broken only by the hum of tires and the unusual stillness of the woman next to him. He was mortally tired—last night, he'd hurt too much and been too distracted by the warm, sweet-smelling body curled next to him to sleep that well. He couldn't turn off his awareness of her last night, and he couldn't do it now. He sighed, glancing over at her.

To his horror, he saw that her eyes were filled with unshed tears. He didn't know what it was about her. He'd seen women cry all his life, far too many women cry. He'd inured himself to tears, knowing that either the woman crying was just trying to manipulate the situation, or else the situation was too bad for him to do anything about it.

But Sally's tears were different. They were like a punch in the gut, and he found himself thinking he'd do anything,

anything to make them disappear, make her smile and babble again.

"Diamond," she said, her voice faintly husky as she glanced over at him.

He closed his eyes quickly so she wouldn't realize he'd been watching her. "Yeah?" he grumbled.

"You are going to find her, aren't you? You're not going to let them hurt her?"

He never made promises. When backed against a wall, he usually managed with a gruff, "I'll do my best" and figured that would have to suffice.

He turned his head and opened his eyes. "I'll find her, kid," he said. "I promise you."

And the smile she gave him was of such a dazzling brilliance, filled with such trust, that it took a full one hundred and twenty seconds to realize what a fool he'd been to promise what he might not be able to deliver.

Chapter Eleven

"You're lost, aren't you?"

Sally plastered her most innocent expression across her face. It was a wasted effort—it was quarter past nine on a dark autumn evening and Diamond wouldn't be able to see well enough to appreciate the nuances of her reaction. "What makes you say that?"

"Because we left at eleven for a place that you assured me was only four hours away. And you, lady, drive too damned fast. So I can only guess that you took a wrong turn somewhere along the way." He pushed in the cigarette lighter and Sally gave it an impotent glare, rolling down her window in exaggerated disapproval.

"Well, I didn't."

"Didn't what?"

"Didn't take one wrong turn. I took several."

"I'm not spending another night in a sleazy hotel with you," he warned.

"There are a number of men who'd consider it a great treat to share a sleazy motel room with me," she said with undaunted cheer.

"I'm not one of them. Where the hell are we?"

"Twenty-seven miles away."

"Oh yeah? Pardon me for sounding skeptical, but..."

"Look at the road sign, Diamond. I made so many wrong turns, I finally ended up where I belonged."

"Only six hours later," he groused.

"Well, maybe if I'd had a navigator instead of someone snoring beside me…"

"I don't snore," Diamond said.

"You do. Both last night and all day long. I hate to think how you'd be if you had any Scotch. You'd probably be comatose."

"Don't count on it. If Isaiah keeps a well-stocked bar in your summer house, you're going to have a chance to find out."

Sally bit her lip. "James…" she said hesitantly. "I don't like people who drink too much."

The silence in the car was oppressive, broken only by the rush of warm night air outside the windows. "Then I guess I'm going to have to live with the fact that you don't like me," he said finally. "Let's leave it at that."

But Sally had never left anything alone in her life. "But why? It can't make you feel good. It makes people stupid and sloppy and sick the next day."

"It dulls the pain."

"What pain? What's hurting so badly that you have to ruin your life—"

"Hey, Carrie Nation, I'm not ruining my life, okay? I like to drink, okay? I'm not hurting anyone but myself, and I figure it's my business."

"You hurt the people who care about you."

He took a deep drag of his cigarette and the tip glowed in the darkness. "Like I said, I'm not hurting anyone but myself."

"Diamond, people care about you…."

"Listen, Sally, my partner's dead, and his family just find me an upsetting reminder of all they've lost. My own family's been gone a long time, my ex-wife is happily remarried, and the guys I used to work with are just as closed up as I am.''

"What about women?''

"What about women?'' he countered, hostility thick in his voice.

"Surely there must be someone…''

"I keep away from women who expect anything of me. My relationships are casual, friendly, expecting nothing but a damned good time in bed. I avoid entanglements, women who fall in love, who dream dreams, who think I'm something I can never be. I avoid women like you.''

It was a direct hit, one she couldn't duck. All she could do was sit there and absorb the blow. "Fair enough,'' she said, her voice deceptively even. "But what about you?''

"What about me?''

"Don't you think you deserve better? Don't you think you're worth more than drinking yourself into an early grave? Don't you think—''

"Give me a break, lady!'' Diamond shot back. "Have you seen me rolling around on the floor? Drooling and staggering? I like Scotch. There are times when I like a lot of Scotch. There are times when I like too much Scotch. But I'm not drinking myself into an early grave, and I can stop anytime I want to.''

"Then stop now.''

"Have I mentioned that I am going to strangle you?''

"Several times. Please don't drink, Diamond. For me.''

"Lady, that's the one thing calculated to get me completely wasted.''

"Diamond…''

"Do you think we could discuss something other than my drinking habits?'' he said in a bored tone of voice. "Like why the Calderinis want the Manchurian falcon. What are they planning to do with it?''

Clearly the subject matter was closed. For now. Sally had no intention of letting it stay off-limits indefinitely, but she was willing to compromise. "I gather they're planning to give it to the Chinese when they have their meeting. At least, that's what it sounded like when I eavesdropped on Vinnie and Alf."

"When and where is the meeting?"

"I don't remember. It was more than six weeks ago when I left for Europe. I thought everything was behind me."

"The Calderinis shouldn't be underestimated. If they're planning to give it the Chinese then they mustn't have had their meeting yet."

"Why do you say that?"

"Because the Chinese would know it wasn't the real falcon, and they'd be after us like fleas on a dog. We've probably got a few more days until they find out they've got a ringer on their hands. But how did they know your father had the falcon in the first place? Was it ever exhibited? Photographed? He said it was the pride of his collection—I would have thought he'd keep it under tighter security."

"There's a little problem with the falcon."

"What's that?"

"It's not really his. He somehow got his hands on it after the war. As far as I know, its existence is a secret."

"Not much of a secret, if he told me the first time he met me."

"That's different."

"Why?" Diamond demanded, tossing his cigarette out the cracked window.

"He liked you."

"So he said."

"He approves of you."

"I'm thrilled."

"He wants you to marry me."

"I'm— What the hell makes you say that? You didn't even know I'd met him."

"Well, if he'd talked to me, I know he would have said so," she said, trying not to sound defensive. "I know Isaiah very well. I know who he approves of and who he doesn't. He's hated every one of my fiancés."

"Is that why you got engaged to them? Some sort of rebellion against Daddy?"

She considered it for a moment. "Actually, no. It always grieved me that he didn't like the men I chose. It didn't surprise me, just grieved me. I tended to pick men I could handle. Isaiah wanted someone who could handle me. That's why I know he approves of you."

The stunned silences lasted only a moment. "Handle you? Are you nuts? You are driving me out of my mind. If I don't find your sister and the falcon in the next couple of days, you can simply drop me at the nearest mental hospital."

Sally laughed, a deep throated chuckle. "You're tougher than that, Diamond. I imagine if it came to a full-scale battle between the two of us, you'd always come out on top." A moment later, the import of what she said came through and Sally choked.

Diamond slid down in the seat. "Oh, not always on top. It gets boring that way."

"You know what I mean."

"I don't understand why you're blushing. You charge through life like a maniac, but all I have to do is mention sex and you suddenly become shy. You brought it up."

"I did not. I just made an unfortunate slip. And I wish you wouldn't do that!"

"Do what?" he asked lazily.

"Make suggestive remarks when you know perfectly well you don't mean it. You have no intention of going to bed with me, so you shouldn't tease me about it."

"I have no intention of doing so," he agreed. "However, you know what the road to hell is paved with."

"Diamond, making love to me is not hell."

"I wouldn't know."

"Diamond...!"

"You still haven't answered my question. How did the Calderinis know about the falcon if it's existence is a secret?"

"I haven't the faintest idea. Maybe the Chinese kept track of it for all these years."

"Don't you care? It might prove to be important. Whoever took the real falcon had to know of its existence. Maybe that's the person who tipped off the Calderinis in the first place. Maybe if we find out who told them we can find out who has it now."

"It doesn't matter. If we get close enough to the Calderinis to find out who told them, then we'll be close enough to get Lucy away."

"Just because we're close enough doesn't mean we'll be able to do it."

"Are you always this pessimistic?" she asked, irritated.

"Naah, sometimes I'm positively morose. Are we ever going to get to Mount Sara?"

Sally jerked the wheel, throwing him against the side of the car as she gunned the engine. They started up a narrow, winding road as fast she could make it, the bumps and ruts making Diamond curse in ill-concealed pain. At the end of the track, she slammed on the brakes, her passenger hurtling forward, restrained only by the seat belt she'd insisted he wear.

"Yes," she said sweetly.

"Yes, what?"

"Yes, we're going to get to Mount Sara. We're here."

Diamond looked up, past the windshield to the silhouette of the gabled and dormered old house. "We're here," he echoed. "And they're not."

Sally's temper vanished abruptly as she stared at the house, a woebegone expression on her face. "No, they're not," she said in a quiet voice. "I hadn't thought that far ahead. What do we do next?"

"We're not going any farther tonight. My ribs couldn't take it. Besides, I didn't really expect to find them here. Did you?"

"Then why did we come here?"

Diamond shrugged. "I was humoring you before we headed back to San Francisco. This was only supposed to take four hours, remember? I don't suppose this place comes equipped with a telephone?"

"It does if it hasn't been turned off for the season. Why? I thought your stool pigeons didn't accept phone calls?"

"Such a sweet tongue," he chided. "There are a few people I can try. Why don't you see if you can rustle up something to eat while I see what I can find out?"

"Women's work?"

"Hey, it's your house. And believe me, you wouldn't want to try my cooking."

"I believe you."

It was a warm night. The air smelled of pine pitch and fresh air and dry leaves, the warm, nostalgic smell that reminded Sally of long summer nights when everything was so much simpler. For a moment, she simply stood by the car and breathed in the earthy aroma, feeling an accustomed tightening in her stomach. Diamond had moved ahead, walking with a bit more ease then he had that morning, and for a moment, she watched him.

When had she thought she was three quarters in love with him? It seemed ages ago. That last twenty-five percent had fallen, and she couldn't imagine why. He was everything she'd been wary of. A cynic, a loner, someone who probably didn't even know how to care. He smoked too much, drank too much, and he lived a life-style that was as foreign as it was romantic. Her fantasy world was dissolving into a reality that she could no longer manage. She wanted James Diamond. She wanted the reality of him. And she didn't even know what that reality was.

The house was cool and faintly musty smelling when she unlocked the front door, dumping their suitcases inside. But the power and water were still on, and moments after Diamond disappeared, she could hear the dialing of the telephone.

She wanted to listen in. She wanted something to eat even more. By the time Diamond appeared in the huge, old-fashioned kitchen, she had canned soup boiling on the stove, blackened toast on the table and a pot of coffee perking cheerfully.

"You aren't much more of a cook than I am," Diamond observed as he sat down at the table.

"Your rib seems much better," she observed in return. "Mind if I punch you in it?"

"I don't think it's cracked, just bruised." He took a sip of soup. "Ever hear of a place called Desert Glory Health Spa?"

She reached into her pocket and tossed the business card onto the table. "You mean this place?"

Diamond set his spoon down with great deliberation. "Where did you get that?"

"On the floor of the office at Lake Judgment." She didn't like the sheer, frustrated rage in his eyes. "Why, do you think it's important?"

"I'm betting that's where your sister is. If you'd had the sense to show me this—"

"You weren't in any condition to listen to me. Besides, I told you I had a clue, and you told me to stop acting like Nancy Drew."

"You were the one who said you wanted to be Nancy Drew."

"Whatever. How was I to know it was important? You don't seem to take my suggestions very seriously."

"We're here, aren't we? Stuck in the middle of nowhere,

with your sister somewhere in the desert, surrounded by gangsters who might just possibly want to do her a great deal of harm. Particularly if they decide she's been playing them for fools.''

''They won't.''

''What makes you so sure of that?'' Diamond reached for his pack of cigarettes.

''I don't suppose I can tell you not to smoke in my house?'' she asked plaintively.

''I don't suppose you can. What makes you think that the Calderinis won't suspect her of double-crossing them?''

''Because she's even more scatterbrained than I am. She couldn't keep a secret if her life depended on it, and by now, Vinnie would know that.''

''*More* scatterbrained than you?''

''A real ditz,'' Sally verified. ''Don't grin like that, Diamond, you look like the Cheshire Cat. I know I don't seem like the epitome of calm reason, but compared to my sister, I'm very sensible.''

''Unbelievable,'' he said, blowing smoke in her direction. ''Where's your father's Scotch?''

It was suddenly too much. She hadn't had much more sleep the night before than Diamond had had, and the long drive with its multitude of wrong turns hadn't improved her state of mind. He sat there so cool, so superior, smoking his blasted cancer weeds and demanding whiskey, and even with his bruised face and swollen knuckles, he still was almost wickedly handsome. The battered face only made him more enticing.

They'd replaced his ripped suit with jeans and a cotton sweater, and the casual clothes made him look less like something out of her silly fantasies and more like a real man. Sally wanted to jump on him and shake him out of his sardonic mood. She wanted... She no longer knew what she wanted, except to have her sister home safe.

She pushed away from the table, knocking her chair over as she went. "Find it yourself," she snapped.

"What's happened to that chirpy Nancy Drew attitude?" he drawled. "Did you finally discover I'm not the man of your dreams?"

"Maybe my worst nightmare."

"Wrong movie. I'd never pass for Stallone. Too wiry."

"There are times, Diamond, when I think I hate you," she announced with deceptive calm. "I'm going upstairs to bed. You can find a room for yourself—feel free to take any of them. You can fill the room with smoke, drink yourself into a stupor and be as unpleasant as you want. I'll see you tomorrow."

"Sally..."

"Don't apologize, Diamond," she said in a voice high-pitched with strain. "It's too late."

"I wasn't going to apologize. I simply wanted to now if you have an alarm clock. If I drink myself into a stupor, I probably won't wake up before noon."

He had that damnable smile on his face, as if he found her temper amusing. "You know, Diamond, I have had quite enough," she said pleasantly. And she tipped the kitchen table over on him, splashing him with soup and burned toast and hot coffee.

She ran then, half hoping he'd follow her. She didn't know what she expected from him, maybe just that he'd put his hands on her and things would take their natural course.

But he didn't follow her, and by the time she reached the second floor, reaction began to set in.

What was happening to her? She tried to treat life as a party, a wonderful feast for her enjoyment. Long ago, she'd learned what pain and loneliness was like, what abandonment and rejection did to one's soul when her feckless mother had left for greener pastures. She'd sworn it would never happen to her again; she'd never care about someone who could twist her around inside.

So why had she fallen for someone like James Diamond when she'd been so careful for so long?

It was too late, she thought as she moved down the second-floor hallway toward the door at the back. She couldn't withdraw into her shell like a cheerful tortoise and pretend that it never happened.

And she sure as hell couldn't make a cynic like Diamond fall in love with her. So she had one choice and one choice alone. To pretend it never happened.

After all, he didn't have to know she'd fallen in love with him. She certainly hadn't given any indication of it—she'd done her best to argue with him night and day. And even though she had kissed him back with enthusiasm, that was acceptable, since he'd been the one initiating the kiss in the first place. It was only polite to kiss back, wasn't it?

The door to the attic creaked loudly in the silent house as she opened it. The musty air was stronger there, staler than in the rest of the house, and she supposed she should be feeling uneasy, stepping into the darkness.

She shut the door behind her and leaned against it, reveling in the sense of safety and peace as it washed over her. It was an unseasonably warm night for autumn in the mountains, and the moon was almost full, shining in the casement windows at the far end of the attic.

She fumbled in the darkness for the table she always kept beside the door. The candelabrum was there, and the matches, and in a moment, she'd managed to create a decent amount of light.

The old iron bed was where it belonged, angled beneath one of the casement windows. The old feather bed was there, the piles of antique quilts that no one knew she'd stolen from the rest of the house, the four pillows and the bookcase full of her favorite books. *The Secret Garden, A Little Princess,* Nancy Drew mysteries from the thirties.

Historical romances published in the early seventies, teeming with sex, Jane Austen novels full of proper courtships. Fantasies, all of them, a world in which nothing could hurt her.

She climbed up onto the high bed and opened the window, letting in the warm night breeze. She could see the Alfa parked below, the moonlight gilding its dark green paint. For a moment, she wondered where Diamond was, and then she put the thought out of her mind. She didn't need to be thinking about Diamond or Philip Marlowe or Rhett Butler. She simply needed a few moments of peace, without thinking about anything or anyone at all. Later, when she'd regained some of her usual amour propre, she could deal with things. Things like Diamond. And the ache inside her. And why the hot water still worked and the phone was still running and the air in the rest of the house barely smelled musty. For now, all she wanted to do was breathe in the warm night air and dream of happy endings.

Even though she knew, in the best of hard-boiled detective novels the endings were always bittersweet and the boy didn't get the girl. For now, she could pretend this was Jane Austen, not Raymond Chandler. And that she was going to live happily ever after. At least for one night.

Chapter Twelve

The house settled down around her. Diamond must have located the shower—Sally could hear the screech of ancient pipes through the attic. And then stillness once more, with only the sound of the soft breeze through the ancient pines, the creak of the bed springs and the ancient stirrings of the old house to break the silence.

In the end, it didn't take that long for him to find her. She was kneeling on the high bed, resting her arms on the sill of the open window, when she heard the door open behind her. She didn't turn; all her attention was focused on the moon.

"When I was young," she said in a dreamy voice, "I used to run away from Lucy and Isaiah and Jenkins. I'd hide up here with bags of cookies and bottles of pop, and piles and piles of books. I'd spend hours up here, listening to them call my name, lost in my own special world. Isaiah says I'm still lost in my own special world."

She heard the creak of the old wood floors as he crossed the attic, but she still kept her back to him. Afraid to look at him. Afraid to let him look at her, to let him read all the longing that consumed her soul.

"What did you think about?" His voice was low, husky from cigarettes, and dangerously beguiling.

She shrugged, pushing her hair back away from her face.

"What every lonely adolescent dreams of. A hero to rescue me from my solitude. A white knight to carry me off. Most hot, summer nights, I'd lie here alone and wish I had some-one to share this bed with me beneath the moonlight." She smiled wryly into the darkness. "Someone to show me the things I read about in books. Someone to take care of me."

He was closer, standing at the edge of the bed. "That's bad politics. Women shouldn't want to be taken care of anymore. They should want equal partners."

"When you're seventeen, you don't worry about politics. You think with your heart."

"Seventeen-year-old boys think with their glands."

"I remember," she said.

"I don't take care of anyone."

"I know," she said, resting her chin on her arms. "But there's nothing wrong with being taken care of. As long as you can take care of the other person in return. Everyone needs a little comfort every now and then."

"I'm not someone to provide comfort."

"I know," she said again.

"How old are you? Twenty-seven? Twenty-eight?"

"Twenty-eight."

"Then I'm ten years older than you. That's too much of an age difference."

"I know," she said, turning from the window to look at him.

The candles beside the bed had guttered down, and the empty attic was lit only with moonlight. He was standing too close, and his body radiated tension. He was wearing his jeans and nothing else. She could see the droplets of water across his bare shoulders. He hadn't replaced his elas-tic bandage, and the bruising across his torso didn't look quite as bad in the moonlight. He still looked battered, tough and very handsome. And very very dear.

"I didn't think you'd be able to find me," she said, her own voice as rough as his.

"I'm a private investigator, remember? It's my job to find missing people." He didn't move. He didn't walk away, as she half expected. He didn't come closer, close enough to touch her, as she half hoped.

"Yes," she said, suddenly patient, suddenly sure.

"I'm going to find your sister—"

"I don't want to talk about my sister."

He was so good at shielding his emotions. "Then I might as well go back to bed."

"Yes," she said, patient as she'd never been before.

"Yes," he said, moving toward her, sliding his hand behind her neck, underneath her hair and pulling her up to him. He held her there for a moment, and in the darkness, his eyes glittered down into hers as his mouth hovered over her parted lips. "This is a mistake," he murmured.

"I know."

His lips brushed hers, gently, soft against her. Softer, sweeter than she would have thought. And then harder, pressing, opening his mouth against her, using his lips, his tongue, his teeth as his other hand snaked around her waist and pulled her up tight against him, her full breasts pressed against his naked, bruised chest.

For a moment, she was afraid to reach out and touch him, afraid to do more than let him kiss her with an intensity that was as devastating as it was practiced. Once she lifted her hands and touched him, she'd be lost. Vulnerable, open to him, with no more defenses or holding back.

He lifted his head and looked down at her in the moonlight. "Put your arms around me, Sally," he said evenly. And her last hesitation was lost.

His skin was smooth, hot beneath her fingers. She could feel bone and muscle beneath his flesh, feel strength and power. She shivered lightly in the night breeze, and then he kissed her again, a full, deep kiss that ended any doubts. This was the man she loved. For some reason, he wanted

her, at least for that night. She would take what she could
get.

He eased her back down on the high bed, against the
welter of quilts, following her down with a fluid grace belied by the bruise on his ribs. Stretching out beside her, he
began unfastening the row of tiny buttons on her silk
blouse, his face in shadows, unreadable. Pushing the fragile
material out of the way, he covered her breast with one
large hand and she realized he planned to take her without
speaking a word.

She didn't expect declarations of love from him. She
wouldn't have believed them. But she needed something
more than this dedicated silence, this attention to business
that had him unfastening her jeans with far too much expertise.

She put her hands over his, stalling him. "Wait," she
begged, her breath coming in short rasps.

"Change your mind?" It was a challenge, pure and simple. He wanted an excuse to stop, to leave her. Before he
got as enmeshed as she was.

"I just wanted..." she began. "I wanted..."

He wasn't going to make it easy for her. "What did you
want?"

"Don't...don't frighten me," she said, putting her hand
over his as she had that morning, unwilling to let him leave.

He froze. "You're forgetting something. Philip Marlowe
isn't a sensitive New Age kind of guy."

"But you're not Philip Marlowe."

"Remember that."

She wouldn't have thought he'd be so deft, sliding her
clothes off her without fumbling, pushing them onto the
floor. She was shivering slightly, but the moonlit night was
still warm and she knew it had to be nerves. And then he
pulled her into his arms, wrapping his body around her, and
the nerves, the doubts vanished. It had been long, too long
since she'd even wanted this. The need she felt for him was

so tense, so rare, that she thought she might explode from it.

He was almost frighteningly efficient about it. He seemed to know just what to do, just where to touch her, how hard, how soft, to elicit the response he wanted. She hadn't known her breasts were so sensitive, but beneath his hands, his mouth, her reactions were astonishingly strong. She lay beside him on the bed, squirming, whimpering, straining to get closer to him as he quickly, cleverly brought her to the edge of explosion, all without letting her touch him.

Just when she thought she'd go mad from frustration, from being so close and yet so far, he pulled her beneath him, spreading her trembling legs with his big hands and filling her with a thrust that belied the distant control he was exerting. She could feel the iron tension running through his body and feel the sweat on his hot skin, and she knew that he was not nearly as removed, as proficient as he would have her believe. He was holding back even as he filled her body, holding back his heart, his soul, his emotions even as he was giving her a kind of pleasure she'd never felt.

She wanted to keep that response from him. She wanted to argue, to force him to break through that control, but the words wouldn't come, her hands could only clutch his sweat-slick shoulder, her body could only move with his, reaching for him, clenching around him in a sudden shower of stars.

She remembered being almost surprised that he followed her, his body going rigid in her arms, his eyes closed tight, his mouth clamped shut as he gave her the one thing he couldn't withhold.

She wanted to cry. She wanted to scream at him, shove him away from her. He'd given her the most profound physical experience of her life, and he'd done it like a scientist, an observer, hardly involved in the act at all until the climax. And she knew that despite everything, after tonight, she'd never be able to break free. No matter how much he wanted her to.

She waited for him to pull away. To roll over and fall asleep, to get up and leave her. To somehow pull his defenses even more tightly around him, leaving her out in the cold.

She could feel his fingers on her temples, pushing her hair away from her face. She could feel the dampness and realized she must have been crying, after all. She waited, patiently, knowing he was going to leave her.

"Sally," he said, his voice husky. "Open your eyes."

She didn't want to. She had her own secrets now, her own love and distrust that she didn't want him to see. But she couldn't resist his quiet request. She couldn't resist anything he asked of her.

His face was in shadows, looming over hers. "Don't look at me like that," he said.

"Like what?"

"Like I just kicked your dog. You came. I felt it. You can't pretend—"

"Do we have to have this conversation?" she demanded, thoroughly embarrassed, pushing at him. She'd never realized quite how big he was until she was trying to shove his almost-two-hundred-pound frame off her much smaller one.

"Yes. Don't tell me you're going to be one of those women who hates any man once she goes to bed with him."

"You've run into that before?"

"A few times."

She stared up at him, willing her expression to be stony. "Then maybe it's your technique."

She waited for him to leave. She knew perfectly well she'd said the one thing calculated to drive any man away. And she wanted to. She wanted him to leave her alone so that she could pull her tattered defenses back around her and somehow deal with the rest of her life.

But he didn't move. To her amazement, he stroked the sides of her face with his thumbs, and his voice was very gentle. "What's wrong, Sally? You didn't want me to tell you I loved you, did you?"

She couldn't tell him. Couldn't tell him that she'd never felt so alone in her life. Couldn't tell him that she didn't want him to say he loved her. She simply wanted him to love her. So she remained silent, trapped beneath him, mute and miserable.

He kissed her then, a gentle brushing of his mouth against hers, a gentle teasing of her passivity into a burgeoning response. He kept on kissing her, coaxing her into participation, until her arms came up around him, and her last conscious thought was that even if it was all a performance designed for her pleasure, there was no denying her pleasure was something she'd never felt before. And right then, she'd rather have misery with James Diamond than a comfortable life without him.

JAMES WAITED UNTIL she slept. The breeze from the open window was cooler now, and he pulled one of the old quilts up around her bare shoulders. She murmured something, sighed and snuggled deeper into the feather bed, and for the moment, her face was smooth, untroubled, even happy.

He sat up carefully. He knew how to move without making a sound, he knew how to leave a bed without disturbing the woman sleeping next to him. He was adept at that particular feat. He didn't like to sleep with the women he made love with. Hell, he'd hated the fact that he'd slept with Sally in the motel, even though that time he'd kept his pants on. That was probably behind his current mess. If he'd just stayed out of bed with her in that motel, he never would have been tempted to make love to her tonight.

He gave a quiet snort, contemptuous of his weak ration-

alizations. Hell, he'd wanted to make love to Sally Mac-
Arthur since the moment she'd showed up at his office.
She'd been arguing with Frankie, and he'd assumed she
was one of his girls and had immediately started considering whether he could break an ironclad rule and pay for
it just once.

It would have been better if she were a hooker. James
didn't have many scruples, but one hard-and-fast rule was
never sleep with a client. It just made things too messy,
particularly when you handed them the bill.

And he kept away from women like Sally, trouble
through and through. But this time, he hadn't kept far
enough away.

And he couldn't even blame it on booze. He hadn't had
a drink in more than two days, and he was thinking of
making it longer. He'd found her father's Scotch with no
trouble at all, even poured himself a generous glass. He'd
poured that generous glass down the old iron sink and
headed upstairs in search of his client.

He didn't know why he went looking for her. Maybe to
do something as asinine as tell her he wasn't going to drink
and see if she'd give him a pat on the head. Maybe to fight
with her enough to goad him into going back downstairs
to the bottle. Or maybe to do exactly what he'd ended up
doing.

Well, he'd done it. Twice, as a matter of fact, and he
could have gone for a third if she hadn't looked exhausted.
He'd managed to keep himself fairly uninvolved the first
time around. It had been sheer cussedness on his part. She'd
spent the past few days being so damned perky, he'd
wanted to see what she looked like in his arms, dazed with
pleasure.

And she was amazingly responsive. No defenses at all
once her clothes were stripped away. She had burned in his
arms like a torch, and it had taken all his wavering control
not to ignite with her.

But the second time, his control had gone. He tried to tell himself he just wanted to pleasure her, but somehow, his own needs became overpowering. Particularly when she pushed him over onto his back and began kissing him, dancing her mouth across his bruised torso with featherlight kisses.

He hadn't realized she'd be so good with her hands. Outside of bed, she was slightly, endearingly clumsy. In bed, she was a gazelle—graceful, sleek, magical. This time, he didn't make love to her. This time, they were in it together and he couldn't choke back his cry of pleasure when he came with her. And he knew he'd called her name.

He looked down at her, sleeping so peacefully now, the tears dried on her pale cheeks, her silky black hair tangled around her. He needed to move away, back to his own bed, back to his own life.

She'd gotten what she'd wanted all along. She'd slept with her vision of Philip Marlowe. She'd gotten Sam Spade into bed—no, she'd gotten Sam Spade to seduce her on the childhood bed where she had her first erotic daydreams. And James had played right into it because he couldn't help himself. Because she made him vulnerable the way no one, man or woman, had managed to in years and years.

But he wasn't Philip Marlowe or anyone remotely like him. And he wasn't here to fulfill her fantasies or be her fantasy lover. This was a one-night stand, and he'd tell her that first thing in the morning.

In the meantime, he was going to find his own bed and forget about her luscious body curled up in that quilt. He was going to forget the way her arms and legs wrapped around him and the soft little noises she made, which were the same and yet different from the noises other women made. Damn, he'd hear those noises in his sleep for a long, long time.

All he had to do was slide out of bed. He wouldn't wake

her; he knew that perfectly well. All he had to do was get away now, fast, before he got any more entangled with her.

His hand moved, almost of its own volition, and pushed the strand of hair away from her mouth. In her sleep, she moved against him, pushing her face against his hand like a contented kitten, and murmured something unintelligible. It sounded hideously close to "love," but he couldn't ask her to repeat it. He could only hope it was his imagination. And not wishful thinking.

It took him almost till dawn to climb out of that bed. There was something so peaceful about the way she slept, at odds with her constant chatty energy during the day. And he didn't move far, only to the sagging director's chair beside the bed.

He sat there, his jeans pulled up but not fastened, and watched her while she slept. Knowing that if he wanted anything like a normal life in the future this would be the last time he could watch her while she slept. It was back to a business relationship when the sun rose. Back to the search for her sister. Back to reality.

Whether he liked it or not.

JAMES AWOKE WITH A START, one of those jerky little movements that come when you're fool enough to try to fall asleep in a chair. The day was colder again, and the air coming in through the open casement window was chilly.

The bed was empty, the pile of quilts on the floor. He could hear the noise of the water pipes—she must be off taking a shower. He looked down his lap. She'd thrown one of the quilts over him. Had tucked it around him, in fact.

He stared at it, running a wondering hand over the faded patchwork design. It had been decades since someone had tucked him in. It gave him a peculiar feeling—uneasy, oddly sentimental.

He yanked the quilt off and stood up, stretching angrily.

He wasn't the kind of man who liked or needed to be tucked in. Why the hell didn't she realize that? Why the hell didn't he realize that?

He passed the first bathroom as he padded down the hallway. He could hear her humming over the noise of the shower, and he felt that old companion, guilt, begin to eat at his gut. She was expecting things from him, he just knew it, and he was going to have to tell her that she couldn't.

He washed up in the downstairs bathroom, throwing on a fresh T-shirt and brushing his teeth. He looked marginally more human in the mirror—the black eye was beginning to turn yellow, and the scrapes on his face were starting to heal. He still looked like someone who'd gone ten rounds with King Kong. He also knew that his slightly swollen lips hadn't come from anybody's fist.

He could smell coffee when he stepped out into the hall. Real coffee, not instant, the sweetest smell in the world. He'd wait to tell her. He'd even put up with sappy glances and good-morning smooches for a decent cup of coffee. Or three or four. Maybe he could even justify a brief return to the creaking iron bed....

Down boy, he ordered himself. There was no justification whatsoever. Last night was last night; this morning was a whole new day. Squaring his shoulders, he marched down the hallway to the huge, old kitchen, then halted in dumbfounded amazement.

"Good morning, handsome," the woman at the kitchen table greeted him saucily, waving her cup of coffee at him. "Want a mug?"

She had Sally's china blue eyes, except Sally's were warmer, happier. She had Sally's mouth, except that he didn't want to kiss this one. She had ash blond hair, and even though he knew she was years younger, she looked to be in her early thirties, older in worldly wisdom if not in years.

"Hello," he said evenly, not giving anything away.

"Sally still in bed? You must have been showing her a hell of a good time—she's usually up with the rooster. I didn't know she knew how to cut loose. I guess there's hope for everyone."

He didn't like this woman. Sibling rivalry was nothing new to a man with two brothers he never even sent Christmas cards to, but he didn't like her. He could hear the steady thud of Sally's footsteps as she came down the stairs at her usual breakneck pace, and to stall for time he headed for the coffeepot, pouring himself and Sally each a mug.

"How long have you been here?"

The woman grinned. "Long enough, handsome. I recognized Sally's car when I came back last night, and I was all set to have a cozy little gossip with her when I heard the bedsprings. So I figured she wasn't alone. What I didn't figure was that her taste would make such a rapid improvement. You're a hell of a lot more man than the usual wimps she hangs around with. Don't tell me it's true love?"

The door to the kitchen slammed open and Sally stood there, shock making her skin whiter than usual, except for the two bright red spots on her cheekbones.

James took a sip of his scalding coffee, stalling for time, telling himself it didn't matter if she was still so damned beautiful he wanted to carry her back upstairs. Last night wasn't going to change anything.

"As you can see," he drawled, "our troubles are over. Sister Lucy's come home to roost."

Sally closed her eyes for a moment, then opened them, shaking her head. "Not quite, Diamond," she said wryly. "What we have before us is the proverbial bad penny."

"Is that any way to put it, darling?" the woman protested in a silky voice.

Sally ignored her. "Diamond," she said flatly, "meet my mother."

Chapter Thirteen

"You might at least sound more welcoming, darling," Sally's mother said in a cheerful drawl. "It's been almost a year since you've seen me. How about a hug?"

"It's been two and a half years since I've seen you," Sally said, mustering her last vestiges of calm. As if this morning wasn't going to be traumatic enough, facing Diamond, she had to contend with her mother's astonishing reappearance. Trust Marietta to show up at the worst possible time. Never when she was needed. "And I learned years ago that hugging you messed up your hair and makeup. I'll blow you a kiss." Her salute was just faintly mocking, and Marietta nodded, accepting the mockery.

For a moment, Sally thought she detected the faint shimmer of hurt in her mother's blue eyes. She dismissed the very notion, just as she had long ago dismissed the vain hope that her mother ever cared more for her child than she did for her own pleasures. She'd always wanted to see pain and hurt in her mother's eyes, some sign of love and caring. They'd always been blank, and she'd learned to accept that.

Diamond was standing beside the counter, a mug of coffee in one big hand. He had that wary expression on his face that she'd been expecting, and she sighed inwardly. He looked too damned handsome in the morning light, and not a bit like a hard-boiled detective in a black T-shirt and jeans. She wanted to cross the room, put her arms around his lean waist and rest her head against his chest. She wanted him to hold her, just for a moment, and make the bad dreams go away.

But that was a mistake she wasn't about to make. "Got some coffee for me?" she asked instead, as casually as if they'd spent the night on different planets.

She'd surprised him, she could see that. Score one for her. Marietta nearly blew it with her arch intervention. "Is that any way for young lovers to greet each other in the morning?" she cooed.

"It's been a long time since you were a young lover, Marietta," Sally said flatly. "It's the way we do things nowadays." She took the mug from Diamond's hand, careful not to touch him. Touching him would set off all sorts of impossible longings, and it was taking every ounce of her concentration to be calm and matter-of-fact. "Thanks," she said, dismissing him, feeling once again his start of surprise.

She moved to the table, sinking down opposite her mother. "So, what brings you here, Ma?" she asked, her voice ironic. "You always hated this place when you were married to Isaiah. What makes you show up here at this particular time? And how did you get a key?"

"Darling, I don't need keys if I want to go someplace. And besides, Isaiah has been very generous, you know that. Unlike you, he doesn't bear grudges. He doesn't expect me to be anyone other than who I am."

"I've heard this before. Why are you here?" Once again, Sally might have imagined the hurt expression in Marietta's eyes.

"Just passing through, darling. I stopped by to see you all in San Francisco and only Isaiah was home. He had no idea where you and Lucy were."

"So you came looking for us?"

"Hardly. I haven't changed that much. I decided I needed some peace and quiet. Some fresh air away from the bustle of the city. It was sheer good luck that you happened to turn up. Where, by the way, is your sister?" It was tossed off almost casually, an afterthought, but Sally wasn't fooled. For some reason, Marietta was just as concerned about Lucy as she was.

"Didn't you hear Diamond when he saw you? He thought you were Lucy. We haven't the faintest idea where she is."

Marietta flashed Diamond her most magnificent smile, the one calculated to make strong men weep. He didn't look teary eyed, but then, he was made of sterner stuff than that. "Darling man," Marietta cooed. "Mind you, I was very young when I had my children—"

"You've also had four bouts of cosmetic surgery," Sally interjected with a daughter's ruthlessness.

"You're behind the times. I'm up to six. It's amazing the things a plastic surgeon can do nowadays." Marietta took a delaying sip of her coffee. "So you're looking for Lucy? Why?"

"Who says we're looking for Lucy?"

"Your gentleman friend. Diamond, you called him. What a delicious name. How did you two lovebirds meet?"

Diamond had understandably had enough of this. He took the third chair at the table, swung it around and straddled it with a casual grace. "Sally and I are old friends," he said. "She's the only one who gets away with calling me Diamond. I prefer James."

Marietta once more tried that high-voltage smile. Diamond blinked in the light for a moment, but resisted. "And I'm Marietta. Heavens, I don't even know what my current last name is. I suppose I'm still Von Troppenburg, but I won't be for long. So you've known my daughter a long time? Are you one of her fiancés? I had word that she was going to marry a gangster."

"How'd you hear that?" Sally demanded.

"Oh, I have my sources," Marietta said, waving an airy hand. "So that doesn't explain who you are, James."

"What makes you think I'm not the gangster?"

Marietta nodded, according him the hit. "I'm assuming you're not. You don't look like a gangster."

"Neither did Vinnie," said Sally. "Besides, how do you know what a gangster looks like?"

"Darling, I've lived a long and adventurous life, despite my extremely youthful good looks." She cast a roguish smile at Diamond. "So, you dumped the gangster and moved on to a private detective. You always were one for extremes."

Sally set her mug down on the table, her eyes meeting Diamond's for one pregnant moment, devoid of any memory of the night before. "How did you know he was a private detective?" she asked carefully.

Marietta didn't even flinch. "Why, you said so, darling."

"No, I didn't."

"Of course, you did. How else would I know?"

"She didn't," Diamond said, his voice deep and raspy.

Marietta simply smiled. "I say she did. You two are both still suffering from the afterglow of your energetic night. Though I must say the two of you don't seem to be glowing."

"Answer my question, Marietta. How did you know what Diamond does for a living?"

Marietta shrugged. "I suppose I have to be honest?"

"If you possibly can."

"I went through his wallet. He'd left it in one of the upstairs bedrooms, and you know how insatiably curious I am." She made a tiny moue. "There, I admit it. I am without honor."

Sally stared at her, immune to the masterful performance. She didn't believe her. Oh, Marietta would certainly go through any wallet that happened to be lying around, and she wasn't above filching spare cash if she happened to need it. But the answer was just a little too easy, and too hard to prove otherwise. "You'll never change," Sally said.

"Lord, I hope you're wrong. How fatally boring to be predictable. I am never predictable."

"Yes, you are. You're never there when you're needed, and you're always around when you're not wanted," Sally said flatly.

This time, there was no mistaking the hurt in Marietta's eyes. "That's a terrible thing to say." Her voice was choked.

"Well, I guess that makes me a terrible daughter. It runs in the family." Sally drained her coffee and pushed back from the table. "This is a waste of time. I'm going to get my things together. Diamond and I are taking off. I don't suppose you want us to drop you anywhere?"

Marietta's pathetic grief vanished instantly. "I have my own car. Where are you going, darling? Off to see Lucy?"

"Nope. We're just going on a round of endless sex in strange places. I think we're going to try for Yosemite next."

Marietta beamed at her. "There's hope for you yet, darling."

Sally looked pointedly at Diamond, who'd been taking this all in without saying a word. "Are you coming?"

"In a minute," he said. "I need another cup of coffee."

The last thing in the world Sally wanted to do was to leave James Diamond alone with Marietta. He was tough, all right, but Marietta had powers unknown to mortal man. She could have him eating out of her hand in a matter of minutes. She could have him…she could have him…

Sally shook herself, disgusted at her paranoia. "I'll meet you in front in ten minutes. See you around, Marietta."

"No goodbye kiss?"

"I thought we settled that." She blew her another mocking kiss. She hadn't touched her mother in seven years, not since Marietta had taken off with the lawyer's clerk Sally had been in love with, and she wasn't about to start now. Not when Marietta was so obviously lying to her.

Besides, Sally was more like her mother than Marietta suspected. Closing the door behind her, Sally moved swiftly, silently through the house, heading with unerring instinct to the master bedroom, where Marietta had set up shop.

Marietta didn't come equipped with anything as organized or mundane as a wallet. Her Gucci purse was stuffed with store receipts, uncashed checks, parking tickets, makeup and airplane ticket stubs. Sally moved fast, pawing through things, looking for some sort of clue to her mother's reappearance. As far as she could tell, her mother had flown in from the Riviera, having spent time in Germany, Italy, and Ireland since the last time she had emptied out her purse.

Within moments, Sally gave up. There was no way of finding out anything about Marietta that she didn't want found out. If she had some hidden agenda, if she knew anything about Lucy's whereabouts, she'd divulge that information on her terms alone. It would do no good to ask, to beg, to plead. Marietta was a law unto herself, and all the longing of a little girl for a real mother wouldn't change the way life was.

Diamond was waiting on the front porch, smoking a cigarette. He had that unreadable expression on his face, the one that hid so many secrets, and Sally was feeling just a bit too fragile to try to work her way past those secrets. She concentrated on the symptoms instead, starting an argument.

"Is that your first cigarette of the day?"

"It is."

"Why are you smoking outside? Don't tell me you finally decided that other people have lungs, too?'' she demanded.

''Marietta's allergic to cigarette smoke.''

Sally had always heard the term ''seeing red,'' and she assumed it had to do with bulls and bullfights. Now she knew it was something far more basic, a bright red color at the back of the eyes when rage exploded. She had two choices—to start screaming, which would benefit no one, particularly herself, or to take deep, calming breaths.

It took her to the count of thirteen before she finally had her temper back under control. ''Marietta smokes unfiltered Gauloises when she's in Europe,'' Sally said flatly. ''It's part of her image.''

She started toward the Alfa, not bothering to look back to see if Diamond was following her.

He climbed into the passenger seat, dumping their meager luggage in back. ''You really hate her, don't you?'' he asked, tossing his half-finished cigarette out the window.

Sally started the car with a vengeance. ''No, I don't. I still love her. And that's the problem.'' She gunned the engine, starting down the driveway with a spurt of gravel, not daring to look back.

She knew exactly what she'd see if she was fool enough to turn around. Marietta would be on the front porch, a faint, sad expression on her face, one she'd perfected years ago, one hand fluttering in a sad farewell. Sally had fallen for it too many times.

Diamond had the extreme good sense to be quiet for the first half hour. When he did speak, his choice of subject matter was not auspicious. ''Exactly where are we going?''

''I don't know,'' Sally snapped back.

''That's a first.''

''Don't mess with me, Diamond. I'm not in a good mood.''

''Neither am I. Why don't you pull over and let me

drive? I have to have a better sense of direction than you have.''

"Everyone has a better sense of direction than I have," she admitted. "But a sense of direction doesn't do much good if you don't know what direction you want in the first place."

"Pull over."

She didn't want to. But she couldn't keep driving aimlessly. She knew perfectly well once she stopped the car, they were going to have the conversation she'd been dreading, and she wasn't quite sure if she was up to dealing with it.

It had all seemed so very simple a few short hours ago. She had woken up in that rumpled bed, feeling better than she ever had in her life. Her body felt as rumpled as the quilts, slightly tender, warm and sated. She'd opened her eyes and had seen Diamond sitting there, sound asleep in the chair, and a rush of tenderness had swept over her.

He hadn't been able to hold back the second time. She'd determined that. And the results had been even more blindingly glorious than before, so overwhelming that she still trembled a little at the thought.

She lay in bed and watched him for a while, cozy and comfortable as she considered her options. He was going to run; she knew it. He was going to push her away, repudiate everything that had gone on the night before. He was going to be cool, distant and professional, and if she brought up the subject he'd inform her that it was a mistake or a one-night stand, or a mutually enjoyable interlude that wouldn't be repeated. She knew him too well.

She could take that kind of dismissal. She could curl up inside and weep. She could respond with angry pride. She could die a little and then move on.

Or she could fight for him. She already had a fair idea of what he was going to do next—she could forestall him, strike the first blow and keep him off balance.

Because she wasn't going to let him get away. She'd known yesterday that she was in love with him. She knew this morning that that love was worth fighting for. Even if the object of her passion was her enemy, she was going to win him over. No more self-pity, no more flight, no more fear and loathing. She'd made up her mind, and when Sally MacArthur's mind was made up, it was a formidable thing.

If only Marietta hadn't shown up when she did, Sally could have dealt the opening salvo. She'd climbed out of bed, tiptoed past the sleeping Diamond, and then, on a whim, had gone back and tucked a quilt around him. It was cold in the room and she wanted more than anything to crawl into his lap and pull that quilt around them both.

But that's what he'd expect and be prepared to reject. The only thing she could do was the opposite of what he thought she'd do. Keep him so off balance, he wouldn't realize he was in love with her until it was too late to do anything about it.

She stopped the Alfa on the side of the road, putting it in neutral. Diamond reached over and turned it off, and Sally allowed herself a long-suffering sigh. Apparently, the confrontation wasn't going to wait any longer.

"I'm in a bad mood, Diamond," she warned him as he pulled the key out of the ignition. "My mother affects me that way."

He was momentarily distracted. "Don't you think you were a little hard on her?"

"Yes, I was a little hard on her. Harder than she deserves? I don't think so. Would you like my opinion on your marriage, Diamond?" she inquired sweetly.

"It's ancient history."

"So is my relationship with my mother. She may have fooled you, but she'll never, ever fool me again."

He reached for a cigarette. "You'd be a lot happier if you didn't feel the need to pass judgment on her. She's human just like the rest of us, with human faults and fail-ings.''

''A little too human, if you ask me,'' Sally said, stifling her pang of guilt.

''Look, I don't want to talk about your mother.''

''Fine. Neither do I. As a matter of fact, I have no in-terest in discussing anything but what our next step in find-ing Lucy is.''

''We've got something else to discuss first.''

Sally sighed again. ''I know what you're going to say, Diamond. And I agree with you completely.''

''Last night we— What?'' He stared at her in amaze-ment.

''A mistake,'' she said airily. ''Hormones running amok, fun and all that, but unwise on both our parts. We won't let it happen again, will we?''

For the first time since they'd met she'd been able to stun him into silence. He just looked at her, his mouth open in voiceless protest, and a sudden spark of mischief over-whelmed her. She couldn't resist it, not this once.

She put a hand on his knee, plastering a solicitous ex-pression on her face. ''Oh, no, Diamond, don't tell me I misunderstood! Please, please don't say that you were go-ing to suggest otherwise! That you might have…'' she al-lowed herself a distressed, dramatic pause ''…have fallen in love with me.''

''Good God, no!'' he said with unflattering haste.

''And you don't want to embark on a *relationship,* do you?'' She put heavy emphasis on the word, waiting with a certain naughty satisfaction for his horrified shudder.

But this time, he surprised her. ''No,'' he said in an even voice. ''I'm not the type for relationships.''

''Well,'' she said brightly, ''neither am I. At least, not the kind you're talking about. I like to get engaged, and clearly you're not candidate number seven. You're much too distracting. So let's leave it at that, shall we?''

"No."

"Come on, Diamond." Her control was beginning to fray just a bit at the edges. "We don't need any postmortems, do we?"

"I just wanted to say I'm sorry."

Oh, God, she thought. "For what?" she said. "Not for last night, I hope. There's nothing to apologize for. We were carried away for a moment, but both of us are much too sensible. Besides, there's no need to make a federal case out of it. I'm sure you've had your share of brief flings, as have I. You simply learn to enjoy them in passing."

She was pushing it, she realized. He'd accept a certain amount of sang froid about the whole thing, but professing a great deal of experience was an easily disproven issue. He'd felt her fall apart in his arms, dealt patiently with a shyness that wouldn't have existed if she'd been through it all too often.

"Sally..." He reached out a hand to touch her, and she jerked out of the way. If he put his hands on her, her control would shatter. She'd fling herself on him, begging him to love her, and all her hard work would have been for nothing.

"Don't, James. Please." Her voice had a telltale rawness, one she couldn't hide, but she kept the cool smile plastered on her face.

For a moment, he didn't move. "All right," he said finally. "We'll leave it at that." He reached for the door handle. "For now."

She watched him walk around the front of the car. She hadn't noticed his walk before. A sexy, slouchy kind of stroll that made her think of Richard Gere at his to-hell-with-you best. She watched him, and wondered whether she'd fooled him at all with her cool renunciation. Maybe the best she could hope for was that he didn't know what to think.

The passenger seat was still warm from his body. She

wriggled into it surreptitiously, drinking in the warmth through her pores, then caught him watching her curiously.

"Got an itch?" he inquired, and she suspected he was deliberately goading her.

She refused to rise to the bait. "Just tired," she said. "Do you mind telling me where we're going? Time might be running out for Lucy while we sit here and bicker."

"If Lucy's anything like the rest of the women in her family, I suspect she can take care of herself. I almost feel sorry for the Calderinis."

"What do you mean by that crack? Marietta and I have nothing in common!" Sally was immediately incensed.

"No," Diamond said, turning the car and heading in the opposite direction. "I don't suppose you do. Other than porcelain skin, blue eyes and better looks than are good for you. Of course, she's too skinny and too old, but you both are hell on wheels at lying, and the performance you just put on had to equal hers at the table this morning."

Sally was speechless. Diamond smiled with devastating sweetness. "None of which matters," he continued. "You can just keep spinning your little fantasies, and I'll do my best to see through them. At least now I can see where you got your talent from."

"Damn you, I'm not like my mother. She doesn't love anyone but herself."

"And who do you love, Sally?"

She wasn't going to let it slip. He was goading her on purpose, maybe because his ego couldn't handle that she wasn't pining with love for him. The fact that she was didn't matter—she'd go through torture before she admitted that fact to him.

"My sister and my father and Jenksy," she said flatly. "That's not very many people, and I can't afford to lose one of them while we sit around and talk absurdities. For the last time, Diamond, where the hell are we going?"

"Isn't it obvious, Sally?" he replied, tapping his long fingers on the leather-covered steering wheel. "We're bound for Glory."

Chapter Fourteen

Sally just stared at him. "Glory?" she echoed.

"Glory, California. The Desert Glory Health Spa. Unless you've got a better idea."

"Aren't we grasping at straws?" she demanded.

"That's what following clues is, lady. People rarely send you engraved invitations when they're hiding out. Besides, it's a little more concrete than that. I made a couple of phone calls before I came upstairs and seduced you." James put it that way on purpose, waiting for her reaction.

He saw her hands clenched together for a moment, but she let the provocation ride over her. "I thought your informants didn't have office hours."

"I still know how to find things out when I need it. Desert Glory's a health spa, all right. Guess who owns it? I mean, after you wade through three different dummy corporations to find out who actually pulls the strings."

"The Calderinis?"

"Obviously. And you can imagine what goes on there along with mud baths and saunas."

"Gambling. But aren't they right near the Nevada border? Why would anybody bother?"

"I told you before—the danger adds spice to the games. Besides, you don't have to pay income tax on money you make on these games, and there's no limit." He pushed in the cigarette lighter. "Your sister is probably going through their seven-day beauty make-over right now, while Vinnie waits for the Bho Tsos to arrive."

"The Bozos?" she echoed in astonishment. "Who the hell are the Bozos? Some clown contingent of the Calderini family? Do they run tickle concessions as a sideline?"

"Bho Tsos," James said wearily, spelling the name. "A very ancient Chinese crime family. They're the ones who want the Manchurian falcon, not the Calderinis. Vinnie's just trying to provide it for them as a gesture of good faith. Probably also as a demonstration of his ability to get things done."

"Vinnie's not very capable," Sally muttered. "I don't think he was cut out for organized crime."

"He was born to it."

"So what? I was born to money and social activities, and I always get bored. What I'd really like to do is work for a living."

She still had the power to surprise him. "Then why don't you?" he countered with little sympathy.

There was something about her rueful smile that always got to him. "I've tried. Everybody keeps firing me. I can't even hold a volunteer job for very long. I tend to destroy office machinery. I don't know why, but photocopiers just fall apart at my fingertips. Faxes explode, computers collapse, even telephones experience core meltdown."

"Yeah, I saw what you did to my office in a few short minutes. Broke the window, the coffeepot and the overhead light."

"I did not break the light!" she protested.

"It hasn't worked since you touched it."

"You might consider changing the light bulb!"

"I don't suppose—" James stopped himself, reaching for his cigarettes instead. She had the power to infuriate him faster than anyone he'd ever known. Even his ex-wife hadn't driven him so nuts. Scratch that. His ex-wife hadn't bothered him in the slightest. He hadn't cared enough to be annoyed.

Not that he cared about Sally MacArthur, he had to remind himself. In fact, he needed to remember that he was relieved that she saw things as clearly as he did. That she grasped the futility of any possible relationship between two such disparate human beings. It was typical of the boneheaded way he'd been going about things recently, that instead of gratitude, he felt out and out annoyance that she was taking the events of the night before with such a cavalier attitude. He'd expected at least a few tears. Possibly an attempt at changing his mind, or at least at making him feel like the world's worst heel.

Instead, he felt as though he was the one who'd been seduced and abandoned. She was sitting next to him, a smug little smile on her slightly swollen lips, and the very memory of what she'd done with that mouth last night made him have to shift his position in the bucket seat.

God, he had to get away from her. They were as different as night and day, and even if either of them wanted to pursue their off-kilter attraction, it would be doomed to failure.

He needed to remember who he was and what sort of woman he did best with. The older, comfortable types who didn't expect much but a good meal beforehand and a good time afterward. Women who'd lost their innocence, their illusions years ago, and were glad of it.

Sally MacArthur was still a virgin of the soul. And he had the hideous, terrifying suspicion that despite her cool avowals, she just might fancy herself in love with him. After all, he fulfilled her favorite fantasies, and he knew better than anyone how well she responded in bed.

She wasn't used to having a man, that much was clear. And most women who didn't sleep around usually had to talk themselves into being in love with their bed partner, at least for as long as the relationship lasted. Then it turned quite abruptly to undying hatred when the man couldn't live up to her impossible expectations. It was a good thing he knew he was beaten before he even tried. Or he might find himself trying to be the man she wanted.

He needed to reunite Sally with her long-lost sister and get the hell away from her, back to the sleazy corridors and mean streets where he felt at home. He didn't belong out in the daylight, in fresh air and sunshine. He didn't belong with a twenty-eight-year-old debutante with a crush on him. And he certainly didn't belong in a life in which he hadn't had a decent drink in three days and was considering cutting back on his cigarettes. She was unmanning him, damn it, and the sooner he got away from her, the better. Because if he waited too long, he wouldn't be able to leave.

James pushed the lighter in for another cigarette; Sally reached over and yanked it out. "My mother may not be allergic to cigarette smoke, but I am," she said pointedly.

"You've been breathing in my secondhand smoke for days now, and I haven't even heard a sniffle." He pushed the lighter in again.

She yanked it out. "If you don't have any consideration for your own lungs, at least think about mine."

He pushed the lighter in. "You'll survive. I've given up Scotch for you, lady. The cigarettes stay."

She stared at him in amazement, and he recognized that telltale fatuous gaze in her blue blue eyes. "You've given up drinking for me?" she echoed in a soft voice.

"Don't get all gooey on me. I figured I couldn't stand the arguments, and you're bad enough when I don't have a headache. If I had to deal with you and a hangover at the same time, I'd probably either slit your throat or mine."

"James…"

"The moment I dump you, I'm getting the biggest, most expensive bottle of Scotch I can buy to celebrate," he warned her.

It didn't do any good. She still looked like a kid who'd

won the prize at the local fair, all shiny eyed and smiling. He never should have said anything, James thought morosely. Maybe the best thing he could do was stop at the next store and buy a bottle, just to convince her that she couldn't believe a word he said.

Problem was, he really didn't want the bottle. And the cigarettes were starting to taste funky, too. The lady was going to reform him and then go on her merry way, and he'd have no happy vices to fall back on.

"There's a simple solution to that," Sally said in a cheerful voice.

"Oh, yeah? What's that?" he grumbled, eyeing the road, forgetting about his need for a cigarette for the time being.

"I simply won't let you dump me."

"That's supposed to cheer me up?" he countered. "An albatross around my neck?" He reached for the lighter one more time.

She put her hand out to stop him, and instead, he grabbed her wrist, forcibly pulling her back. Her cheerful expression vanished, but what lay behind it was even more unsettling. "Are you going to hurt me, Diamond?"

He didn't release her. "I don't hurt women," he said.

"Then let me go."

Of course, he had to. He felt foolish, driving down the highway, his hand wrapped around her slender wrist like a manacle.

He dropped her hand and reached for the cigarette lighter. She was faster than he was, yanking it out of the socket and throwing it out her open window.

He slammed the car to a halt, nearly hurtling her toward the windshield. "What the hell do you think you're doing?" he demanded, enraged.

"Throwing out my cigarette lighter. I don't have any use for the thing, and since my car is for nonsmokers, I don't see any reason to keep it."

"You ever think about forest fires?"

"Not in the middle of the rainy spell."

"I can stop at the next gas station and get matches."

"Go right ahead," Sally said affably. "At least I won't be an enabler."

"Oh, God, psychobabble garbage on top of everything else," James moaned. "What in heaven's name did I do to deserve a pest like you?"

"Just lucky, I guess," Sally said with unimpaired good cheer, keeping her hands folded in her lap.

She hadn't touched him since this morning. He'd been waiting for it, expecting it, bracing himself for it, but she'd kept her hands to herself. No soft caresses, no gentle touches, no accidental brushing of her hand against him.

He couldn't stand it any longer.

Reaching out, he caught her stubborn chin in his hand, turning her face to his. "You think you're pretty funny, don't you?" he grumbled, knowing that his fingers were caressing the smooth line of her jaw, unable to stop them.

He expected her eyes to be bright with triumph. Instead, they were vulnerable, something she was doing her best to hide. "We'll play this any way you want to, Diamond," she said in a quiet little voice.

He couldn't resist. He knew it was absolute madness on his part, but he couldn't stop himself. He leaned forward, across the seat, and kissed her, just a light feathering of his lips across hers, a momentary clinging of his mouth to hers. And then he pulled back, releasing her, and started the car once more.

"Get in the way of me and my cigarettes again," he warned in his calmest voice, "and I'll take up cigars."

James didn't dare glance at her again as he pulled back onto the highway. If he did, he might pull off at the nearest exit and head straight for a motel. The only way he was going to survive was to keep his hands off her. He'd managed for a full three hours since waking up—maybe next time, he could stretch it to six hours. But he didn't know how he was going to make it through the upcoming night.

GLORY, CALIFORNIA, was a small tourist town in the midst of the California desert. Up until the end of the self-absorbed seventies, it had been nothing but a gas station and a mom-and-pop store for the outlying residents. With the advent of the Desert Glory Health Spa, business had boomed. The town was filled with trendy little shops—New Age bookstores, basket shops, health-food restaurants and the like. Sally glanced around her as they drove through, shuddering at the vestiges of California yuppiedom. It was just after five in the afternoon, and Diamond had driven like a demon through the day, stopping long enough for a take-out meal packaged in polystyrene containers.

She'd lectured him for a solid half hour until he turned on the radio full blast. Since he'd found an oldies station with a preference for rhythm and blues, she could hardly complain, and she'd sat back and counted his cigarettes, all the time listening to her body remember the previous night.

She was going to have to do something about birth control, she realized, and probably sooner rather than later. Even if Diamond seemed determined to keep his distance, he still couldn't stop himself from kissing her. She'd kept to her side of the car, curled up and sleepy, but she'd been completely aware of the number of times he'd glanced over at her, his gaze drawn as if he couldn't help himself. She might be sleeping alone tonight. But she doubted it.

The Desert Glory Health Spa was an oasised paradise in the midst of the desert. *The water bills alone must be astronomical,* Sally thought as Diamond pulled up under the canopied front entrance. Maybe self-absorbed health fanatics could support an operation like this. But it was far more likely the Calderini gambling money underwrote the whole thing.

"How are we going to handle this?" she said, finally

breaking the silence that had filled the car, and noting with disapproval that Diamond was lighting his fifth cigarette of the afternoon. "Don't tell me to stay in the car, either, because you should know by now, I'm not going to do any such thing. And are you sure we should just be driving up bold as brass? I mean, think about what happened at Lake Judgment. You may enjoy pain, but I don't find any great pleasure in patching you up."

He glanced at her and she was startled to see the alert brightness in his eyes, the faint twist of a smile at his mobile mouth. "Now I would have thought that right now there'd be nothing you'd like better than having someone beat the hell out of me again."

"Now that you mention it…"

"Forget it. And no, you're not going to wait in the car. You're getting your big chance, kid. We're going in undercover."

Her irritation with him vanished as visions of television cop shows danced in her head. "Undercover?" she echoed in delight.

"Yup. Like Philip Marlowe in *The Big Sleep,* when he first goes to the antique bookstore."

"You mean you're going to pretend to be gay?" she asked, amused at the notion.

"Don't be so literal. We're a married couple. Two professionals looking to improve our life-style. We're here for the Fast-Track Weekend Package. That should be more than enough time to find out where your sister is."

"If it isn't?"

He glanced over at her, and Sally could feel the heat in his eyes. "It will be."

She followed him into the fern-encrusted lobby like a dutiful wife, glancing around her with ill-disguised curiosity. Lucy was there—she knew it with a sixth sense that seldom appeared but was always infallible. She tugged at Diamond's sleeve, but he ignored her, and she realized with amazement that he was someone else entirely. His walk, the set of his shoulders, even his clothes looked different. He looked anonymous, like the thousands of young urban professionals who cluttered the streets of San Francisco at lunch time, moving from bank or law office or stock brokerage to the latest trendy restaurant.

There was no way she could even come close. She stumbled, clumsy, and he reached out and caught her arm, apparently aware of her even as he seemed to ignore her.

The woman behind the vast, teak desk looked like every California blonde who'd ever intimidated Sally. She looked like a Barbie doll—giant smile, perfect teeth, mile-long legs and rippling muscles. She rose as they approached, and Sally watched with ill-disguised fury as the woman took in Diamond's attributes with obvious appreciation, then glanced over and dismissed his dowdy little "wife" as someone of no account.

"Mr. and Mrs. Chandler?" she greeted them, her voice as breathless and phony as the rest of her.

"Please. Raymond and Velma," Diamond said with an easy smirk that reminded Sally of Tom Cruise. And then the names registered. Raymond Chandler, creator of the magnificent Philip Marlowe. And Velma, one of Chandler's quintessential good/bad girls. Sally was going to marry this man if it was the last thing she ever did.

"I see you're here for the Fast-Track Weekend. You look like you're in superb shape. I can't imagine you need any toning," the woman purred.

"Everyone can do with a little refresher," Diamond murmured, eating this up. Reaching behind him, he pulled Sally forward, his arm around her waist in a gesture that was meant to look affectionate. It felt like a stranglehold. "And this is my wife. I'm sure you can do something for her."

"Of course. I recommend the modified fasting and intensive conditioning program. We can at least make a good start at getting rid of those extra twenty pounds she's carrying around.''

Only the pressure of Diamond's arm kept Sally from lunging at the smug creature. "I don't need to lose twenty pounds," Sally said between clenched teeth.

"You're right, thirty would be better. After all, you can't be too thin or too rich, isn't that right?" The blonde let out a high-pitched trill of laughter, and Diamond joined in, a well-bred neigh of a laugh that was perfectly in character. His fingers digging into Sally's waist prompted Sally's own less-than-enthusiastic chuckle.

"I wouldn't want her too skinny," Diamond said in an unctuous voice.

"I wouldn't worry about that, Ray," the Barbie-clone murmured, reaching out and touching his arm with a confiding gesture. "It'll take a lot more than Desert Glory's Fast-Track Weekend to do that." She moved back to the desk, every muscle rippling beneath her skintight black unitard. "Let's see—the two of you are down for one bedroom. Are you certain you wouldn't be happier with two singles? It's always difficult in cases like these, where one partner fasts and the other doesn't."

Diamond patted Sally's clenched fist. "Velma and I couldn't stand to be parted. We haven't been married that long, have we, darling?" There was a devilish light of merriment in his eyes as he looked down at her.

"Not nearly long enough, darling," she responded, reaching her arm around his neck, yanking him down and kissing him hungrily.

She was calling his bluff. His response astonished her. Instead of holding still for her half-playful assault, he simply hauled her into his arms and kissed her back, plastering her body against his aroused one.

The hell with Barbie, Sally thought dizzily, wondering whether she could get away with wrapping her legs around his waist. When he finally broke the kiss, Diamond's expression was dazed. Hers was probably comatose. "One room, one bed," he murmured, still staring down at her.

Barbie sniffed. "Certainly. Though we do recommend that our clients refrain from as much...marital contact as possible during their stay with us. They need to concentrate on their own fitness, be totally centered on strength and wellness. Not, if you'll pardon the expression, on sex. You do understand?"

The woman struck Sally as someone already fixated on sex, particularly with her ersatz husband. "What are you going to do, run a bed check every few hours?" she inquired sweetly.

Barbie managed a strained smile. "As I said, it's just a recommendation. What you do in the privacy of your room is, of course, your business. However, we do have certain rules here at the spa." She waited while they disentangled themselves.

"Such as?"

Barbie held out a golden basket. "No drugs, prescription or otherwise. No alcohol. Drop any pills in here. They'll be returned to you when you leave. Also your car keys."

"Why?" For a moment, the jovial yuppie attitude slipped, and Diamond sounded like his old, suspicious self.

"Why, so the valet can park it," Barbie replied, pushing a button on the desk. She waited while Diamond dropped the keys and his bottle of ibuprofen into the basket, and then she rattled it slightly. "One more thing, Ray."

"Yes?"

"We need your cigarettes."

Sally quickly turned her laughter into a choking sound. Diamond glared at her before turning his attention to Barbie. "Why?"

"Isn't it obvious? We maintain a smoke-free environment—we're very careful about that. And if you're serious about toning and strengthening your body, you must know that cigarettes are the worst thing you can do. Your body is a temple. Smoking is blasphemy.''

"Oh, God," Diamond murmured. "Two of you."

"The cigarettes, Ray?" Barbie was sounding more like a drill sergeant at this point. Diamond glared at her.

"And if I refuse?"

"Then I'm afraid we'll have to cancel your weekend. Regretfully, of course." She smiled at him, wetting her pink lips with her pink tongue. "And I was looking forward to putting you through your paces."

I bet you were, sister, Sally thought, tempted to walk out. And then she remembered why they were there. And who else was there, somewhere in the rambling building.

She reached over, plucked the crumpled pack of cigarettes from Diamond's pocket and dropped it into the basket. "He's been wanting to quit," she said in a dulcet voice.

Barbie even managed a trace of warmth for her. "Then that's settled. I've rung for someone to show you to your rooms. You'll need a chance to settle in before you get started on your program. Dinner's served from six-thirty on. Your diet sheets will already be in place."

"Will you be at dinner?" Diamond inquired.

"Oh, you can count on it," Barbie said. "I'm going to take you on as my personal project."

"I'm looking forward to it," Diamond murmured.

"I wouldn't miss it," Sally said with a growl.

"We're going to have lots of fun surprises for you two," Barbie promised them.

And the first trickles of uneasiness danced down Sally's spine.

Chapter Fifteen

"God, I hate good taste," Diamond muttered when the door finally closed on their suite.

"So I noticed. This is a far cry from your office," Sally said, glancing around her. Much as she wanted to irritate him, she found herself in reluctant agreement with him. The place was so tasteful, it was gaudy, from the southwestern decor, the huge king-size bed, the thick carpeting and the gold fixtures in the bathroom. Everything was very new, very expensive, very soulless, and Sally started to feel nostalgic for the Sleep-Suite Motel, insect livestock, *The Brady Bunch* and all.

"At least there's one good point—no television," Diamond said, dropping down onto the bed.

"I happen to like television."

"That's probably responsible for what ails you." He reached into his pocket, an automatic gesture, seeking cigarettes.

"Nothing ails me."

"There are times, lady, when your grasp of reality is not that strong. I imagine that comes from too many episodes of *Magnum, P.I.*"

"Wrong. It comes from too many old movies. Speaking of which, Raymond Chandler, thank you."

Diamond actually looked embarrassed. "It was spur of the moment. I couldn't think of anything else."

"All my life I've wanted to be called Velma," Sally said with a blissful sigh.

"Now your life is complete." He reached again for the cigarettes, then pulled his hand away in disgust.

"Any particular reason why you insisted on sharing a room?" she asked. "Apart from your insatiable lust for my body." The lightly ironic tone she aimed for failed completely. Probably because of the stormy expression in Diamond's dark eyes.

"Don't let that Barbie doll fool you, kid. This is Calderini turf beneath the fern-bar decor. You saw what they did to me at Lake Judgment. They would be only too happy to carry that one step further if they had the opportunity. We're safer sticking together. We just need to find out whether your sister's here or not, and then we're gone. I don't know—"

"She's here."

He sat up. "You saw her?"

"No. I just know she's here. Instinct, a sixth sense, whatever you want to call it. She's here."

"I like you better as Velma than Shirley MacLaine," he drawled.

"She's here, Diamond. And I'm not leaving until she goes with me."

"If you say so." He came off the bed in one restless move, pacing around the spacious room. He stopped by the tiny refrigerator. "At least there's a bar."

"I thought you'd given up drinking."

"That was before I had to give up cigarettes. I can't do both. If I'm going to make it through the night with clear lungs I'm going to have to make do with Scotch."

"Don't, Diamond. Please."

"Temperance songs, Sally?"

She moved toward him, putting one hand on his arm. "Please, Diamond," she said again.

He shook it off. "My drinking is my own business, lady. All the pleases in the world aren't going to stop me."

She stepped back, admitting defeat. After all, there was a difference between a heavy drinker and an alcoholic. She'd certainly seen him drink a great deal, but he never seemed to show it. And he was probably right. The only person who could make him stop was himself. "All right, get me a diet Coke while you're at it," she said, dropping into the tasteful chair by the full-length windows.

For a long moment, he didn't move, and she could see the battle he was waging within himself, recognize it by the tension in his shoulders, the grim set of his mouth. "Diet Coke isn't a bad idea," he said finally. "Maybe I'll have the Scotch later." And he opened the refrigerator door.

She'd heard enough of his spectacular cursing in the past that his current performance shouldn't have surprised her. The lack of cigarettes must have prompted new inventiveness, however, for the variety and color of his swearing startled even her.

"What's wrong?" she asked when he finally stopped ranting.

"We've got tomato juice, carrot juice, celery juice, and salt-free mineral water. Period."

"No diet Coke?" Sally asked, suddenly galvanized.

"No diet Coke."

She didn't waste time cursing. She headed straight for the phone, regretting the fact that she didn't know Barbie's real name and couldn't very well ask for her by appearance. A few moments later, she hung up, staring at Diamond with a tragic expression.

"It's worse than we thought, James."

"Don't tell me...." he begged.

"No alcohol, no artificial sweeteners," she said. "And no caffeine." Her voice broke slightly on the last.

"No caffeine? As in no coffee?"

Sally swallowed. "That's what the man said." For the first time, she realized how very dangerous Diamond could be. The expression on his face was cold, ruthless, frightening.

"We're finding your sister tonight," he said in a tight voice. "I can do without alcohol. I can even do without the cigarettes. But when they take away my coffee, they're in real trouble. What time is it?"

"Six-fifteen."

"We're going in to dinner promptly at six-thirty. We'll see what our hostess has in mind for us, and then I want you to distract her while I case the joint."

"I think you'd have an easier time distracting her," Sally pointed out with a certain amount of asperity.

Diamond's smile wiped the bleak rage from his face. "You noticed that, did you? Jealous?"

"Of a Barbie doll? Don't be ridiculous. Besides, there's absolutely nothing to be jealous of. I wouldn't make the mistake of assuming there was anything between us, apart from an ill-advised night of sex." She shrugged. "I have no claim on you. If you want to see if you can seduce my sister's whereabouts from Barbie, go right ahead."

His quiet chuckle made Sally want to smack him. "I don't think I've ever managed to seduce anything out of anybody, much as the idea appeals to me. Besides, I doubt Barbie knows anything about your sister. This place is highly segregated—the spa part is completely legit."

"I wouldn't underestimate her if I were you, Diamond. She looks like one tough cookie. God, I'm hungry." Sally quickly shifted gears. "I hope their food is better than their choice of beverages. At least, they'll have fresh fruits and vegetables. After three days on the road with you, experiencing the joys of fast-food and sleazy diners, I feel like I'm about to get scurvy."

"I think scurvy's the disease where your tongue swells up and you can't talk," Diamond said. "If only fate would be so kind."

"Come on, Diamond. Let's go strap on the feed bags," Sally said, holding out her arm in a reluctant truce.

He took it, and once again she saw the light in his eyes, the one that told her he was enjoying himself, the lies, the danger, the subterfuge. "Something tells me we aren't due for steak and potatoes."

"Even a lettuce leaf would look good to me now."

Barbie had given them a brief tour on the way to their room, and Diamond, with his excellent sense of direction, led Sally to the dining room, pulling her back from the several wrong turns she would have made.

The place was packed with a disparate group of people. There were healthy, glowing yuppie couples, plump, determined looking matrons, older, birdlike people who looked as though they ate twigs and branches to survive and might very well burst into warbles at the drop of a hat. These healthy souls were being waited on by people who looked like gym instructors. Sleek, tanned, blond and gorgeous, they moved through the room on perfectly coordinated muscles, carrying trays that looked ominously light.

All those people and waiters were congregated on the main floor of the room. On the right side of the dining area, on a raised platform, sat a very different group of people. The women wore spangles, and each one had a larger bra size than all the health nuts in the rest of the room put together. They were all blond, young and not very bright looking. Sally doubted there was a wedding ring among the lot. The men were older, balding, plump and powerful looking. Their waiters wore tuxedos, and Sally was willing to bet their vegetable-juice cocktails came spiked with a large amount of vodka.

"Ray and Velma?" The toothy jock who served as the spa-side maître d' greeted them. "Glad to have you here. We've got your menu already set up. Just walk this way." He headed toward a small table in the corner of the room, and his gait was a combination mince and swagger.

"I'd like to see you walk that way," Sally muttered to Diamond in an undertone.

"Hell, I'd like to see *you*," he countered.

The waiter who brought their dinners could have been a clone of the maître d', or Barbie's identical, male twin. He flashed a thousand large, white teeth at them as he presented their plates with a flourish. Sally looked at them both and smirked.

Diamond had a plate piled high with boneless chicken breasts, wild rice, fresh asparagus, avocado slices and a huge golden corn muffin. She had a plate with three curly slices of carrot, five green beans arranged like a star, two symmetrical pieces of brown wafer, and pile of something that looked like fish food.

"At least I get an appetizer," she said cheerfully.

She didn't like Diamond's smug expression. "No, you don't," he said, digging into his overloaded plate with gusto.

"What do you mean by that?"

"Look at the menu card, kid. That's the sum total of your dinner."

She stared down at the meager plate in dismay bordering on despair. "No!" she said in real anguish.

"Yes."

"You've got to give me some of yours," she said urgently. "This isn't enough to keep a bird alive. I haven't eaten a thing since you insisted we stop at that disgusting fast-food place, and I'm starving. Starving, do you hear?"

"Sorry. But you know the rules are very strict and you've been put on a modified fast. You want to lose those twenty pounds, don't you?"

"I want to lose you, and fast," she snarled. "I don't need to lose twenty pounds. Ten, maybe..." she admitted with belated honesty, thinking of her beaded dress.

"Well, much as I hate to admit it," Diamond said, chewing thoughtfully on a tender-looking piece of chicken, "I happen to think you're just right."

Her temper vanished in sudden astonishment. "You do?"

"I'd go even further than that," he said, his voice low and his gaze warm. "I think you're perfect."

"Perfect? Me?" Her voice rose in a little squeak of surprise.

He leaned back. "Your body, that is," he drawled. "Your behavior leaves a lot to be desired."

"Go to hell," she said amiably, reaching across the table for an asparagus spear.

He slapped her hand and she dropped the asparagus, scowling at him. "Much as I would love to see how you eat asparagus, I think you'd better behave yourself. Here comes our hostess."

The Barbie clone was weaving her way through the tables, a toothy smile on her face. She'd changed from the spandex she'd been wearing to something even tighter, and her tanned, freckled chest was obviously supposed to be a come-on. Sally wondered whether Diamond had been teasing her. Whether he could really prefer her soft curves to all that toned, rippling muscle. Illogical as it seemed, she believed him. Maybe just because she wanted to.

"You haven't eaten anything, Velma," Barbie cooed. She sank down into one of the empty chairs. "Aren't you hungry? I can have your plate taken if you've decided to go, if you'll pardon the expression, whole hog."

Lucy, Sally thought. *If I attack this woman, I'll ruin all chances of finding Lucy.* She plastered a sickly sweet smile on her face and picked up one crisp carrot curl. "It just looked so beautiful, I hated to wreck the arrangement."

"Our chef prides himself on the presentation. And what about you, Ray? Are you enjoying your dinner?"

Diamond, the pig, had eaten every single morsel on his plate, leaving absolutely nothing for her. Sally started in on the green beans, crunching disconsolately.

Their waiter came up, placing a meaty hand on Barbie's shoulder. "Hey, Barbie," he said. "The boss wants to see you, pronto."

"Duty calls. I'll be right back." She wove her way through the tables with muscular grace, as Diamond and Sally met each other's gaze.

"Don't laugh," she warned him. "If you start, I won't be able to stop."

"Barbie," Diamond said, shaking his head. "Who'd have believed it? I wonder what the boss wanted to talk to her about. And who the boss is?"

"You think they know we're here?"

"Most likely. It doesn't do to underestimate your adversary. The Calderinis do very well for themselves, and they didn't get to their position of power without being on top of things. You finished?"

Sally looked down at her empty plate. There was a tiny flake of fish food left and she scarfed it up with a weary sigh. "I'd say so. They're not giving us dessert, are they?"

"Don't count on it." He rose and pulled her chair out for her, the two of them moving through the crowded room.

The hall was deserted when they stepped outside the dining room. The other inmates had learned to stretch their meager rations. "God, I'm hungry," Sally moaned piteously. "All right, Diamond, what do we do next?"

"Here." He pulled one of the white damask napkins from out of his suit jacket and handed it to her with a flourish.

She took it, opening it with shaking hands to discover the slightly crumbling corn muffin. "Diamond," she said,

"I love you." And she shoved the whole thing into her mouth.

"That's what they all say," he drawled. "If I'd known your price was corn muffins, I would have done something about it days ago."

She swallowed convulsively. "Diamond," she said, her voice low and husky, as she lifted her hands to his chest.

He caught them before they could travel upward. "Don't do it."

"Don't do what?"

"Don't look at me like that, don't touch me, don't kiss me." His fingers tightened reflexively around hers. "If you do, I'm going to carry you back to that disgustingly tasteful bedroom and we're not going to leave until tomorrow morning. We need to find your sister."

She didn't move. "I know that," she said, her fingers caught in his, her heart caught in his.

"There you are!" Barbie breezed by. "I have to check in some new guests, and then we can get you started on your program, Velma. Just a few moderate aerobics, a few laps, just so we can judge how out of shape you really are. Nothing too overwhelming."

The corn muffin hadn't gone far in assuaging Sally's hunger. Diamond's touch had only fanned the flames higher. "Fine," she said with a tight smile.

"After I get Velma started, we can go over your program, Ray," Barbie added over her shoulder as she continued down the hallway at a breakneck pace. "I'll come to your room."

"Over my dead body," Sally muttered.

Diamond had moved away, out of temptation's reach, releasing her hands. "I guess whatever the boss wanted didn't have anything to do with us."

"I guess not," Sally said.

"We have a choice. We follow Barbie and see what she's doing. Or we go back to the room."

Back to the room, Sally's heart cried. "Follow Barbie," her mouth said.

"Good girl. Maybe Vinnie and Lucy have just arrived." He started down the hallway.

"Nope. They're already here," Sally insisted, following him. "And we're going to find her."

They'd just reached the front lobby when Diamond's arm shot out across Sally's chest, blocking her progress. "Well, I'll be damned," he muttered, backing her behind a convenient potted plant.

"Probably." She tried to crane her neck around his larger, obstructing body. "What is it?"

"Bozos," he said flatly, letting her peek.

It was a very large contingent of Chinese. A dozen or so businessmen dressed in silk suits, all looking very disgruntled. They were accompanied by a similar number of women, but unlike their American counterparts, these gentlemen had clearly brought their wives, not their mistresses. The women were regal, elegant and of a certain age not usually associated with chorus girls or bimbos. There must have been two dozen in all, and they were all glaring at the unintimidated Barbie.

"I'm sorry," she said, very loudly, as if speaking to a convention of the hearing impaired. "But this is a smoke-free resort. If any of you smoke, you'll have to leave your cigarettes and lighters here."

No one moved. *High noon at the health spa,* Sally thought irreverently. The future of East-West criminal relations lay in Barbie's hands, and she was about to blow it.

Then one man, a bit older, a bit shorter than the rest, said something in Chinese. With sullen grace, they all moved forward, dumping gold and silver cigarette cases into the little basket.

It was overflowing by the time the last Bozo dropped her emerald-encrusted case on top of the others. She looked like the Dragon Lady, taller than the others, and frankly contemptuous. She ran her dark eyes over Barbie's sturdy frame, said something in a musical Chinese voice that was clearly a great insult, and then stepped back as the other women nodded and laughed.

"These will be returned to you when you leave," Barbie continued at a shout. "In the meantime, you'll be shown to your rooms while we set up a diet and exercise program for you all."

The small man shook his head. "No diet, no exercise. We're here for business, not Western foolishness."

Barbie blinked her huge black eyes that were completely devoid of intelligence. "I'll have to discuss this with my boss...."

"Do that. In the meantime, show us to our rooms and send champagne to each of my people. Dom Perignon '73."

"We don't have champagne," Barbie shouted helplessly. "This is a health spa, not a resort. I think you've made a mistake—"

"I think *you* have made the mistake," the man said in a quiet, stern voice that made the exuberant Barbie turn pale beneath her perfect tan. He clicked his fingers at his assembled entourage and started for the door.

"Mr. Li!" An urgent new voice entered the fray as someone appeared from a doorway at the opposite end of the room. "Forgive my failure to be here to greet you. Welcome to Desert Glory." An elegantly dressed young man, suavely handsome and urbane, moved across the room. Vincenzo Calderini, Vinnie the Viper, smooth and charming as always. Sally slunk backward, hiding behind the potted plant, hoping he wouldn't glance toward the darkened hallway.

Mr. Li was not appeased. "Your employee apparently knew nothing of our arrival."

"She was only just informed, and she was given no details. That's the beauty of Desert Glory, Mr. Li. We keep everything separate. The fewer people who grasp the entire concept, the safer we are. Isn't that right, Barbie?''

Barbie blinked. ''Yes, sir,'' she said automatically, obviously not knowing what he was talking about.

''If you and your people would follow me, I'll do my best to see that you're made comfortable. We've reserved the best rooms, the finest chefs have been flown in...''

The elegant woman said something in a low hiss. Mr. Li grimaced. ''My wife wishes to know about our cigarettes.''

Vinnie looked sorrowful. ''I'm afraid Barbie's right about that. We really can't allow smoking. This is ostensibly a health spa, and cigarette smoke is too difficult to disguise. I thought that was made clear when this meeting was set up.''

Mr. Li simply nodded, neither agreeing nor disagreeing, and Vincenzo charged onward. ''I understand your displeasure. Even my father has to do without his customary cigars when we hold meetings out here, but the inconvenience is more than compensated by the safety and security of our surroundings. We have the finest in athletic equipment, running tracks, exercise machines—''

''We are not here to exercise. We are here for the falcon.''

''Of course. And to sign an agreement.''

Mr. Li's contempt was obvious. ''And to sign an agreement. Assuming your required gesture of good faith is intact. Where is the falcon?''

Vinnie smiled, that easy smile that meant his back was against the wall. ''When my father arrives. At our meeting, tomorrow. In the meantime, let me show you what the finest in American hospitality can mean.''

For a moment, Mr Li didn't move. One of the other gentlemen murmured something, something the Dragon Lady didn't like. She overrode him, her clear strong voice echoing in the cavernous room, and Mr. Li nodded. "You have until tomorrow, Mr. Calderini."

Vinnie smiled his most engaging smile. "I knew you'd be reasonable. This way." He gestured toward the far hallway.

Barbie scurried after them, a worried expression on her face. It wasn't until the sound of footsteps died away that Diamond turned to face Sally.

"Vinnie the Viper?"

"In the flesh. But I wonder where Lucy is," she said, trying not to let her worry overwhelm her. Vinnie looked normal, not like a man in the midst of domestic turmoil. Lucy must still be safe.

"That's what we have to find out. And the sooner, the better. One thing's obvious—he knows he doesn't have the right falcon. If he did, he'd hand it over. The Bho Tsos are already in bad moods, and the longer they go without their cigarettes, the madder they're going to be. Speaking of which..." He started across the deserted reception room, heading straight for the overflowing basket of confiscated cigarette cases.

"Diamond!" Sally said, aghast. "How low can you sink?"

"Pretty low," he admitted, opening the jeweled case. "But not low enough to smoke Chinese cigarettes." In disgust, he dropped the case back into the basket, glancing back toward her with a rueful shrug. And then his expression froze.

"What are you looking like that for?" she asked, irritated.

He glanced away from her toward the front door. It was only a few feet away from him, and outside, under the lights, someone had left a car idling.

It was then that she heard the heavy breathing behind her, and knew their time had suddenly run out. Someone was behind her, someone who meant her no good. Diamond was obviously going to make a run for it, leaving her to get out of this mess any way she could, and she wondered whether she could reach the car when he did and get the hell out of there with him.

But she couldn't leave Lucy behind. She didn't turn around to face the threat behind her. She didn't have to. "Get out of here, Diamond," she said across the room in a clear, calm voice.

He was poised to run. Suddenly the tension drained his body. "I can't, Sally."

"Smart move," said the person behind Sally, one she'd heard before, maybe in a nightmare. "You might have gotten away, but I would have been plenty irritated. And I might have taken it out on the little lady, and then everyone would be mad at me. Turn around, Miss MacArthur."

Sally turned. "Hullo, Alf."

The man chuckled evilly. The gun in his hand was much larger than the one Diamond kept in his shoulder holster, and he looked like a man who knew how to use it. "I thought we'd be seeing you sooner or later. Your friend didn't learn his lesson too well. Guess we'll have to repeat it. Maybe a little harder this time."

"You hurt him," Sally said in a fierce voice, "and I'll... I'll..."

Diamond came up behind her, sliding his arm around her waist. "Don't mess with her, Alf. She's dangerous."

"Yeah, sure. I think you two need a place to cool off. Vinnie's busy right now—I can't tell him you two showed up. Maybe we'll just put you in storage for the time being."

Diamond's hand was moving behind her back. Sally had the truly horrid suspicion that he was reaching for his gun, and she wished she could simply warn him not to. But Alf was watching them too closely, and then it happened so fast, she couldn't even scream.

Diamond shoved her hard, away from him, crashing her against the wall. There was a blinding flash of light, a muffled pop as her head banged against the bleached oak trim. Once more, she heard Diamond's spectacular cursing, and then everything went dark as a welter of pain closed around her head.

Chapter Sixteen

James was a tangled mass of fury and panic. Not three feet away from him lay Sally's still body, and while he thought he could hear fairly regular breathing, he wasn't sure how badly she was hurt. The room Alf and his buddies had dumped them into was some sort of storage room, and Alf wasn't the type to turn on the overhead light once he locked someone in.

He'd certainly done a thorough job of tying James up. No matter how he struggled, he was bound fast to the straight-backed chair. All he could do was sit there and tell himself Sally was breathing as he worked in vain at ropes that held him.

He didn't know whether the low moan that emitted from her was any improvement. "Sally," he hissed in the darkness. "Are you all right? Sally?"

Nothing but silence answered him, and the dim shape on the floor didn't move. "Sally," he tried again, his voice more insistent, bordering on panic. "Are you okay? Speak to me, Sally."

And then miraculously, out of the darkness came a small, grouchy voice. "No, I am not okay. Did you shoot me?"

Relief washed over him. "Of course not."

"Well, don't tell me you haven't been tempted." She

still wasn't moving, but her faint voice was growing infinitesimally stronger. "What the hell happened to me?"

"Alf."

"Alf?" she echoed. "The last thing I remember was you shoving me against the wall while you played shoot-out with the boys." He could hear her moving slightly, possibly rolling over.

"Yeah, well, you were momentarily stunned. You started to get up, and then Alf knocked you out."

"But I don't understand why. I would have thought he'd be much too busy dealing with you to bother with any trouble I might cause."

"That's the way he dealt with me. The moment he had his hands on you, there wasn't a thing I could do."

She considered that in silence for a moment, then he could hear her moving again, struggling to change her position on the floor. "You mean you gave up? Rather than let him hurt me?"

"Something like that." James hated to admit it. He knew she was going to take an admission like that and run with it, jump to all sorts of conclusions. And she was going to be right about every conclusion she jumped to.

But she made no comment. Instead, she asked another question. "Why didn't you run for it when you saw Alf come up behind me? You could have made it. I can't imagine he would have done me that much harm."

"Maybe not. The Calderinis aren't known for their brutality, but this deal with the Bho Tsos is a major step for them. People tend to act impulsively when their livelihood is threatened, and I couldn't count on Alf's restraint."

"Hmm," said Sally, sounding unimpressed. "But wouldn't it have been better to take the chance? That way, you would have been free to rescue me and Lucy."

"Or free to take off and leave you to your own devices. The thought did cross my mind, you know."

"I know," she said, her voice stronger. "But the point

is, you didn't run. You didn't choose either the sensible or the selfish way out. And do you know what that means?''

"I have a horrible feeling I'm about to find out," he said in a wary voice.

"You love me," she said.

"I was afraid you were going to say that."

"You do. You can be as cynical as you want, but it wasn't professional ethics or chivalry that kept you here. You're in love with me, and you just don't want to admit it." She sounded smug, triumphant and almost supremely happy, and James didn't want to burst her bubble. There was a very good chance they weren't going to make it through the next twenty-four hours. The Calderinis were being completely unpredictable, and he had to make things up as he went along.

It wouldn't do her any harm to let her believe what she wanted to believe for a while. It might conceivably make her more malleable, though deep in his heart of hearts, James doubted that anything would accomplish that miracle. At least it would keep her more cheerful and optimistic while he figured out a way to get them out of there. Once they were safe, he'd set her straight. And set himself straight in the bargain.

"Aren't you going to say anything?" Sally demanded. "Aren't you going to tell me I'm crazy? Or even better, admit that I'm right? Why are you just sitting there?"

"I'm just sitting here, lady, because I happen to be tied up," he shot back, relieved not to have to answer her demand. He didn't want to have to comment on her ridiculous assumption. "It wouldn't do any harm if you wanted to come over and untie me."

"Oh, Diamond," she said in a guilty, love-filled voice that tore at his gut. Then she must have half crawled, half flown across the space that divided them, for she was flinging her arms around him and pressing her head against his stomach.

He put up with it in silence for a moment only because there was something unbelievably wonderful about being hugged by Sally MacArthur. And then he drawled, "Not that this isn't real nice, but I'd like to do something about getting us out of here. I can't while you're draped across my lap."

"I don't know, Diamond. I might die happy like this."

"I'd rather live."

She detached herself with a pragmatic sigh. "I guess I would, too." Feeling her way, she crawled around behind him and began busying herself with Alf's fiendish knots. "When did you first realize you loved me?" she asked in a conversational tone.

"January 1999," James said, hoping to prick her bubble just slightly by naming an impossible date.

Wrong answer. "I can wait," she said cheerfully. "Do we get to sleep together until then?"

"Damn it, Sally, could you just concentrate on getting me untied?"

"I'm doing the best I can. I don't think you want to move in with me. Isaiah might like you, but he's a little old-fashioned. He'd probably come to the bedroom door with a shotgun and a parson. No, I think we ought to live at your place. I must say, it looked pretty bland when I followed you that morning when we first came north. I would have thought you'd live someplace a little more colorful. Maybe we could find something we both like. Near the water, with a lot of character."

"Who says we're going to live together?"

"Well, it makes sense." She moved back around on her knees, looking up at him. "After all, the sex is wonderful, and it would be silly to do without until 1999 just because you're so pigheaded."

"Could you please just untie me?" he begged, feeling like his head was about to explode.

"Honey, you're untied."

He yanked at his hands and the ropes fell free. She was already working on the knots at his ankles, but he brushed her hands away and made short work of his bands, mildly embarrassed that he'd been too absorbed in her ridiculous conversation to even notice that she'd loosened the bonds.

A moment later, he was free. He moved as far away from her and temptation as he could get, stretching his cramped muscles, pacing the pitch-dark area they were confined in. As far as he could tell, there was no source of light and the door had no handle on the inside.

"Are we going to get out of here?" Sally asked from her position on the floor. She hadn't moved while he scoped out the place. She sounded oddly at ease.

"Certainly," he snapped, certain of no such thing. "We're just going to have to wait until morning. There's a small window set up high in the wall—that should provide us with enough light. Right now it's too damned dark to see more than a few inches in front of me." He felt his way back to the uncluttered center of the storeroom, moving past the rows of shelving to where Sally sat.

He almost fell over her in the darkness. He squatted down beside her, putting his hands out, telling himself he had to touch her, to make sure she was all right. That was his first mistake.

His hands rested on her shoulders—soft shoulders, melting beneath his hard hands. She rose up on her knees to meet him, putting her arms around his waist and holding onto him in the pitch darkness. He could feel the tension, the fear in her body, a fear she'd tried very hard to disguise.

"Diamond," she said in a quiet voice, "do you think you could just pretend for a little while? Pretend that you love me? I'm a little…frightened."

God, what a sap, what a sucker, what a complete and utter fool he was! He cupped her chin, tilting her face up to his. He couldn't say the words; he still had that much sense of self-preservation. But the way he kissed her, leaning down and brushing his lips across hers, softly, clinging, a reassurance and a benediction, was just as bad.

She sighed then, as some of the tension drained from her body, and her arms tightened around his waist. "If you can't tell me, James," she whispered, "could you show me?"

The floor was cool, cushioned linoleum beneath them as he lowered her to her back. The cotton sweater came off over her head with her assistance, the almost nonexistent scrap of a bra followed. He kissed her, every square inch of her warm, smooth, lush body as he uncovered it. He kissed her collarbone, the soft place behind her ear. He kissed the inside of her elbow and underside of her breast, stripping off his own clothes in awkward haste.

He tried to tell himself he was doing this for her, to reassure her when she was frightened, but he knew that was a lie. He was doing it because he couldn't help himself. It didn't matter that to touch her again would be compromising his independence, his way of life, his very soul. It didn't even matter that she might end up getting even more hurt than he was. There in the darkness on the cool linoleum floor, the only thing that mattered was the moment, the feel of her smooth skin beneath his hands, the tiny little cry she made when he put his mouth on her breast, the restless squirming of her body as he shoved her jeans down her legs and tossed them away in the darkness.

He wanted to take his time. He had no idea what time it was, but chances were they had a long night ahead of them. He wanted to stretch it, make it last, but the more he kissed her, the hotter his own need burned. She threaded her hands through his hair, caressing him as he gently suckled her breasts, and her breath was coming in rapid gusts against his hair. He pulled away, ignoring her little cry of protest, to move his mouth down, across her slightly rounded stomach.

She realized what he intended a moment before he did

it. She made a strangled sound, "Don't," as his mouth found her, and she arched off the floor, digging her heels in.

He held her hips, inexorable, as spasms ricocheted through her body in immediate release. The sound of her choked whimpers of pleasure almost made him explode, and when he finally pulled away, he had every intention of pulling her beneath him and sinking his body into hers.

She stopped him with shaking hands and barely controlled breathing. "No," she said, pushing him onto the floor, onto his back, leaning over him. He couldn't see her expression in the darkness, but he knew it as well as he knew his own heart. She'd be determined, a little dazed and very very sure of herself.

Damn, she was good with her mouth. The little clumsiness only added to the delight, as she kissed his flat male nipples, his stomach, drew her lips across the scars and bruises and war wounds he'd suffered in the past fifteen years. And then she took him into her mouth, her silky hair falling around her face, returning the intimate caress he'd given her, and he was afraid he was going to explode beneath her tender, untutored ministrations.

When he could finally bear no more, he pulled her away with more force than necessary. "Not that way. It's not... fair...."

"But I wanted it," she whispered, and he believed her. He reached for her, but she'd already climbed over his supine body, positioning herself above his aching hardness, sinking down, a bit at a time, until he thought he'd go mad with the sheer pleasure of it. Once more, he caught her hips, helping her with the rhythm of it, and then he couldn't wait any longer and he thrust up into her, hard, filling her with the love he refused to admit existed, holding her as she exploded once more around him, her body squeezing tight.

And then she went limp, all the energy draining out of

her in a rush as she collapsed against him. He caught her as she fell, tenderly, rolling over onto his side and taking her with him. She was gasping for breath like a landed fish, and her heart was pounding against his in triple time.

He held her very tightly for a moment, somehow wanting to absorb her into his skin, his soul. And then he loosened his grip, pushing her damp hair away from her face, following the path his fingers took with his mouth, kissing her eyelids, her cheekbones, her chin, her lips.

Slowly, by infinitesimal degrees, she calmed. Her heartbeat slowed, her breathing steadied, the trembling in her body settled down. She sighed, a deep, shaking sigh, and melted against him, wrapping herself around him like hot wax.

"We're going to surprise the hell out of Alf if he decides to check on us," she said in a rough little whisper. "And I don't care. If he wants to get in the way of true love, then that's his problem."

"Sally," James said, his voice tight with regret, "I'm not the man for you."

"Yeah, I know. You're too old, too broke and too mean. Don't worry about it. I'll get older, I'll give away my money and I'll work on being just as sour as you."

"Sally…"

She put her lips against his and he had to kiss her. There was no way he could stop himself. "Don't argue now, Diamond. Once we're back in San Francisco and my sister's safe, you can give me the brush-off. Or you can try," she added, as if honesty compelled her to. "But for now, just shut up and kiss me."

"You better not expect me to make love to you again," he warned her, drawing his hands down to her breasts and feeling them swell in his hands. "That's one of the problems of being too old." It was a lie. He was ready for her again, and no matter how limited her experience, she probably knew it.

"Diamond, you're thirty-eight, not seventy-eight," she said. "And if you don't want me again, you'd better tell your body that. It seems to have other ideas."

He moved suddenly, pushing her over onto her back and straddling her with breathtaking swiftness. Her black hair was spread out around her on the linoleum floor, and the faint glow of the newly risen moon from the small window shone in her eyes. He cupped her face with his hands, holding her still, and she waited patiently. Waited for what he was willing to give.

As far as he could remember, no woman had ever been patient with him. They'd always been demanding, wanting what he couldn't provide, wanting it immediately.

Sally wanted those things, too. She deserved them. But she was willing to take whatever he could give her. And he could no more see her nagging him than he could imagine her as a yuppie executive. She was crazy, scatter-brained, ridiculous and adorable. And he was absolutely defenseless against her.

"You're going to be the death of me," he said, his voice rough as his insistent body pressed against hers.

She wrapped her legs around him, letting him settle into the cradle of her thighs. "Not for another fifty years," she said, running her hands up his sides.

He couldn't fight any longer. He could fight her. He could fight the lure of sex. But he couldn't fight the lure of his own hungry heart. "I don't believe in happy endings," he muttered against her mouth.

"Tough. You're going to get one anyway." And she opened her mouth against his, and for a while, there were no more arguments as their bodies were in complete accord.

SALLY SLEPT A LITTLE BIT, wrapped in his arms. Diamond slept a little bit, his head on her soft breasts. By the time the first gray light of dawn filtered in through the small, high window, Sally began to stir, aware of every little ache and twinge in her body. She looked at Diamond, still dozing, and she wanted to ignore the pain and wake him up with her mouth. She moved toward him and his eyes flew open, staring at her in unabashed alarm.

"Don't touch me," he warned.

"Why not?"

"Because you know perfectly well what will happen if you touch me, and we'd damn well better get our clothes on and see if we can get out of this place before Alf remembers we're in here."

"Do you think he's forgotten?"

"No. But we can always hope." Diamond was pulling on his clothes with rapid grace, ignoring her wistful expression. A moment later, he was out of reach, stalking around the storage room that was still mostly impenetrable shadows while she started to dress herself, less gracefully, less swiftly, her entire body one mass of aches and pains.

He was examining the door when he whirled around at the moan she was unable to stifle. "Are you all right?" he asked, frowning through the darkness.

"I hurt."

"I'm not surprised. You're not used to so much sex."

"Who says?"

"I say." He turned back to the door, cursing with his usual fluency. "There's no handle on the inside of this door. We're trapped here until Alf comes to get us."

"We can always—"

"Don't even think it," Diamond snapped, obviously in a grumpy mood.

Sally pulled her sweater over her head, pausing long enough to admire the love bite on the top of her breast. She started to struggle to her feet, then sank back down with another groan of pain.

"I have never hurt so much in my entire life," she announced. "My head hurts form where Alf hit me, my back hurts from sleeping on the floor, my...well, my entire body hurts. But you know what hurts most of all?''

''I can imagine,'' Diamond said with a drawl, sinking onto the floor as he abandoned his quest.

''It's not what you think. You know what hurts most of all?'' She clutched at her chest, doing her best to look tragic.

''You're going to tell me,'' he said in a resigned voice.

''I'm going to tell you. It's not my poor bruised and pleasured body. It's not even my fragile heart that's expecting you to stomp all over it.''

''Stomp all over it?'' he echoed, his reserve vanishing in momentary amusement.

''Don't interrupt. It's not even my heart that's tearing me apart. You know what hurts most?''

''What?'' he asked with great patience.

''My stomach.''

She'd managed to drive that dark, almost tortured expression from his face entirely. ''Your stomach?'' he said, not bothering to disguise his incredulity.

''I haven't had a damned thing to eat since that rabbit food last night,'' she said in a loud, unabashed wail. ''I'm starving, Diamond!''

He leaned back against the wall, stretching his long legs out in front of him, and he laughed with real amusement. ''You're in luck, Sally. You were locked into the right place. This isn't just any storeroom. There's food all around you.''

Ignoring her aching body, Sally leapt up, peering through the shadows at the rows of shelving. She grabbed the first thing she saw, a bag of nacho chips, and ripped it apart, sending chips flying around the room as she stuffed a handful into her mouth. Tossing the split bag to Diamond, she went foraging, grabbing anything that took her fancy and shoving it into her mouth. She ate gourmet cookies, dried apricots, semisweet chocolate and Wheat Thins dipped in raspberry preserves, making as big a mess as possible as she went, deriving a small, vengeful satisfaction from her destruction.

"I don't suppose you have a can opener on you?" she said, turning to Diamond and holding aloft a tin of caviar.

He was still leaning against the wall, munching on the nacho chips. "Nope."

"No Swiss army knife?"

"I'm neither a Boy Scout nor MacGyver. On the other hand, I don't suppose you've run across my cigarettes up there on the shelves?"

"No cigarettes. I'm surprised you aren't crankier."

"I've moved beyond cranky to downright murderous. Lucky for you I'm saving my attitude problems for Alf when he decides to reappear."

She tossed the caviar back onto the shelf, listened to it roll off the other side and reached for a box of sugary cereal. Ripping it open, she climbed down from the shelves and sat beside Diamond, offering him the box.

He shook his head, shuddering in disgust as she popped a handful in her mouth. "I worked up an appetite," she said defensively.

"I know you did. I wonder how many residents of the spa get to eat caviar and presweetened cereal," Diamond said, crunching into another nacho chip.

"They're probably part of Barbie's private stash. Diamond, don't you think—" Before she could finish, he'd put his hand across her mouth, silencing her.

"Someone's coming," he hissed in her ear. "Do exactly as I tell you."

She nodded, her eyes wide, and he released her mouth. "Go behind the shelves and lie on the floor," he ordered, barely making a noise.

"Why?"

"I don't want you to get shot."

She shuddered. "I didn't realize you still had a gun."

"I don't. But Alf and his buddies do. Do as I say."

"You're going to take them on without a weapon?" Her whisper got a little louder.

"Do as I say," he said, a little louder himself. "I can handle myself.

"I'm not moving," she said, stubborn and quite loud. "I'm not going to let you get killed in some noble attempt to escape. And don't you threaten me."

"I'm not going to," he said between gritted teeth. "No matter how much I love to. Please," he said, the request sounding more like a warning.

"No."

He stood up, shaking his head as the sounds of footsteps outside the door broke through her panic. "It's too late now," he growled. "Just keep out of the way, and—"

"No," she said, flinging herself against him, wrapping herself around his body like a leech. He wouldn't dare try anything foolhardy if she were in the way.

She simply ignored his fluent curses as he tried to pry her loose. The door opened and Alf stood there, the expected large and nasty gun resting comfortably in his meaty hand.

"Isn't this cute?" he said. "I should have tied you both up."

"What are you going to do, Alf?" Diamond said, trying to sound dignified with a female wrapped around him. "Hasn't this game gone on long enough?"

"Not quite. Not until we have the real falcon."

Sally couldn't quite swallow the little gasp as her worst fears were confirmed.

"We don't know where the real falcon is," Diamond said.

"Now that's just too bad. I guess you'll have to explain that to Don Salvatore. I wouldn't want to be in your shoes then. In the meantime, I've brought you a visitor. Another unwilling guest of Desert Glory's hospitality.'' He shoved a small, slight figure into the room and slammed the door shut.

Sally released her stranglehold on Diamond, rushing toward the small, sagging figure, catching her as she began to sink to the floor. "Lucy!" she cried. "Thank God you're here.''

Chapter Seventeen

"Lucy, darling, have they hurt you?" Sally asked, holding her sister's frail body in her arms.

Lucy looked up, her face woebegone. "Not...not much," she said in a faint voice. "Oh, Sally, I'm so glad you're here. I've been so frightened. I never realized what a brute Vinnie was."

Sally paused for a moment, startled. "A brute? Vinnie? I never would have thought it. You don't mean to say he's hurt you? Actually abused you...?"

Lucy took refuge in another bout of easy tears. James watched the performance, marveling at it, and marveling at how gullible Sally was, taking in every bit of it. "He hasn't actually hit me," Lucy was saying. "Not that it would show. He's just been...so cruel. I'm afraid he's going to kill me."

"My poor baby," Sally crooned, ready tears of sympathy in her own eyes. "I won't let him hurt you, and neither will Diamond. If Vinnie dares to touch you, I'll scratch his eyes out, and Diamond will beat him to a pulp."

"Leave me out of all this bloodthirsty stuff," James said, moving back to the wall and sinking down again.

"Diamond!" Sally protested, shocked and disappointed. "My sister's been hurt, and you're just sitting there being cynical."

"There's not much else I can do at this point until Alf decides to open the door," James pointed out. "You're making more than enough fuss over her for both of us."

Sally glared at him, her tender protestations of love obviously forgotten in the heat of the moment, and then she turned back to her sister. "When did you first realize that Vinnie was after the falcon?"

Lucy obviously wasn't the sort to reply to a straight question. She looked more like her mother than Sally, with the same hard eyes and ash blond hair. She obviously liked lies as much as Sally did, for she was throwing herself into them with a real enthusiasm. There was a difference, however, between her fabrications and Sally's. Sally made up stories mostly for the fun of it. Lucy's lies were for her own advantage.

"Sally, if he doesn't get the real falcon, he's going to kill all of us. He's sworn he will, and I believe him!"

Sally frowned. "Vinnie isn't the killer type. I suppose he's capable of putting a contract out on someone—"

"What makes you think you know more about Vinnie than I do?" Lucy demanded with a certain sharpness that hinted at jealousy. "You never took him seriously. You never cared for him, never even slept with him...."

"And you did," Sally said quietly. "Oh, Lucy, did you love him?"

"She still does," James drawled, deeming it time to interfere with this touching soap opera.

"That's even worse. To love a man who's planning to kill you," Sally said, her blue eyes so like Lucy's, and yet so much more real, filling with easy tears.

"He won't kill me if you tell him where the real falcon is," Lucy said, tossing James a hard glare over her shoulder before returning her attention to her gullible sister. "He's supposed to present it to the Bho Tsos this afternoon in some stupid ceremony. Don Salvatore's arriving this morning, along with his own private army, to witness the deal. If the falcon isn't there, it all falls through."

"So what?" Sally asked, and James was relieved to realize she wasn't being quite as trusting as he'd thought.

"Then the Bho Tsos are going to be very angry and insulted, and the Calderinis are going to be very angry and disappointed, and you and I are going to be very dead. And your pet private detective won't be able to save us."

"How did you know who Diamond is?" Sally asked almost casually.

"Vinnie said something. I guess his father warned him."

"Was that before or after he threatened to kill you?"

Lucy looked up at her sister, her huge eyes swimming in tears, her pale, pretty face defenseless and touching. "Sally," she begged in a sweet, pleading voice, "don't you believe me?"

"Oh, I believe you, Lucy," Sally said, brushing her sister's hair away from her tear-damp face, just as she must have when they were little and sweet sister Lucy fell and skinned her knees. "I believe that the Calderinis want the real falcon and would do just about anything to get it, up to and possibly including murdering me and Diamond. I believe the Bho Tsos will call off the deal if they don't get the real one. But I'm not too sure where you fit in with all this."

"Sally!"

"You and I haven't grown up with too great a respect for telling the truth," Sally said in a meditative tone. "Probably due to Marietta's influence, I suppose, or maybe some internal flaw. But that doesn't mean we can't change. Our lives may depend on it, Lucy. Tell me the truth."

Lucy fluttered her big blue eyes, and her full lower lip trembled enough that even James found himself beginning to believe her. "I'm telling you the truth!" she cried.

Sally's rueful smile was a revelation. She released her comforting hold on her sister and moved across the room, sinking down beside James and taking his hand in hers. He could feel her trembling slightly, and he realized what an effort it had cost her. "Don't waste your time in here, Lucy," she said, resting her head against James's shoulder. It was a nice weight, solid, warm. "Trust me, it's quite uncomfortable. You'll be much better off with Vinnie in his luxurious quarters. You smell of expensive shampoo and perfume, Lucy. If you were being held prisoner, you wouldn't be in such good shape. Go away and spin some lies for Vinnie. Maybe he'll believe you."

The tears in Lucy's eyes vanished. "So you've found true love and that's changed everything," she said in something close to a sneer, taking in Sally's position of trust, leaning against James. He could feel the tension in Sally's body, could feel the tension in his own. Vinnie might not want to hurt Lucy, but James certainly was tempted. He felt a very primitive violence toward anyone who wanted to hurt Sally.

But he didn't move. Sally held him still. "That's changed everything," she agreed.

"Well, I've got news for you. I've fallen in love, too. With Vinnie. And he loves me." Lucy's voice was defiant.

"I'm happy for you."

"I don't believe you. You're jealous!"

Sally laughed, an unfeigned sound of amusement. "Lucy, I have Diamond. What would I want with someone like Vinnie? I didn't want him when I could have him. I certainly don't want him now."

"You could never have him. He was just stringing you along, playing you for a fool while he was trying to get the falcon."

"I thought as much," Sally said, unperturbed. "I'm glad his feelings for you are more sincere."

"You don't think he loves me!" Lucy shrieked.

"I said I'm glad that he does," Sally said patiently.

"If he doesn't get the falcon, our future is ruined!" Lucy wailed.

"Why?"

"This deal with the Chinese has been years in the making. If it falls through at the last minute, all because Vinnie couldn't come up with the goods, then his future with the family will go up in smoke."

"Wouldn't that be for the best?"

"Where is the falcon?" Lucy shrieked.

"I don't know," Sally said, her voice very calm and steady, but her hand shook in James's.

"I hate you," Lucy screeched. "I've always hated you. You're mean and stupid and ugly and I hate you, I hate you, I—"

James had had enough of this. "If you don't shut your mouth, Miss MacArthur, then I'm going to have to shut it for you. And since the only thing I can find to gag you with would be a crumpled up bag that used to hold nacho chips, I don't think you'd find that very pleasant."

Lucy shut up, her blue eyes wide with astonishment as she realized he'd do exactly that. Blessed silence reigned in the storeroom as it grew marginally lighter.

"It's not MacArthur," Lucy said suddenly, in a small, defiant voice. "It never was MacArthur, and it certainly isn't now. It's Calderini. Vinnie and I were married last week."

"Congratulations," James drawled. "Sally and I wish you the best of luck. Count on monogrammed towels from the both of us."

"Go to hell," Lucy snarled, glaring at the two of them.

"After you, Mrs. Calderini," James replied, stroking Sally's hand.

JAMES'S WATCH HADN'T worked in days, and Sally's thin Rolex had disappeared at some point after Alf had knocked her on the head. If Lucy had any idea of the time, she wasn't about to divulge it, so the three of them sat in limbo as the minutes, the hours crawled past.

"I have to go to the bathroom," Lucy announced suddenly, breaking her sulking silence.

"Join the club," Sally said. "I've had to go for the last three hours. This place doesn't come equipped with a private bath."

"Well, I'm not going to sit here any longer and suffer. If you want to die, then that's your choice." Lucy surged to her feet, went to the door and started pounding on it. "Alf, let me out of here! At once!" she shrieked.

"You say she's your younger sister?" James murmured.

"Hard to believe, isn't it? She's always been more mature," Sally said with a ridiculous note of maternal pride.

"I'd say she's more nasty than mature."

"I suppose you could say that, too," she admitted.

Apparently, Alf had gone off duty. No one appeared to answer Lucy's strident demands, and when she began kicking the steel door, James decided he'd had enough.

"If you don't stop that, Mrs. Calderini, I'm going to lift you up and stuff you through the window. I don't expect you'll fit, but I'll put you out head first so we don't have to listen to you shrieking."

Lucy turned on him. "That's the second time you've threatened me, Mr. Diamond. Sally might be impressed by such caveman tactics, but I, for one, am not."

"I'm not trying to impress you, Mrs. Calderini. I'm trying to terrorize you."

"You'd better believe him, Lucy," Sally piped up. "Diamond can be an absolute pig if he wants to be."

"Thank you, dear," James murmured.

"You're welcome, darling," she replied sweetly.

"You two make me sick," Lucy spat out.

James didn't even bother to glance at her. Sally was looking up at him raptly, her big blue eyes shining with a certain guarded adoration. He decided he liked that. Particularly the guarded part. He wouldn't want a woman who was stupid enough to trust anyone implicitly. Given his profession and his nature, he'd never be completely trustworthy in all matters. But he suddenly realized he could be in the area that mattered the most. The area of the heart.

"I sure the hell hope we get out of this mess," he murmured, leaning his head close to hers.

"Why?" she asked. "So you can ditch me and get on with your life?"

"So I can ditch your caterwauling sister and find a real bed where we can spend a couple of days in undisturbed peace."

He liked the light that came into her eyes at the thought. He liked the way her mouth curved into a shy smile. Hell, he liked everything about her, up to but excluding her sister.

"Then I guess we'd better make it through this mess, somehow or other, shouldn't we?" she said, kissing him lightly.

He deepened the kiss gently, and for a moment, they were so absorbed, they didn't hear the heavy, metal door swing open.

"Now ain't love grand?" Alf drawled. "Sorry I had to dump the broad in here to cramp your style, but we ran out of holding places."

"Don't bother, Alf," Lucy said, rising and brushing herself off with haughty dignity. "They didn't believe me." She started toward the door, but Alf's meaty hand shot out, forestalling her.

"Where do you think you're going, little missy?"

Lucy's entire body was rigid. "To Vinnie."

"Nope. You're staying put. The rules of this particular game have changed."

"Vinnie couldn't…?"

"Vinnie didn't. Don Salvatore has taken over, and he's not too pleased with his son and heir. Vinnie's being read the riot act right now, and you're to be kept on ice until the Don decides what to do with all of yous.''

''I'll be dead of a burst bladder before he decides,'' Sally announced in a pragmatic voice.

''The good news is that Don Salvatore is a gentleman. He doesn't believe in holding ladies under adverse conditions. You'll be escorted back to your rooms and locked in. He'd like your word of honor that you won't try to escape. Not that I'd believe it, but the old man has a certain old-fashioned respect for women.''

''I'm not going anywhere without Diamond,'' Sally said flatly.

''Diamond stays here.''

''Then so do I.''

Alf looked torn. Clearly, executive decision making wasn't his forte, but just as clearly, his orders hadn't been engraved in stone. ''You wanna give me your word, copper?''

''Sure, Alf,'' James said in a lazy drawl. ''I won't try to escape. Cross my heart and hope to die.''

Alf spat on the linoleum. ''Up and at 'em, then. You haven't got much time.''

James hadn't really expected he'd be able to get the drop on Alf once they reached the hallway. For one thing, the gun in Alf's hand was much too big, and James couldn't count on being able to keep Sally safe. For another, the expected backup was waiting, a solid phalanx of armed suits waiting to escort them to their rooms.

''A lot of muscle for two women,'' James observed.

''Yeah, well, you were supposed to go, too. I just thought you deserved the storeroom,'' Alf said, his dark, piggy eyes gleaming with hatred.

''I don't know. I have a certain fondness for that storeroom,'' James said, taking Sally's hand and squeezing it lightly.

''Disgusting,'' Alf muttered.

It was too much to hope they'd be taken back to their original rooms. Even if they had been, someone would have gone through their baggage and found the knife James had hidden in Sally's suitcase as extra insurance. Instead, they were locked into two small rooms that must have been reserved for the cleaning staff.

Alf did his best to put the two sisters together, but once more, Sally was having none of that. Once more, Alf backed down and the volubly protesting Lucy was shoved into one room while James and Sally went willingly enough into the other next door.

James leaned against the door and surveyed the cubicle. "I wouldn't call this much of an improvement. There's no window, the door's locked and the bed looks more like a cot."

"There is, however, a toilet and shower," Sally said, heading straight for them. "I'm counting my blessings."

It took all his self-control for James not to join her in the shower. The very sound of her voice, the thumps as she moved around in the tiny shower stall made him hard as a rock. He had to stop thinking with his glands if he was going to get the two of them out of there in one piece, and he had to stop considering whether that tiny cot was really too small.

When she finally emerged from the bathroom, he'd ascertained that there was no way out of the locked cubicle. He looked up when he saw her, frowning as he took in her pale appearance. She'd put her rumpled clothes back on, and her damp hair framed a face white with strain and exhaustion.

"I thought you'd reappear in a towel," he said, moving toward her.

"I decided that might be a bit dangerous. We have to concentrate on getting out of here first."

"You're smart," he said, "and you're gorgeous." He kissed her, hard, and then moved past her to the bathroom.

By the time he emerged fully dressed after his shower Sally was sound asleep, curled up on the tiny cot. He wanted to wrap himself around her, to simply hold her for a while. And that knowledge was the most disturbing of all.

He wasn't ever going to be free. Oh, they might very well get out of this particular mess. He might even be able to get rid of her, drive her away with his complete lack of charm and financial stability. He could start drinking with a vengeance, maybe take up smoking unfiltered cigarettes.

But he didn't think that would get rid of her. The only way he was going to get rid of her was to tell her to go. And when, not if, he did that, he was still going to be haunted by her memory for the rest of his life.

The door was flung open abruptly, and Sally sat up in bed, startled out of sleep.

"Too bad." Alf chuckled unpleasantly. "I was hoping to catch you with your pants down."

"Too bad," James echoed, deciding then and there that Alf wasn't going to get through this unscathed.

"Get on your feet, girly. You're wanted."

"She's not going anywhere without me," James announced.

"Don't get excited. You're going, too. All hell's breaking loose and the Chinese want some answers."

THE FORMAL MEETING between the Calderini crime family and the Bho Tsos was being held in a banquet room that looked better suited to stag parties than high-level criminals. The Bho Tsos were seated at one side of a long table, men only, all of them looking completely disgruntled. At a smaller table sat the wives, with the Dragon Lady firmly in control. She was looking straight at Sally when she entered, and Sally could feel a cold shiver run down her back. She thought Vinnie was essentially harmless and that Don

Salvatore not much more than a sadistic lech, but the Dragon Lady scared the hell out of her.

The Calderinis were at the opposite side of the table, Don Salvatore in the middle, a cowed looking Vinnie beside him, and various midlevel functionaries flanking them. All eyes were on Diamond and Sally when they entered the room. Lucy was already there, sitting in a corner like a naughty little girl.

Sally could feel the tension in the room, the tension radiating from Diamond. She had to be very careful, she thought, or Diamond might make another grand gesture that could get them killed. The phony jade falcon was sitting in the middle of the table, directly in front of Mr. Li and Don Salvatore, and with a sudden surge of energy, Sally pulled away from Alf and sauntered over to it. She reached between Don Salvatore and Vinnie and picked it up, surprised as always by its light weight.

"Do you gentlemen have a problem with my father's falcon?" she asked brightly.

Mr. Li hissed in disapproval, sounding like a fat snake. "We have a problem. The falcon we are looking for was stolen from our country by a thief and a scoundrel. Your father, Miss MacArthur. We want it back."

"You have it." She put the falcon back on the table.

It jumped as Salvatore pounded his fist down. "He does not have it. This is a phony, commissioned by you from Derek Dagradi at the School for Fine Arts. You have no secrets from us, Miss MacArthur. We want to know where the real one is."

"If I had no secrets from you, then you wouldn't be asking," she pointed out with deceptive calm.

Diamond moved then, putting a restraining hand on her elbow. "Sally, watch it," he muttered. "You're not playing with amateurs here."

"Listen to Mr. Diamond, Miss MacArthur," Don Salvatore said. "He's come up against us before. If you don't cooperate, things will go poorly for you. And most particularly, for your baby sister.''

''No!'' Vinnie protested, unquelled by his father's glare. ''She's my wife and I won't let you touch her.''

''Marriages like that can be dissolved.''

''Not mine!'' Vinnie said stoutly. ''She's pregnant.''

Silence filled the room as everyone, the Bho Tsos and the Calderinis, turned to stare at Lucy. ''Whose child is it?'' Don Salvatore asked finally.

Vinnie lunged for his father, knocking the banquet table. The falcon went rolling across the damask cloth, Lucy started screaming, and the Bho Tsos began shouting.

In the midst of all this, the Dragon Lady rose to her full, impressive height and made an announcement in Chinese. It was short and dignified, and had the effect of silencing the place. Everyone was standing, glaring at each other. Mr. Li was taking a step backward, tugging at his suit jacket, when the swinging doors on the lobby side of the banquet room opened.

''Who the hell is that?'' Don Salvatore demanded in a rage, his white hair standing on end.

Alf was already racing toward the door, but he was too late. An elderly figure backed into the room, pulling something behind him. The doors swung shut behind him, and the man turned, wheeling his burden in front of him.

''Oh, God,'' Sally muttered weakly as she recognized Jenkins holding the handles of the wheelchair Isaiah used when he was feeling fragile, or at least, when he wanted to give that appearance.

Isaiah himself was in fine shape, dignified, erect in the chair, his faded eyes glinting with malice. And resting in his lap, beneath his arthritic hand, lay the Manchurian falcon.

''I believe you were looking for this?''

Chapter Eighteen

Dead silence filled the room. Mr. Li moved from behind the table, walking very slowly toward Isaiah's erect figure. "So," he said. "We meet again, Mr. MacArthur."

"We do, Mr. Li," Isaiah said with equal dignity. "It has been many years."

"Many years. You have come to return the falcon to its rightful owners?"

"No, I wouldn't necessarily say the Bho Tsos happen to be the rightful owner of a national treasure like this one," Isaiah said.

"Consider us a representative of the government," Mr. Li said solemnly, an unimaginable glint of humor in his small, dark eyes.

"That would take a stretch of the imagination. Nevertheless, I believe I'm up to it. Assuming my daughters and my future son-in-law are allowed to leave safely."

"Vinnie and Lucy are already married," Sally piped up, before Diamond's hand on her arm could silence her.

Isaiah didn't even glance her way. "I was referring to Mr. Diamond, the private detective." James didn't even bother to wonder how the old man knew who he really was. Obviously, Isaiah MacArthur was a lot more savvy than anyone had given him credit for.

Mr. Li cast a polite glance at Don Salvatore, who nodded with equal dignity. "They are free to leave."

"Then," said Isaiah, lifting the falcon in his swollen hands, "I present to you the Manchurian falcon." He placed it in Mr. Li's slightly trembling hands, and out of the corner of his mouth, he muttered to Sally, "Get the hell out of here."

James grabbed her arm, awash with the sudden sinking suspicion that things were still not what they seemed. He'd just begun dragging a reluctant Sally away from the cluster of men when Mr. Li let out an enraged shout.

"*This* is not the real falcon!"

Immediately two of the Calderini henchmen stepped in front of Sally and James, barring their escape. Sally tried to stare at her father, and Isaiah shrugged. "I tried."

"Where is the real falcon?" Mr. Li demanded, positively vibrating with rage.

"I have no idea. I had this one commissioned from the same man who made the other copy. Your guess is as good as mine as to where the real falcon is."

"You cannot play us for fools," Mr. Li warned. "People do not trifle with the Bho Tsos and come out unscathed. I owe you a debt of vengeance, Isaiah MacArthur, and I rejoice at the chance to pay it." He started toward the wheelchair-bound man as the rest of the crowd watched in fascinated horror. James tensed, ready to step between Li and Isaiah and probably get a bullet in his ear for the trouble. But he had no choice—if he didn't do something to stop it, Sally would.

Suddenly a voice stopped Mr. Li in his murderous tracks. "Behave yourself!" The Dragon Lady said firmly, and Mr. Li hung his head like a naughty little boy.

Isaiah swung himself around in his wheelchair to stare at the woman in surprise. "Why, Bambi," he said, his voice soft with wonder. "I didn't know you were still around."

"Bambi?" Sally echoed in fascination.

The Dragon Lady was a master at dramatics. She strode around the table, her thin, elegant body that of an empress. "I have prospered, Isaiah MacArthur. As have you. I would wish we could share memories together, but this is a day of business, and I'm afraid sentiment is of no value. Where is the falcon?"

"Bambi, I would give it to you if I had it. I truly have no idea where it has gone to," Isaiah said sadly.

"Maybe a random thief?" Sally suggested, but Don Salvatore simply glared at her.

"We would know if anyone had taken something the Calderinis wanted. We would have it by now."

"Then who—"

There was a noise at the door as one more unwanted guest wanted to join the party. Suddenly it all fit together in James's brain, and he laughed with pure pleasure.

The sound of his laughter shocked the room into silence. "What's so damned funny, boy?" Isaiah demanded grumpily.

"Isn't it obvious?" he countered. "Don't any of you know where the damned falcon is?"

"If you know, you'd better inform us immediately. Unless you'd like to lose your fingers one at a time," Don Salvatore said pleasantly.

"I imagine the person who took it is the same person who's making such a fuss right now. If I were you, Don Salvatore, I'd tell Alf to call off his goons and let her in."

"Her?" Several key players echoed as Don Salvatore snapped his fingers imperiously.

"Her," James verified, as a familiar figure sauntered into the room.

"Good God, I should have known," Isaiah moaned, sinking his head into his hands.

"Hullo, mother," Sally said, resigned.

"Hello, darling." Marietta was another player, milking

the scene for all it was worth, and she even managed to put Bambi the Dragon Lady in the shade. She was stunning, dressed in black and crimson, a huge black bag over her arm. She had a cigarette holder that was at least a foot long, with a lit cigarette at the end, and it took all James's strength of mind to ignore it and concentrate on the real falcon.

He almost tackled her for it. Instead, he held still, his hand still protective on Sally's arm, as Marietta reached into her bag and drew forth still another falcon.

To his untrained eyes, it was identical to the other two. But Mr. Li drew in a deep, reverent breath and held out his hands for it.

James was never quite sure how it happened. Mr. Li reached for it; Marietta released it; Bambi lunged for it; Isaiah jerked his wheelchair; and Sally's foot poked out. Mr. Li stumbled; Bambi floundered; Marietta fumbled; and the falcon went flying through the air like a football.

"I've got it," Vinnie shouted, feinting back for the pass, arms overhead like a tight-end receiver. Everyone watched in silence as the statue hurtled toward him, turning over and over in the air. Everyone watched in silence as Vinnie leapt for it. And missed. And the Manchurian falcon crashed to the floor, smashing into a million pieces.

The silence was as intense as a scream. Finally, Sally leaned forward to stare at the rubble, and said in her most prosaic voice, "I never realized jade was so fragile."

Mr. Li straightened himself. He snapped his fingers, and even Bambi pulled herself to attention. "We are leaving," he announced. "The deal is off. If we wish to have a piece of the northern California gambling concession, we will simply take it. In the meantime, the sooner we get out of your benighted country, the happier we will be." He marched toward the door without a backward glance, and the assembled Bho Tsos followed, leaving behind only Bambi.

For a moment, she didn't look like a dragon lady at all as she knelt beside Isaiah's wheelchair. "We should never have grown old, Isaiah," she said in a soft, musical voice.

"You will never grow old, Bambi," Isaiah said, touching her cheek. A moment later, she followed the others, back erect, breathing fire.

Don Salvatore moved slowly, an old man. "I should kill you all for this," he said heavily. "But then I would have to kill my worthless fool of a son, and even I cannot do that. You." He turned to the hapless Vinnie. "You are too weak for the life we lead. Go back to Yale Law School, finish your degree and then come work for me. Maybe you're better at juggling numbers and legal matters than you are at juggling priceless art objects." He glanced over at Lucy's cowering figure, then sighed. "And bring your wife back to the house so that we can welcome her. But not," he said fiercely, pointing at Sally, "that one. She is a plague and a bane."

"I agree," Vinnie muttered, glaring at her.

"So do I," James couldn't resist adding.

Sally stood by her father's wheelchair, and to James's surprise, she didn't even raise her head to glare at him. Her shoulders were bowed, and for the first time, she seemed truly numbed by the events. He wanted to put his arms around her, to lift her chin up and kiss her, to tell her he was only kidding, that she'd done well even if she'd almost gotten them killed. But he didn't move.

It was his chance to break free. Probably his last chance. He couldn't afford to let it pass him by.

The Calderinis marched out, following the old man single file, leaving only Vinnie behind. Alf was the last to leave, and as he did, he turned to glance at James.

James nodded as a silent agreement passed between the two. A cease-fire may have been called between the other warring factions. The battle was still hot between these two men.

"Well, Marietta," Isaiah said finally. "You still manage to surprise me. Why in heaven's name did you steal the falcon?"

Marietta took the handles of the wheelchair from Jenkins's capable hands. "Would you believe me if I told you I heard the Calderinis were after it and I was trying to protect it for you? But when it came to the safety of my daughters and our precious falcon, I had to make the only decent choice."

"Not for one moment," Isaiah replied.

Marietta shrugged, looking very young and very naughty, and James could see where Sally got her love of fantasy from. "Would you believe I heard the Calderinis were after the falcon and I thought I could make a tidy little nest egg by delivering it to them?"

"That sounds more likely. What made you change your mind?"

"I didn't. I knew their reputation well enough to realize my daughters weren't in any real danger. I imagine I could have gotten quite a nice sum from them," she said with misty-eyed regret.

Isaiah reached up and patted her hand consolingly. "Never mind, dearest. You'll find some other get-rich-quick scheme. And don't forget, your daughter just married into a very wealthy family. There must be some profit to be made from all that."

"You always were able to look on the bright side of things, Isaiah," Marietta said fondly, pushing him toward the door. "Every cloud always has a silver lining."

Sally lifted her head for a moment, and James could see a trace of her old fire. "There's even better news, Marietta," Sally called after her rapidly disappearing parents. "Lucy's going to make you a grandmother."

Marietta's scream of anguish echoed long after the doors swung shut. Vinnie had gone to Lucy's side, wrapping her in protective arms, neither of them the slightest bit aware of the other people in the room. James looked at Sally, at the wary, hopeful expression in her eyes, and he hated to douse that flame. But he had no choice.

"Looks like your sister will have her happy ending," he drawled, wishing to hell he had a cigarette. He'd almost forgotten how much he was needing one, but right then, he would have killed for one. Something to keep his hands and eyes busy as he broke Sally's heart.

"What about you?" Her voice wasn't much more than a whisper, but he heard every word, spoken and unspoken.

"You know me. I don't believe in 'em," he said, cool as menthol. "Listen, I need to get back to town. I've got too many other things hanging fire. If you don't mind, I'll take the car and you can catch a ride with one of your parents."

Sally opened her mouth to protest, but that defeated expression blanked over her face and she nodded. "You'll send me your bill?"

"Including seventy-five dollars for my car," he said, wanting to coax a smile out of her.

It didn't work. She looked up at him, and there were tears swimming in her eyes. "Goodbye, Diamond."

He was no good for her, and he knew it even if she didn't. "Goodbye, kid," he said, sounding like Bogart. And he left her standing in the middle of the room, the worthless shards of the priceless falcon at her feet.

"WHY DON'T YOU COME with me? It doesn't do you any good to sit around moping. If that man is foolish enough not to love my daughter, then he's not worth having."

Sally glanced up at Marietta with her customary listlessness. It had been ten days since their return from Glory, California. Ten days of listening to Lucy's blow-by-blow account of her morning sickness, the luxury of the Calderini family compound and what a stupendous lover Vinnie was. Ten days of Marietta and Isaiah flirting and fighting. Ten days of Jenksy's worrying and cossetting and fussing over her. Ten days without word from Diamond.

"You're leaving?" Sally asked her mother, not really surprised. Her mother never stayed in one place for very long—it was one of her major failings and one of her major charms.

"For the Amazon. I have a need for lush, tropical climates. Your father and I aren't going to make a go of it, you know."

"I never expected you would," Sally said, staring out the window into the rainy afternoon. It was a gloomy day in late September. The rain was relentless, and the gray chill filled her soul.

"So why don't you come with me? I know I haven't been much of a mother, but I promise you, I can be a hell of a good companion. We'll have fun."

Sally looked at her with great patience. "Mother," she said, "I don't want to have fun."

Marietta looked startled. "I do believe that's the first time you've called me Mother in years."

"Diamond told me I shouldn't judge you. He's probably right." Sally sighed. "Besides, I don't have the energy to be angry anymore."

"Well, maybe James Diamond isn't as big a fool as I thought he was. Though if he's stupid enough to leave you, he can't be all that bright."

Sally leaned back on the window seat, stretching her long legs out in front of her. They were getting skinnier. For some reason, she hadn't felt like eating, or sleeping for that matter, since they returned from the Calderinis' pseudo spa. At least Diamond had returned her car, though she would have given anything if he'd brought it himself instead of sending it with Frankie the pimp. He still looked like a seminary student, but the assessing looks he'd cast over the MacArthur mansion had been professional, indeed. She'd wanted to count the silver once he'd left.

Diamond hadn't even sent her a bill. And she wanted one desperately. Not so that she could pay it and put some sort of closure on that section of her life. She wasn't nearly so rational and well adjusted.

She wanted the bill because she wanted something of his. Something that belonged to him, even a piece of paper, something that bore his handwriting. She wanted a bill so she could refuse to pay it and make him come and try to collect. She wanted any part of him she could have. And apparently, she could have nothing.

She sighed, glancing up at her mother. Marietta was dressed for travel in a crushed silk suit and rakish hat with a pair of oversized sunglasses on her perfect nose. "Are you leaving now?" Sally asked, rousing herself to curiosity.

"Right this minute. If you think I'm going to wait around while Lucy blossoms, you must be crazy. I'm not ready to be a grandmother. Maybe in another twenty years or so, but not now. I'm simply going to consider the Calderini bambino my godchild."

Sally knew she should be angry with Marietta's blithe self-absorption, but instead, she laughed. "You're hopeless."

"You're certain you won't come? You don't need to pack, you know. We could have a marvelous time shopping."

"No, thank you, Mother. Maybe some other trip."

"You think he'll come back?" Marietta asked shrewdly.

The very thought stabbed hope through Sally's heart. "No," she said, truthfully enough. "But there's a chance in a thousand I'm wrong."

"So you'll sit and wait like some creepy old maid, mourning your lost love?"

For a moment, some of Sally's old energy reemerged. "Of course. For as long as a month, maybe. Then I'll go after him."

Marietta smiled her brilliant, heart-stopping smile. "That's my daughter. Say goodbye to Isaiah for me. I can't do it."

"He doesn't know you're leaving?"

"Oh, he knows, all right. I just haven't told him. He and I came to an understanding years ago. He knows me better than I know myself. I'm just afraid he might have started to hope…" She let the thought trail off, and for once in her life, she looked faintly regretful.

"I'll tell him."

"I left him a little present. Tell him that, darling. And give him my love."

Marietta never hugged Sally or touched her if she could help it. She didn't that day, either. She simply waved, an airy little wave, and ran out the front door.

Sally could imagine the present Marietta had left for her tolerant ex-husband. A stack of bills. A subpoena. Maybe even one of her absolutely awful paintings. The message and the gift could wait.

Night was falling around the old house when the yellow headlights pierced the gathering darkness. Sally watched with her usual apathy, still ensconced on the bench, as the headlights drew closer up the drive. It was some sort of old car, the kind she'd seen in movies, pulling up under the bright lights in front of the house.

Her heart started to pound, loud and hard beneath her breast, and she swung her legs off the window seat. By the time she reached the front door, the car had stopped and someone was walking up the front steps.

She couldn't see his face, but she'd know that body anywhere, even dressed in an old-fashioned dark suit, wing tips and a fedora.

She wanted to run to him, but she couldn't. She was rooted to the spot at the top of the steps, waiting for him.

He looked up and saw her, and she could see the trace of uncertainty on his face. "I looked like hell for an old

Chrysler like Marlowe used to drive,'' he said in a rough voice. "But this '42 Packard was the best I could do. I figured with a swell dame like you, I oughta go for the best."

"James," she said in a broken little voice. "You really do love me, don't you?"

He'd almost reached her. "I thought you'd already figured that out. Who else could make me give up cigarettes and hooch?"

"You said you wouldn't love me till 1999." He'd reached the top step. His face was back to normal now, the bruising gone, and once more, he had his artistic stubble, his beautiful face, his infinitely clever mouth.

"I'm a quick learner. So what's it gonna be, doll? Marriage to a shamus like me, or a life full of empty pleasures? Name your poison."

"Diamond," she said happily, "I'm yours." And she went into his arms, wrapping herself around him, home at last.

She didn't know how much time passed before she heard Jenkins's gentle harrumph. Dazedly she disentangled herself from Diamond, pleased to see that he looked just as shell-shocked as she did. She'd knocked his wonderful fedora off and discovered his hair was still too long, but she liked it.

"What is it, Jensky?" she murmured happily, not bothering to look away from Diamond.

"Your father wants to see you. And may I be the first to offer the two of you my best wishes?"

"You may," Diamond said. "Maybe I'd better ask the old man's permission. Where is he?"

"In the study, sir. And if I may say so, he's been waiting for this quite impatiently."

Sally took Diamond's hand, bouncing along the hallway cheerfully as they headed for the study. "I can be your secretary, Diamond. Hard-boiled detectives always have secretaries who're in love with them.''

''Yeah, but they're usually blond.''

''I'll dye my hair.''

''I'll fire you.''

''That's the nice part about it,'' she said happily. ''You can't fire your wife.''

''What have I gotten into?'' Diamond asked of no one in particular.

''Miss Sally's clutches, sir,'' Jenkins replied gravely, opening the door to the study.

Isaiah was sitting at the desk, an odd expression on his face. He barely acknowledged their arrival. ''Your mother's left,'' he said abruptly.

''Yes,'' Sally said, suddenly less giddy. ''She told me you knew she was going.''

''I figured she would. She always does.''

''Yes, she always does. She told me she left you a present. Is it something quite ghastly?'' Sally took a step toward her father, still holding tight to Diamond's hand.

Isaiah simply shook his head in bewilderment. ''I'm not sure what to make of it. She left me this.'' And his gnarled old hands lifted up a piece of gray-green sculpture. One that looked oddly familiar, and yet different.

''It's not...'' Diamond said.

''It is,'' Isaiah replied, staring at it in wonder and disbelief. ''The Manchurian falcon.''

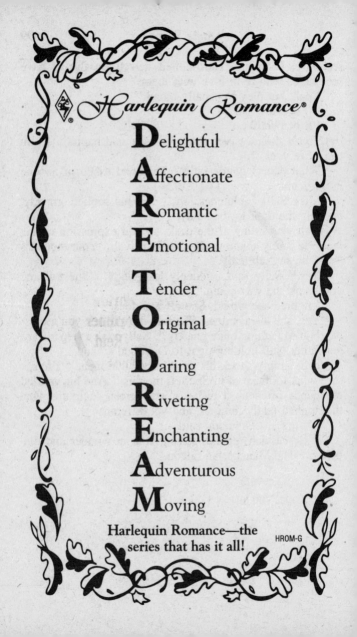

Harlequin Romance ®

Delightful
Affectionate
Romantic
Emotional

Tender
Original

Daring
Riveting
Enchanting
Adventurous
Moving

Harlequin Romance—the
series that has it all!

HROM-G

HARLEQUIN PRESENTS®

The world's bestselling romance series...
The series that brings you your favorite authors,
month after month:

Helen Bianchin...Emma Darcy
Lynne Graham...Penny Jordan
Miranda Lee...Sandra Morton
Anne Mather...Carole Mortimer
Susan Napier...Michelle Reid

and many more uniquely talented authors!

Wealthy, powerful, gorgeous men...
Women who have feelings just like your own...
The stories you love, set in exotic, glamorous locations...

HARLEQUIN PRESENTS,
Seduction and passion guaranteed!

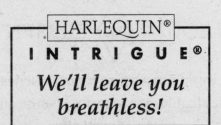

HARLEQUIN®

I N T R I G U E ®

We'll leave you breathless!

If you've been looking for thrilling tales of
contemporary passion and sensuous love stories
with taut, edge-of-the-seat suspense—
then you'll *love* **Harlequin Intrigue!**

Every month, you'll meet four new heroes
who are guaranteed to make your spine tingle
and your pulse pound. With them you'll enter
into the exciting world of Harlequin Intrigue—
where your life is on the line
and so is your heart!

THAT'S INTRIGUE—DYNAMIC ROMANCE AT ITS BEST!

HARLEQUIN®

I N T R I G U E ®

INT-GENR

Harlequin® Historical

From rugged lawmen and
valiant knights to defiant heiresses
and spirited frontierswomen,
Harlequin Historicals will
capture your imagination with
their dramatic scope, passion
and adventure.

Harlequin Historicals…
they're too good to miss!

HHGENR

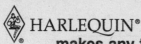